LYLE
OFFICIAL
ANTIQUES
REVIEW 1999

A PERIGEE BOOK

LYLE
OFFICIAL
ANTIQUES
REVIEW 1999

A Perigee Book
Published by The Berkley Publishing Group
A member of Penguin Putnam Inc.
375 Hudson Street
New York, New York 10014

First edition: December 1998
ISBN: 0-399-52450-9
ISSN: 1089-1544

Published simultaneously in Canada.

The Penguin Putnam Inc. World Wide Web site address is
http://www.penguinputnam.com

Printed in the United States of America

10   9   8   7   6   5   4   3   2   1

INTRODUCTION

This year over 100,000 Antique Dealers and Collectors will make full and profitable use of their Lyle Antiques Price Guide. They know that only in this one volume will they find the widest possible variety of goods – illustrated, described and given a current market value to assist them to BUY RIGHT AND SELL RIGHT throughout the year of issue.

They know, too, that by building a collection of these immensely valuable volumes year by year, they will equip themselves with an unparalleled reference library of facts, figures and illustrations which, properly used, cannot fail to help them keep one step ahead of the market.

In its twenty nine years of publication, Lyle has gone from strength to strength and has become without doubt the pre-eminent book of reference for the antique trade throughout the world. Each of its fact filled pages is packed with precisely the kind of profitable information the professional Dealer needs – including descriptions, illustrations and values of thousands and thousands of individual items carefully selected to give a representative picture of the current market in antiques and collectables – and remember all values are prices actually paid, based on accurate sales records in the twelve months prior to publication from the best established and most highly respected auction houses and retail outlets in Europe and America.

This is THE book for the Professional Antiques Dealer. 'The Lyle Book' – we've even heard it called 'The Dealer's Bible'.

Compiled and published afresh each year, the Lyle Antiques Price Guide is the most comprehensive up-to-date antiques price guide available. THIS COULD BE YOUR WISEST INVESTMENT OF THE YEAR!

Anthony Curtis

While every care has been taken in the compiling of information contained in this volume, the publisher cannot accept liability for loss, financial or otherwise, incurred by reliance placed on the information herein.

All prices quoted in this book are obtained from a variety of auctions in various countries during the twelve months prior to publication and are converted to dollars at the rate of exchange prevalent at the time of sale.

The publishers wish to express their sincere thanks to the following for their involvement and assistance in the production of this volume.

ANTHONY CURTIS (Editor)

EELIN McIVOR (Sub Editor)

ANNETTE CURTIS (Editorial)

CATRIONA DAY (Art Production)

ANGIE DEMARCO (Art Production)

NICKY FAIRBURN (Art Production)

SHELLEY HAMILTON

PHILIP SPRINGTHORPE

CONTENTS

ACKNOWLEDGEMENTS

AB Stockholms Auktionsverk, Box 16256, 103 25 Stockholm, Sweden
Abbotts Auction Rooms, The Auction Rooms, Campsea Ash, Woodbridge, Suffolk
Academy Auctioneers, Northcote House, Northcote Avenue, Ealing, London W5 3UR
James Adam, 26, St Stephens Green, Dublin 2
Henry Aldridge & Son, Devizes Auction Rooms, Wine Street, Devizes SN10 1AP
Jean Claude Anaf, Lyon Brotteaux, 13 bis place Jules Ferry, 69456, Lyon, France
Anderson & Garland, Marlborough House, Marlborough Crescent, Newcastle upon Tyne NE1 4EE
Antique Collectors Club & Co. Ltd, 5 Church Street, Woodbridge, Suffolk IP12 1DS
Atlantic Antiques, Chenil House, 181–183 Kings Road, London SW3 5ED
The Auction Galleries, Mount Rd., Tweedmouth, Berwick on Tweed
Auction Team Köln, Postfach 50 11 68, D-5000 Köln 50, Germany
Auktionshaus Arnold, Bleichstr. 42, 6000 Frankfurt a/M, Germany
Barber's Auctions, Woking, Surrey
Bearne's, St Edmunds Court, Okehampton Street, Exeter EX4 1DU
Biddle & Webb, Ladywood Middleway, Birmingham B16 0PP
Bigwood, The Old School, Tiddington, Stratford upon Avon
Black Horse Agencies Ambrose, 149 High Street, Loughton, Essex 1G10 4LZ
Black Horse Agencies, Locke & England, 18 Guy Street, Leamington Spa
Boardman Fine Art Auctioneers, Station Road Corner, Haverhill, Suffolk CB9 0EY
JW Bollom, PO Box 78, Croydon Rd, Beckenham CR3 4BL
Bonhams, Montpelier Street, Knightsbridge, London SW7 1HH
Bonhams Chelsea, 65–69 Lots Road, London SW10 0RN
Bonhams West Country, Dowell Street, Honiton, Devon
Bosleys, 42 West Street, Marlow, Bucks SL7 1NB
Andrew Bottomley, The Coach House, Huddersfield Rd, Holmfirth, West Yorks.
Michael J. Bowman, 6 Haccombe House, Near Netherton, Newton Abbot, Devon
Bristol Auction Rooms, St John Place, Apsley Road, Clifton, Bristol BS8 2ST
British Antique Replicas, School Close, Queen Elizabeth Avenue, Burgess Hill, Sussex
Butchoff Antiques, 229–233 Westbourne Grove, London W11 2SE
Butterfield & Butterfield, 220 San Bruno Avenue , San Francisco CA 94103, USA
Butterfield & Butterfield, 7601 Sunset Boulevard, Los Angeles CA 90046, USA
Canterbury Auction Galleries, 40 Station Road West, Canterbury CT2 8AN
Central Motor Auctions, Barfield House, Britannia Road, Morley, Leeds, LS27 0HN
H.C. Chapman & Son, The Auction Mart, North Street, Scarborough.
Chapman Moore & Mugford, 8 High Street, Shaftesbury SP7 8JB
Cheffins Grain & Comins, 2 Clifton Road, Cambridge
Christie's (International) SA, 8 place de la Taconnerie, 1204 Genève, Switzerland
Christie's Monaco, S.A.M, Park Palace 98000 Monte Carlo, Monaco
Christie's Scotland, 164–166 Bath Street, Glasgow G2 4TG
Christie's South Kensington Ltd., 85 Old Brompton Road, London SW7 3LD
Christie's, 8 King Street, London SW1Y 6QT
Christie's East, 219 East 67th Street, New York, NY 10021, USA
Christie's, 502 Park Avenue, New York, NY10022, USA
Christie's, Cornelis Schuytstraat 57, 1071 JG Amsterdam, Netherlands
Christie's SA Roma, 114 Piazza Navona, 00186 Rome, Italy
Christie's Swire, 2804–6 Alexandra House, 16–20 Chater Road, Hong Kong
Christie's Australia Pty Ltd., 1 Darling Street, South Yarra, Victoria 3141, Australia
Bryan Clisby, Andwells Antiques, Hartley Wintney, North Hants.
A J Cobern, The Grosvenor Sales Rooms, 93b Eastbank Street, Southport PR8 1DG
The Collector, 9 Church St, Marylebone, London NW8 8EE
Collins Antiques, Wheathampstead, St Albans AL4 8AP
Cooper Hirst Auctions, The Granary Saleroom, Victoria Road, Chelmsford, Essex CM2 6LH
Coppelia Antiques, Holford Lodge, Plumley, Cheshire.
The Crested China Co., Station House, Driffield, E. Yorks YO25 7PY
Cundalls, The Cattle Market, 17 Market Square, Malton, N. Yorks.
Clifford Dann, 20/21 High Street, Lewes, Sussex
Dargate Auction Galleries, 5607 Baum Blvd., Pittsburgh PA 15206
Julian Dawson, Lewes Auction Rooms, 56 High Street, Lewes BN7 1XE
Dee & Atkinson & Harrison, The Exchange Saleroom, Driffield, Nth Humberside YO25 7LJ
Garth Denham & Assocs. Horsham Auction Galleries, Warnsham, Nr. Horsham, Sussex
Diamond Mills & Co., 117 Hamilton Road, Felixstowe, Suffolk
David Dockree Fine Art, The Redwood Suite, Clemence House, Mellor Road, Cheadle Hulme, Cheshire
Dorking Desk Shop, 41 West Street, Dorking, Surrey
William Doyle Galleries, 175 East 87th Street, New York, NY 10128, USA
Downer Ross, Charter House, 42 Avebury Boulevard, Central Milton Keynes MK9 2HS
Dreweatt Neate, Donnington Priory, Newbury, Berks.

Dreweatt Neate, Holloways, 49 Parsons Street, Banbury
Hy. Duke & Son, 40 South Street, Dorchester, Dorset
Du Mouchelles Art Galleries Co., 409 E. Jefferson Avenue, Detroit, Michigan 48226, USA
Sala de Artes y Subastas Durán, Serrano 12, 28001 Madrid, Spain
Eldred's, Box 796, E. Dennis, MA 02641, USA
R H Ellis & Sons, 44/46 High Street, Worthing, BN11 1LL
Enchanted House, 18–24 The Roundhouse Industrial Estate, Harbour Road, Par, Cornwall
Ewbanks, Burnt Common Auction Rooms, London Road, Send, Woking GU23 7LN
Fellows & Son, Augusta House, 19 Augusta Street, Hockley, Birmingham
Fidler Taylor & Co., Crown Square, Matlock, Derbyshire DE4 3AT
Finarte, 20121 Milano, Piazzetta Bossi 4, Italy
John D Fleming & Co., The North Devon Auction Rooms, The Savory, South Molton, Devon
Peter Francis,19 King Street, Carmarthen, Dyfed
Fraser Pinney's, 8290 Devonshire, Montreal, Quebec, Canada H4P 2PZ
Galerie Koller, Rämistr. 8, CH 8024 Zürich, Switzerland
Galerie Moderne, 3 rue du Parnasse, 1040 Bruxelles, Belgium
GB Antiques Centre, Lancaster Leisure Park, Wynesdale Rd, Lancaster LA1 3LA
Geering & Colyer (Black Horse Agencies) Highgate, Hawkhurst, Kent
The Goss and Crested China Co., 62 Murray Road, Horndean, Hants PO8 9JL
The Grandfather Clock Shop, Little House, Sheep Street, Stow on the Wold 9L54 1AA
Graves Son & Pilcher, Hove Auction Rooms, Hove Street, Hove, East Sussex
Greenslade Hunt, Magdalene House, Church Square, Taunton, Somerset, TA1 1SB
The Gurney Collection
Halifax Property Services, 53 High Street, Tenterden, Kent
Hampton's Fine Art, 93 High Street, Godalming, Surrey
Hanseatisches Auktionshaus für Historica, Neuer Wall 57, 2000 Hamburg 36, Germany
William Hardie Ltd., 141 West Regent Street, Glasgow G2 2SG
Andrew Hartley Fine Arts, Victoria Hall, Little Lane, Ilkely
Hastings Antiques Centre, 59–61 Norman Road, St Leonards on Sea, East Sussex
Hauswedell & Nolte, D-2000 Hamburg 13, Pöseldorfer Weg 1, Germany
Giles Haywood, The Auction House, St John's Road, Stourbridge, West Midlands, DY8 1EW
Muir Hewitt, Halifax Antiques Centre, Queens Road/Gibbet Street, Halifax HX1 4LR
Hobbs & Chambers, 'At the Sign of the Bell', Market Place, Cirencester, Glos
Hobbs Parker, New Ashford Market, Monument Way, Orbital Park, Ashford TN24 0HB
Holloways, 49 Parsons Street, Banbury OX16 8PF
Hotel de Ventes Horta, 390 Chaussée de Waterloo (Ma Campagne), 1060 Bruxelles, Belgium
Hubbard Antiques, 16 St Margarets Green, Ipswich IP4 2BS
Jackson's, 2229 Lincoln Street, Cedar Falls, Iowa 50613, USA.
Jacobs & Hunt, Lavant Street, Petersfield, Hants. GU33 3EF
P Herholdt Jensens Auktioner, Rundforbivej 188, 2850 Nerum, Denmark
Kennedy & Wolfenden, 218 Lisburn Road, Belfast BT9 6GD
G A Key, Aylsham Saleroom, Palmers Lane, Aylsham, Norfolk, NR11 6EH
George Kidner, The Old School, The Square, Pennington, Lymington, Hants SO41 8GN
Kunsthaus am Museum, Drususgasse 1–5, 5000 Köln 1, Germany
Kunsthaus Lempertz, Neumarkt 3, 5000 Köln 1, Germany
Lambert & Foster (County Group), The Auction Sales Room, 102 High Street, Tenterden, Kent
W.H. Lane & Son, 64 Morrab Road, Penzance, Cornwall, TR18 8AB
Langlois Ltd., Westaway Rooms, Don Street, St Helier, Channel Islands
Lawrence Butler Fine Art Salerooms, Marine Walk, Hythe, Kent, CT21 5AJ
Lawrence Fine Art, South Street, Crewkerne, Somerset TA18 8AB
Lawrence's Fine Art Auctioneers, Norfolk House, 80 High Street, Bletchingley, Surrey
David Lay, The Penzance Auction House, Alverton, Penzance, Cornwall TA18 4KE
Gordon Litherland, 26 Stapenhill Road, Burton on Trent
Lloyd International Auctions, 118 Putney Bridge Road, London SW15 2NQ
Brian Loomes, Calf Haugh Farm, Pateley Bridge, North Yorks
Lots Road Chelsea Auction Galleries, 71 Lots Road, Chelsea, London SW10 0RN
R K Lucas & Son, Tithe Exchange, 9 Victoria Place, Haverfordwest, SA61 2JX
Duncan McAlpine, Stateside Comics plc, 125 East Barnet Road, London EN4 8RF
McCartneys, Portcullis Salerooms, Ludlow, Shropshire
John Mann, Bruntshielbog, Canonbie, Dumfries DG14 0RY
Christopher Matthews, 23 Mount Street, Harrogate HG2 8DG
John Maxwell, 133a Woodford Road, Wilmslow, Cheshire
May & Son, 18 Bridge Street, Andover, Hants
Morphets, 4–6 Albert Street, Harrogate, North Yorks HG1 1JL
Neales, The Nottingham Saleroom, 192 Mansfield Road, Nottingham NG1 3HU
D M Nesbit & Co, 7 Clarendon Road, Southsea, Hants PO5 2ED

John Nicholson, Longfield, Midhurst Road, Fernhurst GU27 3HA
The Old Brigade, 10a Harborough Rd, Kingsthorpe, Northampton NN1 7AZ
The Old Cinema, 157 Tower Bridge Rd, London SE1 3LW
Old Mill Antiques Centre, Mill Street, Low Town, Bridgnorth, Shropshire
Onslow's, The Depot, 2 Michael Road, London, SW6 2AD
Outhwaite & Litherland, Kingsley Galleries, Fontenoy Street, Liverpool, Merseyside L3 2BE
Pendulum of Mayfair, 51 Maddox Street, London W1
Phillips Manchester, Trinity House, 114 Northenden Road, Sale, Manchester M33 3HD
Phillips Son & Neale SA, 10 rue des Chaudronniers, 1204 Genève, Switzerland
Phillips West Two, 10 Salem Road, London W2 4BL
Phillips, 11 Bayle Parade, Folkestone, Kent CT20 1SQ
Phillips, 49 London Road, Sevenoaks, Kent TN13 1UU
Phillips, 65 George Street, Edinburgh EH2 2JL
Phillips, Blenstock House, 7 Blenheim Street, New Bond Street, London W1Y 0AS
Phillips Marleybone, Hayes Place, Lisson Grove, London NW1 6UA
Phillips, New House, 150 Christleton Road, Chester CH3 5TD
Andrew Pickford, 42 St Andrew Street, Hertford SG14 1JA
Pieces of Time, 1–7 Davies Mews, Unit 17–19, London W17 1AR
Pooley & Rogers, Regent Auction Rooms, Abbey Street, Penzance
Pretty & Ellis, Amersham Auction Rooms, Station Road, Amersham, Bucks
Harry Ray & Co, Lloyds Bank Chambers, Welshpool, Montgomery SY21 7RR
Peter M Raw, Thornfield, Hurdle Way, Compton Down, Winchester, Hants SC21 2AN
Remmey Galleries, 30 Maple Street, Summit, NJ 07901
Rennie's, 1 Agincourt Street, Monmouth
Riddetts, 26 Richmond Hill, Bournemouth
Ritchie's, 429 Richmond Street East, Toronto, Canada M5A 1R1
Derek Roberts Antiques, 24–25 Shipbourne Road, Tonbridge, Kent TN10 3DN
Rogers de Rin, 79 Royal Hospital Road, London SW3 4HN
Romsey Auction Rooms, 56 The Hundred, Romsey, Hants 5051 8BX
Russell, Baldwin & Bright, The Fine Art Saleroom, Ryelands Road, Leominster HR6 8JG
Schrager Auction Galleries, 2915 N Sherman Boulevard, PO Box 10390, Milwaukee WI 53210, USA
Selkirk's, 4166 Olive Street, St Louis, Missouri 63108, USA
Skinner Inc., Bolton Gallery, Route 117, Bolton MA, USA
Allan Smith, Amity Cottage 162 Beechcroft Rd. Upper Stratton, Swindon, Wilts.
Soccer Nostalgia, Albion Chambers, Birchington, Kent CT7 9DN
Sotheby's, 34–35 New Bond Street, London W1A 2AA
Sotheby's, 1334 York Avenue, New York NY 10021
Sotheby's, 112 George Street, Edinburgh EH2 2LH
Sotheby's, Summers Place, Billingshurst, West Sussex RH14 9AD
Sotheby's, Monaco, BP 45, 98001 Monte Carlo
Southgate Auction Rooms, 55 High Street, Southgate, London N14 6LD
Spink & Son Ltd., 5–7 King Street, St James's, London SW1Y 6QS
Michael Stainer Ltd., St Andrews Auction Rooms, Wolverton Rd, Boscombe, Bournemouth BH7 6HT
Michael Stanton, 7 Rowood Drive, Solihull, West Midlands B92 9LT
Street Jewellery, 5 Runnymede Road, Ponteland, Northumbria NE20 9HE
Stride & Son, Southdown House, St John's Street, Chichester, Sussex
G E Sworder & Son, 14 Cambridge Road, Stansted Mountfitchet, Essex CM24 8BZ
Taviner's of Bristol, Prewett Street, Redcliffe, Bristol BS1 6PB
Tennants, Harmby Road, Leyburn, Yorkshire
Thomson Roddick & Laurie, 24 Lowther Street, Carlisle
Thomson Roddick & Laurie, 60 Whitesands, Dumfries
Thimbleby & Shorland, 31 Gt Knollys Street, Reading RG1 7HU
Tool Shop Auctions, 78 High Street, Needham Market, Suffolk IP6 8AW
Truro Auction Centre, City Wharf, Malpas Rd., Truro TR1 1QH
Tweedales, 8 Royal Parade, Harrogate HG1 2SZ
Venator & Hanstein, Cäcilienstr. 48, 5000 Köln 1, Germany
T Vennett Smith, 11 Nottingham Road, Gotham, Nottingham NG11 0HE
Garth Vincent, The Old Manor House, Allington, nr. Grantham, Lincs. NG32 2DH
Wallis & Wallis, West Street Auction Galleries, West Street, Lewes, E. Sussex BN7 2NJ
Walter's 1 Mint Lane, Lincoln LN1 1UD
Wells Cundall Nationwide Anglia, Staffordshire House, 27 Flowergate, Whitby YO21 3AX
West Street Antiques, 63 West Street, Dorking, Surrey
Whitworths, 32–34 Wood Street, Huddersfield HD1 1DX
Peter Wilson, Victoria Gallery, Market Street, Nantwich, Cheshire CW5 5DG
Wintertons Ltd., Lichfield Auction Centre, Fradley Park, Lichfield, Staffs WS13 8NF
Woltons, 6 Whiting Street, Bury St Edmunds, Suffolk 1P33 1PB
Woolley & Wallis, The Castle Auction Mart, Salisbury, Wilts SP1 3SU
Worthing Auction Galleries, 31 Chatsworth Road, Worthing, W. Sussex BN11 1LY

ANTIQUES
REVIEW
1999

T HE Lyle Antiques Price Guide is compiled and published with completely fresh information annually, enabling you to begin each new year with an up-to-date knowledge of the current trends, together with the verified values of antiques of all descriptions.

We have endeavored to obtain a balance between the more expensive collector's items and those which, although not in their true sense antiques, are handled daily by the antiques trade.

The illustrations and prices in the following sections have been arranged to make it easy for the reader to assess the period and value of all items with speed.

You will find illustrations for almost every category of antique and curio, together with a corresponding price collated during the last twelve months, from the auction rooms and retail outlets of the major trading countries.

When dealing with the more popular trade pieces, in some instances, a calculation of an average price has been estimated from the varying accounts researched.

As regards prices, when 'one of a pair' is given in the description the price quoted is for a pair and so that we can make maximum use of the available space it is generally considered that one illustration is sufficient.

It will be noted that in some descriptions taken directly from sales catalogues originating from many different countries, terms such as bureau, secretary and davenport are used in a broader sense than is customary, but in all cases the term used is self explanatory.

A Robertson's 1960s illuminated figure, modeled walking wearing red trousers, blue jacket and beige waistcoat, 70cm. high.
(Christie's) $2,576

Handpainted fish-form sign, *Oscar Peterson's Fish Decoys Sold Here*, possibly by Oscar Peterson, 52in. long.
(Eldred's) $1,760

A window display doll, McCoy's Cherokee Smoking Mixture, in the form of a PVC American Indian figure, the motor moves the head and raises the arm with the pipe, 84cm. high. (Auction Team Köln)
$102

An early three colored lithograph poster for the Pittsburg Visible typewriter, by Carl Schnebel, circa 1900, 48 x 71cm.
(Auction Team Köln) $487

A set of three Carltonware Guinness advertising toucans painted in black, white, yellow, red and peach, graduating from 10in. to 6½in.
(Christie's) $320

An enamel sign for Gerster sewing machines, Reutlingen, printed in four colors, 49 x 74cm.
(Auction Team Köln) $160

Morris Trucks, a scarce enameled garage advertising sign depicting radiator motif design, full-color enamel cut-out format, circa 1920s.
(Christie's) $712

Guinness Time, an advertising pocket watch, the face inscribed and printed with a smiling pint.
(Christie's) $730

An enamel sign for Singer sewing machines, in seven colors, by the Frankfurt Enamel Works, 58 x 88cm.
(Auction Team Köln) $218

An advertising teddy bear figure for Pustefix, of yellow plush with glass eyes, air pump operated moving arm, circa 1960, 62cm. high.
(Auction Team Köln) $160

Small painted double sided Tea Room sign, America, 19th century, a black molded frame, 16½in. high.
(Skinner) $3,795

Painted tin violin-form trade sign, 19th century, in red with *Instruments de Musique J. Dussoir* in black letters, 19¾in. long, 10in. wide.
(Eldred's) $605

Marius Rossillon (O'Galop), Nunc est Bibendum, lithograph in colors, 1896, printed by Cornille & Serre, Paris, backed on linen, 61 x 46in.
(Christie's) $10,120

A 19th century Dresden group advertising Yardley's Old English Lavender, depicting a mother and two children carrying baskets of lavender, 12in. high.
(H.C. Chapman & Son) $675

Marius Rossillon (O'Galop), (1867–1946), Le Coup de la Semelle Michelin, lithograph in colors, 1913, printed by Affiches Camis, Paris, on four sheets, 126 x 94in.
(Christie's) $6,992

Guinness advertising enamel sign, rectangular, depicting the drayman, 51cm. high. (Christie's) $208

A Contin poster designed by Gaston Maréchaux, Paris, four-colored lithograph on linen, circa 1925, 60 x 80cm.
(Auction Team Köln) $373

An Allcock fishing tackle display board for the International Fisheries Exhibition 1883, Bronze Medal winner for a 'General Collection of Fishing Tackle', 31in. high.
(Christie's) $3,216

French beauty parlor sign, 19th century, in green and yellow painted iron, double-sided *Coiffeur Service Antiseptique* and *Coiffure de Dames*, 25in. high.
(Eldred's) $330

Milliner's painted iron trade sign, 19th century, 12in. high.
(Skinner) $1,150

'Strike Out Foreign Competition By Buying England's Glory Matches', a lithographed metal sheet showing a boxing match, 18½ x 26½in.
(David Lay) $596

A toyshop advertising poster, 'A La Place Clichy 7 Décembre Étrennes Jouets', French, circa 1900, lithograph, signed *E. Vavasseur,* 36 x 59in., linen backed.
(Sotheby's) $1,457

An original Coca-Cola freezer box, rare pre-war model with two flaps, and electric cooling motor, circa 1938, 105cm. wide.
(Auction Team Köln) $1,016

Noel Fontanet (1898–1982), Adler, lithograph in colors, circa 1935, printed by Sonor S.A., Genève, backed on linen, 50 x 35½in.
(Christie's) $478

John Gilroy, My Goodness My Guinness lithograph in colors, circa 1947, printed by Sanders Phillips & Co., Ltd, London, 30 x 20in.
(Christie's) $1,435

The Graphophone Grand, original display by Sears Roebuck & Co. Chicago, circa 1900, 36.5 x 55.5cm.
(Auction Team Köln) $614

Dick Wilkinson (Wilk), My Goodness My Guinness, lithograph in colors, 1958, printed by Mills & Rockleys Production Ltd., Ipswich, 30 x 20in.
(Christie's) $827

A WW1 period Fokker Eindecker model, possibly by a factory apprentice, 34cm. wingspan.
(Sotheby's) $874

A model propeller driven bi-plane with pilot and gunner, 62in. wing span.
(Ewbank) $1,034

A B type helmet, size 2, with A.M. label, together with a D type mask fitted with 1941 pattern microphone.
(Sotheby's) $461

A Luftwaffe leather flying suit, by Karl Hohenstein, Crailsheim, with sheepskin lining, 1943.
(Auction Team Köln) $323

A scarce, Battle, of Britain period 'Spitfire Fund' collecting box, the top applied with a label bearing stamped/inscribed dates, together with monetary totals, 24 x 19 x 11cm.
(Sotheby's) $388

The flight overalls of Group Captain M.M. Stephens, D.S.O., D.F.C. and 2 Bars, worn by him during the fall of France, The Battle of Britain, in the Western Desert and Malta.
(Sotheby's) $1,749

H. Steiner, Flugtag Bazar, lithograph in colors, 1913, printed by Huber, Anacker u. Cie., Aarau-Luzern, backed on japan, 39 x 27in.
(Christie's) $2,208

A tail turret from a Whitley Mk. V, retaining some perspex to one side panel, front and top, with access doors and section of armor plate, 42in. high.
(Sotheby's) $525

CHP?, Aulnay-Sous-Bois, lithograph in colors, circa 1910, printed by E. Verneau & H. Chachoins, Paris, backed on linen, 58 x 37in.
(Christie's) $1,435

A wheel believed to be from H.M. Airship No. 1, 'The Mayfly', circa 1911, in mahogany with cast metal spokes and frame, 28in. wide overall, sold with a period photograph.
(Sotheby's) $9,218

A WWII R.A.F. operations room clock, by F.W. Elliott Ltd., dial with crest and red, purple and yellow 5 minute sectors, dated 1939, with pendulum.
(Sotheby's) $2,062

An early bomb-release mechanism, possibly from a small airship or WWI period aircraft, with small fabric label inscribed *Zeppelin Bomb Release*, 12in. high.
(Sotheby's) $998

A WWI 'Combats in the Air' report, signed by Major Edward 'Mick' Mannock, dated 13th July 1918.
(Sotheby's) $2,040

A Spitfire instrument panel display, the modern panel fitted with correct instruments.
(Sotheby's) $848

A rare R.N.A.S. pilot's flying log book, relating to E.E. Renaut, an airship crew member, the cover stamped *Naval Airship Station 14 Dec 1917 Wormwood Scrubs*.
(Sotheby's) $712

A Luftwaffe summer weight flying helmet, with original label, complete with throat microphone, and a pair of 'Leitz' pattern goggles.
(Sotheby's) $287

A 1940 Air Ministry bell, cast with Crown, initials and date, with clapper and attached to wrought iron bracket, bell 10¾in. diameter.
(Sotheby's) $1,361

A rare 'Warren' style aviator's flying helmet, brown hardened leather shell with padded ring and leather ear flaps.
(Bosleys) $400

A Luftwaffe mesh flying helmet, Design Lkp N 101, of brown cloth and leather, sheepskin-lined earphones, 1942.
(Auction Team Köln) $91

A Smith's time of trip 24 hour panel clock, Mk.IIIB, WWII period, black dial with luminous numerals and hands, 3in. diameter.
(Sotheby's) $768

A D.H.4 four-bladed propeller, WWI period, tips with green-painted brass sheaths, boss with circular mirror, 120½in. diameter.
(Sotheby's) $1,875

A rare signed menu from a banquet celebrating Louis Blériot's cross-channel flight, held by La Colonie Française, London on 16th September 1909, the four-page card signed in pencil by the aviator on the front, 5½ x 8½in.
(Sotheby's) $922

L. Belloguet, Grande Semaine d'Aviation, lithograph in colors, 1909, printed by La Lithographie Artistique, Bruges, backed on linen, 47½ x 65in.
(Christie's) $4,416

Winston S. Churchill, signed B.E.A. silver wing menu, 25th September 1952, obtained when Churchill was flying to Nice by one of the cabin crew.
(Vennett-Smith) $495

A U.S. type G-1 flying jacket, by Ralph Edwards Sptswear, Inc., the back with artwork entitled The Great Speckled Bird.
(Sotheby's) $1,237

A C type helmet, late pattern, size 3, with non-original zippered earpieces housing type 32 (10A/13466) telephones and wiring.
(Sotheby's) $402

A U.S.A.A.F. type B-15 flying jacket, with original 5th Air Force patch to left shoulder, S.E.A.C. patch to the right, painted leather squadron patch to the left breast.
(Sotheby's) $412

Italian alabaster figure of Apollo, after the Antique, leaning against a tree stump, 29in. high. (Skinner) $977

A French alabaster group of Ariadne and the Panther, after Johann Heinrich von Dannecker, 19th century, 17¼in. high. (Bonhams) $795

An Italian alabaster bust of a young woman, by Antonio Frilli, late 19th century, her veiled face inclined to dexter, 27½in. high. (Bonhams) $3,180

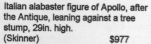

Italian alabaster seated maiden in a bronze Savonarola chair, circa 1880-1900, on a green marble base, 25½in. high. (Skinner) $3,735

A pair of Italian alabaster vases, late 18th/early 19th century, each with circular rim above a pierced waisted dome, 23½in. high. (Christie's) $24,817

A French alabaster bust of a mother and child, circa 1900, she wearing a shawl and with face upraised to sinister, signature R. Goloni, 21¼in. high. (Bonhams) $1,590

A South German partially painted alabaster relief of the Pieta, circa 1500, remainders of polychromy on Christ's head and on base, 6⅞ x 4⅝in. (Sotheby's) $4,025

Carder Steuben double etched mirror black on alabaster vase, large size classic form deeply cameo etched in Shelton foliate Art Deco pattern, 12in. high. (Skinner) $6,900

An alabaster urn on stand, mid 19th century, of campana form, with classical figures carved in relief, circa 188cm. high. (Sotheby's) $25,277

Woodlands Indian beaded saddle bag, deerskin, 17in. square. (Eldred's) $330

Pair of Woodlands Indian child's beaded moccasins. (Eldred's) $176

Pair of Woodlands Indian woman's moccasins. (Eldred's) $110

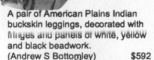

A large Hopi cottonwood kachina doll, probably representing 'The Ogre', with gesturing arms, wearing typical costume, 20in. high. (Sotheby's) $800

A pair of American Plains Indian buckskin leggings, decorated with fringes and panels of white, yellow and black beadwork. (Andrew S Bottomley) $592

Woodlands Indian handled beaded bag, deerskin, 10½ x 10in. (Eldred's) $440

Navajo rug, circa 1920, red and black on an off-white field, 37 x 58in. (Eldred's) $495

Navajo rug, early 20th century, red and black on an off-white field, 41 x 65in. (Eldred's) $330

A North American Indian ceremonial feather head dress, turkey feather plumage, felt crown with embroidered beadwork in patterns, ermine tails to band. (Wallis & Wallis) $239

A Northwest Coast hide suit, probably Nootka, composed of a fur-lined hooded jacket, pants and pair of boots, 59in. high. (Sotheby's) $1,725

A Washoe polychrome coiled basketry jar, finely woven on a single rod foundation in willow, redbud and brackenfern root, 10in. diameter. (Sotheby's) $1,495

A Bell-O-Matic games machine, the works by Mills, Chicago, possibly English case, with large side lever, circa 1960.
(Auction Team Köln) $646

A Fun amusement machine by Brenner of Croydon, black painted wooden case and silvered fittings, lamp holder for electric illumination.
(Auction Team Köln) $808

A Screen Star amusement machine by Mills, Chicago, the drum with film star names instead of symbols, skill button and large side lever, circa 1950. (Auction Team Köln) $550

A Mutoscope No. 2091, with advertising board, cast iron with green and gold decoration, with one roll, 164cm. high.
(Auction Team Köln) $5,873

A Flipper Broadway amusement machine by Bally, Chicago, 177cm. high,circa 1950.
(Auction Team Köln) $162

A cast-iron mussel shell Mutoscope, by the American Mutoscope and Biograph Co., New York, original gold and red paint, with one roll, circa 1890.
(Auction Team Köln) $2,872

An English penny-slide machine, wooden case with brass fittings, front lever, 82.5cm. high, 1920s.
(Auction Team Köln) $614

An English gaming machine, wooden case, brass chute, Christmas decorations of holly and bells, 58cm. wide, 1920s.
(Auction Team Köln) $614

A Ben Hur amusement machine by Caille Bros., Detroit, produced from 1908 until the 1930s, 60cm. high.
(Auction Team Köln) $1,746

A Greek bronze mirror, with border of egg-and-dart motifs and guilloche within beaded rim, 3rd century B.C., 6¼in. diam.
(Bonhams) $2,941

A bronze trefoil-lipped oinochoe, the handle with stylized lion head at the rim and paw at the lower terminal, circa 1st century B.C., 7¾in. and a bronze ladle.
(Bonhams) $1,245

A Boeotian terracotta figure of a horse of stylized form with tail repaired, 5th century B.C., 4¾in. high.
(Bonhams) $726

A Hellenistic dark blue core-formed glass amphoriskos, decorated in opaque blue and yellow trailed decoration, circa 2nd-1st century B.C., 4in. high.
(Bonhams) $2,226

A Proto-Elamite bronze jar with flared sides, on a narrow flattened foot and a smaller undecorated example, circa 3000 B.C., 3in. high.
(Bonhams) $826

An Egyptian fragmentary limestone relief showing a Lector priest, indicated by the hieroglyph above, 26th Dynasty, 664-525 B.C., 8¼in. x 41¼in.
(Bonhams) $697

A red-slip ware amphoriskos, decorated with an appliqué of a couple in erotic embrace, Roman North Africa, 3rd century A.D., 6½in.
(Bonhams) $3,652

An Etruscan Bucchero Ware stemmed chalice set on a flared foot with three grooves around the stem, circa 600-550 B.C., 5¾in. high.
(Bonhams) $2,158

A Sasanian cut glass bottle, the ovoid body with four rows of hexagonal and pentagonal facets, circa 6th century A.D., 3in.
(Bonhams) $1,826

A Roman lead sarcophagus with arched lid, decorated in raised relief, with a frieze of Corinthian columns, 2nd-3rd century A.D., 68 x 20½ x 16¼in.
(Bonhams) $8,063

An Egyptian bronze ibis head with long, curved beak, the eyes hollowed for inlay, Late Period, after 500 B.C., 8in. long.
(Bonhams) $1,613

A Pre-Dynastic slate palette styled as a fish with notched mouth and tail and incised lines, circa 4000-3600 B.C., 6¾in. long.
(Bonhams) $531

A Middle Kingdom circular terracotta offering tray, the larger section with two channels pierced as a run-off for liquids, circa 2050–1786 B.C., 17in. diam.
(Bonhams) $968

A Roman stucco painted fresco in two registers, the lower in bright red with a hound chasing a deer, circa 1st century A.D., 7½in. x 8in.
(Bonhams) $2,258

A Pre-Dynastic black-topped pottery bowl with flat base and gently sloping sides, Nubia, circa 5000–4000 B.C., 6⅛in. diam.
(Bonhams) $564

A large Cypriot Iron Age bichrome ware amphora decorated with two rows of concentric circles around the shoulder, 1050–750 B.C., 25in.
(Bonhams) $4,450

A Roman marble fragmentary female head from a relief, her hair emerging from underneath her diadem, circa 3rd century A.D., 3¼in. high.
(Bonhams) $1,451

A Roman clear blown glass beaker on a pad foot, the body decorated with vertical ribbing, circa 3rd century A.D., 4³⁄₈in.
(Bonhams) $564

A Roman fragmentary hollow bronze left hand, the index finger almost straight, the others bent inwards, circa 1st century A.D., 3½in. long.
(Bonhams) $645

A Roman marble relief fragment carved in the late Archaic style, with naked Apollo on the right, holding a lyre, circa 2nd century A.D., 21½ x 10¾in.
(Bonhams) $5,406

A British Bronze Age copper alloy flat axe with rounded butt, hammered over with crescentic curved cutting edge, early 2nd Millennium B.C., 6⁷⁄₈in. long.
(Bonhams) $6,678

A Roman mosaic glass patella cup, composed of opaque red, yellow and white floral canes set in an amethyst matrix, 1st century B.C./A.D., 1¾in. high. (Bonhams) $6,360

An Egyptian limestone relief fragment, inscribed in raised relief with the hieroglyphic titles of Alexander the Great, after 332 B.C., 28 x 16in. (Bonhams) $7,418

A Roman marble profile head of a bridled horse, the mouth slightly open to take the bit, circa 2nd–3rd century A.D., 7¼in. long. (Bonhams) $1,000

A calcite rectangular four-legged offering table with facing bull's heads carved at one end, circa 5th Millennium B.C., 6½in. long. (Bonhams) $2,258

A Roman marble monumental carving of a bull's head with carved eyes and pupils, circa 2nd–3rd century A.D., 19½in. long. (Bonhams) $9,858

An Egyptian limestone relief fragment with the head of Horus as a falcon in profile, Ptolemaic Period, circa 304–30 B.C., 7¹/8 x 7in. (Bonhams) $3,225

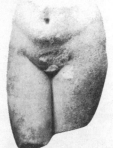

A Roman marble fragment of a naked female lower torso, her right leg slightly forward, circa 2nd century A.D., 5¹/8in. high. (Bonhams) $1,290

A Campanian Red-Figure bell krater showing on side A: a standing female wearing a chiton and wreath, 4th century B.C., 10¼in. high. (Bonhams) $2,338

A Roman marble stela showing a seated female, her himation partially covering her head, circa 2nd century A.D., 14in. high. (Bonhams) $2,096

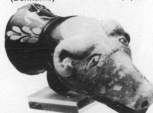

A South Italian Red-Figure Rhyton styled as a ram's head, decorated with the figure of a naked male, 4th century B.C., 9½in. long. (Bonhams) $1,290

A complete Ur III clay tablet with a cuneiform inscription for a receipt of barley received by different named people, 21st century B.C., 3¹/8 x 1⁷/8in. (Bonhams) $1,451

An Etruscan terracotta antefix molded with the facing head of Silenus within a shell niche, 6th century B.C., 7¾in. (Bonhams) $631

A full armor in German Maximilian style, 19th century, hinged visor embossed with a grotesque mask in the manner of Konrad Seusenhofer of Innsbruck.
(Sotheby's) $13,800

An embossed full armor for man and horse in the style of the second half of the 16th century, mostly 19th century, with 16th century small elements.
(Sotheby's) $28,750

A fine miniature armor in the late 16th century German style, 19th century, complete with a swept-hilt rapier with scabbard, 23in.
(Sotheby's) $6,612

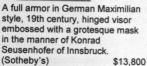

A German fluted full armor in early 'Maximilian' style, 19th century, including a closed helmet with plain skull.
(Sotheby's) $3,162

A miniature armor for man and horse, late 19th century, modeled after the style of the second quarter of the 16th century, height of horse and figure 29½in.
(Sotheby's) $7,475

A German cuirassier armor of blackened steel, circa 1620-30, outer edges turned and predominantly plain throughout.
(Sotheby's) $19,550

An etched half-armor in the style of the third quarter of the 16th century, close helmet, of pronounced 'sparrow's beak' form with stepped centrally divided vision slit, all in the south German style, on a wooden stand. (Sotheby's) $5,888

A composite German armor, mid-16th century, comprising collar, breast-plate, a skirt lame (replaced), movable gussets, early 16th century Italian tassets. (Sotheby's) $6,256

A composite German cuirassier armor, circa 1630, with 19th century blackened finish throughout, on a wooden stand. (Sotheby's) $7,728

A German black-and-white infantry armor, circa 1560, with associated burgonet of mid-17th century construction. (Sotheby's) $7,475

An English pikeman's composite armor, mid-17th century, including pot helmet formed in two halves joined by a low comb. (Sotheby's) $4,600

A full suit of armor, 67½in., comprising close helmet, gorget, articulated pauldrons and enarmes, mitten gauntlets, breastplate, embossed tassets, legharnesses. (Wallis & Wallis) $1,760

A pair of fingered gauntlets, late 16th/early 17th century, each with flared pointed cuff with inner plate, 11¾in. (Sotheby's) $6,900

An extremely rare early parrying manifer, an exchange-piece for the German foot tournament, circa 1500–30, made in one piece for carrying over the left forearm, 24in. (Sotheby's) $17,250

A rare pair of late gothic mitten gauntlets, South German or Austrian (Innsbruck), circa 1490-1500, each with flared gutter-shaped short cuff with medial ridge, 11in. (Sotheby's) $8,050

A mid 17th century Indo Persian chain-mail shirt, with laminar steel plate reinforcements signed on both breastplates, Arabic inscription. (Bonhams) $1,056

A good heavy 17th century Indian mail and lamellar shirt of good quality, 9.6kg., large rectangular front plates applied with six fish shaped buckles. (Wallis & Wallis) $1,243

A contemporary miniature full armor accurately modeled on the Italian style of circa 1460, with visored sallet and two-piece bevor, on metal and wooden stand, 18in. high. (Sotheby's) $1,840

A set of cavalry trooper's breast and backplates, circa 1800, steel stud decoration to borders. (Wallis & Wallis) $640

French Cuirassier's helmet and cuirass, breastplate of heavy polished steel with ten brass studs to the front. (Bosleys) $2,440

A good Household Cavalry other rank's polished cuirass, brass edge binding and studs, leather backed shoulder scales. (Wallis & Wallis) $800

A Japanese face mask mempo, black lacquered with red interior, removeable nose, embossed ears. (Wallis & Wallis) $840

A fine heavy 17th century Indian chainmail and lamellar shirt, the mail of alternate rows of thickly forged solid rings and riveted rings. (Wallis & Wallis) $912

One of a matched pair of Cuirassier trooper's back and breast plates, of bright polished steel complete with original retaining straps. (Bonhams)   (Two) $1,056

Continental steel suit of armor, late 19th century, together with several accessories. (Skinner) $2,185

A good heavy 17th century Indian mail and lamellar shirt, 9.86kg, mail of alternate rows of solid and rivetted links of assorted sizes, long sleeves and skirt, square collar. (Wallis & Wallis) $1,040

A Nimai omadaka-odoshi-do tosei-gusoku, late 19th century, the fifty-six plate russet iron suji-bachi-kabuto of steep sided rounded form. (Christie's) $20,800

An English Civil War period cavalry trooper's breastplate, of typical form with musket ball proof, medial ridge, stamped with Commonwealth and London armorer's marks. (Wallis & Wallis) $572

An unusual Indo Persian chainmail shirt, made of small riveted rings, long sleeves with butted brass rings to cuffs. (Wallis & Wallis) $1,120

A French curassier's breast- and back-plate, 19th century, complete with original brass and leather straps, the interior of the breast-plate etched 'Manuf. R.ale de Klingenthal, Julitte, 1830'. (Bonhams) $723

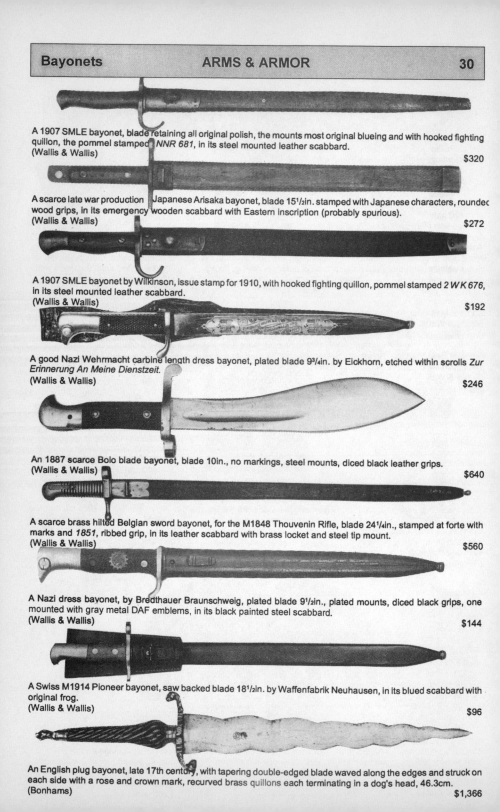

A 1907 SMLE bayonet, blade retaining all original polish, the mounts most original blueing and with hooked fighting quillon, the pommel stamped *NNR 681*, in its steel mounted leather scabbard.
(Wallis & Wallis)
$320

A scarce late war production Japanese Arisaka bayonet, blade 15¹/₂in. stamped with Japanese characters, rounded wood grips, in its emergency wooden scabbard with Eastern inscription (probably spurious).
(Wallis & Wallis)
$272

A 1907 SMLE bayonet by Wilkinson, issue stamp for 1910, with hooked fighting quillon, pommel stamped *2 W K 676*, in its steel mounted leather scabbard.
(Wallis & Wallis)
$192

A good Nazi Wehrmacht carbine length dress bayonet, plated blade 9³/₄in. by Eickhorn, etched within scrolls *Zur Erinnerung An Meine Dienstzeit.*
(Wallis & Wallis)
$246

An 1887 scarce Bolo blade bayonet, blade 10in., no markings, steel mounts, diced black leather grips.
(Wallis & Wallis)
$640

A scarce brass hilted Belgian sword bayonet, for the M1848 Thouvenin Rifle, blade 24¹/₄in., stamped at forte with marks and *1851*, ribbed grip, in its leather scabbard with brass locket and steel tip mount.
(Wallis & Wallis)
$560

A Nazi dress bayonet, by Bredthauer Braunschweig, plated blade 9¹/₂in., plated mounts, diced black grips, one mounted with gray metal DAF emblems, in its black painted steel scabbard.
(Wallis & Wallis)
$144

A Swiss M1914 Pioneer bayonet, saw backed blade 18¹/₂in. by Waffenfabrik Neuhausen, in its blued scabbard with original frog.
(Wallis & Wallis)
$96

An English plug bayonet, late 17th century, with tapering double-edged blade waved along the edges and struck on each side with a rose and crown mark, recurved brass quillons each terminating in a dog's head, 46.3cm.
(Bonhams)
$1,366

A Nazi Police dress bayonet, plated blade 13in., by F.W. Holler, chrome plated mounts, stylized eagle's head slotted for rifle attachment, imitation staghorn grips.
(Wallis & Wallis) $288

An 1840 pattern constabulary carbine triangular socket bayonet, blade 13¼in., with inspection stamp and spring catch, socket marked *80*, in its brass mounted leather scabbard.
(Wallis & Wallis) $144

A Swiss M1914 Pioneer sword bayonet, saw backed blade 18¾in. stamped *HS*, in its blued steel scabbard.
(Wallis & Wallis) $80

A Brown Bess triangular socket bayonet, blade 17in. by I. Salter, Inspection stamp, socket with unusual double socket slot.
(Wallis & Wallis) $120

An 1875 pattern Martini Henry saw back bayonet, blade 18in. stamped at forte with crown above *AS* and knights head trade mark, steel mounts, diced black leather grips.
(Wallis & Wallis) $320

An 1842 Lovells triangular socket bayonet, blade 17in. by S. Hill & Son, inspection stamps, in its brass mounted leather scabbard.
(Wallis & Wallis) $160

A German 1898/05 Mauser Pioneer bayonet, saw backed blade by V.C. Schilling, Suhl, issue mark for 1915, semi muzzle ring, no flashguard, blade retains most polish, in its steel mounted leather scabbard.
(Wallis & Wallis) $136

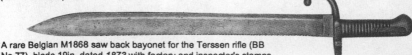

A rare Belgian M1868 saw back bayonet for the Terssen rifle (BB No.77), blade 19in. dated *1873* with factory and inspector's stamps, brass hilt with spring catch, steel guard.
(Wallis & Wallis) $232

An 1879 Artillery bayonet for the Martini Henry carbine, saw backed blade 26in., inspection stamps, issue mark for 1900, steel knucklebow, diced black leather grips, in its steel mounted leather scabbard.
(Wallis & Wallis) $288

A 54 bore English Beaumont Adams percussion revolver, serial number 2146/37047, retailed by Robert Adams, 76 King William Street, London, octagonal barrel, lever rammer, sliding safety bolt and checkered grip, complete in its original oak case, barrel 5¹/₂in.
(Andrew S Bottomley) $960

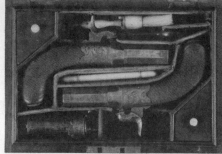

A cased pair of percussion pocket pistols, by W. Mills, approximately 50 bore (.48), with 1⁵/₈in. octagonal turn-off barrels decorated at breech and muzzle.
(Bonhams) $2,275

A very rare 120 bore William Tranter's patent double trigger five shot percussion revolver, retailed by A. Clayton, High Street, Southampton, with barleycorn foresight and notch rear sight, the frame engraved with acanthus foliage, barrel 3³/₄in.
(Andrew S Bottomley) $2,640

A 5 shot .31in. Colt Pocket single action percussion revolver No.208069, 9³/₄in., octagonal breech 5in. London proved, underlever rammer, cylinder roll engraved with stage coach hold up scene.
(Wallis & Wallis) $2,240

A 120 bore British six shot self cocking bar hammer percussion pepperbox revolver, circa 1850, the fluted barrel group with Birmingham proof marks, with recoil shield, scroll engraved side plates and plain varnished walnut grips, barrels 2¹/₂in.
(Andrew S Bottomley) $2,048

A very rare cased pair of Philadelphia style Deringer pocket pistols, the pistols and cased inscribed *W.F. Cody 1866*, with .41 calibre 2¹/₄in. rebrowned barrels, German silver fore-sights, case-hardened breeches inlaid with a pair of German silver bands, 5¹/₄in.
(Sotheby's) $17,250

A cased .31 seven-shot rimfire revolver of Tranter type, late 19th century, with blued octagonal sighted barrel, blued cylinder, scroll engraved brass frame and grip, bright hammer and enclosed trigger, figured checkered walnut grip-scales, 18.5cm.
(Bonhams) $879

A cased Sharp's Patent four-shot rimfire pocket pistol, 19th century, with blued forward-sliding sighted barrels, each rifled with three grooves, brass frame stamped *Tipping & Lawden - Sharp's Patent* one side, checkered hammer with revolving striker, 14.5cm.
(Bonhams) $639

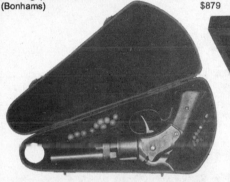

A 6 shot .28in. Maynards tape primed percussion revolver by the Massachusetts Arms Company, 7¼in., round tip up barrel 3in., top strap stamped *Mass Arms Co Chicopee Falls*, foliate engraved frame, two piece walnut grips.
(Wallis & Wallis) $1,080

A very rare 120 bore William Tranter's patent double action pocket revolver, with barleycorn foresight, notch rear sight, Tranter's patent rammer, scroll engraved frame, hook safety and checkered one piece walnut grip, barrel 3¾in.
(Andrew S Bottomley) $2,000

A book cased American .41 rim-fire colt Thuer derringer, No. 1159, circa 1870, with blued sighted barrel engraved '*Colt*' at the breech, 12.5cm.
(Bonham's) $884

A 28 bore double barreled over and under flintlock holster pistol by Grierson of London, 10in., octagonal twist barrels 5in., gold lined vents, roller bearing frizzen springs, engraved trigger guard, silver buttcap, checkered grip, vacant silver escutcheon.
(Wallis & Wallis) $2,720

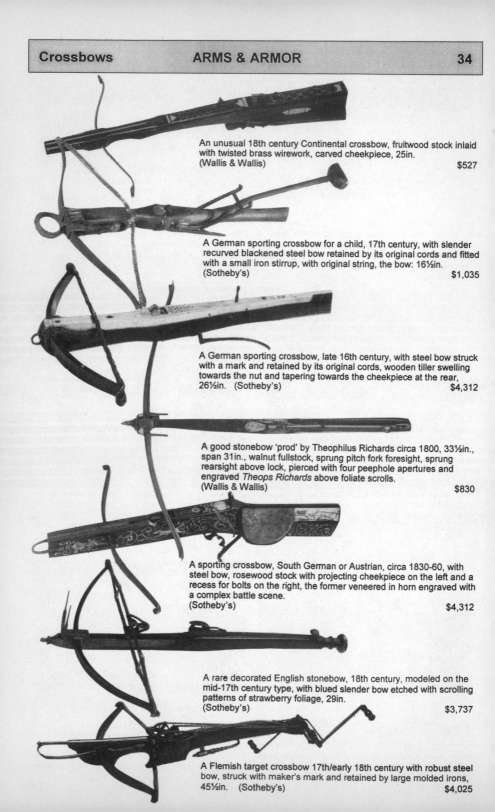

An unusual 18th century Continental crossbow, fruitwood stock inlaid with twisted brass wirework, carved cheekpiece, 25in. (Wallis & Wallis)

$527

A German sporting crossbow for a child, 17th century, with slender recurved blackened steel bow retained by its original cords and fitted with a small iron stirrup, with original string, the bow: 16½in. (Sotheby's)

$1,035

A German sporting crossbow, late 16th century, with steel bow struck with a mark and retained by its original cords, wooden tiller swelling towards the nut and tapering towards the cheekpiece at the rear, 26½in. (Sotheby's)

$4,312

A good stonebow 'prod' by Theophilus Richards circa 1800, 33½in., span 31in., walnut fullstock, sprung pitch fork foresight, sprung rearsight above lock, pierced with four peephole apertures and engraved *Theops Richards* above foliate scrolls. (Wallis & Wallis)

$830

A sporting crossbow, South German or Austrian, circa 1830-60, with steel bow, rosewood stock with projecting cheekpiece on the left and a recess for bolts on the right, the former veneered in horn engraved with a complex battle scene. (Sotheby's)

$4,312

A rare decorated English stonebow, 18th century, modeled on the mid-17th century type, with blued slender bow etched with scrolling patterns of strawberry foliage, 29in. (Sotheby's)

$3,737

A Flemish target crossbow 17th/early 18th century with robust steel bow, struck with maker's mark and retained by large molded irons, 45½in. (Sotheby's)

$4,025

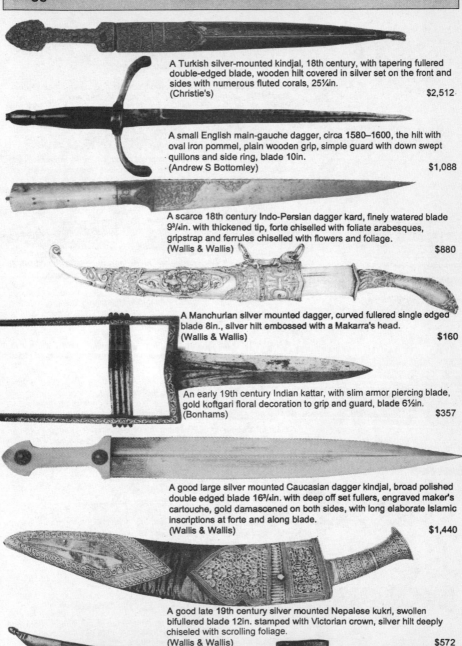

A Turkish silver-mounted kindjal, 18th century, with tapering fullered double-edged blade, wooden hilt covered in silver set on the front and sides with numerous fluted corals, 25¼in.
(Christie's) $2,512

A small English main-gauche dagger, circa 1580–1600, the hilt with oval iron pommel, plain wooden grip, simple guard with down swept quillons and side ring, blade 10in.
(Andrew S Bottomley) $1,088

A scarce 18th century Indo-Persian dagger kard, finely watered blade 9³/₄in. with thickened tip, forte chiselled with foliate arabesques, gripstrap and ferrules chiselled with flowers and foliage.
(Wallis & Wallis) $880

A Manchurian silver mounted dagger, curved fullered single edged blade 8in., silver hilt embossed with a Makarra's head.
(Wallis & Wallis) $160

An early 19th century Indian kattar, with slim armor piercing blade, gold koftgari floral decoration to grip and guard, blade 6½in.
(Bonhams) $357

A good large silver mounted Caucasian dagger kindjal, broad polished double edged blade 16³/₄in. with deep off set fullers, engraved maker's cartouche, gold damascened on both sides, with long elaborate Islamic inscriptions at forte and along blade.
(Wallis & Wallis) $1,440

A good late 19th century silver mounted Nepalese kukri, swollen bifullered blade 12in. stamped with Victorian crown, silver hilt deeply chiselled with scrolling foliage.
(Wallis & Wallis) $572

A Russian artillery kindjal, slightly curved, double fullered blade 17in., Imperial eagle stamp and date 1912 at forte, brass mounted wooden hilt.
(Wallis & Wallis) $224

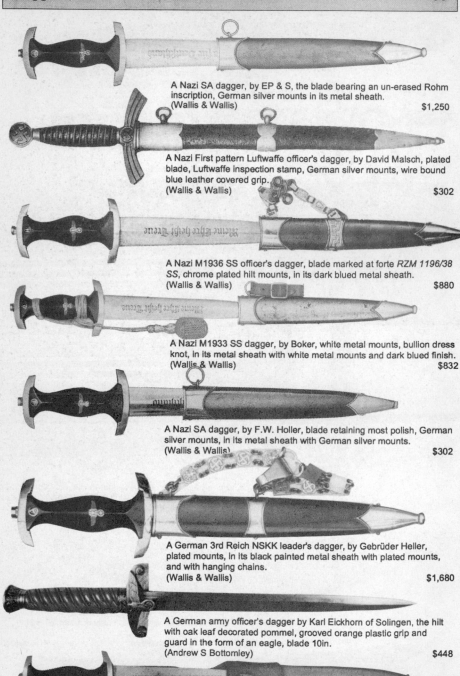

A Nazi SA dagger, by EP & S, the blade bearing an un-erased Rohm inscription, German silver mounts in its metal sheath.
(Wallis & Wallis) $1,250

A Nazi First pattern Luftwaffe officer's dagger, by David Malsch, plated blade, Luftwaffe inspection stamp, German silver mounts, wire bound blue leather covered grip.
(Wallis & Wallis) $302

A Nazi M1936 SS officer's dagger, blade marked at forte *RZM 1196/38 SS*, chrome plated hilt mounts, in its dark blued metal sheath.
(Wallis & Wallis) $880

A Nazi M1933 SS dagger, by Boker, white metal mounts, bullion dress knot, in its metal sheath with white metal mounts and dark blued finish.
(Wallis & Wallis) $832

A Nazi SA dagger, by F.W. Holler, blade retaining most polish, German silver mounts, in its metal sheath with German silver mounts.
(Wallis & Wallis) $302

A German 3rd Reich NSKK leader's dagger, by Gebrüder Heller, plated mounts, in its black painted metal sheath with plated mounts, and with hanging chains.
(Wallis & Wallis) $1,680

A German army officer's dagger by Karl Eickhorn of Solingen, the hilt with oak leaf decorated pommel, grooved orange plastic grip and guard in the form of an eagle, blade 10in.
(Andrew S Bottomley) $448

A scarce Nazi N.P.E.A. dagger, by Karl Burgsmuller, German silver mounts, in its olive green painted metal scabbard with leather frog.
(Wallis & Wallis) $960

A Japanese WWII naval officer's dirk, blade 8¹/₂in. with single fuller, brass mounted hilt with cherry blossom pommel, wire bound imitation sharkskin grip.
(Wallis & Wallis)   **$191**

A Georgian naval officer's dirk, circa 1800, tapering straight double edged blade 13in., etched with crown GR military trophies and foliage, copper gilt mounts, straight crosspiece with finials chiseled with foliage.
(Wallis & Wallis)   **$318**

A Victorian Scottish piper's dirk, Mk II, clipped broad blade 11¹/₂in., by Robt Mole, inspection stamp, etched with thistles, corded wood hilt, German silver studded decoration, German silver base band stamped 3 HLI.
(Wallis & Wallis)   **$239**

A Nazi naval officer's dirk, by Eickhorn, blade retaining most original polish, etched with fouled anchor, entwined dolphins and foliage, gilt mounts, wire bound white grip.
(Wallis & Wallis)   **$366**

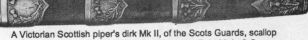

A Victorian Scottish piper's dirk Mk II, of the Scots Guards, scallop backed blade 11¹/₂in., with clipped back tip by Robt Mole & Sons, Birmingham, etched with thistles, corded wood hilt decorated with brass studs.
(Wallis & Wallis)   **$416**

An Imperial Russian naval officer's dirk, plain, diamond section blade 9¹/₄in., brass hilt mounts, reversed crossguard, pommel with cypher of Nicholas II surmounted by laurel spray.
(Wallis & Wallis)   **$232**

A Victorian officer's Highland dress dirk of The Royal Scots, bi-fullered single blade 11¹/₂in. with scalloped back edge, strapwork and 25 battle honors to Pekin, brass mounted strapwork carved wooden hilt with *The Royal Scots* in relief on guard.
(Wallis & Wallis)   **$880**

A Seaforth Highlanders officer's dirk by Kirkwood, Edinburgh, straight single-edged blade 10¾in, together with a ER VII Seaforth Highlander Rosshire Buffs skean dhu.
(Sotheby's)   **$2,332**

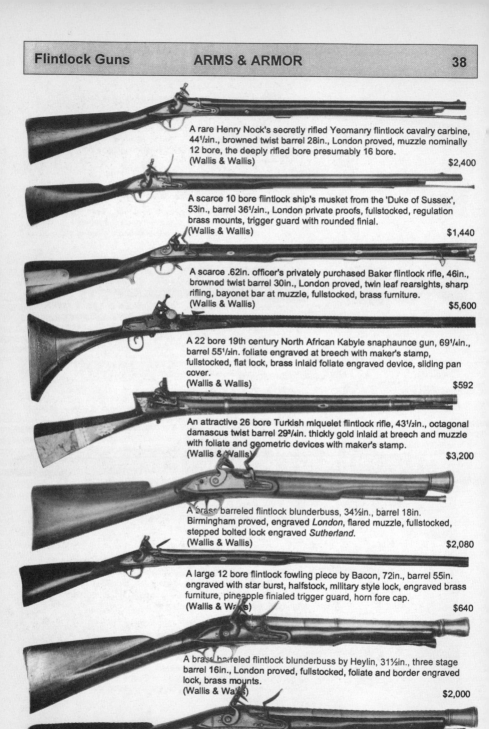

A rare Henry Nock's secretly rifled Yeomanry flintlock cavalry carbine, 44½in., browned twist barrel 28in., London proved, muzzle nominally 12 bore, the deeply rifled bore presumably 16 bore.
(Wallis & Wallis)
$2,400

A scarce 10 bore flintlock ship's musket from the 'Duke of Sussex', 53in., barrel 36½in., London private proofs, fullstocked, regulation brass mounts, trigger guard with rounded finial.
(Wallis & Wallis)
$1,440

A scarce .62in. officer's privately purchased Baker flintlock rifle, 46in., browned twist barrel 30in., London proved, twin leaf rearsights, sharp rifling, bayonet bar at muzzle, fullstocked, brass furniture.
(Wallis & Wallis)
$5,600

A 22 bore 19th century North African Kabyle snaphaunce gun, 69¼in., barrel 55½in. foliate engraved at breech with maker's stamp, fullstocked, flat lock, brass inlaid foliate engraved device, sliding pan cover.
(Wallis & Wallis)
$592

An attractive 26 bore Turkish miquelet flintlock rifle, 43½in., octagonal damascus twist barrel 29¾in. thickly gold inlaid at breech and muzzle with foliate and geometric devices with maker's stamp.
(Wallis & Wallis)
$3,200

A brass barreled flintlock blunderbuss, 34½in., barrel 18in. Birmingham proved, engraved *London*, flared muzzle, fullstocked, stepped bolted lock engraved *Sutherland*.
(Wallis & Wallis)
$2,080

A large 12 bore flintlock fowling piece by Bacon, 72in., barrel 55in. engraved with star burst, halfstock, military style lock, engraved brass furniture, pineapple finialed trigger guard, horn fore cap.
(Wallis & Wallis)
$640

A brass barreled flintlock blunderbuss by Heylin, 31½in., three stage barrel 16in., London proved, fullstocked, foliate and border engraved lock, brass mounts.
(Wallis & Wallis)
$2,000

A brass barreled flintlock blunderbuss by R. Farrall, 32¼in., three stage barrel 16in. with swollen reinforced muzzle, fullstocked, stepped lock, brass mounts, acorn finialed trigger guard.
(Wallis & Wallis)
$1,760

A scarce 20 bore Cossack miquelet flintlock rifle, 53¹/₂in., octagonal barrel 41³/₄in., barrel tang and rearsight thickly gold damascened with foliage and arabesques, fullstocked in striped Circassian walnut, lock of traditional form. (Wallis & Wallis) $1,908

A 10 bore India pattern Brown Bess flintlock musket of the Royal Fusiliers, 55¹/₂in. overall, barrel 39in. with Tower proofs, rounded lock with ring neck cock, walnut fullstock. (Wallis & Wallis) $2,880

A .36in. Kentucky flintlock rifle, 63¹/₂in., octagonal barrel 47¹/₄in., fullstocked, stepped lock faintly engraved *Smith*, roller bearing frizzen spring, brass furniture. (Wallis & Wallis) $2,400

A 32 bore Indian matchlock gun torador, 66in., octagonal barrel 46in. with traces of silver damascened flowers and foliage overall, green painted fullstock with polychrome decoration to butt. (Wallis & Wallis) $480

An unusual steel barreled flintlock blunderbuss, 43³/₄in., flared barrel 28¹/₂in. brass inlaid key pattern at breech, foliate motifs, and borders to flutes at muzzle, fullstocked, Brown Bess lock stamped with crowned GR and Tower. (Wallis & Wallis) $636

A steel barreled flintlock blunderbuss by Richards, fitted with spring bayonet circa 1820, 30¹/₂in., flared barrel 14¹/₂in., engraved *London*, fullstocked, stepped foliate engraved lock, roller bearing frizzen spring and bayonet spring. (Wallis & Wallis) $1,680

A good and unusual flintlock coaching carbine with folding bayonet by Henry Nock, 33¹/₂in., swamped barrel 18in., plain brass furniture, shell carved stock behind barrel tang. (Wallis & Wallis) $2,960

A scarce Dutch doglock flintlock brass barreled grenade thrower or Langridge Gun circa 1700, large cylindrical brass barrel 20in., reinforced muzzle, stepped breech deeply struck with crossed anchors and *AODM* (Admiraliteit Op De Maze). (Wallis & Wallis) $3,680

A .65in. Sergeant's flintlock carbine, of the East Kent Militia, 52¹/₂in., barrel 37in. London proved, with government inspector's stamp, fullstocked, regulation lock and brass mounts. (Wallis & Wallis) $1,600

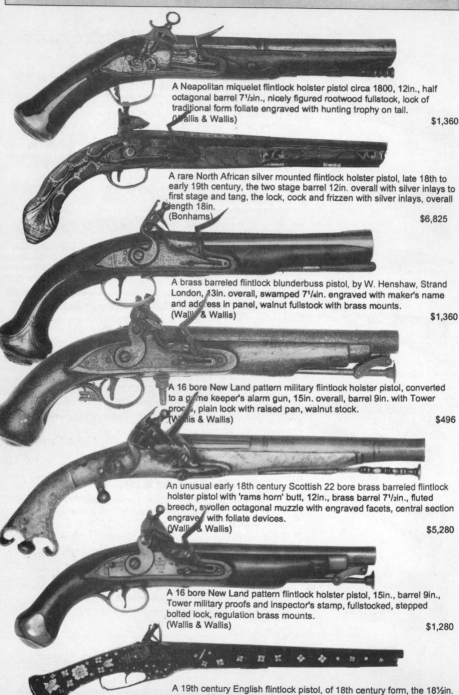

A Neapolitan miquelet flintlock holster pistol circa 1800, 12in., half octagonal barrel 7½in., nicely figured rootwood fullstock, lock of traditional form foliate engraved with hunting trophy on tail.
(Wallis & Wallis) $1,360

A rare North African silver mounted flintlock holster pistol, late 18th to early 19th century, the two stage barrel 12in. overall with silver inlays to first stage and tang, the lock, cock and frizzen with silver inlays, overall length 18in.
(Bonhams) $6,825

A brass barreled flintlock blunderbuss pistol, by W. Henshaw, Strand London, 13in. overall, swamped 7¼in. engraved with maker's name and address in panel, walnut fullstock with brass mounts.
(Wallis & Wallis) $1,360

A 16 bore New Land pattern military flintlock holster pistol, converted to a game keeper's alarm gun, 15in. overall, barrel 9in. with Tower proof, plain lock with raised pan, walnut stock.
(Wallis & Wallis) $496

An unusual early 18th century Scottish 22 bore brass barreled flintlock holster pistol with 'rams horn' butt, 12in., brass barrel 7½in., fluted breech, swollen octagonal muzzle with engraved facets, central section engraved with foliate devices.
(Wallis & Wallis) $5,280

A 16 bore New Land pattern flintlock holster pistol, 15in., barrel 9in., Tower military proofs and inspector's stamp, fullstocked, stepped bolted lock, regulation brass mounts.
(Wallis & Wallis) $1,280

A 19th century English flintlock pistol, of 18th century form, the 18½in. engraved iron barrel, lock plate and cock with gilt overlay, the wheel-lock style stock of full length.
(Bonhams) $487

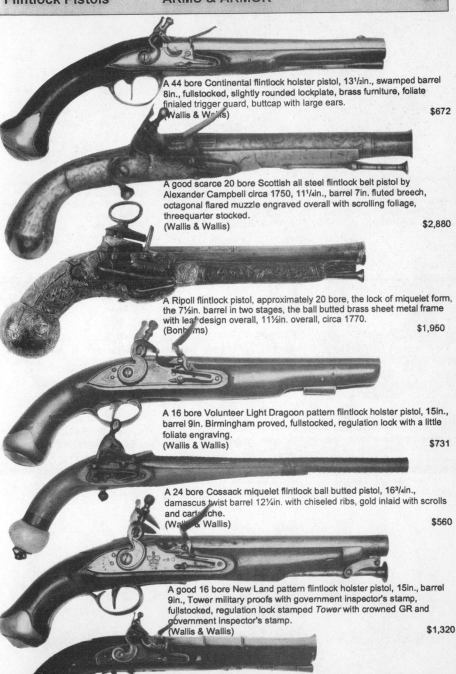

A 44 bore Continental flintlock holster pistol, 13½in., swamped barrel 8in., fullstocked, slightly rounded lockplate, brass furniture, foliate finialed trigger guard, buttcap with large ears.
(Wallis & Wallis)   **$672**

A good scarce 20 bore Scottish all steel flintlock belt pistol by Alexander Campbell circa 1750, 11¼in., barrel 7in. fluted breech, octagonal flared muzzle engraved overall with scrolling foliage, threequarter stocked.
(Wallis & Wallis)   **$2,880**

A Ripoll flintlock pistol, approximately 20 bore, the lock of miquelet form, the 7½in. barrel in two stages, the ball butted brass sheet metal frame with leaf design overall, 11½in. overall, circa 1770.
(Bonhams)   **$1,950**

A 16 bore Volunteer Light Dragoon pattern flintlock holster pistol, 15in., barrel 9in. Birmingham proved, fullstocked, regulation lock with a little foliate engraving.
(Wallis & Wallis)   **$731**

A 24 bore Cossack miquelet flintlock ball butted pistol, 16¾in., damascus twist barrel 12¼in. with chiseled ribs, gold inlaid with scrolls and cartouche.
(Wallis & Wallis)   **$560**

A good 16 bore New Land pattern flintlock holster pistol, 15in., barrel 9in., Tower military proofs with government inspector's stamp, fullstocked, regulation lock stamped *Tower* with crowned GR and government inspector's stamp.
(Wallis & Wallis)   **$1,320**

A flintlock brass barreled blunderbuss pistol, by T. Ketland & Co., 9in. barrel with bell mouth at three stages, fully stocked brass mounted ramrod, length 15in.
(Bonhams)   **$1,056**

A rare Georgian officer's copper gilt gorget of The Royal Marines, engraved with Royal Arms and supporters over fouled anchor. (Wallis & Wallis) $480

A Nazi Feldgendarmerie gorget, luminous painted finish to eagle and caption, with neck chains. (Wallis & Wallis) $152

A Georgian officer's universal pattern copper gilt gorget, engraved crowned GR cypher within laurel sprays. (Wallis & Wallis) $96

A rare officer's hallmarked silver gorget of the Honourable Artillery Company, engraved in the center with the Royal Arms and Supporters, hallmarked London 1787 with maker's mark CH. (Wallis & Wallis) $5,120

Georgian officer's gorget, 1796-1830 Universal Pattern, gilt on copper crescent engraved with crowned GR cypher within a wreath of laurels. (Bosleys) $336

Royal Paisley Volunteers Georgian gorget, burnished gilt on copper crescent with raised rim; engraved around the sides and top of the Royal Arms with GR above, engraved Royal Paisley Volunteers. (Bosleys) $992

A George III officer's copper gilt gorget of the Honourable East India Company, engraved with the post 1709 arms of the United E.I.C. (Wallis & Wallis) $640

Lower Gower Volunteers Georgian gorget, burnished gilt on copper crescent with raised rim. (Bosleys) $400

A good Georgian officer's copper gilt universal pattern gorget, engraved with crowned GR cypher with a spray of laurel either side. (Wallis & Wallis) $288

An Imperial German Wurttemberg NCO's peaked cap (Feldmutze), navy blue cloth, scarlet band and piping.
(Wallis & Wallis)   **$182**

A Fireman's brass helmet, helmet plate with fire fighting devices, comb embossed with dragons.
(Wallis & Wallis)   **$720**

General Staff officer's hat, America, circa 1812, black wool felt bound with black silk ribbon with an inwoven geometric pattern.
(Skinner)   **$1,725**

A fine and rare Italian embossed parade morion, circa 1590, probably Milanese, of so-called 'Spanish form', the skull decorated on its sides with scenes of classical warriors, 8¾in.
(Sotheby's)   **$40,480**

An important Italian parade helmet by Filippo Negroli of Milan, circa 1530-5, with rounded one-piece skull, superbly embossed and chased in high relief, except at the brow and nape, with curly hair, 11½in.
(Sotheby's)   **$178,400**

A north European cuirassier helmet of 'Todenkopf' type, circa 1620-30, with heavy rounded skull formed in two pieces joined along a low roped medial comb, 12in.
(Sotheby's)   **$5,520**

A 19th century US shako of the 64th Massachusetts Light Infantry, black beaver covered patent leather body, patent leather crown and peak.
(Wallis & Wallis)   **$151**

A WWII officer's khaki slouch hat of the 36th Division, silk puggaree with purple flash, cloth badge to turn up brim.
(Wallis & Wallis)   **$166**

A French model 1858 cuirassier trooper's helmet, Second Empire, red horse-hair tuft, black side-mounted crimson ostrich feather plume.
(Sotheby's)   **$1,350**

An Imperial German reservist's Pickelhaube of the Guard Railway Regiment, silver Garde eagle helmet plate with Landwehr cross. (Wallis & Wallis) $688

An Imperial German other rank's shako of a Landwehr Jäger Battalion, black and white oval helmet plate with Landwehr cross. (Wallis & Wallis) $400

An Imperial Wurttemberg infantryman's Ersatz (pressed tin) Pickelhaube, brass helmet plate, spike and mounts, leather lining. (Wallis & Wallis) $416

An Imperial Prussian Jäger Regiment other rank's shako, gray metal helmet plate cloth cockade, single cockade, leather lining and chinstrap. (Wallis & Wallis) $144

An other rank's black patent leather lance cap of The 16th (The Queens) Lancers, cloth sides to top, yellow and red silk band, yellow braid, brass mounts. (Wallis & Wallis) $432

A 16th century Turkish Turban helmet of gently paneled conical form, the spherical knop with 2 bands of 'damascened' calligraphy and motifs. (Graves Son & Pilcher) $8,635

A Victorian officer's lance cap of the 9th (Queen's Royal) Lancers, black patent leather skull and top, brass bound peak. (Wallis & Wallis) $2,560

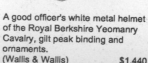

A good officer's white metal helmet of the Royal Berkshire Yeomanry Cavalry, gilt peak binding and ornaments. (Wallis & Wallis) $1,440

A WWI Prussian Infantryman's ersatz (pressed felt) Pickelhaube, gray painted helmet plate, spike and mounts. (Wallis & Wallis) $256

An Imperial Baden Infantryman's Pickelhaube, brass helmet plate spike and mounts, leather chinstrap.
(Wallis & Wallis) $280

A Nazi Infantry officer's peaked cap, bullion cockade, metal eagle, white piping, chin cords.
(Wallis & Wallis) $136

A French model 1913 Chasseur à Cheval officer's helmet, helmet-plate with silvered double-coil bugle, black horse-hair mane.
(Sotheby's) $1,593

A French dragoon trooper's helmet, Third Republic, brass skull with raised comb with Medusa head and felt band printed in leopard skin design.
(Sotheby's) $1,312

A cased Bavarian infantry officer's Pickelhaube with leather skull, brass mounts and central mount complete with black horsehair plume, 28cm. high.
(Bonhams) $965

An 1871 pattern O.R's home service helmet, covered with moss green velvet, helmet-plate of the 39th Norfolk Rifles, Canada, 29cm. high.
(Bonhams) $402

A fine Prussian Garde du Corps officer's helmet, circa 1900, polished tombac skull with nickel edges, silver-plated parade eagle.
(Sotheby's) $7,498

A Nazi Police shako, green cloth covered body, patent leather crown and peaks, large metal eagle helmet plate.
(Wallis & Wallis) $304

A good Senior NCO's busby of the Middlesex Yeomanry Cavalry, black bag with yellow braid trim and button.
(Wallis & Wallis) $429

TOP TIPS

*Collectors and Dealers always prefer to buy items of Militaria in 'as found Condition'.

*Never be tempted to clean metal or other parts of an item as this could destroy the original finish or patination. Many gun parts were originally browned or blued.

*Never handle sword blades or attempt to dismantle Japanese swords. Parts of the sword are delicate and require specialist treatment.

*When buying antique weapons check that all parts match (that decoration is en-suite). Metals used will generally also match e.g. On a pistol, silver trigger guard, silver side plate, silver but-cap and ramrod pipes.

*Never dry-fire a gun (cock and release the hammer) as this can cause damage.

*Never attempt to load or fire a weapon as metal parts can become fatigued with age and old wooden stocks can shatter. You would also be breaking the law!

*If you discover and old gun contact a specialist dealer/auctioneer to find out what you have, NEVER be tempted to sell it to a friend, you could be in breach of the law and liable to a stiff penalty. Ignorance is no defence. Illegal possession of a firearm can result in arrest and imprisonment.

*Always seek specialist advice on old weapons - a mark or a number may hold the key to the weapon's history

*If there is any history uniquely linked to an item this will enhance its value.

Garth Vincent

A cabasset circa 1600, formed in one piece, brass rosettes around base.
(Wallis & Wallis) $239

An Imperial Prussian Infantryman's Pickelhaube, gray metal helmet plate and mounts, leather lining and chinstrap, both cockades.
(Wallis & Wallis) $208

A post-1928 officer's full dress busby of The Royal Regiment of Artillery, plain scarlet bag, gilt grenade with applied badge on the ball.
(Wallis & Wallis) $560

A French 3rd Republic Carabinier officer's helmet, complete with chin scales, stiff horse hair comb and red and white side feather plume.
(Bonhams) $1,950

An Imperial Saxony other rank's Jäger Battalion shako, gray metal helmet plate with addition of light infantry bugle, leather chinstrap.
(Wallis & Wallis) $288

A post 1902 other rank's white metal helmet of the Royal Horse Guards, brass mounts, leather backed chinchain and large ear rosettes.
(Wallis & Wallis) $1,200

A fine Imperial German officer's Pickelhaube of an Adjutant of the Lippe Detmold Infantry regiment, silvered Garde star.
(Wallis & Wallis) $2,000

A Victorian Household Cavalry Officer's silvered helmet, silvered enameled and gilded helmet plate, gilded chinchain.
(Sotheby's) $1,710

A rare and important late Western / early Spring and Autumn period Zhou Dynasty bronze helmet, 800-500 B.C.
(Bonhams) $16,250

An Imperial German parade miter cap circa 1890, silver plated helmet plate with embossed design of Prussian eagle *Pro Gloria et Patria*.
(Wallis & Wallis) $2,080

A Prussian OR's Reservist Pickelhaube, circa 1914, complete with helmet cover.
(Bonhams) $601

A rare Napoleonic tall foul weather shako of the 5th Grenadiers, of card construction covered with light oil-cloth.
(Wallis & Wallis) $1,080

An officer's bearskin of The Royal Scots Fusiliers, Victorian grenade badge with applied Royal Arms to ball.
(Wallis & Wallis) $859

A 19th century Japanese black lacquered retainer's hat Jingasa, 17¹/₂in., nicely red lacquered with a dragon in carved relief, gold Take mon of bamboo.
(Wallis & Wallis) $560

A rare Bavarian officer's Pickelhaube of the Leibgarde Infantry Regiment, circa 1900, with leather skull and leather peaks, 9³/₄in. high.
(Sotheby's) $1,725

An exceptionally fine Victorian officer's blue cloth spiked hemet of The Hampshire Regiment, gilt peak binding, top mount and spike.
(Wallis & Wallis) $1,840

A cabasset circa 1600, formed in one piece, brim struck with armorer's mark, pear stalk finial to crown, brass rosettes around base.
(Wallis & Wallis) $334

A fine post-1902 officer's silver plated helmet of The Life Guards, white hair plume with ball and plain rosette.
(Wallis & Wallis) $3,200

An ERII other rank's uniform of The Blues and Royals, comprising: plated Life Guards helmet, blue tunic with scarlet facings, buckskin breeches.
(Wallis & Wallis) $1,200

An O.R's cap of the 12th Lancers, dated 1908, with helmet-plate, chin-chain and red horsehair plume, 21cm. high.
(Bonhams) $1,254

An unusual early Chinese or Korean war helmet, two piece brazed skull, riveted brow band with eye cut outs, separate shaped peak.
(Wallis & Wallis) $1,200

A good Victorian officer's lance cap of The 21st (Empress of India's) Lancers, gilt and silver plated rayed plate with *Khartoum*.
(Wallis & Wallis) $4,000

A scarce late 16th century peaked cabasset, one piece skull with 'pear stalk' finial, broad brim, probably Italian or Spanish.
(Wallis & Wallis) $912

A good officer's 1878 pattern blue cloth spiked helmet of the Royal London Militia, silver plated peak binding.
(Wallis & Wallis) $880

A Bavarian officer's Pickelhaube, black patent leather skull with gilded brass, helmet plate and mounts, fluted spike.
(Sotheby's) $768

An Imperial Prussian NCO's shako of a Garde Jäger Battalion, cloth state cockade, white metal Garde helmet plate, leather chinstrap.
(Wallis & Wallis) $304

A good scarce officer's blue cloth ball topped helmet, 1902–1908, of the Royal Artillery Militia, gilt mounts.
(Wallis & Wallis) $779

An Imperial Prussian other rank's shako of the 10th Jäger Battalion, gray metal helmet plate with battle honors Waterloo, Peninsula, Venta Del Pozo.
(Wallis & Wallis) $416

An English cavalry trooper's pot helmet, circa 1640, made during the Civil war of 1642–1649, the skull with six radial ridges and small suspension ring to top.
(Andrew S Bottomley) $2,048

An Imperial German Infantryman's Pickelhaube of the State of Mecklenberg Schwerin, brass spike and mounts, brass rayed helmet plate with white metal state badge.
(Wallis & Wallis) $496

A Canadian Dragoon O.R's helmet, with white-metal skull, brass mounts and red horsehair plume, 43cm. high.
(Bonhams) $514

An O.R's cap of the 12th Lancers, dated 1908, with helmet-plate, chin-chain and red horsehair plume, 21cm. high.
(Bonhams) $1,254

A French cuirassier trooper's helmet, circa 1830, crimson horse-hair tuft, black horse-hair crest and mane.
(Sotheby's) $1,875

A Japanese sword katana, blade 64.2cm., mumei, O-suriage, 3 mekugi ana (Shinto, late 17th century), tight mokume hada, gunome hamon, shakudo nanako fuchi kashira, tape bound same tsuka, shakudo menuki as flowers. (Wallis & Wallis)
       $1,160

A Japanese sword ito maki no tachi, blade 67.6cm., signed *Kunisuke*, gunome hamon, fair polish, brass koshirae, tape bound same tsuka, Aoi tsuba nashiji lacquered saya with ito maki no tachi binding. (Wallis & Wallis)
       $1,240

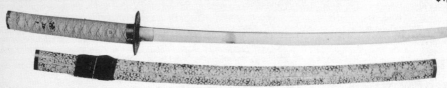

A Japanese sword katana, blade 60.1cm., suriage, mumei, gunome hamon, ito gunome hamon, rebound tsuka, iron mokko tsuba inlaid with soft metal sage beneath tree. (Wallis & Wallis)
       $840

The blade from a Japanese sword katana, 64.2cm., signed *Echizen Noju Harima Daijo Fuji*, gunome hamon. (Wallis & Wallis)
       $1,760

A Japanese sword katana, blade 60.8cm. signed *Kanefusa*, gunome hamon, leather bound same tsuka with gilt shakudo menuki as stylized standing figures. (Wallis & Wallis)
       $1,367

A Japanese sword katana, blade 71.8cm., mumei, 2 mekugi ana, probably Shin-shinto, leather bound same tsuka. (Wallis & Wallis)
       $2,238

A large Japanese sword katana, blade 71cm., signed *Oshu Shirakawa-Shin Tegarayama Masashige* and dated *Kansei 5th year, 8th month, lucky day (=1803)*, ohu suguha hamon, tight itame hada. (Wallis & Wallis)
       $6,464

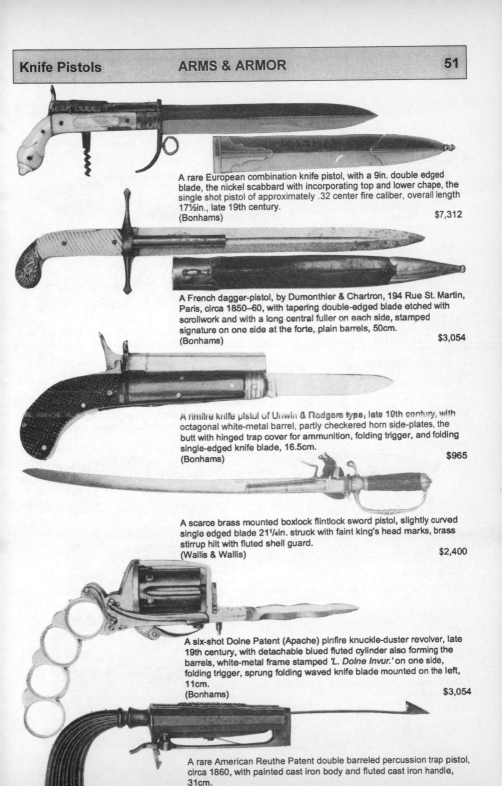

A rare European combination knife pistol, with a 9in. double edged blade, the nickel scabbard with incorporating top and lower chape, the single shot pistol of approximately .32 center fire caliber, overall length 17½in., late 19th century.
(Bonhams) $7,312

A French dagger-pistol, by Dumonthier & Chartron, 194 Rue St. Martin, Paris, circa 1850–60, with tapering double-edged blade etched with scrollwork and with a long central fuller on each side, stamped signature on one side at the forte, plain barrels, 50cm.
(Bonhams) $3,054

A rimfire knife pistol of Unwin & Rodgers type, late 19th century, with octagonal white-metal barrel, partly checkered horn side-plates, the butt with hinged trap cover for ammunition, folding trigger, and folding single-edged knife blade, 16.5cm.
(Bonhams) $965

A scarce brass mounted boxlock flintlock sword pistol, slightly curved single edged blade 21¼in. struck with faint king's head marks, brass stirrup hilt with fluted shell guard.
(Wallis & Wallis) $2,400

A six-shot Dolne Patent (Apache) pinfire knuckle-duster revolver, late 19th century, with detachable blued fluted cylinder also forming the barrels, white-metal frame stamped 'L. Dolne Invur.' on one side, folding trigger, sprung folding waved knife blade mounted on the left, 11cm.
(Bonhams) $3,054

A rare American Reuthe Patent double barreled percussion trap pistol, circa 1860, with painted cast iron body and fluted cast iron handle, 31cm.
(Bonhams) $563

A large Spanish folding knife navaja, swollen single edged blade 11in., etched *No me abra cin razon Ni me ciere cin honor Sevilla 1888*, horn grips with decorative engraving.
(Wallis & Wallis) $432

A Nazi Hitler Youth knife, marked *RZM 7/29—1941*, plated mounts, in its black painted metal sheath with leather strap.
(Wallis & Wallis) $120

A large 19th century Bowie type knife, broad straight shallow diamond section blade 12in. stamped *Wragg & Sons Solly St, Celebrated Cutlery*, white metal hilt with applied pommel embossed with horse.
(Wallis & Wallis) $3,975

A silver-mounted hunting knife, Spanish or South American, 19th century, with single-edged blade doubled-edged towards the point and etched with an inscription within the fuller on each side (illegible), swelling horn grip set with silver studs within silver lines, 45cm.
(Bonhams) $643

An unusually large German deersfoot hilted hunting knife, clipped back blade 7½in., with interrupted fullers, plated crosspiece, line engraved and filigree cut.
(Wallis & Wallis) $64

A good 19th century Malay knife Golok, swollen single edged blade 12in., silver ferrule, nicely foliate carved hilt and sheath.   (Wallis & Wallis) $199

A French WWI Clou Francais, trench stabbing knife, spear shaped blade 6in. (made from barbed wire support post).
(Wallis & Wallis) $127

A Ceylonese knife pia kaetta, blade 8in., copper scroll chiseled ferrule, two piece ivory grips carved en-suite with brass mounts, in its wooden sheath with copper top.
(Wallis & Wallis) $315

A folding Bowie knife, clipped back blade 7½in. by F. Herder Abr Sohn Solingen, German silver mounts, staghorn grips, locking thumb ring.
(Wallis & Wallis) $120

A silver mounted late 19th century Indian Bowie knife, blade 8¾in., clipped back tip, silver crosspiece and bud shaped pommel, spiral carved ivory grip, in its leather sheath with belt loop and silver mounts.
(Wallis & Wallis) $365

A Bowie knife, with broad single-edged blade back-edged towards the point and stamped 'Cameron Cutler Edinburgh' on one side of the forte, oval white-metal quillons, 47.5cm.
(Bonhams) $643

A large Bowie style hunting knife by J. Rodgers and Sons, straight fullered single edged blade 9¾in. with clipped back tip, forte stamped J. Rodgers & Sons No.6 Norfolk St Sheffield England.
(Wallis & Wallis) $448

A good Victorian Bowie knife, tapered double edged blade 7¾in. with traces of etched scrolls and motto, German silver crosspiece with ball finials, embossed German silver hilt decorated with acanthus leaves and shamrock.
(Wallis & Wallis) $232

A Victorian Bowie knife, clipped back blade 7in. by Moillet & Gem, oval German silver crosspiece, silver plated foliate embossed cutlery style hilt, in its leather sheath with belt loop.
(Wallis & Wallis) $288

A 19th century Bowie type knife, broad single edged slightly clipped back blade 10¾in. possibly made from a sword blade, one piece staghorn hilt with iron ferrule and elliptical shaped guard.
(Wallis & Wallis) $228

A late Victorian Bowie knife, straight double edged blade 7½in., of flattened diamond section, by Joseph Mappin 8 Brother St Sheffield , retaining some original polish.
(Wallis & Wallis) $448

A pair of hallmarked silver pepper pots in the form of shell heads, 3¹/₄in. by H.M. Emanuel & Son Portsea, contained in their silk lined red leather covered case.
(Wallis & Wallis)　　　　$350

A flintlock powder-tester of box-lock pistol form, by William Abnett, Windsor, early 19th century, large indicator-wheel with sprung release catch and internal return spring, 15cm.
(Bonhams)　　　　$1,206

A rare Georgian embroidered silk guidon of the York (City) Volunteer Cavalry, violet gray silk bearing the Arms of York with title scroll above.
(Wallis & Wallis)　　　　$4,320

A good pair of 19th century Mexican silver inlaid rowel spurs for the Charro, broad heavy bows inlaid with vine foliage and cable decoration.
(Wallis & Wallis)　　　　$96

A Regimental painted side drum of the 2nd Bn Coldstream Guards, circa 1912, with Royal Arms, badges, titles and battle honors to South Africa 1899–1902.
(Wallis & Wallis)　　　　$580

Battle of Bunkers Hill flag remnant, polychrome decorated flag mounted on paper, 7 x 5in., framed.
(Skinner)　　　　$2,415

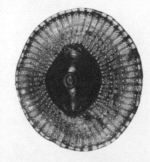

A good EIIR Regimental side drum of the 1st Bn Coldstream Guards, brass frame, wooden painted rims, white cords and wash leather stretchers, 14¹/₂in. diameter.
(Wallis & Wallis)　　　　$716

A scarce Kynoch advertising display board, 26¼ x 20½in. overall, entitled *Kynoch Manufacturer of Military and Sporting Ammunition Central Fire Cartridge Cases.*
(Wallis & Wallis)　　　　$2,240

A 19th century Abyssinian chieftain's shield, made of hardened hippopotamus hide, pressed into a domed circular shape, diameter 18in.
(Andrew S Bottomley)
　　　　$1,120

A large bronze head of Hitler, marked on neck *T.H. Linz G. Wagner Kunstgewbrl Werkst*, 12½in., on marble base.
(Wallis & Wallis) $1,280

A Nazi Naval admiral's cloth car pennant, printed emblem of Nazi eagle upon Iron Cross with crossed batons, 11 x 12in.
(Wallis & Wallis) $672

A scarce Victorian 1880 pattern Royal Navy ratings white duck frock (smock) square collar, blue serge bound, knife pocket to front.
(Wallis & Wallis) $119

A brass snare drum of The 36th (Herefordshire) Regt, plain, with painted rims, the body with maker's name *Kohler and Son., Westminster, London*, and engraved *36th Regt I*.
(Wallis & Wallis) $254

Civil War presentation drum, sticks, and a jacket, drum has a silver plaque *Presented to Samuel H. Proctor by the members of Lincoln Guard · June 12th 1865*.
(Skinner) $17,250

A Nazi DAF standard top, in white metal, traces of plating, base mount stamped *Cosack* and *RZM60*, 10in. overall.
(Wallis & Wallis) $120

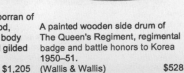

A Scottish officer's dress sporran of the Black Watch by Kirkwood, Edinburgh, white horsehair body with five bullion tassels and gilded brass cantle.
(Sotheby's) $1,205

A painted wooden side drum of The Queen's Regiment, regimental badge and battle honors to Korea 1950–51.
(Wallis & Wallis) $528

A scarce Kynoch advertising display board, 40 x 29in. overall, entitled *Kynoch's Manufacturers of Cordite, Military and Sporting Ammunition*.
(Wallis & Wallis) $1,600

A 26 bore Austrian cadets Augustin System tube lock military carbine, 45in. overall, barrel 32in., plain lock with hinged tube holder, beech wood fullstock, regulation brass mounts.
(Wallis & Wallis) $676

A 10 bore Sea Service 1839 pattern percussion musket, 46in., barrel 30in. Tower military proofs with Government inspector's stamp, WD broad arrow mark to butt, fullstocked.
(Wallis & Wallis) $1,160

A .704in. Tower Brunswick military percussion rifle, 46in. overall, barrel 30in. with Tower proofs, the lock stamped with crowned VR, 1865 Tower and broad arrow over I for India service.
(Wallis & Wallis) $1,153

A scarce World War I German 13mm. Mauser single shot bolt action anti tank rifle, 67in. overall, barrel 39in., halfstocked, pistol grip behind trigger guard.
(Wallis & Wallis) $2,720

A scarce .44in. rimfire Winchester Model 1866 brass framed underlever military rifle with British Government sale marks, 46½in., round barrel 27in., brass frame, steel trigger guard/loading lever.
(Wallis & Wallis) $2,640

A good quality 20 bore double barreled Austrian percussion sporting gun by M. Mayer of Vienna, converted from flintlock, 49in., barrels 33in., halfstocked, fine hallmarked silver furniture, carved cheekpiece, animal's head grip.
(Wallis & Wallis) $1,280

A .577/.450in. Martini Henry Mark III SS military rifle, 49in. overall, barrel 33½in., the frame marked with crowned VR and *Enfield/1883/I*, folding ladder rearsight, walnut stock.
(Wallis & Wallis) $736

A .65in. 1858 pattern Native Mounted Police smooth bore percussion carbine, 37in. overall, barrel 21in. with plain block rearsight, the lock engraved with crowned VR and *1859 Tower*.
(Wallis & Wallis) $528

A scarce .44in. rimfire Winchester presentation engraved carbine, 40in., barrel 20in., stamped *Winchester's – Repeating – Arms. New Haven CT King's Improvement – Patented – March 29. 1866. October 16. 1860.*
(Wallis & Wallis) $5,440

A good .45in. Express Winchester Model 1885 underlever falling block SS sporting rifle, 45½in. overall, round barrel 30in. with two folding leaf rearsights, number 11367, plain walnut stock.
(Wallis & Wallis) $1,600

A scarce .75in. 1842 pattern military percussion musket, 55in. overall, barrel 39in. with Tower proofs and inspectors' stamps, fixed rearsight, line engraved lock with crowned VR, Tower, *1845*.
(Wallis & Wallis) $668

A .577in. Snider 3 band SS military rifle, 55in. overall, barrel 35½in. with military proofs, the lock marked with crowned VR and 1868 Enfield, walnut fullstock with regulation brass mounts.
(Wallis & Wallis) $509

A 6 shot 11mm. double action pinfire revolving rifle by Le Faucheux, Paris, 41in. overall, octagonal barrel 25in. fitted with Enfield military sight, Liege proved, scroll engraved cylinder and frame.
(Wallis & Wallis) $795

A scarce .704in. EIC Brunswick military percussion rifle, 46½in. overall, twist barrel 30in. with two folding leaf rearsights, back action lock with EIC rampant lion, walnut fullstock.
(Wallis & Wallis) $1,600

A good 8 bore percussion rifle, 45in., browned twist octagonal barrel 28½in., stamped *J.S.F. Botha Cape Town*, three leaf rearsight, halfstocked, foliate and border engraved lock with *Wm and Jno Rawbone*.
(Wallis & Wallis) $2,320

A French 11mm. Model 1866 Chassepot bolt action needle fire military rifle, 51½in. overall, barrel 32in., number 21358, the receiver stamped *Manufacture Imperiale Chatellerault*.
(Wallis & Wallis) $445

A 16 bore Bengal Native Police percussion carbine dated *1869*, 37in., barrel 21in., Enfield proofs, standing rearsight, fullstocked, regulation brass mounts, two piece buttcap.
(Wallis & Wallis) $640

A .50in. percussion sporting rifle by Beckwith, 49¼in. overall, round twist barrel 32½in. with deep four groove rifling of Jacobs type, ladder rearsight to 900 yards, walnut halfstock with checkered fore-end and wrist.
(Wallis & Wallis) $960

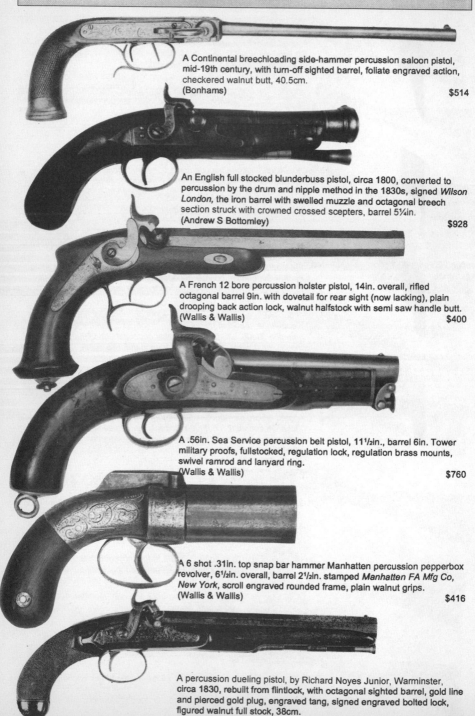

A Continental breechloading side-hammer percussion saloon pistol, mid-19th century, with turn-off sighted barrel, foliate engraved action, checkered walnut butt, 40.5cm.
(Bonhams) $514

An English full stocked blunderbuss pistol, circa 1800, converted to percussion by the drum and nipple method in the 1830s, signed *Wilson London*, the iron barrel with swelled muzzle and octagonal breech section struck with crowned crossed scepters, barrel 5¼in.
(Andrew S Bottomley) $928

A French 12 bore percussion holster pistol, 14in. overall, rifled octagonal barrel 9in. with dovetail for rear sight (now lacking), plain drooping back action lock, walnut halfstock with semi saw handle butt.
(Wallis & Wallis) $400

A .56in. Sea Service percussion belt pistol, 11½in., barrel 6in. Tower military proofs, fullstocked, regulation lock, regulation brass mounts, swivel ramrod and lanyard ring.
(Wallis & Wallis) $760

A 6 shot .31in. top snap bar hammer Manhatten percussion pepperbox revolver, 6½in. overall, barrel 2½in. stamped *Manhatten FA Mfg Co, New York*, scroll engraved rounded frame, plain walnut grips.
(Wallis & Wallis) $416

A percussion dueling pistol, by Richard Noyes Junior, Warminster, circa 1830, rebuilt from flintlock, with octagonal sighted barrel, gold line and pierced gold plug, engraved tang, signed engraved bolted lock, figured walnut full stock, 38cm.
(Bonhams) $399

A French six-shot Mariette Patent percussion pepperbox revolver, No. 552, circa 1850, with browned twist turn-off barrels numbered from 1 to 6, foliate scroll engraved rounded action, 20.5cm.
(Bonhams) $1,206

A rare 18mm Netherlands percussion cavalry pistol of similar form to the French model 1822, originally made as a flintlock, the round steel barrel with round foresight and large percussion nipple fitted to breech extension, barrel 7³/₄in.
(Andrew S Bottomley) $944

A percussion dueling pistol, by Clark, Holborn, London, early 19th century, converted flintlock, with octagonal sighted barrel signed on the top flat, signed engraved flat beveled lock, highly figured walnut full stock, 41.5cm.
(Bonhams) $511

A rare percussion box-lock 'duck's foot' four-shot pistol, by J. Richards, London, early 19th century, converted from flintlock, with turn-off barrels numbered from 5 to 8, signed brass action engraved with a martial trophy, iron trigger-guard and belt hook, 23cm.
(Bonhams) $2,400

A rare Viennese six-shot Grunbaum Patent rimfire pepperbox pistol, No. 417, circa 1860, with rifled fluted sighted barrels in the closed position by an under-lever, foliate engraved action, checkered hammer with revolving nose, folding trigger, 23.5cm.
(Bonhams) $1,447

A 6 shot 70 bore open frame self cocking top snap bar hammer transitional percussion revolver, 12in. overall, half octagonal barrel 5½in., Birmingham proved, plain rounded frame, checkered walnut grips.
(Wallis & Wallis) $384

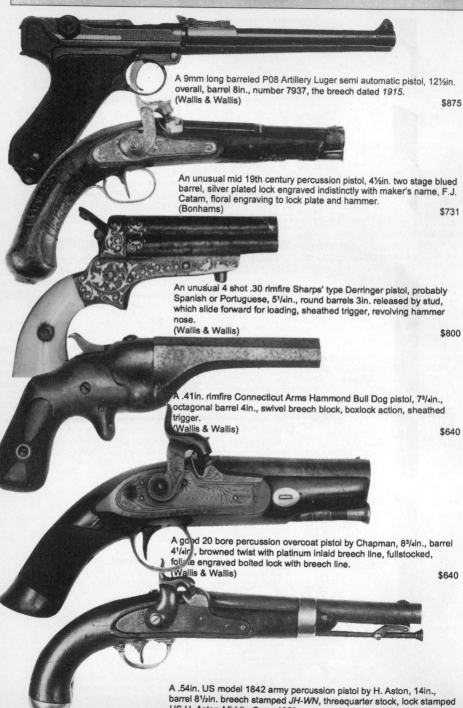

A 9mm long barreled P08 Artillery Luger semi automatic pistol, 12½in. overall, barrel 8in., number 7937, the breech dated *1915*.
(Wallis & Wallis) $875

An unusual mid 19th century percussion pistol, 4½in. two stage blued barrel, silver plated lock engraved indistinctly with maker's name, F.J. Catam, floral engraving to lock plate and hammer.
(Bonhams) $731

An unusual 4 shot .30 rimfire Sharps' type Derringer pistol, probably Spanish or Portuguese, 5¼in., round barrels 3in. released by stud, which slide forward for loading, sheathed trigger, revolving hammer nose.
(Wallis & Wallis) $800

A .41in. rimfire Connecticut Arms Hammond Bull Dog pistol, 7¾in., octagonal barrel 4in., swivel breech block, boxlock action, sheathed trigger.
(Wallis & Wallis) $640

A good 20 bore percussion overcoat pistol by Chapman, 8¾in., barrel 4¼in., browned twist with platinum inlaid breech line, fullstocked, foliate engraved bolted lock with breech line.
(Wallis & Wallis) $640

A .54in. US model 1842 army percussion pistol by H. Aston, 14in., barrel 8½in. breech stamped *JH-WN*, threequarter stock, lock stamped *US H. Aston Middtn Conn 1850*.
(Wallis & Wallis) $597

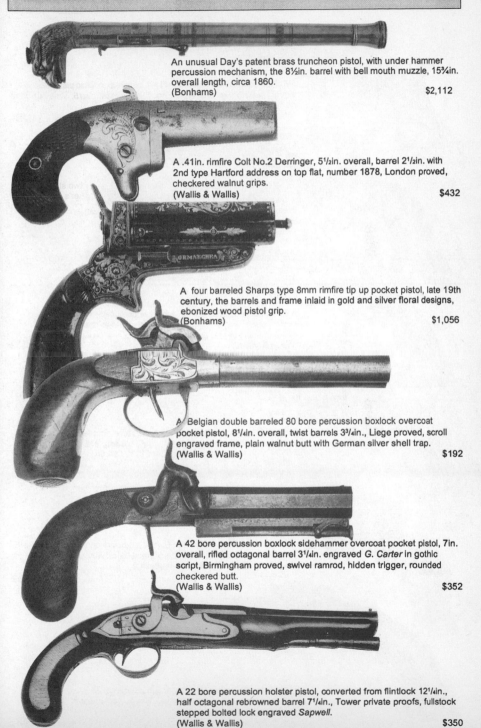

An unusual Day's patent brass truncheon pistol, with under hammer percussion mechanism, the 8½in. barrel with bell mouth muzzle, 15¾in. overall length, circa 1860.
(Bonhams) $2,112

A .41in. rimfire Colt No.2 Derringer, 5½in. overall, barrel 2½in. with 2nd type Hartford address on top flat, number 1878, London proved, checkered walnut grips.
(Wallis & Wallis) $432

A four barreled Sharps type 8mm rimfire tip up pocket pistol, late 19th century, the barrels and frame inlaid in gold and silver floral designs, ebonized wood pistol grip.
(Bonhams) $1,056

A Belgian double barreled 80 bore percussion boxlock overcoat pocket pistol, 8¼in. overall, twist barrels 3¾in., Liege proved, scroll engraved frame, plain walnut butt with German silver shell trap.
(Wallis & Wallis) $192

A 42 bore percussion boxlock sidehammer overcoat pocket pistol, 7in. overall, rifled octagonal barrel 3¼in. engraved G. Carter in gothic script, Birmingham proved, swivel ramrod, hidden trigger, rounded checkered butt.
(Wallis & Wallis) $352

A 22 bore percussion holster pistol, converted from flintlock 12¼in., half octagonal rebrowned barrel 7¼in., Tower private proofs, fullstock stepped bolted lock engraved Sapwell.
(Wallis & Wallis) $350

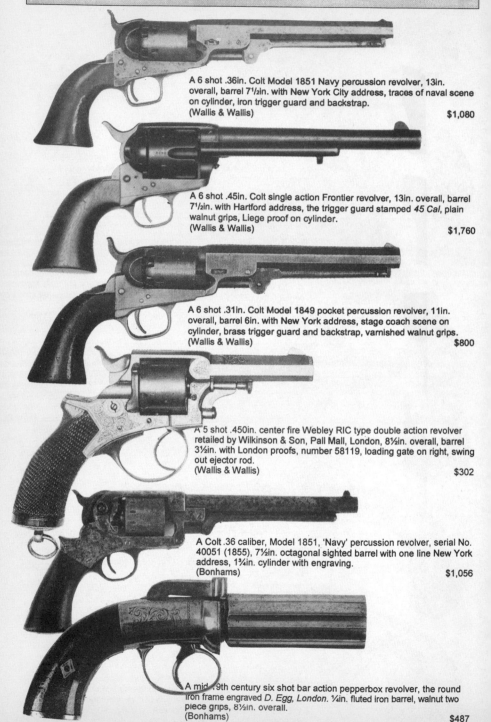

A 6 shot .36in. Colt Model 1851 Navy percussion revolver, 13in. overall, barrel 7½in. with New York City address, traces of naval scene on cylinder, iron trigger guard and backstrap.
(Wallis & Wallis) $1,080

A 6 shot .45in. Colt single action Frontier revolver, 13in. overall, barrel 7½in. with Hartford address, the trigger guard stamped *45 Cal*, plain walnut grips, Liege proof on cylinder.
(Wallis & Wallis) $1,760

A 6 shot .31in. Colt Model 1849 pocket percussion revolver, 11in. overall, barrel 6in. with New York address, stage coach scene on cylinder, brass trigger guard and backstrap, varnished walnut grips.
(Wallis & Wallis) $800

A 5 shot .450in. center fire Webley RIC type double action revolver retailed by Wilkinson & Son, Pall Mall, London, 8½in. overall, barrel 3½in. with London proofs, number 58119, loading gate on right, swing out ejector rod.
(Wallis & Wallis) $302

A Colt .36 caliber, Model 1851, 'Navy' percussion revolver, serial No. 40051 (1855), 7½in. octagonal sighted barrel with one line New York address, 1¾in. cylinder with engraving.
(Bonhams) $1,056

A mid 19th century six shot bar action pepperbox revolver, the round iron frame engraved *D. Egg, London*. ¼in. fluted iron barrel, walnut two piece grips, 8½in. overall.
(Bonhams) $487

A good scarce 6 shot .36in. Colt Navy single action percussion
revolver No.7549 (matching) made for a British Government Contract
with War Department stamp, 13in., octagonal barrel 7¹/₂in., underlever
rammer, steel gripstrap and trigger guard.
(Wallis & Wallis) $2,240

A scarce 6 shot .44in. centre-fire Remington New Model 1874 single
action army revolver, 13¹/₄in. overall, barrel 7¹/₂in., ejector and loading
gate on right, plain walnut grips with traces of inspector's initials on left.
(Wallis & Wallis) $720

A good 6 shot .38in. Colt Lightning double action revolver, 8in overall,
barrel 3¹/₂in. etched *Colt DA .38"* in panel, number 4513, London
proved.
(Wallis & Wallis) $620

A scarce 6 shot .45in. center-fire Adams Mark III double action service
revolver, 11in. overall, barrel 6in., London proofs, checkered walnut
butt with lanyard ring.
(Wallis & Wallis) $166

An early 6 shot .45in. Colt single action Army or Frontier revolver,
12¹/₂in. overall, barrel 7in. with Hartford address, plain walnut grips.
(Wallis & Wallis) $2,560

A good scarce 6 shot .36in. Colt Navy single action percussion
revolver No.187092L (matching) made for the Egyptian Government
contract (1865–1866) with Enfield storekeeper's/inspector's stamp,
13in., octagonal barrel 7¹/₂in. stamped, underlever rammer.
(Wallis & Wallis) $4,000

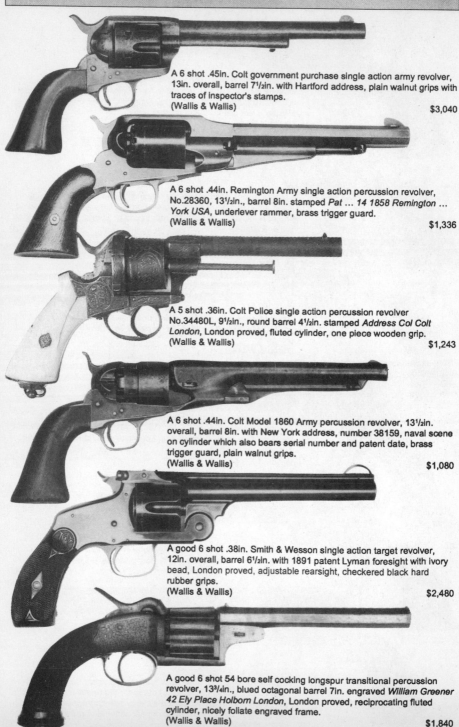

A 6 shot .45in. Colt government purchase single action army revolver, 13in. overall, barrel 7¹/₂in. with Hartford address, plain walnut grips with traces of inspector's stamps.
(Wallis & Wallis)

$3,040

A 6 shot .44in. Remington Army single action percussion revolver, No.28360, 13¹/₂in., barrel 8in. stamped *Pat ... 14 1858 Remington ... York USA*, underlever rammer, brass trigger guard.
(Wallis & Wallis)

$1,336

A 5 shot .36in. Colt Police single action percussion revolver No.34480L, 9¹/₂in., round barrel 4¹/₂in. stamped *Address Col Colt London*, London proved, fluted cylinder, one piece wooden grip.
(Wallis & Wallis)

$1,243

A 6 shot .44in. Colt Model 1860 Army percussion revolver, 13¹/₂in. overall, barrel 8in. with New York address, number 38159, naval scene on cylinder which also bears serial number and patent date, brass trigger guard, plain walnut grips.
(Wallis & Wallis)

$1,080

A good 6 shot .38in. Smith & Wesson single action target revolver, 12in. overall, barrel 6¹/₂in. with 1891 patent Lyman foresight with ivory bead, London proved, adjustable rearsight, checkered black hard rubber grips.
(Wallis & Wallis)

$2,480

A good 6 shot 54 bore self cocking longspur transitional percussion revolver, 13³/₄in., blued octagonal barrel 7in. engraved *William Greener 42 Ely Place Holborn London*, London proved, reciprocating fluted cylinder, nicely foliate engraved frame.
(Wallis & Wallis)

$1,840

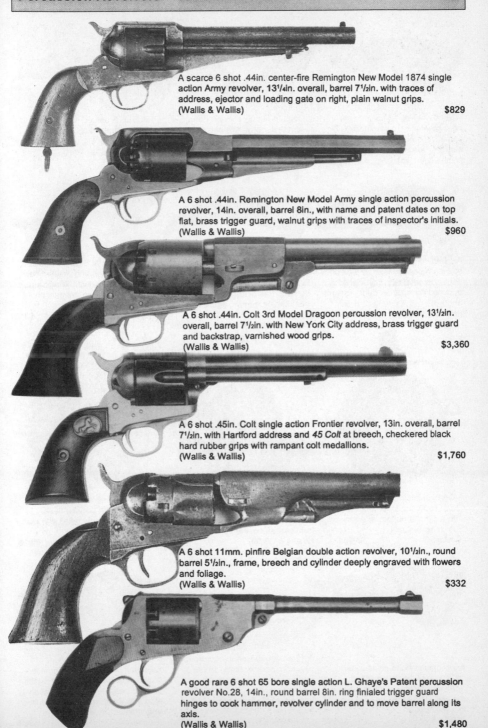

A scarce 6 shot .44in. center-fire Remington New Model 1874 single action Army revolver, 13¹/₄in. overall, barrel 7¹/₂in. with traces of address, ejector and loading gate on right, plain walnut grips.
(Wallis & Wallis) $829

A 6 shot .44in. Remington New Model Army single action percussion revolver, 14in. overall, barrel 8in., with name and patent dates on top flat, brass trigger guard, walnut grips with traces of inspector's initials.
(Wallis & Wallis) $960

A 6 shot .44in. Colt 3rd Model Dragoon percussion revolver, 13¹/₂in. overall, barrel 7¹/₂in. with New York City address, brass trigger guard and backstrap, varnished wood grips.
(Wallis & Wallis) $3,360

A 6 shot .45in. Colt single action Frontier revolver, 13in. overall, barrel 7¹/₂in. with Hartford address and *45 Colt* at breech, checkered black hard rubber grips with rampant colt medallions.
(Wallis & Wallis) $1,760

A 6 shot 11mm. pinfire Belgian double action revolver, 10¹/₂in., round barrel 5¹/₂in., frame, breech and cylinder deeply engraved with flowers and foliage.
(Wallis & Wallis) $332

A good rare 6 shot 65 bore single action L. Ghaye's Patent percussion revolver No.28, 14in., round barrel 8in. ring finialed trigger guard hinges to cock hammer, revolver cylinder and to move barrel along its axis.
(Wallis & Wallis) $1,480

A good Norwegian carved cow horn powder horn dated *1671*, 7in., carved with Adam and Eve, serpent, tree of knowledge.
(Wallis & Wallis)   **$3,200**

Cannon supply powder horn, America, early 19th century, with brass fittings, 26¹/₂in. long.
(Skinner)   **$1,725**

A French carved ivory powder-flask, Dieppe School, mid-19th century, with slightly curved body carved in relief, 10in.
(Sotheby's)   **$1,150**

An 18th century Spanish Colonial cow horn powder horn, 8¹/₂in., body carved in relief with imperial edge, crowned lions, birds, dogs, flowers and sun.
(Wallis & Wallis)   **$480**

A good Norwegian carved cow horn powder horn, dated *1736*, 7in., carved with Adam and Eve, serpent, tree of knowledge, seven mounted horsemen, figure with dragon.
(Wallis & Wallis)   **$2,880**

A good, unusual South American scrimshaw engraved powder horn, 11¹/₂in. engraved with musicians, exotic bird, stylized animals and a couple dancing.
(Wallis & Wallis)   **$318**

A German inlaid priming-flask, circa 1580–1600, the inner face inlaid with a circular pattern of engraved horn foliage, 4³/₈in.
(Sotheby's)   **$3,450**

A large engraved casein powder flask, 11in., well engraved with Diana shooting arrow at boar, tortoiseshell covered back.
(Wallis & Wallis)   **$1,000**

An early 17th century Continental circular wooden powder flask, 4¹/₂in. carved in low relief with four assorted animals.
(Wallis & Wallis)   **$320**

An engraved bone powder flask, 11¹/₂in., well engraved within horizontal bands with Europa and the bull, Diana the huntress, and fantastic birds.
(Wallis & Wallis)   **$840**

A 19th century Spanish engraved cow horn powder horn, 10¹/₂in., engraved with the crowned Spanish arms of Castile and Leon, imperial eagle and scenes of deer hunting and dueling.
(Wallis & Wallis)   **$800**

A French brass-mounted powder-flask, mid 19th century, with bottle-shaped body embossed on each side with a dog mask between two boar's heads, 8¹/₄in.
(Bonhams)   **$284**

A large 19th century engraved cow horn powder horn, 18½in., engraved with naive buildings, musicians, fish, animals, cannons.
(Wallis & Wallis) $520

A 19th century engraved cow horn powder horn, 11½in., engraved with Queen Victoria wearing elaborate regalia, beneath a figure in Shakespearean dress.
(Wallis & Wallis) $880

A brass mounted flattened cowhorn powder flask, 9¼in., common charger stamped *Lesplaut A Paris*, with trade mark of French horn.
(Wallis & Wallis) $127

An engraved cow horn powder horn dated *1841*, 15½in., engraved in naive style with country house, angel, lancer and lady both riding out.
(Wallis & Wallis) $680

A rare scrimshaw decorated American horn, dated *August 1844*, made from a large black tipped cream animal horn, the open end with traces of nickel silver rim binding, overall 14in.
(Andrew S Bottomley)
    $2,400

A French brass-mounted powder-flask, mid 19th century, with shaped body embossed with hanging game on each side, 9in.
(Bonhams) $205

An East European inlaid wooden powder-flask, circa 1720-30, probably Bohemian or Polish, with large flat-sided circular rootwood body, 6¾in.
(Sotheby's) $1,955

A fine German carved ivory powder-flask, third quarter of the 17th century, perhaps Schwäbisch Gmünd, filled on one side with a silver medallion cast in relief, 4⁷/₈in.
(Sotheby's) $6,900

An important Spanish gold-damascened iron priming flask made for the Farnese family, Dukes of Parma and Piacenza, late 16th century.
(Sotheby's) $20,700

An engraved bone powder flask, 13½in., engraved with two hunters with their dogs resting beneath a tree, foliate borders, bullion shoulder cord.
(Wallis & Wallis) $840

A staghorn powder flask dated *1590*, 9in., smooth body engraved with stylized bust portrait above foliage with *BEHE 1590*.
(Wallis & Wallis) $1,120

A French brass-mounted powder-flask, mid 19th century, with shaped body finely embossed with a lion-mask and foliage on each side, 7¾in.
(Bonhams) $300

A Victorian officer's sabretache of the Royal Artillery, bullion embroidered with Royal Arms, foliage and motto. (Sotheby's) $384

A sabretache of the Cavalrie Presidence, circa 1849, of black leather with bound edges and applied brass eagle. (Sotheby's) $525

A Victorian officer's sabretache of the Royal Gloucestershire Hussars, bullion embroidered crown on dark blue felt ground. (Sotheby's) $1,344

Earl of Chester's Yeomanry (Hussars) sabretache, a rare full dress officer's example, dark blue backing cloth with silver embroidery. (Bosleys) $2,080

A Victorian officer's sabretache of the 8th Kings Royal Irish Hussars, battle honors, Leswarree, Hindoostan, Alma, Balaklava, Inkerman, Sevastopol, Central India and Afghanistan. (Sotheby's) $1,728

5th Inniskilling Dragoon Guards officer's sabretache and pouch, circa 1840, of green morocco leather with a dark green velvet face. (Bosleys) $3,600

A Georgian officer's sabretache of the 18th Light Dragoons, bullion embroidered with crowned reversed G.R. cypher and battle honors Peninsula and Waterloo. (Sotheby's) $2,400

West Kent Yeomanry officer's sabretache, red morocco lined scarlet face edged with two inch 'Austrian wave and vellum' silver lace. (Bosleys) $1,200

A Victorian officer's sabretache of the 10th Prince of Wales Own Hussars, battle honors Peninsula, Waterloo, Sevastopol, Ali-Hasjid Afghanistan 1878/79 and Egypt 1882.(Sotheby's) $2,113

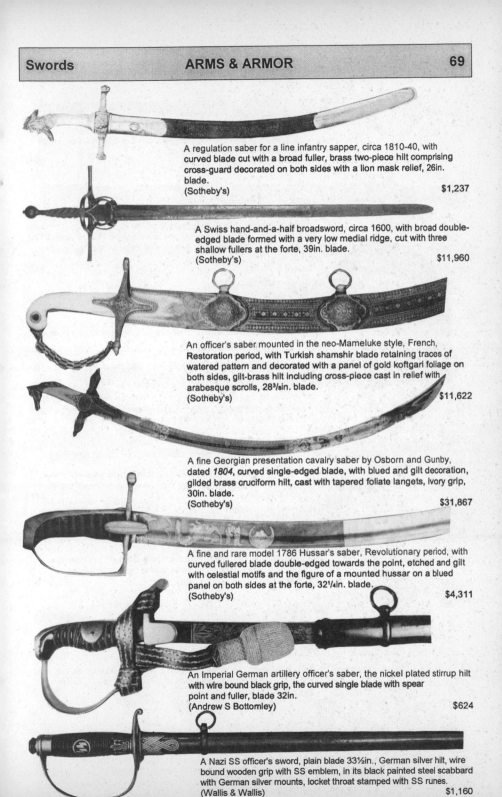

A regulation saber for a line infantry sapper, circa 1810-40, with curved blade cut with a broad fuller, brass two-piece hilt comprising cross-guard decorated on both sides with a lion mask relief, 26in. blade.
(Sotheby's) $1,237

A Swiss hand-and-a-half broadsword, circa 1600, with broad double-edged blade formed with a very low medial ridge, cut with three shallow fullers at the forte, 39in. blade.
(Sotheby's) $11,960

An officer's saber mounted in the neo-Mameluke style, French, Restoration period, with Turkish shamshir blade retaining traces of watered pattern and decorated with a panel of gold koftgari foliage on both sides, gilt-brass hilt including cross-piece cast in relief with arabesque scrolls, 28³/₈in. blade.
(Sotheby's) $11,622

A fine Georgian presentation cavalry saber by Osborn and Gunby, dated *1804*, curved single-edged blade, with blued and gilt decoration, gilded brass cruciform hilt, cast with tapered foliate langets, ivory grip, 30in. blade.
(Sotheby's) $31,867

A fine and rare model 1786 Hussar's saber, Revolutionary period, with curved fullered blade double-edged towards the point, etched and gilt with celestial motifs and the figure of a mounted hussar on a blued panel on both sides at the forte, 32¹/₄in. blade.
(Sotheby's) $4,311

An Imperial German artillery officer's saber, the nickel plated stirrup hilt with wire bound black grip, the curved single blade with spear point and fuller, blade 32in.
(Andrew S Bottomley) $624

A Nazi SS officer's sword, plain blade 33½in., German silver hilt, wire bound wooden grip with SS emblem, in its black painted steel scabbard with German silver mounts, locket throat stamped with SS runes.
(Wallis & Wallis) $1,160

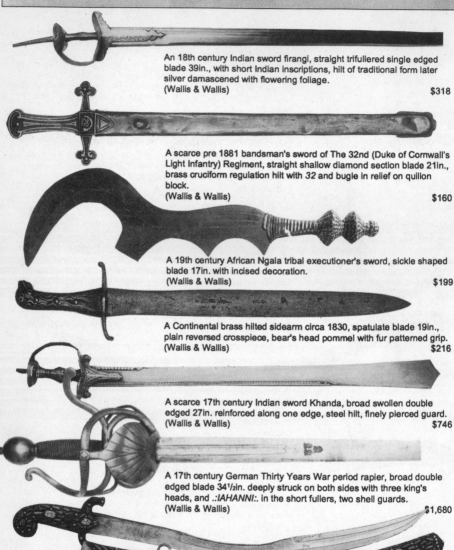

An 18th century Indian sword firangi, straight trifullered single edged blade 39in., with short Indian inscriptions, hilt of traditional form later silver damascened with flowering foliage.
(Wallis & Wallis) $318

A scarce pre 1881 bandsman's sword of The 32nd (Duke of Cornwall's Light Infantry) Regiment, straight shallow diamond section blade 21in., brass cruciform regulation hilt with 32 and bugle in relief on quillon block.
(Wallis & Wallis) $160

A 19th century African Ngala tribal executioner's sword, sickle shaped blade 17in. with incised decoration.
(Wallis & Wallis) $199

A Continental brass hilted sidearm circa 1830, spatulate blade 19in., plain reversed crosspiece, bear's head pommel with fur patterned grip.
(Wallis & Wallis) $216

A scarce 17th century Indian sword Khanda, broad swollen double edged 27in. reinforced along one edge, steel hilt, finely pierced guard.
(Wallis & Wallis) $746

A 17th century German Thirty Years War period rapier, broad double edged blade 34½in. deeply struck on both sides with three king's heads, and .:IAHANNI:. in the short fullers, two shell guards.
(Wallis & Wallis) $1,680

A Turkish kilitch, the hilt and scabbard decorated with corals and semi-precious stones, Turkish blade with gold koftgari overlay, 27½in.
(Bonhams) $6,825

A Venetian 'Schiavona' type sword, circa 1780, with superb parcel gilt silver pommel and original silver binding with leather cover for ricasso, blade 34½in.
(Bonhams) $1,787

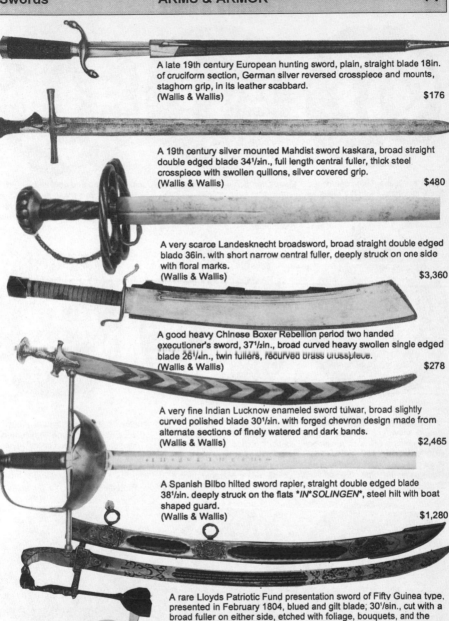

A late 19th century European hunting sword, plain, straight blade 18in. of cruciform section, German silver reversed crosspiece and mounts, staghorn grip, in its leather scabbard.
(Wallis & Wallis) $176

A 19th century silver mounted Mahdist sword kaskara, broad straight double edged blade 34½in., full length central fuller, thick steel crosspiece with swollen quillons, silver covered grip.
(Wallis & Wallis) $480

A very scarce Landesknecht broadsword, broad straight double edged blade 36in. with short narrow central fuller, deeply struck on one side with floral marks.
(Wallis & Wallis) $3,360

A good heavy Chinese Boxer Rebellion period two handed executioner's sword, 37½in., broad curved heavy swollen single edged blade 26¼in., twin fullers, recurved brass crosspiece.
(Wallis & Wallis) $278

A very fine Indian Lucknow enameled sword tulwar, broad slightly curved polished blade 30½in. with forged chevron design made from alternate sections of finely watered and dark bands.
(Wallis & Wallis) $2,465

A Spanish Bilbo hilted sword rapier, straight double edged blade 38½in. deeply struck on the flats *IN*SOLINGEN*, steel hilt with boat shaped guard.
(Wallis & Wallis) $1,280

A rare Lloyds Patriotic Fund presentation sword of Fifty Guinea type, presented in February 1804, blued and gilt blade; 30⅛in., cut with a broad fuller on either side, etched with foliage, bouquets, and the figures of Britannia and Hope.
(Sotheby's) $32,096

An English sword, circa 1610, with iron hilt and original grip, German blade 34½in., marked *SOLINGEN* to one side and *ME FECIT* to the other.
(Bonhams) $1,137

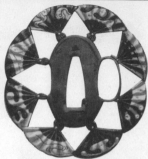

Good iron tsuba, 19th century, finely hammered with the design of an open sickle in the manner of Noritsuki, 3¹/₈in. (Butterfield & Butterfield)　　　$977

Good Onin School inlaid brass tsuba, 17th century, pierced with the chapter marker from the Tale of Genji, 3in. high. (Butterfield & Butterfield)　　　$800

Fine shakudo and gold tsuba, 18th century, rendered with eight open sensu fans, all embellished in gold uttori-zogan, 2¾in. high. (Butterfield & Butterfield)　　　$1,265

Satsuma shakudo tsuba, Meiji period, showing Shoki polishing his sword under a willow by a waterfall; signed *Bunsei Ko Hinoe-inu nigatsu kishi-nichi sasshu Kuwabatake Tadayoshi*, 3in. high. (Butterfield & Butterfield)　　　$3,500

Mixed metal iron tsuba, 19th century, possibly Edo Ito School, cast with gilt cherry blossoms floating on waves, 2⁷/₈in. (Butterfield & Butterfield)　　　$700

Good Minogoto style mixed metal decorated tsuba, late 18th century, rendered in gold and silver on a nanako ground with bamboo, chrysanthemums, bushclover, 3¹/₃in. high. (Butterfield & Butterfield)　　　$1,610

Copper tsuba, Edo period, a Shonai School work rendered in silvered copper with kaki fruit, copper and silver mokume fukurin, unsigned, 2½in. high.(Butterfield & Butterfield)　　　$375

Fine tsuba, 19th century, rendered in gold and shakudo takazogan with crabs swimming in a meandering stream, 3¹/₈in. high. (Butterfield & Butterfield)　　　$2,070

Good Saotome chrysanthemum wheel shape tsuba, mid 17th century, the petal edged iron plate cut into sixty-four spokes, 3⁵/₈in. (Butterfield & Butterfield)　　　$1,725

Silver tsuba, 19th century, rendered with Fukurokuju and Ebisu reading a long scroll, 2¾in. high. (Butterfield & Butterfield) $517

Akasaka School tsuba, early 17th century, cast in the form of a double vajra, unsigned, 3in. long. (Butterfield & Butterfield) $1,380

Fine tsuba, 19th century, rendered in gold and shakudo on a shishiabori ground with kirin in flight, 2¾in. high. (Butterfield & Butterfield) $920

Akasaka School tsuba, 18th century, cast with a crane and minogame in a bamboo landscape, signed *Bushuju Akasaka Tadayoshi saku*, 2³/₈in. long. (Butterfield & Butterfield) $632

An associated set of sword fittings, 19th century, consisting of a pair of Fuchi Kashira, a tsuba and a kozuka, all rendered on a shakudo nanako ground, tsuba 2⁷/₈in. (Butterfield & Butterfield) $3,450

Good Mito School shakudo and gold inlaid tsuba, late 18th century, rendered with a gold dragon emerging from billowing waves pursuing the flaming jewel, 3in. high. (Butterfield & Butterfield) $2,875

Aizu Shoami School tsuba with shell decoration, early Edo period, the heavy iron plate inlaid with copper shells, 3³/₈in. wide. (Butterfield & Butterfield) $805

Gilt copper tsuba, 19th century, cast with an openwork cross containing two pairs of confronted dragons in waves, 2¾in. high. (Butterfield & Butterfield) $450

Kinai School iron tsuba, circa 1750, fashioned as an openwork lozenge-shaped cluster of leaves delicately designed, signed *Yohizen ju Kinai saku*, 3¹/₈in. wide. (Butterfield & Butterfield) $575

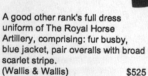

A good other rank's full dress uniform of The Royal Horse Artillery, comprising: fur busby, blue jacket, pair overalls with broad scarlet stripe. (Wallis & Wallis) $525

City of London Yeomanry Rough Riders trooper's uniform, blue gray material with purple facings to the plastron front. (Bosleys) $616

Uniform of ADC to Queen Victoria, comprising cocked hat, tunic, scarlet with ADC pattern waist sash. (Bosleys) $1,360

Royal Engineers Officer's coatee, 1837-1848, scarlet cloth with dark blue velvet facings to the collar and cuffs. (Bosleys) $1,200

56th Punjabi Rifles (Frontier Force) officer's tunic, rifle pattern example of beige melton cloth with dark green facings to collar and cuffs. (Bosleys) $800

A scarce Royal Navy officer's full dress blue tailcoat circa 1840, scarlet facings, double breasted with two lines of ten buttons to chest. (Wallis & Wallis) $496

A good post 1902 Royal Navy Engineer Commander's full dress uniform, comprising: Officer's bicorn hat, tail coat, epaulettes, and sword belt.
(Bosleys) $480

Lancashire Fusiliers 1902 pattern Other Rank's uniform, to the left breast a single medal ribbon of the Military Medal.
(Bosleys) $1,040

A good post 1902 Royal Horse Guards trooper's helmet, tunic cuirass, silvered skull with brass and silvered King's Crown helmet plate to front.
(Bosleys) $2,080

WAAF issue uniform, worn by a sergeant wireless operator, service dress peaked cap, service dress four pocket tunic with sergeant chevrons. (Bosleys) $416

WWII issue Civil Defence Ambulance driver's tunic, attributed to the County of Yorkshire, to the left breast pocket a crowned CD embroidered badge.
(Bosleys) $232

WWII period US Marine Corps uniform & equipment, comprising steel M1 helmet, herringbone stitched jacket, matching trousers and combat service boots.
(Bosleys) $280

A rare German Hauptmann's parade tunic for a Panzer Regiment, with pink piping to the collar, cuffs and epaulettes. (Bosleys) $480

Grenadier Guards Lieutenant Colonel's tunic, of scarlet melton cloth with blue facings to the cuff, collar and epaulettes. (Bosleys) $800

A scarce Imperial German Zeppelin Crew navy blue jacket, double row of plated buttons to front, six ditto to each cuff, with device of Imperial German crown and fouled anchor. (Wallis & Wallis) $795

17th Lancers trooper's plastron tunic, post 1902 example, of dark blue woollen cloth with white plastron to the front. (Bosleys) $512

Austrian Captain's parade tunic, of sky blue cloth, with black velvet facings to the collar and cuffs. (Bosleys) $224

Royal Air Force airman's first pattern blue tunic, of light blue woollen material, to the left breast medal ribbons of the British War and Victory Medal. (Bosleys) $352

56th Punjabi Rifles (Frontier Force) officer's mess jacket, of beige melton cloth with dark green facings to collar and cuffs. (Bosleys) $240

58th CEF WWI other rank's uniform, Canadian manufactured 1902 pattern tunic, khaki woollen breeches, trench cap, Brodie D pattern steel helmet, greatcoat. (Bosley's) $2,567

Rifle Brigade officer's tunic and pouch belt, post 1953, dark green material with plaited mohair shoulder cords bearing Captain's rank insignia. (Bosleys) $320

Yorkshire Dragoons officer's tunic, of dark blue melton cloth edged with silver piping with white facings to the collar and cuffs. (Bosleys) $384

An officer's red serge tropical scarlet frock of The 21st (Royal Scots Fusiliers) circa 1881, blue collar, silver plated grenade collar badges bearing thistle spray on the ball. (Wallis & Wallis) $525

Royal Army Medical Corps 1902 officer's tunic, to each cuff, rank lace denoting the rank of Lt Col. (Bosleys) $520

A silver mounted swordstick, single edged polished fullered blade 23¹/₄in., twist fitting to male malacca cane, foliate embossed silver pommel hallmarked *Birmingham 1890*.
(Wallis & Wallis)   **$760**

A Georgian swordstick, slim diamond section blade 26in. with blued foliate pattern decoration, trace of gold wash decoration, gnarled horn grip.
(Wallis & Wallis)   **$336**

A late 19th century walking stick, rosewood stick, foliate chased silver ferrule, bone grip carved with boar bayed up by dogs, bone tip.
(Wallis & Wallis)   **$464**

A good Georgian swordstick with ivory pommel carved with a bust portrait of Admiral Lord Nelson, single edged fullered blade 28¹/₂in., brass ferrule, copper gilt eyelets for wrist cord.
(Wallis & Wallis)   **$1,640**

A Victorian swordstick, slim, tapering diamond section blade 27in., retaining approximately 60% blued and gilt etched decoration of foliate scrolls, spring catch to malacca hilt.
(Wallis & Wallis)   **$480**

A good 19th century Indian all ivory walking stick, 35¹/₂in., handle in the form of an elephant's head with integral lion's head facing opposite direction.
(Wallis & Wallis)   **$762**

A good quality mid 19th century Continental blued and gilt sword cane, straight single edged fullered blade 26in., ivory handle nicely carved as Napoleon's head.
(Wallis & Wallis)   **$1,360**

A Victorian swordstick, malacca hilt with stud release spring catch, diamond section blade 27in., etched with blued foliate scrolls with gilt background.
(Wallis & Wallis)   **$352**

A Victorian swordstick, straight single edged blade 26in. (from a 1796 Georgian infantry officer's sword), etched with military trophies and foliage, wood hilt.
(Wallis & Wallis)   **$265**

An unusual Georgian swordcane of Dr Syntax, 28¹/₂in. overall, square section blade 17in., pressed horn handle in the form of Dr Syntax, brass ferrule, cane stick.
(Wallis & Wallis)   **$530**

A Georgian malacca swordstick, mounted with blade of an 18th century smallsword, 26in., etched with Turkish bonnet, talisman emblems, etc, malacca hilt, spring catch.
(Wallis & Wallis)   **$176**

An interesting 19th century Indian steel bow, 41½in., etched *Made in Dharampur*, together with an Islamic inscription within rectangular border, two piece riveted horn grips.
(Wallis & Wallis) $560

A finely constructed pipe-tomahawk, circa 1870-90, probably intended for presentation, ax-blade with one face finely engraved with a small buffalo mask, 21⅛in. (Sotheby's) $9,200

An unusual 19th century all steel Indian ax with concealed dagger, 25in., slender crescent head 8in. supported by a wrought framework, octagonal steel haft, pommel unscrews to reveal 10in. stiletto blade.
(Wallis & Wallis) $272

A horseman's hammer, late 16th century, with small ax blade with bearded cutting edge, flat-sided écussons flanking the socket and down-curved rear spike of tapering rectangular section, on its original wooden haft, 21¾in. (Sotheby's) $1,840

A rare German (Saxon) miners guild ceremonial ax, dated 1701, the blade of characteristic form with long pointed edge terminating in small brass acorn shaped cap, the center of the blade pierced with a trefoil device. The sharply recurved bone shaft, finely decorated with six very attractive and interesting vignettes, overall 31in.
(Andrew S Bottomley) $3,520

A scarce Turkish war hammer, early iron head 6¾in. with silver inlaid with geometric shapes and dots, pointed four sided curved tapered beak, swollen hammer head shaped head with extension.
(Wallis & Wallis) $1,680

A rare German horseman's war hammer, early 16th century, the head formed in one piece with small rectangular hammer and slightly downcurved rear beak, 18½in. (Sotheby's) $5,175

A scarce 19th century British Military cavalry farrier's axe, 40in. overall, massive steel head with 10in. crescent blade and 7½in. square section tapered back spike.
(Wallis & Wallis) $1,080

Charles M. Schultz, original 8 x 11½in. color sketch of Snoopy, on card, signed to base.
(Vennett-Smith) $430

B. L. Montgomery, signed 5 x 7in., three quarter length standing in field.
(Vennett-Smith) $132

Gene Roddenbury, signed copy of Star Trek II, writers/directors guide, 12th Aug. 1977 to cover.
(Vennett-Smith) $264

Cricket, Australia, a good signed album page 5 x 4in., by 14 members of the side which played at Nottingham on 12–15th June 1926.
(Vennett-Smith) $248

Horatio Nelson, autographed signed letter, one page, Nelson and Bronte, London 6th November 1801, to Lieutenant Dickinson.
(Vennett-Smith) $825

Duke Ellington, signed and inscribed program for British Tour, Oct. 1971, to full page photo, together with newspaper clippings, photos and related ephemera.
(Vennett-Smith) $157

Nelson Mandela, signed 5 x 6½in., modern reproduction dated 9th Nov. 1996.
(Vennett-Smith) $320

Kathleen Ferrier, 4 x 3½in. photo, with autographed signed letter to reverse, 1953.
(Vennett-Smith) $264

Margot Fonteyn, signed 6½ x 8½in., head and shoulders, in costume.
(Vennett-Smith) $60

Neil Armstrong, signed and inscribed color 8 x 10in., half-length in spacesuit.
(Vennett-Smith) $231

Helen Keller, signed 5 x 7in., three quarter length reading in her study, in usual pencil.
(Vennett-Smith) $462

Martha Graham, signed and inscribed 8 x 10in., head and shoulders.
(Vennett-Smith) $182

Agatha Christie, signed piece 3½ x 1in., overmounted in cream beneath a 9 x 11½in. original sepia photo of Christie, head and shoulders by Salter Bird, framed and glazed.
(Vennett-Smith) $165

Picasso, copy of 9 x 12in. print entitled Cannes, being the poster for an Exhibition 14th August – 30th September 1956, signed in red crayon.
(Vennett-Smith) $1,023

Tyson and Holmes, signed color 8 x 10in., by Larry Holmes and Mike Tyson (gold), both in ring fighting.
(Vennett-Smith) $149

Maria Callas, signed 6 x 4in., head and shoulders, Maria Meneghini Callas.
(Vennett-Smith) $462

David Hockney, signed 8 x 10in., half-length seated smoking cigarette.
(Vennett-Smith) $58

Pope John Paul II, signed color 4 x 6in., head and shoulders, dated 12.V.95.
(Vennett-Smith) $280

Martin Bormann, signed document, 14 pages, most blank, 7th Aug. 1944, relating to Gustav Simon of Koblenz.
(Vennett-Smith) $760

Helena Rubinstein, signed sepia 10 x 8in., head and shoulders standing by sculpture of a horse.
(Vennett-Smith) $140

Yitshak Rabin, signed postcard, head and shoulders.
(Vennett-Smith) $83

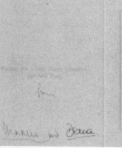

Ulysses Grant, signed document as President, one page, Washington, 28th Feb. 1871, authorising a warrant for the pardon of Otto Andrea (alias Otto Walde).
(Vennett-Smith) $578

Charles and Diana, signed Christmas Greetings Card by both, featuring colored photo of family.
(Vennett-Smith) $1,518

John Chard, V.C., Officer Commanding Rorkes Drift, autograph signed letter, two and a half pages, to the Rev Joy, 15th May 1890, referring to reading a book on a train and sending Joy a duplicate.
(Vennett-Smith) $1,452

Amy Johnson, signed 5 x 7in., head and shoulders in flying cap.
(Vennett-Smith) $132

Mike Tyson, signed color 10 x 8in., full-length fighting against Bruno, certificate from Stans Sports Memorabilia.
(Vennett-Smith) $140

Hoagy Carmichael, signed 8 x 10in., head and shoulders in hat.
(Vennett-Smith) $124

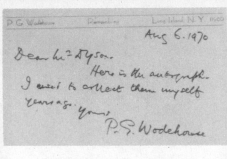

Anna Pavlova, signed sepia postcard, full-length dancing. (Vennett-Smith) **$215**

P.G. Wodehouse, brief autograph signed letter on correspondence card, 6th Aug. 1970, stating that he used to collect autographs years ago. (Vennett-Smith) **$182**

Enrico Caruso, signed postcard, head and shoulders. (Vennett-Smith) **$363**

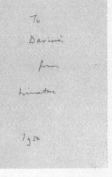

Louis Armstrong, an early 1934 sepia photograph showing the young Louis reading Melody Maker wearing plus fours, signed. (Bonhams) **$560**

Charles and Diana, signed Christmas card, 1983, by both Prince Charles and Princess Diana, with color illustration of them with a baby Prince William. (Vennett-Smith) **$1,155**

Winston S. Churchill, hardback edition of The Grand Alliance, 1st edition, 1950, signed and inscribed to flyleaf to Davina (Duchess of Norfolk?). (Vennett-Smith) **$1,188**

Sigmund Romberg, signed 5 x 7in., head and shoulders. (Vennett-Smith) **$115**

Oscar Wilde, autographed envelope, unsigned, written to A.B. Clifton, in London, in his hand, together with an autographed signed letter written to Wilde, published 1899. (Vennett-Smith) **$314**

Mother Teresa, signed 7 x 9¹/₂in., head and shoulders. (Vennett-Smith) **$230**

Josephine Baker, signed postcard, head and shoulders. (Vennett-Smith) **$248**

Admiral Chester W. Nimitz, a good signed and inscribed 12 x 10½in. signing the Japanese surrender on board USS Missouri, Tokyo Bay, 2nd Sept. 1945. (Vennett-Smith) **$560**

Cole Porter, signed 2¾ x 3¾in., head and shoulders. (Vennett-Smith) **$297**

Brian Epstein, hardback edition of a Cellarful of Noise, 1st edition, 1964, signed and inscribed to flyleaf, *to Jimmy, one of my favourites, Brian.* (Vennett-Smith) **$330**

Richard Nixon, signed and inscribed 8½ x 6in., head and shoulders. (Vennett-Smith) **$149**

General Charles Gordon, autographed signed letter, one page, 9th Jan. 1884, routine content. (Vennett-Smith) **$264**

Count Basie, signed 5 x 7½in., also signed by fifteen members of his band to reverse. (Vennett-Smith) **$102**

Wernher von Braun, signed and inscribed 8 x 10in., half-length seated at desk, signature a little patchy. (Vennett-Smith) **$297**

Ernest Shackleton, signed postcard, full-length in Arctic clothing. (Vennett-Smith) **$230**

Edward VII, signed 7 x 11in., full-length in ceremonial uniform, 1910.
(Vennett-Smith) $346

Britten and Pears, signed postcard, by both Benjamin Britten and Peter Pears individually, April 1953, with additional autographed signed note by Pears to reverse.
(Vennett-Smith) $297

Winston S. Churchill, early signed postcard, Rotary 96A, half-length.
(Vennett-Smith) $1,220

George VI, a fine signed 12½ x 17in. sepia photo, as King, to lower border, dated in his hand 1948, in RAF uniform.
(Vennett-Smith) $346

Muhammed Ali, signed color 8 x 10in., half-length in boxing pose, with certificate from Prince of Cards.
(Vennett-Smith) $215

Louis Armstrong, program for Louis Armstrong & His All-Stars British Tour 1956, signed to full photo page to back cover.
(Vennett-Smith) $145

Robert Baden Powell, signed postcard, head and shoulders as Chief Scout.
(Vennett-Smith) $264

Mikhail Gorbachev, signed 7 x 5in., head and shoulders holding pen.
(Vennett-Smith) $280

Harry Houdini, signed 5 x 7in., head and shoulders with surname only.
(Vennett-Smith) $957

Yuri Gagarin, signed newspaper photo, laid neatly down to postcard and annotated in another hand in Spanish beneath.
(Vennett-Smith) $280

Edward VIII, signed personal crested notepaper, by Edward Duke of Windsor and Wallis Windsor, 5½ x 3½in., together with compliment slip.
(Vennett-Smith) $190

Mark Twain, small signed piece S.L. Clemens, 3½ x ½in., laid down beneath photo album page 4½ x 7½in., scarce.
(Vennett-Smith) $330

Adolf Hitler, large signed 9½ x 14½in. photograph, to lower white border, head and shoulders with chin resting on hand, photo by Kleine of Hanover, circa 1934–7.
(Vennett-Smith) $2,722

Theodore Roosevelt, typed signed letter, one page, to Galvatore Cortesi, Porto Maurizio, 4th April 1910, *I am immensely amused over the law suit against the Herald.*
(Vennett-Smith) $305

General Francisco Franco, signed sepia postcard, head and shoulders in uniform, with covering letter from secretary, 27th May 1953.
(Vennett-Smith) $182

Jimmy Wilde, signed postcard, three quarter length in boxing pose, with champion's belt, 28th May 1941.
(Vennett-Smith) $74

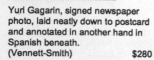

Abraham Lincoln, signed piece cut from the end of a letter, 3¼ x 1in., neatly laid down and annotated in red, *he was born to be great.*
(Vennett-Smith) $1,683

Theodore Roosevelt, signed 14 x 17in. to lower mount, dated 23rd Oct. 1908, as President, head and shoulders wearing spectacles.
(Vennett-Smith) $858

Edward VIII, a fine signed 6 x 8in., as Prince of Wales, dated in his hand, 1929–1935, three quarter length in full guards uniform.
(Vennett-Smith) $495

Nikita Kruschev, signed color postcard of the Kontiki Expedition 1947 to reverse, also signed by Einar Gerhardsten (Prime Minister of Norway).
(Vennett-Smith) $240

Winston S. Churchill, signed bookplate photo, as First Lord of the Admiralty, removed from The World Crisis, 1911–1918, 5¹/₂ x 8in.
(Vennett-Smith) $1,360

Col. Harland Sanders, signed and inscribed 8 x 10in., half-length with hands folded, laid down to 8¹/₂ x 12in. album page.
(Vennett-Smith) $100

Mike Tyson, signed color 8 x 10in., half-length in boxing pose, wearing championship belt, with certificate from Prince of Cards (USA).
(Vennett-Smith) $115

Louis Armstrong, signed and inscribed 8 x 10in., in both forms, half-length playing trumpet, in green.
(Vennett-Smith) $173

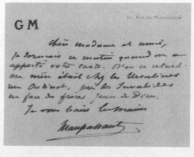

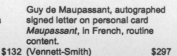

Sarah Bernhardt, signed sepia cabinet photo, 1903, photo by Downey.
(Vennett-Smith) $132

Guy de Maupassant, autographed signed letter on personal card Maupassant, in French, routine content.
(Vennett-Smith) $297

Calvin Coolidge, signed and inscribed sepia 7¹/₂ x 10¹/₂in., head and shoulders.
(Vennett-Smith) $314

HISTORICAL FACTS
Automatons

The earliest automatons were devised in the 18th century by a Swiss family called Jacquet-Droz and they were the wonder of the sophisticated world at that time. Some early automatons were made in the form of animal orchestras with monkeys in powdered wigs and silken jackets playing instruments with musical accompaniments, or elegant singing birds in gilded cages, opening their beaks and turning their heads as they poured out their songs. The first automatons were, like watches, powered by ingeniously coiled springs but other inventors propeled their machines with compressed air, water, sand, mercury or steam. It was the spring however that proved to be the most popular and most efficient.

Early automatons by such famous names as Vaucanson, Robertson or Rechsteiner, particularly the writing and drawing machines, are worth thousands of pounds today. Talking dolls developed by Von Kempelen are in the same price bracket.

In the 19th century German manufacturers saw the possibility of mass producing automatic toys for children and their tin plate industry began to boom around the 1870s. These toys were not so sophisticated as the earlier automatons for they were pressed out by machines and their works were rudimentary but they were cheap and popular and were exported widely, especially to England.

A 'Toothache' musical automaton, the hunched papier mâché figure bending as the music plays, 30 tone cylinder mechanism, 1920s. (Auction Team Köln) $352

A manivelle musician automaton, Germany, circa 1890, with winding handle to one side of the base, 14in. (Sotheby's) $1,288

A musician and clown automaton, French, late 19th century, probably made by Gustave Vichy, the negro musician with composition head, moving mouth and neck, playing a banjo while tapping his foot, 33 x 28in. (Sotheby's) $24,000

A musical automaton of a tightrope walker, attributed to Jean Phalibois, French, circa 1870, stage consisting of ornately carved and gold leaf painted wood in oriental style, 22in. without dome, 18in. wide. (Sotheby's) $48,000

A clockwork dancing negro doll with painted features and red jacket, mounted on wires on a wooden box containing the mechanism, 10in. high. (Christie's) $781

A Vichy bisque-headed automaton of a violinist, with French fashionable doll's head, closed mouth, fixed brown eyes, dark wig, 17½in. high, the head probably Huret. (Christie's) $3,534

Clockwork cobbler, late 19th/early 20th century, composition body, mohair beard and glass eyes, 21in. high. (Skinner) $3,680

A Victorian shipping musical automaton, of painted card sailing ship and windmill, dome painted with coastal scene, 34cm. (Bristol) $504

19th century mechanical gilt birdcage with birds, with wind-up mechanism making birds sing, 21in. high. (Eldred's) $1,430

A Cecile wooden automaton doll, playing a melody from Beethoven's 5th Piano Concerto on a spinet in a red curtained pavilion, Japanese, circa 1965. (Auction Team Köln) $352

A Gustave Vichy nurse and baby automaton, French, circa 1890, the bisque-headed walking figure in original costume with moving legs, 17in. (Sotheby's) $5,888

A shop display automaton, probably French 1920s, the electrically operated movement operating the mechanical figure of a man in evening suit, 39in. high. (Sotheby's) $5,704

A fine and rare Gustave and Henri Vichy musical automaton of 'Sonnette de L'Entracte' with sleeping clown banjo player, French, circa 1890, 29½in. high. (Sotheby's) $56,000

A musical timepiece picture diorama, Swiss, circa 1860, enameled dial, glazed gilt wood and composition framed display case, 24in. high. (Sotheby's) $3,496

A pull along shepherdess automaton, German, probably Gottschalk, circa 1900, in olive green and black velvet dress, 11¾in. (Sotheby's) $1,104

Chrysler - a pair of electric headlamps with seal at the top of retaining ring; chrome-plated, pillar mounting; circa 1929, 11in. diameter (Christie's) $161

Tazio Nuvolari, an original manuscripted telegram post-marked Verona circa 1950, hand-written in blue ink by Nuvolari with regard to a race entry at Silverstone. (Christie's) $562

Rolls-Royce Spirit of Ecstasy, a large showroom display figure of the legendary sculpture created by Charles Sykes, heavy cast-bronze, 24in. high overall. (Christie's) $1,500

Drew and Sons 'En Route' – original picnic set for 4 persons, complete and contained in wicker case. (Christie's) $843

Ayrton Senna, JPS Lotus 1985 – The original race-suit overalls worn by the driver during the British Grand Prix. (Christie's) $33,741

Mille Miglia 1953 – A scarce commemorative printed cotton scarf; decorative silk-screen design incorporating well-known Mille Miglia logo and motif. (Christie's) $1,218

A running board mounted spare-wheel security carrier trunk with three straps to affix to spare tyre stamped *S.C. Simon & Co. Luggage, Phila; U.S.A.* circa 1912, 25in. diameter. (Christie's) $2,070

Jaguar, a silver-plated desk box depicting the XK120, mahogany-lined, with lock and key, by Glyn of London. (Christie's) $1,030

Marchal, - a pair of electric parking side lamps; French, circa 1920s, 4¹/₈in. diameter. (Christie's) $276

Pope Pius XII – A large processional motorcade pennant, double sided silk with leather reinforced edges – Daimler-Benz for a Papal visit, 12 x 13in.
(Christie's) $1,657

A pair of matching wicker-work pannier carriers suitable for running-board near fender mounting.
(Christie's) $1,035

Carl Benz & Co. – A large early bronze carburettor believed to be from early 2 cylinder engine circa 1894; cylinder choke mechanism.
(Christie's) $562

Jackie Stewart, World Champion Driver 1969,1971 and 1983, a rare original race-suit overall; worn by the driver during the 1969 and 1970 seasons.
(Christie's) $5,998

Accident Insurance Coy Ltd., a rare early pictorial advertising showcard for the Commercial Union Assurance Company, color lithograph, circa 1910, 14 x 18in.
(Christie's) $843

James Hunt, Marlboro McLaren World Champion 1976; an original race-used overall suit worn by James Hunt during the 1976 season.
(Christie's) $11,247

Rolls Royce, a decorative drinks decanter in the form of the famous radiator, by Ruddspeed; chrome-plated with definitive grille, English, circa 1960s.
(Christie's) $412

Woodlite - a rare pair of electric head-lamps marked *Western Distributor*, circa 1925,10in. high.
(Christie's) $1,150

Bernd Rosemeyer, a white linen racing wind-cap, given to Neubauer after a race event in 1937.
(Christie's) $6,000

A Victorian oak stick barometer, by A. Reid, Edinburgh, 38in. high. (Christie's) $380

Mahogany veneered barometer with shell and floral inlay by Tarone, Bristol. (Chapman Moore & Mugford) $669

A Victorian oak stick barometer, by Newton & Co., London, 39½in. high. (Christie's) $759

A Victorian mahogany wheel barometer, Burrington, Exeter , circa 1860, 39in. high. (Christie's) $699

A Louis XVI ormolu mounted walnut and mahogany combined cartel timepiece and thermometer, early 20th century, movement inscribed *Bourdon Paris,* 40½in. high. (Christie's) $3,507

A fine mahogany barometer by Dolland, London, circa 1820. (Derek Roberts) $4,400

A Victorian mahogany wheel barometer, mid 19th century, the case with ebony and satinwood stringing and with onion top, 40in. high. (Christie's) $405

A Victorian rosewood marine stick barometer, circa 1850, the case with acorn finial, 41in. high. (Christie's) $6,440

Regency period banjo barometer by Hynes of Lynn, 37½in. long. (G A Key)   £500

A mahogany stick Barometer, J. Smith London, circa 1820, 41in. (Christie's)   £1,155

A Regency satinwood barometer, inlaid with ebony lines, inscribed *J. Fiora/Nottingham*, 40¼in. high. (Christie's)   £0,005

A fine mahogany bow fronted stick barometer, Alexander Adie, circa 1800, 40½in. (Christie's)   £11,550

A fine mahogany bow front stick barometer by Spear, Dublin, circa 1810. (Derek Roberts) $8,800

A gilt-bronze barometer by Susse Frères, Paris, circa 1880, in Louis XVI style, 119cm. high. (Sotheby's) $9,715

A rosewood barometer with 6in. dial by Adie, Liverpool, circa 1850. (Derek Roberts) $2,800

A Regency mahogany and line-inlaid banjo barometer by D. Stampa, Leith St., Edinburgh, No. 14, 43½in. high. (Christie's) $1,138

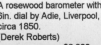

Shaker (?) two-handled splintwork basket, 7in. high, 18in. diameter. (Eldred's) $715

Nantucket basket, early 20th century, 7in. high. (Skinner) $575

Paint decorated two-handled splint basket, America, 19th century, painted pink and black, 15in. wide. (Skinner) $488

Nantucket basket, with turned wooden bottom, 5¼in. high, 9½in. diameter. (Eldred's) $880

Swing-handled apple basket, 19th century, 9½in. high, 14½in. diameter. (Eldred's) $357

Black painted melon basket, America, 19th century, 9in. diameter. (Skinner) $805

Large woven bamboo flower basket, Meiji/Taisho period, signed *Chikuunsai*, fashioned with an irregular but tight weave of bamboo strips rising to a wrapped rim, 17¼in. high. (Butterfield & Butterfield) $2,875

Eastern Woodland Indian paint decorated covered splint basket, 19th century, with salmon and black swab decoration, 15¾in. diameter. (Skinner) $4,312

Nantucket basket, early 20th century, paper label on base, *Lightship Basket made by Fred S. Chadwick Nantucket Mass. 4 Pine St.*, 4⅞in. high. (Skinner) $920

Large Nantucket basket, with wooden swing handle, shows restoration, 13½in. diameter. (Eldred's) $633

Shaker splint basket, probably New England, last quarter 19th century, with circular rim and shaped fixed handle, 7½in. diameter. (Skinner) $250

Nantucket lightship basket, dated 1891, paper label on base *made on board South Shoal Lightship by William Sandsbury*, 8¾in. diameter. (Skinner) $1,495

Trieder 12x binoculars by C.P. Goertz.
(Auction Team Köln) $191

Binoculars by Lemaire, Paris, 8x magnification, 12cm. long.
(Auction Team Köln) $139

Voigtländer 7 x 50 binoculars, both optics adjustable.
(Auction Team Köln) $256

Carl Zeiss Jena marine binoculars, 11cm, adjustable eyepieces.
(Auction Team Köln) $218

Rare Goerz prism binoculars, adjustable eyepieces, 11cm.
(Auction Team Köln) $183

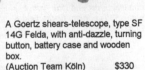

7 x 40 binoculars by Daiichi Seimitsu, gray-beige painted case.
(Auction Team Köln) $159

A Goertz shears-telescope, type SF 14G Felda, with anti-dazzle, turning button, battery case and wooden box.
(Auction Team Köln) $330

D.F. 8 x 60 H binoculars by Carl Zeiss, Jena, both eyepieces adjustable, with contrast filters and end covers, in original metal case.
(Auction Team Köln) $1,454

Zeiss Nedinsco 4 x 28 binoculars, with built in filter change and adjustable optics, 1940.
(Auction Team Köln) $430

7 x 56 binoculars by Hensoldt, Wetzlar, focusing on bridge and right optic, 22cm. long.
(Auction Team Köln) $125

Early binoculars by Hensoldt, Wetzlar, 12.5cm. long, circa 1900.
(Auction Team Köln) $145

A Regency ormolu bust of Bacchus, bearded man with spiraled locks and fillet, 7½in. high.
(Christie's) $4,963

An Italian bronze figure of a rearing stallion, in the manner of Giambologna, cast with flowing mane, 6⅛in. high.
(Sotheby's) $1,725

A French bronze group of a huntsman with his dog, cast by Barbedienne, third quarter 19th century, 17¼in. high.
(Christie's) $1,846

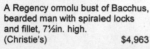

Ferdinand Preiss, Tambourine dancer, 1920s, gilt bronze and ivory figure of a scantily clad female dancer, in mid-step with her arms raised in the air, 13⅝in. high.
(Sotheby's) $6,334

Pair of fine and large archaistic covered 'Sunspot' bronzes, 17th/18th century, each of dou shape with circular lug handles, domical cover and high footed base, 17³⁄8in. high. (Butterfield & Butterfield) $5,750

Hagenauer, Oriental mask, 1930s, patinated metal and ebonized wood, cast as the stylized face of an oriental woman with sleek bobbed hair, 7¼in.
(Sotheby's) $3,457

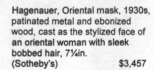

Bronze lion dog, 19th century, cast with his left front paw poised upon a beribboned ball, his tail separately cast, 27½in. long. (Butterfield & Butterfield) $3,450

Pierre le Faguays, Stevedore, 1920s, green patinated bronze, cast as a scantily clad athletic man hauling on a rope, 18⅛in. high.
(Sotheby's) $7,298

Joël and Jan Martel, seated cat, circa 1930, almost black patinated bronze, with stylized features, 15½in. (Sotheby's) $9,602

A Flemish bronze bust of a boy, 17th century, the curly-haired boy laughing with open mouth, 12in. high. (Sotheby's) $12,650

Silvestre, figural clock, 1920s, green patinated bronze, cast as a satyr and a lamb flanking a large ball, 26in. wide. (Sotheby's) $3,073

A bronze and ivory figure of a child skier, in wool hat and jumper, signed *Rarmond*, 7¼in high. (Andrew Hartley) $393

Marcel Bouraine, Fan dancer, 1920s, silvered and cold-painted bronze, cast as a naked female dancer, poised on one foot, holding up a large open fan, 24in. (Sotheby's) $6,146

A pair of French bronze groups of Fame and Mercury, after Antoine Coysevox, late 18th century, each dramatically cast on winged rearing stallions, 16³/₈in. (Sotheby's) $12,650

A pair of gilt-bronze and silvered ewers, in the Mannerist style, each with a scroll handle surmounted by a cherub, 103cm. high. (Sotheby's) $13,024

Good gilt bronze figure of Amitayus, Ming Dynasty, his wide face framed by a crown of five lobes enclosing miniature seated Buddhas, 14½in. high. (Butterfield & Butterfield) $5,462

Demetre H. Chiparus, Warrior, 1920s, green patinated bronze, cast as a semi-draped male warrior holding an oval shield, 18¹/₈in. high. (Sotheby's) $6,914

A Florentine bronze figure of Christ crucified, attributed to Pietro Tacca, first quarter 17th century, 14³/₈in. high. (Sotheby's) $13,800

A gilt-bronze ewer, by Vibert, Paris, circa 1890, cast with a handle in the form of a tree, 42cm. high.
(Sotheby's) $13,892

A pair of bronze tazze, Louis Philippe, circa 1835, each cast in the form of a merchild upholding a shell, 29cm. high.
(Sotheby's) $5,416

A gilt-bronze and silvered toilet mirror, Paris, circa 1880, in the form of a triptych, surmounted by a cartouche centred by a putto, 44cm. high.
(Sotheby's) $5,248

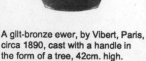

A bronze figure of a clown playing a mandolin, by Bernard-Adrien Steüer (1853–1913), French, late 19th/early 20th century, 56cm. high.
(Sotheby's) $5,055

A pair of gilt-bronze and cut-glass tazze, French, circa 1880, each with a putto upholding the glass tazza and a flower garland, 17.5cm. high.
(Sotheby's) $4,333

A gilt-bronze and onyx jardinière, French, circa 1890, of ovoid form cast with a band of foliage, supported by three cherubs, 38.5cm. high.
(Sotheby's) $8,683

A molded, painted and gilded metal figure of a mermaid, 20th century, resting on her scrolled tail molded with scalework, 35in. high.
(Sotheby's) $28,750

A pair of bronze figures of African musicians by Arthur Strasser (1854–1927), French, late 19th century, male figure 60cm.
(Sotheby's) $17,365

A Gothic bronze mortar, second half 15th century, probably North Italian, with flaring upper rim and stepped foot, with a bronze pestle, 6¼in. high.
(Sotheby's) $5,462

A French bronze model of a bloodhound, cast after a model by A. Jacquemart, the seated hound gazing at a tortoise, 6¼in. high. (Christie's) $1,336

A pair of bronze ewers, Louis Philippe, circa 1845, in the Mannerist style, each cast with a satyr and scroll handle, 51cm. high. (Sotheby's) $5,383

A bronze group of a mare and foal, possibly Polish, early 20th century, the foal suckling, signed *Tap Kirnadmir (?)*, 11½in. high. (Bonhams) $874

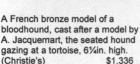

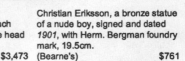

A gilt-bronze strut mirror, French, circa 1890, the rectangular shaped and molded frame surmounted by a cartouche, on hoof feet, 61 x 39cm. (Sotheby's) $2,999

A pair of bronze bison, 20th century, signed *Hofmann*, each standing four square with the head down, 25cm. high. (Sotheby's) $3,473

Christian Eriksson, a bronze statue of a nude boy, signed and dated *1901*, with Herm. Bergman foundry mark, 19.5cm. (Bearne's) $761

A North German bronze lion-form aquamanile 'of Hildescheim type,' 13th century, standing and gazing forward, the spout in his mouth, 9¹⁵/₁₆in. high. (Sotheby's) $233,500

A pair of Napoleon III gilt-bronze and bronze ewers, Paris, circa 1860, each of ovoid form, representing earth and water, 36.5cm. high. (Sotheby's) $9,373

A German bronze three-footed cauldron, late 15th century, one side applied with a relief of Saint George and the dragon, 10½in. high. (Sotheby's) $1,840

A 19th century bronze figure of an Amazon on horseback, on oblong base, signed *Feuchere 1843,* 17in. high. (Andrew Hartley) $2,400

A pair of German bronze bacchic putti, attributted to the workshop of Guillaume de Groff, 18th century, 15¾ and 15½in. high. (Sotheby's) $6,325

A bronze group of a pointer with hare, cast after a model by Pierre Jules Mene, on rounded rectangular naturalistic base, 8in. high. (Christie's) $1,909

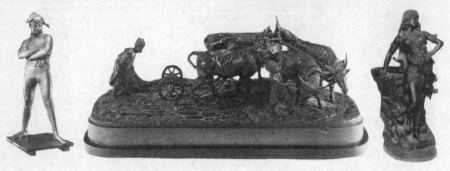

'Harlequin', a gilt-bronze figure, cast from a model by Charles René De St. Marceaux, French, 19th century, 34½in. high. (Christie's) $6,325

A bronze group of farmers, cast form a model by Eugène Lanceray, Russian, 19th century, 22in. long. (Christie's) $3,450

A large, sculptural plant holder held within a bronzed, cast well head, before which stands an exotic Cairene figure, 25in. high. (David Lay) $596

A South German bronze group of two children riding piggyback, after Leonard Kern, circa 1640, 4½in. high. (Sotheby's) $1,955

A pair of 19th century cast metal book ends in the form of books supporting North American Indian figures of boy and girl. (Russell, Baldwin & Bright) $939

A bronze figure of a seated cupid, cast from a model by Alfred Boucher, French, 19th century, 12in. high, light brown patina. (Christie's) $1,380

An Italian bronze figure of the seated Mercury after the Antique, on marble rockwork base, early 20th, century 18in. high.
(Andrew Hartley) $746

A bronze figure of a lion and a serpent cast from a model by Antoine Louis Barye, French, 19th century, 14½in. high, green patina.
(Christie's) $2,875

Russian bronze equestrian group, 20th century, depicting an officer and a lady astride a horse, 14¹/₂in. high.
(Skinner) $863

A pair of late 19th century Italian bronze figures, Diana Chasseuresse and Apollo Belvedere, after the antique, raised on molded black marble bases, 16½in. high.
(Andrew Hartley) $1,920

French bronze figure of a winged nymph, signed *E. Laurent*, 19th/20th century, black marble base, 10¹/₂in. high.
(Skinner) $460

A pair of bronze figures of huntsmen with hounds, cast from models by Alfred Dubucand, French, 19th century, 13½in. high.
(Christie's) $2,875

A late 19th century French bronze figure of the 'Borghese Gladiator, after the Antique, inscribed *Demee Fondeur*, 19in. high.
(Andrew Hartley) $1,962

'Chef Indien', a bronze group cast from a model by Ulpino Checa, Spanish, 20th century, 22in. long.
(Christie's) $2,760

Emile Coriolan Hippolyte Guillemin (French, 1841–1907), 'Arabic Beauty', circa 1900, brown and red patinated bronze sculpture, signed, 21¹/₂in. high.
(Skinner) $5,175

A bronze of a cherub emerging from a shell, by Henri Pernot (1859–1937), signed, 45cm. high. (Sotheby's) **$8,683**

A pair of bronze urns, French, circa 1910, each of ovoid form, cast with swan neck handles and with tendrils and flower heads, 79cm. high. (Sotheby's) **$9,930**

A gilt-bronze vase by Antonin Larroux (1859–1937), of squat form, cast with reapers, signed A. Larroux, 45cm. high. (Sotheby's) **$13,541**

A pair of bronze figures of African women, by Charles Cumberworth (1811-1852), French, late 19th century, 65.5cm. and 63.5cm. high. (Sotheby's) **$9,930**

A pair of gilt-bronze and blue glass tazze, circa 1895, each with later dished tops, on a tripod baluster base, cast with rams' heads, 24cm. high. (Sotheby's) **$2,166**

A pair of bronze figures entitled La Coquette and La Cueillette, by Joseph-François Belin (d.1902), French, late 19th century, 55.5cm. and 44cm. high. (Sotheby's) **$3,611**

A rose granite and gilt-bronze mounted vase and cover, Paris, circa 1890, of baluster form with a molded rim, with rams' head mounts, 35cm. high. (Sotheby's) **$7,873**

A pair of gilt-bronze and marble vases, Paris, circa 1890, each with a pomegranate finial and pierced foliate handles, 42cm high. (Sotheby's) **$5,416**

A gilt-bronze and ivory equestrian group of Julius Caesar on horseback by Raffaello Nannini, Italian, late 19th/early 20th century, signed, group 44cm., base 3cm. (Sotheby's) **$5,557**

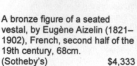

A bronze figure of a seated vestal, by Eugène Aizelin (1821–1902), French, second half of the 19th century, 68cm.
(Sotheby's) $4,333

Franz Bergman Viennese patinated and gilded bronze novelty figure of a long eared owl, figure opening to reveal a further gilded bronze figure of a nude female, signed, 7.75in. high. (Lawrences) $4,185

A French bronze bust of Marie de' Medici, attributed to Guillaume Dupré and Barthélemy Prieur, circa 1600, 10¼in. high.
(Sotheby's) $6,037

A bronze figure of a classical youth, cast from a model by Antonio Canova, the naked figure shown standing with his left arm raised, 26in. high.
(Christie's) $1,700

A pair of Louis XV style ormolu chenets, late 19th century, formed as a semi-nude man and woman kneeling on stylized rockwork bases, 22in. high.
(Christie's) $5,175

A bronze group by Nelson Maclean (1845-1894), cast with two female dancing figures and dated 1881, with brown patination, 72cm. high.
(Sotheby's) $4,694

A bronze group by R. Schnauder (1865–1923), of a naked girl on a horse, on a rocky base and marble plinth, signed and incised, 75.5cm. overall.
(Sotheby's) $7,402

A pair of gilt-bronze candelabra, French, circa 1890, each of baluster form, surmounted by an ionic capital and central sconce, 52cm. high.
(Sotheby's) $8,305

A bronze figure by Auguste Moreau (1834-1917), a girl with a rake and sheath of corn, with dark brown patination, signed, 59cm. high.
(Sotheby's) $3,972

A mahogany and brass-bound plate bucket, first half 19th century, of typical cylindrical outline with brass swing handle, 13¾in. diameter. (Christie's) $1,385

Shaker child's conical form pail, painted yellow with star, bird, flag, shield, and harp decorated, inscribed *Good Girl*, 4½in. high. (Eldred's) $990

Paint decorated leather fire bucket, *Pro: Bono: Publico No. 3 Thomas Briggs 1802*, possibly Duxbury, Massachusetts, 13½in. high. (Skinner) $2,760

A mahogany plate bucket, English, third quarter 19th century, the gilded carrying handle above a well figured cylinder standing on a plinth base, 33cm. wide. (Bonhams) $884

Two mahogany and brass-bound stave buckets, the tapering circular-section body mounted with two brass loop handles, 11in. diameter. (Christie's) $1,018

Shaker wooden covered pail, in pine with a reddish-brown color, swing handle and iron handle, *B* painted on bottom, 7½in. high. (Eldred's) $440

A George III brass-bound mahogany peat bucket, late 18th/early 19th century, of circular form with hinged bale handle, 12in. diameter. (Sotheby's) $1,500

A Dutch mahogany and brass-bound navette-shaped kettle warmer, 19th century, with brass liner and brass swing handle, 14¼in. wide. (Christie's) $1,943

A Regency brass-bound mahogany peat bucket, early 19th century, of oval form with bale handle and similar foot. (Sotheby's) $1,200

A George the IV rosewood bookstand, the raised spindle gallery with 'S' scroll supports and a nulled border, 16in. wide. (Dreweatt Neate) $1,450

A Régence style boulle marquetry ormolu-mounted encrier, center ormolu handle above inkwell compartments and single drawer, 13¼in. wide. (Christie's) $978

An Italian ebonized wood and pietre dure inlaid games box, second half 19th century, the cover inlaid with pietre dure playing cards, 12¼in. (Christie's) $7,383

Bird's-eye maple, tiger maple and cherry miniature blanket box, probably New England, early 19th century, 8in. wide. (Skinner) $2,300

A Victorian brass-mounted curly maple and walnut lap desk, mid 19th century, the rectangular top opening to reveal letter and implement compartments, 12in. high. (Christie's) $2,530

An early Victorian twin-division tortoiseshell and pewter-strung tea caddy, mid 19th century, the interior with twin subsidiary covers, 9in. wide. (Christie's) $3,322

A Victorian brass-bound calamander decanter box, enclosing a velvet and leather lined divided interior with four decanters, 11in. high. (Christie's) $611

A late Victorian oak smoker's cabinet, English, circa 1900, with glazed doors and drawers, 42cm. wide. (Bonhams) $418

Victorian mahogany hexagonal tea caddy, with checker-banded borders, 6½in. long. (Skinner) $373

An Italian pietra dura and ebony jewelry box, circa 1800, the raised top and sides with molded, wavy ebony panels of baroque type, 16in. wide. (Sotheby's) $23,000

A stained fruitwood melon-shaped tea caddy, the hinged lid enclosing a foil-lined interior, 4in. high. (Christie's) $496

A small Nuremberg gilt copper strongbox, by Michel Mann, circa 1600, the lid and sides engraved with figures in contemporary dress, 2⁷/₈in. wide. (Sotheby's) $9,200

Regency blonde tortoiseshell tea caddy, 19th century, with two covered interior compartments, 7¾in. long. (Skinner) $862

Mahogany tea caddy of sarcophagus form, applied with gilt metal mounts and interior fitted with three compartments, 19th century, 9in. (G. A. Key) $800

Italian Renaissance walnut document box, 17th/18th century, carved body and mounted on four paw feet, later cross-banding to hinged lid, 15¾in. long. (Skinner) $1,265

A roironuri ground four-tiered jubako, late 18th century, with indented corners, decorated in gold hiramakie and nashiji with autumnal grasses, 19 x 19 x 26.3cm. (Christie's) $10,764

Pair of red painted alms boxes, 19th century, the dovetail constructed boxes with gilt lettering shaded in black reading *Orphans Fund* and *Widows Fund.* (Skinner) $6,325

A Regency mahogany cutlery-box, banded overall with ebonized lines, the front inlaid with fruitwood lines, 10½in. wide. (Christie's) $754

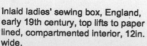

Inlaid ladies' sewing box, England, early 19th century, top lifts to paper lined, compartmented interior, 12in. wide. (Skinner) $1,610

An early 19th century fruitwood tea caddy shaped like an apple, 4¼in. high. (David Lay) $3,454

Carved wood book-form slide top box, signed and dated *Michel Thomas 1759*, chip carved borders centering high relief carved male and female figures, 3⅝in. high. (Skinner) $1,610

Rosewood tea caddy of sarcophagus form, inlaid throughout with boxwood stringing, fitted within for two compartments, 19th century, 7½in.
(G. A. Key) $184

A late-Victorian Aesthetic Movement oak coal scuttle, attributed to Christopher Dresser for Benham and Froud, with brass shovel.
(Christie's) $742

George III fruitwood inlaid mahogany tea caddy, inlaid with shells and leaves, 7½in. long.
(Skinner) $431

Black and gilt lacquer vanity set, 19th century, comprising a four-drawered cosmetic case with tray top, a large mirror case and stand, and four combs with a small storage box. (Butterfield & Butterfield) $1,265

Victorian mahogany apothecary chest, 19th century, with fitted interior of bottles and drawers, 19½in. high.
(Skinner) $1,150

A Transitional George III bright-cut, silver-mounted figured mahogany serpentine-front knife box, second half 18th century, 14¹/₂in. high.
(Sotheby's) $1,380

A treen fruitwood pear-shaped tea-caddy, late 18th/early 19th century, the hinged top enclosing a metal paper-lined interior 6½in. high.
(Christie's) $6,035

Gilt lacquer kondansu with sea life decoration, Meiji period, the surfaces featuring various species of fish, shellfish and crustaceans, 8¾ x 4⁵/₈ x 6in. (Butterfield & Butterfield) $632

A George III mahogany decanter-box, the square stepped hinged lid, enclosing a red velvet-lined compartmentalised interior, 9in. wide. (Christie's) $4,526

A mid 19th century ebonized and boulle inlaid visiting card box of rectangular form, the lid decorated with floral swags above glazed sides, 21cm. wide. (Cheffins Grain & Comins) $608

Rare Roycroft copper box, incised geometric decoration, pyramid rivets, early orb mark, 10½in. wide. (Skinner) $3,450

A Continental fruitwood work-box, 19th century, in the form of a miniature leather trunk with simulated leather straps and handles, 8in. wide. (Christie's) $2,640

A Victorian papier mâché work-box, decorated all over in gilt and mother-of-pearl with bands of foliage, 14½in. wide. (Christie's) $1,049

A paint decorated metal-mounted fruitwood apple-form tea caddy, English, 19th century, 6in. high. (Sotheby's) $2,875

A Colonial (possibly Dutch East Indies) silver-mounted tortoiseshell veneered box, 17th century, 4⅞in. wide. (Sotheby's) $1,610

A Joseph Holdcroft majolica square box and cover, the blue ground painted with birds and mice in Japanese taste, 16.8cm. wide. ((Bristol) $832

A North Italian bone, ivory and ebony-inlaid gamesboard of Embriachi type, circa 1500, the elaborate intarsia designs inlaid alla certosina, 21¼in. wide. (Sotheby's) $16,100

A small French or Spanish iron-mounted cuir ciselé missal box, circa 1500, profusely mounted with iron straps and hinges, 3⅝in. wide. (Sotheby's) $3,450

Bird's-eye maple and polychromed Academy decorated workbox, America, first quarter 19th century, rectangular form with single drawer in base, 14in. wide. (Skinner) $2,990

Oval Shaker swing-handled carrier, in pine with brown stain and shellac finish, labeled, 10½in. long. (Eldred's) $605

An early Victorian rosewood rectangular tea caddy with concave sides, ring handles and two division satinwood lined interior. (Dreweatt Neate) $314

Mahogany inlaid knife box, 19th century, scalloped rim above sloping sides, 15¼in. long. (Skinner) $977

Sailor's valentine, 19th century, octagonal segmented cases with various exotic shells, each case, 9⅝ x 9⅝in. (Skinner) $2,530

Antique American knife box, in bird's-eye maple, 14in. long. (Eldred's) $253

Shaker yellow painted three-finger spit box, possibly New Lebanon, New York, 19th century, maple and pine, 10¼in. (Skinner) $1,955

A Regency brass-inlaid and brass-mounted rosewood inkstand, by R. Dalton, inlaid overall with scrolling foliage, the molded rectangular top with turned spindle carrying-handle, 13in. wide. (Christie's) $3,206

Paint decorated box, America, early 19th century, painted with pinwheel and various sunburst motifs, 9in. wide. (Skinner) $2,185

Baroque silk embroidered jewelry casket, Continental, early 18th century, the cover with a woman in an arbor, 9in. wide. (Skinner) $3,450

A 19th century burr elm and ebonized traveling table top writing desk with brass carrying handles, the slope front revealing a fitted interior, 20½in. (Ewbank) $2,845

Polychrome decorated pine lift top box, attributed to John Colvin, Scituate, Rhode Island, early 19th century, 17¼in. wide. (Skinner) $17,250

A paint-decorated pine utility box, with sliding lid, American, 19th century, the front and sides painted with stylized flowers in red and white, 10¼in. long. (Sotheby's) $2,070

Tortoiseshell and elaborately inlaid wood captain's lap desk, 19th century, the bisected turtle shell opens to a single lift top compartment, 14½in. wide. (Skinner) $4,887

Engraved whalebone jewelry casket, 19th century, the top polychrome decorated with elegant ladies and a child, 10in. wide. (Skinner) $5,462

Leica IIf no. 677920, chrome, red-scale, with a Leitz Summaron 3.5cm. f/3.5 lens no. 1284987. (Christie's) $937

Nikon F no. 6400411, chrome, with a Nippon Kogaku Nikkor-S f/2.5cm. lens no. 523069. (Christie's) $4,873

Contax I no. Z. 25399, Zeiss Ikon, Germany; black, with a Carl Zeiss, Jena Sonnar f/ 1.5 5cm. lens no. 1548061. (Christie's) $792

Kodak Duo Six-20 series II no. 333320K, Kodak A.G., Germany; 620-rollfilm, with a rangefinder and a Kodak Anastigmat f/ 3.5 7.5cm. lens. (Christie's) $487

Super Kodak Six-20 no. 1936, Eastman Kodak Co., Rochester, NY; 620-rollfilm, with a Kodak Anastigmat Special f/3.5 100mm. (Christie's) $2,999

Nikon F no. 7382300, chrome, with a photomic head no. 966762, a Nikon Nikkor 55mm. f/1.2 lens no. 356989, F-36 motor. (Christie's) $899

A Century folding camera by the Century Camera Co., brass-mounted mahogany case, circa 1900. (Auction Team Köln) $702

A Mentor Three/Four by Goltz & Brentmann, Dresden, with Tessar 1:3,5/5cm. lens, in leather case. (Auction Team Köln) $1,321

Halifax camera, Germany; 6½ x 9cm. wood-body, plate-changing mechanism, lens in a sprung shutter. (Christie's) $122

Leica II no. 108396, chrome, 'lavatory seat' top-plate, and a Leitz Summar 5cm. f/2 lens no. 193659. (Christie's) $1,104

Leica M5 no. 1358586, black, side strap-lugs and Leica Camera Ltd repair docket dated 19/06/97. (Christie's) $1,406

Leica IIIg no. 956402, chrome, with a Leitz Summaron 3.5cm. f/3.5 lens no. 751969. (Christie's) $1,687

Leica II no. 112358, chrome, with a Leitz Elmar f/3.5 50mm. lens no. 157953, in maker's ever ready case. (Christie's) $355

Ur-Leica Attrape, the top plate engraved *Nachbildung der Ur-Leica*, in maker's box. (Christie's) $694

Canon 7sz no. 116115 with a Canon 50mm. f/ 1.2 lens no. 43599, in maker's leather ever ready case. (Christie's) $1,232

Kodak Ektra no. 1861, Eastman Kodak Co., Rochester, NY; with a Kodak Ektra f/ 1.9 50mm. lens, a Kodak Ektar f/ 3.3 35mm. lens. (Christie's) $2,811

Leica M6 Platinum no. 1757654, the top plate engraved *150 Jahre Photographie. 1989. 75 Jahre Leica Photographie.* (Christie's) $6,598

Vollenda camera no. 140230, Nagel, Germany; 127-rollfilm, with a Leitz Elmar 5cm. f/3.5 lens no. 109555 in a Compur shutter. (Christie's) $177

An Ermanox camera by Ernemann, with Ernostar 1;1,8/8,5cm. lens, with cassettes. (Auction Team Köln) $2,234

Bessa II, Voigtländer, Germany; 120-rollfilm, with a Voigtländer Apo-Lanthar f/ 4.5 105mm. lens. (Christie's) $3,519

Leica M5 no. 1347662, a Leitz Summicron f/ 2 50mm. lens and lens hood 1976. (Christie's) $1,303

  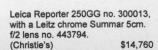

Leica Attrape M5 no. A625, black, side strap-lugs, with a Leitz dummy Summicron f/2 50mm. lens. (Christie's) $1,389

Nikon S2 no. 6170974, black paint, with a Nippon Kogaku W-Nikkor C f/ 4 2.5cm. lens no. 402652. (Christie's) $10,205

Leica Reporter 250GG no. 300013, with a Leitz chrome Summar 5cm. f/2 lens no. 443794. (Christie's) $14,760

Nikon F2 Dummy no. 7109087, chrome, a dummy DP-1 photomic head no. 202008 and a Nikon Nikkor-S Auto f/ 1.4 50mm. lens. (Christie's) $729

A Carte de Visite camera, possibly by Reygondaud, Paris, walnut case, for 11.5cm. square prints, circa 1865. (Auction Team Köln) $1,849

Leica III no. 208743, black, chrome fittings, and a Leitz Elmar f/3.5 50mm. lens no. 152928, in maker's ever ready case. (Christie's) $1,219

Charles Chevalier, Paris, A daguerreian outfit, comprising an 18 x 20cm. walnut body, sliding-box camera; a laquered-brass rack and pinion focusing lens; two walnut single plate holders, three 12 x 16cm. plates. (Christie's) $37,490

Cosmopolite TLR camera, London Stereoscopic Co., London; 9 x 12cm. with a pair of brass bound lenses. (Christie's) $600

Stereflektoskop no. 145254 Voigtländer, Germany; 6 x 13cm., with a Voigtländer Heliar f/4.5 75mm. viewing lens and a pair of Voigtländer Heliar f/4.5 75mm. taking lenses. (Christie's) $525

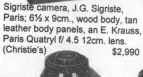

A brass-mounted mahogany portable camera, possibly by Sperling, Berlin, with Zeiss Tessar T 1:4,5/210mm lens, with 6 wooden double cassettes, 1950. (Auction Team Köln) $182

Sigriste camera, J.G. Sigriste, Paris; 6½ x 9cm., wood body, tan leather body panels, an E. Krauss, Paris Quatryl f/ 4.5 12cm. lens. (Christie's) $2,990

Royal Mail copying camera, W. Butcher & Sons, London; quarter-plate, polished mahogany-body and fifteen lenses. (Christie's) $712

Seiki Kogaku, Japan, a Hansa Canon camera, the baseplate numbered 2144, with pop-up viewfinder and a Nippon Kogaku Nikkor f/ 3.5 50mm. lens. (Christie's) $8,446

A Rollei SL66 camera by Franke & Heidecke, with Planar 2,8/80mm lens, with cover and carrying strap. (Auction Team Köln) $1,321

Krügener's Pocketbook Camera', by Haake & Albers, Frankfurt, with periscope optic, for 38mm. square prints, 1890. (Auction Team Köln) $3,632

Alpa model 5B no. 40608, Pignons S.A: chrome, with a Kern Switar AR f/ 1.8 50mm. lens no. 651178, in maker's ever ready case. (Christie's) $2,991

Nikon F4 no. 2223229 sample model, with instruction booklets, in maker's box. (Christie's) $1,477

A black Rollei 35 SE camera, with Sonnar 2,8/40 lens. (Auction Team Köln) $251

Una Traveller no. 130, James A. Sinclair & Co. Ltd., London; 6 x 9cm., polished duraluminium body, a Ross, London patent Combinable 8 inch f/ 11 lens. (Christie's) $4,874

A Reckmeier three-color camera, producing three prints at once in blue, green and red, with Voigtländer Hellar 1:4,5/30mm lens, one of only six cameras produced. (Auction Team Köln) $2,297

Tropical Adoro no. 526017, Contessa-Nettel, Germany; 6½ x 9cm., polished-teak body, tan-leather viewing hood and bellows and a Contessa-Nettel Citonar f/ 4.5 10.5cm. lens no. 177142. (Christie's) $562

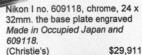

Reflex camera obscura, with hinged top, ground glass and brass bound lens. (Christie's) $1,124

Telephot Button camera no. 2000, British Ferrotype Co., Blackpool; ¾-inch and spring holder. (Christie's) $712

Nikon I no. 609118, chrome, 24 x 32mm. the base plate engraved *Made in Occupied Japan* and *609118.* (Christie's) $29,911

A Zeiss Ikon Contaflex camera with rare Tessar 2,8/5cm. lens, shutter and light meter operative. (Auction Team Köln) $1,585

Stereo sliding box camera, English; 7 x 5inch, mahogany-body, lacquered-brass fittings, a pair of later Taylor, Taylor & Hobson lenses. (Christie's) $2,355

A Zeiss Ikon Miroflex 859/3 U camera with Tessar 1:4,5/12cm. lens. (Auction Team Köln) $218

A fine Tabriz carpet, the shaded brick-red field with overall design of meandering vines 14ft.5in. x 10ft.8in.
(Christie's) $2,584

A fine Tabriz carpet, the indigo field overall design of angular flowering vine issuing polychrome serrated palmettes, 13ft. x 9ft.9in.
(Christie's) $2,399

A fine Heriz carpet, the shaded rust field with various hooked and serrated palmettes and various angular floral motifs, 11ft.7in. x 8ft.3in. (Christie's) $2,769

A Heriz carpet, North West Persia, the terracotta field decorated with angular vines and leaves around a large pendant medallion in pale blue, ivory and jade green, 11ft. 1in. x 8ft. 5in. (Phillips) $1,422

An antique Mahal carpet, the shaded brick-red field with overall design of stylized polychrome palmettes and flowerheads, 14ft. x 10ft.10in.
(Christie's) $2,769

A fine Sarouk-Mahal carpet, the shaded rust-red field with overall design of scrolling floral vines issuing polychrome serrated palmettes and scrolling leaves, 14ft.1in. x 10ft.2in.
(Christie's) $2,769

A fine antique Bijar carpet, the shaded light blue field with stylized polychrome open herati pattern around shaded brick-red large serrated panel, 13ft.5in. x 8ft.9in.
(Christie's) $7,014

A fine Heriz carpet, the shaded brick-red field with overall design of large polychrome hooked leaves enclosing hooked palmettes and angular flowering vine, 11ft.4in. x 8ft.2in. (Christie's) $2,215

A fine European hooked-stitch carpet of Savonnerie design, the shaded sea-green field with overall diagonal rows of alternating wreath and star motifs, 13ft.6in. x 9ft.10in.
(Christie's) $5,906

A fine Aubusson style carpet, the ivory field with flowering and leafy vines issuing from serrated light beige floral inner frame, 11ft.6in. x 8ft. 7in. (Christie's) $2,584

A Turkish carpet of Ushak design, the terracotta field with angular tracery around two green and indigo shaped medallions 12ft.2in. x 9ft.3in. (Christie's) $1,477

A fine Teheran carpet, the blackcurrant-red field with scrolling flowerhead and leaf vine linking polychrome palmettes, 13ft.6in. x 10ft.6in. (Christie's) $4,799

An antique Haji-Jalili Tabriz carpet, the brick-red field with overall design of scrolling polychrome floral vines issuing various multicolored palmettes, flowerheads and scrolling leaves, 15ft.5in. x 11ft.8in. (Christie's) $4,799

A fine north-west Persian carpet of Serapi Design, the ivory field with shaded light coral and light blue stylized large medallion with hooked palmette pendants, 13ft.10in. x 10ft.3in. (Christie's) $6,460

A fine Tabriz carpet, the ivory field with overall design of meandering floral vines connecting various multicolored palmettes, floral sprays and serrated leaves, 11ft.6in. x 8ft.9in. (Christie's) $1,661

An antique Tabriz carpet, the ivory field with delicate scrolling leafy vine issuing small rosettes around large brick-red cusped medallion, 16ft.4in. x 11ft.9in. (Christie's) $7,383

A fine Tabriz carpet, the indigo field with overall design of angular inscription arabesques surrounded by polychrome angular floral vine, 14ft.8in. x 10ft.2in. (Christie's) $4,614

A fine sejed shoghani Tabriz carpet, the light pistachio-green field with scrolling floral vine issuing large multicolored various palmettes and scrolling leaves,12ft.5in. x 9ft.6in. (Christie's) $7,014

An antique Aubusson carpet, the pale green field with scrolling acanthus leaves around ivory shaped large panel, 14ft.3in. x 10ft.6in. (Christie's) $5,537

A fine Kashan carpet, the tomato-red field with meandering floral vine issuing polychrome serrated palmettes, 13ft.6in. x 10ft.5in. (Christie's) $3,138

An antique Mahal carpet, the ivory field with overall stylized large floral vine lattice containing polychrome angular palmettes, 17ft.5in. x 11ft.2in. (Christie's) $5,537

An antique Tabriz carpet, the brick-red field with overall Shah-Abbas design of angular vine linking various multicolored serrated bold palmettes, 16ft. x 12ft.4in. (Christie's) $7,014

A fine Tabriz carpet, the shaded terracotta-red field with overall design of scrolling vines issuing large polychrome serrated palmettes, 14ft.6in. x 11ft.8in. (Christie's) $3,507

A fine Meshed carpet, the raspberry-red field with overall design of meandering floral vine issuing various multicolored floral palmettes, 13ft.2in. x 9ft.9in. (Christie's) $1,477

A fine Javan Tabriz carpet, the tomato-red field with overall design of large stylized polychrome palmettes surrounded by scrolling arabesques 14ft.8in. x 11ft.6in. (Christie's) $5,537

An antique Tabriz carpet of Kashan Mochtasham design, the light blue field with angular vine and sandy-yellow floral palmettes, 10ft.9in. x 8ft.2in. (Christie's) $4,061

An antique Ushak carpet, the shaded moss-green field with polychrome flowerheads and delicate angular flowering vine, 12ft. x 9ft.10in. (Christie's) $6,645

A fine Kashan carpet, the light eau-de-nil field with overall design of scrolling arabesques issuing various polychrome palmettes, 14ft.6in. x 11ft.1in. (Christie's) $8,860

A fine Heriz carpet, the light brick-red field with angular floral vine issuing polychrome serrated palmettes and leaves, 10ft.11in. x 8ft.5in. (Christie's) $4,614

A fine part silk Isfahan carpet, the light beige field with stylized multicolored flowering trees, various floral sprays, birds and animals, 14ft.9in. x 10ft.6in. (Christie's) $5,168

A fine Kashan carpet, the shaded blue field with scrolling leafy vines issuing various polychrome palmettes and leafy sprays, 13ft. 9in. x 10ft.3in. (Christie's) $2,399

An antique Heriz carpet, the shaded brick-red field with angular vines issuing various polychrome floral motifs around large hooked and stepped indigo medallion, 12ft x 8ft 1in. (Christie's) $2,030

A fine Tabriz carpet of Muchtashem Kashan design, the shaded soft-pink field around cusped indigo medallion with palmette pendants,12ft.5in. x 9ft.7in. (Christie's) $1,846

An antique Tabriz carpet, the light dusky-pink field with Shah-Abbas design of meandering vine issuing various large multicolored palmettes, 14ft.9in. x 11ft.3in. (Christie's) $1,846

An antique Khoy Tabriz carpet, the light rust-red field with overall design of polychrome serrated palmettes linked by meandering floral vine, 12ft. x 9ft.4in. (Christie's) $4,061

A fine antique Tabriz carpet, the shaded indigo field with overall design of angular vines linking various multicolored palmettes and flowerheads, 12ft.8in. x 9ft.3in. (Christie's) $3,507

1966 Plymouth Sport Fury Convertible, white with blue interior. Engine: V8, pushrod overhead valves; Gearbox: automatic; Brakes: four-wheel. Left hand drive. (Christie's) $8,625

1922 Velie Touring Car, dove gray and black with leather interior. Engine: straight-six overhead valve; Gearbox: manual three-speed; Brakes: two wheel rear. Left hand drive. (Christie's) $7,475

1952 Porsche 356 (Pre-A) Cabriolet, red with tan leather upholstery. Engine: Air cooled flat (opposed) four cylinder, a replacement engine circa mid-1953; Gearbox: four-speed manual; Brakes: four wheel drum. Left hand drive. (Christie's) $35,650

1927 Chrysler 50 Rumble Seat Roadster, blue and black leather interior. Engine: four cylinder sidevalve, 38bhp; Gearbox: three-speed manual; Suspension: beam axle to front, live to rear, half elliptic leaf springs all round; Brakes: two wheel mechanically operated drum. Left hand drive. (Christie's) $8,050

1905 Peugeot Type 68 Swing-Seat Tonneau with canopy, blue with black mudguards and canopy, gray chassis and wheels. Engine: single cylinder, 883cc, with mechanically operated Gearbox: 3-speed and reverse; Suspension: semi-elliptic front and rear; Brakes: transmission and rear wheels. (Christie's) $29,992

1917 Pierce-Arrow Model 48 Seven Passenger Touring Car, dark brown with black leather interior. Engine: six cylinders in line, 48bhp; Gearbox: manual four speed, shaft drive; Brakes: mechanical by rear wheel drum. Right hand drive. (Christie's) $96,000

1929 Chrysler Model 65 Rumble Seat Roadster, light gray with red vinyl interior. Engine: six cylinder in line, side valve, 195.6 cu. in., 65bhp; Gearbox: three-speed manual; Brakes: four-wheel hydraulically operated drum. Left hand drive. (Christie's) $9,775

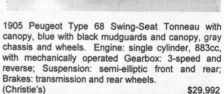

1969 Alfa Romeo 1750 Spider Veloce, red with black interior. Engine: four cylinder in line, twin overhead camshaft, 1,779cc; Gearbox: five speed manual. Right hand drive.   (Christie's) $22,494

1965 Plymouth Valiant Signet 200 Convertible, red with black vinyl interior.   Engine: V8; Gearbox: automatic; Brakes: four wheel drum. Left hand drive. (Christie's) $8,050

1964 Chevrolet Corvair Monza Convertible, maroon with white top and black interior. Engine: six-cylinder horizontally opposed; Gearbox: four-speed all synchromesh manual; Brakes: hydraulically operated drums. Left hand drive.
(Christie's) $8,050

1964 Chrysler Imperial Le Baron Four-Door Hardtop, black with pearl white leather interior.   Engine: V8, 340bhp at 4600rpm; Gearbox: three-speed automatic; Brakes: four-wheel hydraulically operated drum. Left hand drive.
(Christie's) $9,450

1937 Bugatti Type 57 Galibier Pillarless Saloon Parts Car, coachwork by Gangloff, unrestored without any interior.   Engine: very incomplete - Gearbox: cotal type mated to proper Bugatti bellhousing; Suspension: leaf springs front and rear with hydraulic shock absorbers; Brakes: hydraulic drums all round. Right hand drive. (Christie's) $20,125

1926 Rolls-Royce 20 HP Landaulet, coachwork by Hooper of London, black with tan cloth interior. Engine: six-cylinder in-line, 3127cc; Gearbox: manual four-speed with right-hand lever; Brakes: servo-assisted, mechanically operated four-wheel drum. Right hand drive.
(Christie's) $36,800

1926 Pierce-Arrow Series 80 Town Car, coachwork by Derham, gray and blue with tan interior. Engine: six cylinders in line; Gearbox: manual three-speed; Brakes: mechanically operated four-wheel drum. Left hand drive.
(Christie's) $21,850

1911 Chalmers Model M 30 HP, Pony Tonneau, blue with gray frame, black top and black leather interior. Engine four-cylinder, vertical en bloc; Gearbox: 3 speed manual; Brakes: contracting on transmission, expanding on rear wheels. Right hand drive.
(Christie's) $36,800

1958 Rolls-Royce Silver Cloud I Saloon, metallic dark brown over sand with tan leather interior. Engine: six cylinder, 4,887cc; Gearbox: four speed automatic; Brakes: four wheel drum. Left hand drive. (Christie's) $34,500

1920 Rolls-Royce Silver Ghost Landaulet, coachwork by Brewster, black with black leather/gray broadcloth, Engine: six-cylinder 7428cc; Gearbox: four speed manual. Right hand drive. (Christie's) $133,334

1900 Liver 3½ horsepower Phaeton, maroon and black with yellow coachlining. Engine: Benz horizontal single-cylinder, transmission by belts giving two forward speeds plus 'Crypto' extra low gear; Suspension: semi-elliptic front and rear; Brakes: foot operated to rear hubs and handbrake, 'spoon' on rear tyres; Steering by tiller. (Christie's) $84,923

1906 Delage Type B Rear-Entrance Tonneau, red with varnished wood body and mudguards. Engine: De Dion Bouton single cylinder, 699 cc, with automatic inlet valve; Gearbox: 3-speed and reverse; Suspension: semi-elliptic front and rear; Brakes: rear wheels and transmission. Right hand drive. (Christie's) $26,243

1898 Fisson 8 HP Wagonette, yellow and black with varnished wood panels and yellow wheels with black leather interior. Engine: vertical twin-cylinder, 2920 cc; Gearbox: four-speed and reverse; Brakes: transmission from foot pedal, parking brake on rear tyres, plus sprag. Left hand drive. (Christie's) $79,500

1900 De Dion Bouton Type G Vis-à-Vis, red and black. Engine: single cylinder, 4½hp, with automatic inlet valve; Gearbox: two-speeds forwards; Suspension: front semi-elliptic plus transverse leaf, rear three-quarters-elliptic; Brakes: rear wheels and transmission. Handle-bar steering and column gearchange. (Christie's) $33,741

1961 Chrysler 300-G Convertible, black with natural tan leather interior. Engine: V8 pushrod overhead valve; Gearbox: torqueflite automatic; Brakes: vacuum power-assisted four-wheel drum. Left hand drive. (Christie's) $35,650

1958 Jaguar XK 150 Roadster, carmen red with black leather interior. Engine: six cylinder, 3,781cc; Gearbox: four speed manual; Brakes: servo assisted four wheel disk. Left hand drive. (Christie's) $85,000

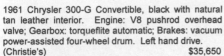

1899 Clément-Panhard Voiture Légère Type VCP Two-Seater, red and black with varnished wood mudguards and yellow wheels. Engine: single-cylinder; Gears: 3-speed; Suspension: full-elliptic rear, front none; Pneumatic tyres; Brakes: transmission and handbrake. Right hand drive. (Christie's) $48,737

1967 Triumph TR4A, dark blue with blue leatherette interior, Engine: four cylinder in-line, 2138cc, Gearbox: manual all-synchromesh fourspeed; Suspension: all-independent; Brakes: hydraulically operated disk to front, drum to rear; Steering: rack and pinion. Left hand drive. (Christie's) $9,372

1912 Mercedes 40HP Phaeton-Tourer, white with black hood and upholstery, varnished wood wheels, Engine: four cylinder, 5.7 litre, T-Head; Gearbox: four-speed and reverse, Brakes: handbrake to rear wheel, two separate on transmission by individual foot pedals. Right hand drive. (Christie's) $145,885

1962 Bentley S3 Continental Drophead Coupe, coachwork by H.J. Mulliner, Park Ward, ivory with red leather interior, Engine: V8, pushrod overhead valve; Gearbox: four-speed automatic; Suspension: independent front, live rear axle; Brakes: hydro-mechanically operated drums with servo assistance. Right hand drive. (Christie's) $53,423

1931 Ford Model A Roadster, green with black fenders and brown leather interior. Engine: four-cylinder, 40hp; Gearbox: standard Model A three-speed; Brakes: four wheel mechanical drum. Left hand drive. (Christie's) $21,850

1973 2.7 Litre Porsche 911RS Carrera Lightweight, blue with red and black interior. Engine: flat six cylinder, 2,687cc; Gearbox: five speed manual; Brakes: ventilated disks all round. Left hand drive. (Christie's) $59,700

1922 Wills Sainte Claire Rumble seat Roadster, polo green with black fenders and black leather upholstery, single overhead camshaft. Gearbox: manual three-speed; Brakes: two wheel rear. Left hand drive. (Christie's) $55,200

1919 Rolls-Royce Silver Ghost Two-Seater Roadster, white with red striping and red leather upholstery. Engine: six-cylinder, 7,428cc; Gearbox: four-speed manual; Brakes: two wheel drum. Right hand drive. (Christie's) $102,600

1937 Bentley 4¼-Litre Drophead Coupe, coachwork by Park Ward, colonial yellow with black fenders and red leather upholstery. Engine: six cylinder, 4,257 cc; Gearbox: four speed manual; Brakes: four wheel drum. Right hand drive. (Christie's) $55,200

1929 Packard 645 Dual Cowl Phaeton, coachwork by Dietrich, blue with black fenders, green wheels and striping and tan leather interior. Engine: straight eight, 120bhp at 3,200rpm; Gearbox: three-speed manual; Brakes: four wheel drum. Left hand drive. (Christie's) $145,500

1941 American Bantam Super Four Hollywood Convertible, red and black with red upholstery. Engine: four cylinders in line; Gearbox: manual three speeds; Brakes: four-wheel mechanical drum. Left hand drive. (Christie's) $10,350

1964 Jaguar E-Type 3.8 Litre Series I Roadster with hardtop, British racing green with tan leather interior. Engine: six cylinder, twin overhead camshafts, 3,781cc; Gearbox: four-speed manual; Brakes: four wheel disk, inboard at rear. Left hand drive. (Christie's) $68,500

1957 BMW 507 Series I Sports Two-Seater, sapphire blue with dark blue interior. Engine: V-8 90 degree overhead valve, 3,168cc; Gearbox: four-speed manual; Brakes: hydraulic front and rear drum. Left hand drive. (Christie's) $156,500

1980 BMW M1, black with black leather checked cloth interior. Engine: six-cylinder in-line, double overhead camshaft, 3,453cc; Gearbox: AF five-speed; Brakes: four-wheel vented disk. Left hand drive. (Christie's) $96,000

1932 Studebaker Commander, dark green with brown mohair interior. Engine: straight eight sidevalve; Gearbox: three speed manual; Brakes: four-wheel mechanical drum. Left hand drive. (Christie's) $34,500

1956 Ford Thunderbird Convertible with removable hardtop, white with red interior. Engine: V-8, overhead valve; Gearbox: Fordomatic three-speed; Brakes: hydraulic servo-assisted drums. Left hand drive. (Christie's) $25,300

1954 Citroen Traction Avant 15 Six Saloon, black with gray cloth upholstery. Engine: six-cylinder in line; gearbox: three-speed manual; Suspension: front, torsion bars, rear, hydropneumatic with trailing arms; Brakes: four wheel drum. Left hand drive. (Christie's) $14,950

1925 Wills Sainte Claire Rumble Seat Roadster, maroon and black with black leather interior. Engine: V8, single overhead camshaft to each cylinder bank; Gearbox: manual three speed; Brakes: four wheel hydraulic drum. Left hand drive. (Christie's) $59,700

1931 Ford Model A 'Woody' Station Wagon, beige and black with natural wood finish and dark brown interior. Engine: four cylinder, in-line; Gearbox: three-speed manual; Suspension: solid axle with leaf-springs; Brakes: four wheel drum. Left hand drive. (Christie's) $55,200

1914 Mitchell Type S6 Speedster, white with black leather interior. Engine: six-cylinder, T-head, 44hp; Gearbox: selective sliding gear transmission with three forward gears and one reverse; Brakes: two wheel drum. Left hand drive. (Christie's) $85,000

1903 Barré Type Y Two-Seater, red with varnished wood body and mudguards, Engine: De Dion Bouton single-cylinder, Clutch: cone; Gearbox: 3-speed and reverse; Brakes: rear wheels and transmission. Right hand drive. (Christie's) $29,054

1912 Renault Type AG-1 Taxi De La Marne, red with black mudguards and chassis. Engine: 2-cylinder monobloc, 1.2 liters, Gearbox: 3-speed and reverse, Left hand drive with central gear and brake levers. (Christie's) $28,117

1907 Premier Model 24 Runabout, cream with black fenders and running gear and black leather upholstery. Engine: four cylinder, T-head, water-cooled, 24cu. in; Gearbox: three speed manual; Suspension: full elliptic leaf springs front and rear; Brakes: two wheel rear. Right hand drive. (Christie's) $42,550

1938/40 Duesenberg Model SJ Long Wheelbase Convertible, coachwork by Rollson, black with violet leather interior. Engine: straight eight with twin overhead camshafts; Gearbox: three-speed; Brakes: servo assisted, hydraulically operated drums on all wheels. Left hand drive. (Christie's) $1,267,500

1957 Jaguar XK150 3.4 Fixed Head Coupe, black with cream leather interior, Engine: straight-six, 3442cc, twin overhead camshaft, Gearbox: four-speed manual synchromesh; Brakes: servo assisted disks; Steering: rack and pinion. Left hand drive. (Christie's) $24,368

1931 Alfa Romeo Tipo 6C-1750 Supercharged Gran Sport Spyder, coachwork by Zagato, red with red leather interior. Engine: six-cylinder, twin overhead camshafts, 1,750cc; Gearbox: four-speed manual; Brakes: four wheel mechanical drum. Right hand drive. (Christie's) $398,500

1924/25 Chrysler Six Rumble Seat Coupe, two toned green and black with brown cloth interior. Engine: six cylinders sidevalve, 68bhp; Gearbox: manual three-speed; Brakes: hydraulically operated four-wheel brakes. (Christie's) $4,370

1914 Trumbull Roadster, green and black with black fenders. Engine: four-cylinder sidevalve, 1.7 liter, 18hp; Gearbox: 3 forward, 1 reverse; Brakes: two wheel drum. Left hand drive. (Christie's) $6,900

1966 Jaguar E-Type 4.2 Series I Two Plus Two Coupe, opalescent silver blue with blue leather interior. Engine: six cylinder in-line, twin overhead camshafts; Gearbox: four-speed synchromesh manual; Brakes: servo assisted disk all round; Centre-lock wire wheels. Right hand drive. (Christie's) $20,619

1954 Aston Martin DB2/4 Coupe, sage green with dark red upholstery. Engine: Six cylinders in line; Gearbox: four speeds, with synchromesh except on first gear; Suspension: independent front by trailing links, rear live axle, coil springs all round; Brakes: hydraulic drum all round. Right hand drive. (Christie's) $27,180

1909 White model O 20 HP Tourer, maroon with white coachlining, black leather upholstery and black top. Engine: 2-cylinder compound double-acting; Suspension: semi-elliptic leaf springs front and rear. Right hand drive. (Christie's) $40,250

1922 Rolls-Royce silver Ghost Pall Mall Tourer, coachwork by Rolls-Royce Custom Coach Works, silver with black leather interior. Engine: six-cylinder, 7,428cc; Gearbox: four-speed manual; Brakes: two wheel drum. Right hand drive. (Christie's) $156,500

A National No. 172 cash register, with four-place lever insertion and side handle, circa 1900.
(Auction Team Köln) $840

A National 41¾ cash register in nickel casing with floral decoration, for English currency, 1908-10.
(Auction Team Köln) $528

An Adler patented German till, with coin carousel, circa 1900.
(Auction Team Köln) $64

A National 442X push button cash register with four-place keyboard, with print-out and till receipt dispenser, decorative bronzed casing, 1903.
(Auction Team Köln) $711

A National Model 37 bronzed brass cast metal cash register with floral decoration, for English currency and with till receipt dispenser, circa 1910.
(Auction Team Köln) $576

A National Model 452-X cash register in silvered Art Nouveau casing, with coin chute and till receipt dispenser, adapted for Swedish kroner, circa 1905.
(Auction Team Köln) $840

A National 442DB push button cash register in silvered cast casing, with side handle and receipt dispenser, circa 1910.
(Auction Team Köln) $528

A National Model 356 cash register with print-out and till receipt dispenser, decorative cast iron casing, circa 1913.
(Auction Team Köln) $614

A National Model 562 X 6C Art Nouveau style cash register with change tills for six cashiers, for German currency, circa 1910.
(Auction Team Köln) $754

A gilt brass hanging lantern in the Moorish taste, the eight glass panels set within a pierced body embellished with models of peacocks and reptiles, 81cm. drop. (Phillips) $664

A rare large pierced tin lantern, American, early 19th century, of conical form with ring finial, the top inscribed *H. HOWARD*, 20in. high. (Sotheby's) $1,437

A Louis XVI style ormolu and cut-glass eighteen-light chandelier with a central etched and cut-glass baluster support, 47in. high. (Christie's) $4,600

Clear blown glass hall candlelight, 19th century, hexagonal format, decorated with wheel-cut and acid-etched alternating panels of gothic arches and geometric shaped enclosing foliate devices, 15¼in. high. (Skinner) $2,530

Gustav Stickley electric lantern, No.202 ½, deep patina to lantern, chain and mount painted, original green glass shade, lantern 14in. high. (Skinner) $10,350

Swedish Neoclassical gilt-metal and cut glass ten light chandelier, early 19th century, with sloped strings of faceted prisms and a circular tier, 45in. high. (Skinner) $7,475

A late 19th century French gilt bronze and ceramic chandelier, the five upturned arms with ceramic candle sconces and candle cups, 61.5cm. drop. (Phillips) $1,343

Tiffany bronze and favrile glass chandelier, striated amber glass segments arranged in large conical brickwork shade, 54in. high in total. (Skinner) $14,950

A 19th century French hanging lantern, the six paneled glazed bulbous body with a pierced domed pediment, 99cm. drop. (Phillips) $1,817

Fulper pottery vase, cylindrical form with two handles under a crystalline green glaze, 7½in. high. (Skinner) $575

Early Van Briggle vase, with incised foliate design, green glaze, incised AA logo, 151, Van Briggle, 1904(?), 4½in. high. (Skinner) $1,495

Silver luster redware circus wagon finial, America, 19th century, recumbent lion finial above belted ball form, 7¾in. high. (Skinner) $1,265

American ovoid redware handled crock, 19th century, in brown on red, with non-matching cover, 8in. high. (Eldred's) $412

Important Marblehead tile in original frame, decoration attributed to Arthur Baggs, landscape scenes with three shades of matte greens, 9¾in. high. (Skinner) $13,800

Cobalt decorated four-gallon two-handled stoneware crock, Somerset Pottery, Pottersville and Boston, Massachusetts, 1882-1909, 14½in. high. (Skinner) $345

Stoneware sponge decorated water cooler, America, 19th century, No. 9, with wooden cover and spigot, 13½in. high. (Skinner) $230

Exceptional Marblehead Pottery vase, incised conventionalised design of trees, dark blue and speckled blue/green glaze, 10½in. high. (Skinner) $10,350

American earthenware covered two-handled crock, with reddish brown glaze, 9¾in. high. (Eldred's) $220

HISTORICAL FACTS
Amphora

The Amphora Porzellanfabrik was established at Turn-Teplitz in Bohemia to make earthenware and porcelain. Much of their porcelain figure output was exported.

The mark consists of three stars in a burst of rays over *RSK* (for the proprietors Reissner & Kessel). They worked in a variety of styles from imitation Dresden and innovative Art Nouveau designs applied with multi-colored glass and cabochons.

An earthenware vase by Amphora, circa 1900, squat form decorated with 'honeycomb' design applied with multicolored glass cabochons, 6¼in. high. (Christie's)
$2,208

An earthenware vase by Amphora, circa 1900, green glaze decorated with multicolored glass centered cobwebs above a frieze of butterflies and bees, 16in. high. (Christie's)
$6,992

Amphora porcelain basket-form vase, Czechoslovakia, early 20th century, three cherubs mounted to one side, 17³/₄in. high. (Skinner)
$230

Pair of Amphora vases, cylindrical form with flared rim and foot, decorated with a carved relief landscape scene, 11³/₄in. high. (Skinner)
$690

Amphora Egyptian vase, tapering cylindrical form decorated with incised panel of an Egyptian theme, 13in. high. (Skinner)
$345

Large Amphora floral vase, bulbous form with two handles, applied floral blooms in soft pink and green on a carved relief green ground, 18in. high. (Skinner)
$402

Amphora centerpiece, with incised decoration and jewel style insets, 9¼in. high. (Skinner)
$345

Important Amphora ceramic bust for the Paris Exposition 1900, swirling portrait of a finely detailed woman in a cream glaze, 10³/₄in. high. (Skinner)
$2,645

An Arita apothecary bottle, late 17th century, decorated in underglaze blue with a continuous band of peonies and foliage with the monogram *RW*, 7½in. high. (Christie's) $3,620

A pair of Arita blue and white models of seated horses, late 17th century, their saddle cloths with flowers and foliage, each 7¹/₁₆in. long. (Christie's) $11,835

A rare Arita model of a cat, 17th century, decorated in iron-red and black enamel, seated with its tail curled about its back, 8½in. high. (Christie's) $51,540

A large Arita tripod ewer, late 17th century, decorated in various colored enamels and gilt with the seven gods and various attributes molded in relief, 18¼in. high. (Christie's) $7,630

A pair of Arita blue and white vases with covers, 17th century, decorated with chrysanthemums in three panels separated by stylized flower motifs, 11¼in. high. (Christie's) $8,590

An Arita porcelain vase of square section and slightly flared form with angled shoulder, decorated in the Kakiemon style, 23.5cm. high. (Bearne's) $1,280

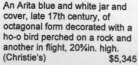

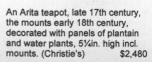

An Arita blue and white jar and cover, late 17th century, of octagonal form decorated with a ho-o bird perched on a rock and another in flight, 20¾in. high. (Christie's) $5,345

A pair of Arita models of cockerels, 18th century, decorated in iron-red, green, blue and black enamels and gilt, minor restoration, each 5⅝in. high. (Christie's) $9,545

An Arita teapot, late 17th century, the mounts early 18th century, decorated with panels of plantain and water plants, 5¼in. high incl. mounts. (Christie's) $2,480

A Berlin K.P.M. oval plaque painted in colors with putti sharpening an arrow on a whetstone, scepter mark, 23cm. wide.
(Christie's) $1,475

A K.P.M. Berlin rectangular plaque, 19th century, painted with a dark-haired beauty, her hair piled in a high chignon, 10³/₄ x 8in., framed.
(Bonhams) $3,498

A Berlin cabinet plate, circa 1820, blue scepter mark, the center painted with a horseguard in a landscape within a broad circular gilt band, 9½in. diameter.
(Christie's) $2,760

A Berlin K.P.M. plaque of Ruth, late 19th/20th century, impressed scepter and monogram mark, painted after Landelle, 16 x 10¼in.
(Christie's) $4,600

A pair of Berlin K.P.M. rectangular plaques each finely painted with a young temptress deshabillée admiring a butterfly, late 19th century, 25 x 19cm.
(Christie's) $10,120

A Berlin K.P.M. rectangular plaque painted by the Wagner workshop with a brunette beauty wearing a wide brimmed hat, signed, circa 1900, 24.5 x 16.5cm.
(Christie's) $4,048

A Berlin K.P.M. rectangular plaque finely painted by J. Bock with a raven haired beauty, with three putti, scepter mark, circa 1900, 25 x 19cm. (Christie's) $3,865

Two Berlin plates each painted with a generous bouquet of flowers and leaves within gilt wells, early 19th century, 21.3cm. diameter.
(Christie's) $995

A Berlin K.P.M. plaque of a drunken bacchante, late 19th/20th century, impressed scepter and monogram mark, signed *Kies*, 13 x 10½in., giltwood frame.
(Christie's) $4,830

HISTORICAL FACTS
Berlin

Berlin ceramics date back to the late 17th century, when from 1678 faience and red earthenware were produced. In 1763 the factory came under royal patronage when Frederick the Great purchased it to become the Königliche Porzellan Manufaktur, and production turned to hard-paste porcelain. From the end of the First World War it became known as the Staatliche Porzellan Manufaktur in Berlin. Throughout its existence it has continued to produce fine tableware with high quality painted decoration, though various designers have also pursued contemporary trends. During the late 19th century, for example, its wares were often characterised by elaborate glaze effects under oriental influence, as seen in the work of H Seeger. Notable figures were designed by Scheurich and in the early years of this century tableware was also produced to Bauhaus designs.

Berlin oval portrait plaque, depicting a bust portrait of a girl in white, after Guido Reni, 8½ x 6¼in.
(Eldred's) $1,430

A Berlin porcelain figure depicting a scholar and his muse, she in purple and yellow dress, he in floral frock coat leaning on a book, raised on square base, 12in. high.
(Andrew Hartley) $560

A pair of Berlin octagonal baluster vases and covers, circa 1720, Funcke's factory, painted with Orientals taking tea, 15¾in. high.
(Christie's) $13,368

A 19th century Berlin style painted terracotta vase and cover, the baluster shaped body decorated with Chinese figures in a garden setting, 53cm. high.
(Phillips) $975

Berlin porcelain oval plaque, early 20th century, depicting a peasant boy with a recorder, impressed marks, 8½in. high.
(Skinner) $977

A Berlin porcelain oblong plaque painted by Walthau and depicting the Rape of the Daughters of Leucippus after Rubens, 9 x 6in.
(Andrew Hartley) $2,480

A Berlin porcelain oval plaque, finely painted with the head and shoulders of a young woman wearing a black mantilla, 23 x 17cm.
(Bearne's) $2,511

HISTORICAL FACTS
Beswick

Beswick are perhaps best known for their highly glazed equestrian and animal figures and for their legendary flying duck wall plaques, which typify 1930s design, and yet were not launched until 1938. James Wright Beswick and his son set up their pottery in Longton in the 1890s and by 1930 employed 400 workers. After the war their expansion continued, until they sold out as a thriving concern to the Royal Doulton Group in 1973.

In addition to their figures, Beswick also made facemasks, vases, cottage ware and salad ware, together with statuettes of such popular figures from literature as Rupert Bear, Alice in Wonderland and Beatrix Potter characters. Their prewar mark is usually *Beswick Ware Made in England*, with its postwar counterpart *Beswick England* in block letters. Models with sufficient room on the base will have the name and number impressed as well as the mark.

Ginger Nutt, a Beswick David Hand Animalland figure, painted in colors, 10cm. high.
(Christie's) $461

'Jiminy Cricket', a Beswick Walt Disney Character, 1952-65.
(Phillips) $416

Beswick large model of a jay, (second version), model number 1219B, painted in colors, 6in.
(G. A. Key) $320

Tommy Brock, a Beswick Beatrix Potter figure, painted in colors
(Christie's) $349

'Frog Footman' and 'Fish Footman' 1975-83.
(Phillips) $512

'Duchess with Flowers', a rare figure, 1954-67.
(Phillips) $2,560

'Tom Kitten', a rare Beswick wall plaque, 1967-69.
(Phillips) $2,160

A Beswick model of a swallow-tail butterfly, 5¼ x 3½in., impressed number *1492*, green mark.
(Anderson & Garland)
                               $188

Beswick model of a seated fox, number 2348, (Fireside Series), impressed marks, 12½in.
(G. A. Key) $416

A Bow blue and white cylindrical mug, the groove strap handle with heart terminal, painted with sampans by huts on islands, circa 1765, 11.6cm. high. (Christie's) $370

A Bow Imari teabowl and saucer painted with stylized lotus, circa 1750. (Christie's) $330

A Bow porcelain sauceboat, of silver shape, with double spurred C shape handle and on three paw feet, 1750–1755, 22.5cm. (Tennants) $1,450

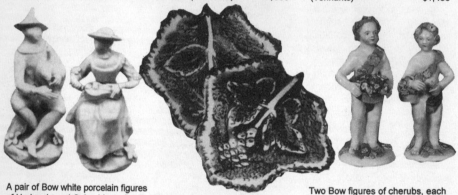

A pair of Bow white porcelain figures of Harlequin and Columbine, after the Meissen originals, he seated playing bagpipes, 13cm. high. (Bearne's) $1,760

Two Bow blue and white leaf shaped pickle dishes, both painted with fruiting vines, circa 1765, 9cm. long. (Christie's) $640

Two Bow figures of cherubs, each with floral headware and garlands and holding baskets of flowers, on circular flower strewn bases, circa 1760, 13cm. (Tennants) $640

A Bow leaf shaped famille rose dish painted with scattered flower sprays within a border band of alternate diaper and flower head panels, circa 1753, 18cm. wide. (Christie's) $480

A Bow figure of a brindled pug dog, resting on a brown and yellow cushion, looking to his rear, 11.2cm. wide. (Bearne's) $1,013

A Bow porcelain shallow dish, painted in polychrome enamels, the center with flowers and bamboo in a garden, 22.2cm. diameter. (Bearne's) $400

A Parianware group of two young children, the one seated on a rock offering a drink in a shell to the other, 11½in. high.
(Andrew Hartley) $251

Royal Winton Grimwades sauce boat, modeled as a cockerel and decorated with the 'Chanticleer' pattern, 7in.
(G. A. Key) $93

Sylvac seated model of a terrier dog, treacle tinted nose and treacle body markings, on a mainly beige ground, 11in.
(G. A. Key) $272

An Elsmore & Forster puzzle jug decorated with a harlequin and cock-fighting scene with inscription, *Joseph Woodman ,1868*, 8in. high.
(Russell Baldwin & Bright) $496

A panel in colors showing a young Spanish woman, the black border inscribed *Colour Books*, 17 x 15in.
(David Lay) $549

Early 19th century English porcelain circular toilet bowl, the center printed in blue with scene 'The Gleaners', within a floral border, possibly Elkin Knight & Co, 14in. (G. A. Key) $144

Charlotte Rhead baluster jug, decorated with bunches of lemons, fruit and foliage in colors, Crown Ducal printed mark, signed, 8½in.
(G. A. Key) $223

An English majolica jardinière on stand, the brown exterior molded with colorful flowering branches, 24cm. overall.
(Bristol) $295

A Charlotte Rhead Crown Ducal pottery vase, of tapering baluster form, decorated with a band of flowerheads and stylized foliage, 10in. high.
(Christie's) $306

A large glazed earthenware cat, designed by Louis Wain, 1920s, hollow to form a vase, 10in. high. (Christie's) $3,749

A Royal Winton chintz 'Orient' pattern tea service for two, comprising teapot and cover, plate, two cups and saucers, milk jug and sugar basin. (H C Chapman & Son) $314

Pratts Italian pattern chamberstick, printed in blue with scene amidst foliage etc, 19th century, 5½in. (G. A. Key) $158

Robinson & Leadbeater white parian bust of Charles Sumner, England, circa 1880, mounted to raised circular plinth, impressed title, verse and manufacturer's mark, 12⁷/₈in. high. (Skinner) $345

A Laura Knight, Foley bone china coffee set, with green feather and copper luster decoration, comprising six cups and saucers, coffee pot - 7in. high, cream jug and sugar basin. (Clarke Gammon) $416

Shorter & Son Ltd. Art Deco pottery jug, formed as a monkey carrying a palm leaf, English, first half 20th century, 11in. (G.A. Key) $159

An English delft posset pot and cover, the two handled body divided into three panels of Chinamen, London or Bristol, circa 1730-1740, 19cm. (Tennants) $1,429

Susie Cooper coffee service, decorated with abstract design of circles with tails, four cups, seven saucers, cream jug and coffee pot. (G.A. Key) $109

Dr Christopher Dresser, a Linthorpe Art Pottery jug, shape 341, incised with band of circled flowerheads, 17cm. (Bristol) $296

Blue and white transfer decorated soup tureen with undertray, W.P. & Co., England, circa 1840, 'Maramora' pattern. (Skinner)   **$632**

A Wade 5in. Disney blow-up model of Jock from Lady and the Tramp, 3½in. high. (Anderson & Garland)   **$596**

Fine English polychrome ironstone platter, 19th century, marked on bottom with shield similar to English Royal Shield, 21½in. long. (Eldred's)   **$1,375**

Charlotte Rhead Crown Ducal circular charger, typically decorated with a central abstract floral motif on a mainly orange and washed ground, signed, 12½in. diameter. (G A Key)   **$313**

A 19th century pair of ironstone vases, of lobed baluster form with twin shoulder handles, painted in an Oriental design in Imari palette, 30.5cm. (Bristol)   **$4,640**

BUYER BEWARE

A guide to determining whether a piece of china has been restored or has a discreet crack — just tap it gently. If a bowl that has been restored or glued together is tapped, it will issue a dull noise. Pieces in perfect condition will always have a ringing sound, and this applies to plates as well. Its not an infallible technique however, and doesn't always work with very tiny cracks.

MARK MEDCALF

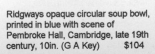

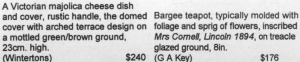

Ridgways opaque circular soup bowl, printed in blue with scene of Pembroke Hall, Cambridge, late 19th century, 10in. (G A Key)   **$104**

A Victorian majolica cheese dish and cover, rustic handle, the domed cover with arched terrace design on a mottled green/brown ground, 23cm. high. (Wintertons)   **$240**

Bargee teapot, typically molded with foliage and sprig of flowers, inscribed *Mrs Cornell, Lincoln 1894*, on treacle glazed ground, 8in. (G A Key)   **$176**

Globular Canton teapot, 19th century, 6in. high. (Eldred's) $187

Pair of Canton candlesticks, 19th century, in trumpet form, 7in. high. (Eldred's) $467

Canton water pitcher, 19th century, with traditional lake scene decoration, 8in. high. (Eldred's) $770

A pair of 19th century Cantonese baluster vases painted with numerous figures in reserves, butterfly and floral surrounds, 23.3in. (Russell Baldwin & Bright) $2,160

Two rose medallion garden seats, China, 19th century, 18¼ and 19in. high. (Skinner) $3,105

A pair of 19th century Chinese Cantonese circular tapered vases, richly painted panels of courtiers, figures in boats and an Emperor on horseback, 24³/₄in. high. (Anderson & Garland) $863

Canton famille rose circular large charger with dished rim, the border decorated mainly in famille rose and verte with bat and butterfly designs, 19th century, 14½in. (G A Key) $296

Pair of rose Canton covered urns, China, 19th century, 19¹/₄in. high. (Skinner) $2,990

Canton covered pitcher, 19th century, in ovold form, architectural lake scene and foo dog finial, 8¹/₂in. high. (Eldred's) $1,870

HISTORICAL FACTS
Capodimonte

The Capodimonte factory near Naples was established by King Charles III in 1742 to make soft-paste porcelain of the French type.

It was not until 1744, however, after numerous failed attempts, that Gaetano Schepers managed to produce a paste which was suitably 'white and diaphanous' and which achieved a brilliance to rival Meissen.

The most famous modeler at the Capodimonte factory was Giovanni Caselli, a former gem engraver and miniature painter. Figurines were among the earliest output of the factory, but snuff boxes, tea services and scent bottles were also made. The small objects were often mounted on gold or silver gilt, and the fine floral decoration was usually painted in finely drawn hair lines.

In 1759 Charles acceded to the throne of Spain, and the factory closed. He set up again at Buen Retiro, but the quality of products produced there is generally inferior to their Italian Capodimonte antecedents.

Capodimonte style painted pottery Stein, late 19th century, with lion finial, the body depicting a continuous hunt scene, 8¼in. high. (Skinner)　$345

A Capodimonte oviform teapot with scroll handle and spout, blue fleur-de-lys mark, circa 1750, 14.5cm. wide. (Christie's)　$1600

Pair of Capo di Monte covered two-handled vases, Italy, 19th century, each with a nautical theme in high relief above dolphin molded plinths, 18in. high, (Skinner)　$2,875

Twelve Capo di Monte style plates, Italy, 19th/20th century, enamel and gilt decorated with classical figures of children in landscape settings., 10½in. diameter. (Skinner)　$2,185

A Capodimonte (Carlo III) shaped gold mounted snuff box, the porcelain circa 1755, 8.5cm. wide. (Christie's)　$1600

Pair of Capo di Monte oval dishes, Italy, 19th century, each in high relief with classical figures among the clouds, 18in. long. (Skinner)　$1,955

Capo di Monte style tankard and cover, Italy, 19th century, continuous scene of classical relief figures enamel and gilt decorated, 9¼in. high. (Skinner)　$805

A Carltonware twin-handled bowl, printed and painted in colors and gilt on a blue ground with stylized flowers and foliage, 31cm. wide.
(Christie's) $736

A Carlton ware 'Guinness is Good for You' lamp, modeled as a black seal balancing a large blue metal revolving ball on his nose, 38cm. high. (Winterton's) $499

A Carlton ware 9¼in. circular bowl, the interior painted a jardiniere of flowers and shrubs, painted flowering boughs and insects on blue ground.
(Anderson and Garland) $360

Carlton Ware luster jug with gilt loop handle, the body painted and gilded with stylized floral and fan decoration, 5in. high.
(Phillips) $400

A Carlton Ware vase of inverted baluster form, painted with polychrome stylized flowers on blue and purple ground, 7¼in. high.
(Dee Atkinson & Harrison)
          $445

Fairy, a Carltonware vase and cover, printed and painted in colors and gilt on a blue luster ground, 17cm. high.
(Christie's) $1,840

Red Devil, a rare Carltonware, ovoid form printed and painted in enamels and gilt in colors on a pale blue ground, 15cm. high.
(Christie's) $1,920

A Carlton ware ginger jar and cover, painted with stylized flowerheads and bell flowers against a mottled burgundy ground, 7½in. high.
(George Kidner) $440

HISTORICAL FACTS
Carter Stabler & Adams

In 1921 John and Truda Adams went into partnership with Harold Stabler and Owen Carter of Carter & Co of Poole Dorset.

Together they made hand thrown and hand decorated pottery, mostly designed either by Stabler and his wife Phoebe, or by John and Truda Adams. Their shapes, mostly tableware and stoneware, were noted for their simplicity and were usually decorated in bold colors under a creamy matt glaze. Around the 1930s candlesticks were also made in the Art Deco style.

It was out of this partnership that the Poole Pottery, as it was renamed in 1963, grew. Poole Pottery products from all periods are much in vogue as collectibles today with some sales being devoted exclusively to their output.

A Poole Pottery jug by Eileen Prangell, painted with stylized flowers and foliage in colors below geometric banding, 19.5cm. high. (Christie's)　　　$405

Poole (Carter, Stabler & Adams) pottery two handled globular baluster vase with blue speckled rim, 1929, 6¹/₂in. (G.A. Key)　　　$251

A Poole Pottery twin-handled vase, shouldered form, by Phyllis Allen, painted with geometric flowers and foliage in colours on a white ground, 13cm. high. (Christie's)　　　$275

A large Carter, Stabler & Adams red earthenware vase, painted in muted enamel colors, the upper section of the ovoid body with a wide band of stylized foliage, 39cm. high. (Bearne's)　　　$5,184

Caughley

HISTORICAL FACTS
Caughley

Around 1772 Thomas Turner established his factory at Caughley in Shropshire. Turner had been manager at Worcester, and had trained as an engraver under Robert Hancock. He persuaded Hancock to join him in his new venture, and set out to rival the Worcester production of blue printed porcelain. He was so successful that by the 1780s Caughley was completely dominating the market, with affordable wares.

A Caughley blue and white leaf molded mask jug printed with the Fisherman and Cormorant pattern, circa 1790, 23.5cm. high. (Christie's)　　　$515

A Caughley quart mug, cylindrical with everted rim and loop handle, 'La Peche' blue transfer pattern to each side, 5¹/₂in., circa 1775. (Russell, Baldwin & Bright)　　　$492

HISTORICAL FACTS
Chelsea

The new Chelsea factory, founded in the 1740s, was largely inspired by Nicholas Sprimont, a Huguenot silversmith from Flanders, and it was probably the first of the six or so soft paste factories which sprang up in England by 1750.

Pieces from this period often carry an incised triangle and have a strong affinity with Sprimont's silverwork, with particular emphasis on shellwork and scroll motifs. Many pieces were left in the white.

The next, or Raised Anchor Period (1749–53) saw the porcelain becoming more opaque as less lead was used. Figures are now more usually colored, this often being done in the London studio of William Duesbury. While oriental influence remained very strong, many decorations of this period are obviously of Meissen origin.

By 1752 a painted Red Anchor Mark was becoming common, and this Red Anchor period, which lasted until about 1758, saw the apogee of Chelsea figure modeling. Table wares still showed oriental and Continental motifs while a new development was the manufacture of handsome vegetable and animal tureens and stands.

The final Gold Anchor period shows a departure towards the opulent and the elaborate, with colored grounds in the Meissen and Sèvres style, and figures in ornate bocages and flowery backgrounds.

Pair of Chelsea figures, English, 19th century, dogs in front of a gumdrop tree with gilt and polychrome decoration, gold anchor mark, 4in. high. (Eldred's) $357

A Chelsea baluster teapot and cover, circa 1756, finely painted in a vibrant palette with exotic birds including two parrots, 5¾in. high. (Christie's) $44,562

A pair of Chelsea porcelain figures, Liberty and Matrimony, depicted seated in front of bocages, on scrolling bases with gilt embellishment, 10¼in. high. (Andrew Hartley) $2,400

A 19th century Chelsea porcelain group of three putti with birdcage, 7½in. high. (Dargate) $200

An attractive Chelsea fluted teabowl and saucer painted in Vincennes style with vignettes of figures and buildings in rustic landscapes, red anchor period. (Phillips) $3200

A Chelsea figure of a shepherd playing the recorder, wearing pink hat, green jacket and his breeches painted in blue, iron-red and gilt, circa 1765, 21cm. high. (Christie's) $1920

HISTORICAL FACTS
Chelsea Keramic

Alexander Robertson founded the Chelsea Keramic Art Works near Boston Mass. in 1872, in partnership with his brother Hugh and later his father James. They produced reproductions of Greek vases, ornamental plaques and tiles, often with decorations in high relief.

Shortly after 1876, Hugh introduced an earthenware with underglaze decoration in colored slip, which was marketed as 'Bourg la Reine' ware, and also turned to oriental glazes and designs. The firm failed in 1888, but a new company, the Chelsea Pottery, was reopened in 1891 and in 1896 moved to Dedham, where it became known as the Dedham Pottery.

Marks include an impressed *CKAW* or the name in full, with artist's marks also incised.

Dedham Ware was made in forty eight patterns and proved very popular. Its mark is Dedham Pottery over a crouching rabbit.

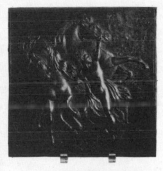

American Chelsea Pottery rabbit facing left pattern plate, raised design, impressed CPUS mark, 10in. diameter. (Skinner) $2,070

Chelsea Keramic Art Works slipper, Massachusetts, circa 1885, mottled olive green and brown glaze, 6in. long. (Skinner) $320

Exceptional Chelsea Keramic Art Works, Robertson & Sons ceramic tile with a copper covered relief of a figure holding two rearing stallions, 10½in. square. (Skinner) $5,750

Late 19th century Chelsea Keramic Art Works pottery vase, Mass., 10½in. high. (Skinner) $2,500

A Chelsea Keramic Art pottery vase with blue-green glossy glaze, circa 1885, 11¼in. high. (Skinner) $800

Chelsea Keramic Art Works pillow vase, incised palm tree decoration under the blue glaze, signed *HCR, Chelsea Keramic Art Works, Robertson & Sons*, 6½in. high. (Skinner) $172

Chelsea Keramic Art Works ewer, mottled sea green glaze, impressed mark, 10in. high. (Skinner) $800

HISTORICAL FACTS
Chinese

The antiquity of Chinese ceramics and their beauty and variety down the ages make their study and collection particularly attractive, and provide scope for every taste.

The earliest unglazed earthenware jars date from as early as 2,000 BC, but it was not really until the Han Dynasty (206BC–220AD) that finer techniques, especially the art of glazing had been definitively mastered.

The next truly great period was the T'ang Dynasty (618–906AD) when the pottery was characterised by a beautiful proportion and vitality. A lead glaze was revived, which was often splashed or mottled, and many decorative themes reflect Hellenistic influence.

It was during the Sung Dynasty (960–1279AD) that the first true porcelain seems to have been made, and this period too saw the production of some of the most beautiful shapes and glazes of all time. It also saw the beginning of underglaze blue painting, which was to be perfected during the Ming period.

During the Ming Dynasty (1368–1644AD) a more or less standardised fine white porcelain body was developed which acted as a perfect vehicle for brilliant color decoration. Glazes tended to be thick or 'fat'. Colored glazes too were introduced and used either together or singly.

The K'ang Hsi period (1662–1722AD) marked a further flowering of the potter's art, which continued under his sons Yung Cheng and Ch'ien Lung (Qianlong).

A Chinese porcelain and gilt-bronze centerpiece, Paris, circa 1870, of oval form, painted in underglaze blue and copper red decoration, 43cm. high. (Sotheby's)   **$9,747**

Fine yellow enameled porcelain deep dish with underglaze blue dragon decoration, Qianlong mark and Period, 8¹⁄₈in. diameter. (Butterfield & Butterfield)   **$4,312**

A pair of Chinese enameled porcelain figure groups, each modeled as two courtesans, in floral and phoenix embellished robes, late 19th century, 31cm. (Tennants)   **$1,111**

Blue and white Nanking two-handled covered urn, circa 1800, decorated with lake scene, 11in. high. (Eldred's)   **$660**

A pair of 19th century Chinese circular tapered vases with raised butterfly decoration, painted with dragons, flowers and berries on turquoise blue ground, 24¹⁄₂in. high. (Anderson & Garland)   **$1,256**

Pair of blue and white porcelain 'Eight Immortals' bowls, Daoguang mark and Period, each with a roundel of Shoulao and the deer of immortality centering the wide curving well, 8¾in. diameter. (Butterfield & Butterfield)   **$862**

Chinese large circular charger, the center painted in underglazed blue with scene of figures on an island, 18th/19th century, 18in.
(G.A. Key) $565

A pair of Chinese famille rose water droppers, each in the form of a lotus flower, the hollow stem forming the spout, 19cm., Guangxu marks.
(Dreweatt Neate) $792

Chinese Nankin canted rectangular dish, typically painted in underglazed blue with motifs of fishermen standing by a shore, 18th century, 10½in.
(G.A. Key) $157

A fine Chinese barrel shaped garden seat richly painted with flowers and foliage, on green ground, 18¼in. high.
(Anderson & Garland) $1,177

A garniture of three Chinese celadon ground porcelain vases, comprising a baluster vase and cover and a pair of gu form side vases, Kangxi, 43.5cm and 41cm.
(Tennants) $5,080

Good painted pottery model of a Bactrian camel, Tang dynasty, hollow molded with its four legs at momentary rest on a rectangular plinth, 22in. high.
(Butterfield & Butterfield) $2,587

A Chinese 17¾in. circular plaque painted with storks, flowers, tree, and gilt clouds.
(Anderson & Garland) $133

A Chinese Meiping vase, painted in enamels with two flowering prunus trees with entangled branches, circa 1900, 21.5cm.
(Tennants) $1,905

A Chinese blue and white bowl with everted rim, the center painted with a woman in a fenced rocky garden, 34.5cm. diameter, Transitional.
(Bearne's) $7,290

Davenport small can shaped cup, printed in puce with 19th century scene of feasting figures around a camp fire, early 19th century, 2½in. (G.A. Key) $104

English blue and white platter, by Davenport with an Oriental scene, 21 x 15½in. (Eldred's) $660

Davenport feeding cup, printed in blue with the 'Muleteer' pattern, circa 1835, 6½in. wide. (G. A. Key) $192

De Morgan

A 'Persian' two-handled vase by William de Morgan, painted by Halsey Ricardo, Fulham Period, 1888-89, painted in Isnik palette, 13½in. high. (Christie's) $3,598

A glazed earthenware 'Persian' vase, by William de Morgan, circa 1885, of shouldered form, decorated in Isnik palette with typically formalized pomegranate flowers, 15in. high. (Christie's) $1,312

A William De Morgan bottle vase, painted with stylized foliage in ruby luster on a white ground, 16cm. high. (Christie's) $368

Dedham

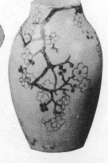

Dedham Pottery stork pattern plate, raised design, blue stamp, 9in. diameter. (Skinner) $5,750

Four Dedham pottery coffee mugs, iris, snowtree, horsechestnut, and magnolia pattern, Dedham mark, 3¼in. high. (Skinner) $690

Dedham Potter prunus decorated vase, tapering cylindrical form, incised *Dedham Pottery*, initialed *BW*, 8½in. (Skinner) $3,105

HISTORICAL FACTS
Derby

Porcelain making in Derby commenced around the mid 18th century and has continued there ever since.

William Duesbury, the London porcelain painter, became a key figure from 1756. He bought the Chelsea factory in 1770 and finally moved to Derby in 1784, where he was succeeded by his son, William II, in 1786. By the 1770s a really perfect porcelain body was being produced at Derby, and the employment of superb landscape and flower painters as decorators ensured that the finished product was of a quality second to none. In 1811 the factory was purchased by Robert Bloor, and production continued until 1848. While the quality of the body declined somewhat during this period, that of decoration remained high, and the factory continued to specialise in Imari and Japanese styles. From 1848 a new factory was opened in King Street, Derby, which continued till 1935 and specialised in copies of earlier Derby pieces. A further factory opened in 1876, called Derby Crown Porcelain Co, and was continued after 1890 by the Royal Crown Derby Co.

Many early period Derby flatware pieces have 'moons' or patches in the paste which look especially bright when held up to the light. Such 'moons' can also be found on some Chelsea and Longton Hall pieces.

A Derby demi-lune bough pot, the central rectangular panel painted with a landscape, late 18th century, 13cm. high. (Christie's) $773

An early Derby porcelain basket with flower encrusted openwork sides, turquoise loop handles, the interior painted with fruit and insects, 7in. wide. (Andrew Hartley) $576

Derby porcelain partial dessert set, of six 8in. plates, oval covered tureen and six-sided dish, circa 1810. (Eldred's) $275

A Derby figure of Sir John Falstaff typically modeled standing holding broadsword and shield, circa 1770, 25cm. high. (Christie's) $368

A pair of Royal Crown Derby ovoid vases with scalloped everted rims, painted with flower sprays in russet and blue, 30cm. high. (Wintertons) $928

A Derby Imari tankard of cylindrical form, painted with alternate panels of a dragon and bird before flowering shrubs, circa 1770, 15.5cm. high. (Christie's) $640

HISTORICAL FACTS
Deruta

The pottery industry in Deruta, Umbria, dates from the late 15th century. At that time wares in the usual high temperature colors were produced, together with some with metallic luster decoration. Some, too, were very distinctive in that, in order to achieve a 'near-flesh' tint, the enamel was scraped away to reveal the pinkish clay body, to which a clear lead glaze was then added.

Early 16th century Deruta luster is brassy yellow outlined in soft blue, often showing a nacreous iridescence. Later wares have a deeper tone, sometimes approaching olive green.

Large plates predominate as a form, with tin glaze on the front only and a colorless lead glaze on the underside. Some dishes and bowls with raised decoration were made using molds. Many of these feature a raised central boss, perhaps to fit the base of a matching ewer.

A Deruta lusterware charger, first half 16th century, Saint Catherine holding the martyr's palm, 15¼in. diameter.
(Sotheby's) $8,050

A Deruta tin-glazed earthenware charger, first half 16th century, a Turk on a charging stallion in the center, 15in. diameter.
(Sotheby's) $11,500

A Deruta double-handled lusterware jar, first half 16th century, with flaring neck fitted with two scrolling handles, 8¼in. high.
(Sotheby's) $2,185

A Deruta (lustred at Gubbio) lusterware charger, first half 16th century, the painted and molded decoration consisting of joined hands with a crown above in the center, 13⅞in. diameter.
(Sotheby's) $10,925

A Deruta tin-glazed earthenware charger, first half 16th century, centered by a hunter with his hound, 15¼in. diameter.
(Sotheby's) $4,025

A Deruta double-handled lusterware jar, first half 16th century, with ear-shaped handles and bulbous body, 10½in. high.
(Sotheby's) $4,600

A Deruta 'peacock feather' lusterware charger, second quarter 16th century, decorated throughout in blue and gold luster 15⅝in. diameter.
(Sotheby's) $17,250

HISTORICAL FACTS
Doulton

The Doulton story began in 1815, when John Doulton, known as the 'best thrower of pint pots in London' set up a pottery business in partnership with a widow called Jones and a journeyman called Watts. The Watts Doulton part of the association continued until the former's retiral in 1853.

In 1835 John's second son Henry joined the company. It was Henry who responded to an approach by John Sparkes head of the newly established Lambeth School of Arts requesting that some of his students should try potting. He set up a pottery studio in a corner of the works, and it is worth noting that George Tinworth and the Barlows, Arthur, Florence and Hannah, were among the first intake.

Henry also acquired an earthenware factory in Burslem, which he renamed Doulton and Co.

Experimentation and constant development were the keynotes for both establishments and they attracted terrific resources of talent. Charles J Noke, for example, joined the company in 1889 and finally became Artistic Director at Burslem. He experimented with Copenhagen and Sèvres type wares and in recreating oriental techniques. The results of the latter were the renowned Flambé , Sung, Chinese jade and Chang pottery. Under Noke, too, the company embarked on one of its most successful lines of all, figure models, the first of which were exhibited at Chicago in 1893.

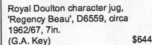

Royal Doulton character jug, 'Regency Beau', D6559, circa 1962/67, 7in.
(G.A. Key) $644

A Royal Doulton figure, entitled 'A Chelsea Pensioner', HN689.
(Bearne's) $518

Pair of Royal Doulton baluster vases with flared rims, the bodies decorated with panels of foliage, impressed marks for late 19th/early 20th century, 12in.
(G.A. Key) $188

A Doulton stoneware jug with silver mount and engraved hinged cover, decorated by Edith Lupton and Mary Ann Thompson, 19.5cm. high, dated 1875. (Bearne's) $598

A Victorian Doulton Lambeth stoneware mug of cylindrical form, relief molded with canoeists in reserves, impressed date 1883.
(Andrew Hartley) $720

A Nelsonian treacle glazed character jug, modeled as the head and shoulders of Horatio Nelson, impressed Doulton & Watts, Lambeth Pottery, London, 7in.
(G A Key) $464

A Doulton figure, Abdulla (*sic*), HN1410, printed mark with *No. 111, mold No. 679A*, initialed *AB*, impressed *4.10.30*.
(David Lay) $445

Royal Doulton large loving cup, made to celebrate the bi-centenary of Nelson's birth, signed by H. Fenton, 10in.
(G.A. Key) $954

A Royal Doulton female figure 'Autumn Breezes', HN1934, 7¹/₂in. high.
(Anderson & Garland) $117

A set of twelve Royal Doulton figures from the 'Middle Earth' series, comprising: 'Gandalf', HN2911, 'Frodo', HN2912, 'Gollum', HN2913, 'Bilbo', HN2914, 'Galadriel', HN2915, 'Aragorn', HN2916, 'Legolas', HN2917, 'Boromir', HN2918, 'Gimli', HN2922, 'Barliman Butterbur', HN2923, 'Tom Bombadil', HN2924 and 'Samwise', HN2925, complete with a matching display stand, 43cm. wide.   (Bearne's) $2,187

Pair of Royal Doulton Art Nouveau period slender baluster vases, elaborately decorated with stylized foliage, by Frank Butler, 10in.
(G.A. Key) $1,485

A Doulton Lambeth round jardinière, decorated by Eliza Simmance and Eliza L. Hubert with scrolling flowers and leaves and stiff leaf bands, 6½in.
(Dreweatt Neate) $363

A fine pair of Hannah Barlow Doulton circular tapered vases incised with bands of cattle with florette borders, 15¹/₂in. high.
(Anderson & Garland) $1,749

A Royal Doulton female figure 'Melanie', HN2271, 8in. high. (Anderson & Garland) $133

A pair of Doulton stoneware vases, by Emily Partington, each globular body decorated with an encircling band of flowers, 40cm. high. (Bearne's) $680

A Royal Doulton female figure 'Fair Lady', HN2193, 7in. high. (Anderson & Garland) $78

Royal Doulton Lambeth Victorian Jubilee ewer of circular baluster form, on a cream foliate and thistle molded blue reserved ground, impressed marks, 7in. (G.A. Key) $471

Twelve Doulton Burslem Shakespeare plates, England, late 19th century, with gilt trimmed scalloped edges and polychrome decorated leafy vines, 9in. diameter. (Skinner) $460

A Royal Doulton stoneware jug applied with a plain silver rim, decorated by George Tinworth, 23.5cm. high, dated *1879*. (Bearne's) $956

Decorative Doulton Burslem plate, the rim molded with rosettes etc, the border with gilt foliage on a deep blue reserve, printed mark, 9in. (G. A. Key) $80

A pair of Royal Doulton stoneware large baluster vases, each decorated by Frank A. Butler and Bessie Newbery, 40.5cm. high. (Bearne's) $2,673

'Mr Pickwick', Jim Beam Whiskey, by Royal Doulton, (Limited Edition of 100). (Gordon Litherland) $300

Decorative Dresden porcelain heart shaped mirror, crested with two putti clutching a garland swag, flower encrusted border painted in colors, on gilt ball feet.
(G. A. Key) $418

Pair of late 19th century, possibly Dresden, Continental porcelain figures of shepherdess and her male companion playing a clarinet.
(G. A. Key) $248

A Dresden porcelain covered portrait vase, oblate form with domed lid and three full bodied ram's horn handles, portrait of Maria Theresa, 21 in. high.
(Dargate) $2,000

Pair of Dresden porcelain covered baluster jars, painted in colors with panels of couples in a garden, printed marks, 7in. high.
(G A Key) $317

A Dresden porcelain jardinière, the cylindrical form painted with polychrome flowers on a gilt embellished trellis ground, 8¼in. high. (Andrew Hartley)
$704

A pair of Dresden gold and black-japanned terracotta urns and covers, early 18th century, each with a turned tapering body with loop handles and pinched neck, 21 in. and 22in. high.
(Christie's) $6,872

Dresden porcelain jardinière, the outer bowl encrusted with flowers and decorated in colors and the pedestal applied with figures of winged putti clutching posies, late 19th century, 17in. high.
(G. A. Key) $798

Dresden porcelain cabinet cup and saucer, two cross swords mark, pink scale border with fruit decoration, German, 19th century.
(G.A. Key) $174

A Dresden pair of baluster jars and covers, with gilt outlined shaped panels of 18th century figures in parkland, on turquoise ground, one restored, 37cm.
(Bristol) $713

A Continental figural group of putti hunting a boar, bearing crowned N mark, modeled as a boar trampling a putto, 7⅝in. high. (Christie's) $460

A pair of Danish 9in. oblong vases, in the shape of urns with lion pattern handles painted with panels of flowers, 7in. high. (Anderson & Garland)

$282

Continental porcelain group of a child seated beside his nodding dog, painted in colors, 4½in. (G.A. Key) $133

A fine 19th century Continental 13¾in. circular plaque richly painted with Europa, the bull and attendant female figure with cherubs. (Anderson & Garland)

$329

A pair of Continental majolica comports, in the form of Nereus and a Mermaid, each on a mound of water plants, 44cm. high. (Bearne's) $637

Wassily Kandinsky for the Imperial Russian porcelain factory, Petrograd, cup and saucer, 1921, porcelain, polychrome enamel decoration, 3in. high. (Sotheby's) $56,235

André-Vincent Becquerel for Etling, 'Venetian', 1920s, glazed earthenware modeled as a caped woman in a tricorn walking a grayhound, 12¾in. (Sotheby's) $1,125

Unusual Continental cheese dish and cover, the triangular cover decorated in colors with puce and lemon foliage, late 19th/early 20th century, 12in. (G. A. Key) $113

TOP TIPS

If you want to disguise hairline cracks or crazy paved stains in your precious china (to enhance your own enjoyment of them, needless to say, rather than prior to selling them!) submerge them in a bowl, containing a solution of water and bleach, overnight. Repeat the process as often as necessary to remove any dirt or staining and all evidence of the cracks has vanished.

WHITWORTHS

A porcelain and gilt-bronze centerpiece, French, circa 1870, the porcelain bowl painted with a Fête Champêtre, 38cm. high. (Sotheby's) $14,444

French painted porcelain moon-shaped vase, painted on both sides with river scenes, one signed *A. Collot* and with gilded twig-form roundels, 14¹/₂in. high. (Skinner) $1,380

A gilt-metal and faience centerpiece, French, circa 1880, of oval form, the pierced border flanked by winged busts, 64cm. high. (Sotheby's) $9,373

A pair of French porcelain vases, late 19th century, of bulbous shape with trumpet necks, applied with summer flower garlands, 15⁵/₈in. (Bonhams) $795

A pair of French ormolu-mounted and Sèvres pattern porcelain vases, late 19th century, the pink-ground bodies painted with panels of courting couples, 17¹/₄in. high. (Christie's) $1,240

Pair of large French porcelain covered ewers, circa 1880, with light blue ground and molded in high relief with foliage, 24in. high. (Skinner) $5,462

A pair of French matte blue-ground vases, late 19th century, Henri Ardant & Cie., Limoges, the ovoid bowls painted in colors with nymphs and putti in flight, 20in. high. (Christie's) $4,600

A pair of gilt-bronze and porcelain jardinières, French, circa 1870, each of ovoid form, the turquoise bodies with kylin and stylized clouds, 28cm. high. (Sotheby's) $3,374

A pair of Paris porcelain baluster vases, late 19th century, painted in polychrome colors with continuous views of a rural idyll, 19¹/₂in. (Bonhams) $1,192

A yellow-glazed faience bulldog by Gallé, decorated with blue/white spots and hearts, 12in. high. (Christie's) $3,084

A large faience clock by Gallé, circa 1895, modeled in full relief with two lions rampant on an elaborate scrolled base, 25in. high. (Christie's) $10,281

Gallé ceramic scenic pitcher, figurative decoration with costumed dancers in pastoral setting, handpainted mark, 8in. high. (Skinner) $920

George Jones

George Jones majolica Stilton dish, the cylindrical cover applied with a branch looped handle and molded with foliage, incised marks, 10in. (G. A. Key) $296

A fine George Jones majolica circular tapered afternoon tea service decorated in the apple blossom pattern with basket weave band on turquoise blue ground, mark for 1873. (Anderson & Garland) $4,960

George Jones majolica rooster teapot, England, circa 1875, 10¾in. long. (Skinner) $3,220

A pair of George Jones majolica vases, molded and colored to both sides with white flowering orchids with green foliage, 1870, 36.5cm. (Tennants) $16,720

A fine George Jones majolica circular shaped tapered teacup with raised floral decoration and square matching saucer. (Anderson & Garland) $627

A George Jones figure of a camel, impressed with monogram, GJ and Kumassie, 23.2cm. high. (Christie's) $2,400

German porcelain figural compôte, late 19th century, the pierced bowl with applied leaves and flowers, printed Thieme mark, 12¼in. high. (Skinner) $460

German porcelain nodding head figure, 20th century, depicting a seated Chinese woman in a floral dress, 7in. high. (Skinner) $1,725

'Spring', a glazed ceramic figure of a putto, designed by Michael Powolny, manufactured by Wiener Keramik, 1907, standing holding a garland of colorful flowers, 15in. high. (Christie's) $12,184

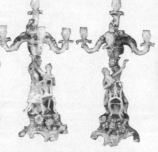

German painted porcelain covered tureen, late 19th century, Carl Thieme Saxonian Porcelain Factory, painted with figural panels and foliate sprays, 12in. high. (Skinner) $517

A pair of Plaue five light candelabra, late 19th/early 20th century, modeled as a couple seated on chairs toasting each other, 22½in. (Bonhams) $2,544

A German 'Vienna' porcelain cabinet plate, the central reserve enameled with two classical women by a pool with swans, inscribed *Wagner*, circa 1900, 24.5cm diameter. (Tennants) $476

Goldscheider

A Goldscheider child figure wearing floral patterned coat, with a Scots terrier, 9¼in. high. (Anderson & Garland) $248

A Goldscheider group of a boy and girl, he wearing a pierrot costume, she wearing a tutu, signed *G. Bouret*, 8¾in. high. (Anderson & Garland) $512

A Goldscheider female child figure wearing a short blue patterned dress and bonnet, with an Alsatian dog, 8¼in. high. (Anderson & Garland) $297

An Iznik pottery dish, Turkey, 17th century, with sloping rim, painted in polychrome with a central saz leaf, 11¾in. diameter.
(Bonhams) $9,750

A fine Iznik pottery jug, Turkey, second half 16th century, with bulbous body, slightly waisted neck and curved handle, painted cobalt blue, green and red, 9in. high.
(Bonhams) $30,305

An Iznik pottery dish, Turkey, 17th century, with sloping rim, decorated in cobalt blue, green, black and raised red, 11¾in. diameter.
(Bonhams) $4,785

A rare Iznik pottery animal dish, Turkey, circa 1580, with sloping rim, decorated on a turquoise ground with two lionesses, a leopard and two birds, 11½in. diameter.
(Bonhams) $41,470

A rare Iznik pottery jug, Turkey, circa 1530-40, with globular body, cylindrical neck and S shaped handle, decorated in sage green, cobalt and turquoise, 7½in. high.
(Bonhams) $71,775

A rare Iznik pottery dish, Turkey, circa 1565, with sloping bracketed rim, decorated in cobalt blue and black in reserve on a raised red ground, 11¼in. diameter.
(Bonhams) $55,825

A fine Iznik blue and white pottery dish, Turkey, circa 1560, with sloping bracketed rim, painted in different shades of cobalt blue, 11¼in. diameter.
(Bonhams) $146,740

An Iznik pottery tankard, Turkey, 17th century, painted in polychrome, slightly tapering body with a small square handle, 8½in. high.
(Bonhams) $10,846

An Iznik pottery dish, Turkey, 17th century, with sloping rim, painted in polychrome, an intricate arabesque design to center, 11¼in. diameter.
(Bonhams) $6,061

A large Japanese Imari dish, the well painted with figures by a terrace among blossoming trees, 24in. diameter.
(Christie's) $1,656

An Imari bowl, the typically patterned design depicting exotic birds and flowering cherry blossom, 9½in. diameter.
(Christie's) $643

A Japanese Imari dish, 19th century, painted with a central roundel of chrysanthemums and foliage within radiating panels, 18in. diam. (Christie's) $827

Pair of Japanese Imari baluster vases with flared necks, elaborately decorated in the typical manner in traditional colors, late 19th/early 20th century, 12in. high.
(G. A. Key) $431

A fine and large 19th century Japanese Imari 24³/₄in. circular fluted plaque painted with panels of storks and animals.
(Anderson & Garland) $1,176

Pair of Japanese Imari large baluster vases, decorated in the typical manner in traditional colors, late 19th century, 14½in.
(G. A. Key) $288

Imari porcelain charger, blue and rust ground with traditional decoration of flowering pots, shrubs and insects etc., circa 1880, 12¼in.
(G.A. Key) $119

A pair of late 19th century Japanese Imari bottle shaped vases, each richly decorated with shaped panels of flowers and phoenix, 14in. high.
(Dreweatt Neate) $1,188

An Imari porcelain shallow circular dish, the center painted with blossom and bamboo within a scroll reserve, 30.5cm. diameter.
(Bearne's) $1,425

A glazed earthenware figure, manufactured by Essevi, circa 1920, modeled as a young melancholic girl weaaring a bonnet and black dress, 11in. high.
(Christie's) $2,400

A fine Lenci female wall face mask wearing floral decorated headsquare, 14in. high. (Anderson & Garland) $1,320

Large Italian tin glazed earthenware basin, late 19th century, with snake handles, decorated with a scene of Perseus and Andromeda, 23in. diameter.
(Skinner) $1,265

A Doccia baluster coffee pot and cover with bird's head mask spout, circa 1780, 22cm. high.
(Christie's) $800

A large glazed earthenware vase, designed by Gio Pontl, manufactured by Ginori, circa 1925/30, decorated with a design of household objects, 10½in. high.
(Christie's) $9,747

TRICKS OF THE TRADE

Has a piece of porcelain caught your eye and are you anxious to find out whether it may have been restored by painting or spraying? If you are not too self conscious about attracting the odd curious glance (the experts of course will know exactly what you're doing) take a gentle bite. If it feels hard to the bite then it will be satisfactory, if it feels slightly soft, it has been painted or sprayed.

MARK MEDCALF

Italian faience circular charger, the border elaborately decorated in typical colors with stylized peacocks, 18th/19th century, 15½in.
(G.A. Key) $363

A Lenci female wall mask wearing a brown ground gilt kashmir style scarf, 12in. high, marked, 1937.
(David Lay) $560

Large maiolica charger, Italy, 19th century, polychrome decorated, recessed central cartouche depicting Neptune with sea nymphs, 24in. diameter.
(Skinner) $805

HISTORICAL FACTS
Liverpool

There were seven porcelain factories in Liverpool in the 18th century, of which three, Chaffers, Christians and Penningtons, are generally regarded as forming the mainstream tradition from 1754–99.

The Chaffers' factory (1754–65) made a bone ash and a soapstone porcelain which are often difficult to tell apart as most of the standard shapes were identically produced in both.

The Christian factory (1765–76) produced examples which were well potted but on which the decoration was competent rather than outstanding. Blue and white tewares are very common but flatware is rare.

The output of the Pennington factory (1769–99) consisted largely of imitations of Christian's wares but was generally of inferior quality as regards both potting and painting. Blue and white predominates, and among the finest examples are ship bowls, which were sometimes named and dated.

Liverpool creamware jug, England, early 19th century, transfer printed reserves of Thomas Jefferson and James Monroe, 9³/₄in. high.
(Skinner) $20,700

Important Liverpool caster set, late 18th/early 19th century, made for the Dutch market, five bottles with black titles and an eagle-handled holder, 11in. high.
(Eldred's) $1,430

Liverpool pitcher, with transfer decoration of a ship on one side and *Washington in Glory* on reverse, 9in. high.
(Eldred's) $220

Liverpool Creamware jug, England, circa 1816, decorated on one side *The Gratitude of Massachusetts follows Caleb Strong to Northampton*, 5³/₈in. high.
(Skinner) $1,610

Limoges

Haviland Limoges porcelain game set, France, circa 1880, including shaped oval platter, twelve plates, shaped cream dish.
(Skinner) $1,495

Limoges painted and parcel gilt punch bowl and matching underplate, circa 1900 with serpentine edge and decorated with grape bunches and leaves, 15 and 18in diameter.
(Skinner) $1,495

Limoges porcelain plate, the centre decorated in colors with portrait of a young lady clutching a posy of flowers, 10in. (G.A. Key) $60

Portuguese majolica circular charger, elaborately molded and decorated in colors with motifs of fish, eel etc., late 19th century, 14¹/₂in.
(G.A. Key) $754

Three 19th century graduated majolica style jugs with basket weave bases, the tops with blackberries in relief, 6in. to 8in.
(Ewbank) $763

Majolica bargee teapot, the whole molded with panels on flowers, birds etc. and inscribed *A Present From Woodville'*, 19th century.
(G. A. Key) $256

Maling

A Maling circular plaque with raised floral and butterfly decoration on blue ground, 11¼in. (Anderson & Garland) $215

A Maling stirrup cup, modeled as a fox mask with tapering red body, 15cm.
(Tennants) $192

A Maling circular plaque with raised floral decoration including tulips on blue ground, 11in.
(Anderson & Garland) $396

A fine Maling 11in. circular plaque with raised cottage, millwheel bridge and floral decoration.
(Anderson & Garland) $320

Maling hexagonal biscuit barrel, decorated with 'Rosine' pattern, circa 1960, 6¹/₂in.
(G.A. Key) $157

A Maling Edward VIII Coronation plaque, designed by Lucien Boullemier, with relief molded central portrait within double ribbon tied wreath edging, 32cm.
(Tennants) $2,816

BUYER BEWARE

There is a large quantity of reproduction Mason's ironstone being placed on the market at present. Some of it has a very plausible mark on the bottom, but looked at closely it actually says *Manon's* rather than *Mason's*. Also, in the case of the typical Mason's ironstone jug of octagonal baluster shape, often with a green snake handle, the handles on the reproductions are much more crudely molded.

MARK MEDCALF

A Masons Ironstone large fluted cylindrical mug, with dragon handle, printed and painted in Imari style with flowers and leaves, 5½in. high, circa 1820.
(Dreweatt Neate) $429

Mason's Patent Ironstone mug, green ground with heavy gilt work to the handle and body, English, circa early 19th century, 4in. high.
(G.A. Key) $198

HISTORICAL FACTS
Martinware

The Martin Brothers co-operative, which set up in 1873, consisted of Robert Wallace Martin, who had worked for the Fulham pottery, and his brothers Walter & Edwin, who had previously been employed by Doulton. Walter was thrower, and Edwin decorator, while a further brother, Charles, became the business manager and ran a shop in Brownlow Street, London.

Martinware comes in a wide variety of shapes. The decoration is mainly incised, with the colours reminiscent of Doulton stoneware. The most common motifs are plants, birds, animals and grotesques, of which perhaps the most notable are R W Martin's 'wally birds'. These are often found as tobacco jars, with the heads forming the lids, and generally have a somewhat menacing air. Some of the later production tended more towards the abstract, relating it to later studio pottery. The works closed in 1914.

A Martin Brothers stoneware face jug, modeled in relief either side with a smiling face, in shades of white and brown on a buff ground, dated *1900*, 17cm. high.
(Christie's) $4,048

A Martin Brothers stoneware bird vase and cover, standing, the wise old bird modeled with a balding head, casting an upwards, knowing glance, 1902, 26cm. high.
(Christie's) $14,720

A large Martin Brothers stoneware bird jar and cover, standing broad beaked creature casting sideways glance, 1897, 29cm. high.
(Christie's) $14,720

A Martin Brothers stoneware vase, incised with scaly fish, in shades of blue and ocher, dated *1879*, 27cm. high. (Christie's) $662

A Meissen figure group emblematic of Peace, late 19th century, after a model by Charles Gottfried Juechtzer, 12in. high. (Christie's) $8,050

Two Meissen figures of a gentleman and companion, late 19th century/20th century, 6½in. high. (Christie's) $2,070

A Meissen figure group of two vintners, 19th century , he with carafe and glass, she with baskets and posy, 6¾in. (Bonhams) $1,192

A pair of Meissen five-light candelabra, late 19th century, each with a central foliate molded candleholder on a spiral twisted branch, 19¾in. high. (Christie's) $4,025

A Meissen figure group emblematic of Love, late 19th century, after Boucher, modeled as a shepherdess, being presented with a garland by a gentleman, 9¼in. high. (Christie's) $2,645

Two Meissen models of jays, each modeled perched on a high tree-stump with cocked wings, 9in. high. (Christie's) $1,380

A Meissen figure group, 19th century, modeled as a male and a female putto and a grinding wheel, preparing the 'arrows of love', 7½in. (Bonhams) $667

A pair of Meissen figures of rabbits, late 19th century, each seated on its haunches, one with right foot raised, 7in. (Bonhams) $3,498

A Meissen figure group of a mother and child, late 19th century, in pink and blue disarrayed drapery, modeled running with her child at her side, 9in. high. (Christie's) $1,150

A Meissen porcelain figural group, Germany, 20th century, depicting a young girl with a spotted dog, 5in. high. (Skinner) **$920**

Pair of Meissen porcelain figures, late 19th century, depicting a fruit seller and a flower girl, 4¾in. high. (Skinner) **$978**

Meissen porcelain hors d'oeuvres dishes, white ground formed as three shells each having scalloped borders, late 19th century, approximately 12in. (G.A. Key) **$302**

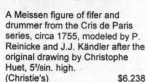

A Meissen model of a ewe, circa 1750, modeled by P. Reinicke, standing to the left with head turned to look back, on a tree-stump molded oval pad base applied with flowers and foliage, 6¾in. wide. (Christie's) **$2,390**

A German porcelain figure group in Meissen style, 19th century, modeled as two musicians seated on a chaise, she with mandolin, he with flute, 8¾in. (Bonhams) **$954**

A Meissen figure of fifer and drummer from the Cris de Paris series, circa 1755, modeled by P. Reinicke and J.J. Kändler after the original drawing by Christophe Huet, 5⅜in. high. (Christie's) **$6,238**

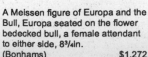

A Meissen figure group of Europa and the Bull, late 19th century, blue crossed swords mark, 8½in. high. (Christie's) **$1,840**

A pair of Meissen porcelain sweetmeat stands, late 19th century, each modeled as a reclining figure of a man or a woman, a large basket held before, 10½in. (Bonhams) **$1,113**

A Meissen figure of Europa and the Bull, Europa seated on the flower bedecked bull, a female attendant to either side, 8¾in. (Bonhams) **$1,272**

HISTORICAL FACTS
Mettlach

The original Mettlach factory was established in 1809 at the Abbey of Mettlach in the Rhineland. In 1836 it merged with the factories of Villeroy and J F Boch and together this group produced earthenwares. Stoneware was also made from 1842 onwards, with a high proportion of the output being exported to America.

Art Pottery, decorated with inlaid clays in contrasting colors (Mettlach ware) was also introduced.

Mettlach two handled balustered jardinière, elaborately molded throughout with panel of dancing figures, 14½in.
(G. A. Key) $222

Mettlach pitcher, incised foliate design in colors of blue, yellow, black and cream, circa 1885–1930, 6¾in. high.
(Skinner) $258

Mettlach book Stein, Germany, late 19th century, .5 litre with inlay lid and body in relief glazed and handpainted with books of law, 5½in. high.
(Skinner) $575

Mettlach pottery covered punch bowl and stand, Germany, early 20th century, with decoration of gnomes working at a winepress and drinking, 16in. high. (Skinner) $747

Mettlach Stein, Germany, late 19th century, .5 liter with pewter lid and etched body of a barmaid holding Steins, 9in. high.
(Skinner) $460

A Mettlach lidded jug with pewter mounts, the green and dark green glazed body molded in white with three figures, 13¾in. high.
(Canterbury) $608

A Mettlach salt glazed stoneware jardiniere, the continuous central band incised and decorated in colors with gnomes cavorting amongst blossoming branches, 23cm. diameter.
(Spencers) $960

Mettlach Stein, Germany, early 20th century, one liter, with inlaid lid and etched body of Tannhäuser in the Venusberg. (Skinner) $345

A Minton majolica flattened barrel shaped ewer, with flared rim and crabstock handle, molded with scrolling vines and putti, 14½in.
(Dreweatt Neate) $1,237

Minton's two handled oval baluster foot bath and matching slop pail, elaborately painted with a line of roses intertwined with a blue ribbon, date cipher for 1897.
(G. A. Key) $471

A Mintons majolica yellow glazed jardinière on stand, the hexagonal paneled vessel molded with scale panels to the rim, year letter 1889, 88.5cm. (Tennants) $1,905

A large Minton Secessionist vase, the bulbous cylindrical form with dominant blood red and lime green coloring, 12½in. high.
(Christie's) $686

A pair of large Minton majolica turquoise-ground jardinières, circa 1875, with six strapwork bands headed by lion mask and fixed ring handles, 17½in. high.
(Christie's) $5,175

Minton majolica flask formed jug with shaped pouring lip and handle, with classical figure design with animals to either side, 11½in.
(G.A. Key) $715

A Minton Parian porcelain group of Ariadne, the bride of Bacchus, riding on a panther, 37cm. high, date code for 1858.
(Bearne's) $583

A pair of 19th century Minton majolica figural fruit dishes, each comprising a pair of cherubs carrying a blue glaze shell, 11in. high.
(Andrew Hartley) $6,996

A Minton majolica jardinière on dish base, turquoise with pink interior, with molded bullrushes to the angles, width of base 21cm.
(Bristol) $672

A Moorcroft vase, Eagle Owl design on a branch with green/blue ground, 12in. high. (Russell, Baldwin & Bright) $596

A Moorcroft pottery jardinière, decorated with a band of freesias, on a shaded blue and pale green ground, dated *1921*, 9³/₄in. diameter. (Christie's) $1,986

Baluster vase, decorated with black tulip pattern, circa 1990, signed *Walter Moorcroft*, 7in. (G. A. Key) $366

A Moorcroft vase, under salt glaze, Leaves & Berries pattern on a green ground, 11in. high, circa 1920. (Russell, Baldwin & Bright) $1,255

A pair of Moorcroft pomegranate pattern vases, navy blue background decorated with fruiting pomegranates and green foliage, dated *1919*, 10¹/₂in. high. (Christie's) $2,075

A fine Moorcroft 12¹/₂in. circular tapered vase, decorated with orchids in blue under flambé glaze, signed in blue. (Anderson & Garland) $2,041

A Moorcroft pottery vase, of baluster form with flared rim and with grape leaf design on deep blue ground, 12in. high. (Andrew Hartley) $1,000

A Moorcroft twin-handled baluster vase, decorated in the 'Wisteria' pattern, in shades of navy blue, lime green and lilac, 8¹/₄in. high. (Christie's) $811

A Moorcroft salt glaze 'Fish' vase with shaped flared body, 7in. high. (Russell, Baldwin & Bright) $1,900

A porcelain and gilt-bronze centerpiece, Paris, circa 1880, the late eighteenth century porcelain punch-bowl painted with figures in a landscape, 54cm. wide.
(Sotheby's) $3,473

A pair of bleu de roi and gilt-bronze vases, Paris, circa 1880, of baluster form, the neck applied with swags of fruit and acanthus leaves, 49cm. high.
(Sotheby's) $10,309

An onyx and gilt-bronze centerpiece, Paris, circa 1900, of oval form, applied with female term figures and masks, 45cm. high.
(Sotheby's) $9,373

A gilt-bronze and porcelain jardinière, Paris, circa 1860, with pierced leaf-cast border and scroll handles, 47cm. high.
(Sotheby's) $4,875

A pair of 19th century Paris porcelain campana shaped vases, with beaded rim, the reserves painted with scenes from the Napoleonic campaigns 8¼in. high.
(Andrew Hartley) $1,472

A parcel-gilt and biscuit porcelain jardinière, Paris, circa 1890, the border molded with cherubs and applied with rams' heads, diameter 55cm.
(Sotheby's) $10,833

A pair of French sang de boeuf and gilt-bronze urns, Paris, circa 1880, each of baluster form applied with foliate scrolls and drapery, 51cm. high.
(Sotheby's) $11,287

A gilt-bronze, porcelain and champlevé centerpiece, Paris, circa 1890, the cream colored ground painted with cherubs playing, 34cm. high.
(Sotheby's) $5,624

A good pair of Napoleon III faience and gilt-bronze vases, Paris, circa 1870, each with a cover with a pineapple finial, 120cm. high including covers.
(Sotheby's) $50,554

English Pearlware oval dish with a pierced rim, the center decorated with Willow pattern, circa 1830, 9in. (G. A. Key) $32

A pearlware purple luster jug, painted on one side with the square rigged ship 'Ann of Malton', 21.4cm. high. (Bearne's) $1,166

A pearlware canted rectangular meat dish, printed in blue with a Chinese gardener and a young boy, 21in. wide. circa 1820. (Dreweatt Neate) $478

A pearlware bull baiting group, the bull modeled standing with a terrier at its feet, early 19th century, 16cm. long. (Christie's) $1,379

A pearlware toby jug typically modeled seated holding a foaming jug of ale on his knee, early 19th century, 24cm. high. (Christie's) $349

Early 19th century English pearlware covered large baluster jug, the rim printed in blue with exotic birds, scrolls and foliage, 7in. (G. A. Key) $640

Poole

Poole pottery large baluster jug, with gray speckled rim, decorated with panels of stylized foliage, flowers etc, by Ruth Paveley, 11½in. (G. A. Key) $288

A Poole Pottery baluster vase painted with flowers in purple, yellow, green and blue within purple, green and yellow banding, 5¾in. high. (Andrew Hartley) $96

Poole pottery large baluster jug, green speckled rim, decorated with central panel of rosettes and flowers and foliage in typical colors, decorators initials 'P.B.', printed mark, 8in. (G. A. Key) $240

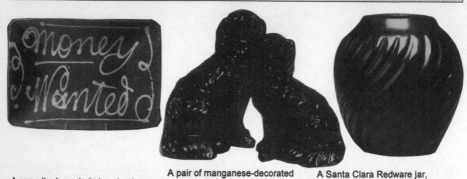

A rare slip decorated glazed redware tray, Pennsylvania, 19th century, of rectangular form inscribed with the legend *Money Wanted,* 14½in. long. (Sotheby's)   **$23,000**

A pair of manganese-decorated Redware spaniels, Brenner Pottery, Hamburg, Pennsylvania, mid-19th century, 8¾in. high. (Sotheby's)   **$1,380**

A Santa Clara Redware jar, signed *Margaret Tafoya*, 20th century, of globular form, the sides molded with swirling lobes, 8¼in. high. (Sotheby's)   **$3,162**

Rookwood

Fine Rookwood Pottery vase, 1932, decorated with wax matte floral decoration in yellow, green and red, 13in. high. (Skinner)   **$2,070**

Rare Rookwood Pottery ale set, tankard and five mugs, decorated by Sturgis Lawrence in 1898, each with a portrait of a different Native American, 5in. high. (Skinner)   **$6,900**

Early Rookwood Pottery vase, pinched cylindrical form, irregular opening, with two handles decorated with butterfly, moon and foliate design, 10¾in. high. (Skinner)   **$1,092**

Rookwood Pottery porcelain vase, Cincinnati, Ohio, 1925, executed by Kataro Shirayamadani (1865–1948), 8in. high. (Skinner)   **$1,300**

Pair of Rookwood Pottery figural bookends, figure of a seated woman reading a book under a matte blue glaze, 6in. high. (Skinner)   **$575**

A Rookwood Pottery ewer, 1903, decorated by Elizabeth Lincoln, standard glaze over floral decoration, 6in. high. (Skinner)   **$230**

Rosenberg coffee service, 1900, comprising: coffee pot and cover, two coffee cups and saucers, sugar basin and tray, coffee pot 7¹/₈in. high. (Sotheby's) $4,927

Sam Schellink for Rozenburg, peacock vase, 1900, eggshell porcelain, decorated in polychrome shades with two peacocks perched on leafy stems, 6¾in. (Sotheby's) $1,921

An octagonal eggshell plate, manufactured by Rozenburg, decorated by J.W. von Rossum, 1901, painted in yellow, orange and green, 8¼in. diameter. (Christie's) $1,195

Royal Copenhagen

Royal Copenhagen polychromed porcelain fairytale group, Denmark, marked April 25, 1955, 8⁵/₈in. high. (Skinner) $1,000

A Royal Copenhagen silver mounted porcelain vase, the silver mounts by Michelsen, Copenhagen 1926, of baluster form, painted with two sailing ships and a steam ship, 12¹/₂in. high. (Christie's) $1,986

Royal Copenhagen porcelain group of milk maid feeding a calf from a bucket, 6½in. (G. A. Key) $328

TOP TIPS

Buyers always like to have a good idea of the period of any piece of china, and the different marks used by potteries at different times in their history are the easiest guide to this. Another good dating sign is if the country of origin is marked on the bottom. If so, it will almost certainly date from after 1880, when a law was passed in the United States that all manufactured imports should have their country of origin stamped upon them.

MARK MEDCALF

Royal Copenhagen porcelain group of pigman and sow, decorated mainly in blue and naturalistic colors, 7in. (G.A.Key) $464

Royal Copenhagen Flora Danica oval soup tureen, cover and stand, modern, enamel painted with botanical specimens, 14¹/₂in. long. (Skinner) $5,750

A Royal Dux porcelain figure of a standing horse, with green saddle and pink rug, on oblong rustic base, 7½in. wide.
(Andrew Hartley) $627

A Royal Dux bust of a lady dressed in lace trimmed decolleté dress and wearing a ribboned hat, applied pink triangle mark, height 56cm.
(Wintertons) $2,640

A fine Royal Dux group of a carthorse with a boy astride its back, 13¾in. high, bearing initials A.D.
(Anderson & Garland)

            $847

Royal Dux figural compôte, Czechoslovakia, 20th century, bowl mounted to a central tree-form support surrounded by three females, 20¼in. high.
(Skinner) $633

A Royal Dux style model of an elephant and a mahout, 12¾in. high.
(Anderson & Garland)

       $722

A Royal Dux group of male and female figures dancing, he wearing a turban, she semi-draped with a flowing blue skirt, 12¼in. high.
(Anderson & Garland) $627

A 19th century Continental Royal Dux style 16½in. group of a female figure, watching an artist decorate urns seated by a column.
(Anderson & Garland)

      $942

A pair of Royal Dux semi-draped female figures, wearing long red dresses, 6in. high, pink tablet marks, No. 3353, printed Czechoslovakia mark.
(Anderson & Garland) $290

Royal Dux figural compôte, Czechoslovakia, early 20th century, modeled with female figure atop a shell-form bowl, 14½in. high.
(Skinner) $748

A pair of Samson porcelain figures of fruit pickers, he with maroon smock and green breeches and carrying two baskets of apples, 9½in. high.
(Andrew Hartley) $816

A Samson Empire-style gilt biscuit figural basket centrepiece, bearing iron-red stenciled marks for Sèvres, the white navette-shaped pierced basket with gilt flowerheads and stiff leaves, 17⁷/₈in. high.
(Christie's) $4,600

Pair of Samson porcelain figures after the Bow Factory, a lady by a bocage and similar courtier figure playing a bagpipe, 19th century, each 9in.
(G.A. Key) $397

Satsuma

Satsuma style cobalt blue ground porcelain tripod censer, Meiji period, signed *Kinkozan*, molded to each side with butterflies, dangling tassels and well painted with figural reserves, 9¼in. high.
(Butterfield & Butterfield) $3,162

Pair of Satsuma pottery cylindrical vases, Meiji, signed *Hotoda*, rim decorated with a pair of full-length panels depicting kingfishers and chidori, 12in. high.   (Butterfield & Butterfield) $1,840

Large Satsuma ware porcelain covered ovoid vase, Meiji period, signed *Hotoda*, painted in gilt and polychrome enamels with numerous rakan, 18in. high.
(Butterfield & Butterfield) $3,737

A Japanese Satsuma square-section vase, the sides with shaped rectangular panels decorated with figures at various pastimes, 12½in. high.
(Christie's) $5,154

Good signed Satsuma pottery dish, Meiji period, the shallow dish depicting three rakan and an attendant holding an ax, 11⁷/₈in. diameter. (Butterfield & Butterfield) $690

Satsuma gilt ground pottery vase with rakan decoration, Meiji period, signed *Hotoda*, its pear form body painted with a continuous panel of Buddhist adepts, 16⁷/₈in. high.
(Butterfield & Butterfield) $2,300

HISTORICAL FACTS
Sèvres

Porcelain production began at Sèvres in 1756 when the Vincennes factory was moved there, and the first 14 years of its output are considered by many to be unsurpassed.

At first, a soft paste porcelain was made, with silky glazes and richly ornate decoration. It was hugely expensive to make, however, and had the further disadvantage that it could not be molded into complex shapes, which tended to fracture in the kiln. Nevertheless, it was dear to the heart of Louis XV, who was wholly responsible for funding the operation, and his mistress Mme de Pompadour. He assisted it further by issuing several decrees granting virtual monopolies in favor of Sèvres, and even acted as salesman in chief, holding annual exhibitions at Versailles and selling off the pieces to his court.

Sèvres products are remarkable for their brilliant ground colors and chemists were constantly at work developing new tones. Honey gilding, then a virtually new technique, was also widely used, while a host of flower and figure painters (Louis engaged fan painters for this) added their designs. With regard to form, tableware shapes largely followed those of the delicate lines of contemporary silver. Sèvres was also famous for its soft-paste biscuit models, notably in the period 1757-66, when Etienne Maurice Falconet was chief modeler.

A pair of ormolu mounted Sèvres pattern dark blue ground porcelain and faience vases and covers, painted by Poitevin, circa 1900, 43in. high. (Christie's) $36,800

A Sèvres coffee-can and saucer, date letter 1767, painted with a blue band gilt with trailing foliage flanked by two bands of garden flowers. (Christie's) $4,634

A pair of 'Sèvres' and gilt-bronze vases, Paris circa 1880, each of ovoid form with an oval reserve painted with a scène galante, 51cm. high. (Sotheby's) $9,930

A 'Sèvres' and gilt-bronze jardinière, Paris, circa 1860, of circular form, the pierced scroll handles supported by cherub masks, 36cm. high. (Sotheby's) $8,060

A pair of gilt-bronze and 'Sèvres' vases, Napoleon III, circa 1860, the body painted with a scenes of lovers and their chaperones, 69cm. high. (Sotheby's) $8,683

A 'Sèvres' and gilt-bronze vase, Paris, circa 1890, of ovoid form, the green and white ground painted with cartouches, 43cm. high. (Sotheby's) $6,373

HISTORICAL FACTS
Sèvres

By 1769, Sèvres was moving over to hard paste manufacture, and this period coincided with a change to more severe, neo-Classical forms, while decoration too became very much simpler. On many pieces, indeed, this was reduced to a simple ground color with gilding. Ground colors changed too, not always for the better. Nor did biscuit figures adapt very well, having a grayer cast in hard paste and becoming more classical in form. After the departure of Falconet for the Russian court, various sculptors were employed to produce reduced size copies of their own works, and they sought to reproduce in the new medium, the appearance of marble, but without surface glaze or shine.

On the abolition of the monarchy Sèvres was taken over by the State in 1793. Under Napoleon's appointee Brogniart, soft paste was finally abandoned (it was revived again in the late 1840s) in favor of a new hard paste formula which was particularly suitable for tableware. Soft paste wares are clearly marked in blue enamel with the usual crossed *Ls* motif and a date letter (doubled after 1777). In hard paste, a crown is placed above the blue mark from 1769-79. After 1793 a date appears instead of the letter.

Genuine Sèvres soft paste porcelain has a virtually clear glaze, not uneven as found in forgeries. On more recent forgeries the colors are not blended with the glaze as was the case with the originals.

Sèvres style celeste blue ground painted porcelain charger, late 19th century, with central figure of Louis XVI surrounded by portrait roundels of notable women, 20in. diameter.
(Skinner) $2,300

A Sèvres biscuit figure group 'La Prairie et le Ruisseau', circa 1900, by Raoul-Francois Larche, signed on the back, 23in. high.
(Christie's) $2,300

A pair of 'Sèvres' and gilt-bronze cache pots, Paris, circa 1870, each painted with a reserve of lovers in a landscape on a blue celeste ground, 34cm diameter.
(Sotheby's) $8,125

A fine pair of 'Sèvres' and gilt-bronze vases, Paris, circa 1890, each of ovoid form, with a bell shaped cover painted in terracotta, 141cm. high.
(Sotheby's) $83,130

A Sèvres style blue-ground part teaset, late 19th century, bearing blue interlaced L's, each piece painted in colors with floral wreaths, tray 8⁷⁄₈in. diameter.
(Christie's) $2,300

Sèvres porcelain portrait vase, France, 19th century, enamel decorated portraits in oval cartouches, 13in. high.
(Skinner) $230

HISTORICAL FACTS
Spode

As early as 1762 Josiah Spode started developing his Staffordshire pottery, which, under his descendants, became the first in England to introduce bone china bodies at the end of the 18th century. Spode's shapes were mostly plain, with correspondingly simple but elegant decoration, or alternatively elaborate Japanese patterns. The bulk of the factory's production consisted of printed pottery and the porcelain was really only a sideline.

In 1833 William Copeland bought the Staffordshire firm of Josiah Spode, and it was in 1842 that Copeland and Garrett of Stoke on Trent first produced statuary in what came to be known as Parian ware.

A variety of marks were used, bearing variations of Copeland and Spode. Most pieces were marked *Spode*, with a pattern number in red. The earliest sometimes have impressed marks.

A Spode blue and white pottery shaped rectangular meat dish, printed with the Bridge of Lucano pattern, 52.2cm. wide.
(Bearne's) $605

Blue and white Spode pottery stool, in Spode Tower pattern with curved top and crescent form legs, 13¾in. long.
(Eldred's) $578

A pair of Spode famille rose 'Bute' teacups and saucers, red marks and pattern no. 868, circa 1820.
(Christie's) $331

Twelve Spode Copeland's china service plates, England, 20th century, embossed gilt bands to either side of a wide blue ground rim, 10¼in. diameter.
(Skinner) $690

Two Spode plates, impressed *Spodes New Stone*, 19th century, 8in. diameter. (Eldred's) $181

A Spode blue and white two-handled oval foot bath, 48cm. wide, and a large jug with leaf molded supporting handle below the spout.
(Bearne's) $2,592

Early 19th century Spode circular plate, (Indian Sporting series), printed in blue with scene of 'Death of the Bear', 9½in.
(G.A. Key) $440

A Staffordshire pearlware pottery rectangular blue and white soup-tureen and cover, circa 1820, printed with a rustic scenery pattern, 13½in. wide.
(Christie's) **$2,640**

A Staffordshire pottery blue and white square bowl, circa 1820, 8½in. wide.
(Christie's) **$717**

A Staffordshire pottery decagonal blue and white soup-tureen and a cover printed with Kirkstall Abbey from the 'Antique Scenery' series, circa 1820.
(Christie's) **$604**

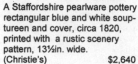

Pair of Staffordshire seated spaniels, naturalistic faces, iron red body markings, gilt collars and leads, black tipped feet, 19th century, 8in.
(G. A. Key) **$384**

A 19th century Staffordshire satyr mask jug, finely molded , also with mask tip and figure surmount to handle, painted in colors, 10in.
(Russell, Baldwin & Bright) **$383**

A pair of rare late Victorian Staffordshire seated pug dogs, each with black markings and a gilt collar, 12¼in.
(David Lay) **$640**

A Staffordshire pearlware figure of a lion, one front paw resting on a ball, and picked out in iron red and black, 6in. high, circa 1825.
(Dreweatt Neate) **$1,237**

Pink and white Staffordshire platter, 19th century, with an Oriental motif and scalloped edge, 20in. long.
(Eldred's) **$247**

A Staffordshire porcelain figure of a seated hound, picked out in black and with a gilt collar and chain, 4¾in., circa 1830-40.
(Dreweatt Neate) **$380**

Historic blue and white Staffordshire teapot, Enoch Wood and Sons, Burslem, England, 1819–46, Washington standing at tomb, scroll in hand, 8in. high. (Skinner) $633

Blue and white Staffordshire platter, England, second quarter 19th century, depicting figures with cows in foreground, waterfalls and ruins in background, 16¾in. long. (Skinner) $489

Staffordshire seated spaniel, iron red ears and body markings, naturalistic face and black tipped feet, 6½in. (G.A. Key) $124

Rare Staffordshire figure, English, 18th century, a cow in front of a floral bocage, signed in a banner on reverse *Walton*, 5in. high. (Eldred's) $742

A pair of Staffordshire creamware pottery realistic models of lions, each beast with a long tousled mane, standing with one foot on a ball, 23cm. high. (Bearne's) $2,309

An early Staffordshire Ralph Wood type figure group of seated couple playing pipes amongst sheep and dogs, 11in. high. (Russell, Baldwin & Bright) $1,099

Staffordshire pink copper luster pitcher, 19th century, in 'Fair Hebe' pattern, 6in. high. (Eldred's) $71

Pair of Staffordshire dogs, in white with worn gilt highlights, 14in. high. (Eldred's) $357

Staffordshire frog mug of cylindrical form, molded and painted in colors with figural decoration, 5½in. (G.A. Key) $86

A figure of Garibaldi standing next to his horse, 7½in. x 8½in. high. (Anderson & Garland) $603

Pair of Scottish figures, Scottish lad and his female companion, he holds a walking stick, she has a purse, 19th century, 10in. high. (G.A. Key) $223

A Staffordshire leopard and cub standing on shaped plinth base, 5in. (Russell, Baldwin & Bright) $704

Blue transfer printed Staffordshire jug, Stevenson, England, second quarter 19th century, 8¼in. high. (Skinner) $747

A Pair of Staffordshire pottery figures of Admiral Sir James Whitley Deans Dundas, and Admiral Sir Charles Napier, 30.5cm. high. (Bearne's) $764

Pink and white Staffordshire milk pitcher, 19th century, in the Abbey Ruins pattern by T. Mayer, 8¹/₂in. high. (Eldred's) $88

A 19th century Staffordshire pottery figure 'Liberty', depicting a soldier in orange tunic holding a banner, 9in. high. (Andrew Hartley) $267

Pair of English Staffordshire spaniels, 19th century, with copper luster decoration, 12in. high. (Eldred's) $742

Staffordshire polychrome figure of Britannia, 19th century, wearing a dress and helmet and seated with a lion at her feet, base marked *Britannia*, 13in. high. (Eldred's) $660

Large gourd formed stoneware bellarmine, molded below the spout with a grotesque mask, 18th/19th century, 16in.
(G.A. Key) $363

Otto Lindig, pitcher and cover, circa 1930, glazed stoneware with light iridescence, 7$\frac{1}{8}$in.
(Sotheby's) $5,061

Two-gallon stoneware pitcher, 19th century, marked *F.B. Norton & Co., Worcester MA*, cobalt flower basket decoration, 13in. high.
(Eldred's) $2,860

A rare cobalt blue-decorated salt-glazed stoneware double-jug, New Haven, Connecticut, circa 1820, each jug with a flared lip and rounded shoulder, 7in. high.
(Sotheby's) $1,092

A stoneware relief molded jug with horsehead handle inscribed *Stop, Stop John Gilpin! Here's the House*, mid 19th century, 24cm. high.
(Christie's) $240

Stoneware wine beer vessel, modeled as the head of Mr Micawber, wearing a night cap and decorated in shades of treacle, 11in. (G. A. Key) $208

BUYER BEWARE

This may sound like good basic common sense, which it is, but it definitely bears repeating.

When handling objects, particularly ceramics and glass, always check for detachable parts and remove them before picking a piece up, then pick it up by the largest part. That way, if anything falls off, you will not be left with a very red face, just holding the handle!

WOOLLEY & WALLIS

A Persian stoneware dish, blue painted with a boteh around a central concave hexagon on white ground, on short foot, 13½in. wide.
(Andrew Hartley) $192

A Danish black stoneware figure of Pan modeled standing, playing a flute, impressed *L P Jorgensen*, late 19th century, 51cm. high.
(Christie's) $1,288

19th century Sunderland luster jug of oval baluster form, the neck moulded and decorated in colors with berries and foliage, 6in. high. (G.A. Key) $176

A Dixon Phillips & Co. Sunderland wall plaque, the center panel decorated with black transfer print of a three masted sailing ship, 8¼ x 7¼in. (Anderson & Garland) $165

19th century Sunderland luster jug of baluster form, elaborately molded with scene of hunting dogs in a landscape, 19th century, 8in. (G. A. Key) $128

A large 19th century pink luster pottery jug, monochrome printed with 'a West View of Iron Bridge over the Wear', dated *1853*, 9in. high. (Russell Baldwin & Bright) $544

A rare set of four early 19th century Sunderland luster sash window stops in the form of King Charles caricatures, purple luster bodies, 4in. wide. (H.C. Chapman & Son) $1,476

A large 19th century luster pottery jug, decorated with the' Great Australian Clipper Ship', 'True Love from Hull' and verse, 9¼in. high. (Russell Baldwin & Bright) $592

A large 19th century pink luster pottery jug, monochrome printed with the 'Iron Bridge at Sunderland' and two verses, 8½in. high. (Russell Baldwin & Bright) $400

Sunderland luster beaker, decorated with a Royal Crest, entwined with 'Let Brotherly Love Continue', with a further verse to the rear, 2in. (G. A. Key) $206

Sunderland luster bridge jug, decorated with central scene in colors of 'West View of the cast iron bridge at Sunderland' also inscribed with rhymes etc, on a puce luster ground, 19th century, 7½in. (G. A. Key) $130

A pair of Vienna style blue-ground covered vases on stands, bearing blue beehive marks, signed *H. Otto*, decorated with maidens in allegories, 15in. high.
(Christie's) $6,325

A 19th century Vienna porcelain plaque of circular form, the center painted in polychrome with 'Tristan's Tod', 15in. wide.
(Andrew Hartley) $800

A pair of Vienna style claret and pink-ground vases, late 19th century, painted in colors with mythological scenes, 20½in. high.
(Christie's) $7,475

Volkstedt

A Volkstedt figure group of a shepherd and his companion, canceled blue monogram mark, he seated on rockwork embracing his companion, 9¾in. high.
(Christie's) $1,150

Volkstedt white glazed porcelain figure group, Germany, 20th century, consisting of eight figures clad in 18th century dress surrounding a piano, 27in. long.
(Skinner) $1,495

A pair of Volkstedt models of parrots, blue monogram marks, one perched on a high leafy trunk, the second eating a cherry, 15½in. high.
(Christie's) $3,680

Walley

Walley pottery covered jar, exceptionally frothy speckled green glaze on a brown ground, impressed marks, 6½in. high.
(Skinner) $173

Fine Walley pottery vase, with a rich speckled green glaze with brown showing through, 7¾in. high.
(Skinner) $1,265

Walley pottery, two-handled vase with frothy green glaze, impressed marks, 6½in. high.
(Skinner) $288

Wedgwood blue and white jasperware pitcher, 20th century, 6in. high.
(Eldred's) $132

Persephone, a Wedgwood part dinner service designed by Eric Ravilious, printed in shades of blue and black, 36 pieces.
(Christie's) $643

20th century Wedgwood vase of tapering cylindrical form with everted rim, 7in. high. (G.A. Key) $152

A Wedgwood majolica double dolphin table centerpiece, with detachable nautilus shell on the tails of the greeny gray dolphins, date code for 1867, 41cm.
(Bristol) $1,271

A rare late 18th century Wedgwood creamware double salt cellar, attached twin cylindrical pots with beaded rims and twin handles, 2¾in. high.
(H.C. Chapman & Son) $667

A rare Wedgwood Fairyland luster malfrey pot and cover, designed by Daisy Makeig Jones, decorated in the Ghostly Wood pattern, 38cm. high.
(Christie's) $40,480

A large gold luster-decorated vase, designed and decorated by Louise Powell, manufactured by Wedgwood, circa 1925, 13³/₈in. high.
(Christie's) $3,374

Near pair of Wedgwood jardinières and stands, typically molded pâte sur pâte with lion mask ring mounts, date ciphers for 1866, 8in. diameter.
(G. A. Key) $232

A Wedgwood Fairyland luster Malfrey pot and cover, designed by Daisy Makeig Jones, decorated in the Bubbles II pattern, 18cm. high.
(Christie's) $20,240

A Wemyss Ware teapot, of squat globular form, painted with cabbage roses and foliage, within green line borders, 4in. high.
(Christie's) $280

Wemyss lidded preserve jar on integral stand, decorated in puce, mauve, green and lemon detail, within green borders, stylized foliate design, green script mark, 5in.
(G.A. Key) $345

A Wemyss ware ewer and basin, painted with peaches, the ewer with printed T. Goode & Co. marks, the basin 15½in. diameter.
(Christie's) $1,049

A Wemyss 4¾in. cylindrical jar and cover painted with strawberries and leaves, blue printed mark of T. Goode & Co., London, 6¼in. high.
(Anderson & Garland) $282

Wemyss balustered jug, green rim and decorated with puce flowers and green leaves on a crackle glazed ground, 9in.
(G.A. Key) $247

Wemyss Ware covered slop bucket, typically decorated in colors with roses, within green borders, applied with a wicker handle, late 19th/early 20th century, 11in.
(G. A. Key) $400

A Wemyss Ware slop-pail and liner, painted with cabbage roses, with swing cane handle, impressed marks, 11in. high.
(Christie's) $351

A Wemyss cylindrical biscuit box and cover painted with purple plums and green foliage, 4¾in. high.
(Anderson & Garland) $215

A Wemyss Ware jug, painted with apples and foliage with green line rim and scroll handle, 5½in. high.
(Christie's) $386

Royal Worcester porcelain model of 'HRH Princess Anne on Doublet', modeled by Doris Lindner, on mahogany socle, 14in.
(G.A. Key) $1,177

A pair of Royal Worcester majolica wall pockets, each in the form of a vintager's basket, 26.5cm., circa 1880.
(Bearne's) $291

Probably Worcester globular teapot with domed cover, decorated in underglazed blue with scene of Oriental figures in a garden, 18th century, 8in.
(G.A. Key) $270

A Hadley's Worcester porcelain jardinière of circular form with pierced rim, reserves painted with peacocks by C V White, 7in. high.
(Andrew Hartley) $1,175

A pair of Royal Worcester two-handled vases, each painted with sprigs and sprays of garden flowers, 17cm. high, printed marks and date code for 1902.
(Bearne's) $875

A Royal Worcester porcelain jardinière with pierced and flared rim, painted pink rose panels by E Spilsbury, on gilt and ivory leaf and scroll molded ground, 8in. high.
(Andrew Hartley) $2,228

Royal Worcester porcelain jug, gilt rim and decorated in colors with panels of garden flowers on a blush ground, date cipher for 1894, 6in.
(G. A. Key) $288

A pair of Royal Worcester pot-pourri jars with inner and outer covers, brightly painted by John Freeman and S. Weston, 25cm. high.
(Bearne's) $2,916

Royal Worcester porcelain two-handled vase, England, circa 1888, molded and pierced foliate panels to neck, ivory ground body, 17in. high.
(Skinner) $978

Mahogany cased bracket clock, circular black chapter ring, eight day movement, strike/silent dial by French, Royal Exchange, London, early 19th century, 11in.
(G.A. Key)　　　$2,512

A mahogany cased bracket clock, unsigned, early 19th century, in chamfered top case with side ring handles, 16½in.
(Bonhams)　　　$2,475

Mahogany bracket clock with domed hood, circular silvered chapter ring, the sides applied with gilt metal trellis apertures, striking movement by Willm Welch, Plymouth, late 18th/early 19th century, 12in.
(G.A. Key)　　　$2,433

Mahogany cased large bracket clock, the domed cover with central pineapple finial, the rectangular face with a silvered circular Roman chapter ring, by Barrie of Edinburgh, late 19th century, 11½in.
(G.A. Key)　　　$2,669

An early 19th century bracket clock by Bennett of 65 Cheapside, London, in walnut and line inlaid break-arch case, 37.5cm.
(Bristol)　　　$787

A Regency brass inlaid mahogany bracket clock by J. and A. McNab with circular enamel dial, 18in. high.
(David Lay)　　　$1,558

An ebonized bracket clock, Thomas Prichard, London, circa 1780, in a bell top case with top carrying handle, cone corner finials, 20½in.
(Bonhams) $4,134

A George III mahogany bracket clock by Eardley Norton, with verge escapement, 15½in. high.
(Derek Roberts) $26,400

A late Victorian brass-mounted quarter-chiming large bracket clock, late 19th century, the case with stepped pediment to the breakarch top, 29¼in. high.
(Christie's) $2,760

A mahogany and gilt mounted chiming bracket clock, English, circa 1880, the triple fusée movement chiming on 8 bells or 4 gongs, 23in.
(Bonhams) $2,703

A fine musical clock with automata, playing four tunes on 10 bells, unsigned, possibly for the Chinese market.
(Derek Roberts) $25,200

A mahogany bracket clock with an enamel dial, signed *Dwerrihouse, Berkeley Square*, the twin fusee movement with engraved backplate, 16¾in.
(Bonhams) $6,270

A Regency bracket clock with two-train fusée movement having repeater mechanism, circular white enamel dial inscribed *John Jefferies, Biggleswade*, 19in. high.
(Russell, Baldwin & Bright) $2,138

A Chippendale mahogany bracket shelf-clock, dial signed *Thomas Parker (1761–1833), Philadelphia*, the upswept domed top centering a brass bail handle above an arched glazed door, 18½in. high.
(Christie's) $2,070

A small mahogany bracket clock with an enamel dial, D. & W. Morice, London, circa 1820, the twin fusée bell striking movement with a signed backplate and engraved border, 14½in.
(Bonhams) $6,996

A Regency bracket clock with cream enamel dial, the eight-day twin-fusée movement striking on a bell, 54cm.
(Bearne's) $1,944

A small early ebony striking bracket clock, circa 1680, the backplate decorated with tulips and signed *Jonathon Lowndes, Londini*, 13½in.
(Christie's) $14,850

A George I ebonized striking bracket clock, first quarter 18th century, signed Francis *Raynsford London*, 20¼in. high.
(Christie's) $6,440

A small size ebonized pull quarter repeating bracket timepiece, Henry Hester, London, circa 1700, in an inverted bell top case with top brass handle, 16in.
(Christie's) $3,960

An early Victorian mahogany striking bracket clock, second quarter 19th century, the arched case carved to the top with leaf scrolls, signed *Dent London,* 118in. high. (Christie's) $2,576

A George I ebonized chiming bracket clock, second quarter 18th century, signed *Thos. Hughes London*, with mock pendulum and date apertures, 21¼in. high.
(Christie's) $7,360

A Chippendale walnut bracket shelf-clock, dial signed *Thomas Daft, New York*, 1786–90, the upswept domed top centering a brass bail handle, 10³/₄in. wide.
(Christie's) $17,250

An early Victorian burr-oak striking bracket clock, second quarter 19th century, signed *Arnold 84, Strand London 546*, 17in. high.
(Christie's) $1,656

A mahogany and gilt-brass mounted quarter-chiming bracket clock, early 20th century, the case with flambeau urn finial and foliate mounts to the waisted pediment, 28in. high.
(Christie's) $2,208

A Regency rosewood and gilt-brass mounted striking mantel clock, circa 1820, pineapple finial to the stepped and chamfered top, 18¾in. high. (Christie's) $2,208

A mahogany padtop bracket clock, circa 1820, painted dial signed *Jeffrey & Ham, Salisbury Square, London,* in a break arch case, 17½in. (Bonhams) $3,960

A late Victorian gilt-brass mounted walnut quarter-chiming bracket clock, late 19th century, signed *Dent,*18¼in. high. (Christie's) $2,944

A rare English Boulle work bracket clock, George Younge, circa 1820, 4½in. enamel dial with Roman numerals, decorated with brass and pewter scroll foliage set in red shell, 17½in. (Christie's) $3,465

A William and Mary ebonised and gilt-brass mounted striking bracket clock with alarm, circa 1690, signed within a foliate cartouche *Edwardus Burgis Londini Fecit,* 13in. high. (Christie's) $6,992

A William and Mary ebonized and brass-mounted quarter-repeating bracket clock for the Turkish market, circa 1700, the central cartouche signed *John Martin Londini fecit,* 15½in. high. (Christie's) $4,784

A George III bracket clock by William Gard, Exeter, with verge escapement and strike/silent regulation, 15in. high. (Derek Roberts) $12,400

Penlington & Co., Liverpool, a George IV bracket clock, in mahogany case carved with foliage and scrollwork, 47cm. (Bearne's) $1,069

A George III bracket clock by John Scott, London, with verge escapement and fast/slow and strike/silent regulation, 15in. high. (Derek Roberts) $20,000

HISTORICAL FACTS
Carriage Clocks

Clocks with their spring driven movements intended for use whilst traveling, had been used to some degree since the sixteenth century but they never really caught on until the French clockmakers began to produce them en masse early in the nineteenth century.

The original concept of the carriage clock was an English innovation, often incorporating such fancy and complex refinements as repeat and date mechanisms, even a dial indicating the phases of the moon.

Most of these clocks have silvered dials and are usually housed in ormolu cases, often embellished with Corinthian columns on the front corners.

Carriage clocks made during the early nineteenth century usually had quite fine cast brass cases, with thick beveled glass windows resting in grooves in the frame. The glass at the top was large; later it became much smaller and was let into a metal plate. Carrying handles are usually round on these early 19th century clocks, tapering toward the ends and, because there is often a repeat button on the top front edge, the handles usually fold backwards only.

The alarm is pretty obvious, having its own small dial with arabic numerals and a single hand situated at the bottom of the face. The driving mechanism for the alarm is the small brass barrel situated about three quarters of the way up the clock and to one side.

A quarter-striking repeater carriage clock, the movement with two hammers striking on two coiled gongs, 6¼in. high. (Christie's) $663

A brass and silvered repeating carriage clock with alarm, French, circa 1890, dark blue enamel dial with gilt Arabic numerals, signed *W. Gibson & Co.*, 7½in. (Bonhams) $1,351

An engraved and jeweled porcelain paneled repeating carriage clock, French, circa 1880, Roman numeral chapter ring on a porcelain dial decorated with putti, 6¾in. (Bonhams) $3,816

A French brass and champlevé enamel carriage timepiece, circa 1890, the corniche case with polychrome enamel foliate decoration to the front angles, 1¾in. high. (Christie's) $368

French gilt bronze and Limoges enamel mounted carriage clock with alarm, circa 1900, in tones of purple and green, the sides with portrait profiles of women, 4½in. high. (Skinner) $7,475

A gilt brass repeating carriage clock, French, circa 1870, 2¾in., lever escapement stamped with the Japy Frères factory mark, in a cannelée molded case 6¾in. (Bonhams) $627

A French brass carriage timepiece with alarm, Henri Jacot, late 19th century, the corniche case with white enamel Roman dial, 5¾in. high. (Christie's) $552

A Drocourt carriage clock, strike, repeat, day, date, alarm, with original box and key, circa 1860. (Derek Roberts) $12,720

A French brass striking and repeating carriage clock, circa 1890, the reeded anglaise case with gilt mask, 6¼in. high. (Christie's) $736

An English engraved silver striking carriage clock, circa 1975, the foliage engraved columnar case on bun feet and with acorn finials, backplate stamped *Mappin & Webb*, 6in. high. (Christie's) $1,325

A French brass carriage timepiece, circa 1910, the boîte riche case with floral trellis mounts to the cornices, white enamel Roman dial, 5¼in. high. (Christie's) $461

A French gilt-brass grande sonnerie striking and repeating carriage clock, Margaine, circa 1885, the gorge case with plain mask to recessed white enamel Roman chapter disc, 6in. high. (Christie's) $2,024

A striking repeater alarm carriage clock, for the Japanese market, the movement striking the hours and half hours on a bell, 6in. high. (Christie's) $1,232

A French brass striking and repeating carriage clock with moonphase, day, alarm and date, L'Epée, 20th century, gorge case, 6in. high. (Christie's) $1,141

A grande sonnerie quarter-striking repeater alarm carriage clock, by Drocourt, the movement with three hammers striking on two coiled gongs, 6in. high. (Christie's) $1,138

A French gilt-brass and champlevé enamel striking and repeating carriage clock, circa 1890, anglaise riche case with columns, 6½in. high. (Christie's) $2,944

A Swiss gilt-brass travel timepiece, Grohe, Genève, late 19th century, the engraved case cast as an heraldic Prussian eagle, 3¼in. high. (Christie's) $552

A French engraved gilt-brass grande sonnerie striking and repeating carriage clock with alarm, Drocourt, circa 1880, 6¼in. high. (Christie's) $4,048

A French gilt-brass and porcelain-mounted striking and repeating carriage clock, the gorge case with porcelain panels to sides and top, 5½in. high. (Christie's) $5,152

A French gilt-brass miniature carriage timepiece, retailed by London and Ryder, late 19th century, waisted rococo case cast with foliate decoration, 4¼in. high. (Christie's) $1,104

A French gilt-brass and Limoges enamel mounted striking and repeating carriage clock, Leroy & Fils, circa 1890, anglaise riche case with Corinthian columns, 7in. high. (Christie's) $7,728

A French gilt and silvered brass striking and repeating small carriage clock with alarm, late 19th century, the anglaise style case on bun feet, 4¾in. high. (Christie's) $883

A French gilt-brass miniature carriage timepiece, Breguet, late 19th century, the waisted rococo case cast with foliate decoration overall, 3in. high. (Christie's) $1,251

A French gilt-brass striking and repeating carriage clock with alarm, circa 1890, the ringed pillars case with stepped base on toupie feet, 6¾in. high. (Christie's) $1,104

A French brass and champlevé enamel striking travel clock, Dufaud, Paris, circa 1890, the case with bud finials to the cupola top, 8in. high. (Christie's) $1,197

A Swiss white metal novelty timepiece, La Cloche Frères, Paris Londres, first quarter 20th century, 5in. high. (Christie's) $10,672

A French engraved gilt-brass and porcelain-mounted striking and repeating carriage clock, late 19th century, corniche case, 5¾in. high. (Christie's) $6,440

A French engraved gilt-brass and porcelain-mounted grande sonnerie striking and repeating carriage clock, circa 1880, the gorge case finely engraved, 6in. high. (Christie's) $15,640

An Austrian ormolu grande sonnerie striking and repeating carriage clock with alarm, second quarter 19th century, the engine-milled drum-shaped case with eagle-headed loop handle, 6½in. high. (Christie's) $4,416

A French gilt-brass and champlevé enamel mignonnette carriage timepiece, circa 1890, the anglaise riche case decorated with bands of polychrome foliate enamel, 3¾in. high. (Christie's) $2,208

A French brass striking and repeating carriage clock with alarm, circa 1890, the anglaise riche case with spiral-twist Corinthian columns, 7in. high. (Christie's') $1,840

A Swiss silver and guilloché enamel sub-miniature travel timepiece, circa 1920, the block case with panels of sky blue enamel between plain white borders, with loop handle and on bun feet, 2in. high. (Christie's) $2,576

A French brass striking and repeating carriage clock with enamel and ivory panels, retailed by Theodore B. Starr, New York., circa 1890, 6¼in. high. (Christie's) $2,392

Ornate ormolu garniture, comprising central clock crested with figure of a putto and pair of matching two handled covered urns also inset with porcelain plaques in the Sèvres manner, 19th century, urns 12½in. (G.A. Key) $1,567

French ormolu and porcelain paneled clock garniture, the clock with drum case striking movement, the side pieces of urn form with porcelain plaques and columns, French, mid 19th century, approximately 14in. (G. A. Key) $604

A late 19th century French champlevé enamel and gilt bronze mantel clock, decorated with panels of polychrome enamel, the circular movement with Japy Freres trademark, 1ft.5.5in. high, together with a pair of similarly decorated vases on griffin monopodiae supports. (Phillips) $3,312

Louis XVI style gilt bronze and marble three-piece clock and garniture, late 19th century, clock height 21in. (Skinner) $2,185

A Louis XVI style ormolu three-piece clock garniture, the clock flanked by lion's masks holding tassel-tied rings, each seven-light candelabrum with a vase cast with vitruvian scrolls, the clock: 27in. high. (Christie's) $7,475

A Louis XV style brass striking mantel clock and garniture, last quarter 19th century, the foliate scroll case cast in relief with musical trophies, and the pair of five-light candelabra en suite, the clock – 25in. high. (Christie's) $920

A French gilt-brass striking mantel clock and garniture, Marti & Cie, the case with arched top centered by female mask and foliate mounts, and the pair of campana side urns on fluted socles en suite, the clock – 12¼in. high. (Christie's) $957

A French gilt-brass clock garniture, late 19th century/early 20th century, the clock movement striking on a single bell, enclosed by a drum case with lion mask and drape-cast loop handles, 21½in. high. (Christie's) $5,727

A French gilt-bronze and white marble striking four-glass mantel clock and garniture, JBD, circa 1880, the arched case surmounted by mounts of a serpent threatening a bird, pair of five light candelabra en suite, the clock – 20¾in. high. (Christie's) $2,392

A French gray bardiglio marble and gilt-bronze mounted striking mantel clock and garniture, last quarter 19th century, the case surmounted by a gilt-bronze figure of a naked young girl with a bow, pair of three-light candelabra en suite, the clock – 16¾in. high. (Christie's) $2,392

A gilt metal mantel clock garniture, French, late 19th century, in an elaborate case decorated with grapevine and foliage swags, the dial flanked by two Bacchanalian female figures, together with a pair of urns similarly decorated, clock 12½in. (Bonhams) $2,623

A gilt ormolu garniture clock set, French, circa 1890, 4¼in. enamel dial with Roman and Arabic numerals with a rubbed signature, in a cast decorated waisted sided case with scrolled acanthus leaves and shells, together with a pair of matching two light candelabra, 15½in. (Bonhams) $2,475

Vieyres & Repingon, Paris, a gilt metal and 'Sèvres' porcelain clock garniture, the bowed breakfront case surmounted by a pair of birds, flowers and draping foliage, 30cm., the side ornaments stamped *P.H. Mourey*, 24.5cm.
(Bearne's) $2,673

A French silvered and gilt-bronze black marble clock garniture, by Pradier, circa 1890, the dial set within a rectangular plinth with a silvered frieze of classical figures, clock 54cm. high.
(Sotheby's) $4,862

An Egyptian Revival rouge and noir marble and patinated bronze three-piece clock garniture, late 19th century, the pyramid form marble clock case flanked by bronze sphinx torso mounts, surmounted by a figure of Cleopatra, matching obelisks of standard form, clock: 30.5in. high.
(Christie's) $10,350

A gilt-bronze and variegated white marble clock garniture, French, circa 1900, the clock of portico form, in a glazed case, clock 49cm. high.
(Sotheby's) $1,910

A bronze and gilt-bronze clock garniture, Paris, circa 1870, the Japy Frères movement with outside countwheel striking on a bell, flanked by a pair of candelabra, each cast as putti, candelabra: 78cm. high.
(Sotheby's) $9,930

A gilt-bronze and 'Sèvres' clock garniture, Paris, circa 1880, the dial with Roman numerals within a bleu celeste border, surmounted by an urn flambeau, flanked by a pair of candelabra, each with six branches, clock: 53cm. high.
(Sotheby's) $6,860

A matched gilt-bronze and porcelain clock garniture, French, circa 1870, the painted dial signed for *Hober, 31 Duke Street, Grosvenor Square London*, flanked by winged harpies, clock 38cm. high.
(Sotheby's) $5,557

An Egyptian Revival three piece noir marble clock garniture set, late 19th century, the clock surmounted by a figural group depicting Cleopatra holding a scepter and seated on a sphinx, the clock: 26in. high. (Christie's) $5,750

A gilt-bronze and porcelain clock garniture, French, circa 1880, the case in the form of a lyre, with gridiron pendulum, flanked by a pair of candelabra in the form of vases with rams' heads, clock: 50cm. high.
(Sotheby's) $8,124

An ormolu-mounted red variegated marble clock garniture, French, late 19th century, the clock movement inscribed *Maple & Co., A Paris,* in lyre-shaped case, and a pair of four-branch candelabra en suite, 15¼in. (Christie's) $5,300

A matched gilt-bronze and jeweled porcelain clock garniture, French, circa 1870, the dial with cartouche numerals painted with figures in a square case, clock: 41cm. high.
(Sotheby's) $6,860

A matched gilt-bronze and porcelain clock garniture, Paris, circa 1870, the base inset with panels painted with cherubs and swags of flowers, flanked by a pair of candelabra, clock: 52cm. high.
(Sotheby's) $8,666

HISTORICAL FACTS
Lantern Clocks

The first truly domestic time-pieces were called lantern clocks. Proper old lantern clocks run for thirty hours and have only an hour hand – the minute hand was not introduced until about 1690. This is not to say that a clock with only one hand dates necessarily from the 17th century, for local clockmakers continued to turn out the less complicated, one -handed timepieces for a further hundred years.

Earliest examples either stood on a bracket or were equipped with an iron hanging ring at the back. The clock was leveled and steadied by means of spikes at the base.

Many of the early lantern clocks had a weight supported on a rope. This was an unsatisfactory arrangement, since the rope often frayed, spreading fluff from the worn parts around the works of the clock, and then snapped, thus the ropes were often replaced with chains.

During the 19th century, these clocks began to be mass-produced, particularly in Birmingham, and, although these have similar cases to the earlier ones, they are fitted with fusee movements and short internal pendulums. These can easily be identified from the front by the winding holes – the others have weights, not springs.

Others, even later – are fitted with a small, eight-day French carriage clock movement which can be seen clinging to the back of the face with the winding key sticking out of the back.

A brass lantern clock, the posted frame surmounted by a bell, signed *Wm. Webster, Exchange Alley, London*, 1ft.3in. high.
(Phillips) $2,208

An early brass cased 30 hour verge lantern clock, English, unsigned, the case with turned corner columns with cup and cover finials, 16½in. (Bonhams) $4,290

A rare brass lantern shelf clock, signed *Peter Closon*, London, 17th century, surmounted by an elaborately shaped finial, now supported on a mahogany wall bracket, 16½in. high.
(Sotheby's) $10,350

A brass cased lantern clock, English, late 19th century, the engraved center signed *J. Booth London*, twin fusee bell striking movement, 16in.
(Bonhams) $1,320

A brass cased 30 hour verge lantern clock, 6½in. brass chapter ring, signed *John Martin Londini Fecit*, 15in.
(Bonhams) $2,640

A brass lantern clock with alarm, silvered alarm disc with sunburst engraving to the center and signature *Edward Stanton in Leaden Hall Street Londini fecit*, 15¾in. high.
(Christie's) $2,392

HISTORICAL FACTS
Longcase Clocks

The faces of early longcase clocks were eight to nine inches square and made of brass, with flowers and scrolls engraved in their centers. These increased to about ten inches square by the 1680s when wider cases were introduced. From the beginning of the 18th century, faces were usually twelve inches square, or larger following the introduction of the arch. The arch was in widespread use by 1720 and, on early examples, was often less than a semicircle.

The silvered brass chapter ring with its engraved roman numerals grew along with the face, and the inner rim was marked with quarter and half hour divisions. The elaborate hour hand reached to the interior of the chapter ring, while the plainer minute hand — if the clock had one — reached to the outer rim.

The earliest spandrels were of cupids' heads between curved wings. Later this became elaborate scrollwork which, by 1700, incorporated a female mask.

Dates of this sort, whilst not infallible, can be useful in establishing an approximate date of birth — or at least ruling out a falsely early date. For instance, the fleur-de-lys, used to mark the half hours, was seldom employed after the 1740s — the same decade in which larger arabic numerals replaced the roman as minute markers. After 1750, an engraved brass or silvered face without a chapter ring was often used, and from 1775, a cast brass or enameled copper face was introduced.

A mahogany longcase clock with moonphase, unsigned, circa 1760, 12in. dial with silvered chapter ring, 7ft. 6in. (Christie's) $5,610

A mahogany longcase clock, N. Davidson, Dunse, early 19th century, 6ft.7in. (Christie's) $2,970

A mahogany and satinwood longcase clock, John Smith, Chester, circa 1753, 7ft.6in. (Christie's) $6,600

A Victorian foliate cut-brass inlaid and gilt-brass mounted rosewood quarter chiming directors' clock, with pedestal, last quarter 19th century, clock – 30¼in. high. (Christie's) $2,760

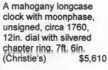

A small mahogany longcase regulator, English, circa 1880, 11½in. silvered dial, signed *Wm Sharp Glasgow*, 6ft. 1in. (Christie's) $7,920

A Victorian mahogany longcase clock, swan-neck pediment centered by an urn finial, inscribed *A. Lang, Larkhall,* spandrels painted with rural scenes, 88½in. high. (Christie's) $2,270

A mahogany drum head longcase clock, Chargois Dublin, early 19th century, 7ft. high. (Bonhams)

$3,180

A Federal inlaid mahogany tall-case clock, dial signed *Effingham Embree*, 1790–1800, New York City, 94½in. high. (Christie's)

$25,300

A Louis XV style ormolu-mounted tulipwood and marquetry pendule réguleuse, late 19th century, dial signed *F. Berthoud Paris*, 102½in. high. (Christie's)

$27,600

A Chippendale figured mahogany tall case clock, John Davis, New Holland, Pennsylvania, circa 1795, 8ft. high. (Sotheby's)

$10,350

An important red-stained pine tall case clock, signed by Nathaniel Dominy IV, Easthampton, Long Island, New York, dated *1809*, 7ft. 3½in. high. (Sotheby's)

$54,625

A French onyx and champlevé pedestal clock, circa 1870, in the Islamic manner, 126cm. high. (Sotheby's)

$7,498

A fine Federal inlaid mahogany tall case clock with rocking ship movement, Aaron Willard, Boston, Massachusetts, circa 1805, 8ft. 7½in. high. (Sotheby's)

$31,050

A fine Chippendale brass-mounted figured mahogany tall case clock, inscribed *Samuel Mulliken, Salem, Massachusetts, 1773*, 7ft. 7in. high. (Sotheby's)

$25,300

A fine and rare Federal grain-painted maple and birchwood tall case clock, Northern New England, circa 1810, 7ft. 4in. high. (Sotheby's)
$10,925

A mahogany and gilt-bronze pedestal clock, French, circa 1890, after Riesener, 227cm. high. (Sotheby's)
$18,055

A Chippendale carved walnut tall case clock, William Reinhardt, Reading, Pennsylvania, circa 1800, 8ft. 7in. high. (Sotheby's)
$11,500

A Federal cherrywood tall-case clock, dial signed *David Wood, Newburyport, Massachusetts*, 1810–20, 86in. high. (Christie's)
$11,500

A kingwood, mahogany and gilt-bronze pedestal clock, Paris, circa 1880, in Régence style, 246.5cm. high. (Sotheby's)
$63,407

A Federal inlaid mahogany tall-case clock, dial signed *Jacob Eby, Manheim, Lancaster, Pennsylvania*, circa 1802. (Christie's)
$11,500

An onyx and champlevé enameled pedestal clock, Paris, circa 1870, 130cm. high. (Sotheby's)
$11,247

A Chippendale cherrywood tall-case clock, dial signed *Christian Eby, Manheim, Lancaster, Pennsylvania*, circa 1795, 92¼in. high. (Christie's)
$14,950

A mahogany longcase clock signed Gabriel *Holland Coventry*, 19th/20th century, 92in. high. (Christie's) $2,208

A mahogany chiming longcase clock, English, circa 1890, 12in. dial. with a silvered chapter ring, 7ft. 9in. (Christie's) $4,290

A George III mahogany longcase clock, G & W Cope, Nottingham, late 18th century, 90¼in. high. (Christie's) $3,312

A fine mahogany quarter chime longcase regulator by John Moore & Sons, Clerkenwell, 6ft. 2¼in. high. (Derek Roberts) $28,000

A rare quarter striking, moon phase mahogany longcase clock by Edward Glaze, Bridgenorth, circa 1820, 7ft. 7in. high. (Derek Roberts) $15,600

A George III mahogany 'London' month going longcase clock by Benjamin Simkin, London, 7ft. 4in. high. (Derek Roberts) $24,800

A mahogany longcase clock, basically 19th century, hood with brass-capped swan-neck pediment, 97½in. high. (Christie's) $2,392

A month going walnut architectural longcase clock with a 1¼ seconds pendulum, Henricus Jones, Londini, circa 1680, 6ft. 5in. (Christie's) $13,200

A 19th century mahogany longcase regulator, signed *Thwaites & Reed, Clerkenwell, London,* 6ft 2in. high. (Phillips) $10,672

A walnut longcase clock in a later case, George Graham London, No. 645, circa 1740 and later, 7ft.1in. (Christie's) $14,025

A fine mahogany regulator by N. Gonshaw, London, circa 1845, 6ft. 10in. high. (Derek Roberts) $14,000

A mahogany and marquetry inlaid longcase clock, case early 20th century, 89in. high. (Christie's) $2,576

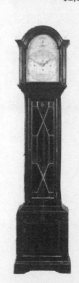

A William and Mary walnut and floral marquetry longcase clock, Nathaniel Birt, London, circa 1700, 88½in. high. (Christie's) $9,200

A George III mahogany longcase clock, Matthew Wylie, Paisley, No.287, late 18th/early 19th century, 85in. high. (Christie's) $3,680

A carved mahogany quarter-chiming longcase clock, Peter Walker, London, first quarter 20th century, 95¼in. high. (Christie's) $5,520

A mahogany quarter-chiming longcase clock, retailed by Mappin & Webb, first quarter 19th century, 90¼in. high. (Christie's) $3,128

A George III mahogany longcase clock, inscribed *John Stewart, Stirling*, 86in. high. (Christie's) $4,232

A Georgian oak longcase clock, inscribed *'Lawfon Newton'*, 84¼in. high. (Christie's) $5,152

A late George III mahogany longcase clock, inscribed *Adam Pringle, Edin*, 92in. high (Christie's) $5,998

A mahogany longcase clock, signed *Jn Belling, Bodmyn*, 89in. high. (George Kidner) $2,359

A Victorian walnut longcase clock, gilt and white painted dial, inscribed *A. T. Espie, Glasgow*, 85in. high. (Christie's) $2,905

Victorian grain painted tall case clock, mid 19th century, painted face, case in tones of reds and yellows, 83in. high. (Skinner) $1,955

An interesting oak cased railway longcase regulator, Dent London, No. 939 for G.W.R., circa 1850, 6ft. 4in. (Christie's) $4,950

An oak and mahogany longcase clock with ship automaton, John Wilson, Peterborough, late 18th century, 6ft.9in. (Christie's) $5,610

HISTORICAL FACTS
Mantel Clocks

As a basic rule French mantel clocks are nearly all decoration while English models are nearly all clock.

Early French makers to look for are Lepine, Janvier, Amand, Lepaute and Thuret, who started to use a great deal of elaborate scroll-work at the end of the seventeenth century. If you find a clock by any of these makers you have certainly found a good clock. Things to look for are a verge escapement – which is loosely indicated by a horizontally turning crown wheel with sharp teeth just above the pendulum – a painted face or porcelain numerals and a winding hole placed in the face where you least expect it. Pendulums should be pear shaped bobs on brass rods.

The word that really matters in any description is 'ormolu' – that is, it is made of a hard metal, such as brass, which is rough cast before being chiseled and engraved by hand and, finally, coated with a thin amalgam of gold and mercury.

Cheaper nineteenth century mass produced clocks have a similar appearance at first glance, but they are made of spelter. This is a soft metal which is simply cast and gilded. The infallible test is to scratch the underside of the clock; if the gold colour comes away to reveal gray metal, it's spelter, if brass is revealed it is ormolu. Another test is to tap the case sharply with a coin. If the sound is sharp and pingy, you have hard metal; if it is a thud, you have soft.

A gilt ormolu and porcelain mounted mantel clock, French, circa 1880, in a case surmounted by crossed burning torches and arrows, 14in.
(Bonhams) $2,145

A German novelty rolling eye dog timepiece, second quarter 20th century, the painted rolling eyes indicating hours and minutes respectively, 7½in. high.
(Christie's) $589

A bronzed mantel clock, French, 19th century, 3½in. enamel dial with Roman numerals, the circular movement striking on a bell, 14in.
(Bonhams) $875

A gilt ormolu and porcelain mantel clock, French, circa 1880, in a cast case surmounted by an urn flanked by two winged putti, 14½in.
(Bonhams) $1,650

An ormolu figural mantel clock, French, circa 1840, enamel dial, signed *Lopin, Palais Royal, No. 143*, 14in.(Bonhams) $1,023

A French gilt brass mantel clock, the bell-striking movement stamped *Japy Frères*, 53cm.
(Bristol) $361

A gilt-bronze and porcelain 'jeweled' mantel clock, French circa 1880, the dial with Roman numerals, painted with an amorino, 51cm. high. (Sotheby's) $9,027

A French gilt-bronze and porcelain-mounted striking mantel clock, circa 1880, the tapering case with shell, dove and flower mounts 15¼in. high. (Christie's) $2,024

A Napoleon III Siena marble and bronze clock, French, circa 1870, the case surmounted by a figure of a classical hero, 64cm. high. (Sotheby's) $2,708

A French gilt-brass four-glass striking mantel clock, late 19th century, the case of typical form with molded top, 12¼in. high. (Christie's) $643

A Directoire ormolu-mounted white marble mantel timepiece, late 18th century, the drum-shaped case modeled with a gilt-bronze figure of Cupid reaching out to a standing Venus, 13¼in. wide. (Christie's) $1,288

A Louis Philippe rosewood and marquetry inlaid striking mantel clock, Le Blanc à Boulogne, circa 1835, 10in. high. (Christie's) $552

A French gilt-bronze and porcelain-mounted striking mantel clock, circa 1880 the case surmounted by an ovoid urn and with pineapple finials, 14¼in. high. (Christie's) $2,392

An unusual French gilt-brass four-glass 400-day mantel timepiece, circa 1900, signed *Grivolas Paris Pendule 400 Jours*, 12½in. high. (Christie's) $1,656

A German tortoiseshell and silver altar clock, second quarter 18th century, the case of typical form with four molded bun feet and multiple layers of moldings 21½in. high. (Christie's) $4,968

A mahogany and walnut lancet top bracket clock with an enamel dial, unsigned, 1820, in a case with molded cornice, 17½in.
(Bonhams) $4,125

A gilt-bronze mantel clock, French, circa 1860, the case cast with the birth of Venus, signed *Lerol à Paris*, 66cm. high.
(Sotheby's) $9,373

A French simulated tortoiseshell red lacquer and gilt-metal mounted striking mantel clock, last quarter 19th century, 9½in. high.
(Christie's) $331

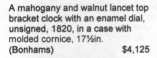

A French brass and glass striking mantel clock, last quarter 19th century, the case of octagonal outline and with beveled glass panels to each side, stamped for Japy Frères, 13½in. high.
(Christie's) $1,472

A Swiss gilt-brass world time desk, timepiece with calendar and moonphase, Jean Roulet, Le Locle, 20th century, the case in the manner of an armillary sphere, 7½in. high.
(Christie's) $920

A French gilt-brass striking four-glass clock, circa 1880, signed *Charles Oudin Hor.Ger de la Marine de L'Etat Palais Royal, 52 Paris,* 11¾in. high.
(Christie's) $1,840

A French foliate cut-brass inlaid and gilt-bronze mounted ebonized striking bracket clock, 19th century, stamped on backplate for *LAGARDA à Paris,* 31¼in. high.
(Christie's) $2,024

An early Victorian mahogany striking four-glass clock, J.W. Benson, 33 Ludgate Hill, circa 1840, the case with beveled glass panel to the stepped top, 12½ high.
(Christie's) $2,944

A French gilt-spelter and porcelain-mounted striking mantel clock, circa 1870, the case with putti caryatid figures supporting columns to the sides, 19¼in. high.
(Christie's) $736

A mahogany and carved case mantel clock, Richard Pickford, Liverpool, mid 19th century, the movement with shaped plates and striking on a bell, 18¹/₂in.
(Bonhams) $1,192

Renaissance Revival black marble mantel clock, circa 1890, incised design with colored marble plaques, 14¹/₂in. long.
(Skinner) $173

Regency gilt bronze mounted mahogany mantel clock, second quarter 19th century, signed *T. Baldwin London*, 19¹/₂in. high.
(Skinner) $1,495

A Louis XV style ormolu and patinated bronze figural mantel clock, second half 19th century, the glazed circular dial beneath a seated female faun and her young, 22¾in. high.
(Christie's) $3,220

A late Victorian nautical clock and combined aneroid barometer, surmounted on a metallic anchor with thermometer and subsidiary 'ship's wheel' day and date dial, 23cm. high.
(Bearne's) $1,231

Rare papier mâché polychrome and gilt mantel clock, The Litchfield Manufacturing Company, Litchfield, Connecticut, circa 1850, the shaped case of two birds above a brass bezel, 14in. wide.
(Skinner) $2,070

A German figural clock and stand, late 19th century, rockwork case surmounted by an Arab horseman, another Arab at his feet and an attacking lion, 24½in. high overall.
(Christie's) $4,025

A late Victorian black slate and green variegated marble perpetual calendar mantel clock, striking on a single bell, 16½in. high.
(Christie's) $1,240

French mantel clock of waisted form, the rims all applied with ebonized scrolled mounts, striking movement by Hy Marc, Paris, 19th century, 15¹/₂in.
(G.A. Key) $1,020

Continental porcelain mantel clock, crested with figure of sleeping Diana and cupid, late 19th century and later, 14in.
(G.A. Key) $329

An onyx marble and gilt-bronze bracket clock, Paris, circa 1890, the onyx dial beneath the muse of music, reclining on a stool, 51cm. high. (Sotheby's) $4,513

A four-glass, ornate, brass-cased clock, the arched top set on arched glass panel, the movement by Japy Frères.
(David Lay) $984

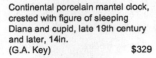

A large mantel clock, possibly designed by J.M. Olbrich, Darmstadt, circa 1905, of architectural form with circular brass face, 20¹/₂in. high
(Christie's) $4,874

A French Art Deco silver mounted and gem set agate bedroom timepiece, maker's mark *EB*, retailed by Garrard & Co. Limited, circa 1930, 4in. wide.
(Christie's) $2,263

Federal mahogany pillar and scroll clock, Seth Thomas, Plymouth, Connecticut, circa 1820, a thirty hour weight driven movement with off center escapement, 30in. high.
(Skinner) $2,415

An English inlaid mahogany eight-day bracket clock, circa 1900, in mahogany lancet-shaped case, 37cm.
(Bristol) $984

Royal Bonn style mantel clock, Germany, late 19th/early 20th century, enamel and gilt decorated dark blue ground with scrolled floral relief, 15½in. high.
(Skinner) $1,035

Regency mahogany bracket clock, London, circa 1800, painted dial, double fusee movement, hour strike with repeat lever, 14in. high.
(Skinner) $1,380

A Napoleon III gilt-bronze and porcelain mantel clock, French, circa 1870, the cover surmounted by a cherub above a revolving annular dial, 87cm. high.
(Sotheby's) $27,082

A gilt-bronze and marble mantel clock, Paris, circa 1880, in Louis XVI style, with white enamel dial, mounted within a fluted column, 35cm. wide.
(Sotheby's) $6,561

A 19th century French mantel clock, with eight day movement, in gilt metal oval case with the inset painted porcelain panels, 16in. high.
(Andrew Hartley) $1,492

A gilt-bronze and marble mantel clock by Denière, Paris, circa 1870, in the form of a lyre, surmounted by a female mask, 68cm. high.
(Sotheby's) $6,860

Peter Behrens for AEG, Berlin, Synchron double sided electric clock, circa 1910, brass, sheet steel, black painted metal, glass, 14³/₈in. diameter.
(Sotheby's) $8,998

A French gilt-bronze mounted scarlet lacquer and foliate cut-brass inlaid striking bracket clock, second half 19th century, case surmounted by the figure of an angel with trumpet, 42½in. high.
(Christie's) $3,312

A Federal inlaid and figured mahogany shelf clock, A. Gooding's, New Bedford, Massachusetts, circa 1800, the arched top with three fluted plinths, 31in. high.
(Sotheby's) $16,100

A French porcelain clock on stand, possibly by Michel-Isaac Aaron, mid 19th century, modeled as a Turk on horseback, holding a pistol in his right hand, 21in.
(Bonhams) $4,134

A Louis XVI style white marble and gilt-bronze mounted striking urn clock, Julien Beliard, Paris, circa 1900, body with mounts to the sides modeled as dolphins, 18¼in. high.
(Christie's) $2,576

A gilt-metal mounted and foliate cut-brass scarlet lacquer striking mantel clock, last quarter 19th century, on toupie feet, 10½in. high. (Christie's) $699

A gilt-bronze and porcelain mantel clock, Napoleon III, circa 1860, the case cast with a shepherd flanked by panels painted with fruits, 46cm. high. (Sotheby's) $3,820

A French ormolu mantel clock, of Louis XV design, 19th century, the cylinder movement with outside countwheel, inscribed *Julien LeRoy,* 19¼in. high. (Christie's) $3,818

A French 19th century enamel and chased gilt lantern shape clock surmounted by a soldier, the watch movement dial painted with a riverscape, 7½in. (Graves Son & Pilcher) $880

Marianne Brandt for Ruppelwerk, Gotha, table clock, circa 1930, black and white painted metal, chromium-plated foot, key, 5⅝in. high.   (Sotheby's) $1,125

A Napoleon III Boulle and gilt-bronze bracket clock, Paris, circa 1870, in Louis XV style, the dial above Apollo in his chariot flanked by caryatids, 110cm. high. (Sotheby's) $5,024

A Louis XV style foliate cut-brass inlaid scarlet lacquer and gilt-metal mounted striking mantel clock, last quarter 19th century, waisted case with floral urn finial, 13½in. high. (Christie's) $1,195

A gilt-bronze and porcelain mantel clock, Napoleon III, circa 1865, the case cast with a lady and two gallants, 51cm. high. (Sotheby's) $6,946

A Restauration style gilt-metal mounted malachite portico clock, the circular dial with Roman chapters within a cylindrical leaf-tip cast case, 19in. high. (Christie's) $3,450

A Napoleon III gilt-bronze mantel clock, French, circa 1860, the white enamel dial in a drum case, 41cm. high.
(Sotheby's) $2,166

Kim Weber for Lawson Time Inc., Alhambra, California, U.S.A., digital clock 'The Zephyr', model no. 304-P:40', 1934, copper, plastic.
(Sotheby's) $1,875

A Boulle and gilt-bronze bracket clock, Paris, circa 1890, in Louis XIV style, the dial above an allegory of Time, 108cm. high.
(Sotheby's) $16,497

A Louis XV style foliate cut-brass inlaid and gilt-bronze mounted scarlet lacquer striking bracket clock, Polti Frères a Tours, circa 1880, 19½in. high.
(Christie's) $1,656

Swiss, yellow gold, enamel travel clock, circa 1913 in 14ct yellow gold, rectangular, hinged 3 bodied, with blue enamel and presentation inscription, signed *Tiffany* on case, 2½ x 3in.   (Butterfield & Butterfield) $1,610

A Louis Philippe bronze and ormolu mantel clock, the arched case flanked by the figure of Psyche crowning Cupid with a floral garland, 28½in. wide.
(Christie's) $4,430

A Meissen bracket clock and stand, late 19th century, the cartouche-shaped clock case encrusted with flowers and with four putti emblematic of the Seasons, 22in. high.
(Christie's) $9,775

Cartier, Paris, alarm clock, circa 1920, in brass case on a bakelite base, white metal bezel, case and bezel decorated with coral, 3½in. high. (Butterfield & Butterfield) $2,588

A Louis Philippe giltwood and porcelain-mounted striking mantel clock, circa 1840, the foliate carved waisted case with floral finial, 20¾in. high.
(Christie's) $829

HISTORICAL FACTS
Skeleton Clocks

It is a widely held belief that skeleton clocks – almost all of which were made during the 19th century – were the work of apprentices, made during their final year of study and designed so that examiners could observe the working and workmanship of each part with a minimum of effort.

While this might well have been the practice from which the style originated, its popularity throughout the Victorian period necessitated the masters' involvement in their manufacture. English models are of fret-cut brass, with silvered brass chapter rings, and are usually to be found on wooden bases beneath glass domes – for they are naturally prone to dust damage.

Some strike the hour with a single 'ping' on the bell at the top. This action is cunningly contrived by means of a pin on the minute hand wheel which, approaching the hour, lifts the hammer and lets it drop as the hour passes. Very rare examples have full striking mechanisms or even chimes. The later Victorian examples show clear Gothic influence, being styled in the shape of a cathedral, say Westminster Abbey, or even the Brighton pavilion. These are elaborate works of art and sell for correspondingly high prices.

Another variety is the French skeleton clock. This is usually much smaller, having solid front and back plates – often engraved on later examples – and with enameled chapter rings.

A mid 19th century portico skeleton clock by Henry Marc à Paris, 18½in. high.
(Derek Roberts) $9,040

A rare skeleton clock by Evans of Handsworth, with detent escapement, circa 1860.
(Derek Roberts) $7,600

A fire-gilt French quarter striking skeleton clock, possibly by Bouchet, with silver rotating ring on top giving days of the week, 1790, 16in. high.
(Derek Roberts) $23,200

A gothic style skeleton clock, chiming and repeating the quarters on eight bells, circa 1845, 22in. high.
(Derek Roberts) $9,200

A Victorian brass skeleton timepiece, third quarter 19th century, with lyre-shaped openwork plates supported on four pillars, 30½in. high excluding dome.
(Christie's) $2,392

A triple plated arabesque skeleton clock by Evans of Handsworth, with enameled numeral plaques and 6 spoke wheelwork, circa 1850, 21in. high.
(Derek Roberts) $7,600

A large brass chiming skeleton clock, English, unsigned, late 19th century, on a white marble base with green velvet center, 23in. (Bonhams) $2,475

A Victorian brass skeleton timepiece, circa 1880, of typical openwork form with spire finials, on stepped oval white marble plinth, 15¾in. high. (Christie's) $736

A Victorian brass skeleton timepiece, circa 1880, of typical openwork form with spire finials, on stepped oval gray marble plinth, 15¾in. high. (Christie's) $645

A brass skeleton timepiece on a mahogany base, English, unsigned, the polished scroll shaped frame with single fusee and four spoke wheels, 11¾in. (Bonhams) $1,403

A Victorian brass skeleton timepiece, T. Gibbs, Stratford-on-Avon, basically mid 19th century, with spire finials, the frame mounted with later gilt-metal relief figures, 12¼in. high. (Christie's) $736

A Continental brass turret clock timepiece movement, 19th century, the single train three-pillar movement with pin-wheel escapement, 18½in. high. (Christie's) $1,197

A Victorian brass skeleton timepiece, circa 1880, the single chain fusee movement with anchor escapement and passing strike on bell, 19¾in. high. (Christie's) $920

A Victorian skeleton clock, the six-pillar architectural movement with single-train fusée drive, mounted on an oval wooden base and set beneath a glass dome, 43cm. high. (Bristol) $918

A French exhibition skeleton timepiece with alarm, Pierret a Paris, mid 19th century, with typical Y-shaped plates mounted on an oval brass base, 9in. high. (Christie's) $829

HISTORICAL FACTS
Wall Clocks

The tax on clocks imposed by Pitt in 1797 was the impetus behind the manufacture of large wall clocks which could be hung in public places for all to see. This is why many large wall clocks are still known today as Act of Parliament Clocks. The earliest of these rather resembled a large headed grandfather clock chopped off at the knees.

By the arrival of the Regency period, wall clocks had reduced in size to about eighteen inches in width, many veneered in rosewood with brass scroll inlay. The larger, Victorian, wall clocks are referred to as Vienna regulators and have a mahogany case and an elaborate pendulum. You will most probably find one driven by means of a spring, but those employing weights are as a rule better quality.

Among the most plentiful are those made by a certain Mr. Chauncey Jerome, of Connecticut, who began mass producing wall clocks with glazed fronts and pretty painted scenes on the lower half. Chauncey made them so cheaply that, when he sent a shipload to Britain, his valuation seemed so low that H.M.'s Customs men decided he was just trying to avoid paying the proper tax. Calling his bluff, or so they thought, they bought the entire cargo for Her Majesty's Government. Chauncey immediately loaded a couple more ships with his cheap clocks in the hope that the Customs men would repeat their generous gesture – they did not.

A mahogany dial timepiece, early 20th century, the white-painted Roman dial with gilt-brass bezel, 15in. diameter.
(Christie's) $552

A late 18th/early 19th century small turret clock, the two-train wrought iron four-post movement with anchor escapement, 54cm. wide.
(Bristol) $1,181

A Gustaf Becker wall regulator, striking on a gong, signed enamel dial with Roman numerals and brass pendulum, circa 1900.
(Auction Team Köln) $246

A 19th century Continental walnut and ebonized Vienna style wall clock, the case with arched top surmounted by turned finials, 4ft.4in. high. (Phillips) $1,139

An early Victorian rosewood and brass inlaid drop-dial wall timepiece, cream enamel dial inscribed H. & E. Gaydon, Brentford, 25in. high. (Christie's) $1,049

An English simulated rosewood drop-dial wall timepiece, early 20th century, the case inlaid with floral designs, 23½in. high.
(Christie's) $736

A Louis XVI style porcelain striking cartel clock, Japy Frères, last quarter 19th century, the shield-shaped case with urn cresting modeled with rams' heads, 26½in. high. (Christie's) $2,208

A late 18th century Act of Parliament clock in japanned case. (Dreweatt Neate) $2,400

A late Gustavian gilt wall clock, dial signed *Jakob Kock, Stockholm*, late 18th century, 100cm. high. (Stockholms Auktionsverket) $1,252

A late Gustavian wall clock, dial signed *Dahlström, Stockholm*, flanked by gilt cornucopiae, late 18th/early 19th century, 85cm. high. (Stockholms Auktionsverket) $1,001

An English mahogany trunk dial wall timepiece, second quarter 19th century, bearing signature *Thos. Harrison London*, 15½in. high. (Christie's) $1,472

A Federal giltwood and églomisé banjo clock, possibly Aaron Willard, Boston, circa 1810, the circular glazed dial door with brass bezel, 34¾in. high. (Christie's) $32,200

A Louis XVI style gilt and patinated bronze striking cartel clock, third quarter 19th century, the shield-shaped case surmounted by an urn cresting, 31½in. high. (Christie's) $1,747

A mahogany weight driven tavern wall timepiece, Handley & Moore, circa 1800, the single train movement with shaped cornered plates, 49½in. (Bonhams) $2,640

A Napoleon III bronze striking cartel clock, third quarter 19th century, the shield-shaped case surmounted by an urn cresting with drapery swag mount, Henry Lepaute, 31½in. high. (Christie's) $5,537

A gilt-bronze late Gustavian wall clock, dial signed *Jakob Kock, Stockholm,* late 18th century, 95cm. high. (Stockholms Auktionsverket) $2,879

An English mahogany wall dial timepiece, first quarter 19th century, signed *Allen Red Lyon St. Holborn,* 14¾in. diameter. (Christie's) $2,208

A Louis XVI style gilt-bronze striking cartel clock, Marti & Cie, last quarter 19th century, the shield-shaped case with swag-hung urn finial, 25¼in. high. (Christie's) $1,840

An early George III giltwood cartel clock in the Chippendale style, signed *William Smith, London,* 77 x 48cm. overall. (Phillips) $4,000

A Louis XVI ormolu clock and barometer set, late 19th century, the clock dial signed *'Popon Père & Fils',* 30¾in. high. (Christie's) $9,200

A Federal figured mahogany wall clock, Massachusetts, inscribed *E. Taber,* circa 1825, of rectangular box form with shaped pediment surmounted by a brass urn finial, 35in. high. (Sotheby's) $10,350

An ormolu-mounted corne verte bracket clock, the circular part-enameled dial with Roman and Arabic chapters inscribed *P.F. Le Doux a Paris,* 34½in. high. (Christie's) $5,693

A black lacquer, shield-shaped Act of Parliament clock by Will Carter, Kingston, five pillar movement and tapering plates, 58½in. long. (Derek Roberts) $18,400

A Louis XV ormolu-mounted and bronze-inlaid corne verte bracket timepiece, inlaid overall with flowerheads and trailing foliage issuing further flowers, 33¾in. high. (Christie's) $7,590

A Black Forest frame clock, black painted softwood frame with glazed door over pressed brass plate with peacocks and flowers, circa 1890. (Auction Team Köln) $149

A French black-painted wood striking wall clock, L. D'Etiveaud a Limoges, second half 19th century, the circular case with octagonal back box. (Christie's) $331

An Art Nouveau light oak striking wall clock, free wooden pendulum with triangular finial, German, circa 1900. (Auction Team Köln) $291

A porcelain mounted wall clock, Black Forest, 19th century, 3³/₄in. enamel dial with Roman numerals with painted porcelain surround decorated with horns of plenty and country church scene above the dial, 8³/₄in. (Bonhams) $302

A Black Forest pictorial clock, the painted and molded wooden dial with Roman numerals, wooden movement, circa 1900. (Auction Team Köln) $78

An early 18th century brass wall clock with engraved dial, roman numerals and subsidiary dial with single steel hand, inscribed *Nathaniel Cavell, Ipswich*, 7¹/₂in. high. (Anderson & Garland) $2,385

A gilt rosewood wall clock, E.N. Welch, Forestville, Connecticut, circa 1840, white-painted dial, 24¹/₂in. high. (Sotheby's) $805

Gilt gesso gallery timepiece, E. Ingraham & Co., Bristol, Connecticut, circa 1870, the circular molded glazed case enclosing white painted metal dial, 20in. diameter. (Skinner) $1,955

Seth Thomas brass ship's bell clock, 19th century, with outside bell, face marked *Chas. C. Hutchinson Boston,* dial diameter 5¹/₂in. (Eldred's) $605

An English octagonal wall clock, the dial signed *A. Hancock, Wetherby*, striking the hours on a gong, the case brass-inlaid, 1844.
(Auction Team Köln) $474

An oak wall clock, striking on a gong, silver colored dial with Arabic numerals, circa 1920, 75cm high.
(Auction Team Köln) $116

An office clock by the Badische Uhrenfabrik, Furtwangen, striking on a gong, painted dial with arabic numerals, circa 1885.
(Auction Team Köln) $129

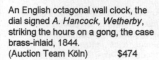

A Victorian walnut and mother of pearl inlaid fusee timepiece with 12in. painted dial.
(Dockree's Auctioneers) $430

A softwood clock case for a Black Forest clock, gilt inner frame, works missing, signed reverse glass painting, circa 1910.
(Auction Team Köln) $259

E. Howard No. 1 banjo clock, American, 19th century, dial signed *E. Howard & Co. Boston*, red, black and gilt glasses, walnut case, 50in. high.
(Eldred's) $2,750

A Victorian large mahogany striking dial clock, C. Keates, Belper, late 19th century, the molded case with sound fret to top of saltbox, 19½in. diameter.
(Christie's) $1,288

Mahogany circular drop dial wall clock, the case inlaid with brass lines and rosettes, mid 19th century, by Heitzman, Wisbeach, 20in.
(G.A. Key) $910

A mahogany cased verge dial timepiece, William Clarke, Rotherhithe, circa 1800, 12in. silvered dial, signed *William Clarke Rotherhithe*, in a case with turned wooden bezel.
(Bonhams) $1,815

A very rare 19th century English verge with a polychrome enamel sun and moon dial in silver pair cases, signed *Geog Cade*, diameter 57mm., 1827.
(Pieces of Time) $3,920

A gilt metal and shagreen verge oignon watch with alarm, Rey A Copet, late 17th century, the case with pierced gallery, diameter 54mm. (Christie's) $2,399

An early 19th century Swiss quarter repeating automaton verge in a silver open face case, diameter 58mm., circa 1810.
(Pieces of Time) $4,400

An 18 carat gold openface lever pocketwatch, signed *J.R. Arnold,* 1840s, the frosted gilt chain fusee movement with monometallic balance, 41mm. diameter.
(Christie's) $576

A Masonic silver triangular timepiece, early 20th century, triangular mother of pearl dial decorated with Masonic symbols, 55mm. high.
(Christie's) $1,840

A verge oignon pocket watch, late 17th/early 18th century, gilt cartouche dial with blue Roman numerals, movement signed *Gavdron a Paris*, 55mm.
(Christie's) $1,840

A 19th century Swiss lever in a gold and enamel full hunter case, signed *Martin & Marchinville a Geneve 44464*, diameter 47mm., circa 1870. (Pieces of Time)
    $2,640

An 18ct. gold openface pocket watch with engine-turned dial and keywound fusée lever movement, signed *Geo. Priest, Norwich, No. 6273.*
(Bearne's) $405

An early 19th century Swiss quarter repeating verge with a fine polychrome enamel dial in a gold open face case, diameter 57mm., circa 1810.
(Pieces of Time) $6,320

A gilt metal and underpainted horn verge pair cased pocket watch with painted dial, Continental, late 18th century, diameter 48mm. (Christie's) $960

A mid 17th century Swiss verge with astronomical indications in a contemporary enamel case, signed *J Girod*, diameter 50mm., circa 1650. (Pieces of Time) $23,200

A late 18th century English verge with polychrome enamel dial, signed *Thos Garnier London 3196*, diameter 48mm., circa 1780. (Pieces of Time) $1,520

A silver pair cased verge pocket watch with painted dial and calendar, Josephson, London, 1786, the border decorated with a scene of a shepherd and shepherdess, diameter 50mm. (Christie's) $831

A 14ct. gold and enamel fan form keyless cylinder fob watch, Swiss, circa 1900, fan shaped case with circular hinged covers decorated with enamel, 40mm. (Christie's) $775

A late 19th century 19th century Swiss minute repeating lever automaton in an engraved gold half hunter case, signed *West End Watch Co. Extra*, circa 1900, diameter 55mm. (Pieces of Time) $7,600

A three color gold keyless lever dresswatch, signed *Hamilton Watch Co., Lancaster, PA*, 1910s, in three color gold chased and engraved case, 55mm. diameter. (Christie's) $1,536

A gilt metal verge oignon pocket watch with alarm, N. Hanet, a Paris, circa 1700, restored cartouche dial with Roman numerals, diameter 60mm. (Christie's) $1,846

An 18 carat gold and enamel perpetual calendar minute repeating and moonphase hunter pocketwatch, signed *J.R. Losada, London*, 1880s., 54mm. diameter. (Christie's) $17,285

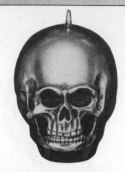

A fine late 17th century English verge clockwatch with gold champlevé dial, signed *Windmills London*, diameter 57mm – depth 18mm., circa 1690. (Pieces of Time) **$9,440**

A silver skull form Masonic watch, Swiss, circa 1910, hinged at the jaw and opening to reveal the white enamel dial, 30mm. approx. (Christie's) **$1,846**

A Continental silver gilt and enamel automaton calendar cylinder pocketwatch, unsigned, so-called Adam & Eve watch, mid 19th century, 57mm. diameter. (Christie's) **$4,993**

An unusual gold and enamel openface cylinder pocketwatch with visible balance, signed *Lebet & Fills*, mid 19th century, in chased and engraved openface gold case with polychrome floral decoration, 46mm. diameter. (Christie's) **$1,632**

A silver astronomical verge paircase pocketwatch, signed *Franciscus Mercier*, Paris, late 17th century, in contemporary silver and tortoiseshell outer case, movement signed, 56mm. diameter outer case. (Christie's) **$10,563**

A wood and bone openface pocketwatch, signed (in Russian) *The Bronnikovs at Viatka*, mid 19th century, the movement made of wood and bone winding through an especially shaped click wheel, 57mm. diameter. (Christie's) **$5,762**

An unusual gold keyless openface dresswatch, signed *Patek Philippe & Co.*, 1900s, in heavily cast gold openface case depicting George and the Dragon, 49mm. diameter. (Christie's) **$6,722**

A good 18 carat gold pivoted detent chronometer hunter pocketwatch, signed *Parkinson & Frodsham*, 1840s, the engine-turned silvered dial with applied gilt floral decoration, 51mm. diameter. (Christie's) **$6,722**

A rare 18th century skeletonised English verge with polychrome enamel dial, signed *Jos Pomroy London 760*, diameter 48mm., circa 1750. (Pieces of Time) **$2,872**

A gilt metal verge oignon pocket watch, Le Siammois a Paris, early 18th century, cartouche dial with gilt brass dial plate, diameter 56mm. (Christie's) $3,138

An 18th century French verge by Le Roy in a fine gold mounted enamel consular case, signed *Jll Le Roy Paris*, diameter 47mm., circa 1760. (Pieces of Time) $4,320

A rare crystal, gold and enamel keyless dresswatch, signed *Cartier, France*, 1920s, in faceted rock crystal case, 48mm. diameter. (Christie's) $9,603

A fine silver paircase verge pocketwatch, signed *Wm. Kipling, London, No. 369*, early 18th century, the frosted gilt chain fusee movement with finely chased and pierced cock, 59mm. diameter. (Christie's) $2,689

A silver gilt triangular Masonic keyless pocketwatch, signed *Montrose*, mid 20th century, the mother-of-pearl dial with colored Masonic symbols, 55mm. length each side. (Christie's) $2,497

A late 18th century gold and enamel verge pair case pocketwatch with outer traveling case, signed *Edw, Scales, London*, outer case back depicting a lady in a garden with Cupid, 51mm. diameter. (Christie's) $3,457

An interesting Swiss gold double dialed triple calendar and moonphase minute repeating chronograph keyless openface pocketwatch, unsigned, 1890s, 54mm. diameter. (Christie's) $9,603

A gold openface minute repeating keyless dresswatch, signed *Patek Philippe*, 1920s, the brushed silvered dial with raised Art Deco style Arabic numerals, 46mm. diameter. (Christie's) $7,682

A rare gold bras en l'air verge pocketwatch, signed *Courvoiser Frères*, No. 12507, 1810s, a gilt female figure on the dial, the time indicated by depressing the pendant which raises the arms, 56mm. (Christie's) $13,444

A Rolex gold self-winding water resistant wristwatch with unusual enamel dial, 1940s, with self-winding movement, 32 x 39mm. (Christie's) $7,682

Bulgari, a gentleman's black plastic automatic wristwatch, limited edition model: New York, 0356/1600, recent. (Christie's) $738

A platinum and diamond set rectangular wristwatch, signed *Hamilton,* 1930s, in rectangular case with stepped bezel, 40 x 21mm. (Christie's) $960

A Rolex stainless steel self-winding water resistant wristwatch, signed *Rolex, Model Oyster Perpetual Chronometer,* 1950s, unusual white textured dial, 35mm. diameter. (Christie's) $1,247

Piaget, a gentleman's 18ct. gold wristwatch with opal and onyx dial, rectangular dial with chamfered corners signed *Piaget*, integral textured Piaget bracelet, 28mm x 32mm. (Christie's) $4,614

A lady's bi-color quartz movement bracelet watch, Cartier Santos Galbee, recent, Swiss made movement in a brushed case with a polished bezel. (Bonhams) $1,081

A World War II pilot's wristwatch, signed *International Watch Co., Schaffhausen,* 1940s, the frosted gilt movement jeweled to the center with screwed chatons, 44mm. diameter. (Christie's) $2,497

Omega, a gentleman's 18ct. gold chronograph wristwatch, 1965, 17-jewel movement with compensation balance, diameter 35mm. (Christie's) $1,656

A stainless steel automatic center seconds bracelet watch, Rolex Datejust, ref. 1601, circa 1960, silvered dial with baton numerals and chamfered edge, 35mm. (Bonhams) $763

Cartier, a lady's stainless steel quartz wristwatch, model: Panthere, 1996, stainless steel Cartier bracelet, 22mm.
(Christie's) $1,472

A lady's gold, diamond and jade wristwatch, signed Piaget, 1980s, the jade dial with gold hands, 28 x 25mm. (Christie's) $4,993

A gentleman's pink gold wristwatch, signed *Jaeger-LeCoultre*, 1950s, the gilt movement with gold alloy balance, 35mm. diameter.
(Christie's) $1,344

A stainless steel and pink gold self-winding water resistant calendar wristwatch, signed *Rolex, Oyster Perpetual Datejust Chronometer*, recent, 35mm.
(Christie's) $3,073

A 9ct gold automatic wristwatch, Rolex Oyster 'Bubbleback', ref. 5015, circa 1937, the automatic movement signed *Rolex Perpetual Chronometer,* 32mm.
(Bonhams) $2,970

A white gold and enamel wristwatch with hinged lugs, signed *Hamilton Watch Co.*, 1930s, in white gold tonneau case with black enamel bezel, 42 x 29mm.
(Christie's) $1,921

An airman's self-winding water resistant chronograph wristwatch, signed *Breguet*, model Aeronavale, recent, with self winding movement.
(Christie's) $4,801

A gold rectangular wristwatch, signed *Omega*, 1950s, in rectangular case with stepped and downturned lugs. 35 x 23mm.
(Christie's) $1,728

A gold self-winding water resistant wristwatch signed *Rolex, Model Oyster Perpetual Chronometer, Bubble-back*, 1950s, 39 x 32mm.
(Christie's) $4,609

Omega, a gentleman's Flightmaster chronograph wristwatch, 1970s, gray dial with baton markers, subsidiary 24-hour dial, 51mm. x 43mm. (Christie's) $831

A stainless steel self-winding water resistant wristwatch signed *Rolex, Oyster Perpetual Chronometer, Bubble-back,* 1930s, 32mm. diameter. (Christie's) $2,113

A stainless steel self-winding and water resistant wristwatch, signed *Rolex, Oyster Perpetual Explorer Chronometer,* 1953, 36mm. diameter. (Christie's) $2,881

A bi-color self-winding mid-size calendar wristwatch, Rolex Oyster Datejust, recent, white dial with Roman and gilt raised block numerals, 30mm. (Bonhams) $2,226

A rare platinum eight day tourbillon calendar wristwatch with power reserve indication, signed *Blancpain,* No. 22, recent, 34mm. diameter. (Christie's) $30,728

An early gold cushion case single button chronograph wristwatch, signed *Rolex,* 1920s, the gold cushion case with chamfered bezel, 32mm. sq. (Christie's) $12,483

A 9 carat gold water resistant wristwatch signed *Rolex, Oyster Precision,* the nickel plated movement with bimetallic balance, 28mm. diameter. (Christie's) $1,921

A gentleman's 18 carat gold self-winding water resistant striking and repeating automaton wristwatch, signed *Ulysse Nardin, Model San Marco,* recent, 40mm. diameter. (Christie's) $23,046

A stainless steel automatic calendar water-resistant wristwatch, signed Blancpain, recent, with flexible steel bracelet and double deployant clasp, 38mm. diameter. (Christie's) $2,881

A white gold rectangular wristwatch, signed *Montres Rolex, Cellini,* 1980s, the nickel plated movement with 19 jewels, 32 x 25mm. (Christie's) $3,457

A gold chronograph wristwatch signed *Longines,* 1950s, the cream enamel dial with applied gold dagger numerals, 37mm. diameter. (Christie's) $2,113

Rolex, a lady's steel and gold Oyster Perpetual date automatic wristwatch, Ref:6917, 1970s, signed gilt dial with baton markers, 25mm. (Christie's) $1,329

A stainless steel and gold triple calendar chronograph wristwatch, signed *Rolex,* 1950s, the nickel plated movement jeweled to the center with gold alloy balance, 35mm. diameter. (Christie's) $8,642

A gold rectangular wristwatch, signed *Rolex,* dial signed *Eaton Prince ¼ Century Club,* 1940s, the silvered dial with the letters ¼ Century Club representing the numerals, 45 x 22mm. (Christie's) $5,762

A yellow gold tuning fork regulated water-resistant wristwatch, signed *Bulova Accutron, model Spaceview,* 1960s, the tuning fork mechanism visible through the (replaced) glass, 33mm. diameter. (Christie's) $615

Breitling, a gentleman's stainless steel Navitimer chronograph wristwatch, 1970s, signed black dial with luminous baton markers, diameter 46mm. (Christie's) $920

A bi-color automatic center seconds wristwatch, Rolex Oyster Perpetual, ref. 6117, circa 1955, silvered dial with dagger and quarter Arabic numerals, 34mm. (Bonhams) $1,033

A stainless steel water resistant chronograph wristwatch, signed *Rolex, Cosmograph Daytona, model Paul Newman,* 1960s, 36mm. diameter. (Christie's) $17,285

A pair of Chinese cloisonné enamel models of cranes, standing in mirror image, the wing feathers multicolored, 22½in. high. (Christie's) $4,784

A Chinese cloisonné and gilt bronze tripod censer and domed cover, elaborately pierced with flowers and scrolling foliage, 16¾in. high. (Christie's) $3,312

Pair of cloisonné enameled metal ground moon flasks, their applied curling dragon handles finished with gilt, 14¼in. high. (Butterfield & Butterfield) $1,840

A cloisonné flattened rectangular snuff bottle and stopper decorated with panels depicting cranes among pine and deer among prunus, Qianlong mark, 2¼in. high. (Christie's) $2,208

A Ming cloisonné and gilt bronze oval box and cover, decorated with a bird perched on a blossoming branch, 16th/17th century, 4¾in. wide. (Christie's) $1,840

A pair of Chinese cloisonné and gilt bronze revolving bottle vases, each with four pierced roundels of dragons among clouds, early 19th century, 13¼in. high. (Christie's) $2,392

Cloisonné covered globular jar with crane decoration, Meiji period, signed *Seitei* [Namikawa Sosuke, 1847-1910], raised on three short feet, 8¹/₈in. high. (Butterfield & Butterfield) $2,875

A large Chinese gilt bronze and enamel cloisonné box and cover, Qianlong Period, 1736-95, 40cm. diameter.
(Galerie Koller) $13,940

A Chinese cloisonné and gilt bronze two handled cup and saucer on short foot, decorated with lotus flowers and foliage, 18th century, 5¼in. diameter.
(Christie's) $588

A Chinese Qing Dynasty bronze and enamel cloisonné censer, 17th century, 31.8cm. high.
(Galerie Koller) $15,931

A late 19th century Russian cloisonné enamel cigarette case, decorated with flowers and foliage on a frosted gilt ground, by Pavel Ovchinnikov, Moscow, 1891, 10.5cm. long.
(Phillips) $1,062

A rare pair of cloisonné enamel square stools, early 19th century, each with a flat top above a narrow waist supported on a thick apron, 19¾in. square,
(Christie's) $22,080

Fine blue ground cloisonné enamel vase, Meiji period, Hayashi Kodenji Studio mark, with continuous scene of birds in cherry trees, 12in.
(Butterfield & Butterfield) $4,312

A Chinese cloisonné and gilt bronze circular box and domed cover on short foot, decorated with three goats amongst plants and rockwork, 18th century, 9.3cm. diameter.
(Christie's) $368

A pair of 19th century Chinese cloisonné circular tapered and fluted vases, decorated with flowerheads on powder blue and black ground, 4½in. high.
(Anderson & Garland) $86

Massive cloisonné enameled metal palace vase, 19th century, the turquoise ground inlaid in 'famille rose' enamels with beribboned emblems of the 'eight Daoist immortals', 67¾in. high. (Butterfield & Butterfield) $6,325

Large cloisonné enamel vase, Meiji period, decorated with alternating phoenix and dragon lappets below an elaborate brocade, 18½in. high. (Butterfield & Butterfield)
$1,840

Melon form cloisonné enamel covered jar, Meiji period, the elongated ovoid body enameled with alternating bands of mustard and brown enamels, 7¾in. high. (Butterfield & Butterfield)
$920

Large Japanese sky blue ground, cloisonné enamel vase, early 20th century, the body decorated with a continuous design of cranes and parrots, 24½in. high. (Butterfield & Butterfield)
$1,610

Fine Japanese blue ground cloisonné enamel vase with floral decoration, Meiji period, finely decorated to the front with four birds in flight, 14½in. high. (Butterfield & Butterfield)
$1,495

Grey ground cloisonné enamel two handle vase with butterfly design, Meiji period, signed Ota, decorated with reserves of butterflies and chrysanthemums, 5⅝in. high. (Butterfield & Butterfield)
$1,380

Yellow ground cloisonné enameled metal vase, Meiji period, signed Ota, inlaid in delicate silver wire outline and with blue birds and autumn blossoms, 12¼in. high. (Butterfield & Butterfield)
$1,380

Large cloisonné vase, enameled with large flowering chrysanthemums before a blossoming prunus tree, 14½in. high. (Butterfield & Butterfield)
$862

Cloisonné enameled covered globular jar with flying crane decoration, Meiji period, enamelled at the rounded shoulder with a continuous band of cranes in flight, 7¼in. high. (Butterfield & Butterfield)
$920

Japanese cloisonné enameled dragon vase, early 20th century, Ota Tameshiro cipher, enameled with a coiled dragon on a graded blue enamel ground, 6in. high. (Butterfield & Butterfield)
$488

A German brass alms bowl, circa 1500, the well with crowned mask issuing stylized fruit and flowers, 15¼in. diameter.
(Sotheby's) $2,587

City of Glasgow, a graduated part set of four copper and brass conical measures by Alexr. Ramsay, Maker, Glasgow, comprising: two gallon, one quart, four gill and two gill. (Christie's) $370

A pair of Argentinian brass shoe stirrups, circa 1860, embossed with horse motifs.
(Bonhams) $130

Stickley Brothers copper umbrella stand, #168, hexagon-form with hammered finish, original dark patina, 26in. high.
(Skinner) $800

City of Glasgow, a graduated set of six copper and brass check pumps, comprising: up to ten gallons.
(Christie's) $1,943

A Herrengrund partially gilt-copper double beaker, dated 1759, in the form of a barrel, each end engraved with German miner's inscription, 3½in. high.
(Sotheby's) $920

Fine Tibetan copper repoussé figure of Gautama Buddha, 17th/18th century, seated dhyanasana on a double lotus pedestal base, with hands in bhumisparsa mudra, 20¾in. high.
(Butterfield & Butterfield) $3,162

Burgh of Coatbridge, canceled from county of Berwick, a graduated part set of nine brass bushel measures by Bate, London, maker of the Exchequer Standards, 1824.
(Christie's) $4,999

A large brass sheave, American, 20th century, cast G.M. Mfg. Co 408–1, for ⁵/₁₆in. cable, 53cm. high, together with a brass anchor shackle and brass winch.
(Bonhams) $402

A brass newspaper rack by Margaret Gilmour with circular beaten panel depicting a peacock within a wreath of leaves, 31¾in. high.
(Christie's) $737

A WMF brass inkstand, of oblong form with two indented pen holders, the back flanked by two inkwells, 11¼in. long.
(Christie's) $351

A Georgian bell metal rectangular footman, with turned handles, shaped apron and cabriole front supports, 39½cm. wide.
(Bristol) $248

A Hughes Owens and Co. pattern 0183 compass binnacle, Canadian, early 20th century, with floating compass, gimbaled mount, brass binnacle with side illuminant, 47cm. high.
(Bonhams) $563

A German embossed brass alms dish, 17th century, the center embossed with bunches of grapes, the border with lozenge decoration, 17½in. diameter.
(Bonhams) $448

Unusual brass dinner gong with horn supports, joined to a domed base, applied throughout with brass mounts, circa late 19th/early 20th century, 13in.
(G. A. Key) $200

A pair of Flemish brass pricket candlesticks, 17th century, each with deep drip-pan fitted with iron pricket, prickets 26¾in. high.
(Sotheby's) $2,300

Unusual Victoria copper tea set, includes teapot, sugar, creamer, and tray, impressed *Victoria, Taxco, Mexico*, coffeepot 8½in. high.
(Skinner) $230

Two Jarvie-style brass candlesticks, signed *F*, 12½in. high.
(Skinner) $172

Copper conical shaped measuring jug. (Chapman Moore & Mugford) $140

A Benham & Fround copper and brass mounted Arts & Crafts kettle. (Academy) $144

Early 19th century copper samovar of oval form, the four fluted supports molded with mask designs, 9in. (G.A. Key) $165

George Prentiss Kendrick copper tea caddy, circa 1892, repoussé foliate design, marked *GPK*, 3¼in. high. (Skinner) $2,300

A pierced gilt brass jardinière, early 20th century, of cylindrical form with pierced lattice frieze and molded base on paw feet, 14in. high. (Christie's) $7,383

A Dutch embossed brass alms dish, early 18th century, with plain center and stylized border, 15½in. diameter. (Bonhams) $512

Designed and executed by Hans Przyrembel, tea caddy, circa 1932, part-textured brass, 4½in. (Sotheby's) $1,687

A Continental brass oval jardinière, late 19th century, decorated with repoussé ornament, the sides with a pseudo armorial device, 28½in. wide. (Christie's) $2,215

Rebajes copper wall plaque, abstract figure of a woman, signed *Rebajes*, 14in. high, 7in. wide. (Skinner) $173

Wood duck decoy, A. Elmer Crowell, East Harwich, Massachusetts, with raised crossed wings, 12¾in. long. (Skinner) $7,187

Wigeon drake decoy, Joe Lincoln, Accord, Massachusetts, stamped *F.B. Rice* on base, 15½in. long. (Skinner) $1,380

White winged scoter drake decoy, Monhegan Island, 7½in. high x 17½in. long. (Skinner) $1,495

Common pintail drake, Ward Brothers, Crisfield, Maryland, marked on base made and painted by Lem Ward 1930, 17½in. long. (Skinner) $1,840

Barnacle goose decoy, 19½in. long. (Skinner) $632

Hollow carved canvasback hen decoy, Dodge factory, Detroit, Michigan, 15in. long. (Skinner) $747

Long bill curlew, Chief Coffey, Long Island, New York, 8in. high x 15½in. long. (Skinner) $1,380

Partridge family group, branded on base *R.G. Jansson Cape Cod*, on a driftwood base, 9¾in. high x 22in. long. (Skinner) $488

Canada goose decoy, 15¼in. high x 28in. long. (Skinner) $1,265

Shore bird decoy, 14in. high x 15in. long. (Skinner) $460

Black-bellied plover decoy, 11¼in. (Skinner) $747

Dowitcher decoy, John Dilley, Quoque, Long Island, 10¼in. long. (Skinner) $9,200

A goldeneye hen decoy, attributed to 'Shang' Wheeler, Stratford, Connecticut, circa 1900, the full-carved solid figure with carved bill detail. (Sotheby's) $1,495

A carved wood swan, New Jersey, the full-carved hollow figure with carved bill detail and inset glass eyes. (Sotheby's) $460

A Delaware River black duck decoy, circa 1900, the full-carved hollow figure with carved bill and wing detail. (Sotheby's) $230

Herring gull decoy, New Jersey style, with delineated wing tips, 18¾in. long.
(Skinner) $2,760

Eider drake decoy, probably Maine, 7in. high x 17½in. long.
(Skinner) $920

Canada goose decoy, A. Elmer Crowell, East Harwich, Massachusetts, 23in. long.
(Skinner) $12,650

Wigeon drake decoy, Madison Mitchell, Havre de Grace, Maryland, 13⅝in. long.
(Skinner) $316

Goldeneye drake decoy, Benjamin Schmidt, 14in. long.
(Skinner) $632

Mallard hen decoy, Charles Perdew, Henry, Illinois, with later varnish, 17½in. long.
(Skinner) $2,012

Red breasted merganser drake decoy, marked *LB* on base, 14in. long. (Skinner) $373

Pair of hooded merganser decoys, Hurley Conklin, Manhawkin, New Jersey, marked *H. Conklin* on base, 14 and 14¼in.
(Skinner) $920

White winged scoter drake decoy, Roswell Bliss, Stratford, Connecticut, stamped on base *R. Bliss*, 5½in. high. x 16in. long.
(Skinner) $287

Green heron, A. Elmer Crowell, East Harwich, Massachusetts, 13in.
(Skinner) $6,325

Black bellied plover, A. Elmer Crowell, East Harwich, Massachusetts, rectangular stamp, 8½in. long.
(Skinner) $6,325

Yellow legs decoy, Elisha Burr, Hingham, Massachusetts, 11½in. long. (Skinner) $2,760

A Canada goose decoy, Eugene Hendrickson, Lower Bank, New Jersey, circa 1930, the full-carved hollow figure with carved bill detail and tack eyes.
(Sotheby's) $1,380

Red-breasted merganser drake decoy, in the style of Monhegan Island, 15½in. long.
(Skinner) $517

A Merganser hen decoy, probably Maritime Provinces, early 20th century, the full-carved solid body with cut sheet-metal comb and inset lead weights.
(Sotheby's) $460

HISTORICAL FACTS
Bru Dolls

The doll making factory of Bru Jne & Cie was established in 1866 by Casimer Bru. He remained with the company until 1883. It then passed through a series of directorships before amalgamating with a number of other French firms to form the Société Française de Fabrication de Bébés et Jouets (SFBJ) in 1899. Bru dolls, though less costly than their Jumeau counterparts, were luxury items, with bisque heads and composition, wood or kid bodies. Casimer was a great experimenter, and he invented many mechanical devices.

His designs were many and varied and included crying dolls, feeding dolls and two-faced dolls, which showed a happy and a crying or sleeping face.

With regard to bodies, Bru designed types in jointed wood, gusseted and jointed kid and combinations of composition and kid. Early models had bisque shoulder-heads or swivel heads mounted on gusseted kid bodies, and were often adult in shape. These Bru lady dolls tend to have smiling faces with strikingly upturned mouths. The eyes are usually of glass, fringed by long, densely painted lashes.

In 1872 the Bébé Bru line was introduced often with open molded mouths revealing teeth and tongue. Like other manufacturers of the time, Bru made dolls representing different nationalities. The most common Bru mark is Bru J$^{ne\,R}$.

'König Wernicke's lovable black doll', googly eyes, open mouth with two glass teeth, original wig, composition head and body.
(Auction Team Köln) $149

A fine Emile Jumeau bisque doll, French, circa 1880, with fixed blue paperweight eyes, open/closed mouth, 23in.
(Sotheby's) $6,256

An Étienne Denamur bisque doll, French, circa 1895, jointed wood and composition body, stamped in blue *Bébé Jumeau*, 15¼in.
(Sotheby's) $552

A Bébé Schmitt bisque doll, French, circa 1880, in original white lace and ribbon trimmed gauze gown and hat, 13¾in.
(Sotheby's) $6,256

A rare pair of small all-bisque swivel neck character dolls of 'Max & Moritz' probably by J.D Kestner, German, circa 1920, with smiling closed mouths, painted blue eyes, 4¾in. (Sotheby's) $2,483

A Jules Steiner walking/talking baldhead bisque doll, French, circa 1885, walking key wind body with composition forearms and lower legs, 17¾in.
(Sotheby's) $1,195

A bisque doll, probably Kestner, German, circa 1890, impressed *1361*, long blonde curly hair on fabric and card pate, 13¾in. (Sotheby's) $920

A rare and unusually large Kammer & Reinhardt googly eyed doll, German; circa 1915, with jointed wood and composition body, 17¼in. (Sotheby's) $11,592

A Kämmer & Reinhardt bisque doll German, circa 1890, jointed wood and composition body, in ivory silk dress, 25½in. (Sotheby's) $736

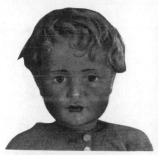

A Kämmer & Reinhardt bisque character doll, German, circa 1910, with blue intaglio eyes, closed mouth, short blonde wig, 19in. (Sotheby's) $4,784

A Louis Vuitton doll, miniature wardrobe trunk and collection of costume, French, circa 1950, of hard plastic, 17in. (Sotheby's) $2,760

A Simon & Halbig bisque character baby doll, German, circa 1910, jointed five piece composition body, 23in.   (Sotheby's) $4,048

An Oriental Schoenau & Hoffmeister 4900 character with fixed brown slanting eyes, black mohair wig and jointed body, dressed in a kimono, 10in. high. (Christie's) $781

A fine Kestner bisque doll, German, circa 1880, with weighted dark brown paperweight eyes, closed mouth, in flounced gown, 17¾in. (Sotheby's) $2,944

A bisque doll, French, probably Jumeau, circa 1900, with fixed pale blue glass eyes, closed mouth with white line visible between lips, 12¼in. (Sotheby's) $827

HISTORICAL FACTS
Pierre Jumeau Dolls

Pierre Jumeau opened his family doll making enterprise in Paris in 1842. They had a factory complex at Montreuil-sous-Bois where they made not only the wood and kid bodies, but also the clothes, and in 1873 kilns were opened, enabling the manufacture of heads as well. The company continued until 1899, when it became part of the SFBJ. After that time the SFBJ continued to produce Jumeau dolls, reissuing them as late as the 1950s.

Initially, Jumeau used heads by other manufacturers, such as Simon & Halbig. Original bodies were shaped kid or jointed wood, but after 1870 these were made also of composition, and it was then too that bébé-type dolls began to be made. (Though bébé refers to representations of children from babyhood to about 6 years, most Jumeau examples are of the older type.)

Jumeau dolls were very much at the top end of the quality scale, and won many international awards in the 1880s and 90s. The eyes are often particularly fine, while other characteristics include rather heavily drawn eyebrows and somewhat chunky bodies.

In addition to lady and child dolls, many character dolls were produced, perhaps modeled on real children. Two-faced dolls and those representing other nationalities were also made, together with a few mechanical types.

A life size Simon and Halbig bisque china head doll, impressed *S.H. 18. 949*, with socket head and shoulder plate, 3ft. high.
(Bearne's)   **$4,212**

A large and fine smiling Bru fashion doll, French, circa 1875, blonde wig, on white kid leather body with gusseted joints, 25in.
(Sotheby's)   **$11,040**

A Jumeau Triste bisque doll, French, circa 1880, accurately molded ball jointed wood and composition body with straight wrists, 22in.
(Sotheby's)   **$9,200**

A Bru Jeune pressed bisque swivel head doll, French, circa 1880, with open/closed mouth and dimple in chin, 26in.
(Sotheby's)   **$13,800**

An early American autoperipatetikos, porcelain head and leather arms, with original dress, box and key, in working order, 1862.
(Auction Team Köln)   **$1,865**

A swivel neck fashion doll, French, possibly Etienne Denamur, circa 1890, cork pate, gusseted kid leather body, 17¾in.
(Sotheby's)   **$699**

A Roullet et Decamps/Simon & Halbig flirty eyed walker bisque doll, French, circa 1900, 17in. (Sotheby's) $920

A fine Steiner A series Bébé bisque doll, French, circa 1890, with fixed blue paperweight eyes, 21¼in. (Sotheby's) $3,680

An Armand Marseille 341 baby doll with closed mouth, blue sleeping eyes and bent limbed body, dressed in cream woollen outfit, 18½in. high. (Christie's) $558

An Étienne Denamur bisque doll, French, circa 1890, with a jointed wood and composition body, 15½in. (Sotheby's) $827

A fine and rare Jumeau A mold bébé, French, circa 1885, short blonde wig on cork pate, on a jointed wood and composition body, 24½in. (Sotheby's) $9,200

An S.F.B.J. bisque character boy, French, circa 1910, lightly painted hair, fixed blue glass eyes, slightly open mouth with teeth, 17in. (Sotheby's) $1,288

A fine and original Tête Jumeau bisque doll, French, circa 1885, long, curly blonde real hair wig on cork pate, jointed wood and composition body, 14in. (Sotheby's) $9,568

A fine Gaultier bisque doll, French, circa 1890, on a jointed wood and composition body, 30in. (Sotheby's) $4,784

Hertel, Schwab & Co., a bisque china head 'Googlie' eyed doll with closed mouth, having silver blonde wig and blue paperweight glass eyes, 35cm. (Bearne's) $3,888

'Grenville House', a fine ¹/₁₂-scale doll's house of Georgian style with nine furnished and decorated rooms.
(Anderson & Garland)
$2,119

Irene's miniature kitchen, German, late 19th century/early 20th century, with blue and cream painted checkerboard floor, 39¾ x 17 x 16in. (Sotheby's)
$4,232

A painted wooden fort, German, late 19th century, the fort mounted on two islands with painted bark to sides, 21½ x 13in.
(Sotheby's)
$643

A painted wooden butcher's shop, English, late 19th century, the facade of a Georgian house with three windows above, 27½ x 17in.
(Sotheby's)
$2,208

Architectural model of a house, New England, 19th century, the house with yellow clapboard sides and brown trim, the front porch with turned supports, 6½in. wide.
(Skinner)
$2,645

A wooden doll's house, circa 1860, painted cream and blue with gold detailing, containing four rooms.
(Sotheby's)
$1,120

Irene's miniature salon and bedroom, late 19th/early 20th century, the two rooms with dividing wall and connecting door, 34½ x 18 x 16½in.
(Sotheby's)
$6,624

A late 19th century painted Noah's Ark, with sloping roof decorated with a dove and containing about 160 carved animals, 44cm. wide.
(Cheffins Grain & Comins)
$960

Doll's kitchen, circa 1920, wood, with one glazed window, fully furnished, and including a quantity of doll's crockery, 82 x 36 x 52cm.
(Auction Team Köln)
$242

A hand-forged puzzle lock, the door of the lock opening when one of the flanking decorations is pushed up, circa 1880.
(Auction Team Köln) $175

A late Victorian Kent's patent knife cleaner, English, late 19th century, on green painted wrought iron stand, 49cm. wide.
(Bonhams) $289

Cast iron washboard with heart cutout, Pennsylvania, 19th century, original surface, 22½ x 12½in.
(Skinner) $2,415

Gerhard Marcks for Schott & Gen. Jena'er Glassworks, Jena, coffee machine 'Sintrax' and hot ring, circa 1925, clear, heat-resistant glass, chromium-plated metal, 15¹/₈in.
(Sotheby's) $1,875

Bell metal and wood candlemold, Massachusetts, 19th century, the molded stamped *A.D. Richmond New Bedford, patent*, 10¹/₄in. high.
(Skinner) $805

Designed and executed by Herbert Schulze, Fachhochschule, Dusseldorf, tea maker, 1990, silver-colored metal, glass, ebony, cork, 11¼in.   (Sotheby's) $3,374

A large Peugeot coffee grinder, wooden base and cast handle, with brass coffee container, French, circa 1900.
(Auction Team Köln) $246

A Victorian paint-decorated pine birdcage, third quarter 19th century, the demilune-shaped top fitted with a hanging ring, 16in. high.
(Sotheby's) $1,380

A large fan by Marelli, Milan, with brass blades and black cast base, three stage adjustment, 44cm. diameter.
(Auction Team Köln) $141

A set of Irish Victorian brass and japanned metal mechanical bellows, circa 1860, mounted on a mahogany baseboard with bun feet, 25½in. long.
(Christie's) $1,477

A set of 19th century boulle postal scales by Aspreys of London, the scales on fretted brass support, 24.5cm. wide.
(Bristol) $886

An oversized burlwood ladle, American, 18th/19th century, with slightly arched tubular handle, 39in. long.
(Sotheby's) $2,875

Decorative cast-iron household scales, enamel dial, scale 0-10 kg.
(Auction Team Köln) $103

A large wooden, brass-mounted Dubois coffee grinder, steel grinder, Belgian.
(Auction Team Köln) $129

An outsize antique padlock, with original key, circa 1850, 26cm. high.
(Auction Team Köln) $157

A coppered and brass bound pitcher, early 20th century, 61cm. high.
(Bonhams) $257

An Enterprise Mfg. Co. Model 35 large fruit press, cast iron painted black with gold decoration, 8 quart capacity, circa 1880, 53cm. high.
(Auction Team Köln) $305

An unusual table fan-lamp with vertical fan beneath conical glass bulb, circa 1935.
(Auction Team Köln) $323

An unusual cast-iron and brass puzzle padlock, German, circa 1872, lacks key.
(Auction Team Köln) $169

A Heeley & Sons brass kingscrew corkscrew, English, late 19th century, the turned bone handle with ring and later brush, the barrel mounted with a badge.
(Bonhams) $418

A French hand-forged padlock, in pentagonal sheet-iron casing, the flap over the keyhole opening on pressure on the handle below right, circa 1850.
(Auction Team Köln) $97

HISTORICAL FACTS
Enamel

Real Battersea enamel was made in Battersea, at York House for only three years from 1753 to 1756, and it would be an understatement to say that pieces produced there at that time are extremely scarce. The term Battersea has come into popular use by the trade to describe most enamel boxes and trinkets, despite the fact that they are more likely to have been made at Wednesbury, South Staffordshire, Bilston or even last week in Czechoslovakia. Old examples should be surfaced with a substance similar to opaque glass applied over a copper base.

Pieces with any age are expensive trinkets but extremely pleasing. Decorated with a wide variety of subjects encompassing landscapes and seascapes, the most tender-hearted of these are love tokens and souvenirs from popular resorts.

Battersea enamel snuff box, with molded spaniel cover and landscape painted base, 3in. long. (Skinner) $1,265

Decorative enamel vase and cover, (non-matching), painted in colors with portraits of historical and allegorical figures, 19th century, 6½in. (G A Key) $320

A pair of George III enamel plaques, signed *W.H Craft, 1788*, each oval and depicting female allegorical figures in interior settings, 5½in. high. (Christie's) $5,762

An important silver and enamel exposition vase, Tiffany & Co. New York, 1893, made for the Columbian Exposition, design attributed to John T. Curran, 56oz 10dwt. gross, 14½in. high. (Christie's) $85,000

An enameled vase by Eugene Feuillatre, circa 1898, the copper body in midnight blue puzzled with pale lilac, decorated with a pink and ocher moth, 3½in. high. (Christie's) $3,312

A French ormolu and champlevé enamel strut toilet mirror, late 19th century, decorated with stylized flowering vine, 15¾in. high. (Christie's) $1,846

A silver and enamel card tray, Tiffany & Co. New York, circa 1910, raised on a foot rim, the field engraved with scrolling foliage radiating from a lozenge in the center, 9oz. gross, 6¾in. diameter. (Christie's) $3,450

A fan signed *Billotey*, the pink silk leaf painted with blue tits, bees and hydrangea, 14in., circa 1890. (Christie's) $1,288

Venus in her chariot drawn by dolphins, a painted fan, the ivory sticks carved and pierced, 10in., circa 1770. (Christie's) $662

Owl, signed *A. Thomasse*, a fan, the shaped silk leaf signed on verso *Duvelleroy, Paris*, with pierced gilt wooden sticks, circa 1918, 10in. (Christie's) $3,321

A fine fan signed *Gimbel inv et fec*, painted with a noble couple in a carriage attended by putti, 12in. circa 1880. (Christie's) $2,760

An ivory brisé fan lacquered in various golds with hiramakie and takamakie enriched with kirigame, 10in., Japanese, circa 1890. (Christie's) $6,440

Chemins de Fer de L'Ouest, a chromolithographic fan signed *E. Nerme,* with circular views of Trouville, Dinard, Dieppe, Dinan, Chateau de Combourg and Mont St. Michel, 13in., 1893. (Christie's) $1,749

A fan signed *Marie Peiler*, the silk leaf painted with eight cats watching a mouse, smokey gray mother of pearl sticks, 14in., late 19th century. (Christie's) $368

A fine fan by Alexandre, the leaf painted with a theatrical scene of lovers and attendants, the guardsticks carved in high relief, 11in., French, circa 1865. (Christie's) $18,400

An unusual tortoiseshell brisé fan, lacquered in silver with figures and buildings, 9in., Canton, mid-19th century. (Christie's) **$9,200**

A Canton ivory brisé fan with monogram *A.O.*, finely carved and pierced recto with figures, buildings and boats, 8in., circa 1820. (Christie's) **$736**

A chinoiserie fan, the leaf painted with three vignettes in the manner of Pillement, 11in., circa 1760. (Christie's) **$1,840**

A Canton ivory brisé cockade fan, carved and pierced with figures and a border of shells, 7in., circa 1820. (Christie's) **$1,472**

A silver handscreen, chased with flowers, and trimmed with peacock feathers, 15in. high, Indian, late 19th century. (Christie's) **$3,312**

Frederick, Prince of Wales, a printed fan, the leaf a hand-colored etching decorated with mother of pearl, ivory sticks, 11in., English, 1751. (Christie's) **$9,200**

A fan, the leaf painted with a classical scene, the verso with two figures in a landscape, ivory sticks painted, carved and pierced with putti, mid 19th century, 12in. (Christie's) **$664**

The Colosseum, Grand Tour fan, the chickenskin leaf painted with the Colosseum, 11in., Italian, with English sticks, circa 1770. (Christie's) **$1,749**

A printed silk dress, the textile produced by the Wiener Werkstätte, 1920s. (Christie's) $1,874

A short sleeved evening overdress of black tulle embroidered with self-colored beads forming geometric patterns, circa 1910-12. (Christie's) $1,650

A cocktail dress of gold colored tulle, embroidered with vertical bands of gold sequins, beads and opalescent sequins, mid 1920s. (Christie's) $640

A printed silk dress, textile designed by Max Snischek, 1926, produced by the Wiener Werkstätte, circa 1926. (Christie's) $2,999

A cocktail overtunic of jade green crepe embroidered in gold and silver sequins and beads with asymmetrical banding, 1920s. (Christie's) $645

A summer dress en princesse of ecru linen tamboured in ivory silks with stylized floral roundels and foliage, late 1870s. (Christie's) $330

A strapless cocktail dress of bottle green velvet appliqué with black cord and feathers, edged with a tulle frill, labeled *Christian Lacroix, Luxe, Paris.* (Christie's) $400

A cocktail dress of wine colored chiffon, the skirt embroidered with zigzags in bugle beads, 1920s, and a collar and skull cap. (Christie's) $1,147

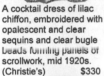

A cocktail dress of lilac chiffon, embroidered with opalescent and clear sequins and clear bugle beads forming panels of scrollwork, mid 1920s. (Christie's) $330

A short sleeved dress of ivory wool printed with various sprigs including thistles, roses and tulips, 1840s. (Christie's) $640

A cotton day dress, the white ground printed with small floral cones against a sawtooth ground, with pagoda sleeves, early 1850s. (Christie's) $400

A day dress of purple, bottle green and black striped shot silk, 1850s, with carriage parasol. (Christie's) $640

A very small unusual dress of mushroom and beige colored silk, labeled *Newberry*, circa 1876-8. (Christie's) $770

A cocktail overdress of black chiffon, embroidered all over with silver bugle beads forming a vermicular pattern, circa 1923. (Christie's) $1,100

A day dress of brown and ivory checked silk, late 1850s, and another of pale blue striped silk, circa 1860. (Christie's) $405

A cocktail dress of black muslin, embroidered with black, silver, ivory and clear beads and sequins, mid 1920s. (Christie's) $700

A short sleeved cocktail dress of black tulle embroidered in black beads and blue sequins, with shaped hem, circa 1926. (Christie's) $288

A dress of emerald green, black and white checked silk, the skirt with black velvet ribbon trimmed flounces, late 1850s. (Christie's) $440

A sleeveless cocktail dress of midnight blue velvet embroidered with copper colored, blue, green and pink beads. mid 1920s. (Christie's) $280

A sleeveless cocktail dress of ivory tulle embroidered with ivory bugle beads and opalescent sequins, circa 1926-7. (Christie's) $280

A long sleeved black tulle overdress with integral shaped waistcoat, embroidered in ivory cotton, with matching purse, early 1920s. (Christie's) $480

A long trained dressing sacque of lemon yellow nainsook, the outer layer with Valenciennes lace inserts, circa 1898. (Christie's) $405

An opera coat of emerald green satin, the sleeves and deep hem border of black velvet, labeled *Premet, Paris*, circa 1920. (Christie's) $272

A quilted dressing gown of emerald green silk lined in sugar pink silk, with open pleat at the back, 1890s, Japanese for Western export. (Christie's) $331

Continental metallic thread 'jeweled' bishop's miter, 19th century, filigree work depicting scrolling foliage, inset with paste stones, 16in. high.
(Skinner) $690

French embroidered bishop's robe, with floral designs and metallic threads, 18th century.
(Eldred's) $385

Parade fire hat, 19th century, painted leather, front with eagle and harp with banner above Hibernia, 6½in. high.
(Skinner) $3,335

A fine 'Paisley' shawl woven with a residual criciform center, the ends with cones and vegetation, probably French, circa 1863-5, 64 x 128in.
(Christie's) $560

Silk and gold threadwork dalmatic, in a brilliant flower and urn design, Italian, 18th century.
(Eldred's) $1,100

A cape of ivory satin woven with a grid of roundels enclosing pairs of doves in gilt colored threads, the hood and orphrey tamboured in colored silks, 20th century, Continental. (Christie's) $368

A black silk chiffon jacket, single tie opening, open half sleeves edged in black velvet, probably Austrian, 1920s. (Sotheby's) $1,480

An opera cape of rose pink velvet trimmed with a wide band of gold lamé, painted and applied with glitter forming stylized flowers, 1920s.
(Christie's) $560

A young child's dress of silk tartan, with short sleeves and pointed waist, with multicolored fringe and black silk braid trim, circa 1860.
(Christie's) $552

Johnny Guitar, 1953, Republic,
19½ x 14in.
(Christie's) $284

The Seven Samurai, 1954, Toho,
Japanese one-panel, 29 x 20in.
(Christie's) $4,554

King Kong, 1933, R.K.O., U.S. three-sheet, 81 x 41in., style A, linen backed, framed.
(Christie's) $47,438

The Maltese Falcon, 1941, Warner Bros., U.S. one-sheet, 41 x 27in., linen backed.
(Christie's) $5,313

Harvey, 1950, Universal, 22 x 14in.
(Christie's) $1,043

The Man Who Knew Too
Much/L'Homme Qui En Savait
Trop, 1956, Paramount, 15 x
21½in. (Christie's) $380

West Side Story, 1961, U.A., U.S.
one-sheet, 41 x 27in., linen backed.
(Christie's) $417

Goldfinger, 1964, U.A., complete set of four U.S. door panels, each – 60 x 20in., all linen backed. This is the
only known complete set for this title. (Christie's) $24,668

The Mummy/La Malediction des
Pharaons, 1958, Hammer, French,
63 x 47in., linen backed.
(Christie's) $950

An Affair To Remember, 1957,
T.F.C., British quad, 30 x 40in.,
linen backed.
(Christie's) $607

Lolita, 1962, M.G.M., German, 33 x
23in., linen backed.
(Christie's) $760

The Suspect/Le Suspect, 1944, Universal, 20 x 14in., linen backed. (Christie's) $342

It's A Wonderful Life, 1946, R.K.O., U.S. title card, 11 x 14in. (Christie's) $1,233

Houdini, 1953, Paramount, 22 x 13½in., paper backed. (Christie's) $530

Dial M For Murder, 1954, Warner Bros., U.S. one-sheet, 41 x 27in., linen backed. (Christie's) $2,087

A Dog's Life/Une Vie De Chien, 1918, First National, 10¼ x 16½in. (Christie's) $950

Brighton Rock, 1947, Associated British, British one-sheet, 40 x 27in., paper backed. (Christie's) $853

Vertigo, 1958, Paramount, U.S. one-sheet, 41 x 27in., linen backed. (Christie's) $2,657

Lawrence of Arabia/Lawrence D'Arabie, 1962, Colombia, French two-panel, 63 x 94in., linen backed. (Christie's) $3,226

Rear Window, 1954, Paramount, U.S. one-sheet, 41 x 27in., linen backed. (Christie's) $3,795

Key Largo, 1948, Warner Bros., 22 x 14in.
(Christie's) $1,422

Breakfast At Tiffany's, 1961, Paramount, U.S. quad, 30 x 40in., linen backed.
(Christie's) $2,277

Casablanca, 1942, Warner Bros., 15¼ x 11in.
(Christie's) $2,087

Destination Moon/Destination Lune! 1950, Universal, French, 63 x 47in. linen backed.
(Christie's) $1,422

The Spy With My Face, 1966, M.G.M., British quad, 30 x 40in.
(Christie's) $912

Battleship Potemkin/Potemkin, 1925, Goskino, German, 51 x 35in., linen backed.
(Christie's) $4,744

The Great Dictator/Le Dictateur 1940, U.A., 16 x 11in.
(Christie's) $1,043

Cover Girl/La Reine de Broadway, 1944, Columbia, French, 63 x 94in. linen backed.
(Christie's) $1,139

Raging Bull, 1980, U.A., advance U.S. one-sheet, 41 x 27in., linen backed. (Christie's) $1,100

Dr. Jekyll And Mr. Hyde, 1941,
M.G.M., 16 x 10½in.
(Christie's) $474

La Belle et la Bête, 1946, Discina,
French two-panel, 63 x 94cm., linen
backed.
(Christie's) $10,436

Dr. Cyclops, 1940, Paramount,
Italian four-foglio, 79 x 55in.
(Christie's) $1,518

A Hard Day's Night/Quatre Garçons
Dans Le Vent, 1964, U.A., 25 x
16in.
(Christie's) $760

Titanic, 1953, T.C.F., British quad,
30 x 40in.
(Christie's) $1,328

Reach For The Sky, 1956, Rank,
British three-sheet, 80 x 40in. linen
backed. (Christie's) $663

Hangmen Also Die, 1943, Arnold
Pressburger, U.S. one-sheet, 41 x
27in., linen backed.
(Christie's) $760

Moscow Nights/Noches De Moscu,
1936, London Films, Argentinian
two panel, 43 x 58in., linen backed.
(Christie's) $474

Les Enfants Terribles, 1947,
Gaumont, French, 63 x 47in., style
B, linen backed.
(Christie's) $13,283

La Belle et la Bête, 1946, Discina, French, 63 x 47in., style A, linen backed. (Christie's) $3,416

The Hunchback Of Notre Dame/Der Glöckner von Notre-Dame, 1923, Universal, German, 56 x 74in., linen backed. (Christie's) $4,934

Raffles, 1939, U.A., Argentinian, 43 x 29in., linen backed. (Christie's) $531

Fantasia, 1940, Disney, Swedish, 39 x 27in. (Christie's) $1,328

Goldfinger, 1964, U.A., British quad, 30 x 40in. (Christie's) $1,708

Dr. No, 1962, U.A., U.S. one-sheet, 41 x 27in., linen backed. (Christie's) $2,087

La Dolce Vita, 1960, Cineriz, Italian four-foglio, 79 x 55in., linen backed, style A. (Christie's) $5,693

Get Carter, 1971, M.G.M., British quad, 30 x 40in., paper backed. (Christie's) $797

To Have And Have Not/Le Port De L'Angoisse, 1945, Warner Bros., 15½ x 17in. (Christie's) $2,087

Montgomery Clift, signed postcard, head and shoulders.
(Vennett-Smith) $346

Silkwood, signed 8 x 10in., by Kurt Russell, Meryl Streep and Cher.
(Vennett-Smith) $82

Grace Kelly, signed 8 x 10in., head and shoulders.
(Vennett-Smith) $560

Mario Lanza, signed program, to photo front cover, British Concert Tour 1958, annotated in another hand to cover.
(Vennett-Smith) $248

Elizabeth Taylor, signed color magazine photo, 7$^{1}/_{2}$ x 9$^{1}/_{2}$in., half-length in fifties dress, with small diamond shape piece of matching pink paper.
(Vennett-Smith) $255

Bette Davis, signed 7$^{1}/_{2}$ x 9in., head and shoulders, from All About Eve, modern reproduction signed in later years.
(Vennett-Smith) $148

Eddie Murphy, signed color 8 x 10in., head and shoulders from Coming to America.
(Vennett-Smith) $100

Johnny Weissmuller, signed and inscribed 8 x 10in., head and shoulders, signed in later years.
(Vennett-Smith) $132

Robert Redford, signed color 8 x 10in., head and shoulders in evening suit.
(Vennett-Smith) $115

Carole Lombard, signed 5½ x 7in., in green, head and shoulders. (Vennett-Smith) $858

Keanu Reeves, signed color 8 x 10in., from Speed. (Vennett-Smith) $132

Stan Laurel, signed sepia 8 x 10in., head and shoulders. (Vennett-Smith) $346

Gene Kelly, signed 8 x 10in., head and shoulders in navy uniform, modern reproduction signed in later years. (Vennett-Smith) $115

Hoffman and Cruise, color 8 x 10in., from The Rain Man, signed by both Tom Cruise and Dustin Hoffman. (Vennett-Smith) $149

Ethel Merman, signed 8 x 10in., half-length in cocktail dress, modern reproduction signed in later years. (Vennett-Smith) $82

Noel Coward, signed 6 x 8in., head and shoulders, 1937, photo by Dorothy Wilding. (Vennett-Smith) $148

Audrey Hepburn, signed and inscribed 8 x 10in., head and shoulders. (Vennett-Smith) $182

Johnny Weissmuller, signed and inscribed postcard, full-length as Tarzan. (Vennett-Smith) $107

Gloria Swanson, signed 7½ x
9½in.
(Vennett-Smith) $206

Clara Bow, signed and inscribed
7 x 9in. sepia magazine photo.
(Vennett-Smith) $88

Jane Darwell, signed 8 x 10in.,
head and shoulders.
(Vennett-Smith) $875

Roscoe Fatty Arbuckle, signed and
inscribed sepia 7 x 9in., Paris, 2nd
April 1928.
(Vennett-Smith) $627

Shirley Temple, signed and
inscribed sepia 5 x 7in., as
teenager, head and shoulders in
hat.
(Vennett-Smith) $116

Harry Langdon, signed and
inscribed sepia 8 x 10in., sitting on
bench, first name only, rare.
(Vennett-Smith) $198

Helen Morgan, signed sepia 8 x
10in., head and shoulders, photo
by James Hargis Connelly.
(Vennett-Smith) $135

Thomas Michell, played Scarlett
O'Hara's father in Gone With the
Wind, small signed piece.
(Vennett-Smith) $91

Julia Roberts, signed and inscribed
color 8 x 10in., half-length in
brown dress, 1993.
(Vennett-Smith) $132

Ingrid Bergman, signed 6 x 4in., head and shoulders. (Vennett-Smith) $149

William Hurt, signed color 8 x 10in., head and shoulders, in silver. (Vennett-Smith) $66

Audrey Hepburn, signed 7 x 9½in., head and shoulders smiling. (Vennett-Smith) $225

Astaire and Rogers, signed 8 x 10in., head and shoulders, by Ginger Rogers and Fred Astaire. (Vennett-Smith) $462

Rita Hayworth, signed and inscribed 5 x 7in., head and shoulders smiling, together with typed signed letter, one page, 1958. (Vennett-Smith) $264

Jeanette Macdonald, signed and inscribed sepia 8 x 10in., full-length from The Girl of the Golden West. (Vennett-Smith) $173

Gary Cooper, signed sepia 5 x 7in., head and shoulders, partially in darker portion. (Vennett-Smith) $83

Stanley Baker, signed and inscribed 8 x 10in., head and shoulders in army uniform. (Vennett-Smith) $149

Audrey Hepburn, signed 8 x 10in., head and shoulders, signed in later years. (Vennett-Smith) $264

Douglas Fairbanks Snr., signed sepia 8 x 10in., head and shoulders.
(Vennett-Smith) $165

Harold Lloyd, signed and inscribed 10 x 8in., three quarter length standing alongside two young girls in bathing costumes, inscribed to his physician, 1932.
(Vennett-Smith) $180

Anna Paquin, signed 8 x 10in., head and shoulders from The Piano.
(Vennett-Smith) $58

Vivien Leigh, signed sepia 4½ x 6½in., head and shoulders in hat.
(Vennett-Smith) $264

Cary Grant, autographed signed letter, one page, 11th Dec. 1933, stating that he has no photos whilst in England, centerfold.
(Vennett-Smith) $264

Orson Welles, signed sepia 5 x 7in., head and shoulders, early.
(Vennett-Smith) $248

Joan Crawford, signed and inscribed 9 x 12½in. half-length seated in large hat.
(Vennett-Smith) $96

Indiana Jones, signed 8 x 10in., by both Harrison Ford and Sean Connery, from Indiana Jones and the Last Crusade.
(Vennett-Smith) $338

Fred Astaire, signed 8 x 10in., half-length smoking, reproduction signed in later years.
(Vennett-Smith) $132

Clara Bow, signed and inscribed
8 x 10in., full-length holding mink
stole.
(Vennett-Smith) $149

Errol Flynn, signed 7 x 9in. color
magazine photo, head and
shoulders.
(Vennett-Smith) $215

Mae West, signed sepia 8 x 10in.,
head and shoulders wearing black
hat.
(Vennett-Smith) $165

Katharine Hepburn, typed signed
letter, one page, 26th May 1976,
on Houghton Hepburn notepaper.
(Vennett-Smith) $165

Wizard of Oz, signed 8 x 10in., by
Ray Bolger and Jack Haley,
signed in later life, showing them
from the Wizard of Oz.
(Vennett-Smith) $230

Ingrid Bergman, signed and
inscribed 9 x 6¹/₂in. bookweight
photo.
(Vennett-Smith) $120

Harry Langdon, signed and
inscribed 7 x 9in., half-length in
comical pose.
(Vennett-Smith) $182

Richard Gere, signed color 8 x
10in., full-length squatting, 1992.
(Vennett-Smith) $107

Shirley Temple, signed and
inscribed sepia 5 x 7in., as
teenager.
(Vennett-Smith) $90

Lionel Barrymore, signed sepia
7¹/₂ x 9¹/₂in., head and shoulders.
(Vennett-Smith) $140

Will Rogers, signed postcard, head
and shoulders in profile.
(Vennett-Smith) $140

Errol Flynn, signed and inscribed
sepia 5 x 7in., head and shoulders.
(Vennett-Smith) $495

Mae West, signed and inscribed
8 x 10in., head and shoulders in
white furs.
(Vennett-Smith) $157

Laurel and Hardy, signed sepia
8 x 10in., by Stan Laurel (inscribed)
and Oliver Hardy, head and
shoulders in characteristic pose.
(Vennett-Smith) $842

Clark Gable, signed postcard, head
and shoulders, partial ink skipping
and bad contrast, corners clipped.
(Vennett-Smith) $248

Judy Garland, early signed sepia
5 x 7in.
(Vennett-Smith) $726

Will Rogers, signed 7¹/₂ x 10in.,
three quarter length in polo gear.
(Vennett-Smith) $215

Charles Boyer, signed 8 x 10in.,
head and shoulders.
(Vennett-Smith) $100

Lucille Ball, signed 6¹/₂ x 8¹/₂in., half-length, with rarer full signature. (Vennett-Smith) $140

Robert Donat, signed 6 x 8¹/₂in., head and shoulders. (Vennett-Smith) $85

John Wayne, signed postcard, head and shoulders. (Vennett-Smith) $248

Hugh Griffith, signed postcard, head and shoulders. (Vennett-Smith) $148

Marilyn Monroe, an 8 x 10in. black and white photograph signed and dedicated *To David, Marilyn Monroe*. (Bonhams) $4,480

Ward Bond, signed sepia 5 x 7in., head and shoulders. (Vennett-Smith) $85

Patrick Swayze, signed color 8 x 10in., head and shoulders, 1994. (Vennett-Smith) $63

Peter Lorre, signed 8 x 10in., half-length leaning against ladder. (Vennett-Smith) $206

Basil Rathbone, signed sepia postcard, head and shoulders. (Vennett-Smith) $264

Gary Cooper, signed postcard, head and shoulders.
(Vennett-Smith) $198

Lon Chaney Jnr., signed 10 x 8in. by Lon Chaney Jnr. and Evelyn Ankers.
(Vennett-Smith) $363

Bela Lugosi, signed postcard, head and shoulders as Dracula in red.
(Vennett-Smith) $545

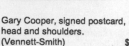

Margaret Rutherford, signed postcard, head and shoulders seated, photo by Vivienne.
(Vennett-Smith) $124

Steve McQueen, signed and inscribed 10 x 8in., on still from Love With the Proper Stranger.
(Vennett-Smith) $1,023

Laurel and Hardy, signed illustrated handbill, for the Garrick Theatre Southport, August 18th n.y., 5½ x 8½in.
(Vennett-Smith) $710

Shirley Temple, signed color postcard, as child, advert to reverse for Central Hall South Norwood.
(Vennett-Smith) $215

Ingmar Bergman, signed 10 x 8in., half-length alongside camera, with Sven Nykvest on the set of Fanny and Alexander.
(Vennett-Smith) $140

Cary Grant, signed and inscribed postcard, head and shoulders, dated to reverse 20.2.58.
(Vennett-Smith) $230

Harpo Marx, signed sepia postcard, half-length playing harp. (Vennett-Smith) $230

John Wayne, signed and inscribed colour 8 x 10in., full-length standing in costume as Rooster Cogburn. (Vennett-Smith) $627

Richard Burton, signed postcard, head and shoulders. (Vennett-Smith) $157

Bob Kane, original black ink sketch of The Joker, on 7 x 4½in. white card, signed. (Vennett-Smith) $297

Laurel and Hardy, signed and inscribed 9½ x 7½in., by both Stan Laurel and Oliver Hardy individually, half-length in characteristic pose. (Vennett-Smith) $760

Ingrid Bergman, color 10 x 13in., signed and inscribed to mount *Bob Woolfe 1945*, head and shoulders as Nun. (Vennett-Smith) $165

Veronica Lake, signed and inscribed postcard *Ronni*, head and shoulders looking over shoulder. (Vennett-Smith) $215

The Marx Brothers, a scarce early 8 x 10in., signed by all four, in a scene from one of their movies. (Vennett-Smith) $842

Sean Connery, signed and inscribed postcard, early, head and shoulders, dated to reverse *2.2.60*. (Vennett-Smith) $85

A cast-iron fire surround, designed by Hector Guimard, circa 1900, with red marble top, 31in. wide. (Christie's) $11,408

An early George II white statuary marble chimneypiece, attributed to Daniel Harvey (Hervé), the design attributed to James Gibbs, the rectangular shelf above a stiff-leaf and acanthus covered egg-and-dart molded cornice, 66¾in. wide. (Christie's) $40,089

Thomas Jeckyll for Barnard, Bishop and Barnard, fire surround, 1873, bronze frame cast with Japanese style badges, inset with Doulton tiles decorated with apple-blossom, iris blooms and butterflies, 45⁵∕₈in. (Sotheby's) $23,046

A cast iron fireplace designed by Hector Gummard, circa 1904, cast with typically stylized floral designs and floral motifs, 39in. wide. (Christie's) $12,851

A George II white statuary marble chimneypiece, attributed to Daniel Harvey (Hervé), the design attributed to James Gibbs, the foliate-molded rectangular shelf above a tapering egg-and-dart bed molding, 61¾in. wide. (Christie's) $258,130

A George II white statuary and Siena marble chimneypiece, attributed to Sir Henry Cheere, the foliate molded double-breakfront rectangular shelf supported by scrolled acanthus brackets punctuated by rosettes, 84¾in. wide. (Christie's) $367,690

Federal carved mantel, Hudson, New York, circa 1790, with raised panel of two carved fans, 87in. wide. (Skinner) $2,760

George III stripped pine and composition mantelpiece, late 18th century, central decoration depicting the flight of Athena, 74½in. wide. (Skinner) $2,990

A white painted pine and shell-decorated fireplace mantle, American, possibly New York, 1800–30, the reverse-breakfronted overhanging mantle above a recessed frieze, 5ft. 6in. wide. (Sotheby's) $10,925

Dixon & Sons cast iron fireplace surround, scroll design, impressed *Dixon & Sons, Philadelphia*, 34in. wide. (Skinner) $1,380

A carved mahogany overmantel and fireplace, designed by Louis Majorelle, circa 1900, carved with branches of pineapples, the upper section with large mirror surmounted by further carved details of pineapples supporting twin shelves, 54¼in. wide. (Christie's) $34,040

A pair of cast-iron owl andirons, American, 20th century, each cast in the half-round, perched on an arched branch, 21⁵/₈in. high. (Sotheby's) $690

Pair of 19th century brass andirons, crested with rosette motifs, 7½in. (G. A. Key) $112

Large pair of Scottish baroque style wrought iron and brass andirons, late 19th century, 36in. high. (Skinner) $1,093

A pair of French gothic style silver plated andirons of large size, French, early 20th century, the fronts with fleur de lys shields, 82cm. high. (Bonhams) $1,575

Gilbert Poillerat, pair of fire irons, circa 1930, wrought iron, each with a design of intertwined loops surmounted by a highly stylized crest, 13in. high. (Sotheby's) $23,046

A pair of Chippendale brass andirons, Rhode Island, third quarter 18th century, each with ball finial above a bulbous-ended shaft, 19½in. high. (Christie's) $4,830

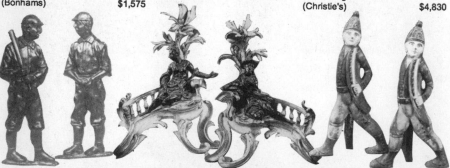

Pair of painted cast iron baseball player andirons, dated 1909, painted black, each with molded front depicting a baseball player in profile, 9¾in. high. (Eldred's) $1,430

A pair of Louis XV style ormolu and patinated bronze chenets, late 19th century, each cast as a Chinese man and woman seated against a balustrade, 19¼in. high. (Christie's) $2,760

A pair of polychrome-decorated cast iron Hessian soldier fireplace andirons, 19th/20th century, each figure looking left and holding a sword in mid-stride, 19½in. high. (Sotheby's) $575

A French bronze adjustable fender, last quarter 19th century, the uprights with flambeau and flowering urns, torches, bow and wreath mounts, on toupie feet, 48¼in. wide. extended. (Christie's) $1,292

A Victorian gilt brass and steel fender, the scrolling foliate pierced frieze centered with a cherub playing a lute, 42½in. wide. (Christie's) $2,030

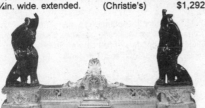

A French bronze adjustable fender, last quarter 19th century, the uprights modeled in relief as seated sphinxes, the rail with openwork running scroll frieze above a gadrooned border, 51in. wide extended. (Christie's) $2,399

A late Victorian brass fire-surround, the padded seat covered in nailed red leather, above turned supports on a molded plinth base 67in. wide. (Christie's) $6,601

Set of Egyptian Revival gilt bronze fireplace equipment, comprising a pair of andirons and a set of tools. (Skinner) $2,760

Edgar Brandt, cobra fire irons, circa 1925, black patinated wrought iron, fashioned as rearing serpents with spread hoods, 41in. wide. (Sotheby's) $61,289

A rare and early pair of brass and wrought-iron fireplace andirons, second half 17th century, each having a ball-and-steeple finial, 25½in. high. (Sotheby's) $2,587

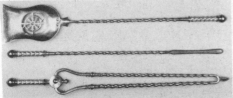

A set of Victorian steel and brass fire irons, mid 19th century, the lattice-work grips with knop pommels, with barley-twist shafts, the pierced shovel – 30in. long. (Christie's) $1,754

A set of Regency steel fire irons comprising; poker, shovel and tongs, the cylindrical shafts with knopped intersections, the baluster grips with urn-shaped finials. (Christie's) $1,570

A Napoleon III bronze adjustable fender, third quarter 19th century, the uprights modeled as swag-hung urns on square section plinths mounted with portrait roundels, 48½in. extended. (Christie's) $2,584

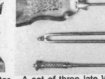

A set of three late William IV or early Victorian steel and brass fire irons, comprising ; poker, shovel and tongs, the grips cast with lappeted leafy panels below conforming mushroom-shaped pommels. (Christie's) $1,570

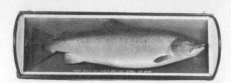

A pike by F. T. Williams & Co. of London, with gilt inscription *Pike, weight 11lbs., taken by E.E. Bunn at Stoke Newington. February 16th 1911,* case 40¾in. x 16½in. (Bonhams) **$547**

A P.D. Malloch mounted salmon within a barrel fronted black painted case inscribed *Salmon (Female) 39lbs. Caught by Archd. Coats, Stobhall, Sept. 3rd 1907,* 52in. wide overall. (Christie's) **$2,742**

A barbel by Gibson, mounted in a setting of grasses inscribed *Barbel – taken by Mr. H Lane at Cookham, 11th Dec 1886, wgt. 1lb. 14oz.,* case 22⅝ x 12¼in. (Bonhams) **$1,768**

A fine chub by W.F. Homer, mounted in a setting of reeds and grasses inscribed *Chub, 5lb. 3ozs. Caught by R. McIntosh in the River Thames, March 10th 1902,* case 26 x 13¾in. (Bonhams) **$1,366**

A very large Common Bream, mounted in a setting of reeds and grasses, *Bream – caught in Oxon gravel Pit, July 28th 1984, weight 11lbs. 11oz,* case 36 x 19¾in. (Bonhams) **$611**

A large and rare case by J. Cooper & Sons, containing eight roach and two chub, 50⅝ x 30½in., card inscribed *caught by J. Ambley on the River Thames at Bray Lock, Oct 6th 1908. Total weight 17lbs. 6ozs.* (Bonhams) **$4,180**

A fine brown trout by J. Cooper & Sons, mounted in a setting of grasses bearing inscription *Trout, caught by R. Mead, Sept. 1938, weight 7lbs,* case 29 x 13½in. (Bonhams) **$1,447**

A rare treble case of trout by J. Cooper & Sons, the three different species of trout mounted swimming in different directions, case 33 x 15½in. (Bonhams) **$2,251**

A pike by J. Cooper & Sons, with inscription *Pike taken by Lewis Cotton from 'The Dyke' Wycombe, June 19th 1896, weight 18¼lbs.* 44 x 17½in. (Bonhams) $788

A pike, attributed to Cooper, mounted in a setting of reeds and grasses, gilt inscription *Pike. Caught by W. Webster in the River Lovett, March 3rd 1912. Weight 9lbs. 8oz.* Case 38 x 15¼in. (Bonhams) $965

A Roach by J. Cooper & Sons, mounted in a setting of reeds and grasses inscribed *Roach, caught in the Avon, Malmsbury, Wilts – October 1904 – weight 2½lbs,* case 20¾ x 13½in. (Bonhams) $1,206

Four roach, mounted in a setting of grasses, bearing inscription *Roach – caught at Tring reservoir by Mr. W. Cheeld,* case 37¼ x 22½in. (Bonhams) $772

A fine grayling by J. E. Miller of Leeds, mounted in a setting of reeds and grasses, reading *Grayling 1lb. 8ozs., caught by S. Millward. Leeds City Angling Club, 10th Sept. 1907.,* case 20¾ x 12¼in. (Bonhams) $2,250

The current British Record wild brown trout, mounted against a green background, *British Record wild Brown Trout (Salmo Trutta) Caught by A. Finlay – Loch Awe, 7th April 1996. Wgt. 25lbs. 5¾ozs.,* case 44¾in. x 19¾in. (Bonhams) $5,466

A mirror carp by J. Cooper & Sons, mounted in a setting of reed and grasses, inscription *Mirror Carp. Caught by W. Webster, October 1933, weight 14lbs. 8ozs.,* case 36¾ x 17½in. (Bonhams) $965

A fine Roach by W. F. Homer, mounted in a setting of reeds and grasses, inscription *Roach, 1lb. 14oz. caught at Oxted by E. Smith Jnr. 15th July 1930,* case 21½ x 12½in. (Bonhams) $1,286

A perch by J. Cooper, mounted in a setting of reeds and moss against a light blue background, case 19¾ x 12½in. (Bonhams) $1,286

A zander, details to case *Zander; caught in the Serpentine, Sept. 1984, weight 9lbs. 12ozs.*, case 33¾ x 16in. (Bonhams) $482

A tench by W. F. Homer, mounted in a setting of reeds and grasses with red groundwork against a green reed painted background in a gold lined bowfronted case. Gold inscription to case *'Tench 5lbs. 4 ozs. caught in "Daventry Reservoir" by J. Parker. July 8th 1908'*, case 25¾ x 14½in. (Bonhams) $1,120

An early pair of brown trout by J. Cooper & Son, mounted one above the other in a setting of reeds, 21¼in. x 19½in. x 5¼in. (Bonhams) $1,366

A common bream by Saunders, mounted in a setting of reeds and grasses against a reed painted blue background, 21 x 13in. (Bonhams) $402

A carp by J. Thorn, mounted in a setting of reeds against a green background in a gilt lined bowfronted case with card to interior inscribed *Carp - taken at Walton on Thames by J. Woodhouse, July 2nd 1899, weight 4½ lbs.*, case 29¾ x 12½in. (Bonhams) $1,120

A carved wooden and painted salmon mounted on a stained wooden backboard inscribed, *46½lbs/caught by H.J.T./ in Two Stones pool, Delfur/ April 29, 1922, in one hour/ Length 52inches./ Girth 25½inches*, 60in. wide. (Christie's) $3,784

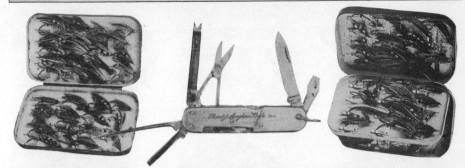

A Hardy black japanned fly box, containing 37gut-eyed dressed salmon flies, 3 to 6/0 size.
(Christie's) $454

A Hardy Bros. No. 4 angler's knife, with large blade marked *Taylor Sheffield,* screw driver/bottle opener, scissors, tweezers, stiletto, file/discorger, together with a Hardy discorger.
(Bonhams) $354

A Malloch's black japanned salmon fly box, containing 30 gut-eyed and 15 metal-eyed salmon flies.
(Christie's) $434

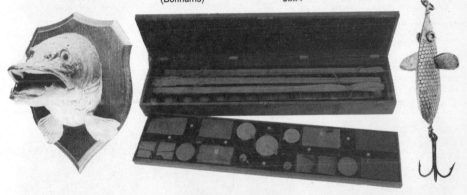

A pike head on a wood shield by Rowland Ward of Piccadilly, with Roland Ward Ltd labels to reverse of shield.
(Bonhams) $547

A fine and rare fisherman's brass-bound mahogany tackle case by J. Jones, circa 1850; the lift-out tray with velvet lined compartments, 52½in. long.
(Sotheby's) $17,492

A rare late Victorian unnamed glass-eyed spinning bait, attributed to Gregory.
(Bonhams) $547

A rare late Victorian 'Wheeldon' type spinning bait attributed to Gregory, the 2½in. brass lure gilded to the underside.
(Bonhams) $1,206

A fitted brown leather covered tackle case, containing two Ogden Smiths built cane trout fly rods, the base compartments with an Ogden Smiths 'Reversa' net.
(Bonhams) $576

A Hardy's No. 1 angler's knife, with stainless steel blade marked *Howill & Sons, Sheffield,* stiletto and scissors.
(Bonhams) $482

An Abu Abassadeur 6000 Baitcaster, red finish, cased. (Christie's) $130

All brass clamp-foot winch, 2in. diameter, lacking handle. (Christie's) $400

An Abu 5001 C, red finish, cased. (Christie's) $130

A Farlow, 3¾in., brass salmon reel, 191 Strand address, ivory handle and reduced foot, engraved with name. (Christie's) $207

A Hardy, the 'Bougle Mark II' 3in., alumin alloy reel, ebonite handle, reduced brass foot, three pillars, one with roller. (Christie's) $984

A Hardy, The 'Perfect', 4in. alloy reel, wide-drum, post-war double-check, straightline logos, grooved brass foot. (Christie's) $303

A Hardy, The 'Silex Major' 4in. alloy reel, twin black handles, grooved brass foot, shortened on one side, ivorine brake handle. (Christie's) $207

A Hardy, The 'Perfect', 3¾in., alloy reel, wide drum Eunuch with 1912 check, short fat ivorine handle, brass foot, central circular logo. (Christie's) $650

A Hardy, The 'Perfect Taupo', 3⅞in., alloy reel, black handle, straightline logo, smooth chrome foot, rim tension adjuster. (Christie's) $530

A Yawman and Erbe automatic fly reel, marked with patent Feb 28th 1888 and June 16th 1891; with four others. (Christie's) $359

A Hardy, The 'Field', 2⅞in. alloy reel, wide drum, smooth brass foot (bent), ivorine handle, stamped *The 'Field'* (Christie's) $795

A Hardy's 2¾in. brass faced 'Perfect' trout fly reel, circa 1900, with brassbridged rim tension regulator screw, ivorine handle. (Bonhams) $804

An all brass clamp-foot winch,
2¼in. diameter, with crank winding
arm, no handle.
(Christie's) $420

An Abu Ambassadeur 9000
Baitcaster, red finish, cased; and
boxed. (Christie's) $245

An ABU Ambassadeur 5000c De-
luxe multiplier, complete with spare
spool and instruction leaflet in
maker's teak case.
(Bonhams) $386

A Hardy The 'Perfect', 4¼in., brass-
faced reel, ivorine handle, strapped
rim-tension adjuster with a turk's
head locking nut, 1906 check.
(Christie's) $719

A rare 2⅝in. Hardy all brass
Transitional 'Perfect' trout fly reel,
circa 1894-5, with open ball race
and brass bearings.
(Bonhams) $1,010

A Hardy, The 'Super Silex', 4in.,
alloy reel, twin ebonite handles,
grooved brass foot, ivorine
quadrant casting regulator, ivorine
brake handle.
(Christie's) $434

A Hardy, The 'St. George', 3in. fly
reel, slim ivorine handle, chrome
foot, three rivet drum latch, single
check mechanism, circa 1920, with
a Hardy box. (Christie's) $661

An Edward Vom Hofe '504', 4¼in.,
6/0 multiplier reel, ebonite and
German silver, balanced S-shaped
handle, check button and
adjustable tension dial.
(Christie's) $2,081

A Holroyd 4¼in., brass-faced
salmon reel, ebonite with brass rims
and foot, horn handle, inscribed
*Holroyd / Maker / 59 Gracechurch
St / London.* (Christie's) $378

A Hardy's The 'Perfect' 3⅛in. alloy
trout fly reel, 1896 check, ivorine
handle, bridged rim tension
regulator. (Bonhams) $241

A Charles Farlow, 4¼in., brass
salmon reel, ivory handle, foot with
fish logo, 191 Strand address.
(Christie's) $303

A Hardy, The 'St. George', 3in. fly
reel, black handle, chrome foot, two
screw drum latch, double check
mechanism. (Christie's) $434

A Spanish gilt and painted wood frame, 17th century, the inner border with beaded decoration, outer dimensions 17¹/₂ x 14³/₄in. (Sotheby's) $3,450

A Louis XVI giltwood frame, 18th century, with beaded inner border and stylized acanthus outer border, outer dimensions 39¹/₂ x 19in. (Sotheby's) $7,475

An Italian giltwood frame, 17th century, boldly carved with deep, strapwork and foliate scrolls, outer dimensions 42 x 36in. (Sotheby's) $2,875

An Italian (Veneto?) octagonal giltwood frame, early 17th century, with punched design of undulating foliage within two molded borders, outer dimensions 19¹/₂ x 15in. (Sotheby's) $1,150

A French 19th century carved and gilded Louis XIV style frame, with foliate sight, sanded frieze and cross-hatched ogee, 56.5 x 47.6 x 15.5cm. (Bonhams) $1,120

A Flemish ebony-veneered wood frame, 17th century, elaborately worked with various wavy, patterned and basket-weave borders, outer dimensions 34 x 26¹/₂in. (Sotheby's) $2,875

A Règence carved and gilded frame with strapwork and palmette sight, plain ogee with scallopshell cartouche centers, 71.5 x 58.7 x 13.3cm. (Bonhams) $1,280

A Spanish gilt and painted frame, 17th century, the broad border of corrugated motif and faux-tortoiseshell decoration, 31 x 25¹/₄in. (Sotheby's) $4,887

A Florentine 19th century carved, pierced and gilded frame, with foliate sight, cavetto, double bead and reel, 77.8 x 62.2 x 14cm. (Bonhams) $1,920

A French Provincial cream painted and parcel-gilt decorated armoire, 19th century, decorated with foliate carvings, 36½in. wide. (Christie's) $3,322

A William and Mary paneled gumwood kas, New York or New Jersey, 1730–80, in three parts, 6ft. 4½in. wide. (Sotheby's) $4,600

A French Provincial oak armoire, 19th century, decorated with foliate and stiff-leaf carvings, 58in. wide. (Christie's) $3,322

A French ebonized armoire, probably Normandy, in Baroque style, the molded overhanging bracketed and dentiled cornice over a pair of doors, 56½in. wide. (Sotheby's) $5,520

A Napoleon III ormolu and pietra dura mounted ebonized armoire, third quarter 19th century, by Charles-Guillaume Diehl, 60in. wide. (Christie's) $5,175

A kingwood gilt-bronze and parquetry armoire, by François Linke, Paris, circa 1890, with a pair of quarter-veneered paneled doors, 160cm. wide. (Sotheby's) $22,575

A pair of Louis XV style gilt-bronze mounted black lacquer bas d'armoires, French, late 19th century, each with a later molded gray and red mottled marble top, 75cm. wide. (Sotheby's) $9,373

A Napoleonic III ormolu-mounted brass inlaid black-lacquer armoire, third quarter 19th century, with an egg-and-dart molded rectangular cornice above a leaf-tip cast frieze, 49in. wide. (Christie's) $5,750

A classical figured mahogany armoire, labeled by Joseph Meeks & Sons, New York, circa 1835, two lancet-arched paneled doors flanked by free-standing columnar supports, 5ft. 9in. wide. (Sotheby's) $6,325

A Continental walnut bed, 19th century, the headboard centred by a blank cartouche flanked by dolphin grotesques, 61½in. wide. (Sotheby's) $4,600

A marquetry and gilt-bronze bed, French, circa 1880, in the manner of Riesener, the head board with a guilloche border, 171cm. wide. (Sotheby's) $12,184

A kingwood and gilt-bronze bed, Paris, circa 1880, with a shaped crossbanded and quarter-veneered headboard, 134cm. wide. (Sotheby's) $5,958

A Jacobean oak full tester bed, 17th century, the underside of the canopy with recessed panels supported on a headboard, 50½in. wide. (Sotheby's) $4,312

A George III oak metamorphic bureau-bed, the rectangular top above a hinged slope and four simulated long drawers enclosing a folding bed, 43½in. wide. (Christie's) $12,825

A fine Federal figured mahogany four-post bedstead, Philadelphia, circa 1800, the horizontal box tester on flaring ring-turned supports, 6ft. 8in. long. (Sotheby's) $2,300

A late Federal turned maple bedstead, Pennsylvania, circa 1830, with acorn finials on reel- and vase-turned posts, 4ft. 4in. wide. (Sotheby's) $2,587

A 17th century oak crib with canopy and carved floral panels decorated with turned finials and raised on splay feet, 17½ x 40in. long. (Anderson & Garland) $1,431

A Portuguese Colonial Baroque mother-of-pearl and ivory inlaid jacaranda bedstead, mid-18th century, with elaborately carved and shaped headboard, 6ft. 4½in. wide. (Sotheby's) $9,200

A William IV mahogany bookcase, the molded and tasseled cornice above two sections of six open adjustable shelves, 130in. wide.
(Christie's) $14,996

A Victorian oak breakfront bookcase, the molded cornice with swan-neck pediment, carved with scrolling vines centered by a cartouche, 85in. wide.
(Christie's) $7,378

A George III style mahogany breakfront library bookcase, on a base with acanthus leaf carved cabriole legs and ball and claw feet, 98in. wide.
(Hy. Duke & Son) $2,880

Edwardian rosewood serpentine shaped revolving bookcase the top inlaid with bows and arrows and scrolling foliage, fret cut end brackets, 20in.
(Ewbank) $1,980

A large Victorian mahogany breakfront bookcase with a flared cornice above seven glazed panel doors enclosing adjustable shelves, 156in. wide.
(Anderson & Garland) $13,038

An early 20th century chinoiserie black lacquer revolving bookcase, the black and gilt decorated top with gadrooned edge, 46cm. wide.
(Bristol) $705

A George IV ivory-inlaid rosewood bookcase, the molded rectangular cornice above a plain frieze inlaid with lozenges and a pair of glazed doors, 69½in. wide.
(Christie's) $10,373

One of a pair of George IV rosewood breakfront low open bookcases, each with a rectangular top above a plain frieze, the central section with two shelves flanked by panels, 60¼in. wide.
(Christie's) (Two) $47,150

A late Victorian oak bookcase, the molded and dentiled cornice fitted with three glazed doors, the base with three frieze drawers above three paneled cupboard doors, 71in. wide.
(Christie's) $2,024

A Dutch walnut and floral marquetry breakfront bookcase, the molded cornice above an ogee frieze, 126in. wide.
(Christie's) $15,272

An Edwardian mahogany and crossbanded revolving bookcase, the top with central fan inlaid decoration, 20in.
(Dreweatt Neate) $785

An early Victorian mahogany breakfront bookcase, the architectural pediment above a molded cornice, 120in. wide.
(Christie's) $8,539

A mahogany bookcase, the molded cornice with a scrolling foliate-carved frieze above a pair of astragal glazed doors, 45in. wide.
(Christie's) $3,322

A pair of rosewood and parcel-gilt dwarf open bookcases, 20th century, each with a white marble top above adjustable shelves, 48in. wide. (Christie's) $11,997

A carved painted and parcel-gilt bibliothèque, French, circa 1890, with a scroll cresting above a pair of doors, carved with arrows and with grills, 100cm wide.
(Sotheby's) $3,430

An early Victorian mahogany breakfront bookcase, the stepped molded cornice above four astragal glazed doors enclosing adjustable shelves, 102in. wide.
(Christie's) $13,289

A rosewood dwarf open bookcase, early 19th century, of broken outline, with two simulated rosewood open shelves between acanthus-carved column uprights, 43in. wide.
(Christie's) $2,399

A kingwood and gilt-bronze bookcase, Paris, circa 1880, the bleu turquin molded top above a frieze cast with foliage, 91cm. wide.
(Sotheby's) $7,583

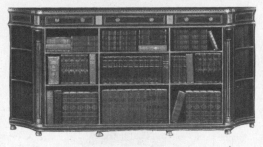

An ebonized and scarlet veneered brass-inlaid bookcase, late 19th/early 20th century, decorated with premier partie scrolling foliage palmettes and C-scrolls, 51¾in. wide. (Christie's) $5,537

A parcel-gilt and bronzed dwarf open bookcase, the shallow shaped breakfront green leather-inset top with three-quarter pierced ormolu gallery, 76½in. wide. (Christie's) $11,454

A satinwood bookcase, 19th century, decorated with lines and tulipwood crossbanding, 54in. wide. (Christie's) $9,229

A walnut glazed bookcase, attributed to J.G. Crace after a design by A.W.N. Pugin, circa 1852/3, 74in. wide. (Christie's) $19,682

A 19th century mahogany and ebony line inlaid bookcase with dentil cornice above four astragal glazed doors, 96in. wide. (Ewbank) $9,600

An early Victorian mahogany bookcase, the projecting base fitted with six panel doors between paneled angles, 135in. wide. (Christie's) $12,920

A 19th century mahogany bookcase with two glazed doors enclosing shelves, one drawer under, 49in. wide. (Ewbank) $2,378

An Edwardian satinwood, cream-painted and parcel-gilt breakfront side cabinet, on acanthus-carved legs with bun feet, 78in. wide. (Christie's) $6,460

An oak bookcase, designed by E.W. Godwin for Dromore Castle, Ireland, manufactured by William Watt, circa 1869/70, 49in. wide maximum. (Christie's) $28,117

HISTORICAL FACTS
Bureau
Bookcases

The earliest Queen Anne bureau cabinets had paneled doors to the upper section, often containing Vauxhall mirror glass, which enclosed a multitude of small drawers and pigeon holes.

Since bureau bookcase carcasses tend to be very similar, the pattern made by the glazing bars is a good aid to establishing the date of a piece. Unfortunately, however, it is not infallible, since many of the designs were used throughout the different periods.

Broadly, however, in the late 17th century, the glazing was of plain rectangles secured with putty behind substantial, half round moldings. In the 1740s, the glass was mounted in a wavy frame and the establishment of mahogany soon after meant that, by the 1740s, the glazing bars could be finer and more decorative - usually forming 13 divisions or shaped in the fashion of Gothic church windows.

At the end of the 18th century, Hepplewhite introduced diamond glazing and also flowing curves and polygonal shapes, often enriched with foliate designs, in the glazing of his furniture. Sheraton too, used similar forms, often enhanced by their super-impositions on pleated silks.

Most reproductions of this period are of plain mahogany enhanced with a boxwood string inlay and a conch shell in the center of the bureau flap.

A George III mahogany bureau-bookcase, crossbanded with string inlay, on bracket feet, 48in. wide. (Andrew Hartley) $4,800

George II burl walnut secretary/bookcase, second quarter 18th century, 39½in. wide. (Skinner) $5,750

A Provincial George I carved oak double bonnet-top bureau bookcase, first quarter 18th century, on cabriole legs ending in square pad feet, 36in. wide. (Sotheby's) $2,530

A Chippendale carved cherrywood secretary bookcase, New England, probably Connecticut, circa 1780, in two parts, the upper section with shaped cornice, 44in. wide. (Sotheby's) $5,462

A William and Mary walnut bureau-cabinet, inlaid overall with ash feather-banding, the arched bolection cornice above a pair of doors inlaid with arches, 40in. wide. (Christie's) $16,974

A Chippendale figured cherrywood secretary bookcase, Connecticut, circa 1780, in two parts, on ogee bracket feet, 38in. wide. (Sotheby's) $4,312

A George III mahogany bureau, the later bookcase top with molded cornice fitted with a pair of geometrically glazed doors, 48in. wide. (Christie's) $4,773

A Dutch walnut and floral marquetry bureau cabinet, 19th century, the architectural pediment above an arched mirrored door, 42in. wide. (Christie's) $16,560

A North European black and gilt-japanned and ebony bureau-cabinet-on-stand, decorated overall with Chinese rural and fishing scenes, 26¼in wide. (Christie's) $20,999

A mid-Georgian mahogany bureau bookcase, the molded cornice fitted with a pair of paneled cupboard doors, 38in. wide. (Christie's) $5,520

A George I stained field-maple bureau-cabinet, in the manner of Coxed and Woster, inlaid overall with pewter lines and crossbanded in walnut and rosewood, 40in. wide. (Christie's) $28,635

A Chippendale carved and figured walnut secretary bookcase, Pennsylvania, circa 1770, in two parts, on ogee bracket feet, 39in. wide. (Sotheby's) $24,150

A George III mahogany bureau bookcase with molded and drop bead decorated cornice, a pair of astragal glazed doors enclosing, adjustable sliding shelves, 41in. wide. (Dreweatt Neate) $9,578

A fine and rare Federal inlaid and figured mahogany secretary bookcase, attributed to John Shaw, Annapolis, Maryland, circa 1795, in three parts, 42in. wide. (Sotheby's) $19,550

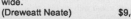

The writing desk was born in the monasteries of the Middle Ages, originally as a small, Gothic style oak box with a sloping lid hinged at the back like old fashioned school desk tops.

As time passed and men of letters increased their output, the writing box grew and was made a permanent fixture in the copying rooms of the monasteries, being built upon a stand, usually high enough to be used by a man standing or seated on a high stool.

Later, the hinges of the lid were moved from the back to the front, allowing the lid to fall forward on supports and form a writing platform in the open position. The practice on the Continent was to cover this area with a 'burel' or russet cloth, probably named from the Latin *burrus* (red), the color of the dye used in its manufacture. It is doubtless from here that we gain the word bureau, though the connotations of the word have changed somewhat since it was first coined.

The bureau remained little more than a box on a stand until the close of the 17th century when it was married to a chest of drawers for obvious practical reasons. From that time onward, there have been few changes in the design beyond relatively small stylistic alterations, which were reflections of the changing tastes of the fashionable rather than modifications dictated by practical usage.

A kingwood and tulipwood crossbanded cylinder desk, of Louis XV style, on slender cabriole supports, 31in. wide.
(Christie's) $1,233

An 18th century Dutch marquetry bureau, the fall front enclosing stepped interior with well.
(Jacobs & Hunt) $4,960

A Federal inlaid and figured mahogany slant-front desk, Baltimore, Maryland, circa 1805, the molded hinged rectangular lid inlaid with a central oval reserve, 39½in. wide.
(Sotheby's) $3,737

A Wylie & Lochhead Arts & Crafts oak and stained glass bureau, by E.A. Taylor, two rectangular doors inset with leaded and stained glass panels, 30in. wide.
(Christie's) $16,660

Chippendale maple slant lid desk, New England, late 18th century, with a stepped interior of small compartments, flanking a prospect door, 36½in. wide.
(Skinner) $4,600

A Chippendale figured walnut slant-front desk, Pennsylvania, circa 1780, the case with four graduated thumbmolded long drawers, 40in. wide.
(Sotheby's) $4,887

American Chippendale four-drawer slant-lid desk, in tiger maple, ogee bracket base, 38³/₄in. wide. (Eldred's) $12,650

Edwardian paint decorated satinwood lady's slant front writing desk, circa 1900–10, 24¹/₄in. wide. (Skinner) $2,415

George III style mahogany and marquetry slant lid desk, 19th century, 33in. wide. (Skinner) $1,840

Chippendale maple and tiger maple slant lid desk, New England, late 18th century, the fall front opens to an interior of valanced compartments and drawers, 37in. wide. (Skinner) $2,415

A Federal cherrywood slant-front desk, Mid-Atlantic States, circa 1800, the rectangular top with hinged slant-front lid opening to a shell-carved prospect door, 45in. wide. (Sotheby's) $4,025

Chippendale mahogany carved fall front desk, probably Newport, Rhode Island, circa 1750, the fall front above a case of four thumbmolded graduated drawers, 37in. wide. (Skinner) $29,900

Chippendale painted maple fall front desk, probably Massachusetts, circa 1750, on bracket feet centering a carved fan pendant, 38in. wide. (Skinner) $4,312

Art Deco period limed oak bureau cabinet, the fall front enclosing a fitted interior, flanked on either side by two open shelves over cupboards, possibly by Heal & Co., 41½in. (G. A. Key) $704

Chippendale maple slant lid desk, Rhode Island, 18th century, the interior with scrolled and valanced compartments above two tiers of small drawers, 36³/₄in. wide. (Skinner) $6,325

A black lacquer and gilt-bronze bureau en pente after Vanrisamburgh, Paris, circa 1880, the shaped hinged front decorated with landscapes, 66cm. wide. (Sotheby's) $16,871

A fine mahogany, marquetry and gilt-bronze cylinder bureau, Paris, circa 1870, after a model by Jean Henri Riesener, 144cm. wide. (Sotheby's) $31,867

A parquetry and gilt-bronze bureau de dame, Paris, circa 1880, in the manner of Charles Cressent, surmounted by a cherub upholding a timepiece, 100cm. wide. (Sotheby's) $65,383

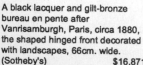

A late 18th century colonial padouk wood bureau, the sloping flap with an indistinct description, on bracket feet, 42¾in. wide. (Bearne's) $3,078

A George I walnut bureau, cross and feather-banded overall, the rectangular top above a sloping fall-front enclosing a green leather-lined writing-surface, 38in. wide. (Christie's) $18,136

A Queen Anne burr-walnut and walnut bureau, feather-banded to the front and top, the rectangular top above a sloping fall-flap, 38¼in. wide. (Christie's) $43,378

A rare William and Mary mahogany slant-front desk, Philadelphia, 1730–50, the rectangular top with molded gallery above a slant-front, 39in. wide. (Sotheby's) $49,450

A Chippendale carved walnut slant-front desk, Philadelphia, 1760–80, the rectangular hinged thumbmolded slant-lid opening to a fitted interior, 39¼in. wide. (Christie's) $5,750

A George I walnut bureau, decorated with feather bandings enclosing a fitted interior, above two short and two long drawers, 31in. wide. (Christie's) $5,906

An early 18th century burr yew-veneered bureau, upper section on later stand, with boxwood line inlay, 38¹/₂in. wide.
(Bearne's) $1,490

A bois satiné and gilt-bronze cylinder bureau, French, circa 1890, the shaped top centered by a clock with a white enamel dial signed *Leroy, Paris*, 107cm. wide.
(Sotheby's) $9,551

An Italian rosewood, fruitwood and marquetry bureau en pente, late 19th century, decorated with meandering floral sprays, 30in. wide. (Christie's) $4,614

A South German walnut serpentine bureau, 18th century, decorated with crossbanding, the fall front enclosing a fitted interior, 40in. wide.
(Christie's) $6,276

A fine and rare Chippendale carved walnut and cherrywood serpentine-front slant front desk, signed by John Shearer, Martinsburg, Virginia, dated *1805*, 39in. wide.
(Sotheby's) $28,750

A very fine and rare Chippendale carved and figured mahogany slant-front desk with blocked lid, Salem, Massachusetts, circa 1765, 41¹/₂in. wide.
(Sotheby's) $101,500

A George III mahogany bureau, the sloping flap enclosing a simple fitted interior, four graduated long drawers below, 38¹/₂in. wide.
(Bearne's) $1,944

A George I walnut bureau, crossbanded overall and feather-banded to the top and front, 37½in. wide. (Christie's) $7,544

A good Chippendale carved and figured mahogany slant-front desk, Newport, Rhode Island, 1770–80, 39¹/₄in. wide.
(Sotheby's) $8,050

A Victorian walnut and boxwood strung music cabinet, the top with a pierced brass gallery, enclosed by a glazed door, 22½in. wide. (George Kidner) $1,573

A chinoiserie lacquered black ground cabinet in early 18th century style, with ornate chased brass mounts, 36in. wide. (David Lay) $1,884

A Victorian walnut and gilt metal mounted pier cabinet, circa 1880, the boxwood strung top above a conforming frieze, 31in. wide. (Bonhams) $874

A French red Boulle work cabinet with black marble top above the leaf molded frieze, a panel door below, 30in. wide. (Anderson & Garland) $1,381

A 19th century burr walnut side cabinet by Marsh, Jones and Cribb, of inverted breakfront form, 70in. wide. (Andrew Hartley) $3,360

A Louis XVI style kingwood bombé cabinet with a marble top above the single drawer and paneled door decorated with vernis martin style panels, 40in. wide. (Anderson & Garland) $2,067

A fine quality burr walnut collectors' cabinet with five drawers enclosed by a pair of panel doors, 13½ x 17¼in. (Anderson & Garland) $826

A Continental gothic style walnut side cabinet, French or Italian, with two-part hinged top opening to a well, 52in. wide. (Sotheby's) $4,887

A French walnut cabinet à deux corps in Renaissance style, 19th century, the molded overhanging cornice above a frieze, 65½in. wide. (Sotheby's) $5,462

Continental gothic style carved oak cabinet, late 19th century, 40¾in. wide.
(Skinner) $2,300

A Dutch Renaissance oak two-part cabinet, the molded rectangular top over a paneled door flanked by fluted stiles, 38½in. wide.
(Sotheby's) $3,737

Napoleon III ormolu mounted boulle marble top side cabinet, third quarter 19th century, 33in. wide.
(Skinner) $575

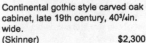

One of a fine pair of French Boulle pier cabinets, in the manner of Pierre Etienne Levasseur, circa 1840, with carrara marble slabs above concealed frieze drawers, 34½in. wide.
(Bonhams) (Two) $7,632

A 19th century Continental ebonized and ivory inlaid pedestal side cabinet, the lower center section with turned ivory balustrade, 94in. wide.
(Andrew Hartley) $2,240

American two-part kitchen cabinet, in walnut, upper section with beveled cornice and beaded molding above two three-light doors, probably Pennsylvania, 48in. wide.
(Eldred's) $1,100

An Art Deco bird's-eye maple cocktail cabinet, 1930s, by S. Hille & Co. Ltd., with large silvered carved shell motif support, 94.5cm. wide.
(Bristol) $3,936

A French marquetry inlaid breakfront side cabinet, circa 1890, the top with a gilt metal molded edge above a scrolled floral inlaid frieze, 47in. wide.
(Bonhams) $5,406

An Italian walnut two-part cabinet in Renaissance style, with molded rectangular top over a pair of paneled doors, 33in. wide.
(Sotheby's) $11,500

A Dutch mahogany and checker lined opflaptafel, the hinged rectangular top with canted angles, enclosing a divided interior and a shelf, 50in. wide.
(Christie's) $3,680

A mid 18th century Dutch mahogany and marquetry cabinet, the bombé base with two brushing slides and a recessed central door, 54¹/₂in. wide.
(Bearne's) $25,110

A rosewood, parquetry and gilt-bronze meuble d'appui, Paris, circa 1880, the molded bréche d'Alep top above two frieze drawers, 147cm. wide.
(Sotheby's) $9,373

A pair of Victorian walnut and gilt-bronze side cabinets, English, circa 1850, each with a shaped white marble top above a crossbanded panel door, 69cm. wide.
(Sotheby's) $12,638

A pair of late Victorian ebonised side cabinets, each fitted with a paneled cupboard door, inlaid in pewter and tortoiseshell, 42in. wide.
(Christie's) $8,280

A stenciled pine cabinet, probably American, 1870s, the top with stenciled upper panel above three recessed compartments, 36¹/₈in. wide.
(Christie's) $3,561

A Victorian rosewood side cabinet, enclosed by a fretted door, flanked by applied floral chains, 34in. wide.
(George Kidner) $1,337

A 19th century walnut cabinet, inlaid with flowers and scrolling foliage and with gilt metal mounts, 35in.
(Ewbank) $3,105

A kingwood and porcelain side cabinet, French, circa 1860, the molded white marble top above a pair of doors, 113cm. wide.
(Sotheby's) $7,222

A kingwood marquetry and gilt-bronze side cabinet, by Schmit, Paris, circa 1900, with a brêche violette marble top, 155cm. wide. (Sotheby's) $78,671

A gilt-bronze and kingwood side cabinet, French, with a pair of paneled doors, centered by figures of Diana and Venus, 127cm. wide. (Sotheby's) $9,373

A Napoleon III ebonized, gilt-bronze and hardstone mounted side cabinet, Paris, circa 1870, 102cm. wide. (Sotheby's) $14,444

A mid-Georgian walnut and herringbone banded cabinet-on-chest, the molded cornice fitted with a pair of arched beveled mirrored doors, 42in. wide. (Christie's) $13,800

A pair of George III satinwood dwarf side cabinets, banded overall in amaranth and boxwood lines, one 40in. wide. (Christie's) $13,363

An Anglo-Indian ebony and ivory-inlaid satinwood cabinet, early 19th century, inlaid overall with ebony lines terminating in ivory-centered roundels, 27in. wide. (Christie's) $8,018

An oak and parcel-gilt gun cabinet, Victorian, circa 1850, the cresting carved with foliage and centered by a sheaf of corn, 194cm. wide. (Sotheby's) $23,431

A late Victorian ebonized and brass inlaid side cabinet, the breakfront top with in-curved sides, 57in. wide. (Christie's) $3,680

A parcel-gilt and painted side cabinet, Italy, circa 1840, the upper part with two tiers surmounted by an anthemion, 146cm. wide. (Sotheby's) $5,624

A red and gold lacquer cabinet, 19th century, decorated with Chinoiserie scenes, with brass escutcheon and lock, 34½in. wide. (Christie's) $4,048

Gothic Revival walnut collector's cabinet, third quarter 19th century, the molded top with a glazed velvet lined compartment, 26½in. wide. (Skinner) $2,530

A Regency mahogany side cabinet with veined marble top, pair of doors with brass mesh to panels, 4ft. wide. (Russell, Baldwin & Bright) $6,966

An Arts and Crafts oak cabinet, the rectangular top above seven graduated drawers and two graduated shelves, 25¾in. wide. (Christie's) $3,772

A George IV mahogany breakfront side cabinet with a pair of arched paneled cupboard doors flanked on either side by a glazed door, 82in. wide. (Christie's) $4,416

An Alpine gothic style pine cabinet, with molded roof top above a conforming tall door carved with St. George and the Dragon, 63 x 33 x 23¼in. (Sotheby's) $575

An Italian Provincial chestnut cabinet, 19th century, with two tall cupboard doors with incised decoration, 40in. wide. (Sotheby's) $1,035

A Victorian walnut and floral marquetry side cabinet, the rounded rectangular breakfront top above an inlaid frieze, 57½in. wide. (Christie's) $2,291

A North Italian inlaid walnut cabinet on stand, surmounted by a later balustrade above a pair of central panel doors, 43in. wide. (Anderson & Garland) $2,857

A Federal inlaid mahogany canterbury, American, circa 1810, of rectangular form, the upper section with five slightly arched transverses, 17½in. wide. (Sotheby's) $1,495

A Victorian mahogany canterbury. (Tweedales Commissions) $1,920

A Regency mahogany three-division canterbury, with slatted open slides, above a drawer fitted to one end on ring-turned legs, 18in. wide. (Christie's) $1,754

A George III mahogany four-division canterbury, with slatted compartments, above a drawer, on square legs, 18in. wide. (Christie's) $4,430

A mahogany canterbury, late 19th century, with four divisions with lyre ends above a lower tier, 41cm. wide. (Sotheby's) $3,775

A William IV rosewood canterbury, after a design by John C. Loudon, with four X-shaped divides joined at the top by ring-turned spindles, 19in. wide. (Christie's) $8,487

A Georgian mahogany canterbury with cut-out center handle, one long drawer to the base, 20 x 19½in. high. (Anderson & Garland) $2,146

A classical figured maple canterbury, New York, mid/late 19th century, the rectangular frame headed by ring-turned ball finials, 19in. wide. (Christie's) $6,900

A Federal inlaid mahogany canterbury, American, probably Boston, Massachusetts, circa 1810, of rectangular form, on ring-turned tapering legs, 19in. wide. (Sotheby's) $4,600

The Hepplewhite style is renowned for its flowing curves, shield, oval and heart-shaped backs and straight lines broken by carved or painted wheat ears and corn husks, all of which Hepplewhite adapted from the work of Robert Adam, the distinguished architect/designer and published in his famous guide: *The Cabinet Maker and Upholsterer*.

Though his designs have much in common with those of Hepplewhite, Thomas Sheraton (1751–1806), a drawing master from Stockton on Tees, much preferred straight lines to the curves favored by Hepplewhite, his chairs achieving their feminine delicacy with their fine turning and slender frames.

Sheraton served his apprenticeship as a cabinet maker but he never actually manufactured furniture himself, concentrating on creating designs which he published in his *Cabinet Maker's and Upholsterer's Drawing Book (1791–1794)*.

Thomas Chippendale designed and made furniture for the wealthy in his premises in St. Martin's Lane, London, establishing styles of his own rather than copying and adapting those of others. Like Sheraton and Hepplewhite, Chippendale published his designs, which were used by cabinet makers throughout the country, with the result that a considerable number of 'Chippendale' chairs were produced in a variety of qualities and a medley of styles.

A rare William and Mary turned maple upholstered-back side chair, Boston, Massachusetts, 1722–35. (Sotheby's) $2,300

Two of a set of eight 'Chippendale' mahogany dining chairs, by James Phillips and Sons Ltd. of Bristol. (Bristol)   (Eight) $1,488

A brace-back Windsor side back, branded *M.BLOOM/N.YORK*, 1787-93, the hooped and molded crestrail centering nine swelled spindles. (Christie's) $2,760

Two of a set of six mahogany dining-chairs, of George III design, including two armchairs, on molded square supports joined by square stretchers. (Christie's)   (Six) $2,024

A good Queen Anne walnut side chair, Pennsylvania, 1730–60, the yoke-form crest above a vase-form splat. (Sotheby's) $3,795

A pair of Franco-Flemish walnut upholstered armchairs, in Baroque style, on similarly turned legs and stretchers resting on pad feet. (Sotheby's) $1,680

Two similar Queen Anne carved maple side chairs, Massachusetts, 1730–50, each with a carved yoke-form crest above a vasiform splat. (Sotheby's) **$3,737**

Chippendale mahogany carved side chair, Massachusetts, circa 1780, the serpentine crestrail with carved terminals. (Skinner) **$2,300**

Two of a harlequin set of twelve Victorian oak dining chairs, shaped molded toprails above padded seats. (Christie's) (Twelve) **$3,818**

Two of a set of eight mahogany dining chairs, of George III style, including one armchair, the yoked toprails above pierced vase-shaped splats. (Christie's) (Eight) **$6,072**

One of a set of four classical mahogany carved dining chairs, probably Massachusetts, circa 1820, the slightly rectangular crest bordered by carved beading. (Skinner) (Four) **$1,610**

Two of a set of eight mahogany dining chairs in George I style, each shaped back with a carved crest and carved vase splat. (David Lay) (Eight) **$7,632**

Two of a set of twelve late Victorian mahogany dining-chairs, of George III design, including two pairs of armchairs. (Christie's) (Twelve) **$8,832**

American Country Chippendale side chair, in maple with tiger maple crestrail, pierced splat, box stretcher, and rush seat. (Eldred's) **$440**

Two of a set of six Regency mahogany dining chairs, with reeded backs above Gothic style slats, 87cm. (Bristol) (Six) **$2,160**

Two of a set of twelve mahogany dining chairs, eight chairs early 19th century, four chairs 20th century, including two open armchairs.
(Christie's) (Twelve) $8,860

Peter Behrens, side chair for the house of the poet Richard Dehmel, Hamburg, 1903, white painted wood, with original tapestry seat cover. (Sotheby's) $4,499

Two of nine George III mahogany dining-chairs including two open armchairs, each with an undulating top-rail and pierced splat.
(Christie's) (Nine) $20,303

A pair of Chippendale carved mahogany side chairs, Boston, 1760–80, each with serpentine crestrail with molded ears above a pierced interlaced splat.
(Christie's) $13,800

Joseph Hoffmann for Jacob & Josef Kohn, Vienna, side chair for the dining room of the Purkersdorf Sanatorium, 1904, stained bentwood and plywood, studded black leather upholstery.
(Sotheby's) $18,745

A pair of Queen Anne carved cherrywood side chairs, Philadelphia, circa 1750, each with a serpentine crest centering a shell-and leaf-carved device.
(Sotheby's) $10,925

Two of a set of six Dutch floral marquetry dining chairs, 19th century, each decorated with meandering floral stems, birds and flower filled urns.
(Christie's) (Six) $7,383

One of a set of six William IV rosewood dining chairs, each with a bowed bar top-rail above a horizontal splat.
(Christie's) (Six) $4,430

Two of a set of eight Regency mahogany dining chairs, the reeded rectangular backs with bowed toprails and shaped stick splats.(Bearne's) $3,564

Two of a set of eight walnut dining chairs, early 20th century, including two open armchairs, each back decorated with crossbandings.
(Christie's) (Eight) $13,289

A carved pearwood side chair, designed by Hector Guimard, circa 1903, open back with padded top.
(Christie's) $39,364

Two of a set of ten mahogany dining-chairs, of George III style, including two armchairs, each with waved acanthus-scrolled toprail.
(Christie's) (Ten) $24,817

Two of a set of ten Regency black and gilt decorated dining chairs, including two open armchairs, each with a pierced back with a tablet centred top-rail.
(Christie's) (Ten) $18,458

One of a set of six Regency mahogany dining chairs, each with a chaneled bow bar top-rail above reeded uprights.
(Christie's) (Six) $2,953

Two of a set of ten mahogany dining chairs, 20th century, including two open armchairs, each with an undulating top-rail carved with paterae to the corners.
(Christie's) (Ten) $13,843

A set of four Genoese cream and green painted dining chairs, 19th century, decorated with floral stems, figures and butterflies.
(Christie's) $1,661

A rare William and Mary black-painted carved maple cane-seat side chair, Boston, Massachusetts, 1717–30.
(Sotheby's) $14,950

A pair of George IV mahogany hall chairs, each with a scallop-shell carved waisted back painted with a lion's helm.
(Christie's) $3,138

Two of a set of six Regency simulated rosewood dining chairs, the bobbin-turned toprails above similar horizontal splats.
(Christie's)   (Six) $1,431

A William and Mary turned and carved maple cane-back side chair, North-eastern Shore, New England, 1720-1740. (Sotheby's)
        $2,500

Two of a good Victorian set of four rosewood dining chairs, with kidney-shaped carved bar backs, 84cm.
(Bristol)   (Four) $992

A pair of Chippendale carved walnut side chairs, Philadelphia, 1760–80, the serpentine crest with incised edge and ears above a pierced vasiform splat.
(Christie's) $9,200

One of a set of four Victorian walnut dining chairs, the marquetry inlaid arcaded spindle backs with arched crest.
(Andrew Hartley) (Four) $840

Two of a set of six Regency dining chairs with simulated rosewood finish, gilt leaf twist top rails, pierced cross frame center bar.
(Russell, Baldwin & Bright)
       (Six) $2,138

Two of a Harlequin set of six early 19th century North Country spindle back dining chairs with rush seats, turned stretchers and pad feet.
(Dreweatt Neate)
     (Six) $1,570

A good green and gray painted bow back brace-back turned Windsor side chair, New England, circa 1780.
(Sotheby's) $1,150

Two of a set of four William IV
mahogany dining chairs, the bar
back above lotus molded uprights,
together with two similar chairs.
(Bristol)   (Six) $853

Chippendale mahogany side
chair, Western Massachusetts, 18th
century, with shaped crest ending in
scroll-back terminals.
(Skinner) $1,265

Two of a set of eight mahogany
dining chairs, of George III style,
including two armchairs.
(Christie's) (Eight) $7,636

A rare pair of Federal inlaid
mahogany shield-back side chairs,
New York, circa 1800, each with a
horizontal line and bellflower-inlaid
crest.
(Sotheby's) $1,610

A rare Chippendale mahogany side
chair, Portsmouth, New
Hampshire, attributed to Robert
Harrold, circa 1780, the serpentine
crest above a strapwork splat.
(Sotheby's) $5,750

Two of a set of eight mahogany
dining chairs, of George III design,
including two armchairs, the yoked
toprails above pierced and
interlaced vase-shaped splats.
(Christie's) (Eight) $3,562

Pair of birch Transitional side
chairs, 18th century, Newburyport,
Massachusetts area, raked
molded terminals and broad splat.
(Skinner) $1,840

One of a set of six 19th century
rosewood dining chairs, the open
backs surmounted by carved
flowers and foliage.
(Ewbank)   (Six) $1,425

A pair of Chippendale painted
maple rush-seat side chairs, New
England, 1750–80, each with a
serpentine crest.
(Sotheby's) $1,150

One of a pair of carved and giltwood armchairs, French, circa 1870, in Louis XVI style, the seat rail with edged border. (Sotheby's) (Two) $7,222

An early Victorian mahogany library chair, the padded back and outswept arms with reeded U-shaped front-rail. (Christie's) $3,692

A Louis XVI gray-painted bergère, with a chaneled frame, the arched top-rail above a padded back and arms. (Christie's) $3,046

Ludwig Mies van der Rohe for the Berliner Metallgewerbe Joseph Müller, Berlin, cantilever armchair 'MR 20', 1927, chromium-plated tubular steel, stained cane seat and arms, 32⅜in. (Sotheby's) $16,871

A pair of Florentine Renaissance walnut Dantesque chairs, early 16th century, each with boldly curved scrolling arms. (Sotheby's) $14,950

A beech open armchair, early 20th century, the outswept arm rests with foliate-carved scrolled terminals, on scrolled supports. (Christie's) $2,769

One of a pair of carved giltwood bergères, Paris, circa 1870, each in Louis XVI style, with a padded back and elbow rests. (Sotheby's) (Two) $6,499

A William IV mahogany metamorphic library chair/steps, with a reeded frame, with a close studded red-leather padded back and downswept arm rests. (Christie's) $5,168

A William IV mahogany library bergère, the bowed scrolled top-rail above downswept arms with scroll terminals. (Christie's) $7,383

A George II mahogany armchair, on serpentine supports, on cabriole legs with bud-feet, restorations, possibly Scottish.
(Christie's) $30,544

A pair of giltwood open armchairs, 19th century, the waisted buttoned back surmounted by a pierced foliate and scrolled top-rail.
(Christie's) $2,953

A Scottish George II laburnum armchair, the chaneled cartouche-shaped back with foliate angles.
(Christie's) $24,817

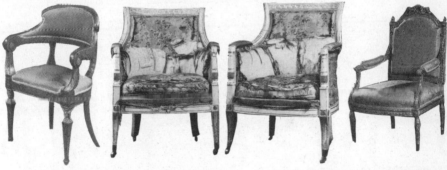

A walnut and parcel-gilt chair, late 19th/early 20th century, applied with neo classical mounts, the shaped arched top-rail above a padded back.
(Christie's) $1,754

A pair of Regency white-painted and parcel-gilt bergères on square tapering saber legs headed by roundel panels.
(Christie's) $28,635

One of a pair of carved giltwood armchairs, French, circa 1880, in Louis XVI style, the frame surmounted by a torch and quiver.
(Sotheby's)
(Two) $3,126

A Federal mahogany lolling chair, New England, circa 1790, the shaped crest with peaked ears above a padded back.
(Sotheby's) $19,550

A pair of French beech fauteuils, early 20th century, each with a ribbon-tied reeded frame carved with foliage and rocaille.
(Christie's) $5,537

A George II mahogany armchair, the outcurved scrolled arms on serpentine supports decorated with acanthus.
(Christie's) $36,271

A George III mahogany open armchair, the scrolled arms on paneled supports, on fluted and paneled square tapering legs. (Christie's) $8,487

A matched pair of George I walnut chairs, each with padded back and seat on cabriole legs, terminating in pad feet. (Christie's) $2,030

A William IV mahogany bergère, chaneled overall, the arms with lion-mask terminals on downswept supports, on reeded baluster legs. (Christie's) $2,640

A Regency mahogany tub bergère, the scrolled padded back and squab cushion covered in later polychrome tapestry. (Christie's) $4,963

A pair of Irish William IV oak bergères, by Jones & Co., Dublin, on ring-turned legs, headed by square foliage patera. (Christie's) $24,518

A George III mahogany tub bergère, the chaneled back and arms covered in close-nailed black horsehair, on square tapering legs. (Christie's) $5,658

One of a pair of giltwood armchairs, Paris, circa 1890, each with a padded back within a molded frame. (Sotheby's)   (Two) $3,126

A matched pair of George III mahogany open armchairs, each with a cartouche-shaped padded back, serpentine-fronted seat and arms. (Christie's) $12,259

A George III mahogany library armchair, the arched rectangular padded back above an upholstered seat flanked by padded armrests with downswept foliate-carved stiles. (Christie's) $4,416

A mahogany and gilt-bronze bergère, with padded back, the arms terminating in ram's heads. (Sotheby's) $4,499

A pair of giltwood armchairs, each with leaf-carved oval back, centered with floral posy, on fluted tapering legs. (Christie's) $6,412

A late Victorian mahogany bergère, on turned and fluted tapering supports with brass caps and castors. (Christie's) $1,747

One of a set of six George III cream-painted and parcel-gilt side chairs, the back centered by a spray of flowers and with a carved husk edge. (Christie's) (Six) $11,693

A pair of mid-Victorian library armchairs, each with a rounded rectangular padded back, arms and concave seat, the arms terminating in lion-masks. (Christie's) $35,834

A George II giltwood side chair, the scrolled seat-rail centered by acanthus, on cabriole legs headed by acanthus. (Christie's) $28,290

A walnut open armchair, early 20th century, the shaped arm rests with outswept terminals carved with eagle masks. (Christie's) $3,322

A pair of ebonized and parcel-gilt mahogany open armchairs, modern, of George I style, the front seatrail centered by a cartouche with a scallop shell. (Christie's) $25,461

A William IV mahogany library bergère, the bowed scrolled top-rail above a waisted back. (Christie's) $11,997

Empire style gilt bronze mounted mahogany armchair, late 19th/20th century.
(Skinner) $4,025

A Chippendale mahogany lolling chair, Massachusetts, circa 1780, the serpentine crest above a padded back.
(Sotheby's) $2,070

A 19th century elbow chair with spoon back, crested with ribbon mount, on fluted tapering cylindrical supports.
(G.A. Key) $693

A tufted Turkish Revival upholstered armchair, American, 19th century, the rounded stuffed and shirred crestrail above a tufted and reclining barrel back.
(Christie's) $2,070

One of a pair of 19th century French easy chairs with buttoned backs and floral upholstery, the bow-fronts decorated with carved scallop shell motifs and scrolls.
(Anderson & Garland)
(Two) $3,816

A Federal mahogany lolling chair, Massachusetts, circa 1790, the serpentine crest flanked by shaped arms on molded downswept supports.
(Sotheby's) $4,600

A Victorian rosewood framed salon chair, the spoon back with floral needlework covering in a pierced and carved scrolling foliate surround.
(Andrew Hartley) $1,099

Lifetime Morris chair, pegged construction, through tenons on arms, four vertical side slats, quartersawn oak.
(Skinner) $2,875

A Victorian walnut show frame open armchair with extensive scroll and leaf carving, red leather upholstered back, arms and serpentine fronted seat.
(Dreweatt Neate) $1,020

American Egyptian Revival ebonized and parcel-gilt armchair, circa 1865, 39½in. high. (Skinner) **$8,050**

Pair of Renaissance Revival walnut, burl walnut, and marquetry armchairs, circa 1865, 44½in. high. (Skinner) **$1,840**

A longhorn armchair, attributed to Wenzel Friedrich, San Antonio, Texas, circa 1889. (Christie's) **$5,175**

One of a set of four giltwood armchairs, Paris, circa 1890, each with a padded back within a molded frame, carved with leafy tendrils. (Sotheby's) (Four) **$9,551**

A pair of Regency mahogany open armchairs, each with a padded rectangular back, arms and seat covered in close-nailed blue leather. (Christie's) **$14,145**

A Classical Revival ebonized and rosewood veneer chair, attributed to Herter Brothers, New York City, 1870–85. (Christie's) **$7,475**

An Edwardian rosewood and ivory inlaid easy armchair, decorated with lines, meandering foliage and inlaid with pewter paterae. (Christie's) **$2,399**

A pair of massive Venetian baroque style upholstered walnut armchairs, each with scalloped arched open back above bold scrolled and fluted arms. (Sotheby's) **$920**

An early 19th century mahogany-framed and cane-paneled bergère with reeded rectangular back and downswept arms. (Bearne's) **$1,620**

One of a set of four green painted and parcel-gilt salon hairs, by Sormani, Paris, circa 1890. (Sotheby's) (Four) $5,777

A pair of oak armchairs, Belgian, circa 1900, open back and sides with sweeping detail and lightly carved with whiplash motifs. (Christie's) $3,374

A walnut armchair, designed by Ernest Gimson, circa 1905, open lattice back with fine chamfered detailing. (Christie's) $6,373

Erich Dieckmann for Weimar Bau und Wohnungskunst GmbH, child's chair, designed and manufactured circa 1928, red and cream painted beech and plywood, 25⅝in. (Sotheby's) $2,437

A pair of George III mahogany hall chairs, each with pierced oval back with lozenge-centered cross splat and scrolled base. (Christie's) $45,816

A Queen Anne figured maple armchair, Philadelphia, 1740–60, the serpentine crestrail with molded ears above a solid vasiform splat, 45½in. high. (Christie's) $134,500

Richard Riemerschmid, executed by Dresdener Werkstätten for Handwerkunst, Dresden-Hellerau, armchair, 1902, beech and pearwood, upholstered seat. (Sotheby's) $5,624

A pair of Italian baroque walnut and parcel gilt upholstered armchairs, each with rectangular padded back, the stiles surmounted by gilded acanthus finials. (Sotheby's) $7,475

A Queen Anne carved and figured walnut armchair, Pennsylvania, circa 1750, the serpentine shell-carved crest with molded ears above a vasiform splat. (Sotheby's) $8,625

Painted maple and ash armchair, New England, early 18th century, the four arched slats joining turned stiles with ball finials. (Skinner) $5,175

Painted turned roundabout chair, New England, 18th century, the shaped backrest continuing to circular handholds. (Skinner) $1,495

A good Queen Anne carved maple armchair, Philadelphia, 1730–50, the yoke-form molded crest above a baluster splat. (Sotheby's) $23,000

A painted and gilded cabriole armchair, Philadelphia, 1790–1810, the arched crest above an upholstered tablet back. (Christie's) $81,700

A pair of Regency white-painted and parcel-gilt armchairs, each chaneled overall with a Greek-key pattern toprail above a padded horizontal splat. (Christie's) $8,591

A George III mahogany open armchair with interlaced splat back with scroll carving, shaped arms with scroll terminals. (Ewbank) $3,680

The Jacob Meyers fine and rare Queen Anne carved and figured walnut open armchair, Philadelphia, Pennsylvania, circa 1750. (Sotheby's) $519,500

A fine Queen Anne walnut balloon-seat corner armchair, Boston, Massachusetts, circa 1760, the shaped crest on a concave armrest. (Sotheby's) $13,800

A Chippendale carved and figured walnut open armchair, Pennsylvania, circa 1780, on shell-carved cabriole legs ending in ball-and-claw feet. (Sotheby's) $20,700

Arts and Crafts armchair, quartersawn oak, nine vertical back spindles, dark original finish. (Skinner) $633

Rosewood reclining chair, 19th century, movable curving back, stationary seat and adjustable leg support, 36½in. high. (Butterfield & Butterfield) $862

One of a set of six Edwardian mahogany and strung dining chairs, with satinwood banded toprails. (George Kidner) (Six) $1,337

Chippendale mahogany carved roundabout chair, New England, circa 1780, the shaped back rest continuing to scrolled arms. (Skinner) $2,530

Gerrit Rietveld, executed by G.A. van de Groenekan, child's high chair, designed circa 1921, executed circa 1938, red and cream painted wood. (Sotheby's) $22,494

A rare green-painted low-back Windsor armchair, Philadelphia, circa 1765, the concave line-incised arms with outscrolled terminals. (Sotheby's) $2,875

A steel electric chair, ex Dept of Penal Correction, California State, once owned by Andy Warhol then Pietro Psaier, entitled 'Rest in Peace, PAX', 169cm. high. (Bristol) $7,440

Pair of Gustav Stickley armchairs, No.360, original finish with good quarter-sawn oak, Gustav red decal on both. (Skinner) $3,450

HISTORICAL FACTS
Elbow Chairs

Possibly the greatest problem confronting a designer of chairs has always been that of creating a style robust enough to survive while retaining a degree of elegance.

Very few designers achieved this happy blend, most coming down on the side of strong practicality and a few, such as Sheraton and Hepplewhite, concentrating on a fashionable delicacy at the expense of strength. Chippendale was the man who came closest to combining the two elements and it is this which has made chairs based on his designs among the most popular.

Beside the elegance of his designs, Hepplewhite is to be remembered for the explicit instructions given in his book regarding the materials to be used for the purpose of covering his chairs: for japanned chairs with cane seats, cushions covered in linen; for dining chairs, horse hair material which may be either plain or striped; for upholstered chairs, red or blue morocco leather tied with silk tassels.

While most surviving Sheraton chairs are made of mahogany, they can also be found in satinwood, painted white or gold or even japanned. The delicacy of his design demands that a fine fabric be used to cover the upholstery, green silk or satin being generally considered the most suitable. Not being a manufacturer himself, Sheraton concerned himself more with the aesthetics of design than with the practicalities of use.

A pair of black-painted turned and carved bow-back Windsor armchairs, New England, probably Rhode Island, early 19th century. (Sotheby's) $5,462

An early Georgian walnut and elm armchair, the waved toprail centered by confronting stylized eagle-heads above a pierced vertical tapering splat. (Christie's) $3,018

A pair of Spanish walnut leather upholstered armchairs in Baroque style, each with rectangular open back above a suspended leather seat. (Sotheby's) $1,265

A William and Mary brown-stained maple and turned ash bannister-back rush seat armchair, New England, probably Connecticut, 1730–70. (Sotheby's) $1,840

Emile-Jacques Ruhlmann, two of a set of four armchairs 'Ledroua', 1924, palisander, each with small upholstered rectangular back rests with scroll top. (Sotheby's) (Four) $40,330

A combed pine and elm Windsor armchair, the rectangular toprail above a sparred back and solid seat flanked by out-curved armrests. (Christie's) $916

A fine Queen Anne carved mahogany corner chair, Massachusetts, circa 1750, the reverse-scrolling crest above concave spurred arms. (Sotheby's) $43,700

A pair of painted open armchairs, early 20th century, each decorated with bellflower swags and floral sprays. (Christie's) $3,692

A mahogany open armchair, late 19th/early 20th century, decorated with foliate carvings, on cabriole legs. (Christie's) $1,570

A walnut open armchair, 20th century, with a pierced scrolling top-rail and vertical splats between turned uprights. (Christie's) $775

A pair of William IV brass-mounted mahogany open armchairs by W. Turner & Son, the acanthus-scrolled toprail centered by a roundel with a crest of a liver bird holding a branch of oak leaves. (Christie's) $15,088

An inlaid birch armchair, designed by Mackay Hugh Baillie Scott, manufactured by the Dresdener Werkstätten für Handwerkskunst, circa 1903. (Christie's) $7,123

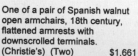

One of a pair of Spanish walnut open armchairs, 18th century, flattened armrests with downscrolled terminals. (Christie's) (Two) $1,661

A pair of mahogany open armchairs, late 19th century, each with a wheel-back carved with radiating leaves. (Christie's) $3,507

A George III mahogany open armchair, the waved scroll-carved toprail above a pierced interlaced-scroll vase-shaped splat. (Christie's) $10,373

A rare Chippendale carved walnut armchair, Philadelphia, circa 1760, the shaped crest above a pierced gothic splat and serpentine arms. (Sotheby's) $10,350

A pair of walnut open armchairs, 20th century, each carved with foliage with a pierced top-rail. (Christie's) $1,570

One of a pair of Spanish upholstered armchairs, 19th century, decorated with foliate brass mounts, on square legs joined by stretchers. (Christie's) (Two) $1,107

Carlo Bugatti, corner chair, circa 1900, the two circular back panels centered by a star motif, inlaid throughout with bone and gray metal. (Sotheby's) $6,146

Two of a set of eight white and polychrome-decorated open armchairs, six George III and two later, each with a rectangular back with stepped toprail. (Christie's) (Eight) $43,378

A mahogany clerk's chair, mid 19th century, the shaped bowed top-rail padded with a close-studded red-leather buttoned panel. (Christie's) $2,584

A George II walnut chair, the paper-scrolled undulating top-rail above a pierced vase splat. (Christie's) $738

A pair of small Regency mahogany caned bergères, each reeded overall, with a carved back and sides, the arms terminating in paterae. (Christie's) $16,974

An Anglo-Indian ebony open armchair, first half 19th century, with caned back and seat, the rectangular back with carved foliate tablet toprail. (Christie's) $7,921

Fine L. & J.G. Stickley high-back rocker, V-sided arms and back over six vertical slats, drop in spring cushion.
(Skinner)   **$977**

Adirondack rocking chair, bent oak slats with natural timber frame.
(Skinner)   **$833**

L. & J.G. Stickley rocker, inverted V-back over five vertical slats, original finish, branded mark.
(Skinner)   **$460**

Shaker child's cherry armless production rocking chair, marked *#1, Mount Lebanon, New York*, circa 1875, with early cherry finish and an old splint seat.
(Skinner)   **$1,092**

A Victorian steel and brass rocking chair, after a design by R. W. Winfield & Co. for the Great Exhibition of 1851, the serpentine frame flanking a buttoned green suede back and seat.
(Christie's)   **$4,904**

Painted and decorated ladder-back rocking armchair, Providence, Rhode Island, early 19th century.
(Skinner)   **$747**

Limbert rocking Morris chair, original light brown finish with overcoat.
(Skinner)   **$4,025**

President Lincoln's rocking chair, claimed to the one in which he was sitting at the Ford Theatre in Washington when he was assassinated, 1865.
(Auction Team Köln)   **$338**

Adirondack rocking chair, bentwood oak slats with natural timber supports.
(Skinner)   **$1,840**

HISTORICAL FACTS
Wing Chairs

Wing chairs have been made since the 17th century, this being one of the few designs to have remained virtually unchanged since its conception, only the legs changing shape according to the dictates of fashion.

The Queen Anne wing chairs had high cabriole legs canted from the corners which demanded extra stretchers for strength. The legs were later straightened and squared off with the inside edges chamfered, before the Georgian influence saw a return of the cabriole legs, but shorter this time and terminating in ball and claw feet.

The armchair by Thomas Chippendale is one of the best chairs ever made. Beautifully constructed to a superbly elegant design, it is strong, graceful and comfortable; a truly classic example of everything a chair should be.

The strong rectangle of the back is softened by the flow of the humped top rail and the arm supports, molded and richly carved with feathers, terminate in cabochon ornament above the graceful acanthus carved cabriole legs with claw and ball feet.

The mid Victorian period abounds with furniture showing the exaggerated curves and floral and leaf carving which clearly reflect the Louis XV rococo influence and beautifully designed chairs of this period simply cry out to be sat in. Earlier examples had filled-in arms of rather plain frames of mahogany or rosewood.

Queen Anne wing chair, 18th century, in mahogany with red upholstery.
(Eldred's) $1,760

A Chippendale mahogany easy chair, New England, circa 1780, the serpentine crest flanked by ogival wings and outscrolled arms.
(Sotheby's) $4,025

A Federal inlaid mahogany wing chair, New York or New England, circa 1800, the serpentine crest with peaked ears flanked by ogival wings.
(Sotheby's) $4,887

A mid Georgian mahogany wing armchair, with golden embroidered fabric upholstery, projecting hand rests and sliding footrest.
(Bristol) $1,804

A Chippendale mahogany wing chair, Philadelphia, circa 1780, the serpentine crest flanked by ogival wings with outscrolled arms.
(Sotheby's) $6,325

A Federal mahogany easy chair, New England, circa 1810, on ring-turned tapering legs, ending in peg feet.
(Sotheby's) $8,625

A Chippendale carved mahogany wing armchair, New York, circa 1770, the serpentine crest flanked by ogival wings continuing to scrolled supports. (Sotheby's)　　$13,800

A mahogany wing armchair on cabriole legs headed by scrolled angles and foliage, on pad feet. (Christie's)　　$3,018

A Queen Anne beech and walnut wing armchair, on cabriole legs joined by an H-stretcher and on hoof feet. (Christie's)　　$10,120

A good Chippendale carved mahogany easy chair, circa 1770, the arched crest flanked by ogival wings and outscrolled arms. (Sotheby's)　　$32,200

A Chippendale carved mahogany easy chair, Philadelphia, 1760-80, the arched crestrail flanked by shaped wings continuing to outward C-scrolled arms, on ball and claw feet. (Christie's)　　$244,500

A Queen Anne turned walnut easy chair, New England, circa 1730, the arched crest flanked by ogival wings on conical supports. (Sotheby's)　　$4,600

A Federal mahogany wing armchair, probably New York, circa 1800, the arched back flanked by ogival wings and scrolled arms. (Sotheby's)　　$4,312

A George I walnut wing armchair, with scrolling arms and on cabriole legs and pad feet. (Christie's)　　$5,600

A rare Queen Anne carved walnut easy chair, the arched crest flanked by ogival wings and downswept arms. (Sotheby's)　　$50,000

A mahogany wing armchair, 19th century, with a paper scroll arched top-rail, outsplayed sides and arms.
(Christie's) $2,584

A George I walnut ratchet-back wing armchair, the cabriole legs headed by a scallop-shell and shaped brackets.
(Christie's) $166,830

A George I walnut wing armchair, cabriole legs with shaped brackets terminating in pad feet.
(Christie's) $14,318

A rare Chippendale carved and figured mahogany easy chair, Philadelphia, circa 1770, the arched crest flanked by ogival wings.
(Sotheby's) $310,500

A George III mahogany wing armchair, the chaneled arm-supports carved with a patera and trailing foliage, on square chamfered legs.
(Christie's) $6,601

A fine Queen Anne carved and turned walnut easy chair, Boston, Massachusetts, 1740-60, the arched crest flanked by ogival wings continuing to conical supports.
(Sotheby's) $79,500

A George III mahogany wing armchair, on square legs and H-shaped stretcher.
(Christie's) $12,880

A George II walnut wing armchair, with padded back, arms and seat, on cabriole legs joined by stretchers.
(Christie's) $4,061

A George III mahogany wing armchair with stuffover serpentine arched back and C scroll arm supports.
(Phillips) $1,920

HISTORICAL FACTS
Chests of Drawers

Throughout the transitional period from coffer to chest of drawers, there were a great many variations on the basic theme but, eventually, a practical and attractive formula emerged about 1670. Not slow to respond to the demand, cabinet makers produced vast quantities of chests of drawers, employing, as a rule, the familiar native wood, oak, for the purpose.

The fine architectural geometric moldings proved popular as decoration and these were glued and bradded in position - a practice with continues to the present day.

The use of veneers made the manufacture of molded drawer fronts impractical and, consequently, more emphasis was placed on the figuring of veneers as a decorative feature. The oyster design was particularly popular and results from careful cutting of the veneer from a tree bough. This is glued vertically on to the drawer front, the figuring being meticulously matched, and it is crossbanded on the edges, often with an intermediate herringbone inlay.

The drawers are now found to slide on the horizontal partitions which separate them and they are finely dovetailed, where earlier they were more crudely jointed or even nailed together.

Walnut continued as the most favored wood for chests of drawers until the middle of the 18th century.

A Federal inlaid and figured birchwood chest of drawers, New England, circa 1815, the rectangular top above four crossbanded graduated long drawers, 42¾in. wide.
(Sotheby's) $5,175

Chippendale red painted cherry chest of drawers, New England, late 18th century, the rectangular overhanging top above case of four graduated drawers, 40¼in. wide.
(Skinner) $1,265

A Federal grain-painted birchwood chest of drawers, Northern New England, possibly Maine or New Hampshire, circa 1820, the rectangular top surmounted by a recessed superstructure, 42in. wide.
(Sotheby's) $2,070

A good Federal inlaid mahogany bow-front chest of drawers, Mid-Atlantic States, circa 1800, the oblong crossbanded top above four graduated line-inlaid long drawers, 39in. wide.
(Sotheby's) $3,737

A Chippendale stained birchwood chest of drawers, New England, circa 1780, the rectangular thumbmolded top with four graduated long drawers, 38¼in. wide.
(Sotheby's) $2,587

Federal bird's-eye maple veneer and cherry bowfront bureau, New England, circa 1820, four cockbeaded graduated drawers, 39½in. wide.
(Skinner) $1,380

A Regency mahogany chest of four long graduated, crossbanded drawers, on dwarf saber legs, 3ft.11in. wide. (Russell, Baldwin & Bright) $1,727

Fine Gustav Stickley nine-drawer chest, six small drawers over three, bowed side, arched base, original finish, 48in. high. (Skinner) $10,350

Federal birch inlaid bowfront chest of drawers, attributed to Joseph Clark, Portsmouth or Greenland, New Hampshire, 1810–14, 39¼in. wide. (Skinner) $8,050

A Federal inlaid and figured walnut chest of drawers, Pennsylvania, circa 1810, the rectangular top with projecting cornice above four graduated molded long drawers, 42in. wide. (Sotheby's) $2,070

Chippendale mahogany serpentine chest of drawers, eastern Massachusetts, 1760-80, with a molded and blocked top overhanging a conforming case of graduated drawers, 36in. wide overall. (Skinner) $24,150

A fine Chippendale carved and figured walnut reverse-serpentine block-front chest of drawers, Massachusetts, circa 1780, the shaped molded top with four graduated long drawers, 37in. wide. (Sotheby's) $35,650

Federal birch mahogany and bird's-eye maple chest of drawers, New England, circa 1820, rectangular overhanging top above a case of four cockbeaded graduated drawers, 39in. wide. (Skinner) $1,610

A late George III mahogany bowfront chest, the satinwood crossbanded and ebony lined top above four similarly lined long graduated drawers, 37½in. wide. (Christie's) $1,656

Grain painted pine chest, New England, 1843, inscribed on reverse Elihu Nye May 10, 1843, with scrolled splash board above graduated drawers, 30¾in. wide. (Skinner) $1,495

A George III mahogany chest, fitted with a slide and four graduated long drawers, on bracket feet, 30 in. wide. (Christie's) $2,953

Chippendale cherry serpentine bureau, probably Massachusetts, circa 1780, the overhanging molded top with serpentine front, 19³/₄in. wide. (Skinner) $42,550

An early 18th century walnut and burr walnut-veneered chest of two short and three graduated long drawers, 41in. wide. (Bearne's) $3,240

A Chippendale birchwood reverse-serpentine chest of drawers, Massachusetts, circa 1780, the oblong molded top with reverse serpentine front, 39¹/₂in. wide. (Sotheby's) $6,900

A Dutch walnut serpentine chest, 19th century, the shaped top with projecting rounded angles above four drawers, 32in. wide. (Christie's) $7,014

A Chippendale mahogany serpentine-front bombé chest-of-drawers, Boston, 1760–80, 36in. wide. (Christie's) $27,600

A George II mahogany serpentine-fronted dressing chest with a brushing slide, four graduated long drawers and on bracket feet, 29in. wide. (Bearne's) $2,268

Chippendale mahogany oxbow serpentine chest of drawers, Massachusetts, last quarter 18th century, 34in. wide. (Skinner) $17,250

A late 17th century oak chest, with two short and three long geometrically paneled drawers, 37in. wide. (Bearne's) $1,264

A George III mahogany chest fitted with two short and three long graduated drawers, on bracket feet. 43in. wide.
(Christie's) $2,953

A Federal inlaid mahogany and flame-birch veneered chest-of-drawers, Portsmouth, New Hampshire, 1805–15, 41¼in. wide.
(Christie's) $18,400

A very fine and rare Chippendale mahogany serpentine-front chest of drawers, Boston, Massachusetts, circa 1780, 36in. wide.
(Sotheby's) $82,250

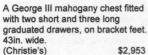

A George III burr-yew bachelor's chest, banded overall in rosewood and boxwood, the rectangular folding top above two simulated drawers functioning as lopers, 36in. wide. (Christie's) $102,920

A Victorian simulated-bamboo and yellow-painted chest, decorated overall with black and green lines, 31¾in. wide.
(Christie's) $1,225

A Dutch oak serpentine chest, early 19th century, fitted with four serpentine fronted drawers, on bracket feet, 34½in. wide.
(Christie's) $2,399

A William and Mary walnut oyster-veneered and marquetry chest, decorated with crossbanding, lines and panels inlaid with meandering floral sprays, urns and birds, 38in. wide. (Christie's) $20,303

Chippendale mahogany carved veneer serpentine chest of drawers, Boston or Salem, Massachusetts, 18th century, with molded top with canted corners, 41½in. wide overall.
(Skinner) $74,000

A north European satinwood and parquetry bowfronted chest, late 18th century, the ebony-banded top with a central oval medallion, probably Swedish, 28¼in. wide.
(Christie's) $10,373

A George II oak and pine chest of unusual configuration, having two rows of small drawers, two short and two long drawers under, 96cm. wide. (Tennants) $4,000

A George III mahogany chest of slide, two short and three graduated long drawers, 33½in. wide. (Ewbank) $6,080

A Chippendale figured walnut chest of drawers, probably Connecticut, circa 1780, rectangular thumbmolded top, 33½in. wide. (Sotheby's) $8,625

A Chippendale figured maple serpentine front chest of drawers, New England, probably Massachusetts, circa 1790, the oblong top with thumbmolded edge, 38¼in. wide. (Sotheby's) $8,050

A Queen Anne walnut and herringbone banded bachelor's chest with folding top above two short and three graduated long drawers, 30in. wide. (Ewbank) $10,880

A Queen Anne walnut and laburnum oyster veneered chest of drawers, circa 1710, the rectangular holly strapwork inlaid top with cushion molded edge, 37½in. wide. (Bonhams) $11,200

A mahogany and bird's eye maple chest, 20th century, of small size, with a white marble top above three drawers, on bracket feet, 28½in. wide. (Christie's) $1,600

A fine George III mahogany serpentine chest of drawers, circa 1780, the shaped top with molded edge above a brushing slide, 44½in. wide. (Bonhams) $9,600

A George II mahogany chest, with molded edge to the top and a slide with two short and three long drawers under, 87cm. wide. (Tennants) $6,400

A rare Chippendale carved and figured mahogany serpentine front chest of drawers, Boston area, Massachusetts, circa 1770, 39¾in. wide.
(Sotheby's) $60,250

A Scottish fruitwood and brass-bound military chest, 19th century, in two sections, on turned bulbous supports, 39in. wide.
(Christie's) $2,483

An early 18th century walnut veneered bachelor's chest with chevron banding throughout, on splayed feet with scrolled toes, 78.5cm. wide.
(Bearne's) $6,647

A good Chippendale figured mahogany chest of drawers, Philadelphia, circa 1770, the rectangular molded top above four graduated thumbmolded drawers, 37in. wide.
(Sotheby's) $23,000

A walnut veneered bachelor's chest, with baize lined fold-over top over three drawers, on bracket feet, 18th century, 75cm. wide.
(Tennants) $8,000

A Dutch burr and figured walnut chest, early 18th century, the serpentine molded quarter veneered top above a bombé front, 32¾in. wide.
(Christie's) $47,840

A George III mahogany chest of four graduated long drawers, with molded edge to the rectangular top, and on shaped bracket feet, 95cm. wide.
(Bearne's) $1,741

A late George III mahogany serpentine chest, the centered rectangular top above four long drawers, 37in. wide.
(Christie's) $14,720

A George III mahogany serpentine front dressing chest, the molded overhanging top with canted corners and a frieze drawer with a baize slide, 108cm. wide.
(Phillips) $6,400

In the early 18th century, the tallboy, or chest on a chest, began to replace the chest on a stand and, by about 1725, had virtually superceded it.

Early examples were veneered in finely grained burr walnut and often sport a sunburst decoration of boxwood and holly at the base, which usually has the fashionable bracket feet.

As an added bonus, buyers of these superb pieces of furniture often get a secret drawer in the frieze as well as the brushing slide fitted above the oak lined drawers in the lower section.

Despite the obvious difficulty in reaching the top drawers and the competition from wardrobes and clothes presses, tallboys were made in vast quantities throughout the second half of the 18th century. So common were they, in fact, that George Smith, in his Household Furniture observed that the tallboy was an article ". . . of such general use that it does not stand in need of a description".

As a rule, tallboys were made of mahogany and ranged in quality from rather plain, monolithic but functional pieces to magnificent, cathedral-like specimens with elaborate cornices, fluted pillars flanking the upper drawers, low relief carving on the frieze and fine ogee feet.

Their popularity lasted until about 1820 when the linen press, with cupboard doors to the upper section, proved to be more practical.

A Queen Anne carved and figured walnut bonnet-top chest on chest, Goddard Townsend School, Newport, Rhode Island, circa 1775, 42½in. wide.
(Sotheby's) $85,000

A figured walnut chest on chest, the lower part with a brushing slide over two short and three long drawers, parts associated, both 18th century, 114cm. wide.
(Tennants) $6,400

A fine George II walnut chest on chest, circa 1730, the concave molded cornice above three short and three long feather banded drawers, 41¾in. wide.
(Bonhams) $24,000

A walnut chest-on-stand, early 18th century, decorated with crossbandings, the later top above a molded cornice, 39½in. wide.
(Christie's) $4,799

A George III mahogany chest on chest, circa 1770, the dentil molded cornice above a pair of short drawers, 44½in. wide.
(Bonhams) $8,000

A fine Queen Anne highly figured walnut chest on chest, Philadelphia, 1750-70, the upper part with a rectangular overhanging cornice, width of cornice 45in.
(Sotheby's) $40,250

A walnut chest on stand, decorated with crossbandings, the molded cornice above three short and three long graduated drawers, 41in. wide. (Christie's) $4,800

A William and Mary walnut and marquetry chest-on-stand, the crossbanded rectangular molded top above two short and two long drawers, 43¾in. wide. (Christie's) $6,440

An important Queen Anne carved, parcel-gilt, figured walnut bonnet-top high chest of drawers, Boston, Massachusetts, 1730-50, 38in. wide. (Sotheby's) $937,500

A rare William and Mary sycamore and turned cherrywood high chest of drawers, New York, 1710-40, on an arcaded apron and 'trumpet' turned legs, 41in. wide. (Sotheby's) $25,875

A Queen Anne oyster veneered walnut chest-on-stand, the rectangular molded top inlaid with circles and fleurs de lys, 38¾in. wide. (Christie's) $12,880

A Queen Anne burr elm and walnut chest on stand, the upper part with projecting cornice over two short and three long drawers, 106cm. wide. (Tennants) $8,000

A William and Mary oyster veneered chest on stand, late 17th century and later, the whole crossbanded in holly, on five bulbous turned supports, 34½in. wide. (Bonhams) $4,800

Early 18th century oyster veneered olive wood chest of two short and two long drawers with geometrically patterned top, on later bobbin turned stand, 36½in. (Ewbank) $5,120

A Queen Anne figured cherrywood flat top high chest of drawers, Rhode Island, circa 1760, the upper section with molded projecting cornice, 38in. wide. (Sotheby's) $28,750

A Victorian rosewood chiffonier, the mirrored back with a shelf, carved gallery and female mask brackets, 50½in. (David Lay) $2,640

An early Victorian rosewood chiffonier, the pedimented back with single shelf, 101cm. wide. (Bristol) $1,148

A Regency ormolu mounted and brass inlaid chiffonier in the manner of John MacLean & Son, the rectangular top with a two tiered mirror backed superstructure, 35¾in. wide. (Christie's) $12,880

A Victorian walnut chiffonier with carved and scrolled crest to back above a single shaped shelf support on scrolled carved brackets above an oval panel, 42in. wide. (Dee Atkinson & Harrison) $990

A small Regency rosewood chiffonier, the raised back with shelf having pierced brass gallery, 25½in. wide. (Andrew Hartley) $3,925

A mid Victorian mahogany chiffonier, the shaped and scrolled edged back with carved leaf and flower surmount, 50in. wide. (Andrew Hartley) $1,138

HISTORICAL FACTS
Commode Chests

Most early French commodes had their basic rectangularity softened by subtle curves in the rococo manner – a popular style from the accession of Louis XV in 1715. Good examples are often beautifully inlaid with birds, garlands of flowers and musical instruments beside having superb ormolu mounts and handles made by such masters as Cressent, Gouthière and Caffieris.

Just after the mid century, a number of commodes were made to blend with the Chinese style rooms which had become fashionable, and decorated panels were imported – portraying domestic scenes – for inclusion in their manufacture.

By the 1780s, many commodes appeared with fine decoration after the styles of Angelica Kaufmann and Pergolesi – often painted in the form of cupids set in ovals surrounded by painted flowers and scrolls. Another style, particularly favored by Adam, was that of a white ground on which were colored urns set amid wreaths and surrounded by friezes of gilt molding. Toward the end of the century, however, the commode slipped somewhat from its former importance in fashionable drawing rooms and the quality took a predictably downward turn.

Early in the 19th century, commodes lost their flamboyance altogether, returning to a rectangular form and resembling more the chiffonier.

Edwardian paint decorated satinwood commode, circa 1900–10, 42¼in. wide.
(Skinner) $6,325

A German Baroque walnut and fruitwood marquetry commode, first half 18th century, the molded rectangular top of undulating form, 46¼in. wide.
(Sotheby's) $9,775

A Victorian satinwood, rosewood, Goncalo-Alvez and marquetry demi-lune commode, inlaid overall with boxwood ebony lines crossbanded in kingwood, 49in. wide.
(Christie's) $8,487

Unusual paint-decorated commode, 19th century, with 20th century hand-painted decoration of hunting and sporting scenes, 29in. wide.
(Eldred's) $935

Pair of George III style paint decorated satinwood commodes, 19th century, 51in. wide.
(Skinner) $25,300

A George III mahogany, fiddleback-mahogany and satinwood serpentine dressing-commode, inlaid overall with fruitwood lines and crossbanded in amaranth, tulipwood and satinwood, 41¼in. wide. (Christie's) $8,298

A rosewood, marquetry and gilt-bronze bombé commode, French, circa 1880, of serpentine outline, with a shaped rouge marble top above three long drawers, 129cm. wide.
(Sotheby's) $8,124

A walnut kingwood and floral marquetry bombé petit commode, the molded serpentine crossbanded top above a frieze fitted with two drawers, 29in. wide.
(Christie's) $2,100

A George III ormolu-mounted padouk serpentine commode, attributed to John Cobb, the eared molded serpentine-fronted rectangular top crossbanded overall, 49in. wide.
(Christie's) $84,660

An Italian walnut commode, late 18th century, decorated with later crossbanding and lines, on collared square tapering legs, 49in. wide. (Christie's) $2,769

A mahogany commode, late 18th century, applied with later gilt-metal mounts, gray veined marble top, 46in. wide. (Christie's) $1,661

A North European walnut and kingwood banded serpentine commode with molded gray marble serpentine top, 49½in. wide. (Christie's) $6,992

An Italian walnut serpentine commode, decorated with crossbanding, the top previously hinged above a drawer, 25½in. wide. (Christie's) $4,430

A pair of kingwood and gilt-bronze petites commodes, French, circa 1890, each with a verde antico shaped marble top, 45cm. wide. (Sotheby's) $13,024

A French kingwood and foliate marquetry petite bombé commode, 20th century, the mottled serpentine marble top above three drawers inlaid with floral sprays, 27½in. wide. (Christie's) $4,799

A Dutch tulipwood serpentine commode, late 18th/early 19th century, applied with gilt-metal mounts, the later shaped marble top above two drawers, 30in. wide. (Christie's) $4,430

A bronze and parquetry commode en tombeau, French, circa 1880, with a molded brèche d'Alep marble top, 100cm. wide. (Sotheby's) $5,777

A parquetry, marquetry and gilt-bronze commode, Paris, circa 1880, in the Transitional style, with a brèche d'Alep molded marble top, 113cm wide. (Sotheby's) $4,514

A North Italian walnut serpentine commode, late 18th century, decorated with meandering floral stems and crossbanding, 52in. wide. (Christie's) $7,752

A kingwood and gilt-bronze bombé commode, French, circa 1880, with molded rouge marble serpentine top, 119cm wide. (Sotheby's) $6,319

A mahogany, tulipwood and inlaid commode, early 19th century, decorated with checkered banding, lines and simulated fluting, 47¼in. wide. (Christie's) $8,860

A French kingwood and foliate marquetry petite bombé commode, 20th century, applied with gilt-metal mounts, the rouge marble top above three drawers, 27½in. wide. (Christie's) $4,430

A George III mahogany serpentine commode, the molded serpentine-fronted rectangular top with canted angles above four long graduated drawers, 36¼in. wide. (Christie's) $20,999

A French kingwood and marquetry breakfront commode, late 19th/early 20th century, the top inlaid with a lakeside scene, 32in. wide. (Christie's) $11,997

A George III mahogany serpentine-fronted dressing commode with a baize-covered slide and compartments to the top drawer, 38½in. wide. (Bearne's) $3,726

A kingwood and gilt-bronze commode, French, circa 1890, in Louis XV style, of bombé form, 116cm. wide. (Sotheby's) $5,416

A Swiss walnut and parquetry commode, late 18th century, decorated with fruitwood banding and lines, rectangular brêche violette marble top, 45in. wide. (Christie's) $4,430

A mahogany night cupboard, by Whytock and Reid of Edinburgh, the rounded rectangular galleried top above a brushing-slide, 16in wide.
(Christie's) $1,240

A mahogany serpentine bedside commode, 19th century, the later top above a pair of tambour shutters with an adapted pull-out front, 21½in. wide.
(Christie's) $1,754

A George III mahogany serpentine commode with a hinged top above the open arms and serpentine front raised on chamfered square legs, 22in. wide.
(Anderson & Garland)
                                 $826

A George III mahogany night commode, 23in. wide.
(Dreweatt Neate) $2,400

A George III mahogany tray top bedside commode, the undulating gallery pierced with carrying handles above a pair of paneled doors, 21½in. wide.
(Christie's) $5,537

A George III mahogany commode, the shaped galleried top with pierced handles above fallfront door and pull-out seat, on square supports, 52cm. wide.
(Bristol) $1,536

A George III mahogany bedside cabinet with rectangular tray top above a hinged flap, 19¾in. wide. (Bearne's) $1,426

A Regency mahogany step commode, decorated with ebonized lines, the three gilt-tooled red leather lined treads, 17in. wide. (Christie's) $2,584

An English 18th century style oak tray-top bedside cabinet, 19th century, profusely inlaid with Dutch floral marquetry, 49cm. wide. (Bristol) $722

Henry van de Velde for Hofkunsttischlerei H. Scheidemantel, Weimar, bedside cabinet, 1902-3, white painted pine, brass grip handle, on castors, 15½in. wide. (Sotheby's) $3,562

Pair of Continental neoclassical faux marbelized pot cupboards, early 19th century, the paint of later date, 26¾in. high. (Skinner) $920

A George III mahogany bedside commode, the shaped galleried tray-handled rounded rectangular top above a pair of doors crossbanded in tulipwood, 22in. wide. (Christie's) $4,715

A George III mahogany tray top night commode, with a pair of ebony strung doors, above one ebony strung dummy drawer, 19¾in. wide. (Dreweatt Neate) $1,491

A George III mahogany and boxstrung tray top night commode, with cupboard door above two pull out dummy drawers to reveal a chamber pot, 19¾in. wide. (Dreweatt Neate) $1,067

A George III mahogany tray top bedside commode, the galleried rectangular top above a hinged fall flap with an adapted pull-out front below, 24in. wide. (Christie's) $2,215

An early 18th century painted pine corner cupboard, the two doors depicting an allegorical scene, 60cm. wide.
(Bearne's) $981

A pair of mahogany and gilt-bronze encoignures, Paris, circa 1880, each with a white marble top above a frieze, 75cm. wide.
(Sotheby's) $20,838

19th century mahogany standing corner cupboard, the top with pierced cornice and a central panel with palms and ribbon ties, 49in. wide. (Ewbank) $5,760

A late Federal maple-inlaid cherrywood corner cupboard, probably Pennsylvania, circa 1820, in two parts, the upper section with molded cornice, 53in. wide.
(Sotheby's) $9,200

A pair of gilt-bronze and ebony encoignures, French, circa 1870, each with a nero antico molded top, above a frieze with foliate scrolls, 72cm. wide.
(Sotheby's) $18,957

A paneled yellow pine hanging corner wall cupboard, Pennsylvania, 1750–70, the molded cornice above a double-paneled hinged door opening to shelves, 34in. wide.
(Sotheby's) $39,100

A Chippendale cherrywood corner cupboard, Pennsylvania, circa 1790, in two parts, the upper with molded cornice above glazed doors, 52in. wide.
(Sotheby's) $7,475

A pair of Louis XVI jacaranda veneered encoignures, with mottled gray marble tops, 100cm. high, French.
(Stockholms Auktionsverket) $3,257

An important Queen Anne carved and blue- and red-painted pine corner cupboard, New York, probably Long Island, circa 1760, 43in. wide.
(Sotheby's) $18,400

A George III mahogany corner cupboard, with molded and dentil breakfront cornice, two arched doors each, 38½in. wide. (Andrew Hartley) $2,433

An early 18th century walnut veneered hanging corner cupboard with arched broken pediment and canted corners, 75cm. wide. (Bearne's) $1,456

Painted corner cupboard, New England, circa 1790, the flat molded cornice above four cupboard doors, 49in. wide. (Skinner) $4,025

American one-piece corner cupboard, in cherry, molded cornice with dentil decoration, two eight-light doors above two paneled doors, 82in. high. (Eldred's) $3,740

A pair of late 18th century walnut and fruitwood inlaid corner cupboards, 65cm. wide. (Finarte) $5,902

A Chippendale pine corner cupboard, Pennsylvania, 1760–1800, in two parts, the reverse-breakfronted overhanging cornice with canted corners, 4ft. 5in. wide. (Sotheby's) $3,162

Glazed pine paneled corner cupboard, Middle Atlantic States, 19th century, glazed doors open to a three-shelved interior, 48½in. wide. (Skinner) $2,415

A mid 18th century German walnut veneered bowfront hanging corner cupboard, with cavetto cornice, 67.5cm. wide. (Bearne's) $1,662

American architectural corner cupboard, late 18th/early 19th century, in yellow pine with molded surround, probably Mid-Atlantic States, 87in. high. (Eldred's) $880

An English oak press cupboard, 17th century, the upper section with overhanging cornice decorated with blind fret-work, 70½in. wide.
(Sotheby's) $3,450

A figured maple and birchwood hutch cupboard, New England, early 19th century, in two parts, the overhanging cornice above glazed doors, 5ft. wide.
(Sotheby's) $9,200

A Victorian carved oak gothic style cupboard with a gray marble top above two short drawers, 57½in. wide.
(Anderson & Garland)
     $15,700

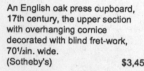

A Victorian walnut breakfront credenza decorated with inlaid stringing and honeysuckle motifs, 59in. wide.
(Anderson & Garland)
     $3,532

A fine and rare paneled walnut hanging wall cupboard with drawer, Pennsylvania, circa 1760, the molded cornice above a paneled molded door, 29in. wide.
(Sotheby's) $28,750

An Italian baroque walnut credenza, probably Emilian, with overhanging molded top above a molded door, 29½in. wide.
(Sotheby's) $1,380

An early George III mahogany low cupboard with molded top and two fielded paneled doors, 49½in. wide.
(David Lay) $1,360

A red- and brown-painted pine and poplar two-part cupboard, first half 19th century, in two parts, 4ft. 4in. wide.
(Sotheby's) $3,450

A fine and rare William and Mary paneled pine and turned maple valuables chest, Massachusetts, 1700–40, 19¾in. wide.
(Sotheby's) $20,700

American hutch cupboard, early
19th century, in pine with molded
cornice and three shelves above
two paneled doors, 52in. wide.
(Eldred's) $1,100

American cupboard, in pine with
single door, shaped bracket feet,
38½in. wide.
(Eldred's) $550

A French oak cupboard, fitted with
a fielded paneled cupboard door,
the stylized scrolled uprights on bun
feet, 28½in. wide.
(Christie's) $1,288

A Chippendale blue-painted pine
hutch cupboard, Pennsylvania,
circa 1780, in two parts, the
projecting lower section with three
short drawers and two field-
paneled cupboard doors, 5ft. 1in.
wide.
(Sotheby's) $33,350

A fine pair of ormolu mounted and
marquetry inlaid meubles d'appui,
by Henry Dasson, circa 1885, the
rectangular breakfront griotte
marble tops with canted corners,
31¾in. wide.
(Bonhams) $25,440

A fine grain-painted poplar step-
back cupboard, Pennsylvania,
1790–1810, in two parts, the
overhanging cove molding above
a case with chamfered corners, 5ft.
2in. wide.
(Sotheby's) $44,850

An ocher-painted pine cupboard,
American, probably New York
State, 1730–80, the dramatically
stepped overhanging cornice
above a cupboard door, 39in. wide.
(Sotheby's) $4,025

A carved oak press cupboard,
with molded cornice and frieze on
baluster turned supports, 62in.
wide, 17th century and later.
(Andrew Hartley) $4,800

A red and gray-painted paneled
pine cupboard, probably New York,
1730-60, the projecting molding
above two large raised panel
doors, 4ft. 6in. wide.
(Sotheby's) $2,645

HISTORICAL FACTS
Davenports

This is a very delightful little desk which originated during the final years of the 18th century.

Earlier davenports were usually made of rosewood or satinwood and were boxlike in structure apart from the sloping top, which would either pull forward or swivel to the side in order to make room for the writer's lower limbs. They stand on bun, small turned or, occasionally, bracket feet and better examples sport a fine brass gallery to stop pens and small objects from falling down the back.

While most examples are about two feet wide, it is well worth looking for the smaller ones (about 15 inches to 18 inches wide), for these can fetch twice as much as the larger models even though they usually have only a cupboard at the side instead of drawers.

It was during the William IV period that the davenport gained its name and its popularity.

The story goes that one Captain Davenport placed an order for one of these writing desks with Gillows of Lancaster, a well-known firm of cabinet makers at the time. Known during its manufacture as 'the Davenport order', the first desk was completed and the name stuck, being applied to all subsequent orders for a desk of this particular style.

Davenports were, at the middle of the 19th century, at the height of their popularity and at peak quality. Therafter standards of workmanship declined.

A Victorian walnut davenport, the raised back with pierced brass gallery, 21in. wide.
(Andrew Hartley) $3,768

An Edwardian mahogany and boxwood inlaid davenport, fitted with three drawers to one side, 26in. wide.
(Christie's) $1,125

A Victorian ebonised and burr walnut crossbanded davenport, the hinged sloping leather-lined writing surface surmounted by a hinged pencil-box.
(Christie's) $1,593

A mid-Victorian figured walnut harlequin davenport, the counter-balanced rising compartment with fret framed fronted drawers.
(David Lay) $5,088

A Victorian walnut davenport, the leather inset top enclosing maple interior with four true and four false drawers, 54cm. wide.
(Bristol) $704

A Victorian walnut davenport, the paneled front flanked on one side by four short drawers and by four false drawers to the other, 23in. wide. (Christie's) $2,081

A fine William IV burr walnut veneered davenport, the sliding top with a brass gallery.
(David Lay) $5,120

A Victorian walnut veneered harlequin davenport, the piano front opening to reveal a sliding adjustable writing surface.
(David Lay) $2,080

A Victorian rosewood davenport, with shaped three-quarter gallery and harlequin action, 21in. wide.
(Christie's) $3,888

A Victorian walnut davenport, with ebony inlay and stringing, the hinged stationery compartment above leather inset writing slope, 86cm. wide.
(Bristol) $2,170

A Victorian rosewood-veneered piano-front davenport with rising stationery compartment, 22 1/2 in. wide.
(Bearne's) $5,022

Fine quality rosewood davenport with sliding top, four graduated drawers to the right hand section, dummy drawers to the left, English, circa 1800, 1ft. 8in. wide.
(G.A. Key) $2,862

A Victorian walnut davenport, with pierced brass gallery and secret stationery compartment, 22in. wide.
(Andrew Hartley) $3,360

A Regency rosewood square davenport with carved fan corners and gadrooned borders, the sliding top with pen tray and inkwells, 19 1/2 in.
(Ewbank) $2,560

A 19th century French ebonized and ormolu side cabinet.
(Christopher Matthews) $1,248

A mahogany and gilt-bronze display cabinet, Paris, circa 1890, on turned tapering fluted legs, 176cm. wide.
(Sotheby's) $9,551

A Sheraton style satinwood serpentine cabinet inlaid with ebony lines and with swags of flowers, on square legs, 44in.
(Ewbank) $1,208

A Louis XVI ormolu-mounted tulipwood and mahogany vitrine, with a chamfered rectangular molded brèche violette marble top, 37½in. wide.
(Christie's) $17,250

An Edwardian mahogany and inlaid display cabinet, the breakfront cornice with inlaid dentiled molding, above a frieze with satinwood crossbanding, 53in. wide. (Christie's) $5,108

An Edwardian serpentine front satinwood display cabinet, the molded cornice with a boxwood strung frieze above a single glazed and paneled door, 58in. wide.
(Bonhams) $6,996

A late Victorian mahogany and boxwood inlaid drawing room display cabinet, with scrolled pediment, above a glazed door, 48in. wide.
(Christie's) $1,422

An Edwardian satinwood and inlaid bowfronted display cabinet, the arched top with dentil cornice, 80in. high.
(George Kidner) $12,895

A Victorian gilt-brass and ebonized display cabinet, English, circa 1890, the upper part with a door enclosing three shelves, 78in. wide.
(Sotheby's) $2,888

An Empire style ormolu-mounted mahogany vitrine, late 19th/early 20th century, with an eared D-shaped case, 43¾in. wide.
(Christie's) $7,475

Small Art Deco china cabinet, two doors, glass shelves, electrified, burl walnut, 44½in. wide.
(Skinner) $546

A Syrian mother-of-pearl inlaid walnut vitrine with a scrolling broken arch pediment centering a raised shaped panel 50in. wide.
(Christie's) $11,500

An Edwardian satinwood, rosewood banded and boxwood and ebony line inlaid display cabinet, the raised back with pierced scrolling foliage, 48in. wide.
(Ewbank) $3,520

Rare L. & J.G. Stickley china cabinet, No.746, chamfered backboards, interior original finish, exterior overcoated with good color, 44in. wide.
(Skinner) $5,175

Tiger maple glazed cabinet, New York or New Jersey, circa 1825, the flat carved molded cornice above two glazed doors, 41in. wide.
(Skinner) $5,175

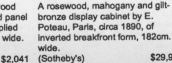

A 19th century French kingwood vitrine with serpentine glazed panel and sides decorated with applied ormolu foliate banding, 34in. wide.
(Anderson & Garland) $2,041

A rosewood, mahogany and gilt-bronze display cabinet by E. Poteau, Paris, circa 1890, of inverted breakfront form, 182cm. wide.
(Sotheby's) $29,992

A late Victorian mahogany and satinwood inlaid display cabinet, the broken pediment with checker lines, above a frieze inlaid and engraved with foliage, 58in. wide.
(Christie's) $17,480

A Chinese carved hardwood cabinet with a flared cornice above a large glazed panel door enclosing shelves, 45in. wide. (Anderson & Garland)

$785

A gilt-metal-mounted rosewood and floral marquetry vitrine table, of Louis XV style, on slender cabriole supports joined by a shaped platform, 23½in. wide. (Christie's)

$2,100

A French kingwood display cabinet with a single glazed door and glazed sides, on turned and fluted legs, 36in. wide. (Ewbank)

$1,250

An Edwardian inlaid mahogany bow fronted china display cabinet with satinwood stringing, fitted single glazed door on square tapering legs and spade feet, 3ft. wide. (Russell, Baldwin & Bright)

$2,229

One of a pair of 19th century ebonized and boulle display cabinets in the Louis XIV manner, each applied throughout with gilt-brass moldings, 45¼in. wide. (Bearne's)

(Two) $2,187

An Edwardian mahogany display cabinet with raised back and bow-front central panel door enclosing lined shelves, 48in. wide. (Anderson & Garland)

$1,431

A Sheraton Revival painted satinwood display cabinet, profusely painted with floral garlands, scrolling tendrils and urns, 53½in. wide. (Andrew Hartley) $8,300

L. & J.G. Stickley two-door bookcase, attributed, original finish with vibrant quarter-sawn oak, replaced back, 45in. wide. (Skinner) $1,610

A kingwood serpentine vitrine cabinet of Louis XV style, the molded domed top above two glazed doors painted with Vernis Martin style panels, 40in. wide. (Christie's) $5,345

A late Victorian mahogany and satinwood crossbanded display cabinet, the D-shaped top above a paneled frieze, 48in. wide. (Christie's) $3,562

A 19th century French Empire rosewood vitrine with pierced brass gallery over single glazed door with beveled glass panel, 2ft. 8in. wide. (Russell, Baldwin & Bright) $2,397

A satinwood and marquetry display cabinet, Edwardian, circa 1905, of serpentine outline, 118cm. wide. (Sotheby's) $9,551

Rare Limbert two-door bookcase, tapered sides, arched base, paneled sides, corbels, three adjusting shelves, 36in. wide. (Skinner) $3,105

A Victorian ebonized and burr walnut pedestal cabinet, the central glazed panel door enclosing lined shelves and flanked by fluted Corinthian pilasters, 33½in. wide. (Anderson & Garland) $1,507

Edwardian mahogany display cabinet inlaid with ribbon ties and foliage, two part glazed doors enclosing shelves, 45in. wide. (Ewbank) $1,320

A late Victorian mahogany display cabinet, with foliate-carved pierced and scrolled superstructure and shaped mirrored back, 59in. wide. (Christie's) $3,562

Unusual Art Nouveau period mahogany china display cabinet, the frieze inlaid with stylized tulip motifs, over a leaded glass door, late 19th century, 36in. (G.A. Key) $858

An 18th century Dutch marquetry glazed cabinet, with domed pediment over pair of quarter-glazed doors, 142cm. wide. (Bristol) $5,115

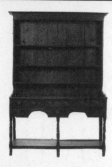

An oak dresser, the molded cornice above a three open shelves, on turned baluster supports joined by a platform undertier, 55in. wide.
(Christie's) $4,582

Diminutive George III oak dresser, late 18th century, the top and bottom associated, 55¹/₂in. wide.
(Skinner) $2,415

An antique oak Welsh dresser having open plate rack, the base fitted with two frieze drawers, 4ft. 7in. wide.
(Russell, Baldwin & Bright) $3,807

An elmwood and pine step-back cupboard, English or Continental, mid-18th century, the rectangular molded cornice above three shelves, 5ft. 4in. wide.
(Sotheby's) $3,737

An oak dresser, the later molded cornice above a fluted frieze fitted with five open shelves, 76in, wide.
(Christie's) $3,818

A late 18th century style oak Shropshire type dresser, crossbanded in mahogany, 189cm. wide.
(Bristol) $3,565

A brown- and blue-painted pine step-back cupboard, American, 19th century, the overhanging cornice above three conforming shelves, 5ft. wide.
(Sotheby's) $8,050

A mid-Georgian oak dresser, 18th century, with associated plate rack back, the shaped frieze above three open shelves, 84in. wide.
(Christie's) $6,810

A good George III elm dresser, the bordered delft rack with molded cornice and two shelves flanked by fluted pilaster uprights, 79in. wide.
(Anderson & Garland) $6,908

HISTORICAL FACTS
Dumb Waiters

Dumb-waiters were extremely fashionable during the final quarter of the 18th century and throughout the Regency period, although there is evidence that they were available as early as 1727, when Lord Bristol purchased one from a cabinet maker named Robert Leigh.

It was Sheraton, with a turn of phrase as elegant as one of his own chairlegs, who described the dumb-waiter as 'a useful piece of furniture to serve in some respects the place of a waiter, whence it is so named'.

Generally consisting of three or four graduated shelves revolving around a central column, dumb-waiters were usually made with a tripod base terminating in feet whose style varied with the transient fashions of the period. The shelves, largest at the bottom, were sometimes made from single pieces of wood and sometimes constructed with flaps.

A French walnut metamorphic dumb waiter, late 19th century, fitted with three tiers, the central with a molded frieze, 39½in. wide.
(Christie's) $5,537

An early 19th century mahogany dumb waiter with two tiers each later carved and inlaid, 22in. wide.
(Andrew Hartley) $1,749

An early Victorian mahogany two tier 'Lazy Susan', the round top and undertier with dished piecrust border, 18 x 14in.
(Dreweatt Neate) $495

A Victorian mahogany three-tier dumb waiter surmounted by carved foliated motifs and raised on scrolling brackets, 53½in. wide.
(Anderson & Garland) $1,813

A Georgian mahogany dumb waiter with three graduated tiers, the bottom two revolving, 44½in. high.
(Anderson & Garland) $2,119

A Regency mahogany dumb waiter, with three rectangular tiers fitted with pierced brass galleries and decorated with molded studs, 45in. wide.
(Christie's) $2,953

Regency period mahogany three tier dumb waiter of circular form, with central balustered and ring turned shaft, 25in.
(G. A. Key) $2,400

Queen Anne cherry bonnet top high chest of drawers, Concord, Massachusetts, last quarter 18th century, 38in. wide.
(Skinner) $17,250

American Queen Anne highboy, 18th century, in walnut, on cabriole legs and duck feet, 36½in. wide.
(Eldred's) $5,500

A fine Queen Anne carved cherrywood bonnet-top highboy, Connecticut, circa 1760, on cabriole legs ending in pad feet, 40in. wide.
(Sotheby's) $31,050

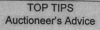

TOP TIPS
Auctioneer's Advice

Early, pre 18th century, pieces can often be distinguished by their drawer linings, the grain of which usually runs from front to back. After that date the grain usually runs from side to side.

Drawers lined in oak rather than pine usually indicate that a piece is of superior quality. It is also a good sign if the wide drawer on a chest has a center splat, again indicating a better quality piece.

Thomson Roddick & Laurie

Queen Anne walnut chest on frame, Pennsylvania, circa 1760–80, the top section with flat molded cornice above a case of three thumbmolded short drawers, 38in. wide.
(Skinner) $26,450

Queen Anne tiger maple high chest of drawers, Massachusetts, circa 1760, the top section with flat molded cornice above case of four thumbmolded graduated drawers, 37¾in. wide.
(Skinner) $28,750

Queen Anne tiger maple high chest of drawers, Newburyport, Massachusetts, circa 1760, the top section with flat molded cornice, 38⅜in. wide.
(Skinner) $20,700

A Queen Anne figured maple flat-top highboy, New England, 1750–70, on cabriole legs centering a shaped apron, lower case 28in. wide.
(Sotheby's) $13,800

Queen Anne painted pine high chest of drawers, probably Hartford, Connecticut, circa 1740, the top sections with flat molded cornice, 37in. wide.
(Skinner) $35,650

A Queen Anne carved cherrywood high chest-of-drawers, in two sections, on cabriole legs with pad feet, 39in. wide.
(Christie's) $8,625

A fine and rare Queen Anne richly figured maple flat top highboy, Delaware River Valley, 1740–60, in two parts, 42in. wide.
(Sotheby's) $68,500

A Queen Anne maple flat-top highboy, probably Oyster Bay, Long Island, New York, circa 1750, in two parts, 39½in. wide.
(Sotheby's) $18,400

A good Queen Anne carved maple flat-top highboy, New England, probably Eastern Connecticut, circa 1750, in two parts, 39¼in. wide.
(Sotheby's) $26,450

The Mifflin family matching Chippendale carved mahogany high chest-of-drawers and dressing table, Philadelphia, 1750–55, chest 44¼in. wide; dressing table 34in. wide.
(Christie's) $717,500

A Queen Anne carved and figured cherrywood flat-top highboy, Massachusetts, circa 1750, in two parts, on cabriole legs ending in pad feet, 39½in. wide.
(Sotheby's) $9,775

A Chippendale carved and figured walnut highboy, Pennsylvania, circa 1780, in two parts, on shell-carved cabriole legs ending in claw-and-ball feet, 44½in. wide.
(Sotheby's) $6,900

A Queen Anne carved and figured walnut chest-on-frame, Pennsylvania, circa 1755, in two parts, 42in. wide.
(Sotheby's) $21,850

Queen Anne maple carved high chest of drawers, Salem or Newburyport, Massachusetts, circa 1760, the top section with flat molded cornice, 36¼in. wide.
(Skinner) $24,150

A Victorian mahogany cylinder desk with a fitted interior including a pull-out writing surface, 59¾in. wide.
(Hy. Duke & Son) $4,320

Dutch neoclassical style walnut and floral marquetry kidney-shaped desk, late 19th century, 51in. wide.
(Skinner) $2,760

A Victorian mahogany desk with a central drawer flanked by four bowfronted drawers on each side, 48in.
(Ewbank) $1,920

A Swedish rolltop desk, circa 1900, 149 cm. wide, with original matching swivel chair.
(Auction Team Köln) $508

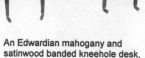

An Edwardian mahogany and satinwood banded kneehole desk, the top with inset red leather, 48in. wide.
(George Kidner) $2,123

A late 19th century oak roll top desk, hinged sides above eight drawers on plinth base, 66in.
(Ewbank) $1,242

A Smith Premier mahogany roll-top desk with integral, adjustable height, typewriter table, complete with Royal No. 5 typewriter, American, circa 1895, 122cm. wide.
(Auction Team Köln) $970

A George II kingwood kneehole desk, the crossbanded brown leather-lined rectangular top, above a central kneehole with foliate and trellis-work border,47in. wide.
(Christie's) $16,227

An 18th century mahogany kneehole desk with molded top over one long frieze drawer, 2ft. 6in. wide.
(Russell, Baldwin & Bright)
   $5,338

A late Victorian mahogany twin-pedestal partner's desk, the molded rectangular leather-lined top above a frieze fitted with three drawers, 63in. wide.
(Christie's) $3,680

An 18th century mahogany double-sided twin pedestal desk, one side with nine drawers, the other with two doors beneath three drawers, 32½ x 60in.
(David Lay) $24,600

A late Victorian walnut twin-pedestal partner's desk, the molded rectangular leather-lined top above a frieze fitted with three drawers to either side, 60in. wide.
(Christie's) $4,048

Walnut veneered small partner's desk, twin pedestal, on cabriole legs, English, turn of the century, 5ft. 3in. wide.
(G.A. Key)   **$2,544**

Campaign-style desk, in mahogany with inlaid gilt brown leather top, ebonized finish with brass-bound top and pedestals, 54in. long.
(Eldred's)   **$1,045**

Good quality mahogany kidney shaped ladies writing desk, kneehole type with nine drawers, English, circa 1900, 4ft. 3in.
(G.A. Key)   **$2,782**

A mahogany and gilt-bronze writing desk, English, 1890, in the Directoire style, the leather-inset top with a molded border, 149cm. wide.
(Sotheby's)   **$7,123**

A good Moorish Revival suite, early 20th century, comprising a pedestal desk, an ensuite envelope card table, armchair and five single chairs, pier mirror, lidded jardinière and open bookcase.
(Bonhams)   **$6,360**

An oak and curled oak pedestal desk, late 19th century, the rectangular top inset with redleather writing surfaces, the central panel fitted with hinged compartments, 72in. wide.
(Christie's)   **$3,070**

A George III mahogany architect's pedestal desk, attributed to Gillows, the green leather-lined rectangular hinged top on ratchet supports, 49¼in. wide.
(Christie's)   **$19,090**

A George III mahogany library desk with a hinged burgundy leather writing surface opening to an interior with secretaire drawers and pigeon holes, 49½in. wide.
(Hy. Duke & Son)   **$1,840**

A walnut kneehole desk, diagonally-banded to the top and front, the molded rectangular top with cut front corners, 30in. wide.
(Christie's)   **$5,281**

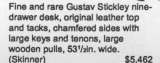

Fine and rare Gustav Stickley nine-drawer desk, original leather top and tacks, chamfered sides with large keys and tenons, large wooden pulls, 53¹/₂in. wide.
(Skinner)   **$5,462**

Italian Renaissance-style walnut desk, late 19th century, 61¼in. wide.
(Skinner)   **$2,530**

A mahogany pedestal desk, the molded rectangular green leather-lined top above three frieze drawers, 19th century, 50in. wide.
(Christie's)   **$3,206**

Dutch neoclassical mahogany and marquetry linen press, late 18th century, with three interior shelves, 63in. wide.
(Skinner) $9,200

A George III mahogany linen press, the dentil-molded cornice above a blind fret-carved frieze with two paneled doors below, 53in. wide.
(Christie's) $2,953

A Regency mahogany linen press, the molded cornice above pair of a panel doors enclosing four slides, 140cm. wide.
(Bristol) $2,015

TOP TIPS
Auctioneer's Advice

There are many ways of dating furniture. One, if you have an accurate measure to hand, is by the thickness of the veneer on a piece.

Thin veneers of up to 1mm thick indicate machine cutting and this would imply that the piece dates from about 1850 onwards. Before that, veneers had to be cut by hand and were rarely less than 2mm thick.

Thomson Roddick & Laurie

A George III mahogany linen press, the molded rectangular top above a pair of paneled doors enclosing three later sliding trays, 47½in. wide. (Christie's) $3,507

A late George III mahogany secrétaire linen press, the molded checker lined cornice fitted with a pair of boxwood lined and crossbanded paneled doors, 48in. wide. (Christie's) $3,128

An early 19th century mahogany linen press, with cotton reel cornice, pair of oval inlaid panel doors, 129cm. wide.
(Bristol) $2,403

A George III mahogany linen press, the molded and blind-fretwork-carved cornice fitted with a pair of paneled cupboard doors, 49in. wide. (Christie's) $4,416

A Regency mahogany linen press, the molded cornice above flamed mahogany paneled doors, 119cm. wide.
(Bristol) $1,920

The Rodman family Queen Anne figured cherrywood lowboy, Rhode Island, circa 1750, the rectangular molded top with notched corners, top 37³/₄in. wide.
(Sotheby's) $35,650

A fine and rare William and Mary walnut veneered, inlaid and turned oak or ash lowboy, New England, circa 1730, 32¹/₂in. wide.
(Sotheby's) $18,400

A George III walnut and elm lowboy, the molded rectangular quarter-veneered and crossbanded top above a pair of short drawers and a long drawer, 30in. wide.
(Christie's) $13,202

A Queen Anne carved and figured cherrywood lowboy, Massachusetts, 1750–70, the rectangular thumbmolded top above one long drawer and three short drawers, case 30¹/₂in. wide.
(Sotheby's) $8,050

A fine and rare Chippendale carved and figured walnut lowboy, Philadelphia, circa 1780, the rectangular thumbmolded top above one long and three short drawers, 38in. wide.
(Sotheby's) $60,250

A fine Chippendale carved mahogany lowboy, Philadelphia, circa 1770, the rectangular molded top above a case with one long and three short molded drawers, 35¹/₄in. wide.
(Sotheby's) $32,200

A good Queen Anne walnut lowboy, New England, probably Massachusetts, circa 1740, the rectangular thumbmolded top with notched corners, 35in. wide.
(Sotheby's) $20,700

A fine Queen Anne carved and figured walnut lowboy, Philadelphia, circa 1750, on volute-carved cabriole legs, case 31in. wide.
(Sotheby's) $107,000

A William and Mary black-painted maple and walnut lowboy, Massachusetts, 1720–50, the rectangular top with molded edge, 33in. wide.
(Sotheby's) $63,000

HISTORICAL FACTS
Screens

Screens have been in widespread use since at least the fifteenth century, for warding off draughts, for protecting sensitive complexions from the fire's heat or for privacy.

It is hardly surprising perhaps, that the quality of screens' manufacture has varied but little from those early days, and the materials used are still very much the same too; from simple buckram, wickerwork, wood and needlework to extravagant finishes for royalty, including gold lace and silk. During the reign of Charles II, some fine examples, having up to twelve folds, and decorated with superb lacquer work were imported from the East. Today, of course, one of these would cost many thousands of pounds.

By the William and Mary period, small screens fitted with sliding panels of polished wood or embroidery had become popular and these developed into the cheval screens of the 18th century. Small pole screens also put in an appearance at this time, though these became more numerous as the eighteenth century gave way to the nineteenth.

Some of these are particularly fine, having delicately carved tripod bases, but they are more decorative than practical.

Interesting and fairly reasonable Victorian screens to look for are those in the Chinese style with applied mother-of-pearl or ivory birds and foliage, or those decorated with scraps.

Whimsical Victorian painted tin candle screen, 19th century, depicting girls with cats, 10in. high. (Skinner) $1,610

Polychrome decorated pine fireboard, possibly New England, last quarter 19th century, 38 x 39in. (Skinner) $1,840

A Flemish four-fold tapestry screen, the tapestry circa 1600, each framed panel resting on foliate carved feet, each panel 73 x 22in. (Sotheby's) $5,750

Paul Etienne Saïn, four panel abstract screen, circa 1930, each panel with gold leaf decoration on a red and brown ground, each panel 68¼ x 17½in. (Sotheby's) $19,205

A mahogany three-leaf screen, 1880s, each leaf with upper geometric fretwork detailing, enclosing a finely embroidered silk panel, 68¼ x 22¼in. each panel. (Christie's) $10,872

A three fold lacquer screen, by Leonor Fini, circa 1930, decorated with three dancing figures, against a black ground, 57 x 15¾in. each panel. (Christie's) $14,996

A William IV rosewood firescreen and writing table, adjustable glazed screen above a hinged writing surface and single drawer, upholstered foot pad and scroll legs, 15½in. wide.
(Hy. Duke & Son) $928

A fine three-fold painted screen, probably early 18th century, the central domed fold painted with a garden scene, 250.5cm. wide.
(Sotheby's) $23,920

A carved giltwood and tapestry firescreen, French, circa 1880, with a late 18th century oval tapestry reserve, 65cm. wide.
(Sotheby's) $4,515

A Louis XV style giltwood three-panel screen, third quarter 19th century, with a central cartouche shaped silk and velvet embroidered panel decorated with trellis work, 91in. wide.
(Christie's) $17,250

A pair of mahogany table fire-screens, one George II and one of later date, each with a rectangular back with twin-hinged semi-circular flaps, 20in. wide.
(Christie's) $13,579

Classical rosewood carved and rosewood grained parcel-gilt ormolu mounted firescreen, probably New York, circa 1830, 38in. high.
(Skinner) $21,850

A threefold carved walnut screen, circa 1890, with central mirrored section within a molded frame, largest fold 193cm. high.
(Sotheby's) $3,126

A Louis XVI style parcel-gilt white-painted four-panel screen, third quarter 19th century, each panel inset with a cartouche allegorical of the four elements, each panel 20½in. wide.
(Christie's) $13,800

Paul Etienne Saïn, four panel abstract screen, circa 1930, each panel with white gold leaf decoration on a black ground, each panel 67¾ x 16½in.
(Sotheby's) $6,914

A Dutch marquetry secretaire, fitted with a drawer over a fall front enclosing drawers, 37¾in. wide. (George Kidner) $3,460

George III mahogany writing chest, 45in. wide. (Skinner) $3,450

A Dutch mahogany and floral marquetry secrétaire, 19th century, later top above a frieze drawer with a fall front below, 36in. wide. (Christie's) $5,168

A French mahogany secrétaire semainier, mid 19th century, fitted with two drawers above a fall front simulated as two drawer fronts, 32in. wide. (Christie's) $3,322

Tiger maple fall-front desk, New England, early 19th century, the fall front reveals an interior of seven valanced compartments and twelve drawers, 20¾in. wide. (Skinner) $3,450

A William and Mary walnut escritoire, featherbanded to the front, the molded rectangular cornice above a cushion frieze-drawer and a fall-front, 42½in. wide. (Christie's) $24,518

A Spanish Renaissance inlaid walnut iron-mounted vargueño on stand, first half of the 16th century, the plain rectangular top above a fall-front, 39¾in. wide. (Sotheby's) $18,400

American Sheraton six-drawer bureau, in mahogany with tiger maple drawer fronts, scrolled backsplash, and turned legs, 47in. wide. (Eldred's) $770

An Empire mahogany secrétaire à abattant, with rectangular mottled black marble top, the frieze fitted with a drawer above a leather-lined fall-flap, 32in. wide. (Christie's) $4,963

Spanish baroque iron mounted walnut, bone inlaid and parcel-gilt vargueño, 44¹/₂in. wide. (Skinner) $10,925

American Sheraton blind-front secretary, Massachusetts, circa 1810–20, in mahogany and mahogany veneers, upper section opens to reveal shelves, drawers and pigeonholes, 40¹/₂in. wide. (Eldred's) $1,650

An early 19th century mahogany secrétaire campaign chest in two sections, with Bramah locks, 39³/₄in. wide. (Bearne's) $2,916

An early 18th century walnut secrétaire chest, the lower section fitted two short and three long drawers, raised on bun feet, 3ft. wide. (Russell, Baldwin & Bright) $3,218

A Federal inlaid and figured mahogany chest of drawers, New York, circa 1815, the rectangular top above a crossbanded frieze, 46¹/₂in. wide. (Sotheby's) $1,840

A lacquer and gilt-bronze secretaire à abattant, French, circa 1880, after the celebrated model by Henri Riesener, with a later marble top above a frieze drawer, 117cm. wide. (Sotheby's) $17,808

A walnut fall-front writing cabinet, designed by Edward Barnsley, 1933, fully paneled front, top, sides and back, 33in. wide. (Christie's) $20,619

A George III mahogany secrétaire chest, decorated with lines, the crossbanded top above a fall front enclosing an inlaid interior, 42¹/₂in. wide. (Christie's) $2,030

A Biedermeier mahogany secrétaire, the shaped stepped pediment above a long drawer, with a paneled fall front below, 42in. wide. (Christie's) $3,692

Secrétaire bookcases were developed at about the same time as bureau bookcases and were dictated by the same fashionable taste.

A useful, though not absolutely reliable guide to dating a piece is to look closely at the interior fitting of the secrétaire drawer; generally speaking, the better the quality the earlier the date. It is often disappointing to find that, among the late 19th century reproductions of earlier furniture, the rule was, 'what the eye doesn't see, the heart doesn't grieve over' – finely finished exterior surfaces concealing a considerable amount of scrimping on the small drawers and pigeon holes in the fitted compartments of secrétaires and bureaux.

Attention should also be centered on the oak lined drawers as a guide to date of manufacture, for it was in about 1770 that a constructional change occurred.

Until this time, the drawer bottoms were made with the grain of the wood running front to back but, from this time onward, the grain will be found to run from side to side, the bottom often being made of two separate pieces of wood supported by a central bearer.

The secrétaire bookcase, dating from 1820, still has the basic shape of an 18th century piece but the classical pediment with its scroll ends and the delicate carving are typical of the Regency period as is the delicate carving on the curved pilasters.

A Regency brass-mounted rosewood secrétaire-cabinet, decorated overall with spirally-twisted lines, 36¾in. wide. (Christie's) $8,018

Empire two-part secretary, in mahogany veneers, upper section with two glazed cathedral doors, 40in. wide. (Eldred's) $1,595

Classical mahogany and mahogany veneer glazed desk/bookcase, New England, circa 1830, the flat molded cornice above two glazed doors, 45½in. wide. (Skinner) $4,600

A Victorian mahogany secrétaire bookcase with a flared cornice above a pair of glazed paneled doors enclosing adjustable shelves, 48in. wide. (Anderson & Garland) $2,260

Federal mahogany veneer carved and glazed desk bookcase, New England, 1815–25, the cornice above glazed doors opening to movable shelves. (Skinner) $1,495

A George III mahogany secrétaire bookcase, the later molded cornice and frieze above a pair of later astragal glazed doors, 50in. wide. (Christie's) $4,614

A good Federal inlaid and figured mahogany secretary bookcase, New England, circa 1805, in two parts, 41¼in. wide.
(Sotheby's) $4,025

A George III mahogany secrétaire bookcase, the fall front with a fitted interior, above three graduated long drawers, 50in. wide.
(Christie's) $6,460

American Sheraton/Empire two-part secretary, in mahogany and mahogany veneers, bonnet top with brass urn finials, 37½in. wide.
(Eldred's) $1,320

A late Regency mahogany secrétaire bookcase, the base fitted with a secrétaire drawer, above a pair of paneled cupboard doors, 40½in. wide.
(Christie's) $4,416

A Victorian mahogany breakfront secrétaire bookcase with a flared cornice above two pairs of glazed paneled doors enclosing adjustable shelves, 78in. wide.
(Anderson & Garland)
    $2,904

Important American Federal secretary, New York State, circa 1800–20, in mahogany, upper section with scrolled and inlaid cornice above two astragal glazed doors, 43in. wide.
(Eldred's) $14,300

A Victorian mahogany library cylinder bookcase, the upper section with glazed doors enclosing interior shelves, 50in. wide.
(Hy. Duke & Son) $2,400

American Sheraton two-part blind-front secretary, in mahogany veneers with satinwood inlaid panels, 40in. wide.
(Eldred's) $1,430

HISTORICAL FACTS
Settees & Couches

Settle, settee, sofa, chaise longue or daybed – they are all basically alike yet each has its exclusive character and shape and its exclusive place in the scheme of things.

There are a number of Regency couches, all of which are influenced by the styles of Egypt, Rome or early Greece.

It was Sheraton in his *Cabinet Dictionary* who first introduced a couch of this style to England and its scroll ends and lion's paw feet made it one of the most elegant fashions to have been seen at that time. Inevitably, the style became popular and exerted considerable influence, not only on the furniture of the period but on the whole conduct of domestic life in that it seemed to embody the spirit of gracious living.

Until the decline of the Regency period, the upholsterer played a very minor role in the production of home furnishings and was really not in the same league as the cabinet maker, his work consisting mainly of hanging curtains and tapestries and lining walls with material.

Around the 1840s, however, there was a small, bloodless revolution within the furniture factories, the upholsterer rising to hitherto unheard of heights in his craft, virtually dictating the shape and style of chairs and settees and leaving the cabinet maker only the responsibility for making relatively simple frames of birch or ash.

An oak settle, 18th century, the molded toprail above a back, carved and molded with four arched panels, 72in. wide.
(Christie's) $2,944

A mid Georgian oak hall settle, the molded toprail, carved with panels of interlaced flowerheads and foliage, above five arched panels, 70½in. wide.
(Christie's) $1,240

Edwardian two seater cottage sofa, banded throughout in boxwood and satinwood with ebonized stringing, 45½in.
(G.A. Key) $659

Continental gothic oak bench, comprising antique elements, 43¾in. wide.
(Skinner) $6,325

A Charles II style two-part oak corner settle, incorporating early elements, with tall back panels formed with a cornice, each section: 70 x 41 x 20¾in.
(Sotheby's) $805

A mahogany twin-chair back settee, late 19th century, carved overall with floral sprays, the back with pierced vertical splats.
(Christie's) $1,570

A Georgian oak settle, the molded rectangular paneled back above a planked seat, flanked by down-scrolled armrests, 62in. wide.
(Christie's) $1,173

An elm tavern settle of curved form with a plank back and 'winged' arm supports, 18th century, 75½in. wide.
(Hy. Duke & Son) $3,680

Victorian mahogany chaise longue, shaped back, scroll molded top rail joining a splayed scroll molded back rest, mid to late 19th century.
(G. A. Key) $1,120

A classical carved mahogany settee, attributed to Duncan Phyfe, 1768–1854, New York, 1820–40, 91½in. long.
(Christie's) $40,250

A fine classical ormolu-mounted figured mahogany récamier, probably New York, circa 1820, with a reverse-scrolling headrest and shaped, padded backrest, 7ft. 8in. long.
(Sotheby's) $3,450

An early amboyna and ivory inlaid boudoir canapé, the design attributed to Jules Leleu, circa 1920-25, the curved top inlaid with ivory with a design of swags, the front with small detailed ivory scrolls, 58½in. wide.
(Christie's) $10,281

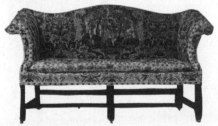

A George III mahogany sofa, the serpentine padded back, outscrolling arms and squab cushion covered in gross and petit point floral needlework, on square chaneled legs joined by H-shaped stretchers, on later brass and leather casters, 68in. wide.
(Christie's) $60,188

Painted and decorated settee, Pennsylvania, 1830s, with old light green ground paint, accented by gold and green striping, with polychrome fruit stencil decoration, 72in. wide.
(Skinner) $1,955

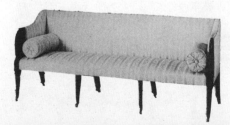

A Federal mahogany sofa, New England, circa 1815, the upholstered back flanked by reeded baluster arm supports, 6ft. 6in. long.
(Sotheby's) $1,840

A mahogany and needlework sofa, the serpentine padded back, outscrolled arms and serpentine fronted cushion covered in gros and petit floral needlework, 68¼in. wide. (Christie's) $12,259

A close-studded brown leather upholstered mahogany sofa, late 19th century, the padded hump-back and outswept sides above a blind-fret carved frieze, 90in. wide. (Christie's)   **$14,766**

A Victorian upholstered sofa, the padded back, arms and seat covered in buttoned floral patterned yellow fabric, with tasseled fringes, 100in. wide. (Christie's)   **$4,430**

A Chippendale mahogany camel-back sofa, Philadelphia, Pennsylvania, circa 1770, the upholstered and serpentine back flanked by outscrolled arms, 8ft. 5in. long.
(Sotheby's)   **$16,100**

A Louis XV beech serpentine canapé, the frame carved with scallop shells and floral sprays, the undulating top-rail above a padded back, sides, seat and squab cushion, 80in. wide.
(Christie's)   **$2,399**

A Regency ebonized and gilt-framed sofa with padded rectangular back and conforming sides, turned arm supports painted with leaves and foliate motifs, 76in. wide.
(Bearne's)   **$1,425**

A walnut and Aubusson canapé, 20th century, in Régence style, with a shaped back and open arms, the rail carved with shells and foliage on a diaper, 173cm. wide.
(Sotheby's)   **$3,647**

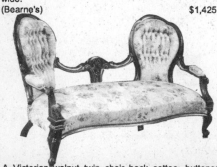

A Victorian walnut twin chair back settee, buttoned padded chair backs between a pierced foliate-carved back, the padded arms with foliate-carved terminals, 70in. wide. (Christie's)   **$2,215**

A Louis XV beechwood lit à repos, the shaped arched outcurved channeled ends above a channeled seat-rail, on cabriole legs terminating in scroll feet, 75in. wide. (Christie's)   **$4,799**

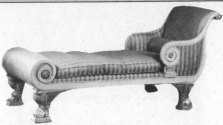

A Regency cream and white-painted and parcel-gilt daybed, on paw feet headed by reeding and terminating in a block on castors, 74in. long. (Christie's) $7,254

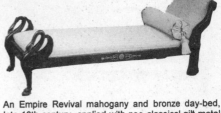

An Empire Revival mahogany and bronze day-bed, late 19th century, applied with neo classical gilt-metal mounts, the raised outswept end carved with dolphin masks and foliage, 22in. long. (Christie's) $5,168

A William IV rosewood settee, the scrolled and molded toprail above a cushioned seat with two bolsters, 86in. wide. (Christie's) $3,818

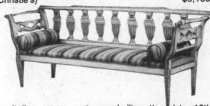

An Italian cream and parcel-gilt settee, late 18th century, the back with a stiff-leaf carved top-rail and pierced vase splats, 94in. wide. (Christie's) $6,645

A walnut sofa, early 20th century, with padded back, outswept arms, on cabriole legs terminating in foliate-carved feet, 55in. wide. (Christie's) $4,799

A Dutch mahogany and floral marquetry triple chair back settee, 19th century, decorated with meandering floral stems, musical trophies and chequer lines, 60in. wide. (Christie's) $3,507

A rare Federal carved mahogany cane-seat settee, attributed to Duncan Phyfe or one of his contemporaries, New York, circa 1815, 6ft. long. (Sotheby's) $9,775

A Louis XV walnut serpentine canapé, with a foliate, carved channeled frame and undulating top-rail, on cabriole legs terminating in scroll feet, 84in. wide. (Christie's) $4,061

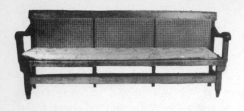

American settee, 19th century, in bird's-eye maple with cane seat and back, 76½in. long.
(Eldred's) $990

George III style paint decorated satinwood settee, late 19th century, upholstered with striped silk, 54in. long.
(Skinner) $3,738

An early Victorian sofa, the back with a plain mahogany veneered arch rail, each arm with a fruit-and-cornucopia shaped and carved front support.
(Ewbank) $820

A Scottish Regency mahogany sofa, in a reeded frame and reeded scroll supports with foliate terminals ending in later brass castors 78in. wide.
(Christie's) $3,054

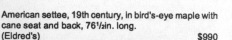

A Federal carved mahogany sofa, school of Duncan Phyfe, New York, first half 19th century, the crestrail carved with a central panel decorated with a pair of cornucopia, 6ft. 2in. long.
(Sotheby's) $4,600

A Federal carved mahogany sofa, attributed to Duncan Phyfe or one of his contemporaries, New York, circa 1810, the reversed scrolling horizontal crest carved with a central tablet, 6ft. 2in. long.
(Sotheby's) $10,350

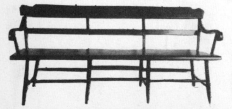

American deacon's bench, Pennsylvania, early 19th century, in brown paint with stenciled decoration, 75in. long.
(Eldred's) $1,430

A mahogany sofa, of early George III style, in a molded frame carved with scrolling acanthus divided by stylized shells, 73in. wide.
(Christie's) $2,392

Sheraton sofa, in mahogany with scrolled arms and turned legs, 72in. long.
(Eldred's) $825

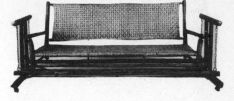

Rare old hickory swing settee, original finish, webbing in excellent condition, 90in. wide.
(Skinner) $6,612

A Victorian satinwood day bed, circa 1880, with bowed top rails continuing to scrolled channeled downswept padded arms, 71¼in. long.
(Bonhams) $2,544

American Empire-style sofa, 19th century, in mahogany with allover carved decoration, bowed crestrail, scrolled arms, and paw feet, gold upholstery, 88in. long.
(Eldred's) $1,045

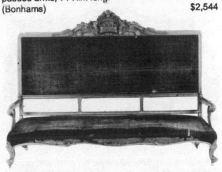

A Victorian walnut settee, with rectangular padded back and upholstered seat, in a molded frame, the cresting carved with a coronet, 87in. wide.
(Christie's) $1,840

George III mahogany double chair back settee, third quarter 18th century, 48¼in. long.
(Skinner) $7,475

A Federal carved mahogany sofa, attributed to Slover and Taylor, New York, circa 1795, the horizontal molded crest with projecting fluted tablet, 6ft. 6in. long.
(Sotheby's) $9,200

Paine Furniture settle, fifteen vertical back spindles, five vertical side spindles, painted black, paper label, 64½in. wide.
(Skinner) $500

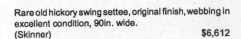

Painted and decorated settee, Pennsylvania, early 19th century, the yellow ground with gold and olive-green fruit and floral stencil decoration.
(Skinner) $1,725

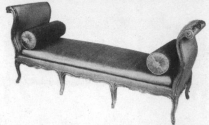

Swedish rococo giltwood day bed, third quarter 18th century, upholstered in blue silk with two bolster cushions, 82¼in. long.
(Skinner) $3,738

Jacques Adnet, bed, circa 1925, black lacquered wooden frame veneered with galuchat, 91in. wide.
(Sotheby's) $30,728

A French Empire Revival mahogany daybed, late 19th century, with outswept ends, above a paneled front above paterae, 74in. wide.
(Christie's) $3,322

A Coalbrookdale medallion pattern cast iron seat, circa 1870, with iron front rail, the back centered with a panel of a reclining classical maiden, 65in. wide.
(Andrew Hartley) $13,188

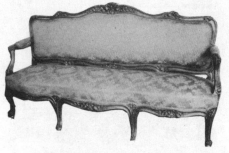

A 19th century giltwood settee, the crestrail shaped, molded and foliate carved, the part-upholstered arms with molded and flowerhead terminals on molded similar supports.
(Dee Atkinson & Harrison) $1,485

A French beechwood canapé, the frame with C-scrolls and one high end, on cabriole legs headed by a fan motif, 75½in. wide. (Christie's) $2,277

A large Flemish oak choir stall, late 15th/early 16th century, the three seats divided and flanked by differing grotesque masks, 105¾in. wide.
(Sotheby's) $10,925

Blue painted wall shelf, probably New England, first third 19th century, 20½in. wide. (Skinnner) $1,380

A pair of rococo giltwood phoenix wall brackets, probably English, circa 1760, each having a scalloped platform supported by a spread-wing phoenix, 16in. high. (Sotheby's) $16,100

A Black Forest ebonized pine wall bracket, late 19th century, the shaped bowfront shelf supported by a displayed eagle resting on a branch, 43in. high. (Christie's) $493

Grain painted standing shelves, New England, circa 1830, five rectangular graduated shelves, 42¼in. wide. (Skinner) $1,495

Lacquered wood sword stand, 19th century, fitted with tiers for three swords above a bi-level shelving unit containing four small drawers, 17⅞ x 7½ x 15in. (Butterfield & Butterfield) $2,300

A set of mahogany hanging book-shelves, the arched boxwood-line inlaid pediment above two adjustable open shelves, 18th century, 36in. wide. (Christie's) $1,176

Shaker pine and poplar sewing steps, New Lebanon, New York, 1850-1875, with arched sides and varnished stain, 15¼in. high x 15¾in. wide. (Skinner) $2,645

A pair of Régence giltwood brackets, first quarter 18th century, each carved with scroll and acanthus decoration, 8½in. high. (Sotheby's) $5,750

A pair of tulipwood and porcelain hanging shelves, Napoleon III, circa 1865, above a mirrored back and a pair of crossbanded doors, 48cm. wide. (Sotheby's) $6,860

HISTORICAL FACTS
Sideboards

Most pieces of furniture have clearly traceable roots planted firmly in the distant past. Not so the sideboard. As we know it today this particular item first appeared on the scene in or around 1770.

Prior to that time, certainly, there were sideboards (Chaucer – and who could argue with his evidence? – mentions a 'sytte borde') but these were no more than side tables, sometimes marble topped, which contained neither drawers nor cupboards.

The introduction of a sideboard as a piece of furniture designed for storage came about for one main reason; the hard drinking habits of 18th century Englishmen established a need for a convenient hidey hole in which to keep large quantities of drink close by the dining table.

It is thought that Robert Adam was the first to couple the drawerless side table with a pair of pedestals, one to either end, often placing knife boxes on the top.

Although Shearer, on the other hand, usually takes the credit for joining the three sections together, as illustrated in his Guide of 1788, there are records of Messrs. Gillows informing one of their customers in 1779 that ". . . we make a new sort of sideboard table now, with drawers, etc., in a genteel style, to hold bottles."

Chippendale, Sheraton and Hepplewhite, too, are all contenders for the title "Father of the Modern Sideboard".

American Hepplewhite sideboard, in mahogany with three drawers over three cupboard doors, the central one recessed, 53½in. wide. (Eldred's) $1,980

A mahogany sideboard, 19th century, of broken outline, decorated with lines and crossbanding, 86½in. wide. (Christie's) $2,584

A Scottish Regency mahogany breakfront sideboard, decorated with lines and checker bandings, the superstructure fitted with two doors and two sliding compartments, 78in. wide. (Christie's) $4,061

An early 18th century oak low dresser, with a central tier of three graduated drawers, 66½in. wide. (David Lay) $5,576

A Regency mahogany breakfront sideboard, of 'D' shaped outline, decorated with ebonized lines, the frieze fitted with a drawer above a tambour shutter, 56½in. wide. (Christie's) $4,984

Classical mahogany and mahogany veneer sideboard, probably New England, circa 1820, veneered peaked backboard and scrolled gallery, 58in. wide. (Skinner) $3,105

Emile-Jacques Ruhlmann, meuble Rasson, amboyna, with ivory stringing and ivory and brass mounts, the slightly bombé front with two doors, 55⅞in. wide. (Sotheby's) $66,800

A Victorian walnut credenza with shaped top, brass banding, inlaid leafage and husk designs, 3ft. 5in. wide. (Russell, Baldwin & Bright) $3,321

Art Deco burl wood dresser, original maple finish, 48in. wide. (Skinner)   **$431**

An oak dresser, the molded rectangular top above a frieze fitted with three drawers and shaped apron, partly 17th century, 72in. wide. (Christie's)   **$4,784**

An Italian Renaissance walnut credenza, 16th century, with molded dentiled overhanging top, 84in. wide. (Sotheby's)   **$19,550**

A George III mahogany bowfront sideboard, decorated with ebonized lines, with a central frieze drawer above an arched apron, 70½in. wide. (Christie's)   **$7,000**

A 19th century mahogany inverted breakfront pedestal sideboard, the raised back with scroll and foliage carving, 72in. (Ewbank)   **$1,200**

A Federal inlaid walnut bow-front sideboard, Southern, circa 1800, the oblong top with projecting and bowed center section, 5ft. wide. (Sotheby's)   **$13,800**

Fine L. & J.G. Stickley sideboard, original hardware with deep patina, plate rail backsplash, original interior, 54in. wide. (Skinner)   **$4,887**

Robert Thompson of Kilburn, 'Mouseman' sideboard, 1934, oak, of rectangular form, central section with three drawers, 53¾in. wide. (Sotheby's)   **$6,914**

A George III mahogany serpentine sideboard, decorated with lines, with a crossbanded top, above a central drawer, 42½in. wide. (Christie's)   **$11,075**

A George II mahogany serving-table, the eared serpentine rectangular top above a blind gothic fretwork frieze on pierced gothic three-sided legs, 51½in. wide. (Christie's)   **$22,908**

A William IV mahogany pedestal sideboard, the raised paneled back supported by scrolled brackets, flanked by cylindrical pedestals, 102in. wide. (Christie's)   **$12,843**

A mid-18th century oak dresser fitted with three short drawers to the center, flanked by a pair of arched paneled doors, 54½in. wide. (Anderson & Garland)   **$4,452**

A Regency mahogany breakfront sideboard, with paneled sliding superstructure, on turned and fluted tapering baluster supports, 88in. wide. (Christie's) $4,963

A Victorian mahogany sideboard, fitted with three shaped frieze drawers over two pairs of doors, 7ft. wide. (Russell, Baldwin & Bright) $1,099

A late George III Scottish mahogany and boxwood lined barrel-front sideboard, with stepped and fitted superstructure, 78in. wide. (Christie's) $7,636

A good Federal inlaid and figural mahogany sideboard, Baltimore, Maryland, circa 1795, the oblong top with astragal corners, 6ft. 2in. wide. (Sotheby's) $14,950

A mahogany serving-table of George III style, the indented floral-carved top above a frieze fitted with five variously-sized drawers, and a pair of matching pedestals, the table 72in. wide. (Christie's) $5,888

An Arts and Crafts oak sideboard, by Liberty & Co., the molded rectangular top with pierced three-quarter gallery, 75½in. wide. (Christie's) $2,545

Limbert sideboard, with plate rail, two drawers over two doors and long bottom drawer, original light oak finish, 48in. wide. (Skinner) $2,185

A Victorian mahogany pedestal sideboard, the mirrored back with straight molded crest and carved scrolled brackets, 82in. wide. (Andrew Hartley) $2,320

Fine Limbert sideboard, No. 1320, paneled sides, through tenons, hardware with deep patina, arched apron, 45in. wide. (Skinner) $2,530

An Edwardian mahogany and banded serpentine fronted sideboard, decorated with paterae and festoons of bell husks, 54in. wide. (George Kidner) $1,494

Rare L. & J.G. Stickley server, three drawers above lower shelf, signed *The work of ...*, 44in. wide. (Skinner) $2,070

A George III mahogany veneered sideboard of small proportions, the bow front fitted with two central drawers, 52¼in. wide. (David Lay) $7,155

Federal mahogany inlaid sideboard, probably Massachusetts, circa 1790, the bowfront top flanked by concave ends, 64in. wide.
(Skinner) $7,475

A Scottish William IV mahogany sideboard, the rectangular indented top with ledged back and scrolled pediment, 84in. wide.
(Christie's) $6,440

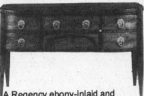

A Regency ebony-inlaid and figured mahogany bow-front sideboard, first quarter 19th century, the rectangular top with bowed center section, 5ft. wide.
(Sotheby's) $2,300

A mahogany bowfront sideboard, 19th century, deep drawer, on square tapering supports and block toes, 69in. wide.
(Christie's) $3,245

An early Victorian mahogany twin-pedestal sideboard, the reverse-breakfront top fitted with three drawers, 85½in. wide.
(Christie's) $1,049

A late Regency rosewood sideboard of inverted breakfront form with a reel molded frieze above a central drawer, 65in. wide.
(Hy. Duke & Son) $1,920

Grain painted sideboard, possibly New England, early 19th century, the rectangular top with shaped gallery, 40¾in. wide.
(Skinner) $1,840

Rare and exceptional Limbert 'Ebon-oak' server, fine original finish and patina to metal fittings, inlaid ebony, paneled sides with through tenons, 38in. wide.
(Skinner) $2,587

Harden sideboard, attributed, original medium brown finish, quarter-sawn oak, felt lined center drawer, arched backsplash, interior shelf, 52⅛in. wide.
(Skinner) $805

A Georgian mahogany bowfront sideboard with central drawer, arched frieze under, flanked by single drawers, 3ft. 8in. wide.
(Russell, Baldwin & Bright) $2,075

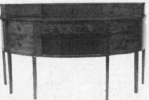

A mahogany and chequer lined bowfront sideboard, by Gardner & Sons, Glasgow, the superstructure fitted with a sliding tambour shutter, 80in. wide.
(Christie's) $2,291

A Federal inlaid mahogany serpentine-front sideboard, New York, the oblong serpentine top above a conformingly-shaped case, 65½in. wide.
(Sotheby's) $8,050

HISTORICAL FACTS
Stands

Such was the ingenuity of past craftsmen and designers that there is a purpose built stand for just about everything from whips to cricket bats.

The 17th century ancestor of the anglepoise lamp was the candlestand. Its purpose was to supplement the general lighting, and the ordinary style was made of walnut or elm and consisted of a plain or spiral turned shaft supported on three or four plain scrolled feet.

At the turn of the 18th century a vase shape was introduced at the top of the pillar. This was often as much as a foot across and elaborately decorated with acanthus.

There were a number of delicate little stands made during the second half of the 18th century for the purpose of supporting books or music. The earliest of these resemble the mahogany tables which were popular at the time, having vase-shaped stems and tripod bases but with the addition of ratchets beneath their tops which permitted adjustment of the surface angle.

Ince and Mayhew improved the design by adding candle branches either side of the top and Sheraton made his stands adjustable for height by means of a rod through the center column which was clamped or released by the turn of a thumb screw.

The Victorian walnut duet music stand is particularly good with its turned central column and carved cabriole legs.

A Chippendale mahogany tilt-top candlestand, New England, 1760–80, on three downswept legs ending in snake feet, 22in. wide. (Sotheby's) $1,610

Windsor cherry candlestand, New England, early 19th century, the circular top on vase and ring-turned post, 18½in. diameter. (Skinner) $1,840

Federal maple candlestand, southeastern New England, late 18th century, the square top on a vase and ring turned post and tripod cabriole leg base, 25in. high. (Skinner) $805

A Federal turned mahogany candlestand, Massachusetts, circa 1800, the rectangular top with shaped corners, 28¼in. high. (Sotheby's) $1,035

A William and Mary red-painted maple and oak candlestand, New England, 1700–50, the circular top above a square flaring pedestal and an X-form base, 15in. diameter. (Sotheby's) $1,035

A Federal turned and figured mahogany tilt-top birdcage candlestand, Pennsylvania, circa 1810, on a ring-turned standard with urn-form support, 20in. diameter. (Sotheby's) $575

Federal cherry inlaid tilt top candlestand, Concord, Massachusetts area, circa 1780, 14½in. wide.
(Skinner) $5,462

Tiger maple candlestand, New England, 19th century, the square molded top above a turned pedestal, 16¼in. wide.
(Skinner) $1,150

A rare Federal lignum vitae tilt-top candlestand, New England, circa 1800, the square top with shaped sides, 19¾in. wide.
(Sotheby's) $3,737

A Chippendale carved mahogany dish-top birdcage candlestand, Philadelphia, circa 1770, on three downswept legs ending in snake feet, 23in. diameter.
(Sotheby's) $1,725

Classical cherry carved tilt-top candlestand, New England, circa 1825, vase and ring turned and spiral carved post on three scrolled legs, 22in. wide.
(Skinner) $1,150

A Federal cherrywood candlestand, Connecticut River Valley, 1790–1810, the circular porringered top above a ring and baluster-turned support, 17½in. diameter.
(Christie's) $8,050

A Chippendale mahogany tilt-top candlestand, Salem, Massachusetts, circa 1790, the hinged oval top tilting above a ring-turned standard and urn-form support, 27½in. high.
(Sotheby's) $1,150

A fine and rare red-painted and turned tripod candlestand, Northeastern New England, 1750–75, the octagonal molded top above a tapered urn-form and ring-turned standard, 17½in. diameter.
(Sotheby's) $24,150

TOP TIPS
Auctioneer's Advice

Always treat furniture in transit with every possible care. Damage may be caused by even the most careful of handlers who would never dream of leaving a pet in a hot car, but might unthinkingly leave a piece of furniture locked into a scorchingly hot, stationary vehicle. A few hours in these conditions and frames might warp, veneers lift and the piece might never be quite the same again.

MICHAEL J. BOWMAN

A carved giltwood easel, Venetian, mid 19th century, the pierced folding frame with a border of scrolls, flower heads and foliage, 70cm. wide.
(Sotheby's) $7,222

A French stained wood saddle stand, with three cylindrical rails above a cane shelf, between twin column uprights, 43in. wide.
(Christie's) $1,107

A late 19th century Italian walnut étagère of serpentine outline, the four shelves above a divided compartment, 27in. wide.
(Bearne's) $1,215

A carved and stained wood jardinière, probably Black Forest, of rectangular form, the panels carved with flowers on a ground of trailing ivy, 34½in. high.
(Christie's) $2,584

A pair of oak Gothic Revival stands, 19th century, each with a rectangular top above an undulating apron, supported on pierced and bracketed panel, 34in. wide.
(Christie's) $4,061

A French kingwood, gilt-bronze and porcelain jardinière, Napoleon III, circa 1870, the top with a crossbanded cover of shaped outline with 'Sèvres' plaques, 67cm. wide.
(Sotheby's) $7,293

A brass and simulated rosewood folding magazine stand, late 19th/early 20th century, with two serpentine tiers with brass handles.
(Christie's) $1,477

A French cream and green-painted umbrella-stand, of semi-elliptical outline with laurel-leaf cresting and caned back, 27½in. wide.
(Christie's) $1,036

A gilt-bronze jardinière, French, circa 1890, of oval form, the frieze applied with ribbons cornucopiae and flowers, 62cm. wide.
(Sotheby's) $6,138

A William IV rosewood folio stand, with pierced adjustable sides, on an X frame support joined by ring-turned stretchers, 26in. wide.
(Christie's) $5,906

A mahogany and gilt-bronze meuble d'appui, French, circa 1890, in Louis XV style, of bombé form, beneath a molded white marble top, 89cm. wide.
(Sotheby's) $4,341

A kingwood and burr-walnut jardinière, English, circa 1860, the rectangular top with an inset cover enclosing a liner, 64cm. wide.
(Sotheby's) $4,874

A Chinese Export gilt-decorated red lacquer candlestand, mid 19th century, the scalloped top, turned standard and shaped legs decorated in gilt, 27in. wide.
(Sotheby's) $4,025

A pair of Louis XVI style ormolu-mounted inlaid-brass tortoiseshell and ebony pedestals, third quarter 19th century, in the manner of André-Charles Boulle.
(Christie's) $10,350

An Anglo-Indian hardwood folding charger-stand, 18th century, the associated circular mahogany removable top above three scrolling interlinked supports, 25¾in. diameter.
(Christie's) $24,817

A two-tier marquetry stand, designed by Emile Gallé, circa 1900, the upper and lower shelf inlaid with chestnut leaves, 45in. high.
(Christie's) $3,561

A mahogany and gilt-bronze jardinière, French, circa 1890, of rectangular form with a pierced gallery above panels cast with Venus and Cupid in relief, 91cm. wide.
(Sotheby's) $9,373

A kingwood, gilt-bronze and marquetry pedestal, Paris, circa 1890, of bombé form, with a molded fleur de pêcher marble top, 41in. wide.
(Sotheby's) $7,222

A mid-Victorian carved oak font, the circular molded top above a foliate-carved frieze, 29in. wide. (Christie's) $1,500

A Regency mahogany pedestal, of pylon shape, the rectangular top above a paneled door enclosing a shelf, 19¼in. wide. (Christie's) $2,640

Federal birch one-drawer stand, Loudon, New Hampshire, early 19th century, the top overhangs a drawer, 17¾in. wide. (Skinner) $747

A late Victorian oak post-box, the rectangular top with turned baluster gallery, above a letter division and a glazed door, 12½in. wide. (Christie's) $2,576

A pair of Venetian blackamoor torchères, each painted in blue, red and gilt, 80in. high. (Christie's) $3,627

Rosewood carved and rosewood veneer classical double-sided music stand, probably England, circa 1830, on leaf carved octagonal post, 18in. wide. (Skinner) $1,955

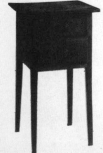

A Federal inlaid birchwood two-drawer stand, New England, circa 1820, each drawer with a compass-star inlaid knob, 16½in. wide. (Sotheby's) $920

An unusual painted and parcel-gilt bird cage, probably French, circa 1860, of octagonal, architectural form with a balustrade and copper roof above brass grills, 135cm. wide. (Sotheby's) $22,568

Michigan Chair Company magazine stand, No.K125, two vertical slats, keys and tenons, 16½in. wide. (Skinner) $978

A classical carved mahogany piano stool, attributed to Duncan Phyfe or one of his contemporaries, New York, circa 1810.
(Sotheby's) $1,725

Pair of classical mahogany and mahogany veneer window benches, probably Boston, circa 1820, 33½in. wide.
(Skinner) $4,945

An Italian baroque upholstered walnut stool, with padded rectangular seat above slanted turned legs.
(Sotheby's) $1,035

A William IV rosewood piano stool, the circular revolving seat on a lotus-carved bulbous turned column. (Christie's) $1,477

A pair of upholstered walnut stools in Italian Baroque style, supported on four boldly turned legs.
(Sotheby's) $2,875

A Charles X rosewood piano stool, decorated with lines, the circular revolving seat on a bulbous turned column.
(Christie's) $738

A beechwood window seat, late 19th/early 20th century, carved with foliage and C-scrolls, 30in. wide.
(Christie's) $1,292

A rare pair of green-painted turned birchwood upholstered stools, American, probably New England, 1720–50, each having a rectangular seat on vase- and ring-turned splayed legs.
(Sotheby's) $8,050

Attributed to Marcel Breuer, for Thonet, stool, 'B37', designed 1932, manufactured 1932–33, chromium-plated tubular steel, original brown eisengarn seat.
(Sotheby's) $1,875

A George IV rosewood stool, the rectangular padded seat on X-framed end-supports centered by a roundel, 37½in. wide.
(Christie's) $12,825

A Victorian rosewood stool of large size, upholstered rectangular top, scrolled frieze on leaf carved cabriole legs and brass castors, 82cm x 132cm.
(Wintertons) $3,360

A Victorian rosewood center stool, with rectangular gros point needlework upholstered top, 35in. wide. (Christie's) $1,875

An early Victorian rosewood X-frame stool, the rectangular padded seat upholstered in green fabric, on X-frame legs centered with a patera, 28in. wide.
(Christie's) $2,399

A mahogany stool, of early George III design, the rail with egg-and-dart molding, on cabriole legs carved with shells. (Christie's)
    $351

A 19th century mahogany framed dressing stool having pink figured silk top on cabriole legs with leafage carved feet, 21 x 20in. (Russell, Baldwin & Bright)
    $596

A Charles X mahogany piano stool, inlaid with meandering florals stems and lines, bowed back pierced with carrying handle, circular revolving seat on stiff-leaf bulbous turned column and outswept legs.
(Christie's) $1,754

A pair of Louis XV style giltwood tabourets, each with a circular padded seat in a shaped rope twist molded frame, 24in. diameter.
(Christie's) $2,760

A rare William and Mary turned maple and birchwood joint stool, New England, 1710–50, the oval chamfered top above a rectangular frieze.
(Sotheby's) $11,500

A 19th century gilt wood stool, the seat probably with the original upholstery, the short cabriole legs molded with rosettes and terminating in peg feet, 21in.
(G.A. Key) $314

A classic photo-studio 'Roman bench', wood with red velvet-upholstered seat, circa 1870.
(Auction Team Köln) $452

Shaker pine footstool, Enfield, Connecticut, mid 19th century, with shaped sides above the slanted footrest and arched sides, 20⅜ in.
(Skinner) $230

Italian Neoclassical style giltwood bench, 19th century, 44½in. wide.
(Skinner) $2,530

One of a pair of gilt metal stools, 20th century, of large size, each with a buttoned red-leather drop-in seat, 78in. wide.
(Christie's) (Two) $14,766

A banquette, Italy, circa 1840, with a padded seat above a rail with a carved rosette, 110cm. wide.
(Sotheby's) $13,496

A mahogany stool, 19th century, the rectangular upholstered top above a molded and shell-carved frieze, 19½in. wide.
(Christie's) $827

An 18th century mahogany square dressing stool with upholstered seat on floral carved French scroll supports, stamped *TC*.
(Russell, Baldwin & Bright) $1,036

A Dutch mahogany and floral marquetry X-frame stool, 19th century, with turned arm rests with scrolled terminals, 27in. wide.
(Christie's) $2,584

19th century mahogany circular adjustable piano stool, raised on octagonal tulip baluster column, spreading circular base terminating in scrolled feet, 13½in.
(G. A. Key) $352

A pair of walnut stools, second quarter 19th century, on ring-turned and faceted baluster legs joined by a shaped H-shaped stretcher, 15¾in. square.
(Christie's) $3,395

One of a pair of beadwork and giltwood stools, French, circa 1860, each with a padded top, worked with a dragon and scrollwork.
(Sotheby's) $2,708

A George III mahogany window seat, on square tapering legs joined by an H-shaped stretcher, on block feet, restorations to the stretcher, 54¾in. wide.
(Christie's) $4,904

A Victorian oak X-frame hall bench, the paneled seat with chamfered arm rests and a raised outswept back, 22½in. wide.
(Christie's) $738

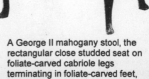

A George II mahogany stool, the rectangular close studded seat on foliate-carved cabriole legs terminating in foliate-carved feet, 26in. wide.
(Christie's) $2,030

Marcel Kammerer for Thonet, bentwood salon, circa 1906, comprising: sofa, two armchairs and center table, stained beech, brass sabots, blue leather studded and stitched upholstery, the table with square top with rounded corners inset with glass and with hammered brass base. (Sotheby's) $6,722

Victor Horta, salon, circa 1900, comprising: banquette, two armchairs and four side chairs, the mahogany frames with curvilinear outlines and carved with organic scroll details, banquette: 36¾in. (Sotheby's) $38,410

A Victorian carved satin birch bedroom suite, circa 1880, comprising a bed, a commode with a marble top, and a pair of bedside cupboards, each with a carved upper section, and a similar paneled cupboard, bed 191cm. wide. (Sotheby's) $23,431

A five-piece mahogany salon suite, by Louis Majorelle, circa 1900, comprising canapé and four side chairs, the backs pierced and carved with floral details, the legs similarly carved. (Christie's) $7,873

A fine parcel-gilt and painted salon suite, Italy, circa 1840, comprising two armchairs and six sidechairs, the armchairs with a padded back, within a reeded frame, surmounted by acanthus leaves and scrolls. (Sotheby's) $26,243

A dining room suite, French, 1940s, seven chairs and large sideboard en suite, the table supported on elaborate lyre-end legs with bracket stretcher applied with gilt bronze scroll detailing, table 78³/₄in. wide. (Christie's) $15,933

Paul Follot, four piece Art Deco salon suite, circa 1925, comprising: sofa and three armchairs, giltwood frames, each with shaped oval back and reeded cylindrical supports, with cushioned backs and seats, sofa: 50⅝in. wide. (Sotheby's) $11,907

Dining room suite, 1930s comprising: extending dining table, sideboard, serving table, two armchairs, six side chairs, blonde burrwood. (Sotheby's) $15,360

Paul Follot, Art Deco bedroom suite, circa 1925 comprising: bed, wardrobe, chest of drawers, dressing table, two side chairs and bedside cabinet, oak, the bed with paneled headboard and footboard with stylized floral motif, wardrobe: 55½in. wide. (Sotheby's) $4,225

An Irish Regency mahogany breakfast table, the rounded rectangular top crossbanded in rosewood, on a faceted column, 58in. wide.
(Christie's) $4,061

A Victorian walnut and marquetry breakfast table, the circular tilt top decorated with floral marquetry, 53in. diameter.
(Christie's) $10,705

A George III mahogany breakfast-table, the rounded rectangular top crossbanded in partridgewood and inlaid with boxwood lines,60in. wide. (Christie's) $9,545

A Scottish William IV mahogany breakfast table, the circular top with egg and dart molded border and similar frieze, 48in. diameter.
(Christie's) $3,312

A rosewood breakfast table, early 19th century, applied with later gilt-metal mounts, the circular tilt top on a turned column, 50in. diameter.
(Christie's) $7,014

A Victorian rosewood breakfast table, the circular tilt top with an undulating apron, on a faceted bulbous column, 53in. diameter.
(Christie's) $4,614

A good Victorian inlaid walnut breakfast table, circa 1860, the circular top profusely inlaid with floral designs, 54in. wide.
(Bonhams) $5,883

A Regency oval mahogany snap top breakfast table with crossbanding, inlaid lines and reeded edge, 53 x 44in.
(David Lay) $4,991

A William IV burr elm breakfast table, the circular segmented and crossbanded top above a molded frieze, 56in. diameter.
(Christie's) $15,272

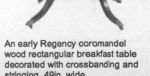

A William IV mahogany breakfast table, the circular gadrooned top, on a tapering triangular stem, 46in. diameter.
(Christie's) $2,482

A Victorian rosewood breakfast table, the oval molded top on foliate carved turned baluster stem, 56in. wide.
(Christie's) $5,152

An early Regency coromandel wood rectangular breakfast table decorated with crossbanding and stringing, 49in. wide.
(Anderson & Garland) $2,305

A Victorian burr walnut serpentine card table, applied with gilt-metal mounts and decorated with lines, 37in. wide.
(Christie's) $2,399

A Regency brass-inlaid rosewood-veneered card table, with cut brass stylized foliate motifs and roundels throughout, 36¼in. wide.
(Bearne's) $4,698

An Edwardian rosewood and inlaid card table, the playing surface above a frieze inlaid with bone and marquetry floral stems, 36in. wide.
(Christie's) $2,769

A William IV rosewood card table, the rounded rectangular hinged top above a fluted and scroll carved shaped frieze. 36in. wide.
(Christie's) $5,727

An important pair of Federal satinwood-inlaid figured mahogany demi-lune card tables, attributed to William Whitehead, New York, circa 1800, 36in. wide.
(Sotheby's) $151,000

A Regency rosewood-veneered card table inlaid with brass lines, 36in. wide.
(Bearne's) $2,673

A George III satinwood and floral-painted card table, of broken D-shaped outline, the hinged top crossbanded in tulipwood, 36¼in. wide. (Christie's) $5,906

A Regency mahogany D-shaped card table decorated with ebonized lines, the hinged top enclosing a leather-lined writing surface, 36in. wide. (Christie's) $1,846

A William IV rosewood card table, the D-shaped hinged tip enclosing a green baize lined playing surface above a shaped frieze, 36in. wide. (Christie's) $2,215

The Hubbard family Queen Anne mahogany concertina-action gaming table, Boston, 1730–50, 34in. wide. (Christie's) $29,900

A rosewood and brass-inlaid D-shaped card table, early 19th century, decorated with cut foliate motifs, 36in. wide. (Christie's) $4,430

A very fine Federal birchwood-inlaid mahogany card table, Northern Coast of Massachusetts, circa 1810, 37in. wide. (Sotheby's) $17,250

A mid Victorian walnut serpentine card table with burr walnut-veneered fold-over top, 35½in. wide. (Bearne's) $1,490

A late Victorian calamander and boxwood lined card table, the hinged D-shaped top on boxwood lined square tapering supports, 30in. wide. (Christie's) $4,048

A satinwood demi-lune card table, late 18th century, decorated with tulipwood crossbanding, the hinged top with meandering floral marquetry border, 35¼in. wide. (Christie's) $3,322

A Chippendale carved mahogany card table, New York, 1760–80, the serpentine hinged top with square corners above a conforming apron, 34¼in. wide. (Christie's) $46,000

A fine Federal inlaid and figured mahogany bow-front card table, New York, circa 1810, the oblong top with conformingly shaped hinged leaf, 36in. wide. (Sotheby's) $3,162

A William IV rosewood-veneered center table, the acanthus-carved stem with gadrooned collar, 49³/₄in. wide.
(Bearne's) $2,997

An Italian Renaissance style mother-of-pearl inlaid ebony, fruitwood and marquetry center table, late 19th century, attributed to the Falcini workshop, 50in. wide.
(Christie's) $8,050

A Victorian burr walnut-veneered center table with well-matched segmentally-veneered circular top, 50in. diameter.
(Bearne's) $2,187

A mahogany and ormolu-mounted center table, of French Empire design, 19th century, with circular green variegated marble top above a molded frieze, 37in. diameter.
(Christie's) $20,045

A rosso antico, Siena and brèche marble center table, 20th century, the square geometrically veneered top on a turned column, 26in. wide.
(Christie's) $2,399

A gilt-bronze mahogany center table, Paris, circa 1890, in the manner of François Linke, white veined marble top, 102cm. diameter.
(Sotheby's) $20,838

A mahogany serving table, 20th century, the rectangular top above a frieze with pounced and cross-hatch ground, 60in. wide.
(Christie's) $12,920

A giltwood and micromosaic center table, circa 1870, the circular top inset with views of Rome, 57cm. wide.
(Sotheby's) $5,210

A center table, Italy, circa 1840, with an oval velvet lined top, above two frieze drawers on supports in the form of sphinxes, 173.5cm. wide.
(Sotheby's) $3,749

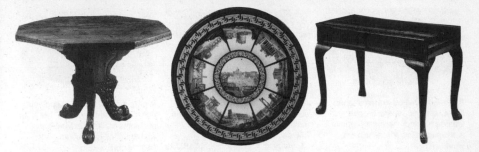

An Italian Renaissance walnut octagonal center table, first half 16th century, the molded top with a carved geometric frieze. (Sotheby's) $10,925

A micromosaic and ebonized center table, Italian, circa 1860, the circular top with a central view of St. Peter's, surrounded by further Roman views, 88cm. diameter. (Sotheby's) $36,110

An Anglo-Indian calamander center table, late 18th/early 19th century, the molded rectangular top above two frieze drawers, on cabriole legs and claw feet, 44in. wide. (Christie's) $10,939

A burr-walnut and marquetry center table, designed by Oskar Kaufmann, circa 1918, the circular top with carved ebonized border, 41½in. diameter. (Christie's) $14,058

A pair of gilt-metal center tables, 19th century, each tier fitted with gray veined black marbles, 41in. wide. (Christie's) $7,014

An Italian giltwood center table, 19th century, decorated with foliate carvings and beaded and cable moldings, 28¼in. wide. (Christie's) $3,692

A mahogany and gilt-bronze center table, the top veneered en soleil, on cabriole legs, 81cm. diameter. (Sotheby's) $5,416

A burr-veneered and mahogany sepentine center table, applied with later associated gilt-metal mounts, 35½in. wide. (Christie's) $1,385

A fine gilt-bronze and kingwood center table by François Linke, Paris circa 1895, the 'X'-form stretcher centered by a winged cupid, diameter 103cm. (Sotheby's) $45,137

A carved giltwood console table, Paris, circa 1880, the brêche violette molded marble top above a shaped lattice frieze, 201cm. wide.
(Sotheby's) $20,620

A polished steel and gilt-metal console table, 20th century, with a molded verde antico marble top, 228cm. wide.
(Sotheby's) $18,233

A parcel-gilt, marble and painted console table, Italy, circa 1840, the rectangular Siena marble top above a frieze, 163.5cm. wide.
(Sotheby's) $21,557

A Spanish baroque style walnut console table, incorporating early elements, with D-shaped molded top, 65in. wide.
(Sotheby's) $4,025

A wrought iron and marble console table, designed by Edgar Brandt, circa 1925, four scrolling straps supporting marble top with pierced foliate apron, 59in. wide.
(Christie's) $46,862

A carved giltwood console table, French, circa 1890, in the form of a commode in the manner of Charles Cressent, 172cm. wide.
(Sotheby's) $7,814

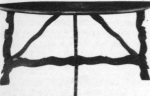

A Napoleon III gilt-bronze and Boulle console table, Paris, circa 1860, after a model by André-Charles Boulle, the white marble top above a frieze drawer, 119cm. wide.
(Sotheby's) $11,247

A George III style painted satinwood console table, late 19th century, the demi-lune top above a frieze painted with floral garlands, 48¼in. wide.
(Bonhams) $4,452

An Italian green painted and parcel-gilt console table, 19th century, the frieze decorated with flower filled cornucopiae and anthemion decoration, 26¼in. wide.
(Christie's) $4,799

A mahogany and bronze console table, French, circa 1890, in Empire style, rectangular gray fossil marble top, 145cm. wide.
(Sotheby's) $9,373

A giltwood console table, 20th century, the verde antico rectangular marble top above a frieze decorated with fluting and paterae, 74½in. wide.
(Christie's) $4,430

Raymond Subes, console, circa 1925, patinated wrought iron, the base with openwork frieze of stylized swags and tassels, on four scrolled supports, 59in. wide.
(Sotheby's) $24,966

A 19th century mahogany extending dining table on turned reeded and fluted legs with castors, 46 x 73½in. with one leaf. (Ewbank) $2,800

A Victorian walnut loo table, the quarter veneered top with molded undulating outline, 58½in. (Dreweatt Neate) $1,570

A Victorian mahogany oval dining table, the top with a molded edge and a plain frieze, on ring-turned bulbous reeded tapering legs, 72in. long. (Christie's) $4,614

A Victorian mahogany extending dining-table, the circular molded top opening to enclose four extra leaves, 152in. long, extended. (Christie's) $17,480

A late Regency mahogany concertina-action extending dining table, the rounded rectangular hinged top opening to enclose three extra leaves, 110in. long. (Christie's) $12,409

A late 19th century mahogany extending dining table on turned legs, 50 x 106½in. maximum with four leaves. (Ewbank) $3,200

A Victorian mahogany extending dining table, with one extra leaf, on ring-turned lotus lappeted tapering supports, 190cm. long overall. (Bristol) $3,760

A Regency mahogany oval dining table with satinwood and ebony stringing on turned center column, 4ft. 11in. (Russell, Baldwin & Bright) $2,952

An early Victorian mahogany extending dining table, the molded top above four turned and reeded legs, 131cm. wide. (Bristol) $4,264

An early 18th century oak refectory table raised on turned and square legs with later understretchers, 92in. wide. (Anderson & Garland) $4,134

An early Victorian rosewood snaptop table with fluted vase pedestal, the tripod base with carved knees and scroll carved feet, 46½in. diameter. (David Lay) $1,884

A Regency mahogany dining table, the extending rectangular top with a molded edge and rounded corners, 138¾ x 47¾in. extended. (Hy.Duke & Son) $5,760

Large dressing tables complete with mirrors were, if we are to judge from the design catalogs, made in profusion throughout the eighteenth century and some, Chippendale's in particular, were very fine indeed.

Designers of the period vied with each other to see who could cram in the greatest number of ingenious little fitments, each designer claiming every innovation as his own and decrying all others for having pinched his ideas. Sheraton, in particular, was fascinated by the challenge and his designs became more and more complex as he progressively widened the scope of his ideas until, towards the end, it would seem that he was attempting to develop the ultimate, all-purpose item of furniture. One of his later creations was a superbly eccentric construction incorporating hinged and swing mirrors, numerous drawers, a washbasin, compartments for jewelry, writing materials and cosmetics, not to mention the commode.

By far the most popular dressing tables to come from the second half of the eighteenth century were described by Shearer as 'dressing stands'. These were usually of quite small size, standing on fine, elegant legs and fitted with hinged box lids.

During the Victorian period, there were a few small dressing tables but, as a rule, the Victorians preferred them rather more solidly proportioned.

A high Victorian dressing chest, in oak, veneered and inlaid with yew, pollard oak, ebony, purple wood and holly, 60in. wide. (David Lay) $2,880

Portneuve, Lady's dressing table, 1920s, oval mirrored top above frieze with two small drawers, 31½in. (Sotheby's) $2,497

Attributed to Paul Follot, dressing table, circa 1925, gold lacquered wood, rectangular section, with central pivoting mirror, 55in. wide. (Sotheby's) $3,457

A late George III mahogany dressing-chest, the mahogany rectangular section, the top inlaid with an oval panel of crossbanding, 28in. wide. (Christie's) $2,576

A Queen Anne carved mahogany dressing table, Philadelphia, 1730–50, the rectangular top with thumbmolded edge with cusped corners, 35½in. wide. (Christie's) $10,350

Attributed to D.I.M., dressing table, circa 1930, macassar, of rectangular section, the top with swivel mirror flanked by two small cabinets, 43in. wide. (Sotheby's) $3,457

A Louis Philippe mahogany dressing table, the circular swing plate on a U-shaped support, on X-frame supports, 26½in. wide. (Christie's) $2,308

A Scottish late Regency mahogany sofa/dressing table, the rounded rectangular twin-flap top above a frieze fitted with five variously-sized drawers, 52in. wide. (Christie's) $2,576

An early Victorian mahogany dressing table, decorated with gothic tracery panels, arcading and quatrefoils. (Christie's) $7,014

Federal mahogany veneer dressing chest, New England, 1810–20, the dressing glass supported by scrolled supports above two-tiered drawers, 38¼in. wide. (Skinner) $862

The Morris family Chippendale carved mahogany dressing table, Philadelphia, 1760–80, the rectangular top with molded edge and cupid's-bow front corners, 35½in. wide. (Christie's) $59,700

A very fine and rare Federal, ormolu-mounted figured mahogany dressing table with mirror, attributed to Duncan Phyfe, New York, circa 1810, 36½in. wide. (Sotheby's) $25,300

Queen Anne walnut dressing table, Massachusetts, 18th century, with molded top above a case of thumbmolded drawers, 33¼in. wide overall. (Skinner) $8,970

A Louis Philippe rosewood and marquetry poudreuse, the stepped rectangular hinged top centered with floral sprays above a frieze drawer, 21½in. wide. (Christie's) $1,846

A Queen Anne carved cherrywood dressing table, Connecticut, 1740–60, the rectangular thumbmolded top above one long thumbmolded drawer, 35½in. wide. (Christie's) $13,800

George III mahogany and bird's-eye maple Pembroke table, last quarter 18th century, 37in. wide. (Skinner) $2,530

Good quality oak drop leaf dining table with bow ends and oval leaves, English, early 18th century, 2ft. 9in. wide. (G.A. Key) $1,272

A Queen Anne mahogany drop leaf dining table, New England, probably Massachusetts, 1750–70, the oblong top with bowed ends. (Sotheby's) $4,887

Queen Anne maple dining table, southeast New England, late 18th century, the overhanging rectangular top on four block turned legs, 38¾in. wide. (Skinner) $2,760

A late George III mahogany Pembroke table with a pair of rectangular hinged flaps above a single drawer to the frieze, 39in. wide. (Anderson & Garland) $826

Maple Queen Anne drop leaf dining table, Massachusetts, mid 18th century, with shaped skirt above cabriole legs, 46in. wide extended. (Skinner) $2,530

A Queen Anne walnut drop-leaf dining table, Pennsylvania, 1740–60, the circular hinged top with two drop leaves above a shaped apron, 48in. wide. (Christie's) $2,760

Queen Anne maple dining table, probably Massachusetts, circa 1770, the overhanging rectangular top with cutout corners on four cabriole legs, 36in. wide. (Skinner) $1,495

American diminutive Queen Anne drop-leaf table, in cherry, top 11in. wide with two 11in. drop leaves. (Eldred's) $7,040

A Queen Anne cherrywood drop-leaf dining table, New York, 1750–80, the oblong top with bowed ends flanked by D-shaped leaves, 4ft. 2in. wide open. (Sotheby's) $5,175

A fine Chippendale carved and figured walnut drop-leaf dining table, Pennsylvania, circa 1760, on cabriole legs, 4ft. 9in. wide open. (Sotheby's) $40,250

A rare Queen Anne figured mahogany drop-leaf dining table, New York, 1750–80, the oblong top with bowed ends, 48in. wide open. (Sotheby's) $3,737

A Chippendale carved and figured walnut drop-leaf dining table, Philadelphia, circa 1770, the shaped skirt continuing to cabriole legs, 4ft. 11½in. wide extended. (Sotheby's) $20,700

Federal pine and cherry harvest table, New England, early 19th century, the rectangular overhanging top on four square tapering legs on casters, 72in. wide. (Skinner) $4,025

A George II mahogany drop-leaf dining table, the oval twin flap top above a gate-leg action, with foliate-carved cabriole legs, 54½in. long. (Christie's) $4,614

A Queen Anne maple drop-leaf table, New England, 1740–60, the rectangular hinged top with molded edge above a cyma-shaped carved apron, 42in. wide. (Christie's) $2,990

A large late Georgian mahogany drop-leaf table with a pair of semi-circular hinged flaps raised on turned and square legs, 60in. wide. (Anderson & Garland) $1,304

A Federal figured mahogany drop-leaf dining table, Baltimore, circa 1815, the rectangular top flanked by hinged leaves with reeded edges, 5ft. 3in. wide open. (Sotheby's) $4,025

A Queen Anne carved and figured walnut drop-leaf dining table, Pennsylvania, 1730–50, the rectangular top flanked by notched leaves, 4ft. 6½in. wide open. (Sotheby's) $3,737

William and Mary cherry butterfly table, probably Connecticut, early 18th century, the overhanging oval drop leaf top on four splayed block vase and ring-turned legs, 40in. wide. (Skinner) $2,415

An Italian Baroque walnut trestle-form drop-leaf table, the oval top with twin hinged leaves over two opposing drawers, 43¼in. wide. (Sotheby's) $3,450

Federal mahogany drop leaf table, New England, early 19th century, the squared leaves fall over turned tapering legs, 46¼in. wide extended. (Skinner) $460

Rare and early Gustav Stickley drop-leaf table, No.443, unsigned, through tenons and pegs, deep reddish-brown original finish, 40in. (Skinner) $5,462

Painted Queen Anne maple drop leaf table, southern New England, 18th century, with old red stained top above darkened straight cabriole legs, 40in. wide. (Skinner) $8,625

HISTORICAL FACTS
Drum Tables

The drum table, also known as the 'library' or 'rent' table, first made its appearance during the later half of the 18th century, becoming widely popular throughout the entire Regency period and remaining in favor until about the middle of the 19th century.

Earlier drum tables are of mahogany, Regency manufacturers also using rosewood. The Victorians continued to make them of both these woods but seemed to prefer burr walnut.

Often having revolving tops, drum tables were widely used in estate offices and the idea was that the agent could swivel the table top round in order to reach all eight or so drawers without moving from his seat (each drawer relating to a portion of the estate).

Although there are some eight to twelve drawer fronts round the circumference of the top, do not be surprised to find that a number of these are false – had they all been used to hold the rent money it is probable that craftier tenants would have paid their rent with one hand and dipped into someone else's drawer with the other!

Due to its having been in constant use as an item of office furniture, you may find that an otherwise sound drum table is marred by a badly damaged top. Even though the wood itself is beyond repair, a transformation may be effected by having the top covered in tooled leather as many of the original pieces were.

A George III mahogany and ebonized octagonal library table, the green leather-lined top above four paneled drawers and four simulated drawers, 41½in. wide. (Christie's) $11,454

A French mahogany drum table, mid 19th century, the circular top inset with a gilt tooled black-leather lined writing surface, 38½in. diameter. (Christie's) $4,430

A brass-mounted and brass-inlaid calamander drum table, the octagonal crossbanded revolving top with green leather-lined surface and reeded edge, 31in. diameter. (Christie's) $17,181

George III mahogany and inlay circular library drum table, circa 1800, with alternating working and faux drawers, inset gilt tooled green leather top, 31in. high, 42in. diameter. (Skinner) $8,625

A Regency mahogany drum table, the circular top above a frieze fitted with four true and four dummy drawers, 38in. wide. (Christie's) $11,997

A Regency mahogany drum table, the circular top with inset leather and fitted with five frieze drawers, 36¼in. diameter. (George Kidner) $5,120

An English oak gate-leg table in late 17th century style, the oval hinged top with twin leaves, 41½in. long extended. (Sotheby's) $920

A small oak gateleg table, designed by Edward Barnsley, circa 1926, on two pairs of chamfered leg supports, 30½in. wide. (Christie's) $4,784

A Charles II oak joined small gateleg table, the rectangular top with molded edge, 24in. wide. (David Lay) $1,200

Victorian walnut Sutherland table, the two drop flaps with pie crust edges, raised on elegant slender reeded and ring turned baluster supports, 31½in. (G. A. Key) $880

A Flemish baroque oak gateleg table, 17th century, with twin semi-circular hinged leaves above a plain frieze with a single drawer on baluster-form legs joined by plain stretchers, 28¾in. high x 37in. wide x 62½in. long (extended). (Sotheby's) $3,737

A walnut gate-leg tea table, designed by Edward Barnsley, circa 1930/35, shaped rectangular top set on substructure of finely chamfered gate-legs, 40in. wide. (Christie's) $4,499

An English oak gate-leg table in late 17th century style, the oval top with twin hinged leaves over a single drawer, 37½in. long extended. (Sotheby's) $517

A late 17th century oak, oval gateleg dining table, at each end a shaped frieze, one end with a drawer, 68 x 57in. (David Lay) $6,440

A late 17th/early 18th century walnut gateleg table, fitted with a single drawer on eight, plain, turned tapering supports. (David Lay) $443

An oak rectory table in Jacobean style, partly composed of early elements, the rectangular planked top above a dentiled frieze on six baluster-form legs, 132in. long. (Sotheby's)   **$7,475**

Early Victorian mahogany two-pedestal dining table, mid 19th century, with a crossbanded top and additional leaf, 80in. long. (Skinner)   **$2,300**

A George IV mahogany extending dining table, with pedestal ends and drop leaf center section, with the molded edges on ring turned columns, 2.71m. x 126cm. extended. (Phillips)   **$10,500**

A George IV mahogany extending dining table with reeded top on four slender turned and fluted tapering supports, 4ft. x 8ft. full extension. (Russell, Baldwin & Bright)   **$7,693**

A mahogany and boxwood lined dining table, Gardner & Sons, Glasgow, the circular top opening to enclose four extra leaves, 144in. long, extended. (Christie's)   **$13,363**

A Continental baroque walnut refectory table, Provincial, 17th century, the massive rectangular top supported on six faceted columnar legs joined by plain rectangular stretchers, 109½in. long. (Sotheby's)   **$9,775**

A walnut draw-leaf table, early 20th century, the paneled rectangular top on bulbous ring-turned legs joined by similar stretchers and supports, 125in. fully extended. (Christie's)   **$8,860**

George III style mahogany two-pedestal dining table, late 19th century, 74in. long. (Skinner)   **$1,725**

A George III mahogany triple-pillar dining-table, with molded rounded rectangular end-section enclosing two extra leaves, on ring-turned baluster stems and molded splayed quadripartite supports, 141in. long, extended. (Christie's)   **$40,480**

A late Regency mahogany extending dining-table, the rounded rectangular crossbanded and ebony lined top opening to enclose five extra leaves, 134in. long, extended. (Christie's)   **$12,880**

An early 19th century mahogany extending dining table with reeded edge, on six fluted, turned, tapering legs, approximately 5ft. x 12ft. 6in. open.
(Russell Baldwin & Bright) $9,792

A Regency mahogany serving table, the rectangular top with a raised back above a plain frieze fitted with a drawer, on lotus-carved gadrooned turned tapering legs, 91in. wide. (Christie's) $11,997

An English oak extending refectory table in Jacobean style, with rectangular planked top above a frieze carved with a guilloche pattern, 157¹/₂in. long extended.
(Sotheby's) $9,200

A Regency mahogany concertina action extending dining table, including three extra leaves, with an extending D-end section fitted with a hinged leaf, 111 in. extended. (Christie's) $13,843

Federal cherry and walnut veneer dining table, New England or New York, circa 1825, with shaped reveneered skirt, above spiral carved legs ending in turned feet, 84¹/₄in. wide extended.
(Skinner) $1,380

An early Victorian plum-pudding mahogany dining-table, by Holland & Sons, comprising two D-shaped end-sections which extend to accommodate six further leaves, 299in. long, extended.
(Christie's) $30,544

A mahogany triple-pillar dining table of Regency design, opening to enclose two extra leaves and with breakfast table fittings to the end sections   150in.   long   extended.
(Christie's) $4,582

A fine and rare Federal inlaid and figured mahogany diminutive two-part dining table, New England, circa 1805, comprising two D-shaped end sections, 8ft. 3in. wide extended.
(Sotheby's) $43,125

Georgian style mahogany and beechwood two-pedestal dining table, late 19th century, 72in. wide, with two additional leaves, each measuring 24 x 48in.
(Skinner) $5,175

Painted pine and maple stretcher base table, New England, 18th century, the top with bread board ends overhangs a single drawer, 69¹/₄in. wide.
(Skinner) $10,925

A George II mahogany tripod table, the rounded rectangular tilt-top above a spirally-fluted turned baluster shaft, 26¼in. wide.
(Christie's) $4,200

A late Regency simulated rosewood coaching table, the oval hinged top on a collapsible X-frame support, 49in. wide.
(Christie's) $4,614

A George III mahogany pie-crust tripod table, the circular tilt top with shaped edge above a bird cage action, 24½in. diameter.
(Christie's) $1,661

A George III mahogany tripod table, the circular tilt top on a ring-turned reeded column and downswept cabriole legs, 35in. diameter.
(Christie's) $2,806

Ludwig Mies van der Rohe, for Bamberg Metallwerkstätten, serving trolley, designed 1927–29, manufactured circa 1930, nickel-plated steel, tubular steel, wood handle, glass, 28^{7}/₈in. high.
(Sotheby's) $27,180

A kingwood marquetry and gilt-bronze occasional table by Grohe, Paris, circa 1870, the oval top with a pierced gallery, crossbanded and centered by a spray of flowers, Paris, 61cm wide.
(Sotheby's) $6,319

An octagonal rosewood and pietre dure occasional table, French or Italian, circa 1860, the top inlaid, with a lapis lazuli border, 73cm. high.
(Sotheby's) $9,027

An oak and pine occasional table, the oval planked top, above a frieze fitted with a drawer to one side, partly 18th century.
(Christie's) $530

A porcelain and gilt composition guéridon, Paris, circa 1850, the circular dished top with a central plaque depicting Napoleon, 55.5cm. diameter.
(Sotheby's) $9,373

A French mahogany tray top occasional table, early 20th century, the top with a gallery pierced at the ends with carrying handles, 30½in. wide. (Christie's) $2,399

A rare maple hutch table, New York or New England, 1720–50, the hinged oval top tilting to reveal a well, 42in. wide. (Sotheby's) $10,350

A walnut, burr-elm and inlaid occasional table, early 20th century, the rounded rectangular top decorated with foliate sprays, 24in. wide. (Christie's) $2,215

A black slate specimen marble topped octagonal table, 20th century, the top decorated with a border of trailing foliage and flowers, 34½in. wide. (Christie's) $6,460

Alvar Aalto for Oy. Huonekalu-ja-Rakennustyötehdas AB, Turku, Finland, tea cart, model '98' 1935–36, bent laminated and solid birch, plywood, lacquered wood, 35½in. wide. (Sotheby's) $5,624

A Louis Philippe mahogany guéridon, the circular mottled gray marble top with a molded edge, above a plain frieze, 39in. diameter. (Christie's) $2,769

A French kingwood bijouterie table, mid 19th century, the rectangular glazed hinged top enclosing a green velvet lined interior, 25½in. wide. (Christie's) $2,584

A French kingwood, amaranth and marquetry table de nuit, late 19th century, the top with projecting angles, 16¼in. wide. (Christie's) $5,537

A George III mahogany silver table, the shaped canted rectangular molded top with later pierced fretwork gallery, 37½in. wide. (Christie's) $32,453

A 19th century walnut round table, the top inlaid with central flowers and ribbons and with a surrounding garland of similar flowers, 24in.
(Ewbank) $984

An Italian baroque walnut trestle table, 17th century, with moulded rectangular top, supported on carved scrolling trestles, 62in. wide.
(Sotheby's) $7,475

A George III oak tripod table, the tilt top above baluster turned support on three outswept cabriole legs, 73cm. wide.
(Bristol) $416

A mahogany and gilt-metal mounted two-tier occasional table, the rectangular top with baluster three-quarter gallery and frieze drawer, French, 22in. wide.
(Christie's) $2,087

A late Victorian mahogany and box strung tea table, the top with removable glass bottomed tray, the sides with four similarly inlaid retractable panels falling to form plate stands, 21in.
(Dreweatt Neate) $1,415

A 19th century Portuguese rosewood rectangular shaped occasional table with a gadrooned edge, 25½in. wide.
(Anderson & Garland)
                          $1,017

A mahogany occasional table, of mid Georgian design, the circular molded top on a ring-turned baluster shaft, partly 18th century, 34in diameter.
(Christie's) $1,069

A 19th century French kingwood and marquetry veneered table à ouvrage, the hinged lid opening onto a mirror and compartments, 23in. wide.
(David Lay) $1,020

An early 19th century oak tilt top table on turned column on downswept tripod base, 40in. diameter.
(Dreweatt Neate) $628

A mahogany, bronze and gilt-bronze guéridon, Paris, circa 1880, in the Empire style, the circular verde antico marble top on three legs, 69cm. diameter.
(Sotheby's) $11,247

An Italian walnut low table in Renaissance style, the oval top on a central columnar support, 19¹/₂in. high.
(Sotheby's) $690

A Victorian Aesthetic Movement inlaid burr-walnut occasional table, the circular top on turned and gilt-metal mounted column with splayed legs, 21in. wide. (Christie's) $629

A pair of mahogany and gilt-metal guéridons, French, circa 1890, each with a pierced gallery and oval onyx top, 51cm. wide.
(Sotheby's) $6,319

One of a matched pair of Louis XV style mahogany and marquetry oval occasional tables, each with an oval top with a pierced brass gallery, 19¹/₂in. wide.
(Bonhams) (Two) $4,770

Eugène Gaillard, two tiered table, circa 1900, fruitwoods, shaped rectangular top with gilt bronze handles on shaped incurved legs, 27¹/₈in. wide. (Sotheby's) $4,575

Queen Anne cherry and maple tea table, New England, 18th century, the oval top on four block turned legs, 34³/₄in. wide.
(Skinner) $4,888

A good Transitional style marquetry and gilt metal mounted inlaid table ambulante, circa 1900, the circular top inlaid with trellis within a ribbon tied foliate border, 29in. diameter.
(Bonhams) $5,400

A George III mahogany Pembroke table, with molded edge to the rectangular top, 37in. wide. (Bearne's) $680

An early 19th century satinwood and rosewood-banded Pembroke table, later painted with trailing briars, 37¾in. wide. (Bearne's) $2,349

A good Federal inlaid mahogany Pembroke table, Connecticut, circa 1810, the rectangular top flanked by D-shaped leaves, 40in. wide open. (Sotheby's) $2,875

A fine Federal satinwood-inlaid mahogany single-drawer Pembroke table, New York, circa 1800, the oblong top with two hinged D-shaped leaves, 44in. wide open. (Sotheby's) $14,950

A late George III polychrome-decorated and stenciled Pembroke table, the oval top with a band of oval landscape medallions divided by flowerheads 36¼in. wide. (Christie's) $6,109

A late George III mahogany Pembroke table, with reeded edge and rounded flaps, one drawer and one false drawer, 35in. wide. extended. (Dreweatt Neate) $405

A George III burr-walnut Pembroke table, crossbanded overall in rosewood and banded with ebony and fruitwood lines, 40½in. wide. (Christie's) $11,454

A George II mahogany Pembroke table, the rectangular twin-flap above a blind fret-paneled frieze enclosing a drawer, 31½in. wide, open. (Christie's) $7,254

A Federal inlaid mahogany Pembroke table, New York, 1790–1810, the circular hinged top with two drop leaves, 31¼in. wide. (Christie's) $10,350

A George III mahogany serpentine Pembroke table, the rectangular twin-flap top above a frieze drawer and simulated drawer to the reverse, 35¼in. wide, open. (Christie's) $49,634

A George III ebony-inlaid satinwood and marquetry Pembroke table, possibly by Mayhew and Ince, crossbanded overall in tulipwood and inlaid with boxwood and checkerbanded lines, 46½in. wide. (Christie's) $24,817

A late George III mahogany Pembroke table decorated with crossbanding and ebony stringing fitted with a single drawer to the frieze, 36in. wide. (Anderson & Garland) $922

A Federal inlaid mahogany Pembroke table, New York, circa 1795, the line-inlaid top flanked by rectangular leaves, 40in. wide open. (Sotheby's) $2,587

A good Chippendale mahogany Pembroke table, New England, possibly Rhode Island, circa 1780, the oblong top with bowed ends, 36½in. wide open. (Sotheby's) $4,600

Federal mahogany breakfast table, probably New York area, circa 1815, the rectangular top with shaped leaves above a beaded skirt, 34in. wide. (Skinner) $1,610

One of a pair of Italian giltwood pier tables, 20th century, serpentine molded light brown marble top, 177cm. wide.
(Sotheby's)
(Two) $15,629

A giltwood and gesso pier table, the verde antico marble top above a frieze centered by an acanthus and c-scroll cast cartouche, 70in. wide.
(Christie's) $4,200

A Victorian carved giltwood pier table, of Louis XV style, the molded serpentine carrara marble top (damaged) above a shaped frieze, 75in. wide.
(Christie's) $2,760

A classical carved parcel-gilt rosewood marble-top pier table, Boston, 1820–40, 45in. wide.
(Christie's) $6,900

An important Queen Anne carved walnut serpentine-front marble-top pier table, Boston, Massachusetts, circa 1745, 27½in. high overall.
(Sotheby's) $200,500

A fine George II carved and figured mahogany marble top pier table, English, mid-18th century, on cabriole legs ending in claw-and-ball feet, top 30in. wide.
(Sotheby's) $6,900

A Victorian gilt framed pier glass and matching table, the table of serpentine outline with red veined marble top, 36 x 106in. high.
(Canterbury) $1,280

Late 19th century neo-classical style marble topped painted pier table, the gray veined marble top over serpentined frieze, 38½in.
(G. A. Key) $1,152

Continental baroque walnut writing table, second quarter 18th century, 38in. wide.
(Skinner) $2,530

A George III fruitwood side table with molded border, with one drawer, on square chamfered legs, 30in. wide.
(Dreweatt Neate) $452

A giltwood side table, the later verde antico marble top above an egg-and-dart molding and vitruvian-scrolled frieze, 50½in. wide. (Christie's) $20,746

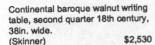

A Louis XV style kingwood and parquetry occasional table, the shaped top inlaid with geometric stylized flower heads, 21in. wide.
(Bonhams) $2,067

A pair of mahogany and ormolu-mounted side tables of French Empire design, 19th century, D-shaped green variegated marble tops, 34½in. wide.
(Christie's) $30,544

A small ebonized console table, circa 1905, open rectangular frame, semi-circular top with single frieze drawer, 20in. wide.
(Christie's) $4,874

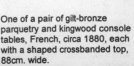

Classical mahogany and mahogany veneer side table, probably Massachusetts, circa 1825, the rectangular top with scrolled gallery, 39in. wide.
(Skinner) $2,530

A matched pair of Scottish boxwood tree tables, mid-19th century, each with two tiers and decorated on all sides with knotted pieces of wood, 32in and 31in. wide.
(Christie's) $16,031

One of a pair of gilt-bronze parquetry and kingwood console tables, French, circa 1880, each with a shaped crossbanded top, 88cm. wide.
(Sotheby's) (Two) $6,860

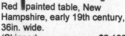

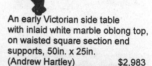

Pine and maple stretcher base table, New England, 18th century, tapering ring-turned legs joined by stretchers, 36in. wide. (Skinner)   **$2,645**

Red painted table, New Hampshire, early 19th century, 36in. wide. (Skinner)   **$2,185**

An early Victorian side table with inlaid white marble oblong top, on waisted square section end supports, 50in. x 25in. (Andrew Hartley)   **$2,983**

An 18th century oak side table, the rectangular molded edge top enclosing frieze drawer, on turned legs united by stretchers, 38in. (Dreweatt Neate)   **$1,491**

A late 19th century Chinese hardwood side table, the rectangular top with pierced flower head and branch frieze. (Dreweatt Neate)   **$628**

A maple single-drawer stretcher-base side table, American, probably New York or New England, 1770–1800, 34in. wide. (Sotheby's)   **$1,380**

Important American Queen Anne side table, in walnut with one drawer, reeded side panels, 30in. high. (Eldred's)   **$12,650**

A pair of tortoiseshell and bone side tables, French, circa 1840, in 17th century style, on barley twist legs, 79cm. wide. (Sotheby's)   **$10,833**

A Spanish baroque walnut side table, with overhanging top above a frieze drawer 24¼in. wide. (Sotheby's)   **$1,495**

A Victorian burr walnut side table with inset leather top above two short and one long drawers, 36in. wide. (Anderson & Garland)   **$1,538**

An Italian baroque ebonized side table, the molded rectangular overhanging top above a single frieze drawer, 37¾in. wide. (Sotheby's)   **$4,887**

An early period Robert Thompson of Kilburn oak table of good color and patination having an oblong adzed top with shelf undertier, 42in. long. (H.C. Chapman)   **$2,496**

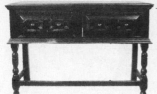

Italian baroque walnut side table, 18th century, 47½in. wide. (Skinner) $2,300

A Louis XVI style walnut table à milieu on pierced S-scrolling legs crisply carved with rocailles, drapery and putti masks, 64½in. wide. (Christie's) $10,925

A Victorian grained and composition side table, in the Adam style, the rectangular white marble top inlaid with bluejohn, 61in. wide. (Christie's) $90,138

A 19th century mahogany side table with molded rounded oblong top, two frieze drawers with inset turned wood handles, 51 x 25in. (Andrew Hartley) $1,312

One of a pair of Louis XVI style gilt-bronze and blue-painted steel side tables, circa 1890, each with a 'D'-shaped bleu turquin marble top, 123cm. wide. (Sotheby's) (Two) $15,629

A fine and rare Chippendale figured mahogany one-drawer side table, Rhode Island, circa 1780, on square molded legs. (Sotheby's) $32,200

An oak side table, the molded rectangular top above a deep drawer, on bobbin-turned legs, partly 18th century, 23in. wide. (Christie's) $661

A pair of bamboo side tables, 20th century, each with a demi lune top above a pierced lattice work frieze, 42in. wide. (Christie's) $3,322

Thonet two-tiered side table, 'MM3', 1932 chromium-plated tubular steel, black painted laminated wood, 15¾in. wide. (Sotheby's) $337

An Italian mahogany and marquetry side table, 20th century, decorated with meandering floral sprays, lines and crossbanding, 29½in. wide. (Christie's) $1,846

An Irish Regency mahogany side table, the grained brown marble top above a paneled frieze, on reeded spiral-turned legs, 48½in. wide. (Christie's) $3,322

A George II gilt-gesso side table, the later Regency Portor marble top with fluted edge, 38¼in. wide. (Christie's) $14,318

A Regency sofa table in mahogany with satinwood/ebony stringing, fitted with two drawers, 3ft.1in. closed.
(Russell, Baldwin & Bright)
$2,142

George III mahogany and inlay sofa table, late 18th/early 19th century, 49in. wide.
(Skinner)
$1,265

A George IV ebony-inlaid satinwood sofa-table, the rounded rectangular twin-flap top above a pair of frieze drawers, 56in. wide.
(Christie's)
$18,136

A Regency rosewood sofa table, the rounded rectangular twin-flap top above a frieze fitted with two drawers, 60in. wide.
(Christie's)
$4,061

A Regency rosewood sofa table, decorated with lines, the crossbanded rounded rectangular twin-flap top above two frieze drawers, 63in. wide.
(Christie's)
$4,061

A Regency mahogany sofa table on trestle-end supports with rosewood crossbanded and boxwood lined splayed feet, 60in. wide, open.
(Christie's)
$11,040

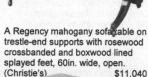

Classical painted sofa table, Baltimore, Maryland, circa 1830, the rectangular drop leaf top above two short drawers, 31in. wide closed. (Skinner)
$1,725

A Regency rosewood sofa table, with line-inlay and rounded rectangular top with two frieze drawers and dummy drawers to the reverse, 58in. extended.
(Christie's)
$2,639

A Regency mahogany sofa table with crossbanded rounded rectangular top, two frieze drawers, 60½in. wide.
(Bearne's)
$4,212

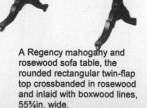

A Regency rosewood and marquetry sofa table, the rounded rectangular twin-flap top bordered by meandering floral inlay above two frieze drawers, 60in. wide.
(Christie's)
$7,752

Continental Neoclassical brass and ivory inlaid rosewood sofa table, second quarter 19th century, 52½in. wide extended.
(Skinner)
$3,335

A Regency mahogany and rosewood sofa table, the rounded rectangular twin-flap top crossbanded in rosewood and inlaid with boxwood lines, 55¾in. wide.
(Christie's)
$7,918

Grain painted chair table, probably New England, early 19th century, the rectangular top above baluster and ring turned supports, 42¼in. wide.
(Skinner) $4,887

Pine and maple chair table, northern Europe, 46½in. wide.
(Skinner) $2,990

Pine and maple stretcher base table, New England, 18th century, the top overhangs a painted block and ring turned base, 43⅜in. wide.
(Skinner) $3,737

William and Mary painted tavern table, New England, early 18th century, the rectangular overhanging top on four block, vase and ring-turned legs, 43in. wide.
(Skinner) $6,325

Pine and ash shoe foot hutch table, New England, late 18th century, on demi-lune cut-out ends, 46¾in. diameter.
(Skinner) $16,100

A turned and figured walnut two-drawer tavern table, Pennsylvania, 1740–80, the rectangular removable top above a frieze, 4ft. 10in. wide.
(Sotheby's) $6,900

A fine and rare William and Mary red-painted pine, hickory, and maple tavern table, New England, 1730–50.
(Sotheby's) $5,462

A Continental baroque style rectangular oak table, with overhanging top raised on baluster-turned legs joined by an H-form stretcher, 45in. wide.
(Sotheby's) $690

A grey-painted and turned pine tavern table, New England, 1730–60, the oval top above a rectangular frieze, 21in. wide.
(Sotheby's) $3,162

Red painted pine and maple chair table, New England, early 19th century, on ring-turned tapering legs, 41⅛in. wide.
(Skinner) $4,312

Walnut tavern table, Pennsylvania, early 18th century, the overhanging rectangular top above a molded skirt containing a thumbmolded drawer, 32in. wide.
(Skinner) $2,530

A turned walnut two-drawer stretcher-base tavern table, Pennsylvania or Mid-Atlantic States, 1775–1800, 4ft. 6½in. wide.
(Sotheby's) $4,312

A good Queen Anne figured maple oval-top splayed-leg tea table, New England, 1760–90, 35½in. wide. (Sotheby's)　　**$9,775**

A Scottish William IV rosewood tea table, the rounded rectangular hinged top, above a molded frieze with bobbin-turned border, 41in. wide. (Christie's)　　**$2,905**

A good Queen Anne red- and green-painted maple and pine tray-top tea table, New England, 1740–60. (Sotheby's)　　**$13,800**

A rare Chippendale carved and figured mahogany tilt-top birdcage tea table, New York, circa 1770, 31¾in. diameter. (Sotheby's)　　**$11,500**

A George III mahogany serpentine tea-table, the hinged molded top above a frieze inlaid with a checker-band, 35¼in. wide. (Christie's)　　**$2,087**

The Edwards family Chippendale carved mahogany tilt-top tea table, Boston, 1760–80, 36in. diameter. (Christie's)　　**$46,000**

A Queen Anne cherrywood tray top tea table, New England, 1740–60, the rectangular top with cove molding, 28¾in. wide. (Sotheby's)　　**$32,200**

A very fine and rare Chippendale turned and carved cherrywood tilt-top tea table, Lancaster County, Pennsylvania, circa 1765, 33¾in. diameter. (Sotheby's)　　**$288,500**

A rare Queen Anne gumwood tea table, New York, circa 1750, the rectangular thumbmolded top above a plain molded frieze, 30¼in. wide. (Sotheby's)　　**$6,325**

A good Queen Anne maple and
pine tea table, New York State,
probably Long Island, 1780–1800,
the rectangular top above a cyma-
shaped skirt, 25½in. wide.
(Sotheby's) $2,875

A mid-Georgian mahogany tea
table, the hinged D-shaped top
above a plain frieze, 32in. wide.
(Christie's) $1,379

A Chippendale mahogany tray-top
tea table, probably New York,
1750–70, the rectangular dished
top with cusped corners, 32in.
wide.
(Christie's) $63,000

Chippendale walnut dish-top tea
table, Pennsylvania, 18th century,
the top tilts above the birdcage and
pedestal on cabriole leg base,
33½in. diameter.
(Skinner) $863

A pair of Regency ebony-inlaid
mahogany swivel-action tea-tables,
crossbanded overall in rosewood,
each with rounded rectangular
hinged top, 36in. wide.
(Christie's) $16,227

A Chippendale carved and figured
maple piecrust tilt-top tea table, in
the Pennsylvania manner, on
acanthus leaf-carved cabriole legs,
29in. high.
(Sotheby's) $5,462

A Chippendale carved mahogany
tea table, Philadelphia, 1765–85,
the circular top with molded
scalloped edge tilting and turning
above a birdcage support, 35½in.
diameter.
(Christie's) $121,300

A good Queen Anne carved walnut
tray-top tea table, Boston,
Massachusetts, 1740–60, slender
cabriole legs ending in pad feet,
27½in. wide.
(Sotheby's) $63,000

A Victorian rosewood tea table with
a rectangular hinged swivel top and
plain frieze raised on an octagonal
bulbous column, 38in. wide.
(Anderson & Garland)
    $1,240

HISTORICAL FACTS
Workboxes
& Games Tables

Well before the introduction of playing cards, in the 15th century, proficiency at chess, backgammon and dice was considered to be an essential part of the education of anyone intending to take his place in society. Indeed, all forms of gaming were so popular that *The Complete Gamester* was felt to be almost compulsory reading and, in the edition of 1674, we find the declaration . . . he who in company should appear ignorant of the game in vogue would be reckoned low bred and hardly fit for conversation." Since there were, at the time, dozens of games widely played, including glecko, primero, ombre, picquet, basset, quadrille, commerce and loo, to name but a few, there must have been a considerable number of people wandering about with inferiority complexes.

Early games were played on marked boards (as chess and draughts) which were placed either on the floor or on a table. Towards the end of the 17th century, however, the business of losing a fortune was civilised somewhat by the introduction of beautifully made gaming tables specifically designed for players of particular games.

Although a few earlier pieces do exist, it was during the 18th and 19th centuries that gaming tables really came into their own, more often than not being combined with a workbox.

A French kingwood and cube parquetry serpentine table à ouvrage, late 19th/early 20th century, 25in. wide.
(Christie's) $3,138

A French table à ouvrage veneered with cube work and kingwood, the body of very slight bombé shape, 18½in. wide. (David Lay) $981

A papier-mâché, ebonized and mother-of-pearl inlaid work-table, Napoleon III, circa 1850, the oval shaped hinged top centered by a chinoiserie landscape with figures, 59cm. wide.
(Sotheby's) $5,416

A Regency ormolu-mounted and brass-inlaid mahogany work/games-table, inlaid overall with boxwood, ebony and ebonized lines, 19½in. wide.
(Christie's) $11,454

A Napoleon III walnut worktable, Paris, circa 1865, the hinged crossbanded top with a gilt-bronze foliate border, 55cm. wide.
(Sotheby's) $7,583

A Regency brass-inlaid rosewood work table with brass lines, star motifs and quatrefoils throughout, 19in. wide.
(Bearne's) $5,022

A George IV rosewood-veneered card and work table with rectangular fold-over top, frieze drawer and sliding work compartment, 20¼in. wide. (Bearne's)   **$1,587**

A walnut, kingwood, marquetry and gilt-bronze work table, Napoleon III, circa 1850, the shaped, hinged top centered with a spray of flowers, 62cm. wide. (Sotheby's)   **$8,435**

A French rosewood and marquetry work table, 19th century, decorated with meandering floral stems and lines, the oval drop-leaf top above a frieze, 29in. wide. (Christie's)   **$4,799**

A Regency brass-inlaid and mounted rosewood games-table, inlaid overall with lines, the hinged and sliding ratcheted square top with removable book-stop, 18¾in. wide. (Christie's)   **$6,035**

Renaissance Revival ebonized and parcel-gilt drop-leaf games table, A. Cutler & Son, Buffalo, New York, circa 1874, 36in. long. (Skinner)   **$690**

A kingwood and rosewood work table, English, circa 1860, the shaped hinged top inset with an oval panel painted with lovers in a landscape, 44cm. wide. (Sotheby's)   **$5,624**

A William IV rosewood worktable, decorated with gadrooned moldings, the circular hinged top enclosing a baize lined well, 17in. diameter. (Christie's)   **$2,769**

A Regency mahogany drop-leaf worktable, the rounded rectangular twin-flap top above two drawers opposed by two dummy drawers, 30in. wide. (Christie's)   **$2,584**

A Dutch mahogany and floral-marquetry work table, 19th century, decorated with floral sprays and lines, 18½in. wide, 29in. deep. (Christie's)   **$2,769**

A Federal figured mahogany work table, New York, circa 1810, the rectangular top with reeded edge, 21³/₄in. wide.
(Sotheby's) $4,025

Victorian walnut fold top games table with chessboard and baccarat board to either leaf, English, circa 1840, 2ft. 4in.
(G.A. Key) $2,544

A William IV rosewood work table with a single plain drawer over a rosewood sliding bag.
(David Lay) $2,226

A Federal inlaid and figured mahogany serpentine sewing table, Massachusetts, circa 1820, the shaped oblong top with turret corners and checker-inlaid edge, 20in. wide.
(Sotheby's) $10,350

Victorian burr walnut games/work table, the folding and swiveling top inlaid for checkers, backgammon and cribbage, mid 19th century, 20¹/₂in.
(G.A. Key) $1,374

Extremely rare American Sheraton two-drawer drop-leaf stand, in pine with allover decoupage decoration, 27¹/₂in. high.
(Eldred's) $1,760

A rare classical stencil-decorated and parcel-gilt carved mahogany swivel-top work table, New York, circa 1820, 25in. wide.
(Sotheby's) $1,955

A Victorian walnut and boxwood inlaid games/work table, the hinged rectangular sliding tip with molded canted angles, 29in. wide.
(Christie's) $2,673

A classical inlaid and veneered mahogany worktable, New York, 1815–30, on tapering reeded legs, 22¹/₄in. wide.
(Christie's) $6,900

A Federal figured mahogany sewing table, Massachusetts, circa 1810, the rectangular top above a drawer and a slide, 20in. wide.
(Sotheby's) $2,587

A Damascus games table, the swivel hinged top revealing sunken compartment and inlaid backgammon board, 87cm. wide.
(Bristol) $1,395

A classical mahogany worktable, Massachusetts, 1800–20, on four baluster-turned reeded legs, 18³/₄in. wide.
(Christie's) $3,450

Classical mahogany carved and mahogany veneer work table, Massachusetts, circa 1825, the rectangular top above two cockbeaded drawers, 22³/₄in. wide.
(Skinner) $2,070

A 19th century mahogany work table, the shaped casket top with hinged lid, on waisted tapering column with leaf collar, concave platform, base with lion paw feet, 20½in. wide.
(Andrew Hartley) $910

Federal mahogany carved, bird's-eye maple and mahogany veneer work table, probably Massachusetts, 1815–20, 20½in. wide.
(Skinner) $2,875

Victorian mahogany pedestal sewing table of octagonal form, inlaid in the center with neo-classical motif and the borders with Tunbridgeware inlay, 17½in.
(G.A. Key) $753

A Victorian walnut games/work table with string and marquetry inlay, on baluster turned twin end supports, 28in. wide.
(Andrew Hartley) $3,840

Classical tiger maple work table, Middle Atlantic States, circa 1825, the rectangular top above two graduated drawers, 21in. wide.
(Skinner) $1,092

A Louis XV style kingwood bureau rognon, circa 1890, the curved superstructure with an arrangement of five drawers, 41in. wide.
(Bonhams) $3,816

A mid-Georgian oak desk, the molded rectangular fall-flap enclosing a fitted interior, partly 18th century, 35in. wide.
(Christie's) $1,195

Federal tiger maple and mahogany inlaid desk, Massachusetts, circa 1820, the top section with crossbanded cornice board above two tambour doors, 39¹/₄in. wide.
(Skinner) $19,550

An ebonized and porcelain bonheur du jour, Germany, circa 1870, the upper part with a balustrade above a cupboard flanked by small drawers, 112cm. wide.
(Sotheby's) $45,149

American Sheraton desk, probably northern New England, early 19th century, in cherry, scrolled backsplash with rosettes above three side-by-side drawers, 38¹/₂in. wide.
(Eldred's) $4,840

A late Victorian ebonised and thuya ladies writing table, by Gillows, circa 1890, with a leather inset sliding easel writing surface above rectangular folding leaves, 44in. wide open.
(Bonhams) $2,862

A Napoleon III rosewood and marquetry bonheur du jour in the Louis XV manner, the superstructure with brocatelle marble top, 35½in. wide.
(Andrew Hartley) $4,000

Paine Furniture Co. drop front desk, two over two drawers with pyramid wooden pulls, three interior drawers and twelve pigeonholes, 38in. wide.
(Skinner) $460

A George III architect's mahogany desk with a hinged rising top above tuck away candlestands and a drawer fitted, 33in. wide.
(Anderson & Garland) $3,657

A late Victorian rosewood and boxwood and bone inlaid writing desk, shaped toprail above a mirrored back, 38in. wide. (Christie's) $2,100

A Regency brass- mounted and inlaid ebony, ebonized and parcel-gilt bonheur-du-jour, inlaid overall with brass lines and stylized foliate sprays, 30¼in. wide. (Christie's) $7,636

An Edwardian mahogany writing desk with raised back decorated with inlaid stringing, 42in. wide. (Anderson & Garland) $1,081

Pierre Chareau, small desk, circa 1925, sycamore, of rectangular form with pull-out shelf above five short drawers. (Sotheby's) $6,146

Federal mahogany veneer lady's desk, New England, early 19th century, the doors open to an interior of small drawers and valanced compartments, 39¼in. wide. (Skinner) $1,725

A Regency brass-mounted rosewood cheval writing-table, by John McLean, the crossbanded hinged rectangular top on an adjustable ratcheted support, 22½in. wide. (Christie's) $57,270

A Napoleon III kingwood, gilt-bronze and porcelain bonheur du jour, English, circa 1870, the upper part with a pierced metal gallery, above a pair of doors, 76cm. wide. (Sotheby's) $7,123

American Empire bureau, 19th century, in pine with bird's eye maple drawers, scrolled backsplash, two stepped drawers over four drawers, 45½in. wide. (Eldred's) $550

American schoolmaster's desk, in pine under original blue-green paint, upper section with slant lid and applied molding rail, 31½in. wide. (Eldred's) $1,265

A Victorian walnut library writing table, the rounded rectangular top inset with a gilt tooled leather writing surface, 48½in. wide. (Christie's) $5,537

A George III harewood and fiddleback-mahogany harlequin table, checkerbanded overall and inlaid with boxwood lines, 25in. wide. (Christie's) $16,227

A French kingwood bureau plat, late 18th century, applied with later gilt-metal mounts and decorated with crossbanding, 61in. wide. (Christie's) $6,276

A kingwood and gilt-bronze bureau plat, by François Linke, Paris, circa 1890, the leather inset shaped top within a gilt-bronze border, 190cm. wide. (Sotheby's) $68,705

A carved pearwood desk, designed by Hector Guimard, circa 1903, the back with low upper panel with shaped shelves at each end, 63⁷/₈in. wide maximum. (Christie's) $68,786

A German rosewood library table, late 19th century, the top with bowed ends, inset with a black leather lined writing surface, 60in. wide.   (Christie's) $3,507

An Edwardian satinwood bonheur du jour, the stepped superstructure with a pierced three-quarter gallery, 29½in. wide. (Christie's) $3,322

A French kingwood and parquetry oval writing table, late 19th century, the crossbanded top with rounded projecting angles, 40in. wide. (Christie's) $2,953

A Victorian mahogany clerk's desk, fitted with a sloping hinged fall with gilt-tooled red leather writing surface, 36.12in. wide. (Christie's) $1,292

A French mahogany kidney-shaped bureau plat, early 20th century, on ring-turned fluted tapering legs raised on brass toupie feet. (Christie's) $5,168

A parquetry and gilt-bronze bureau de dame, the upper section fitted with a clock, flanked by small drawers, 182cm. wide. (Sotheby's) $27,082

A mahogany desk, 20th century, carved with scrolling foliage, ribbon-tied swags, bellflowers, paterae and rams masks, 48½in. wide. (Christie's) $3,322

A kingwood and gilt-bronze bureau plat, probably French, circa 1880, with a shaped crossbanded top, 159cm. wide.
(Sotheby's) $6,499

A William IV mahogany library table, decorated with gadrooned moldings, the frieze fitted with four drawers, 60in. wide.
(Christie's) $7,014

A kingwood and gilt-bronze bureau plat, Paris, circa 1890, the leather inset top within a crossbanded and molded border, 181cm. wide.
(Sotheby's) $20,838

A mahogany and gilt-bronze bureau plat, English, circa 1880, the rectangular leather-inset writing surface within a molded gilt-bronze border, 180cm. wide.
(Sotheby's) $11,247

An ormolu mounted bureau plat, by Jules Leleu, 1940s, three frieze drawers, the legs and central drawer with ormolu mounts, 50$\frac{1}{4}$in. wide.
(Christie's) $9,372

A late George III brass-mounted satinwood Carlton House desk inlaid overall with boxwood and ebonized lines and crossbanded in tulipwood, 55$\frac{1}{2}$in. wide.
(Christie's) $112,050

A French kingwood serpentine bonheur du jour, late 19th century, superstructure fitted with two glazed doors, 24in. wide.
(Christie's) $3,322

A French kingwood and cube parquetry bureau plat, late 19th/early 20th century, the kidney-shaped crossbanded top above a central frieze drawer, 54in. wide.
(Christie's) $5,906

An Edwardian mahogany and marquetry secrétaire bonheur du jour, on square tapering legs, 36$\frac{1}{2}$in. wide.
(Christie's) $4,799

A small tropical hardwood writing desk, designed by Edward Barnsley, late 1930s, shallow central drawer flanked by two fall-front compartments, 41$\frac{5}{8}$in. wide.
(Christie's) $7,123

A kingwood and gilt-bronze bureau de dame, Paris, circa 1880, the upper part with two small drawers beneath a gallery, 120cm. wide.
(Sotheby's) $31,257

A mahogany, gilt-bronze and marquetry writing table by Sormani, Paris, circa 1880, the shaped top within a gilt-bronze border, 102cm. wide.
(Sotheby's) $11,194

Queen Anne maple tall chest of drawers, probably Rhode Island, circa 1750, on bracket feet, 33¾in. wide.
(Skinner) $2,645

Chippendale maple tall chest, Rhode Island, late 18th century, the flat molded dentil cornice above the thumbmolded drawers, 36in. wide.
(Skinner) $8,337

A crossbanded walnut chest, the rectangular top above five graduated long drawers and a shaped apron, on bracket feet, 23¼in. wide.
(Christie's) $661

A good Chippendale walnut tall chest of drawers, Pennsylvania, circa 1780, the overhanging stepped cornice above three short and five long graduated molded drawers, 45in. wide.
(Sotheby's) $13,800

Chippendale tiger maple tall chest, Rhode Island, late 18th century, the cornice molding over a seven-drawer thumbmolded case, 37in. wide.
(Skinner) $10,350

Chippendale maple tall chest of drawers, southeastern New England, late 18th century, case of two thumbmolded short drawers and five long drawers on bracket feet, 36in. wide.
(Skinner) $1,725

An Empire period mahogany and brass strung tall chest, containing six long drawers between tapered stiles, possibly Dutch, 103cm. wide.
(Phillips) $2,550

Cherry and maple tall chest of drawers, New England, circa 1800, the case of six thumbmolded graduated drawers on cut-out bracket base, 36in. wide.
(Skinner) $1,840

Chippendale applewood carved tall chest of drawers, probably Concord, Massachusetts, circa 1780, the flat molded cornice above a case of six graduated drawers, 35½in. wide.
(Skinner) $4,025

HISTORICAL FACTS
Teapoys

The word teapoy comes from the Hindi tin and ter, three, and the Persian Pai, a foot. It started life therefore as a small tripod table, and only by erroneous association with tea did it arrive at its final form, a small tea chest or caddy standing on a small three-footed stand. The teapoy is mentioned in inventories as early as 1808, by which time taking tea was well established as an elegant social habit.

Teapoy, English, 19th century, in fruitwood with pedestal base, 13in. high.
(Eldred's) $357

A Victorian rosewood teapoy, the hinged lid enclosing a fitted interior.
(Jacobs & Hunt) $960

A George IV rosewood teapoy, the lappeted stem on a concave quadripartite base ending in turned feet, 18½in. wide.
(Christie's) $955

A George IV mahogany teapoy, the hinged rectangular top enclosing an interior fitted with two tin lidded compartments and two cedar-lined compartments, 19¾in. wide.
(Christie's) $1,362

A rosewood teapoy, early 19th century, decorated with gadrooned and ripple moldings, the rectangular hinged top inset with a glazed molding, 20½in. wide.
(Christie's) $2,215

A Regency rosewood teapoy, sarcophagus shaped box, the hinged lid enclosing four canisters and two later glass mixing bowls, 45cm wide.
(Wintertons) $1,600

Early Victorian walnut and burl walnut teapoy, mid-19th century, fitted with two storage containers and two cut glass mixing bowls, 29in. high.
(Skinner) $1,265

An early Victorian rosewood teapoy, the sarcophagus hinged top on a faceted column and concave sided quadripartite platform with bun feet, 15in. wide. (Christie's) $750

Painted and stencil decorated six-board chest, probably Schoharie County, New York, first quarter 19th century, 39¾in. wide.
(Skinner) $2,070

Rare Roycroft bridal chest, mortise and tenons on sides, cast iron hardware, orb mark on front, 39¼in. wide.
(Skinner) $17,250

A paint-decorated pine diminutive blanket chest, New York State, dated 1829, the rectangular molded hinged lid opening to a well with a till, 43in. long.
(Sotheby's) $67,400

A cedar chest-on-frame, Bermuda, 1750-70, the rectangular molded hinged top opening into a single compartment fitted with a till, 52in. wide.
(Christie's) $5,175

American blanket chest, in pine with old brown finish, moulded upper and lower edges, paneled sides and front, 41½in. wide.
(Eldred's) $1,760

A grain-painted and stencil-decorated pine blanket chest, Pennsylvania, circa 1825, the hinged rectangular top opening to a well fitted with a till, 4ft. 1in. wide.
(Sotheby's) $4,312

A carved giltwood and painted cassone, Italian, circa 1860, in High Renaissance style, the hinged top carved above a panel painted with figures beneath an awning within an Italian town scene, 180cm. wide.
(Sotheby's) $13,122

American lift-top blanket chest, in old brown grain paint with stenciled decoration, 38in. long.
(Eldred's) $770

An Italian baroque walnut credenza, Bologna, incorporating 17th century elements, with later rectangular top above a tapering well, 51¼in. wide.
(Sotheby's) $2,587

Antique American lift-top sea chest, in pine with canted front, original painted decoration, painted on front Daniel W. Brewster, 44in. long.
(Eldred's) $688

An unusual carved and red-painted pine blanket chest, New England, circa 1800, the hinged rectangular top above a conformingly-shaped case, 4ft. wide.
(Sotheby's) $3,450

A carved pine blanket chest, signed Ship Eagle, E. O'Brien, Curling Master, dated 1859, the rectangular hinged lid opening to a well, 43½in. long.
(Sotheby's) $12,650

An Italian walnut cassone in late Renaissance style, of sarcophagus form, the molded two-stage top with dentiled edges, 67½in. long.
(Sotheby's)   **$4,025**

An Italian giltwood cassone, 19th century, the hinged rectangular top above a paneled front, painted with an Italianate scene, 71in. wide.
(Christie's)   **$7,360**

A Regency green-painted ottoman with hinged rectangular upholstered top and fabric covered sides, 44in. wide.
(Christie's)   **$1,379**

Small grained pine six-board chest, New England, 19th century, the hinged lid opens to an interior with lidded till, 37½in. wide.
(Skinner)   **$1,495**

Grain painted and paint decorated poplar six-board chest, Schoharie County, New York, first quarter 19th century, 37¾in. wide.
(Skinner)   **$1,265**

An English oak chest in 16th century style, the hinged paneled rectangular top over four recessed panels, 46in. wide.
(Sotheby's)   **$8,625**

An English inlaid oak chest in Charles II style, the hinged molded top over two square recessed panels, 47¾in. wide.
(Sotheby's)   **$1,380**

Painted pine wood box, northern New England, first half 19th century, original light green paint, 40in. wide.
(Skinner)   **$1,725**

A Continental baroque beechwood chest, probably a North Italian madia, with slanted roof-shaped top with zigzag ends, 42in. wide.
(Sotheby's)   **$1,380**

A good late 17th century carved oak chest, the molded top above three-panel front with architectural and foliate carved decoration, 131cm. wide.
(Bristol)   **$640**

A Charles II oak coffer with triple paneled front and hinged lid, on groove molded block legs, basically late 17th century, 45½in.
(Hy. Duke & Son)   **$672**

Chinese camphorwood chest, late 19th/early 20th century, original label inside reads *Wah Tuck Chan, Canton,* brass mounts, 38in. long.
(Eldred's)   **$715**

A red, green and yellow-painted pine blanket chest, Pennsylvania, circa 1790, the hinged rectangular top decorated with two pinwheels, 43in. wide.
(Sotheby's) $5,750

A polychrome-decorated brown-painted pine blanket chest, signed by Johannes Rank or Ranck, Jonestown, Pennsylvania, circa 1795, 4ft. 3½in. wide.
(Sotheby's) $9,775

A fine and very rare blue-green and white-painted pine blanket chest, attributed to Johannes Spitler, Shenandoah County, Virginia, circa 1800, 4ft. wide.
(Sotheby's) $74,000

A Queen Anne brass-nailed leather trunk, in the manner of Richard Pigge, decorated overall with geometric patterns in nails, 39¼in. wide. (Christie's) $5,345

Federal walnut inlaid dower chest, Pennsylvania, circa 1800, the rectangular molded top opens to an interior with till, 49in. wide.
(Skinner) $1,495

A fine Italian Renaissance inlaid walnut cassone of sarcophagus form, first half 16th century, 71¾in. wide.
(Sotheby's) $19,550

A rare William and Mary green- and brown-painted poplar and pine one-drawer blanket chest, Long Island, New York, 1700–50, 41½in. wide.
(Sotheby's) $8,050

American lift-top blanket chest, 18th century, in maple with tiger maple top, three drawers with molded fronts and brass escutcheons, 39in. wide.
(Eldred's) $935

Vinegar putty painted chest over drawers, Southeastern New England, circa 1835, the molded hinged top above a deep well, 40in. wide.
(Skinner) $6,325

Painted pine and poplar chest over drawer, New England, early 18th century, the molded lift top above a half-round molded case, 36in. wide. (Skinner) $4,600

American two-drawer lift-top blanket chest, in pine with old red stain, molded top edge, shaped bracket base, 45in. wide.
(Eldred's) $302

Red painted pine chest over drawers, Milton, New Hampshire, area, circa 1830, with molded hinged top above a cavity, 38in. wide. (Skinner) $3,450

A classical carved mahogany wardrobe, New York City, 1820–40, the molded cornice above a veneered band over an inset veneered frieze, 64in. wide. (Christie's) $2,990

An Empire period cherrywood wardrobe with straight molded pediment, plain frieze, the two paneled doors flanked by column supports. (Galerie Moderne) $1,750

A walnut wardrobe designed by J.S. Chapple after William Burges, 1891, with pierced and castellated cornice, twin tall cupboards, 72½in. wide. (Christie's) $49,677

A bamboo-turned figured maple wardrobe, attributed to R.J. Horner & Company, New York City, 1870–85, in three parts, 33in. wide. (Christie's) $10,925

An Art Nouveau Liberty style mahogany bedroom suite, comprising wardrobe with central arched mirror door and matching dressing table on spiral turned supports. (Russell Baldwin & Bright) $3,040

An Aesthetic Movement painted ash compactum wardrobe, 19th century, the cavetto cornice above single mirror door, 127cm. wide. (Bristol) $869

A walnut and crossbanded wardrobe, by Whytock and Reid of Edinburgh, the molded rectangular top above a foliate-carved and molded frieze, 50in. wide. (Christie's) $3,531

An inlaid mahogany neo-gothic wardrobe, attributed to Christopher Pratt & Sons, circa 1860, the mirrored central door opening to reveal drawer-lined interior, 81in. wide. (Christie's) $2,760

A Dutch mahogany and floral marquetry wardrobe, early 19th century, decorated with meandering floral sprays, lines and flower-filled urns, 54½in. wide. (Christie's) $6,460

American Sheraton stepped vanity, in old yellow and black paint with stenciled decoration, 33½in. wide. (Eldred's) $550

A Regency mahogany washstand with raised gallery, the base fitted with five drawers around leafage carved apron on cheval base, 3ft. 8in. wide. (Russell Baldwin & Bright) $2,880

A George II mahogany washstand, the pierced square top with two hinged flaps, one associated large circular dished bowl and one associated small circular bowl, 14in. wide. (Christie's) $4,526

A French cream-painted simulated bamboo tole washstand, the rounded rectangular top with later circular basin and brass taps, 28¼in. wide. (Christie's) $3,395

A late Victorian mahogany washstand, by Maple & Co, London, the boxwood lined toprail above a marble splashboard back, 51in. wide. (Christie's) $1,328

A satinwood bowfront corner washstand, 19th century, the molded and dentiled cornice above an open shelf, four pigeon holes and two cupboard doors, 28in. wide. (Christie's) $2,195

A late George III mahogany and boxstrung bow fronted corner washstand with central frieze drawer flanked by a dummy drawer either side. (Dreweatt Neate) $910

An Art Nouveau oak part bedroom suite, comprising a mirror back dressing chest, together with matching marble top and raised tile back washstand, 42in. wide. (Dreweatt Neate) $720

A Federal figured maple washstand, Mid-Atlantic States, circa 1830, the three-quarter scrolling back-splash above a rectangular top, 23in. wide. (Sotheby's) $4,600

A late 19th century mahogany Chinese Chippendale style étagère, the pagoda top with carved hanging bells in each corner, 81cm. wide. (Phillips) $2,686

An early Victorian mahogany two tier buffet, the molded edge top with shaped gallery on turned supports and brass castors, 45in. wide. (Dreweatt Neate) $1,402

A late Georgian mahogany four-tier square shaped whatnot with turned supports terminating in brass castors, 50in. high. (Anderson & Garland) $1,908

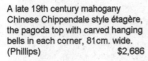

A Napoleon III ebonised whatnot/music stand, with pierced gallery, the four shelves supported on turned column supports. (Galerie Moderne) $250

Pair of mahogany whatnots, galleried tops, inset below with brushing slides, supported by ring turned uprights, 20th century, 19in. (G. A. Key) $1,360

A mahogany whatnot, early 19th century, the upper two caned tiers on ring-turned supports surmounted by turned finials, 15½in. wide. (Christie's) $1,846

A Victorian oak four-tier what-not, the molded rectangular tiers with canted corners and three-quarter galleries, 30½in. wide. (Christie's) $1,111

A mahogany four tier serpentine whatnot, the two rear supports encrusted with urn finials and joined by a fretwork pierced gallery, 39in. wide. (G A Key) $2,216

A Victorian burr walnut and inlaid canterbury whatnot, the inlaid top on turned supports. (Bristol) $1,680

A George III mahogany and brass bound callaret on stand, of oval tapering form with hinged crossbanded lid, 24½in. wide. (Andrew Hartley) $7,040

A George III mahogany and brass-bound, octagonal cellaret-on-stand, with a hinged top and brass carrying handles, 20in. wide. (Christie's) $3,138

A plain 18th century mahogany cellaret with hinged square section lid, the base with plain, brass carrying handles and bracket feet, 14in. wide. (David Lay) $984

A George III mahogany cellaret with dome lid and side brass drop handles, above a later cupboard base, 54cm. wide. (Dreweatt Neate) $1,408

A mahogany two division cellaret, with an undulating border, enclosing six divisions with an arched central division pierced with a carrying handle, 16in. wide. (Christie's) $2,584

A rare Federal inlaid cherrywood cellaret, Southern, circa 1795, the hinged rectangular top with molded edge opening to a well, 31¾in. wide. (Sotheby's) $4,600

A George II brass-bound mahogany wine-cooler, of oval tapering shape, the lead-lined interior with two plugs, 23½in. wide.
(Christie's) $4,149

A Federal inlaid mahogany and maple cellaret, Rhode Island, 1790–1810, the rectangular hinged lid with central inlaid fingured maple oval, 17½in. wide.
(Christie's) $1,725

A late classical carved mahogany cellaret, New York, 1820–40, the rectangular peaked or hinged lid with rounded edge, 39¾in. wide.
(Christie's) $3,450

A Federal inlaid and figured mahogany cellaret, Mid-Atlantic States, circa 1795, the rectangular molded top section fitted with a crossbanded door, 19¼in. wide.
(Sotheby's) $2,185

A pair of George III ormolu-mounted mahogany wine-coolers, each of oval shape with a gadrooned rim above a guilloche frieze, 30in. wide.
(Christie's) $45,816

An early George III mahogany and brass-bound oval wine cooler-on stand, with brass carrying handles to the sides, on channeled square legs, 25in. wide.
(Christie's) $4,430

A Sheraton Revival satinwood cellaret, crossbanded with string and checker inlay, of oblong form, 16in. wide.
(Andrew Hartley) $6,123

A late Georgian mahogany cellaret, with hinged sloping bowfront lid, on molded bowfront plinth, 19in. wide.
(Christie's) $1,049

A William IV/early Victorian mahogany cellaret with sarcophagus top enclosing two compartments, 25¾in. wide.
(Bearne's) $1,101

A Bohemian transparent enameled beaker, painted in colors with a continuous river landscape, 20th century, 13.5cm. high. (Christie's) $459

A South Bohemian hyalith chinoiserie beaker, Count Bouquoy's Glasshouse, with everted gilt rim, circa 1830, 6cm. high. (Christie's) $736

A Bohemian transparent-enameled beaker, on amber stained flange foot, gilt lining, late 19th century, 11.6cm. (Bristol) $102

A North Bohemian faceted lithyalin shaped beaker, circa 1835, attributed to the workshop of Friedrich Egermann, the exterior of marbled blue, green and yellow, 4½in. high. (Christie's) $1,600

A Bohemian engraved beaker engraved with a man standing in a field holding a wine glass, early 18th century, 11.5cm. high. (Christie's) $643

A Bohemian transport enameled cog wheel beaker, painted with an oval portrait medallion of Napoleon Bonaparte, 12.5cm. high, late 19th century. (Christie's) $1,573

A Bohemian dated stained ruby hexagonal spa beaker, cut with five titled reserves engraved with buildings and the sixth inscribed *Von Jacob Josephn 1846,* 15cm. high. (Christie's) $874

A Bohemian transparent enamel flared beaker (Ranftbecker) painted with a sprig of orange blossom and gilt inscribed *Mein Liebstes,* 20th century, 11.5cm. high. (Christie's) $736

A Bohemian fluted tapering beaker, engraved with a bacchic putti merrymaking within branches of fruiting vines, 15cm. high, 19th century. (Christie's) $436

A Lalique bowl, with vertical stylised leaf molded decoration with scrolled ends, molded mark *R.Lalique France*, 1930s, 22cm. (Tennants) $445

A Sabino glass bowl, on three foliate feet, molded with flowerheads, 12in. diameter. (Christie's) $160

New England Agata Art Glass bowl, ten-ruffle rim on shaded rose pink color with overall blue and gold 'oil spots', 2½in. high. (Skinner) $546

Bohemian cameo glass covered jar, frosted colorless base and top cased to off-white and layered on enameled orange and black, 5¼in. diameter. (Skinner) $575

Webb Cameo tricolour bowl and undertray, brilliant red layered in sapphire blue and overlaid white, diameter 5⅛ and 6in. (Skinner) $1,380

'Papillon', a pâte de verrè bowl, by Gabriel Argy-Rousseau, circa 1915, decorated with large moths below the rim, 3in. high. (Christie's) $6,748

Important Carder Steuben rose quartz Cintra applied and etched bowl, scalloped rim on mottled and crackled pink, blue and frosted colorless glass body, 7in. high. (Skinner) $1,495

Mount Washington Napoli glass and silver plated compote, colorless glass dish reverse painted maroon with blue and yellow blossoms, 5½in. high. (Skinner) $403

'Lierre', a pâte de verre bowl, by Gabriel Argy-Rousseau, circa 1915, with a cluster of green berries with purple leaves below the rim, 3⁹⁄₁₆in. high. (Christie's) $5,623

Orrefors cut crystal leopard centerbowl, Gunnar Cyren design of caged animals achieved by cut and faceted 'bars', 6in. diameter. (Skinner) $1,380

Dale Chihuly contemporary studio glass bowl, early sea-form vessel of seedy colorless glass shaded to smoky topaz color, 6¾in. high. (Skinner) $1,035

Austrian Steinschonau Art Glass compôte, attributed to Karl Massanetz, colorless and amber bowl on faceted pedestal, 5¼in. high. (Skinner) $1,840

Pair of Sandwich canary glass candlesticks, 19th century, loop base with petal socket, 7in. high. (Eldred's) $302

Sandwich pressed glass candlestick, 19th century, in turquoise, loop base with petal socket, 7in. high. (Eldred's) $1,045

Pair of Carder Steuben blue Aurene candlesticks, early design with ropetwist shaft, 10in. high. (Skinner) $1,840

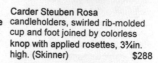

Pair of Carder Steuben Amethyst Silverina candleholders, mica flecked light amethyst with controlled bubble pattern, 5in. high. (Skinner) $863

Rare Carder Steuben Cyprian candelabrum, aquamarine tinted verre de soie with celeste bleu accent rims on three arm candle holder, 19in. high. (Skinner) $1,840

Carder Steuben Rosa candleholders, swirled rib-molded cup and foot joined by colorless knop with applied rosettes, 3¾in. high. (Skinner) $288

Three Carder Steuben jade and alabaster candlesticks, flared cups and bases of pale green jade, alabaster double bulbed shafts, 12in. high. (Skinner) $1,725

A composite-stemmed candlestick, circa 1750, the ribbed nozzle with everted rim supported on a central octagonal tapering pedestal stem, 10in. high. (Christie's) $1,650

T.G. Hawkes cut and engraved crystal bowl and candlesticks, bright cut floral and webbed motif on bowl, 14in. high. (Skinner) $3,105

Tiffany & Co. cut glass decanter with Sterling top, 1902-07, 11½in. high. (Skinner)   **$1,725**

Fine Victorian presentation silver three bottle tantalus, the rectangular shaped frame with rope twist edges, Sheffield circa 1880, 13 x 6½in. (G. A. Key)   **$3,120**

Orrefors engraved crystal decanter, designed by Nils Landberg, domed rectangular form with sailor playing accordion at reverse, 10¼in. high. (Skinner)   **$1,150**

Silver overlay crystal decanter, star-cut base on squat colorless glass stoppered pitcher heavily overlaid in silver, 7½in. high. (Skinner)   **$546**

Thomas Webb rock crystal cut and engraved pair of decanters, faceted and bulbed vessels with stylized ocean waves below five fish swimming, 14¾in. high. (Skinner)   **$2,875**

An electroplate-mounted 'crow's foot' decanter, designed by Dr Christopher Dresser, manufactured by Hukin & Heath, circa 1878, 9½in. high. (Christie's)   **$5,483**

A Victorian silver mounted molded glass decanter, maker's mark of William Comyns, 1898, the foot and shoulder mounts pierced with flower heads and c-scrolls, 9¾in. high. (Christie's)   **$342**

A Victorian brass bound oak tantalus, the shaped back containing three cut glass decanters above lidded fitted cigar compartment, 34cm. (Bristol)   **$508**

A Georgian spirit decanter of Hexagonal form, the rounded shoulders printie cut in the form of flowers, circa 1780, 10in. high. (Andrew Hartley)   **$224**

Handel Opalware pug dog tray, collectible metal mounted glass dish handpainted with red collared pug dog, signed *Bauer*, 4¾in. high. (Skinner) $632

Tiffany blue floriform compôte, deep ruffled broad blossom rim enhanced by stretched bright blue iridescence, 4½in. high. (Skinner) $2,070

Daum, wisteria jardinière, circa 1905, clear glass internally decorated with pale apricot around the neck and pale green towards the base, 11¼in. maximum width. (Sotheby's) $4,993

A cameo glass marine platter, by Gallé, circa 1900, in clear electric blue overlaid with milky blue, white and caramel, 15in. diameter. (Christie's) $8,225

A gilt and enamel glass coupe by Daum, circa 1906, the bowl etched and gilded with patterned field and enameled with a cockerel, eagle, thistles and oak leaves, 4½in. high. (Christie's) $6,440

Good aubergine Peking glass dish, 18th century, the shallow dish molded with radiating petals on the cavetto below the floriform rim, 11¼in. diameter. (Butterfield & Butterfield) $9,775

American flint glass compote, in diamond thumbprint pattern, 11in. diameter, 9½in. high. (Eldred's) $242

Schneider compote on wrought iron stand, broad shallow mottled pink and aubergine centerbowl raised on striped glass stem, 14in. diameter. (Skinner) $978

A cut circular center dish, the turnover rim with star band, late 19th century, 20cm. high. (Christie's) $368

A Bohemian ruby-cased goblet, the octagonal bowl engraved with flower sprays, second half 19th century, 19cm. high.(Christie's) $1,104

Two European Art Glass goblets, attributed to Bimini, cups with delicate orange and white swirls above bubble stems, 7¼in. high. (Skinner) $316

Carder Steuben oriental poppy goblet, flared rib-molded water goblet with fine pink-opal colour, applied Pomona green straight stem. 8¼in. high. (Skinner) $489

A large cut armorial goblet, the coat of arms within an oval cartouche, the reverse with racehorse and jockey, mid 19th century, 19cm. high. (Christie's) $1,195

A pair of Victorian wine goblets, the bucket bowls engraved with a continuous hunting scene, circa 1860, 8in. high. (Andrew Hartley) $192

Steuben Crystal 'Lust' exhibition goblet, Sidney Waugh design, first in the 'The Seven Sins' series, 7½in. high. (Skinner) $1,380

A Bohemian ruby flash goblet, the flared bowl engraved with a continuous band of deer in a forest landscape, third quarter 19th century, 28.5cm. high. (Christie's) $3,312

A pair of 19th century Bohemian ruby flashed goblets, with faceted finial on domed lid, the body etched with a stag hunting scene, 13in. high. (Andrew Hartley) $3,200

A large Harbridge commemorative engraved and cut baluster goblet, for the coronation of His Majesty King George VI, 32.5cm. high. (Christie's) $436

Cobalt blue overlay white Peking glass jar and cover, 19th century, carved to one side with an ox beneath a pine tree gazing back at the sun, 5in. high. (Butterfield & Butterfield)　　$1,380

Pair of five colour overlay Peking glass jars, decorated with blossoming sprays issuing from rockwork, 5¼in. (Butterfield & Butterfield)　　$4,312

Painted cranberry cylindrical gilt metal mounted glass jar, star cut lid and base, raised on three foliate molded gilt metal paw feet, 7½in. (G.A. Key)　　$128

Jugs

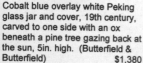

Cut glass claret jug with a silver mounted handle, lid and pourer, hallmarked for London 1898. (G.A. Key)　　$235

Smith Brothers decorated Mount Washington sugar bowl and creamer, ribbed melon-form set with matching yellow centered white aster/daisy like blossoms, 4in. (Skinner)　　$431

An electroplated mounted cut-glass claret jug with leaf capped scroll handle, mask spout and engraved decoration, 28cm. high. (Bearne's)　　$340

Late Victorian glass claret jug with wheel engraved decoration of leafy scrolls and concentric rings, 8½in. high, Birmingham 1900. (G.A. Key)　　$668

Brilliant cut glass jug, spherical body with offset stoppered spout, applied notched handle in the Sinclaire manner, 7in. high. (Skinner)　　$518

A rare enameled glass jug 'parlant' by Gallé, circa 1900, the body internally streaked with red and green, with an exotic fish, 5½in. high. (Christie's)　　$8,096

A cut punch urn, the tapering bowl with a field of stars within borders of fluted squares, late 19th century, 43cm. high. (Christie's)　　**$552**

Pair of green opaque glass lustres with hanging prism drops, second half 19th century, 12¹/₂in. (G.A. Key)　　**$349**

American amethyst blown glass handled bottle, rough pontil, applied handle and collared lip, 7³/₄in. high. (Eldred's)　　**$687**

Murano Studio glass ritorte coppa, design attributed to Fulvio Bianconi for Venini, oversize brandy snifter form, raised on cobalt blue pedestal stem and foot, 12in. high. (Skinner)　　**$1,725**

A leaded glass panel, designed by David Gauld for McCulloch & Co., Glasgow, 1891, the rectangular panel depicting a full-length female figure with auburn hair, 31¹/₂ x 18¹/₂in. (Christie's)　　**$26,404**

An American silver and cut-glass flask with Columbian Exposition mark, Tiffany & Co., New York, circa 1893, the glass body cut with grapevine and scrolls, 7³/₄in. high. (Sotheby's)　　**$1,725**

A large silver-gilt and enamel ornament, by George Frampton, 1898, circular panel depicting a single tree in vibrant blue and green enamels, 3³/₈in. diameter. (Christie's)　　**$15,933**

Pair of Venetian style overlaid glass lusters, the bowls alternately decorated with panels of painted stylized flowers, 19th century, 13in. (G.A. Key)　　**$1,567**

Gabriel Argy-Rousseau and Bouraine, sculpture 'Papillon', 1928, modeled as a standing female nude, her back arched over her butterfly wings, 10in. (Sotheby's)　　**$43,351**

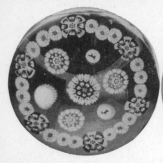

Antique Baccarat concentric paperweight, unusual arrowhead and star canes and three 'Gridel' animal silhouettes, 3¼in. diameter.
(Skinner) $1,380

A St Louis faceted upright bouquet paperweight, the bouquet with central white flower, 7cm. diameter.
(Christie's) $3,128

Antique Baccarat millefiore paperweight, close pack intricate canes, including B1846, 3in. diameter.
(Skinner) $1,725

New England poinsettia paperweight, ten-petal red blossom with blue and white center cane, faceted edging, 2¾in. diameter.
(Skinner) $402

Antique Clichy swirl paperweight, rose, green and white pinwheel swirl with pink centered turquoise center, 3in. diameter.
(Skinner) $1,035

Baccarat antique floral paperweight, two red and yellow star centered striped blossoms, one purple, one white, 2½in. diameter.
(Skinner) $1,610

A St Louis pompom paperweight, the flower with many recessed white petals about a pale yellow center, mid 19th century, 7cm. diameter.
(Christie's) $1,840

Victor Trabucco magnum snake paperweight, green and yellow bellied black snake on silvered rocky sanded ground, 3¾in. diameter.
(Skinner) $690

Ken Rosenfeld bouquet paperweight, spray of exotic lavender bellflowers and dark centered yellow flowers on leafy stems, 3½in. diameter.
(Skinner) $488

Webb cameo glass double cap footed perfume, cased red oval bottle with white cameo etched blossom motif overall, 5in. high.
(Skinner) $1,840

Webb cameo glass figural teardrop perfume, turquoise blue flattened oval bottle overlaid in white cameo, etched and carved overall with a downcast boy carrying faggots, 4¼in. long.
(Skinner) $13,800

Webb cameo glass nautical perfume bottle, ruby red sphere decorated by shell and seaweed motif, with hallmarked silver rim, 3in. high.
(Skinner) $2,070

Webb cameo glass apple blossom perfume, white cased to colorless glass round bottle overlaid in white over rose red cameo, 3½in. high.
(Skinner) $1,500

Pair of blue Czechoslovakian perfumes, heart shaped cut crystal bottles with colorless stoppers framing intaglio portrait of woman picking bouquet, 8½in. high.
(Skinner) $632

An English cameo glass globular scent bottle, the red ground overlaid in white and cut with a dog rose and foliage, the silver cover by Sampson Mordan & Co., London,1887, 10.5cm.
(Tennants) $508

René Lalique blue Marquila perfume flaçon, frosted 'navy' blue with molded artichoke lappet design, matching stopper, 3¹/₂in. high.
(Skinner) $1,955

Silver overlaid green perfume, sphere of teal green glass layered at shoulder with floral decorated motif, 5½in. high.
(Skinner) $345

A small mounted iridescent glass bottle by Tiffany Studios, the lobed body with delicately feathered peacock trails, 5in. high. (Christie's)
                $11,040

Handel/Pittsburgh-style ceiling shade, round crackle glass ball transfer printed with Art Deco parrots front and back, 9in. diameter.
(Skinner) $633

An etched glass hanging shade, by Daum, 1920s, large shallow smoked glass shade etched with simple linear design, 24¹/₈in. diameter.
(Christie's) $2,436

A bronze and frosted glass plafonnier, early 20th century, the domed shade cut with stellar and stiff leaf designs, 14¾in. diameter.
(Christie's) $2,584

Daum, fuchsia plafonnier, circa 1905, gray glass internally streaked with white and royal blue and etched and enameled in shades of violet, red and green, 13in. diameter.
(Sotheby's) $20,165

Two American cameo glass fluid lamp shades, attributed to Gillander Glass of Philadelphia, crimped rim on flared cased body, 4½in. high.
(Skinner) $345

Emile Gallé, campanula plafonnier, circa 1900, gray glass internally decorated with yellow, overlaid with blue and etched with flowering stems, 13⁵/₈in. diameter.
(Sotheby's) $9,987

A bronze and frosted glass plafonnier, early 20th century, the domed shade cut with stellar and stiff leaf designs, 12in. diameter.
(Christie's) $3,322

A gilt bronze mounted glass ceiling light, 20th century, the circular faceted dish with cone terminal suspended from a berried laurel circlet, 17in. diameter.
(Christie's) $2,215

A French brass and frosted glass plafonnier, early 20th century, the domed shade cut with stellar and stiff leaf designs and with budding terminal, 14½in., diameter.
(Christie's) $2,953

A Bohemian Zwischengold glass tumbler, 18th century, the faceted vessel decorating with gilt foliate scrolls, 3⁵/₈in. high. (Sotheby's) $1,035

A Bohemian amber and blue flash octagonal tumbler, each panel with a flash reserve variously engraved and named in gothic script, 10cm. high. (Christie's) $600

A Victorian blue dipped tumbler, engraved with a continuous scene of fishermen, circa 1860, 5in. high. (Andrew Hartley) $152

Clear etched blown glass tumbler, John Frederick Amelung, New Bremen Glass Manufactory, near present day Frederick, Maryland, circa 1788–89, 6¹/₈in. high. (Skinner) $83,900

A Bohemian cylindrical tumbler with a verre eglomisé panel, circa 1800, with an oval double-walled panel gilt with the monogram *AR* on a ruby-ground, 4¼in. high. (Christie's) $1,650

An engraved colorless handblown flip glass, English or Continental, mid 18th century, decorated with flowers, leaves, and berries and a shield, 8¹/₄in. high. (Sotheby's) $2,587

Tankards

European blown glass tankard, 19th century, with enameled decoration, 5in. high. (Eldred's) $165

A Bohemian glass tankard, octagonal cut with roundels of stained amber, gilded and enameled with arabesques, 5¼in. high. (Andrew Hartley) $32

A Bohemian opaque blue faceted mug and a cover, of slender tapering form, gilt and silvered with spiral bands of fruiting vine, mid 19th century, 20cm. high. (Christie's) $555

René Lalique opalescent Ceylan vase, extended rim on press molded vessel with four pairs of lovebirds in high relief, 9in. high. (Skinner) $4,025

Emile Gallé cameo glass vase, flared jarre form of colorless glass cased to opalescent and fiery amber interior, 6in. high. (Skinner) $1,150

G. Argy-Rousseau pâte-de-cristal vase, golden-amber and brown glass with central conical bud vase on oval plinth, 5¼in. high. (Skinner) $4,025

Rare Thomas Webb cameo glass figural vase, translucent green glass body in gourd-form with solid applied top stem as handle, 7¼in. high. (Skinner) $3,220

An Art Nouveau turquoise ovoid vase, with dimples and overall gilt painted with trailing flowering plants, 11.5cm. (Bristol) $208

Mount Washington Crown Milano vase, flared eight-lobed rim on ribbed sphere decorated with polychrome spring blossoms on peach colored background, 6in. high. (Skinner) $1,725

Carder Steuben etched mansard vase, oval of frosted colorless crystal cut in repeating stylized Art Deco blossoms, etched fleur-de-lis, 6in. high. (Skinner) $1,495

Sabino Art Glass vase, colorless elliptical body with full-bodied nude women at each side among frosted blossoming flower beds, 7½in. high. (Skinner) $1,495

Tiffany blue iridescent vase, raised folded rim on dark bulbous vessel decorated by pulled and hooked swirls of iridescent devices, 8in. high. (Skinner) $4,887

A Laliqué opalescent glass vase, of flared cylindrical form, moulded with upright stiff leaves, 6½in. high. (Christie's) $505

Pair of American flint glass celery vases, in diamond thumbprint pattern. (Eldred's) $187

An Art Nouveau turquoise shoulder ovoid vase, with brown combed panels and painted with flowering plants, 11.5cm. (Bristol) $416

Venini Pezzato 'Istanbul' vase, Fulvio Bianconi 1952 design, flared model with patchwork squares of purple, gray, colorless and pale yellow, 8in. high. (Skinner) $6,900

A pair of Austrian streak glass vases, the clear ovoid bodies colored with blue, green and yellow, 9in. high. (Andrew Hartley) $160

Tiffany favrile striped Cypriote vase, broad bulbous oval of iridescent ambergris decorated by alternating wide and narrow vertical stripes of metallic Cypriote texture, 12in. high. (Skinner) $4,600

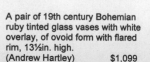

Carder Steuben mirror black engraved vase, polished raised rim on broad glossy oval decorated by five repeats of foliate panels and scrolling devices, 12in. high. (Skinner) $1,495

A pair of 19th century Bohemian ruby tinted glass vases with white overlay, of ovoid form with flared rim, 13½in. high. (Andrew Hartley) $1,099

Moncrieff Art Glass vase, attributed to Monart/Ysart studios, bulbous angular bright orange body, with gray powered overlay crackled on surface, 8in. high. (Skinner) $431

Emile Gallé 'blow out' aquatic vase, circa 1900, amber/green-blue slightly opalescent glass, overlaid with amber and etched with fronds of seaweed and starfish, 13¹/₈in. high. (Sotheby's) $14,956

Hans Bolek for Glashütte Lötz Witwe, Klostermühle/Böhmen vase, 1915–17, glass, 4¹/₈in. (Sotheby's) $2,437

Emile Gallé, two-handled vase, 1880's, smoked glass, enameled in polychrome shades with delicate floral sprigs and with two cartouches, 4in. (Sotheby's) $2,487

Emile Gallé, chrysanthemums vase, circa 1900, opaque cream glass, overlaid with orange and etched with two large blooms, 9¼in. (Sotheby's) $7,682

A pair of George Jones & Sons dark-olive ground pâte-sur-pâte globular vases, last quarter of the 19th century, each with putti in flight, 6in. high. (Christie's) $2,070

Tiffany mahogany floriform vase, blossom composed of translucent brown 'petals' outlined in ruby red against opal glass border rim, 9in. high. (Skinner) $3,738

René Lalique, vase 'Oranges', after 1926, frosted glass, molded with fruits amidst leaves, 11¼in. (Sotheby's) $21,126

Pair of decorative lusters, the hipped rims with gilt borders and decorated with heart shaped motifs, 14in. (G. A. Key) $992

René Lalique, vase 'Perruches', after 1919, electric blue glass, molded with a design of pairs of budgerigars on leafy branches, 10in. (Sotheby's) $14,404

A marquetry glass vase, by Gallé, circa 1900, rectangular section, internally colored with purple from half height, 8¹/₈in. high. (Christie's) $33,741

A pair of Bohemian faceted vases, each with ovoid bowl overlaid with ruby panels, late 19th century, 20cm. (Bristol) $508

Austrian Art Glass mounted vase, Loetz-type emerald green bulbed vessel with overall indentations, 12¹/₂in. high. (Skinner) $632

An etched and enameled glass vase, by Daum, circa 1905, shouldered with raised foot, mottled lime green shading to blood red, 10³/₈in. high. (Christie's) $3,561

Two English dark-olive green-ground pâte-sur-pâte vases, late 19th/early 20th century, probably George Jones & Sons, 8¹/₈in. high. (Christie's) $1,150

An etched, carved and enameled glass 'mushroom' vase, by Daum, circa 1900, lightly ribbed with squared rim, 10in. high. (Christie's) $20,619

Mount Washington Royal Flemish covered vase, squat bulbous colorless vessel heavily decorated with butterflies and colourful stylized blossoms, 6¼in. high. (Skinner) $3,737

Pair of green Peking glass vases, 19th century, each high shouldered baluster form with a short waisted neck and everted rim, 9½in. high. (Butterfield & Butterfield) $3,450

Gabriel Argy-Rousseau, vase 'Tragi-Comique', 1922, molded with roundels centered by flowerheads above a frieze of six sealing wax red laughing and crying masks, 10¼in. (Sotheby's) $8,066

A Saxon engraved wine glass, the thistle bowl with a man in a garden landscape above facets, mid 18th century, 16cm. high. (Christie's) $699

A pair of French 19th century champagne flutes, cut and gilded with festoons, circa 1840. (Andrew Hartley) $232

An engraved armorial baluster wine glass, the bell bowl with a coat of arms of a horse head and tower, circa 1730, 17.5cm. high. (Christie's) $1,104

TOP TIPS
Auctioneer's Advice

Glass is a very sensitive medium and that doesn't just mean that it's likely to break if you drop it! Ambient conditions too can wreak havoc. Never place a piece of glass that you care about in direct sunlight on a window ledge. The extremes of temperature and humidity could one day cause the item to crack.

MICHAEL BOWMAN

Ten cobalt blue overlay cut to clear glass wine stems, decorated with birds and foliage, 8in. high. (Skinner) $1,035

A hollow stemmed wine glass, with hammered round funnel bowl cut and engraved with a band of fruiting vines, 16.5cm. high, circa 1760. (Christie's) $800

An engraved facet stemmed wine glass, the waisted bowl with two perched birds and baskets of flowers, circa 1790, 15cm. high. (Christie's) $736

A small commemorative wine glass, the drawn funnel bowl inscribed *WILKES & LIBERTY*, on conical foot, perhaps late 18th century, 7.5cm. high. (Christie's) $331

A Dutch engraved light baluster armorial wine glass, the funnel bowl with a coat of arms and a griffin to reverse, circa 1740, 17.5cm. high. (Christie's) $920

HISTORICAL FACTS
Gramophones

It was Thomas Alva Edison who launched the phonograph in America in 1876 and in 1887 Emile Berliner patented the first gramophone, also in the U.S.A.

The early Edison machine consisted of a box structure housing the works, surmounted by a spindle, a needle lever and a horn. The record in the form of a cylinder, is fitted to the spindle and when the works are cranked up, upon the release of a catch, the cylinder begins to turn, the needle moves onto the cylinder and sound issues from the horn.

The first machines were jerky because of hand cranked powering but in 1896 the techniques of clockwork mechanisms were worked out and shellac discs replaced the old zinc coated rubber disks. From the time of the First World War, every family wanted a gramophone in the parlor and there were many manufacturers vying for their business. They gave their machines wonderful names like Aeolian, Vocalion, Deccalion and Oranoca.

These early machines had big horns, some of which looked very elegant and could be made of brass, painted tin (sometimes decorated with flowers inside), or papier mâché, but as people began to look on the gramophone as a piece of furniture, the horns shrank and were concealed inside the sets which were disguised as cabinets.

A Swiss Paillard Concertola Superfonica portable gramophone, with built in horn and space for disks in lid, circa 1930.
(Auction Team Köln) $194

A Victor III mahogany gramophone with horn by the Victor Talking Machine Co., Camden, NJ.
(Auction Team Köln) $2,576

A Klingsor coin-operated gramophone by Krebs & Klenk, Hanau, with concealed integral metal speaker and leaded glass doors, circa 1915.
(Auction Team Köln) $1,627

A Columbia Model 701 standard gramophone, with automatic turn-off, closable speaker front and two side compartments for disks, American circa 1912, 81cm. wide.
(Auction Team Köln) $582

An Edison Bell portable gramophone, the wooden case covered in red paper, with Edison Bell Electrotone sound pick-up, circa 1920.
(Auction Team Köln) $78

A Decca child's portable gramophone with integral speaker, covered and lined with brightly colored oilcloth, circa 1940.
(Auction Team Köln) $149

An early American Stewart Phonograph Co. tinplate gramophone, painted to simulate wood, 1916.
(Auction Team Köln) $218

An extremely small Swiss portable Mikiphone, by Vadasz Brothers, Geneva, silvered case with original black celluloid resonator.
(Auction Team Köln) $420

A Deutsche Grammophon horn gramophone in richly carved oak case. (Auction Team Köln)
                                    $1,492

An American Victor V-1 horn gramophone by the Victor Talking Machine Co., Camden, NJ, 1906.
(Auction Team Köln) $485

A miniature Japanese MikkyPhone gramophone, in a crinkled painted metal case, for disks under 30cm. diameter, 12 x 10 x 15cm., circa 1947.
(Auction Team Köln) $226

A Pathé Diamond portable gramophone with integral speaker.
(Auction Team Köln) $135

A brass Dual gramophone, with intergral horn for second Pathé arm, French, circa 1910.
(Auction Team Köln) $840

A Kolibri Belgian black painted tinplate portable gramophone, the smallest box-camera gramophone, 9 x 9 x 12cm.
(Auction Team Köln) $190

A German Rex gramophone, the base with sliding glass panels to three sides, with large bronzed horn, circa 1905.
(Auction Team Köln) $614

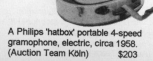

A Philips 'hatbox' portable 4-speed gramophone, electric, circa 1958.
(Auction Team Köln) $203

A Bing Pigmyphone tinplate toy gramophone, with wind-up mechanism and key, 1924.
(Auction Team Köln) $291

A Union portable gramophone, red suitcase cover, with original sound pick-up and door for horn.
(Auction Team Köln) $129

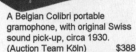

A Valora child's gramophone by Bing Bros. Nürnberg, tinplate case lithographed to simulate wood, circa 1925.
(Auction Team Köln) $305

A rare Laryphone small portable gramophone with folding disk plate, Swiss amplifier and integral speaker.
(Auction Team Köln) $338

A Belgian Colibri portable gramophone, with original Swiss sound pick-up, circa 1930.
(Auction Team Köln) $388

A large Klingsor standard gramophone, with marble top and glazed Art Nouveau doors, by Krebs & Klenk, Hanau, 1907
(Auction Team Köln) $2,134

A Bingola-type tinplate gramophone, with Mignonphone tone-arm, circa 1920.   (Auction Team Köln)
        $338

A German portable Polyphon Musik gramophone, with chrome horn in the lid, circa 1920
(Auction Team Köln) $175

An Apollo table gramophone, with built-in wooden horn, with flap side and top, British, 1909.
(Auction Team Köln) $452

A portable Victor Victrola gramophone with integral wooden horn, automatic switch off, and swing-out disk holder, circa 1925.
(Auction Team Köln) $142

A mahogany standard Columbia Harmony Consolette No.20, with integral disk storage and horn, circa 1920.
(Auction Team Köln) $582

A Deutsche Grammophon early German horn gramophone, circa 1900.
(Auction Team Köln) $408

A rare Dukephone tin record player by Carl Lindstrom, Berlin, 1913.
(Auction Team Köln) $2,263

A Pathéphone No. 6 gramophone with red tin convolvulus horn and decorative wooden case, circa 1908.
(Auction Team Köln) $1,084

Silver evening chain bag, 1909, La Secla, Fried & Co., bright-cut scroll foliate border and central medallion, monogram, 5¼in. long, approx. 5 troy oz. (Skinner) $230

Pucci silk shoulder bag, rectangular-form covered in silk twill in fuchsia, greens and blues, signed *Emilio Pucci*. (Skinner) $287

Silver evening bag with chain, circa 1900, American, acid-etched scroll foliate design, monogram, 6¾in. long, approx. 10 troy oz. (Skinner) $747

Emilio Pucci handbag, circa 1950s, in silk twill with a cream background, blues, turquoise and fuchsia Aztec-style design. (Skinner) $345

Emilio Pucci rectangular box purse, cream background abstract design of browns and grays, signed. (Skinner) $374

A white 'wet look' patent handbag, trimmed with a large composition jewel on metal geometric cut outs, Pierre Cardin, 1968-70. (Christie's) $454

Judith Leiber pink reptile leather shoulder bag, compartmented interior containing change purse and comb, chain handles, signed. (Skinner) $488

Art Deco diamond, sapphire, seed pearl, platinum & gold purse, featuring a 14ct gold framed mesh pouch, enhanced by European-cut diamonds. (Butterfield & Butterfield) $3,450

Gucci brown alligator shoulder/hand bag, stylized *Gucci* on closure, with yellow metal and alligator shoulder straps and alligator handle, marked *made in Italy by Gucci*, with Gucci chamois pouch. (Skinner) $1,610

Four case gilt and black lacquer inro, 19th century, each side decorated with temple rooftops, together with a 19th century marine ivory netsuke, inro $2^7/8$in. (Butterfield & Butterfield) $690

Good four case gilt lacquer inro, 19th century, decorated to either side with chrysanthemums growing beside a bamboo fence, together with a marine ivory ryusa manju, height of inro $2\frac{3}{4}$in. (Butterfield & Butterfield) $4,312

Fine lacquered two-case inro, Meiji period, executed with a seascape of shells floating on undulating waves, $2\frac{1}{4}$in. high. (Butterfield & Butterfield) $1,610

Three case inlaid lacquer inro depicting sea life, 19th century, decorated to the front with a large inlaid aogai fish, together with an ivory netsuke of a woodcutter in a forest, inro $3^1/8$in. (Butterfield & Butterfield) $3,450

Good large ivory three-case inlay decorated inro, Meiji period, shaped as a lidded wine jar, the underside signed *Yoshitoshi* within an inlaid aogai plaque, $4\frac{1}{2}$in. high. (Butterfield & Butterfield) $3,450

Good four-case gilt lacquer inro, Meiji period, humorously decorated with a scene of three men running for cover from the rain, together with a carved nut ojime and stag antler cap netsuke, inro height $3^3/8$in. (Butterfield & Butterfield) $3,450

Good black and gilt lacquer four-case inro, Meiji period, the ro-iro ground worked with sparse nashiji and hiramaki-e to depict wind chimes swinging from cherry tree, $3\frac{3}{4}$in. high. $1,840

Good five case lacquer inro, 19th century, depicting a spring landscape, signed *Kakyosai*, $3\frac{1}{2}$in. (Butterfield & Butterfield) $5,462

Good Koma school four-case inro, 19th century, signed *Kansai*, the dense nashiji ground displaying a hawk perched on a rock, $2\frac{1}{4}$in. high. (Butterfield & Butterfield) $2,070

A Philips cinema low voltage projection lamp with integral mirror, 9.4cm. diameter, circa 1950.
(Auction Team Köln) $38

Set of mother of pearl barreled gilt metal opera glasses with handle by Iris of Paris, 19th century, 4in.
(G.A. Key) $102

An Exacta six-dial adding machine, in hammered green metal case, Swedish, circa 1955.
(Auction Team Köln) $141

Oak cased barograph by Redferns of Sheffield, No. H11528, English, circa 1900.
(G.A. Key) $525

An 18th century English brass graphometer, the frame with two sights and double scales from 0 to 180 and 180 to 360 degrees, 22.5cm. wide.
(Phillips) $6,992

A late Victorian barograph, the seven stacking movement with brass fittings, in beveled glazed mahogany framed case, 14¼in. wide. (Christie's) $916

A Griffin & George, London, Wimshurst machine, gilt conductor balls and connections, on painted plywood base, circa 1950.
(Auction Team Köln) $373

An Augsburg brass equinoctial dial, by Lorenz Grassl, 18th century, square shaped plate engraved with foliate scrolls, cornucopia, birds and hounds, 3⁵/₁₆in. square.
(Sotheby's) $3,162

Cased transit, marked *W. & L.E. Gurley, Troy, NY* and *C.C. Hutchinson, Boston, MA*, fitted case with accessories and tripod.
(Eldred's) $413

A late Victorian rosewood two-day marine chronometer, by Alexander Dobbie, No. 65, the dial 4in. diameter.
(Christie's) $4,200

An American aluminium slide rule, 19.5cm. diameter, with carry-ten facility.
(Auction Team Köln) $194

A Eureka Automatic calculator, with lithographed calculating wheel and moving pointer for all four functions, French, circa 1900.
(Auction Team Köln) $1,227

A well made and seldom found solid brass and rosewood serving mallet.
(Tool Shop Auctions) $91

A most unusual brass stemmed mortise gauge, the points are adjustable both ends with a threaded rod running up the middle of the stem.
(Tool Shop Auctions) $66

A fantastic 22 x 4in. 18th century slick, handle forged separately from its blade, with trefoil decoration.
(Tool Shop Auctions) $231

A tinplate Consul - The Educated Monkey reckoner by the Educational Toy Manufacturing Co, Springfield, MA., with original instructions, 1918.
(Auction Team Köln) $305

English telescope, 19th century, by Dolland London, wooden barrel with extra 10½in. extension tube and brass table-top tripod.
(Eldred's) $1,980

A French calculating wheel in original wooden box, circa 1870, 15.5cm. diameter.
(Auction Team Köln) $380

A Thomas Jones hygrometer, English, 1820s, signed on the white enamel dial with scale from 0°–100°, 4.5cm. high.
(Bonhams) $884

A large green enamel theodolite, American, early 20th century, with 42cm. telescope 'U'-shaped support above enclosed horizontal circle, 36cm. high.
(Bonhams) $1,125

An Augsburg brass equinoctial dial, by Andreas Vogler, second half 18th century, the octagonally shaped plate engraved with foliate scrolls, 2³⁄₈ x 2¹⁄₄in.
(Sotheby's) $3,162

A late 18th century/early 19th century lacquered brass twin pillar double action vacuum pump, on a molded mahogany base, 28cm. wide. (Phillips) $699

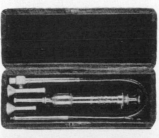

A Read's patent hydraulic machine, English, second quarter, 19th century, with accessories in green plush lined morocco case, 23cm.
(Bonhams) $193

A tangential compass by Baird of Edinburgh, wooden , with brass compass housing, circa 11cm. diameter, circa 1890.
(Auction Team Köln) $142

Stereo-graphoscope, wood-body, with 6in. magnifying lens, a pair of stereo viewing lenses and photograph stage.
(Christie's) $139

The Filoscope, built under licence from the British Mutoscope & Biograph Co., founded by Henry Short, 1898.
(Auction Team Köln) $382

A lacquered and oxidized brass compound monocular microscope, with rack and pinion and micrometer focusing, 11½in. high.
(Phillips) $272

A Waltham mahogany cased eight day gimbaled deck watch, American, circa 1940, the 55mm. silvered dial with subsidiary seconds, bowl 12.5 x 12.5cm.
(Bonhams) $932

Regency terrestrial 12in. globe on stand, by Bardin of London, corrected to 1817, with an ebonized four leg stand, 16in. high to meridian.
(Skinner) $1,380

A rare Matthew Berge miniature sextant, English, first quarter 19th century, signed, the anodized brass frame with beveled silvered scale from 0°–140°.
(Bonhams) $2,411

An Adams stereo viewer for 9 x 18cm. stereo cards or slides, on brass foot.
(Auction Team Köln) $479

Rowsell-pattern stereo-graphoscope, wood-body, with hinged swinging magnifying lens, a pair of stereo lenses and slide stage. (Christie's) $221

City of Glasgow, a set of blue and gold enamel and brass 56lb scales by De Grave & Co., Makers, London, no. 1595, in fitted pine box.
(Christie's) $407

An early 19th century pocket globe by Beuler, the sphere applied with a printed map of the world, in fishskin covered case, 7cm.
(Bearne's) $1,782

A William De Silva ebony octant, English, circa 1850, signed, 28cm. radius index arm, bone scale from 0°–105°, bone vernier.
(Bonhams) $836

A fine wooden desktop stereo viewer by H.C. White, with porcelain base and foliate decorated column.
(Auction Team Köln) $256

A Hearn & Harrison blackened brass transit theodolite, Canadian, late 19th century, signed, with 28cm. telescope, rack adjustment, bubble, vertical circle with vernier engraved on the reverse, 47cm. high.
(Bonhams) $514

A pair of William IV mahogany globes, by William and Alexander Keith Johnston, Edinburgh, the 18 in. terrestial globe made up of two sets of twelve chromolithographed gores, each 45½in. high.
(Christie's) $52,808

A French silver 'Butterfield' dial by P. Le Maire, 18th century, octagonal plate with adjustable engraved gnomon and degree pointer in the shape of a bird, $2^7/8 \times 2^5/16$in.
(Sotheby's) $2,300

A fine mid 19th century Newton's terrestrial globe, on mahogany stand with reeded baluster column, globe 60cm. diameter.
(Bearne's) $18,468

A De Grave Short and Co. lacquered brass beam balance, English, 1930s, No. 4218, 42cm. high, dismantling into a mahogany traveling case.
(Bonhams) $225

A Georgian lacquered brass 'Improved' compound monocular microscope by Dollond, London, 45cm. high, in a fitted mahogany box. (Phillips) $4,232

The Original Knox Fluter fluting iron, with brass roll, American, circa 1880. (Auction Team Köln) $122

A French iron doorknocker, 16th century, elaborately wrought in the form of two dolphins swallowing a bearded mask, knocker 5¹/₂in. long. (Sotheby's) $1,840

A French steel doorknocker, late 16th century, the s-shaped body of an amphisbaena with grotesque masks, knocker 7¹/₈in. long. (Sotheby's) $1,150

A German Bolzen iron No.8 by L. Schröder, Schalksmühle, with ceramic handle, circa 1910. (Auction Team Köln) $271

An extremely early French anvil, probably 16th century, museum quality. (Tool Shop Auctions) $2,228

A Knox Imperial fluting iron with portrait photograph and floral decoration, American, 1877. (Auction Team Köln) $213

An Adam style cast iron and brass fire grate, 19th century, the pedimented back above serpentine fronted basket, 74cm. wide. (Bristol) $713

A cast-iron fireback, Pennsylvania, 18th century, of rectangular form depicting a minister in a pulpit with inscription below, 29¹/₄in. wide. (Sotheby's) $1,840

Mixed metal inlaid iron tetsuban with orchid design, Meiji period, the tall handled teapot finely finished with a deep chocolate brown patina, 7½in. high.(Butterfield & Butterfield) $1,380

An Anker Heegaad heaxgonal cast iron iron stove, on three lion's paw feet, with five various irons. (Auction Team Köln) $420

Large cast iron butterfly maedate, Edo period, constructed with two front and two back wings each pierced with three stylized prunus mon, 10¾in. high. (Butterfield & Butterfield) $2,587

A Berlin cast carbon 'dragon' iron, plate 17cm. long, circa 1900. (Auction Team Köln) $156

A brass iron with forged iron grip, circa 20cm. long, heating grid consists of three grooves, circa 1900. (Auction Team Köln) $129

A French Gothic iron-mounted cuir ciselé wood coffer, 15th century, of sarcophagus-form, the whole worked with various panels of floral designs, 13½in. wide. (Sotheby's) $12,650

Iron and brass food chopper, English, late 18th/early 19th century. (Eldred's) $138

Two large Italian wrought-iron keys, 17th century, perhaps originally used for shop signs, 18in. and 20¼in. high. (Sotheby's) $2,300

 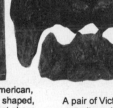

A rare cast-iron waffle iron depicting the Great Seal of the United States, American, circa 1800, of traditional scissor-form with loop handle catch, 27½in. long. (Sotheby's) $5,462

An American Planetary Pencil Pointer pencil sharpener, by A.B. Dick, Chicago, with original drawer, lacking cover, 1896. (Auction Team Köln) $291

A cast iron fireback, American, early 19th century, the shaped, arched and molded crest above the Great Seal of the United States, 30½in. high. (Sotheby's) $3,162

A pair of Victorian cast iron lion portrait masks, each realistically modeled in relief, with detached jaws, 12in. wide. (Christie's) $1,240

Cast iron hitching post, in the form of a jockey with lantern, 35in. high. (Eldred's) $357

A French iron doorknocker, 16th century, of the oblong shape and worked in the form of addorsed sea creatures, knocker 6¾in. long. (Sotheby's) $1,725

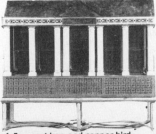

A fine cast iron and copper bird cage, English, in the form of an orangery, the pitched roof centered by the Royal arms, 230cm. wide. (Sotheby's) $28,118

A pair of 19th century cast iron campana shaped garden urns, the body with frieze of cornucopia within scrolled surrounds, 24in. high. (Andrew Hartley) $1,177

Important carved ivory tusk vase, circa 1890, depicting Northwest Coastal totem poles, dog sledding, gold panning and railroading scenes, 9¼in. high.
(Eldred's) $2,310

Pair of tinted ivory brush pots, Meiji period, signed *Toshihide*, carved with scenes of country life unfolding under pine branches, 14in. high overall. (Butterfield & Butterfield) $5,750

Shibayama inlaid ivory brushpot, early 20th century, signed *Masamitsu*, inlaid to one side with a pair of pheasants perched in a flowering peony tree, overall height 10¼in. (Butterfield & Butterfield) $2,070

An Oriental carved ivory female figure, carrying a basket of fruit with insect on her shoulder, 10in. high.
(Andrew Hartley) $928

Large carved ivory and wood okimono group of travelers, meiji period, depicting three figures crossing a bridge, signed *Kozan*, 39in. long. (Butterfield & Butterfield) $16,100

A Japanese ivory okimono figure of a man, trampling an eagle and fighting off a snake, 9¾in. high.
(George Kidner) $535

A French or German ivory comb, 15th century, one side carved with two jousting knights, 4⅞ x 5¾in.
(Sotheby's) $28,750

A Japanese ivory okimono figure of a fisherman, with an eagle perched on his arm with fish in its mouth and claws.
(George Kidner) $535

A Siculo-Arabic copper-mounted ivory casket, 13th century, the whole mounted with multiple gilt-copper straps, 2⅝in. wide.
(Sotheby's) $6,900

Ivory study of a Sennin, 18th century, the laughing Chokaro dressed in mugwort leaves, 2½in. (Butterfield & Butterfield) $690

Three ivory okimono studies, 19th century, depicting the simians in their humorous 'See-no-evil, speak-no-evil, hear-no-evil' poses, 1⅜in. high. (Butterfield & Butterfield) $2,070

A Japanese ivory netsuke in the form of a fox disguised as a Buddhist priest, 19th century, unsigned, 3in. high. (Skinner) $546

Gilt and polychromed ivory figure of Guandi reading the Classics, 19th century, the figure wearing the robes of an official over his armor as he sits reading a book, 5⅞in. (Butterfield & Butterfield) $1,035

Good ivory okimono of a dragon headed carp, Meiji period, with a fluttering tail, textured scales, fins and barnacle-encrusted gills, 16in. long. (Butterfield & Butterfield) $10,350

An Oriental carved ivory figure of a man with a child on his back, and two monkeys at his feet, 9in. high. (Andrew Hartley) $704

A pair of Dieppe carved ivory and paste gem set figures of Renaissance ladies, mid 19th century, 11¾in. and 11½in. high. (Christie's) $11,997

An ivory diptych relief of the Nativity, 14th century, probably Rhenish, the Holy Family surrounded by various revelers and animals, 3⅞ x 3⅝in. (Sotheby's) $6,325

A South German ivory group of frolicking putti, from the Kern workshop, first half of the 17th century, 5¼in. high. (Sotheby's) $11,500

Fine spinach nephrite circular disk screen, carved and undercut in relief with immortals and attendants amid pavilions, 5in. diameter. (Butterfield & Butterfield) $8,625

Nephrite carving of a recumbent horse, carved with its head forward and alert, with inlaid cubic zirconia eyes, 9½in. long. (Butterfield & Butterfield) $1,380

Jadeite carving of children on a boat, the children shown playfully overtaking a junk, hoisting in the sail, 4½in. high. (Butterfield & Butterfield) $1,955

Fine and large jadeite figure of Guanyin, circa 1900, the elegant figure depicted standing with eyes downcast and both hands before her holding a double gourd vase, figure 21½in. high. (Butterfield & Butterfield) $40, 250

Fine pair of jadeite birds, each elegant bird perched on a gnarled trunk, its crested head turned to one side, 7½in. high. (Butterfield & Butterfield) $11,500

Large pale celadon nephrite bi disc, 19th century, well carved to either side with a central section of raised spiraled bosses, $7^{13}/_{16}$in. diameter of bi. (Butterfield & Butterfield) $4,887

Fine Mughal style spinach nephrite tray, the circular shallow tray carved at the well in low relief with a mounted horseman, 8¼in. diameter. (Butterfield & Butterfield) $7,475

Turquoise carving of two boys, 18th/19th century, one shown climbing onto the back of the other, 3 and 1¾in. high. (Butterfield & Butterfield) $1,150

Good nephrite hat ornament, Ming dynasty, the openwork ornament carved as cranes among a cluster of lotus leaves and blossoms, $2^1/_8$in. (Butterfield & Butterfield) $1,265

Carved coral figural group of two immortals, early 20th century, dressed in flowing robes and high chignons, one holding a ceremonial wine vessel, 8³/₈in. (Butterfield & Butterfield) $3,450

Good white nephrite covered jar with floriform handles, the globular jar carved with a foot as overlapping petals of a fronted flower, 3½in. high. (Butterfield & Butterfield) $3,450

Soapstone figure of an immortal, the caramel colored stone carved with an immortal in a rocky landscape, 4¼in. high. (Butterfield & Butterfield) $632

Coral carving of a female immortal and a dragon, the standing female immortal supported on a base carved as a ferocious dragon, 6¾in. high. (Butterfield & Butterfield) $1,840

Green jadeite Qilong form covered vase, the winged beast standing supporting a vase on its back, 7½in. high. (Butterfield & Butterfield) $1,150

TRICKS OF THE TRADE

Which is it, glass or jade? Jade feels much colder to the skin. Hold the piece against your cheek, which is the most sensitive part of your body. Glass will warm up much more rapidly on contact than jade ever will.

MARK MEDCALF

Which is it, ivory or resin? Genuine ivory can be distinguished by holding the item to the light. Ivory has a grain like pattern not evident in resins.

WHITWORTHS

Pale celadon nephrite figural group of the Hehe twins, 19th century, one boy carved seated and holding a small bird, the other boy standing beside him, 5in. high. (Butterfield & Butterfield) $6,325

Nephrite footed cup with archaistic decoration, the cylindrical cup carved to the exterior with dragons emerging from a squared scroll design, 3½in. high. (Butterfield & Butterfield) $632

White nephrite carving of a Buddha's hand citron, 19th century, the large pebble deeply undercut with leafy stems supporting the multi-fingered citron, 6¼in. high. (Butterfield & Butterfield) $2,587

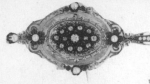

Diamond, seed pearl, cultured pearl, gold pendant-brooch, accented by seed pearls. (Butterfield & Butterfield) $1,092

Enamel 18ct. bicolor gold brooch. (Butterfield & Butterfield) $805

Edwardian 14ct. yellow gold buckle, decorated with floral and foliate engraving, 18.10dwt. (Skinner) $489

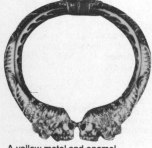

A yellow metal and enamel hinged bangle formed as two hinged open-work yellow metal half-moons, each surmounted by a realistically modeled lion's head. (Christie's) $562

Victorian diamond, sapphire, gold and silver brooch, featuring European-cut diamonds, enhanced by keystone, shield, epaulet, and trapeze-shaped sapphires, set in 14ct. gold. (Butterfield & Butterfield) $6,900

Antique diamond, green beryl, gold, silver pendant-brooch, centering one emerald-cut green beryl measuring approx. 20.20 x 19.50mm, surrounded by single-cut diamonds. (Butterfield & Butterfield) $3,450

Italian carved shell cameo of a child reading a book, mid 19th century, in a gilt metal frame, 2³/₄in. long. (Skinner) $374

Pair of Art Deco diamond, emerald and platinum clip-brooches, including one clip section featuring two European-cut diamonds, highlighted by baguette and trapeze-cut emeralds. (Butterfield & Butterfield) $24,150

Battersea enamel oval portrait medallion of George II, third quarter 18th century, painted en grisaille, 4in. long. (Skinner) $1,265

Diamond, platinum brooch, featuring full-cut diamonds, enhanced by single, baguette, and marquise-cut diamonds, set in platinum. (Butterfield & Butterfield) $2,070

Pair of garnet, diamond, platinum, gold earrings, each featuring one carved garnet plaque, enhanced by tapered baguette-cut diamonds weighing a total of approx. 1.00ct. (Butterfield & Butterfield) $1,380

Victorian amethyst, pearl, enamel, gold pendant-brooch, centering one oval-cut amethyst, enhanced by half-pearls, accented by black enamel. (Butterfield & Butterfield) $1,495

Victorian carved coral bracelet, designed as two flowers in a ribbon-like frame with applied beads, wiretwist and foliate accents. (Skinner) $805

14ct. yellow gold brooch, designed as a horse's head, 3.60 dwt. (Skinner) $345

Retro 14ct yellow gold clips, double clips, abstract scroll and fan motifs, hallmark for Larter & Sons. (Skinner) $1,265

14ct. gold hair comb, having plastic teeth. (Butterfield & Butterfield) $1,092

A Victorian pearl and enamel bracelet, formed as an oval section snake-link bracelet, with a pearl-set and blue enamel decorated triple coil. (Christie's) $1,087

An enamelled gold baroque pearl turkey pendant, possibly Spanish, circa 1600, the body in the form of a baroque pearl, 3in. (Sotheby's) $28,750

14ct. yellow gold and enamel comb, designed as a Victorian lady decorated with opalescent enamel, with a hinged comb encased in her skirt, signed *Cartier, N.Y.* (Skinner) $2,278

A French gold and diamond cluster brooch designed as a swirling cluster of textured oval beads with diamond-set ribbon tails. (Bearne's) $680

A pair of 19th century gold pendant drop earrings with bead and engraved decoration. (Bearne's) $364

Diamond, enamel, cultured pearl, platinum-topped 18ct. gold pendant-brooch, Masriera y Carreras, designed as a winged female, with polychrome enamel wings. (Butterfield & Butterfield) $8,050

A 19th century gold brooch, the trumpet-shaped reservoir with seed-pearl set foliage lip and ribbon bow motif. (Bearne's) $981

A George Jensen pierced oval brooch depicting a deer amongst stylized foliage, stamped with maker's mark, *Sterling, Denmark* and *256,* 45mm long. (Bearne's) $443

Burmese ruby, diamond, platinum, gold ring, centering one heart, shaped Burmese ruby, flanked by pear-shaped diamonds. (Butterfield & Butterfield) $34,500

Diamond, sapphire, black onyx, platinum brooch, designed as a ship featuring full, single, baguette, and square-cut diamonds, enhanced by buff-top calibré-cut sapphires. (Butterfield & Butterfield) $5,750

Edwardian diamond brooch, pierced design with a row of diamonds set throughout with smaller diamonds, approx. total wt. 3.00cts., platinum mount. (Skinner) $1,840

Antique diamond and citrine bow brooch, centered by a citrine, in a diamond-set bow, approx. total wt. 9.00cts., silver mount. (Skinner) $5,750

Pair of amethyst, diamond, gold earrings, each featuring two amethyst cabochons, accented by full-cut diamonds, set in 18ct gold. (Butterfield & Butterfield) $1,265

Diamond, ruby, gold ring set, including one ring, featuring full-cut diamonds, accented by round-cut rubies, gold ring guard. (Butterfield & Butterfield) $633

Ruby, diamond, emerald, gold ring, chaumet, centering one oval-shaped ruby cabochon enhanced by full-cut diamonds, accented by round-cut emeralds. (Butterfield & Butterfield) $2,185

Antique shell cameo, depicting a female in high relief with grapes and grape leaves in her hair and a stole, simple 14ct. yellow gold frame. (Skinner) $489

Jadeite, diamond, platinum brooch, centering one jadeite cabochon, enhanced by full-cut diamonds, accented by baguette and single-cut diamonds, set in platinum. (Butterfield & Butterfield)

$2,070

Enamel, diamond, gold clip-brooch, A.J. Hedges & Co., featuring polychrome enamel, enhanced by one European-cut diamond, set in 14ct gold. (Butterfield & Butterfield) $1,610

18ct. gold brooch, featuring round-cut rubies, accented by round-cut sapphires. (Butterfield & Butterfield) $1,092

Diamond, ruby, enamel, gold brooch featuring single-cut diamonds, accented by one round-cut ruby, enhanced by polychrome enamel, set in 18ct yellow gold. (Butterfield & Butterfield) $1,035

Diamond, platinum, gold double clip-brooch featuring baguette-cut diamonds, enhanced by European, full and single-cut diamonds, total diamond weight is approx. 3.80cts. (Butterfield & Butterfield) $6,325

Gent's diamond, enamel, gold dress set, including one tie bar, centering one round brilliant-cut diamond, together with one matching pair of cuff links, Soviet hallmarks. (Butterfield & Butterfield) $4,312

Diamond, onyx and ruby automobile brooch, designed as a 1950s Jaguar XK120, onyx side panels, crystal windows, pavé-set diamond hood and top. (Skinner) $6,325

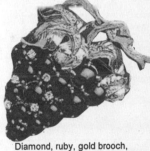

Diamond, platinum clip-brooch, featuring marquise and baguette cut diamonds, total diamond weight approx. 14.70cts. (Butterfield & Butterfield) $23,000

Pair of diamond, coral, lapis lazuli, mother of pearl, black onyx, 14ct. gold earrings, having plated white accents. (Butterfield & Butterfield) $1,265

An Art Nouveau Continental gold-colored and baroque pearl brooch of openwork foliate design. (Bearne's) $891

Diamond, gold convertible brooch, featuring full-cut diamonds weighing approx. a total of 3.85cts., set in a 14ct white gold brooch, set within a detachable 18ct yellow gold frame. (Butterfield & Butterfield) $1,955

A rare cameo brooch, the carved oval shell cameo depicting George III within a blue enamel and seedpearl frame, 33mm. wide overall. (Bearne's) $1,539

Diamond, ruby, gold brooch, featuring round and oval-shaped ruby cabochons, accented by full-cut diamonds, set in 14ct tricolor gold. (Butterfield & Butterfield) $862

Diamond, polychrome enamel, gold clip-brooch featuring polychrome enamel, enhanced by full-cut diamonds, accented by one oval-shaped black onyx cabochon. (Butterfield & Butterfield) $1,265

Pietra dura and 14ct. rose gold bangle bracelet, set with a large pietra dura plaque depicting a bouquet of spring flowers, flanked by two leaves. (Skinner) $460

Diamond and 18ct. yellow gold brooch, designed as a textured gold Pegasus with diamond-set platinum wings, tail and hooves, signed *Tiffany & Co., Italy*. (Skinner) $4,600

Diamond, cultured pearl, gold clip-brooch, featuring full-cut diamonds, set in 18ct white gold, enhanced by one cultured pearl. (Butterfield & Butterfield) $748

Etruscan Revival lapis lazuli and gold bracelet, featuring five lapis lazuli cabochons, set in circular 15ct gold frames. (Butterfield & Butterfield) $3,737

Diamond, sapphire, ruby, silver-topped gold brooch, featuring single-cut diamonds, enhanced by round-cut sapphires. (Butterfield & Butterfield) $5,750

An 18ct. gold and synthetic ruby mounted spray brooch of stylized design, signed *Kutchinsky*. (Bearne's) $1,426

Multi-color 14ct. gold brooch, designed as a parrot's head with textured feathers and a diamond-set eye, boxed. (Skinner) $863

Diamond brooch, set with two diamonds, approx. total wt. 2.33cts., within a diamond openwork 14ct. white gold mount. (Skinner) $3,105

18ct. yellow gold and sapphire brooch, designed as a frog set with sapphires, gold granulation accents, cabochon-cut ruby eyes, English hallmarks. (Skinner) $3,450

A 19th century gold and rock crystal triple swivel seal of scroll design, the seal engraved with a crest, coat-of-arms and a monogram. (Bearne's) $778

Antique enamel and diamond bracelet, graduating oval sections set with old mine-cut diamonds and seed pearls within a blue enamel background. (Skinner) $4,600

Diamond, mabe cultured pearl and platinum brooch, Cartier, centering one mabe cultured pearl, enhanced by European-cut diamonds. (Butterfield & Butterfield) $10,350

Victorian diamond, ruby, demantoid garnet, pearl, silver-topped gold, gold brooch, centering one pearl measuring approx. 7.00mm, flanked by two insects. (Butterfield & Butterfield) $2,300

Silver brooch, designed as a winged dragon, signed *Taxco*, hallmark for Spratling. (Skinner) $374

Diamond, sapphire, enamel, 18ct. gold brooch featuring full-cut diamonds, accented by sapphire cabochons. (Butterfield & Butterfield) $2,185

A diamond mounted floral spray brooch with circular brilliant-cut diamonds in claw and pavé setting. (Bearne's) $2,430

Silver brooch, 1933-44, designed as dove within a foliate wreath, hallmark for Georg Jensen. (Skinner) $431

An 18ct. gold, ruby and diamond ribbon spray brooch of rope-twist basket work design, claw-set with circular rubies and brilliant-cut diamonds. (Bearne's) $599

Silver brooch, an open circle set with a naturalistic design of flowers and butterflies, hallmark for Georg Jensen. (Skinner) $403

Art Deco diamond, emerald, enamel, platinum pendant-brooch, featuring single-cut diamonds, enhanced by emerald cabochons, accented by enamel. (Butterfield & Butterfield) $3,450

South Sea cultured pearl, diamond, sapphire, gold brooch, featuring one baroque South Sea cultured pearl enhanced by single-cut diamonds, accented by round-cut sapphires. (Butterfield & Butterfield) $805

Diamond, emerald, sapphire, gold clip-brooch, featuring single-cut diamonds, enhanced by sapphire cabochons, accented by square-shaped emeralds. (Butterfield & Butterfield) $2,587

Bradley and Hubbard bent glass paneled table lamp, octagonal flame motif in green-black metal frame for eight emerald green slag glass panels, 23½in. high. (Skinner) $575

Tiffany bronze and damascene favrile glass student lamp, decorated with spiral beading and smocked diamond design on urn-form font, 21in. high. (Skinner) $9,200

Wilkinson leaded glass pansy lamp, amber and green slag alternating brickwork conical shade with belted scalloped border, 26in. high. (Skinner) $2,990

Pittsburgh reverse painted lamp, labeled conical glass shade painted orange amber and pink inside with black Arts and Crafts geometric motif, 18in. high. (Skinner) $1,265

Leaded glass floral table lamp, scalloped border with pink and green blossom and leaf design below amber caramel slag brickwork dome, 22in. high. (Skinner) $747

Rare Handel reverse painted wild rose lamp, textured glass domed shade handpainted overall with delicate wild roses and varicolored leaves, 24½in. high. (Skinner) $5,462

Handel obverse painted daffodil lamp, conical glass shade handpainted with green and yellow naturalized blossoms, 23½in. high. (Skinner) $5,750

Austrian Art Glass table lamp, Loetz-type molded mushroom cap colorless glass shade with iridescent raised honeycomb design, 16in. high. (Skinner) $575

Handel oversize reverse painted scenic lamp, eight ribbed domed glass shade extensively enamel painted with naturalized landscape scene, 24½in. high. (Skinner) $8,050

Reverse painted Taj Mahal scenic lamp, textured and glue-fired glass dome shade attributed to Pittsburgh, 26in. high. (Skinner) $2,415

Tiffany gilt bronze and drapery glass bell lamp, fitted with nine-sided shade of gold-amber linenfold glass panels, 12in. high. (Skinner) $5,175

Handel paneled table lamp, octagonal bronzed metal brickwork shade frame with eight amber slag bent panels, 23in. high. (Skinner) $2,185

Bent glass paneled table lamp, octagonal metal frame of floral and latticework with eight amber slag bent panels, 24in. high. (Skinner) $575

Leaded bent panel table lamp, domed shade composed of caramel and green slag sections with rippled red accent glass above scalloped border, 21in. high. (Skinner) $633

Handel reverse painted parrot lamp, textured glass domed shade with three brilliantly colored bright-eyed macaws, 23½in. high. (Skinner) $16,100

Bigelow Kennard iris blossom lamp, deep domed shade of leaded glass to depict overall clusters of yellow iris buds and blossoms, 24in. high. (Skinner) $12,650

Tiffany Studios 'Blue' daffodil table lamp, broad conical favrile glass shade leaded to depict five clusters of yellow daffodil blossoms, 24½in. high. (Skinner) $26,450

Wilkinson leaded glass waterlily lamp, dome shade with pink and white blossoms interspersed with green and red ripple glass leaves, 24½in. high. (Skinner) $3,450

Tiffany acorn desk lamp, leaded green and white glass segments with green-amber acorn-shaped leaf and vine border, 17in. high. (Skinner)　　　　　　$4,600

A rare pair of olive green and opaque glass fluid lamps, New England, circa 1840, each with a brass collar, 12³/₄in. high. (Sotheby's)　　　　　　$402

Handel obverse painted teroma lamp, unusual molded octagonal glass shade with dropped apron, 22¹/₂in. high. (Skinner)　　　　　　$2,645

Handel reverse painted scenic lamp, especially fine colorful riverside summer scene handpainted on glass dome shade, 22¹/₂in. high. (Skinner)　　　　　　$4,600

Marianne Brandt and Hin Bredendieck for Körting & Mathiesen AG, Leipzig, adjustable bedside lamp '702', 1928, brown lacquered steel, silver painted interior, black plastic, 12⁵/₈in. max. height. (Sotheby's)　　　　$675

Handel reverse painted scenic lamp, textured glass dome shade handpainted in colorful riverscape with tall green trees under sunset orange skies, shade 18in. diameter. (Skinner)　　　　　　$4,025

Handel reverse painted lamp, textured domed glass shade handpainted with realistic pastel rose blossoms and three crystal yellow butterflies, 23¹/₂in. high. (Skinner)　　　　$10,350

Pair of unusual plated oil lamps, (now converted to electricity), with green spreading shades, 20¹/₂in. (G.A. Key)　　　　　　$330

Reverse painted grist mill scenic lamp, attributed to Pittsburgh, textured glue-fired domed glass shade with water wheel mill scene on interior, 22in. high. (Skinner)　　　　　　$2,070

Handel lamp with rose panels, white slag glass with painted red and green florals, base with good patina signed *Handel*, 19in. high. (Skinner) $373

Tiffany Studios bronze and gold damascene piano lamp, ten prominent ribs in amber favrile glass shade with golden iridized damascene decoration, 9½in. diameter. (Skinner) $4,600

Puffy poppy lamp, blown out reverse painted glass shade raised on foliate cast iron lamp base with 10-inch ring support, 22in. high. (Skinner) $1,035

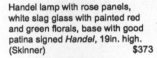

'Coupe Fleurie', a pâte de verre lamp, by Gabriel Argy-Rousseau, 1923, modeled as a cluster of stylized flowerheads, 5⅝in. high overall. (Christie's) $9,935

Christian Dell for Zimmermann GmbH, Frankfurt am Main, table lamp 'Type K', 1929 black painted and nickel-plated steel, black painted iron sheet, 20⅞in. max. height. (Sotheby's) $1,405

Rare Roycroft table lamp, four-sided trapezoidal shade with curvilinear supports and stepped base framing panels of slag glass, 26in. high. (Skinner) $4,600

Duffner Kimberly leaded glass lamp, sixteen-panel amber caramel slag conical shade with Prairie School-type gold square belt border, 23in. high. (Skinner) $2,530

Patinated bronze figural lamp base, probably American, in the form of a leering bacchante, black marble base, 29in. high. (Skinner) $1,725

Tiffany Furnaces enamel and mesh table lamp, green favrile glass vasiform shaft mounted in gilt bronze two-socket base, 20½in. high. (Skinner) $3,220

Fulper pottery vase with lamp mount, tapering form with square handles under a mottled blue/green glaze, 6³/₄in. high.
(Skinner) $546

Daum, geometric lamp, 1920s, frosted glass, etched throughout with abstract designs, 17in.
(Sotheby's) $13,444

Tiffany Studios, Tulips lamp, 1899-1920, the leaded glass shade decorated with tulip heads, 20⁷/₈in.
(Sotheby's) $7,298

Emile Gallé, vine lamp, circa 1900, gray glass internally decorated with pink and spring green, overlaid with brown and olive green, 24in.
(Sotheby's) $15,364

A bronze and onyx figural lamp centerpiece, cast from a model by Guigner, formed as two bronze kneeling female figures decked with garlands of foliage with arms raised, 21¼in. high.
(Christie's) $14,030

Muller Frères and Reiss-Joeuf, two-handled lamp, circa 1920, ovoid body in gray glass internally mottled with green, purple, blue and orange, 25³/₈in.
(Sotheby's) $4,801

Muller Frères and Chapelle, heron lamp, 1920s, wrought iron armature cast as a bird balanced on one foot, the body blown with raspberry pink glass, 15³/₈in.
(Sotheby's) $23,046

A rare pâte de verre lamp by Gabriel Argy-Rousseau, circa 1928, flat fan shaped panel molded with two tigers stalking through foliage, 8in. high.
(Christie's) $23,989

An early 19th century French silvered brass hurricane lamp, the faceted stem raised on a stepped circular petal shaped base, 28.5cm. high. (Phillips) $225

A Doulton Lambeth stoneware oil lamp base, by Mark V. Marshall, incised with panels of stylized owls and butterflies, circa 1885, 34cm. (Bristol) $853

A doll lamp, with porcelain bust and legs, on plinth, original dress/shade, 41cm. high, circa 1925. (Auction Team Köln) $238

Emile Gallé, flowerform lamp, circa 1900, patinated bronze base cast as a leafy stem, gray glass shade overlaid with mauve and green, 20^{5}/8in. $28,808

Daum and Edgar Brandt for Goldscheider, thistle lamp, circa 1920s, patinated bronze cast as a curved thistle stem with pendant flower, 16^{n}/8in. (Sotheby's) $9,218

Marcel Bouraine, 'Vestal' lamp, 1920's, modeled as a standing female figure, her arms held out over two short flared pillars, 15¾in. (Sotheby's) $2,881

Tiffany lamp base with Handel shade, unsigned bronze lamp base with twelve raised foliate elements on shaft and font, 25in. high in total. (Skinner) $4,025

Daum, geometric lamp, 1930s, opaque glass, etched with a geometric design against a textured ground, heightened with blue staining, 17¼in. (Sotheby's) $9,987

Albert Cheuret, pair of tulip lamps, circa 1900, gilt bronze and alabaster, each cast as three tulip stems rising from a foliate base, 15in. (Sotheby's) $11,139

Floriform leaded glass table lamp, bent green slag glass panels arranged in lappet blossom form with red granite diamond border glass, 23in. high. (Skinner) $517

A magic lantern by Jean Schoenner, brassed tin case, for 4.5cm. wide strips, with 9 original strips, 26cm. high.
(Auction Team Köln) $430

A red-painted tin magic lantern, by Max Dannhorn, with swollen base to chimney, 1880, 34cm. high.
(Auction Team Köln) $479

A Newton magic lantern for 13cm. strips, brass fronted with screw focusing, with Newton Refulgent Lamp for Magic Lanterns, 1880.
(Auction Team Köln) $179

A magic lantern by Jean Schoenner, on wooden base, painted blue with gold decoration, for 35mm strips, with burner, six strips and original box.
(Auction Team Köln) $106

The Monarch Ethopticon biunial lantern, Riley Brothers, Bradford; mahogany body, a pair of lacquered-brass bound 9¾in. condensing lenses, and a limelight burner.
(Christie's) $2,062

A magic lantern, possibly by Jean Schoenner, with red-painted, drum-shaped, tin casing with gold decoration, 1890. for 4cm. strips.
(Auction Team Köln) $179

A No. 291A magic lantern by Jean Schoenner, red-painted tin casing, for round disks and 3.5cm. strips, 1890.
(Auction Team Köln) $319

A magic lantern by Jean Falk, for 4cm. strips, with seven strips, some home-made.
(Auction Team Köln) $185

A brass magic lantern by Jean Schoenner, with black and gold decoration, for 4cm. strips, and with cassette for round disks, 29.5cm. high.
(Auction Team Köln) $479

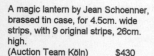

A French magic lantern, by Demaria Lapierre, Paris, hardwood body with black tinplate lamp housing, with unusual condensor, circa 1900. (Auction Team Köln) $103

A gray metal Lanterne carré, for 7cm. strips, 26cm. high. (Auction Team Köln) $133

A Walter Tyler mahogany magic lantern with brass optics, fitted for electricity, with ventilator flap on the lamp housing. (Auction Team Köln) $541

Magic lantern, W. Watson & Son, London; mahogany-body, lacquered-brass fittings, brass lens section, lens chimney and slide-carrier. (Christie's) $478

A rare German magic lantern, by Fritz Neumeyer, Nürnberg, blue tinplate case with brass optics, for 35mm rolls, with burner, 35cm. high. (Auction Team Köln) $85

Pathérama viewer, Pathé, France; comprising a hand-held viewer and Cocorico projector with lens and four film strips. (Christie's) $88

A Système Demeny projector by Gammout, Paris, on cast metal base, black painted tinplate body, with brass lens, lens barrel, and slide holder, 1920. (Auction Team Köln) $179

Cinématographe no. 91, Auguste et Louis Lumière, France; 35mm., wood-body, internal film mechanism stamped J. Carpentier, Paris, side-mounted film holder, and a brass bound lens with wheel stops. (Christie's) $11,776

A Gloria magic lantern by Ernst Plank, Nürnberg, with some original glass plates, lacking burner but with original wooden case, circa 1900. (Auction Team Köln) $198

Cesare Fantacchiotti (1844-1922) a white marble sculpture of Cupid reclining holding an arrow and quiver, 1864, 32½in. high.
(Hy. Duke & Son) $12,000

A pair of baroque Italian marble wall brackets in the form of cherubim, late 18th century, 23¼in. high.
(Sotheby's) $4,887

'The Sacrifice of Isaac', a marble figure by Randolph Rogers, American, 19th century, signed, 43½in. high.
(Christie's) $6,325

A French white marble bust of Benjamin Franklin, after Jean-Antoine Houdon, 19th century, his head slightly bowed, 25¼in. high.
(Sotheby's) $18,400

A fleur de pêcher centerpiece, Paris, circa 1880, the lobed body applied with scroll handles cast with foliage and bullrushes, 46cm. high.
(Sotheby's) $14,059

An Italian white marble bust of Apollo after the Antique, late 18th/19th century, on waisted marble socle, 26¾in. high.
(Sotheby's) $8,625

A sculpted white marble allegorical group, by J. Clesinger, late 19th century, the figures of a semi-naked nymph and youth shown astride a panther, 29in. high.
(Christie's) $7,383

One of a pair of gilt-bronze and marble side tables, circa 1890, each with a pink veined marble top, 66cm. wide.
(Sotheby's)
(Two) $10,872

Italian carved Carrara marble bust of The Greek Slave, after Hiram Powers, circa 1850-70, nude with head and leaf tip molded edge on a circular socle, 25½in. high.
(Skinner) $8,050

A marble bust of Jules Hardouin, after Antoine Coysevox (original 1698), late 19th/20th century, 34¾in. high.
(Sotheby's) $3,910

A white marble group of Ganymede and the Eagle, after Bertel Thorvaldsen (Danish, 1770–1844), the youthful Ganymede wearing a Phrygian cap, 45cm. high.
(Sotheby's) $8,435

Italian carved Carrara marble bust of Venus, with clamshell, pearl headdress and shell covered bust, 25½in. high.
(Skinner) $5,750

A large Italian marble group of Menelaus and Patroclus, after Pietro Tacca, the helmeted Greek hero dragging the dying, naked youth across the rocks, 49½in. high. (Sotheby's) $9,200

An Italian marble baptismal font, 12th century, carved with rampant beasts and birds within interlocking circlets, 18⁷/₈in. high.
(Sotheby's) $9,775

A white marble group of a bacchanalian dance, French, late 19th century, in the manner of Clodion (French, 1738–1814), 92cm. high.
(Sotheby's) $33,741

A German sculpted white marble bust of a young Lady, by Emil Wolff, circa 1842, 18¼in. high.
(Christie's) $5,168

A Southern French Romanesque marble capital, late 12th century, perhaps from Saint Pons de Thomières (Narbonne), 11³/₈ x 10¼in. (Sotheby's) $10,350

A white marble bust of Cleopatra by A. Testi, with her head uplifted, an asp emerging from her bodice, signed, 62cm. high.
(Sotheby's) $8,998

A marble group of young lovers by Professor Felli, Italian, 19th century, signed, 61½in. high. (Christie's) $32,200

A pair of gilt-bronze and Fleur de Pêcher marble lamps, French, circa 1890, each in the form of an ovoid vase, 59cm. high. (Sotheby's) $9,027

A white marble bust of an Arab woman, Continental, 19th century, 20in. high. (Christie's) $2,300

A marble figure of a young girl, Continental, 19th century, 26½in. high. (Christie's) $2,760

A pair of bronze and black-marble urns, 19th century, each with a low-relief sacrificial scene with maidens below a lappeted and turned neck, 16in. high. (Christie's) $2,829

One of a pair of marble wall fountains, Continental, 19th century, 64½in. high. (Christie's) (Two) $20,700

An Italian white marble bust of Augustus Caesar after the Antique, 19th century, inscribed below *Augusto*, 23¼in. high. (Sotheby's) $2,300

A pair of French gilt-bronze mounted Marmo Cippolino ornamental urns, last quarter 19th century, 15¼in. high. (Christie's) $4,430

A marble figure of putto emerging from an egg, by Emanuele Caroni, Italian, 19th century, signed *Firenze 1888*, 25½in. high. (Christie's) $11,500

A carved white marble bust of 'Winter', by I.A Fontana, late 19th century, depicting a bearded man wrapped in drapery, 20in. high.
(Christie's) $6,035

A white marble group of a boy with a dog, Continental, 19th century, 13¾in. high.
(Christie's) $2,530

A French sculpted white marble bust of a young woman, by Albert Carrier-Belleuse, mid 19th century, 26¼in. high.
(Christie's) $3,507

A white marble group of a boy with a cat, Continental, 19th century, 24in. high.
(Christie's) $2,070

A pair of verde antico and gilt-bronze jardinières, each in the form of Roman baths, 38cm. wide.
(Sotheby's) $6,599

An early 19th century white marble figure of Apollino, after the antique, one hand raised above his head, 31½in. high.
(Andrew Hartley) $3,840

An Italian marble bust of a young Roman Emperor, attributed to Giovanni Maria Mosca, early 16th century, 21in. high.
(Sotheby's) $23,000

A marble group of three frolicking children, by Benoit Rougelet, French, 19th century, signed, 24in. high.
(Christie's) $10,350

A marble bust of William Pitt, workshop of Joseph Nollekens, circa 1807, classical drapery about the shoulders, 29¼in. high.
(Sotheby's) $4,312

A model 134M Russian Air Force two-day chronometer, First Moscow Watch Factory, No. 5879, circa 1960, 101mm. dial diameter.
(Christie's) $1,840

Cunard Line Album the Official Guide & Album of the CUNARD steamship Service, Revised Edition, 1877-8, 12 x 9in.
(Christie's') $840

A Korean diving helmet, constructed in spun tinned copper and brass, air intake valve, side valve, 16in. high.
(Christie's) $840

A compass binnacle, British, late 19th/early 20th century, with compass and gimbal mounts, brass cover and cylindrical wooden plinth, 114cm.
(Bonhams) $643

An admiralty Pattern 6-bolt diving helmet by C.E. Heinke & Co. Ltd, No. 120 (all matching), circa 1920-1930, constructed in copper and bronze, 19in. high.
(Christie's) $6,446

A Sestrel brass binnacle on wooden pillar, by Henry Brown & Son, Essex, with side lamps for electricity and paraffin, red and green painted iron compensation balances.
(Auction Team Köln) $582

A Henry Brown & Son brass compass binnacle, English, early 20th century, with 9cm floating compass rose, gimbal mount and brass housing, 30.5cm.
(Bonhams) $354

H.M.S. 'Britannia', a pair of tri-focal aluminium and leather binoculars signed on the eye-pieces J. *Coombs. Devonport*, 7½in. fully extended.
(Christie's) $643

A three-bolt Russian diving helmet, circa 1975, hand beaten with three face plates, each threaded, front with pags for removal, 19in. high.
(Christie's) $3,312

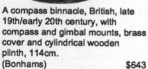

A replica U.S. Navy Mark IV diving helmet, 20th century, copper and brass, 48cm. high.
(Bonhams) $450

Two mahogany rudders, 20th century, each with brass mounts, largest 117cm.
(Bonhams) $482

A brass ship's bell, English, 1940s, with GVIR cypher and marked 3–5, with clapper, 24cm. diameter.
(Bonhams) $209

A Chadburn brass ship telegraph, English, 20th century, signed *Chadburns*, 80cm., together with a brass panel.
(Bonhams) $804

U-boat 20 Bell, the submarine responsible for the torpedoing of R.M.S. Lusitania in the spring of 1915.
(Christie's) $22,080

A Miller-Dunn Co. copper style II navy standard diving hood, American, 20th century, with brass angled glazed visor, arched shoulders air inlet and handle, 61cm. high.
(Bonhams) $1,929

A twelve-bolt Siebe Gorman & Co. Ltd diving helmet, late 1940s, hand beaten with three face plates, the front one threaded for removal, 18in. high.
(Christie's) $2,576

A souvenir plate from S.S. Normandie designed and signed *R. Liftreau*, by Haviland of France, 9¾in. diameter.
(Christie's) $552

A Siebe Gorman & Co 12 bolt diving helmet, circa 1890-1895, constructed in copper and brass, the hand beaten bonnet with three face plates with brass grills, 17in. high. (Christie's) $5,059

A Höhner Multimonica II two-manual electro-pneumatic organ with 3½-octave range, black painted wood and plastic case, circa 1950.
(Auction Team Köln) $541

A Q.R.S. Play-A-Sax mechanical saxophone with three rolls.
(Auction Team Köln) $238

A Serinette musical box with a 15cm. wooden cylinder, playing six airs, circa 1870.
(Auction Team Köln) $323

A Wurlitzer 750 juke box for 24 disks, with bubble tubes to right and left by Paul Fuller, 1941.
(Auction Team Köln) $9,154

A Steck Player Piano, a German version of the American model by the Aeolian Company, New York, inlaid Empire-style case, circa 1910.
(Auction Team Köln) $5,424

A Wurlitzer 1100 juke box for 24 disks, 1948, with some disks.
(Auction Team Köln) $6,466

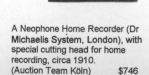

A rotating musical Christmas tree stand, for 11.5cm. disks with external drive, with three disks.
(Auction Team Köln) $271

A Bols ballerina Danziger Goldwasser bottle with integral musical mechanism, containing a red-haired dancer in a white dress, circa 1958.
(Auction Team Köln) $45

A Neophone Home Recorder (Dr Michaelis System, London), with special cutting head for home recording, circa 1910.
(Auction Team Köln) $746

An unusual musical photograph album, playing 2 airs on a 32-tone comb, containing original photographs, circa 1880.
(Auction Team Köln) $194

An Ariston tabletop wind-up organ for 29cm. cardboard disks, with 11 disks, German circa 1895.
(Auction Team Köln) $711

A rare German Trombino silvered tin 18-tone mechanical trumpet, with 4 paper rolls, circa 1900.
(Auction Team Köln) $1,152

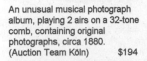

A Seeburg Symphonola Type B early juke box by the Seeburg Co. Chicago, Art Deco style wooden case, for 12 shellac disks, 1936.
(Auction Team Köln) $1,219

A Wurlitzer 1080 24 disk juke box, with a few disks, 1947.
(Auction Team Köln) $9,700

A Belgian mirror-front barrel piano, playing 10 different melodies, together with 8-tone xylophone and 3-tone Glockenspiel, 130cm. wide, circa 1900.
(Auction Team Köln) $576

A Baby Tanzbaer Concertina, by Zuleger, Leipzig, with external handle to advance the paper roll, circa 1900.
(Auction Team Köln) $846

A Swiss Paillard musical photograph album, playing 4 airs on a 36 tone comb, for cabinet size photographs, circa 1880.
(Auction Team Köln) $905

A French musical box, with silvered brass case and brass handle with porcelain finial, circa 9cm. diameter.
(Auction Team Köln) $129

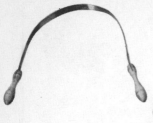

A Georgian tongue scraper with turned ivory handles.
(Anderson & Garland) $251

A 19th century silver metal penis, with plunger and valve, 3¼in. long.
(Christie's) $1,563

A doctor's bag of small size, brown leather with crocodile trim, textile lining.
(Auction Team Köln) $72

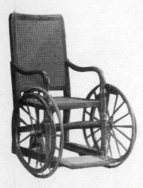

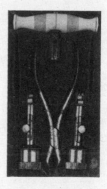

An Invalid's wheel chair, with cane seat and back, iron-tyred wheels with hand-driving outer rim, and adjustable foot slide, 42½in. high.
(Christie's) $221

A rare 19th century papier mâché, plaster and wood veterinary anatomical model of a standing horse, delicately colored to show organs, veins and muscles, 81in. long. (Christie's) $47,840

An ivory handled brass and steel trephine, with two heads, and forceps signed Weiss, in plush lined part case, 7in. long. (Christie's) $827

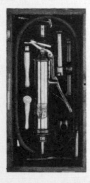

A brass enema syringe by Evans & Wormull, London, with ivory and ebony fittings, in plush lined mahogany case, 12in. wide.
(Christie's) $478

A 19th century dental demonstration model by Vecabe, the nickel jaw with twenty eight teeth and others in a velvet lined fitted box, 25cm. wide.
(Phillips) $662

A fine reproduction porcelain leech jar, the blue ground decorated in gilt, with cover, 14½in. high
(Christie's) $736

A painted pine miniature blanket chest, probably Pennsylvania, circa 1830, the rectangular hinged lid opening to a well, 17½in. long.
(Sotheby's) $3,162

Doll's tester bed, 19th century, in walnut with carved cornice, turned columns and carved legs, 18in. long.
(Eldred's) $687

A rare Federal birchwood-inlaid rosewood miniature chest of drawers, North Coastal New England, circa 1810, 19¼in. wide.
(Sotheby's) $4,887

A Victorian mahogany miniature chest, the reverse breakfront top above an ovolo frieze, three short and three long graduated drawers below, 11¼in. wide.
(Christie's) $850

A Dutch walnut and marquetry miniature bureau of bombé form, the crossbanded fall front with a brass rococo key escutcheon inlaid with flowers, 14½in. wide.
(Hy. Duke & Son) $2,880

A classical turned cherrywood and figured maple miniature chest of drawers, Ohio, dated 1822, on turned tapering legs, 18in. wide.
(Sotheby's) $1,725

A good miniature Federal maple chest of drawers, probably Philadelphia or New Jersey, circa 1800, on bracket feet, 14in.
(Sotheby's) $2,587

A rare Federal mahogany miniature chest of drawers, signed by Haskell & Card and Co. Massachusetts, possibly Salem, circa 1800, the rectangular top above three short drawers, 16¼in. wide.
(Sotheby's) $2,300

Biedermeier style walnut miniature chest of drawers, late 19th century, fitted with two short over three long drawers on bun feet, 11½in. wide.
(Skinner) $172

A Neo-Grec giltwood console mirror, New York City, 1870–90, the broken pediment centering a bust-carved cartouche, 88in. high.
(Christie's) $5,175

A good classical giltwood and part-ebonized convex four-light girandole, New York, circa 1825, surmounted by a spreadwing eagle finial, 48in. high.
(Sotheby's) $10,350

American Chippendale mirror, with scrolled pediment, apron and ears, 18¹⁄₂ x 12in.
(Eldred's) $605

Monumental Renaissance Revival carved oak pier mirror, circa 1875, finely carved throughout with game, putti, and centered by Ceres, with glass shelves to the sides, 124in. high, 85in. wide.
(Skinner) $9,200

A Chinese-export black and gilt-lacquer dressing-mirror, 18th century, decorated overall with Chinese landscape scenes and foliage, 15in. wide.
(Christie's) $1,225

A Napoleon III Boulle and gilt-bronze strut mirror, French, circa 1870, after the model by André-Charles Boulle, the shaped plate within a molded frame, 71cm. high.
(Sotheby's) $4,124

A 19th century Continental repoussé mirror, the central rectangular beveled plate within an ebonized ripple molded frame, 37in. wide.
(Andrew Hartley) $544

A painted mirror frame, by Ben Nicholson, 1930, stained and painted with zig-zags, dots and stripes, 29 x 29in.
(Christie's) $29,992

A large boulle and porcelain overmantel, French, circa 1880, frame of alternating tortoiseshell and brass panels and porcelain plaques 257cm. high.
(Sotheby's) $18,055

Italian micromosaic, inlaid and giltwood mirror, serpentine outline, 21½in. high.
(Skinner) $1,265

A classical carved pine giltwood convex mirror, possibly New York, circa 1825, the spreadwing eagle above a spherule-mounted circular frame, 4ft. 4in. high.
(Sotheby's) $3,162

A Regency mahogany, crossbanded and line inlaid dressing-table mirror, bowfront box-base fitted with three drawers, 21in. wide.
(Christie's) $663

A 19th century Dieppe bone and ivory wall mirror with oval beveled plate surrounded by foliage, cherubs and coats of arms, 33in. high.
(Ewbank) $3,520

A George III giltwood and gesso overmantel mirror with triple divided plate surmounted by leaf carved cornice and frieze, later painted with classical figures, 42 x 56in.
(Andrew Hartley) $4,160

Fine Victorian silver mounted dressing table mirror with heart shaped glass, the surround pierced and embossed, 11 x 9½in. maximum, London 1905 by William Comyns.
(G.A. Key) $759

A gitlwood and composition overmantel mirror, late 19th century, the arched rectangular plate within an imbricated leaf inner edge, 62in. wide.
(Christie's) $2,584

A polychrome-decorated églomisé and red stained pine courting mirror, Continental, 18th/19th century, 17in. high.
(Sotheby's) $575

A Chippendale parcel-gilt mahogany wall mirror, circa 1760, the shaped crest centering a pierced volute- and leaf-carved gilt reserve, 28in. high.
(Sotheby's) $1,495

A George II mahogany toilet mirror, the beveled rectangular plate within a molded frame with a parcel-gilt foliate slip, 16½in. wide.
(Christie's) $459

A shagreen and ivory dressing mirror, probably English, circa 1925, swing-mounted with turned ivory knobs and finials, 16¾in. high.
(Christie's) $3,749

A Louis XIV giltwood marginal mirror, the later arched rectangular central beveled plate bordered by marginal plates, 23in. wide.
(Christie's) $2,399

A carved giltwood and composition mirror, French, second half 19th century, in Louis XV style, the beveled plate within a molded frame, 191cm. high.
(Sotheby's) $14,760

An Italian giltwood mirror, late 17th century/early 18th century, the later rectangular plate within an ovolo carved central plate bordered by a pierced frame, 21½in. wide.
(Christie's) $2,399

Gilt and black painted split baluster looking glass, New England, circa 1830, the mirror with tablet showing a standing figure of lady against a draped background, 32in. high.
(Skinner) $747

A large wrought iron mirror, the design attributed to Raymond Subes, circa 1935/40, surmounted by scrolled ribbon work, 37in. wide.
(Christie's) $3,749

An early Victorian carved giltwood overmantel, with arched rectangular plate and molded sides, 66in. wide.
(Christie's) $2,291

A silvered bronze strut mirror, French, circa 1890, cartouche shaped molded border cast with foliage, flowerheads and a putto, 61cm. high.
(Sotheby's) $4,874

An early Victorian mahogany
dressing-table mirror, the oval plate
enclosed by a molded frame,
28½in. wide.
(Christie's) $531

Parquetry inlaid stepped frame,
probably England, 19th century, old
surface, 36 x 32in.
(Skinner) $978

A William IV mahogany toilet mirror,
decorated with a lotus-carved
spiral-turned frame with urn finials,
25½in. wide.
(Christie's) $923

A classical giltwood pier mirror,
American, 1810–20, the
rectangular frame headed at each
corner with applied fleurs-de-lys,
61½in. high.
(Christie's) $1,955

A William IV giltwood and part-
ebonized convex mirror, the circular
plate within a rope-twist border,
36½in. diameter.
(Christie's) $7,383

One of a pair of Dieppe mirrors,
circa 1840, each with an oval
beveled plate, surmounted by a
coat of arms and the motto
Montoiye St. Denys, 58cm wide.
(Sotheby's) (Two) $7,222

A good George III parcel-gilt walnut
mirror, labeled *Thomas Phipps,
London,* mid-18th century, the
incised swan's neck pediment with
leafy terminals, 27in. wide.
(Sotheby's) $6,325

A giltwood and composition mirror,
the later beveled rectangular plate
within a foliate-carved frame, 23in.
wide.
(Christie's) $3,507

An ivory Dieppe mirror, Napoleon
III, circa 1870, the shaped beveled
plate within a molded frame, with
a cartouche and foliate cresting,
64cm. high.
(Sotheby's) $4,862

Classic cased model of the American steam tug 'Cleveland', glass display case with marquetry inlay simulating a rope pattern, model length 25in. (Eldred's) $1,760

Cased planked bone model of the New Bedford whaleship 'Sunbeam', whaleboats hanging from davits and tryworks on deck, model length 11in. (Eldred's) $1,760

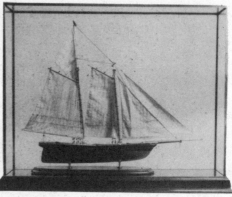

Cased model of a three-masted American clipper ship, hull painted black above waterline and bronze below, standing and running rigging, model 24in. high. (Eldred's) $1,210

Cased model of the schooner yacht 'America', rigged with a full suit of sails, plank-on-frame hull with copper sheathing, 29in. long. (Eldred's) $990

Cased planked model of the American clipper ship 'Flying Cloud', launched from the shipyard of Donald McKay in East Boston, MA in 1851, model length 37in. (Eldred's) $1,760

Cased bone model of a three-masted warship, with polychrome decoration, some restoration, model length 12in. (Eldred's) $2,860

Cased wooden model of the H.M.S. 'Victory', built by Fred R. Henderson, height 37in., length 51in., depth 19in.
(Eldred's) $715

Cased plank-on-frame model of the Revolutionary warship 'Rattlesnake', rigged with standing and running cords, 27in. long.
(Eldred's) $1,430

Cased plank-on-frame model of the whaleship 'Charles W. Morgan', five fully-equipped whaleboats hang from davits, glass case, model length 31in.
(Eldred's) $2,090

Cased plank-on-frame model of Henry Hudson's 'Half Moon', planked in all natural woods, mounted into an inlaid case, model 22in. high.
(Eldred's) $990

Cased model of the steam tug 'Bath', planked deck carries a brown deckhouse with brass portholes and a mahogany wheelhouse, 24in. long.
(Eldred's) $2,750

A carved whalebone whaleship model, American, 19th century, fitted with slung whaleboats and complete standing rigging, 16½in. long.
(Sotheby's) $2,875

A well detailed O gauge two rail electric model of an LMS 4-6-0 'Rooke' locomotive and tender, modern, professionally finished in gloss LMS maroon, 17¾in. (Sotheby's) $552

A Bub gauge 1 American market locomotive and tender, German, 1920s, 110-volt 0-4-0 locomotive, lithographed in green and red, with a four wheel tank wagon. (Sotheby's) $147

A Marklin O gauge live steam NBR 4-4-2 Atlantic locomotive and tender, German, circa 1920, handpainted in brown with red, yellow and black lining. (Sotheby's) $2,760

A Hornby O gauge 20 volt 'Princess Elizabeth' locomotive and tender, English, circa 1939, the 4-6-2 locomotive finished in LMS maroon with matching six wheeled tender, 20¾in. (Sotheby's) $1,803

A Hornby series E320 Royal Scot locomotive finished in LMS red with 6100 to cab, LMS to tender, boxed. (Andrew Hartley) $288

5 Wrenn 00, an 0-6-2 tank in LMS red livery RH2274 and four maroon LMS bogie coaches, all boxed. (Wallis & Wallis) $152

A Wrenn Brighton Belle, Southern Electric motorcoach two car set, Pullman coaches in brown and cream, nos. 88 (powered) and 89, in original box. (Wallis & Wallis) $496

A scarce Marklin HO gauge 3017, electric three unit express, German, circa 1955, finished in red and ivory, comprising electric Bo-Bo locomotive and two coaches. (Sotheby's) $4,784

A Wrenn 40602 loco and six wheel tender, Dorchester, BR green livery RN34042, in original box. (Wallis & Wallis) $192

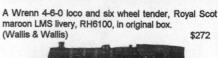

A Wrenn 4-6-0 loco and six wheel tender, Royal Scot maroon LMS livery, RH6100, in original box. (Wallis & Wallis) $272

A Hornby Dublo G25 goods set, class 8F locomotive, open wagon, bogie well wagon, refrigerator van and BR (LMR) goods brake van. (Christie's) $480

A Hornby Dublo 3218 4MT 80059 tank locomotive, nickel silver wheels, in original box. (Christie's) $405

A Bassett-Lowke electric 4-6-2 LNER 'Flying Scotsman' locomotive and tender No. 103, lithographed in lined apple green, circa 1949. (Christie's) $1,403

A Bassett-Lowke electric 4-6-2 LMS 'Duchess of Montrose' locomotive and tender No. 6232, painted in lined lake, in original box and packing with sales docket, circa 1948. (Christie's) $2,280

A Bing for Bassett-Lowke Gauge I 4-6-0 'King Arthur' locomotive and tender, German, circa 1920, number 453, the live steam model finished in green Southern Railway livery with matching eight wheeled bogie tender. (Sotheby's) $1,152

Aster for Fulgurex BR 4-6-2 A4 Pacific 'Sir Nigel Gresley' locomotive and tender, Japanese, 1984, professionally assembled by Mike Pavey, made for 45mm. gauge, live steam model built to scale 1:32in. (Sotheby's) $3,265

A Wrenn 4-6-2 streamline A4 class locomotive and 8 wheel tender, Golden Eagle, in green LNER livery, RN 4482, in original box. (Wallis & Wallis) $224

An O-gauge 4-4-0 clockwork locomotive and tender by Bassett-Lowke in B.R. livery. (Anderson & Garland) $408

A Wrenn 4-6-0 locomotive and six wheel tender Cardiff Castle in green BR livery, in original box. (Wallis & Wallis) $96

A Wrenn 4-6-0 and six wheel tender, Black Watch in black LMS livery, in original box. (Wallis & Wallis) $256

A Wrenn 4-6-2 loco and six wheel tender, City of Stoke on Trent, in black LMS livery, RN6254, in original box. (Wallis & Wallis) $104

A Wrenn 2-6-4 tank loco, BR green livery, RN 80135, in original box.(Wallis & Wallis) $248

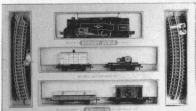

A Hornby Trains 4-6-2 Princess Elizabeth locomotive, finished in LMS red with gold lining and lettering, complete in green lined wood case. (Andrew Hartley) $2,880

A rare Hornby Dublo final issue 2019 2-6-4 tank goods train set, with three leaflets and guarantee in original blue and white picture box. (Christie's) $552

HISTORICAL FACTS
Money Banks

Modern type money boxes began to appear in Europe in the 17th century and in the 18th, Staffordshire pottery money banks in the form of cottages were popular. 19th century Prattware examples also fetch good sums.

It was the 19th century that saw the manufacture of money boxes designed especially for children Understandably, these had to be of a tougher material than pottery, and the first were of cast iron. Often, these were in the shape of animal or human heads, open mouthed to receive the coins, or of figures and buildings with slits in the top.

In comparison with the United States or even Europe, British versions were fairly unimaginative. Few mechanical versions were produced (though find one by John Harper & Co. and it could be worth a considerable amount).

It is however American money boxes which fetch the highest prices today. During the last 30 years of the 19th century such firms as Shephard Hardware and J & E Stevens of Cromwell, CT produced cast iron banks in such forms as acrobats, bucking broncos, and Punch & Judy. Most were mechanical, some operated simply by the weight of the coin, while others had a lever or catch action. The Jolly Nigger was a favorite example, and when a coin was placed on the tongue the eyes would roll. This 'Sambo' type was copied in the UK, though usually as a 'still bank' with no mechanical action.

Stevens mechanical bank, 'Tammany', old repaint, 6in. high. (Eldred's) $137

Stevens mechanical bank, circa 1872, frog on lattice, 4½in. high. (Eldred's) $77

An Artillery Bank mechanical money bank, coin fired from the cannon to land in the tower. (Auction Team Köln) $360

Stevens mechanical bank, 'Always Did 'Spise a Mule', original paint, 9in. high. (Eldred's) $467

Painted tin architectural form still bank, American, mid 19th century, in the form of a brick home 7in. long. (Skinner) $4,025

A J & E Stevens 'Bulldog' cast iron bank, American, circa 1880, the seated dog's neck shrinking and mouth opening when tail is pressed, 7¾in. high. (Sotheby's) $640

A J & E Stevens 'Eagle and Eaglets' cast iron bank, American, circa 1885, adult eagle feeds its offspring when the snake at the opposite end is pulled downwards, 8in. (Sotheby's) $275

A J & E Stevens 'William Tell' cast iron bank, William shoots the coin from his gun when his foot is pressed, knocking the apple from a young boy's head, American, circa 1900, 10¼in. (Sotheby's) $478

A well-restored cylinder musical box, with 23.5cm. cylinder and 53-tone comb, circa 1890.
(Auction Team Köln) $1,164

An Adler No. 225 musical box for 21cm. disks, with 40-tone comb, by Zimmermann of Leipzig, circa 1900.
(Auction Team Köln) $338

A Swiss musical box, with 13in. brass barrel, in rosewood, crossbanded and floral marquetry case, 22¾in. wide.
(Christie's) $949

A 19th century Swiss musical box playing six classical airs, with comb and drum movement, in walnut and ebonized case.
(Andrew Hartley) $2,240

A Symphonion No. 10N musical box for 19.5cm. disks, with 41-tone comb, circa 1900.
(Auction Team Köln) $183

A 19th century Swiss musical box playing ten airs as listed on the tune sheet, inscribed *Pap Leon & Co. Paris, 1261A,* in ebonized and grained case, 25½in. wide. (Andrew Hartley)
    $2,945

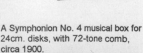

A Symphonion No. 28 musical box, for 14.5cm. disks, with external manual drive and 40-tone comb, circa 1900.
(Auction Team Köln) $129

A Swiss cylinder musical box by J.H.Heller, Bern, with 27.5cm. brass cylinder and 74-tone comb, circa 1890.
(Auction Team Köln) $1,164

A Symphonion No. 4 musical box for 24cm. disks, with 72-tone comb, circa 1900.
(Auction Team Köln) $420

A Dutch violin by Johannes Cuypers, The Hague, 1782, with original label, l.o.b. 14in. (Phillips) $27,600

A violin by Szepessy Bela, London, 1885, with maker's label, l.o.b. 359mm. (Phillips) $8,464

Cello in tigermaple and other woods, by F A Tenny, 19th century, 50in. (Eldred's) $121

An English violin of the Chanot School by John Byrom, dated *May 1890*, l.o.b. 358mm. (Phillips) $7,360

An Italian violin by Giovanni Grancino, Milan, 1707, with original label, l.o.b. 14in. (Phillips) $53,360

Orpheum four-string tenor No 3 banjo, fretboard and peghead with mother of pearl inlay, fretboard 13½in. long. (Eldred's) $880

A fine English violoncello by William (Royal) Forster, London, circa 1780, l.o.b. 29in. (Phillips) $22,650

An interesting violoncello, circa 1780, the two-piece back of small curl, the ribs similar, the length of back 28¹/8in. (Christie's) $8,855

A Quinton or Pardessus, Paris School, circa 1760, l.o.b. 14¾in. (Phillips) $3,004

Gibson mandolin, mother of pearl inlaid neck and peghead, 26¼in. long. (Eldred's) $1,265

An English violin by W.E. Hill & Sons, London, 1895, l.o.b. 357mm., in case. (Phillips) $10,304

A Dutch violin by Johannes Cuypers, The Hague, 1797, with label, l.o.b. 14in. (Phillips) $36,800

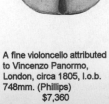

A fine violoncello attributed to Vincenzo Panormo, London, circa 1805, l.o.b. 748mm. (Phillips) $7,360

A 19th century giltwood and rosewood harp, signed *Erard, no. 2103*, with eight pedals, 70in. high overall. (Dockree's) $4,960

A violin by Bela Szepessy, in London 1889, the two-piece back of medium curl, l.o.b. 14in. (Phillips) $4,832

An Italian violoncello by Giovanni Baptista Morassi, Cremona, 1971, l.o.b. 758mm. (Phillips) $22,080

Fine ivory study of an ox, 18th century, the recumbent bovine shown with tethered bridle, signed *Tomotada*, 2¾in. (Butterfield & Butterfield) $3,162

A Japanese ivory netsuke of a nicely patinated man holding a badger down, 1¾in. high. (Skinner) $546

Fine ivory study of a recumbent deer, 19th century, in a recumbent pose with head turned in on his back flank, 2in. long. (Butterfield & Butterfield) $747

Ivory study of Daikoku, late 19th century , carved with the Lucky God astride an ox led by a karako, 1½in. high. (Butterfield & Butterfield) $862

Ivory study of a clam dream, 19th century, signed *Fuji Masanobu*, carved as a cluster of partially open shells housing landscapes with figures, 2in. long. (Butterfield & Butterfield) $1,840

Fine boxwood study of a toad, 19th century, signed *Masanao* (Ise/Yamada), the masterfully carved toad with inlaid eyes, 1¼in. (Butterfield & Butterfield) $1,380

Fine ivory zodiac Ryusa Manju, signed *Kaigyokusai Masatsugu*, carved with a continuous depiction of the twelve zodiac animals, 1½in. diameter. (Butterfield & Butterfield) $16,100

Fine wood study of a badger, signed *Yuzan* (Masatoshi), accompanied by a tomobako reading Netsuke Renyori (badger) signed *Jikishi-in Masatoshi* with kaki-han, 2¼in. (Butterfield & Butterfield) $3,450

Good boxwood shellfish group, early 19th century, comprising an awabi, a scallop, and six clam shells all naturalistically carved, 1¾in. wide. (Butterfield & Butterfield) $920

Good boxwood figural study, 19th century, depicting Rishi leaning on his tiger, signed *Soju*, 1¾in. (Butterfield & Butterfield) $690

Fine boxwood study of a recumbent goat, 19th century, finely rendered with realistic detailing and masterful hair work, 1⁷/₁₆in. (Butterfield & Butterfield) $3,450

Ivory netsuke of a dog with a bell, 19th century, 1¼in. high. (Skinner) $1,380

A hardwood netsuke of a rakan weaving a giant sandal of straw, a charm for porters representing a wish for strength and endurance. (Skinner) $1,150

Ivory study of a bamboo shoot, 19th century, the take no ko realistically carved and well patinated, signed *Gohosai*, 2½in. high. (Butterfield & Butterfield) $575

An ivory netsuke as a pair of quail with millet pods on a straw hat, signed *Okatomo, 81* (years old), 1½in. high. (Skinner) $1,495

Ivory study of a deer, Meiji period, signed *Ranichi*, in a recumbent pose with his head turned back over his spine, 1³/8in. (Butterfield & Butterfield) $546

A 19th century ivory netsuke of two men locked in combat, a tattooed bandit and an armored samurai, signed *Garaku*. (Skinner) $863

Ivory study of a rabbit, 20th century, signed *Kangyoku*, delicately modeled with pink coral inlaid eyes, 1½in. (Butterfield & Butterfield) $1,495

Amber netsuke, a dozing figure of a rotund Hotei with a fan, covered with finely aged engraving, indistinctly signed, 19th century, 2in. high. (Skinner) $460

Good boxwood rabbit group, 20th century, signed *Masanao*, depicting a mother rabbit with two babies, 1⁵/8in. (Butterfield & Butterfield) $1,495

A 19th century Japanese ivory netsuke in the form of a stylized phoenix, 3in. long. (Skinner) $287

Ivory study of a carp, 19th century, depicting Kinko riding on the mythical fish through foaming waves, 2¹/8in. (Butterfield & Butterfield) $575

Ivory study of a tiger crouching on a bamboo section, early 19th century, with inlaid horn eyes and darkly stained coat, 1⁷/8in. long. (Butterfield & Butterfield) $1,610

Ivory study of two shishi, late 19th century, depicting a shishi and cub playing with an elaborate reticulated ball, signed *Kanegawa*, 1¹/8in. high. (Butterfield & Butterfield) $920

An Agaphone tape recorder by Haycraft of England, circa 1955.
(Auction Team Köln) $135

Automatic Pencil Sharpener, an American pencil sharpener with three rotary blades, 1906.
(Auction Team Köln) $203

An early German Parlograph dictaphone, export model for the Spanish market, with original wooden cover, with microphone and cable.
(Auction Team Köln) $323

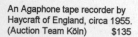

A Gould & Cook pencil sharpening machine, with rotary sandpaper wheel as sharpener, circa 1886.
(Auction Team Köln) $678

An extremely rare Pathépost machine for recording and playing 11 and 14cm. wax disks, French, 1908.
(Auction Team Köln) $3,880

A cast iron notary's seal blindstamp, with gold and colored decoration, circa 1900.
(Auction Team Köln) $97

A Webster Electronic Memory Model 80-1 RMA 375 tape recorder, with mocrophone, cable, three tapes and instruction booklet, circa 1935.
(Auction Team Köln) $213

A Victorian copy press for Alexanderwerk, Berlin, Art Nouveau design, plate size 28 x 25cm., circa 1870.
(Auction Team Köln) $177

A Williams Automatic Bank Punch check writer, very decorative check perforating machine with gold decoration and automatic paper feed, 1885.
(Auction Team Köln) $238

A Gaumont redwood stereo viewer for 45 x 107mm slides, with one cassette of slides of the Andes, 1920. (Auction Team Köln) $830

Stereo Kromaz viewer, mahogany body, with colored glasses, viewing lenses and rear diffusing screen. (Christie's) $562

Taxiphote stereoscope, Jules Richard, Paris; 45 x 107mm., wood-body, with a pair of dividing and focusing lenses. (Christie's) $515

Stéréo-Relieur viewer, C. Fougert, France; 6 x 13cm., wood body, plate-changing mechanism and a pair of rack and pinion focusing lenses. (Christie's) $461

A walnut mechanical viewer by Jules Richard, for 6 x 13cm. slides, with adjustable optics, storage drawer and cupboard under. (Auction Team Köln) $1,085

A desktop stereo viewer by ICA, Dresden, redwood, metal-mounted case, with five magazines of 25 slides of Argentina, 1910. (Auction Team Köln) $702

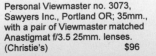

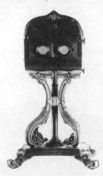

A French stereo viewer for 45 x 107 slides, in tropical wood case, with cassette for 50 slides, together with 32 contemporary slides of nudes, 1910. (Auction Team Köln) $574

Personal Viewmaster no. 3073, Sawyers Inc., Portland OR; 35mm., with a pair of Viewmaster matched Anastigmat f/3.5 25mm. lenses. (Christie's) $96

Natural stereoscope, C. H. Charlesworth, Huddersfield; the walnut-veneered case with hinged top and inset mirror, on an adjustable brass column and four scrolling legs. (Christie's) $7,498

An English pressed steel Triang pedal car, with rubber tires and windshield, 105cm. long, circa 1950. (Auction Team Köln) $170

An Austin J40 Pedal Car, blue finished, 57in. long. (Bristol) $644

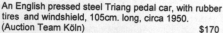

A Porsche Formula 1 pedal car, sheet-steel, plastic steering wheel with simple horn, 87cm. long, circa 1960. (Auction Team Köln) $181

A rare Kirk-Latty pedal car, red livery with yellow trim, American, circa 1915. (Auction Team Köln) $1,132

A J40 Austin pedal car, painted in pale blue with dark blue upholstered seats and dashboard, two way light switch. (Andrew Hartley) $672

A J40 Austin pedal car painted in red with 'Austin' bonnet badge, cream upholstered seats and pull punch dashboard light switch. (Andrew Hartley) $608

A Renault Dauphine of sheet steel construction, electric headlamps, rubber wheels, circa 1960. (Auction Team Köln) $213

A Buick sheet steel pedal car, massive cast aluminium steering wheel, rubber tires circa 1952. (Auction Team Köln) $291

A Chrysler New Yorker pedal car, 137cm. long, newly repainted red, circa 1950. (Auction Team Köln) $356

A '7' early American tinplate pedal car by American National, hand painted in red and black, with cream and green trim, 114cm. long, circa 1910. (Auction Team Köln) $2,587

A 1940s metal model pedal aeroplane. (G E Sworder) $640

An early child's pedal car with bell in excellent original condition; wooden frame chassis with steel springs, red paint with gold lining; circa 1910. (Christie's) $4,140

A Lines Bros. painted wood and metal Bullnose Morris pedal car with aluminium radiator cover, painted in green and red lines, with first aid box and petrol can, 48in. long. (Andrew Hartley) $1,120

A Eureka painted metal Bugatti Type 35 pedal car with chain drive, adjustable seat and hand brake, in blue and red, 61in. long. (Andrew Hartley) $1,040

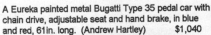

A Ferbedo pedal car by Ferdinand Bethäuser, Nürnberg, early sheet steel model, rubber tires, circa 1940. (Auction Team Köln) $646

A Mors wooden-framed, pressed tin pedal car, red livery with yellow lines, 114cm. long, circa 1907. (Auction Team Köln) $2,490

A Parker 9ct. gold Flamme 61, with medium nib, London, 1968.
(Bonhams) $825

Conklin, a black Duragraph Crescent filler, with no. 7 Toledo nib, American, circa 1924.
(Bonhams) $1,680

Mont Blanc, a black No. 6 size pen and a black 46 pencil, the pen with No. 6 nib, Danish, 1940s.
(Bonhams) $286

Mont Blanc, a red and black mottled [4K] M safety, with no 4 Simplo nib and original gold plated snake clip, German, 1920s.
(Bonhams) $2,856

An Omas special edition Vermeil Jerusalem, marked *925*, the terracotta body decorated with a frieze of Jerusalem and with 18ct. Jerusalem nib, Italian, 1996.
(Bonhams) $1,270

A Pilot Maki-E lacquer cartridge-filler, decorated with bamboo shoots and leaves and decorated with iroe-hira Maki-e, nashiji and mura nashiji on a roiro-nuri ground, 14ct. Pilot nib, Japanese, 1970s.
(Bonhams) $313

A Namiki Maki-E lacquer ring-top lever-filler, decorated with a flowering basket and a pair of butterflies, executed in iroe-hira maki-e on a roiro-nuri ground with silver mounts and a No.2 Namiki nib, Japanese, Taisho period, 1920s.
(Bonhams) $495

Waterman's, a black hard rubber 'Smallest Pen in the World' safety filler, with small nib and barrel imprint, American, circa 1910.
(Bonhams) $756

A Mabie Todd, silver Swan leverless, with chevron design and stub No.2 ETN nib, London, 1938.
(Bonhams) $214

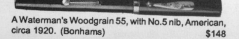

A Waterman's Woodgrain 55, with No.5 nib, American, circa 1920. (Bonhams) $148

Mont Blanc, a red and black mottled 2M safety, with no 2 Simplo nib and original accommodation clip, German, 1920s. (Bonhams) $3,024

Parker, a limited edition RMS Queen Elizabeth 75 no. 1598/5000, with medium nib, American, circa 1974.
(Bonhams) $756

Mont Blanc, a platinum striped 246 M pen set, the pen with Mont Blanc nib, German, 1950s.
(Bonhams) $1,008

Kritikson Bros Inc, a black 'Security' self filler with check protector, with gold plated 'Security Clip' and no. 6 size Security nib, the check protector located in the cap, American, 1920s. (Bonhams) $118

A Waterman's rare black combination desk pen and pencil, with flared cap, gold plated trim and No.2 nib, American, circa 1920.
(Bonhams) $297

A Visconti limited edition set of Uffizi No.315/500, the matched pens with turquoise marble bodies and with silver and vermeil filigree barrel overlays and each pen with two-color 18ct. Visconti nib, Italian, 1993.
(Bonhams) $3,424

A Reicife limited edition Andy Warhol's Marilyn pen No.35867500, the body in pink, yellow and black Mystique echoing Warhol's famous silk screen prints of Marilyn from 1967 and with two-color 18ct. Reicife nib, French, 1995.
(Bonhams) $429

A Waterman's gold plated 42 Safety, with floral cap crown and cap band set with blue stones, with No.2 nib, probably Italian, 1920s.
(Bonhams) $313

Waterman's, a Red Ripple 76, with extra broad oblique Waterman's no. 6 nib, American, 1920s.
(Bonhams) $805

A Le Boeuf black Holy Water Sprinkler, American, 1920s. (Bonhams) $148

A Waterman's 18ct. gold CF, with navy line and fluted design and medium 18ct. inlaid nib, London, 1973.
(Bonhams) $660

Carey(?), a white metal filigree eyedropper, marked *Sterling* with no. 3 Carey nib, American, circa 1920.
(Bonhams) $319

Wahl Eversharp, a pearl and black oversize Gold Seal Deco Band, with flexible Gold Seal nib, American, circa 1929. (Bonhams) $218

Inkograph Co, a black Mickey Mouse pen, the barrel transfer decorated with a picture of Mickey, American circa 1935.
(Bonhams) $504

A Mabie Todd and Bard gold plated 'Snail and Twist' Swan eyedropper, with under-over fed nib, American, circa 1910.
(Bonhams) $627

Sheaffer, a limited edition W A Sheaffer Commemorative Pen no. 4787/6000, the brass, lever filling pen decorated with low relief foliate design and two-color 18ct. nib, American, 1996.
(Bonhams) $437

A Bion-pattern fountain pen, the brass body of tapered cylindrical form decorated with red hard wax and copper foil glass, both incorporating black 'dragged' lines, closed 125mm., probably French, but possibly English or Italian, mid 18th century.
(Bonhams) $3,024

An unmarked pen holder, with tortoiseshell and piqué body decorated with flowers and plain holder, English, early 19th century.
(Bonhams) $437

Mont Blanc, a red and black mottled hard rubber 0-F Safety, with '0' nib, German, 1920s.
(Bonhams) $4,368

Parker, a black 51 Aerometric with Betty Grable clip, American, 1950s. (Bonhams) $134

CC/Waterman, a bi-color 18ct. gold CF, with inlaid 18 medium nib, English, 1970s.
(Bonhams) $2,352

Parker, a 9ct. gold 'Waterdrop' 61, with 9ct gold clip cartridge/convertor filler, London, 1970.
(Bonhams) $504

A gold plated Waterman's 42 Safety, with detailed rose design, ring-top and No.2 nib, probably Italian, 1920s.
(Bonhams) $594

A Wahl Eversharp yellow metal Command Performance pen and pencil set, both marked 14ct. solid gold, pen with Skyline nib, American 1940s.
(Bonhams) $429

Mordan, a bone pen/pencil thermometer/compass combination, with engraved white metal mounts, the compass set into the finial, English, 1860s/1880s.
(Bonhams) $672

A Mont Blanc gold plated 0–M baby Safety, the barrel decorated with alternating columns of plain and wavy line design and with twin bands decorated with a blue enameled floral pattern and with Mont Blanc '0' nib, German, circa 1920. (Bonhams) $1,815

A Mont Blanc limited edition Lorenzo de Medici No.2734/4810, marked *925*, the black resin body covered by an octagonal overlay with alternating panels of engine turned and engraved design and with two-color 18ct. 4810 nib, German, 1992.
(Bonhams) $5,652

A yellow metal and glass pen holder and propeling pencil set, each with octagonal bodies decorated with a snake, with red stone eyes, the pen holder with sprung grip, English, circa 1900. (Bonhams) $470

An Aurora black Selene ring-top, with platirido-extra Aurora nib, Italian, 1940s.
(Bonhams) $148

Parker, a gold plated 'Rainbow' 75, with broad nib, American, 1970s. (Bonhams) $840

Mont Blanc, a tiger's eye 242, with Mont Blanc nib, German, late 1950s. (Bonhams) $706

Wahl Eversharp, a rosewood Gold Seal Personal Point, with roller clip and medium flexible Gold Seal nib, American, 1920s. $336

Omas, a platinum striped Extra, the twelve sided body with gold plated trim and Omas Extra nib, Italian, 1950s. (Bonhams) $605

Mont Blanc, a black L139/ Masterpiece, with two silver cap bands surrounding a gold plated cap band and with two-color 18ct. 4810 nib, German, mid to late 1940s. (Bonhams) $1,428

Namiki, a maki-e lacquer pen, decorated with a quail eating from a branch, with no. 3 Namiki nib, Japanese, Showa-Taisho period, 1920s. (Bonhams) $1,680

Pilot, a maki-e laquer FK, decorated with the Imperial ox cart and cherry blossom and executed in iro-taka maki-e and iroe-hira maki-e with two-color 18k Pilot nib, Japanese, circa 1990. (Bonhams) $2,520

Dunhill Namiki, a maki-e lacquer pen, decorated with a tiered pagoda behind pine trees and executed in iroe-hira maki-e with a broad no. 3 Dunhill Namiki nib, Japanese, Showa-Taisho period, circa 1930. (Bonhams) $336

Waterman, a gold plated [0552], decorated with stylized pansies in alternating diamonds and semi circles and with no. 2 nib, probably American, 1920s. (Bonhams) $706

Waterman's, a 412½ S filigree, with no 2 nib, American, circa 1920. (Bonhams) $571

A Chilton pearl and black Senior, with warranted nib, American, circa 1924. (Bonhams) $148

Parker, an 18ct gold 'Fine Barley' 61, with broad nib, London, 1966. (Bonhams) $470

Waterman, a 9ct gold combination pen/pencil, with fine barley design and later Waterman nib, London, 1939. (Bonhams) $437

Namiki, a black Luccanite balance lever filler, with no. 2 Pilot nib and Namiki clip, Japanese, 1930s. (Bonhams) $151

Pilot, a maki-e lacquer eyedropper, decorated with a tatsu (dragon) holding a Buddhistic flaming pearl, manifold Pilot nib, Japanese, 1960s. (Bonhams) $1,428

Epenco, a spinach green Popeye pen, the cap decorated with a picture of Popeye and his adoring Olive Oyl and with Epenco nib, American, 1937. (Bonhams) $168

Zerollo, a black 'Unic Duocolour' Double pen, the pen with gold plated trim and twist action that advances the nibs in a clockwise or anticlockwise direction, Italian, circa 1930. (Bonhams) $2,520

Dunhill Namiki, a maki-e lacquer balance, decorated with hasli (lotus flowers) and executed in iroe-hira maki-e and mura nashiji on a roiro nuri ground, Japanese, Showa period, 1930s. (Bonhams) $1,176

De La Rue, a turquoise enamel over silver Onoto, with wavy line etching and under-over fed nib, English, circa 1920. (Bonhams) $2,856

Waterman, a gold plated 42 Safety, with floral cap crown and clip and no. 2 nib, Italian, 1920s. (Bonhams) $336

A Parker fuchsia pink 51 Custom, cap and guard marked *Industria Argentina*, South American, probably 1960s. (Bonhams) $214

Waterman, a woodgrain 55, with no. 5 nib, American, circa 1920. (Bonhams) $302

Waterman, a [445] 'Barleycorn', with no. 5 nib, London, 1926(?). (Bonhams) $1,092

Waterman, a black hard rubber 'Smallest Pen in the World' safety pen, with small gold nib, American, circa 1920. (Bonhams) $8,400

Parker, an 18ct. gold filled 75 Rainbow ballpen, with gold plated trim, American, 1970s. (Bonhams) $437

De La Rue, a red hard rubber Onoto, with etched body and nib with red hard rubber under and over feeds, English, 1920s. (Bonhams) $1,142

Mont Blanc, a black 20M Masterpiece Safety, with Mont Blanc nib, German, 1920s. (Bonhams) $1,042

Omas, a limited edition Guglielmo Marconi '95 QSL pen no 081/340, marked 750, the body with rings to represent radio waves, two-color 18ct "1895-1995" Omas nib, Italian, 1995. (Bonhams) $2,856

Pilot (?), a black maki-e lacquer piston filling pen, the cap decorated with a Chinese style landscape, with no. 3 Pilot nib, Japanese, circa 1960. (Bonhams) $588

Namiki, a green maki-e lacquer pen, the barrel decorated with a basket of peonies and the cap with four butterflies, no. 2 Namiki nib, Japanese, Taisho-Showa Period, late 1920s. (Bonhams) $4,368

Salz Bros., a scarlet red Peter Pan ring top lever filler, with black cap bands, the cap set with a ring of flowers and with warranted nib, American, 1920s. (Bonhams) $118

An unsigned ebony and ivory Penner, the tapered bulbous body with screw-in knife blade, ivory point, covered by a screw-on French language perpetual calendar, 121mm, French, late 18th century. (Bonhams) $538

Mont Blanc, a limited edition Oscar Wilde fountain pen no. 06478/20000, with pearl and black marbelized body, vermeil clip and trim, and engraved 18ct. 4810 nib, German, 1994. (Bonhams) $420

Mont Blanc, a fine and rare Italian style gold plated lever filler, cap marked Mont Blanc 18KR, with alternating plain columns with a single line of dots and columns, German, 1920s. (Bonhams) $2,520

A Barrett & Sons, a large silver and enamel double ended pencil, the plain body with sliding colored enameled bands to each porte crayon signed A BARRETT & SONS 63 & 64 PICCADILLY Birmingham, 1897. (Bonhams) $538

Mont Blanc, a black hard rubber octagonal 4M safety, cap marked Max Weidler Wien, with no. 4 nib, Austrian, mid to late 1920s. (Bonhams) $672

Mont Blanc, a silver striped 42 piston filler, with gold plated trim, the cap engraved Fabricado en Espana por e Wiese and with 14ct Mont Blanc nib, Spanish, 1950s. (Bonhams) $336

Waterman, a 9ct gold 'Barleycorn' half overlaid 12, with stub no. 2 nib, London, 1931. (Bonhams) $134

Waterman, a sterling silver [452] Barleycorn, with later no. 3 Waterman nib, London, 1925. (Bonhams) $840

A Parker 9ct. gold Chevron 61, with broad italic nib and 9ct gold clip, London, 1969. (Bonhams) $525

A Parker burgundy pearl vacuum-filler, with Arrow nib, Canadian, circa 1933. (Bonhams) $280

A Dutch Urania Art Nouveau pewter water jug with shaped handle and short spout, decorated with sinuous foliage, 8in. high.
(Christie's) $105

A WMF style Art Nouveau pewter dish with central circular panel, stamped and applied with a woman's head facing right, 9¼in. diam.
(Christie's) $262

A pewter flat-top quart tankard, attributed to Frederick Bassett, New York City, active 1761–1800, 6½in. high.
(Christie's) $575

Liberty & Co. Tudric pewter ice bucket, raised foliate design, impressed *Made In England, Tudric Pewter 0705*, 6in. high.
(Skinner) $747

A pair of pewter candelabra, designed by Hugo Leven, manufactured by Kayserzinn, circa 1903, organic form with double branches, 10½in. high.
(Christie's) $4,416

A pewter quart dome-top tankard, attributed to Thomas Danforth II, 1731–82, Middletown, Connecticut, or Thomas Danforth III, 1756–1840, Stepney, Connecticut, 7in. high.
(Christie's) $1,495

A pewter teapot, attributed to William Will, 1742–98, Philadelphia, the pear-shaped body with domed lid and disk finial, 7½in. high.
(Christie's) $1,380

A pair of polychrome decorated pewter figures of Westerners, China, late 18th/19th century, 7½in. high. (Skinner) $575

Cardeilhac, tureen and cover, circa 1925, silver-colored metal, the deep bowl ringed with silver-colored metal band joining the large shaped ivory handles, 9½in. high.
(Christie's) $24,006

A pewter creamer, attributed to William Will, 1742–98, Philadelphia, with curved and beaded spout, 4¹⁄₂in. high. (Christie's) $6,900

An Art Nouveau pewter five-piece tea service in the "Orivit" pattern, comprising: hot-water jug, lidded sugar basin, and tea tray, tray 16¾in. long. (Christie's) $613

Liberty & Co. pewter owl pitcher, incised decoration with ceramic blue eyes, 8in. high. (Skinner) $373

A pewter teapot, by Liberty & Co., circa 1910, and a coffee pot, sugar basin and cream jug of similar form. (Christie's) $168

A pair of WMF pewter syphon stands, on spreading base with Secessionist style pierced sides and reeded tapering feet, 4in. high. (Christie's) $240

An early 20th century pewter inkwell in the form of a 'Martin Brothers' grotesque bird with three legs, 11cm. (Bearne's) $388

A Modernist cocktail shaker, designed by Sylvia Stave, manufactured by Hallberg, Sweden, spherical with loop handle, 7¼in. high. (Christie's) $10,624

A WMF pewter centerpiece, formed as a winged nymph holding a dove, the dish formed as two lily pads, 8¾in. high. (Christie's) $964

A German pewter Art Nouveau punch bowl and cover, with happy and sad face masks and allover floral decoration, 44cm. (Bristol) $736

A fine replica of an Edison tinfoil phonograph. (Auction Team Köln) $582

A Nymph phonograph by Georges Carette of Nürnberg, the cast iron base in the form of a mermaid, with convolvulus horn, circa 1910. (Auction Team Köln) $711

An Edison Home phonograph, No. H68907, model C, latest patent date 1898, in oak case; with black horn and approx. 75 cylinders. (Bristol) $720

An Edison Fireside phonograph, Model A No. 31916, now with Diamond B reproducer, Model R and Model K reproducers with adapter ring. (Christie's) $1,120

A Graphophone Type BE early American phonograph for standard cylinders, in decorative case, 1906. (Auction Team Köln) $711

Edison Triumph phonograph Model E, for two and four minute cylinders, with Music Master horn and original wooden cover, circa 1910. (Auction Team Köln) $1,164

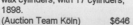

An Edison Fireside phonograph, Model A No. 25426, the K reproducer, crane and 36 two-minute and four-minute wax cylinders in cartons. (Christie's) $1,120

An Edison Standard phonograph for wax cylinders, with 17 cylinders, 1898. (Auction Team Köln) $646

An Edison Triumph phonograph, Model A No. 45259, in 'New Style' green oak case, with 14in. witch's hat horn. (Christie's) $1,200

An Edison Diamond Disc phonograph, Model H19, with built in loudspeaker and drawer for disks under, circa 1918.
(Auction Team Köln) $626

An Edison Amberola 30 phonograph with wooden case and integral horn, with three disks, circa 1915.
(Auction Team Köln) $646

American The Graphophone Type BC, in decorative oak case with bronze mountings and original wooden cover, 1905.
(Auction Team Köln) $1,423

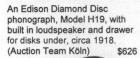

Edison Standard Phonograph Model F, with large, gallows-held swan-neck horn, and original wooden cover,circa 1911.
(Auction Team Köln) $644

An early French Pathé Nr. 1 phonograph for standard cylinders and adaptor for Pathé's Inter cylinders, with original wooden cover, circa 1903.
(Auction Team Köln) $452

Edison Home Phonograph Model B for two- and four-minute cylinders, with Music Master mahogany horn and wooden cover, circa 1907.
(Auction Team Köln) $1,322

A Pathé IV phonograph, with aluminium horn, for standard disks with adaptor for Inter-disks, with a few of each, 1904.
(Auction Team Köln) $627

An Excelsior Pearl phonograph, with silvered tin horn, wooden cover and one disk, German, circa 1905.
(Auction Team Köln) $452

An American Edison Home Phonograph, Model A - Type 2, with original cover, 1896.
(Auction Team Köln) $517

Richard Avedon, 'Marella Agnelli, New York Studio, December 1953', printed later, gelatin silver print, 24 x 20in., signed, titled, dated.
(Christie's) $10,373

Roger Fenton (1819-69), 'The Alexander Column & Winter Palace, St. Petersburg', 1852, salt print from a waxed paper negative, 6¾ x 8³/₈in. (Christie's) $32,062

Heinrich Kuhn, 'Study in Tones III (Miss Mary)', 1910, gum over platinum print, 11½ x 9³/₈in., signed in ink on recto.
(Christie's) $13,202

Albert Renger-Patzsch, Industrial study, 1920s, gelatin silver print, 7 x 5 in., numbered in pencil.
(Christie's) $3,018

Jacques-Henri Lartigue 'Renée Perle allongée sur un canape, Paris', 1931, gelatin silver print, 2³/₈ x 3½in., annotated later on verso.
(Christie's) $22,632

Henri Cartier-Bresson, 'Interlude in Bali - The Dancing Island', 1950, six glossy silver prints, each approx. 6¾ x 9¾in.
(Christie's) $4,526

Lewis Carroll (Charles Lutwidge Dodgson), 1832-98, 'Rachel Morrell', circa 1865, albumen print 6³/₈ x 4¹³/₁₆in. numbered 2401 in the negative.
(Christie's) $3,395

Robert Doisneau (1912-1994), 'Le Baiser de l'Hotel de Ville, 1950s', printed later, gelatiin silver print, image size 9½ x 11¾in., signed in ink in margin.
(Christie's) $3,772

Attributed to A. De Bonis, The gardens of the French Academy, 1858, two albumen prints, 9⁷/₈ x 7¾in. and 7³/₈ x 10in., each stamped DB on recto.
(Christie's) $1,358

William Klein (born 1928), 'Simone + Nina, Piazza di Spagna, Rome, 1960 (Vogue)', printed later, gelatin silver print, image size 17½ x 13½in. (Christie's) $3,018

Anonymous, Two gentlemen by a bench in front of Niagara Falls, circa 1866, half-plate ambrotype, decorative gilt-metal mount. (Christie's) $717

Brassai (Gyula Halász) (1899-1984), Portrait of Matisse in his studio, 1939, gelatin silver print, 10 x 7¾in. inscribed *Matisse*. (Christie's) $7,544

Anonymous (American), 'Kaloma', 1914, warm-toned hand-tinted gelatin silver print, 12 x 5in., blindstamped with title. (Christie's) $4,904

Jacques-Henri Lartigue, Femme aux renards ou Arlette Provost dite 'Anna la Pradvina' avec ses chiens Cogo et Chichi (Avenue des Acacias), Bois de Boulogne', 1911, gelatin silver print, 2⅝ x 4³/₈in. (Christie's) $74,620

Walery (Paris), Josephine Baker, circa 1925, warm-toned gelatin silver print, 9 x 6½in., signed in ink on recto. (Christie's) $1,602

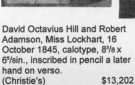

David Octavius Hill and Robert Adamson, Miss Lockhart, 16 October 1845, calotype, 8³/₈ x 6⅝in., inscribed in pencil a later hand on verso. (Christie's) $13,202

Leonard Misonne, Les Pecheurs, circa 1935, mediobrome, 9³/₈ x 11¾in., inscribed and initialed by the photographer's grandson in pencil on verso, matted. (Christie's) $1,886

David Octavius Hill and Robert Adamson, James Linton, Newhaven, June 1845, calotype, 7⅞. x 5⅝in mounted at top corners on paper. (Christie's) $3,772

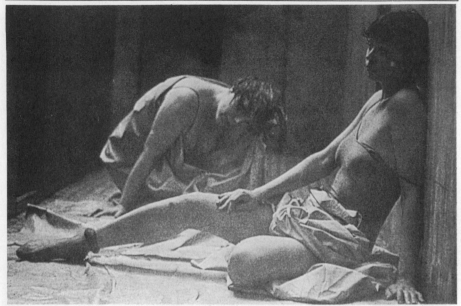

Deborah Turbeville, (b.1937), Bowery Bath House, circa 1974, two cibachrome prints, each approximately 8½ x 12½in., photographer's and publisher's credit *Polo Editions Inc.* as blindstamp in margin, each signed and inscribed *Edition 10* in ink on verso. (Christie's) $2,829

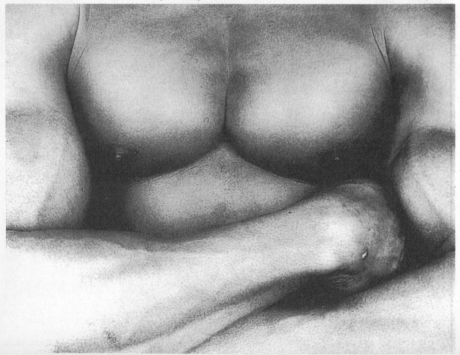

Robert Mapplethorpe, Chest, 1987, gelatin silver print, 19 x 22¾in., signed and numbered *1/10* and with ink stamp on verso, matted, framed, titled and dated on verso. (Christie's) $7,544

Willy Kessels, Profile of a woman wearing a large-brimmed hat, 1939, matt gelatin silver print, 11³/₈ x 9in., mounted on card.
(Christie's) $1,509

Jacques-Henri Lartigue 'Dani et ses flirts', 1922, gelatin silver print, 4³/₈ x 6¹/₈in., dated 20 Mars 1922 in pencil on verso.
(Christie's) $7,167

Horst P. Horst (born 1906), Marlene Dietrich, New York, 1942, printed later, platinum print, image size 9¼ x 7½in., signed in pencil in margin.
(Christie's) $3,772

Horst P. Horst, Coco Chanel, Paris, 1937, printed later, platinum palladium print, 15¼ x 14¾in. signed in pencil in margin.
(Christie's) $12,259

Jacques-Henri Lartigue, J.H. Lartigue and Richard Avedon, 1966-68, gelatin silver contact print, 2⁷/₁₆ x 2⁷/₁₆in., dated and annotated in pencil on verso.
(Christie's) $3,206

Jacques-Henri Lartigue, 'Premier vol de Gabriel Voisin de l'Aeroplane 'Archdeacon', Merlimont', 1904, gelatin silver contact print, 2⁵/₁₆ x 2½in. (Christie's) $18,860

Anonymous, Family group, 1850s-60s, ambrotype, visible image 11¾in. x 9½in., hand-tinted in white on lace and with gilt highlights.
(Christie's) $1,886

Leonard Misonne, Winter river scene, 14 June 1920, oil print, 9¼ x 11½in., dated, annotated.
(Christie's) $1,509

André Kertesz, 'Au bon Coin', 1929, printed later, gelatin silver print, 13¾ x 10¾in., signed, dated and inscribed. (Christie's) $2,075

Andy Warhol (1928-87), 'Self Portrait, 1983', unique Polaroid print, 4¼ x 3½in., matted, framed, titled, dated, credited. (Christie's) $9,053

Benjamin Brecknell Turner (1815-94), 'Scotch Firs, Hawkhurst', circa 1852, albumen print from a waxed paper negative, 11¼ x 15³/₈in. (Christie's) $35,834

Heinrich Kuhn (1866-1944), Gentleman seated, holding a pipe, 1898, pigment transfer print over pre-existing print, 11¾ x 9¼in. (Christie's) $2,829

Anonymous, Leo Tolstoy, 1904, gelatin silver print 10¾ x 8¼in., signed and dated in Cyrillic in pencil. (Christie's) $8,487

Willy Kessels, Woman reclining in leather dress, 1934, matt gelatin silver print, 6½ x 9in. photographer's blindstamp *W. Kessels Brux.* on recto. (Christie's) $1,320

Dorothea Lange (1895-1965), 'Bridie O'Halloran', 'Linked Hands', Ireland 1955, two gelatin silver prints, 10 x 7¾ and 8¼ x 8in. (Christie's) $1,697

Heinrich Kuhn, Portrait of Hans, the photographer's son, circa 1906, platinum print, 11⁷/₈ x 9³/₈in., pencil annotations on verso. (Christie's) $4,526

Jacques-Henri Lartigue (1894-1996), 'Ma premiere photographie, Pont de l'Arche (Portrait de ma famille)', 1902, printing-out-paper print, 4⁷/₈ x 6⁷/₈in., flush-mounted on card. (Christie's) $9,430

Charles Jones, 'Bean Runner', circa 1900, gelatin silver print, 10 x 8in., signed *C.J.*, titled and annotated in pencil on verso. (Christie's) $2,640

Bruce Weber, 'Three men in a reflecting pool, Santa Barbara, 1989', platinum print, 12½ x 10¼in., matted, framed, titled and dated.
(Christie's) $1,132

Jacques-Henri Lartigue, 'L'envol de ma cousine Bichonade, (40, Rue Cortambert), Paris', 1905, gelatin silver contact print, 2¹/₈ x 2⁹/₁₆in.
(Christie's) $30,176

Jeremiah Gurney, Portrait of two children, 1850s, daguerreotype, 5 x 4in., delicately hand-tinted, gilt matt with arched corners.
(Christie's) $1,602

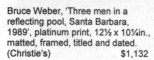

Richard Avedon, 'Carmen (Homage to Munkacsi), Paris, 1957', printed later, gelatin silver print, 18 x 14in., signed and numbered 17 on verso.
(Christie's) $10,939

Bert Stern (born 1929), Marilyn Monroe, 1962, printed later, platinum print, image size 14½ x 22in. signed, dated and titled *Marilyn*. (Christie's) $3,206

Julia Margaret Cameron, Thomas Carlyle, 1867, albumen print, 13 x 10in., mounted on card, trimmed to edge of print, matted.
(Christie's) $15,088

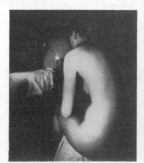

Bill Brandt (1904-83), 'Nude, Campden Hill', London, 1949, printed later, gelatin silver print, 13½ x 11½in., surmounted on card, signed in ink on mount.
(Christie's) $2,392

Jacques-Henri Lartigue, 'Promeneuses (Avenue du Bois), Bois de Boulogne', 1915, gelatin silver print, 4½ x 4¹⁵/₁₆in., dated later in pencil on verso.
(Christie's) $18,860

Robert Howlett (1831-58), Soldiers in front of a gun carriage at Greenwich Hospital 1855, light albumen print, 9¼ x 7³/₈in., arched top, mounted on card.
(Christie's) $1,320

Classical mahogany and rosewood veneer piano, Wilkins & Newhall, Boylston Street, Boston, early 19th century, 72in. wide. (Skinner) $805

A Steinway mahogany Model M grand piano with non-matching bench, 1937, 66in. long. (Du Mouchelles) $10,000

A fine marquetry and 'ivory' inlaid satinwood Steinway grand piano, serial No. 114666, circa 1904, the case decorated with 'ivory' inlaid oval medallions of classical figures, 87in. long, together with an en suite box duet piano stool. (Bonhams) $35,000

A drawing-room grand pianoforte, overstrung, seven octaves, in rosewood case, 5ft. 6in. long, by Schiedmayer, Stuttgart, circa 1922. (Russell, Baldwin & Bright) $2,512

Steinway & Sons mahogany grand piano, 1915, with ivory keys, 7ft long. (Du Mouchelles) $10,000

A marquetry, gilt-bronze porcelain and lapis lazuli upright piano by Declercq, Paris, circa 1865, the hinged top with a parquetry lattice ground, 164cm. wide. (Sotheby's) $67,981

Polyphon No. 42 D musical box for 28.1cm. disks, with 108-tone double comb, inlaid wooden lid, circa 1910.
(Auction Team Köln) $1,099

A Polyphon No. 71 musical box for 20.7cm. disks, with 41-tone comb, circa 1900.
(Auction Team Köln) $291

A Polyphon No. 41C musical box for 20.7cm tin disks, with 41-tone comb, with 5 disks, circa 1895.
(Auction Team Köln) $323

A Polyphon No. 42 musical box by Polyphon, Leipzig, with 54-tone comb, for 28.1cm. disks, circa 1904, with 8 disks.
(Auction Team Köln) $508

A Swiss Stella No. 84 musical box for 43.8cm. disks, with 84-tone comb and tempo regulator and automatic stop/start lever, in inlaid walnut case, circa 1885.
(Auction Team Köln) $3,557

A Kalliope No.60 musical box for 34cm. disks, with 61-tone comb, the lid with inlaid Art Nouveau motif, circa 1900.
(Auction Team Köln) $1,164

A Kalliope No. 26 musical box for 14.5cm. disks, with 26-tone comb, circa 1900.
(Auction Team Köln) $194

A Polyphon No. 72 G musical box for 28.1cm. disks with 47-tone comb and eight bells, circa 1900.
(Auction Team Köln) $970

A Polyphon No. 41 C musical box for 20.7cm disks, with 41-tone comb, circa 1900.
(Auction Team Köln) $356

Daniel O'Keefe (1740-1787), a Lady, facing right in blue dress with lace cuffs, oval, 2¹⁵/₁₆in. high. (Christie's) $1,255

George Engleheart (1750-1829), Lady Betty Foster, facing right in white dress, oval, 2in. high. (Christie's) $11,592

English School, circa 1785, an Officer, facing right in scarlet coat with buff facings, oval, 2¾in. high. (Christie's) $3,671

George Engleheart (1750-1829), an Officer believed to be Lieutenant-Colonel Henry Conran of the 52nd (Oxfordshire) Regiment of Foot, signed and dated *1800*, oval, 3³/₁₆in. high. (Christie's) $8,114

Henry Bone, R.A. (1755-1834) after Andrew Robertson (1777-1845), Mrs Robert Hawthorn, facing right in white dress, and blue lined purple cloak, signed, enamel on copper, oval, 3¼in. high. (Christie's) $4,830

John Oliver (1616-1701), Samuel Desborough, facing right in black gown and white lawn collar, black skull cap, long curling brown hair, blue background, oil on copper, oval, 2³/₁₆in. high, gilt-metal frame. (Christie's) $5,410

Philip Jean (1755-1802), a young Gentleman, facing right in blue coat with large gold buttons, oval 1¹³/₁₆in. high. (Christie's) $4,250

John Smart (1742/43-1811), an Officer, facing right in scarlet coat with silver epaulette and primrose facings, signed with initials and dated *1801*, oval, 3¹/₈in. high. (Christie's) $21,252

Anne Mee, née Foldsone (circa 1770/75-1851), a young Lady, facing right in white dress, oval, 3½in. high. (Christie's) $2,125

Isaac Wane Slater (1784/85-1836), Mrs Power, facing right in white dress, signed and dated *1808*, oval, 3in. high. (Christie's) $1,352

Nathaniel Hone, R.A. (1718-1784), a young Boy, facing right in red coat, signed, oval, $1^{3}/16$in. high. (Christie's) $1,835

George Engleheart (1750-1829), a young Officer, facing left in scarlet coat with gold edging, oval, $1^{3}/8$in. high. (Christie's) $2,125

Christian Friedrich Zincke (1683/84-1767, a young Lady, facing left in open white dress with white underslip, enamel on copper, oval, $2^{7}/16$in. high. (Christie's) $4,250

Attributed to Sir Antonio Mor (1512/19-1575/77), an important historical portrait miniature of William, 1st Marquess of Winchester, K.G., facing left, oil on card, $2^{1}/16$in. diameter. (Christie's) $17,388

English School, circa 1660, a Gentleman, facing left in black cloak, white frilled shirt and black bow tie, on vellum laid down on card, oval, $2^{1}/8$in. high. (Christie's) $1,739

William Wood (1769-1810), Mrs Hope, facing right in white dress with frilled collar, white turban in her dark brown hair, oval, $3^{1}/16$in. high. (Christie's) $21,252

Jean-Théodore Perrache (1744-after 1789), Dr. Benjamin Franklin, facing right in russet-colored coat, signed, enamel on copper, oval, $1^{3}/4$in. high. (Christie's) $30,912

George Engleheart (1750-1829), a young Gentleman, facing right in blue coat with large gold buttons, oval, $1^{13}/16$in. high. (Christie's) $3,478

Charles Boit (1662-1727), a young Lady, facing right in open blue velvet day-gown, signed, enamel on copper, oval, 2in. high.
(Christie's) $7,728

Richard Cosway, R.A. (1742-1821), Mrs Floyd, facing right in loose white dress with blue sash, oval, 2^{1}/16in.
(Christie's) $6,762

Charles Bestland (b. 1764), a young Gentleman, facing right in brown coat, white waistcoat and tied cravat, oval, 3^{1}/8in. high.
(Christie's) $1,352

Susannah-Penelope Rosse (circa 1655-1700), Cosimo III of Medici, Grand-Duke of Tuscany, facing right in gilt-studded armor, on vellum, oval 3^{5}/16in. high.
(Christie's) $14,490

Alexander Cooper (circa 1605-1660), Lord William Craven, facing right in embroidered white doublet, signed with initials, on vellum, oval, 1^{7}/8in. high.
(Chrsitie's) $59,808

Franciszek Smiadecki (fl. circa 1664), Sir Anthony Cope, facing right in black gown, lawn collar with tassels, oil on copper, oval, 2^{5}/16in. high, silver-gilt frame.
(Christie's) $5,410

William Wood (1769-1810), a Gentleman, facing right in blue coat with black collar and gold buttons, white cravat, signed, oval, 3in. high.
(Christie's) $289

John Thomas Barber Beaumont (1774-1841), a young Lady, facing right in white dress, signed with initials, oval, 3in. high.
(Christie's) $4,830

English School, a young Officer, believed to be Michel Descartes of the 5th Regiment of the Chevaux-Légers, oval 2^{5}/8in. high.
(Christie's) $3,864

John Smart (1742/43-1811), a young Lady, facing left in salmon pink dress, signed, *1788,* oval, 2¼in. high. (Christie's) $38,640

N. Freese (fl. 1794-1814), Jack George Dalbiac of the 11th Light Dragoons, facing left in blue uniform, oval, 3in. high, silver-gilt frame. (Christie's) $13,524

William Wood (1769-1810), after Richard Cosway, R.A. (1742-1821), a young Lady, facing left in white dress, oval, 3³/₁₆in. high. (Christie's) $1,739

Henry Bone, R. A. (1755-1834), Elizabeth Shutz, in profile to left in white dress with high collar, signed, dated *1831,* enamel on copper, oval 2³/₈in. high. (Christie's) $2,898

Gervase Spencer (d. 1763), George, 3rd Duke of St. Albans, facing left in gold-embroidered light blue jacket, signed, enamel on copper, oval, 1¾in. high. (Christie's) $2,705

R. Fortin (fl. circa 1792-1794), John Conslade, facing right in black coat and waistcoat, frilled cravat, signed and dated *Fortin / 1792,* oval, 2⁵/₁₆in. high. (Christie's) $3,864

Samuel Lover, R.H.A. (1797-1868), a young Girl, facing right in white dress with pale pink sash, signed, oval, 4¹/₁₆in. high. (Christie's) $2,512

George Engleheart (1750-1829), Captain A. Mackay, facing left in scarlet coat with blue collar, oval, 3in. high. (Christie's) $14,490

Robert French (fl, circa 1720-1740), a young Lady, facing left in yellow-bordered white dress, on vellum, signed and dated *1742,* oval, 1⁵/₈in. (Christie's) $1,062

Paul, Colin (1892–1986), Dunlop, lithograph in colors, circa 1950, printed by P.P.P.P., Paris, backed on linen, 31 x 24in.
(Christie's)　　　　　$1,380

Fraikin, Ce Michelin est Indechirable, lithograph in colors, 1908, printed by Ch. Verneau, Paris, backed on linen, 35¹/₂ x 30in.
(Christie's)　　　　　$1,840

F de Prado, Rafaga La Campeon de Aragon, published by Friedrichs Barcelona, 112 x 77cm., on linen.
(Onslow's)　　　　　$156

Anonymous, Vermouth Perucchi, lithograph in colors, circa 1935, printed by J. Ortega, Valencia, backed on linen, 42 x 30in.
(Christie's)　　　　　$368

Georges Dola (1872–1950), Kina-Lillet, lithograph in colors, circa 1900, printed by Imprimeries Reunies de Levallois, backed on linen, 55 x 38¹/₂in.
(Christie's)　　　　　$478

Adolphe Mouron (Cassandre), Mentor, lithograph on colors, 1949, printed by Andreasen & Lachmann, Copenhagen, 34 x 24¹/₂in.
(Christie's)　　　　　$1,840

Percival Pernet (1890–1977),
Grand-Prix, 1948, lithograph in
colors, 1948, backed on linen,
39 x 25½in.
(Christie's) $1,380

Paul Nash, Footballers Prefer
Shell, lithograph in colors, circa
1935, printed by Waterlow & Sons,
Ltd., London, backed on linen,
20½ x 45in.
(Christie's) $2,944

Anonymous, Rosee Creme,
lithograph in colors, circa 1900,
printed by Charles Verneau, Paris,
55 x 39½in.
(Christie's) $478

Adolphe Mouron (Cassandre),
Miniwatt, Philips Radio, lithograph
in colors, 1931, printed by
Alliance Graphique, Paris, 22 x
15½in.
(Christie's) $2,392

Ben Nicholson (1894–1982), These
Men Use Shell, lithograph in
colors, 1938, printed by Waterlow
& Sons, London, 30 x 45in.
(Christie's) $1,747

Anonymous, Michelin, Confort-
Bibendum, lithograph in colors,
circa 1930, backed on linen, 77 x
49in.
(Christie's) $1,563

Ludwig Hohlwein (1874–1949), Dr.
Klopfer-Nudeln und Maccaroni,
lithograph in colors, 1912, printed
by J. Aberle & Co., Berlin, backed
on linen, 35½ x 23in.
(Christie's) $680

Hans Schleger, (Zero) (1898–
1976), Journalists, You Can Be
Sure of Shell, lithograph in colors,
1938, printed by Waterlow & Sons,
Ltd., London, backed on linen,
29½ x 44½in.
(Christie's) $5,520

After E. Vulliement, Cycles
Peugeot, lithograph in colors,
circa 1910, printed by L. Revon &
Cie, Paris, backed on linen, 63½
x 47in.
(Christie's) $736

Albert Solon, Farman Airlines, published by Publicité West, 90 x 61cm., 1926.
(Onslow's)　　　　$597

Albert Brenet, Afrique Occidentale Air France, 1952.
(Onslow's)　　　　$148

Fly Safari To Africa Operated Jointly by Airwork Ltd and Hunting-Clan. (Onslow's)　　　　$48

T A, Swedish Air Lines AB Aero Transport, published by Rokotryck Stockholm, 94 x 60cm.
(Onslow's)　　　　$625

Anonymous, From The Cold and Foggy North to the Glowing Blue and Gold of Majorca Fly Iberia Airlines of Spain; and Seville Easter Fair Fly Iberia.
(Onslow's)　　　　$33

Roger de Valerio (1896–1951), Air France, Paris Londres en 1h30, lithograph in colors, 1936, printed by Perceval, Paris, backed on linen, 19½ x 12in.
(Christie's)　　　　$643

HISTORICAL FACTS
Aeronautical Posters

Airline posters of the 1920s and 1930s are probably the most difficult of all to find. Good examples for Imperial Airways depicting their Empire Flying Boats fetch high hundreds whilst those for BOAC or BEA from the '40s and '50s by Frank Wootton, Lee-Elliott, Abram Games are more common and affordable at $160–$480 and many from the 1960s sell at under $160.

John Jenkins (Onslow's)

W.H.A. Constable, India By Imperial Airways (Handley Page HP42 Hannibal), printed by Stuarts, double crown, circa 1935.
(Onslow's)　　　　$1,398

Harold McCready, Imperial Airways (Armstrong Whitworth Argosy 1 City of Wellington), printed by John Horne, double crown, 1929.
(Onslow's)　　　　$2,468

Lewitt-Him, AOA to USA, lithograph in colors, 1948, printed by W.R. Royle & Son, Ltd., 38 x 24in.
(Christie's) $165

Anonymous, Fly TWA To Chicago.
(Onslow's) $230

Anonymous, Pan American World Airways The System of the Flying Clippers Paris A New York, color photographic, double royal, framed.
(Onslow's) $173

Mart Kempers, Fly The Sapphire Service To Ceylon Air Ceylon.
(Onslow's) $33

Jean Walther (1910–), Douglas DC-3, offset and photography in colors, circa 1935, 24 x 29½in.
(Christie's) $1,010

Bernard Villemot, French Riveria Air France, 1952.
(Onslow's) $214

H.M. Burton, South African Airways "The Blue and Silver Way" (Junker Ju 52), published by Hortors, Cape Town, double royal.
(Onslow's) $444

Anonymous, KLM Amsterdam Batavia Twice Weekly Speed Comfort Reliability Fokker-Douglas DC2, double royal.
(Onslow's) $247

Jules Isnard Dransy (1883–c.1945), Air France, lithograph in colors, 1933, printed by Joseph-Charles, Paris, 39½ x 27½in.
(Christie's) $275

'Virages' - Original film poster featuring Paul Newman: known otherwise as 'Winning'. (Christie's) $1,030

From the studio of Alfred Lambart, The Morris Eight From £118 Buy British and Be Proud Of It, printed by J. Howitt & Sons, Nottingham, 62 x 86cm., conserved on linen. (Onslow's) $855

Fangio – 'Una Vita a 300 All'ora'., two original film posters; large and small formats; differing images. (Christie's) $1,030

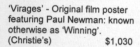

Anonymous, Michelin, offset and lithograph in colors, circa 1940, 47 x 31½in. (Christie's) $2,024

Melnikoba, The Youth on Cars and Motorcycles, lithograph in colors, 1937, printed in Moscow, backed on linen, 27 x 40in. (Christie's) $643

Hans Liska, Mercedes Benz French Grand Prix 1954 – A large victory achievements poster depicting Fangio's winning streamlined W196 car; full-color lithograph design, 33 x 23in. (Christie's) $1,312

Le Mans 'Scorciatioa per L'inferno' – an original film poster featuring Lang Jeffries and Erna Schurer, large format, circa 1970. (Christie's) $280

From the studio of Alfred Lambart, Vauxhall Light Six The Car For Happy Days, printed by J. Howitt & Sons Offset, Nottingham, double crown, conserved on linen. (Onslow's) $724

Mundorff, Grosser Preis von Deutschland Nürburgring 2nd August circa 1950, full color lithograph design, 32 x 23in. (Christie's) $655

'Le Mans' - Original film poster featuring Steve McQueen; Le 24 Ore di Le Mans, Italian text.
(Christie's) $1,217

E. A. Hermans, Grosse Preis Von Belgien Spa Francorchamps; full color lithograph design, 20 June circa 1952. 22 x 28in.
(Christie's) $655

Jacques Ramel, Monaco, 22 Mai 1955, lithograph in colors, 1955, printed by Editions J. Ramel, Nice, 47 x 31½in.
(Christie's) $1,570

André Galland ((1900–1989), Le Mans, lithograph in colors, circa 1930, printed by A. Demoulin, Paris, 39½ x 24½in.
(Christie's) $920

M,S, Cabanne-Nirouet, lithograph in colors, circa 1910, printed by Ch. Wall & Cie., Paris, 39½ x 55in.
(Christie's) $1,440

George Hamel (Geo. Ham), (1900–1972), 6eme Grand Prix Automobile, Monaco, lithograph in colors, 1934, printed by Monegasque-Monte-Carlo, backed on linen, 47 x 31in.
(Christie's) $4,600

Mundorff, Grosser Preis von Deutschland – Nürburgring 29 Juli 1951: a scarce original poster: full color lithograph, 32 x 23in.
(Christie's) $1,030

From the studio of Alfred Lambart, The Vauxhall Light Six with Independent Springing, printed by Howitt Offset, Nottingham, double crown, conserved on linen.
(Onslow's) $790

Anonymous, Le Chauffeur – 'A Moi la Coupe'; an early humorous motoring print; color lithograph French circa 1905, 10 x 30 in. approx. (Christie's) $749

Hass, I Always Travel Union Castle (Neptune), Quoits On Deck, color photographic.
(Onslow's) $109

Et. Bauer, Hamburg–Amerika Linie, lithograph in colors, circa 1920, 33 x 23½in.
(Christie's) $590

Charles Hallo (Alo), (1884–1969), Red Star Line, New York–Southampton, lithograph in colors, circa 1920, 38 x 25in.
(Christie's) $700

Albert Sebille (1874–1953), Comple. Genle. Transatlantique, lithograph in colors, circa 1920, printed by Buttner & Thierry, St. Ouen, 36 x 25½in.
(Christie's) $883

Norman R.I. Wilkinson, The New T.S. "Falaise". Southern Railway, lithograph in colors, 1947, printed by The Baynard Press, London, 40 x 50in.
(Christie's) $957

P. Irwin Brown, LMS Express & Cunard Liner The Highest Standard of Comfort In Rail and Ocean Travel, published by LMS, printed by Forman, double royal, dry mounted on board, framed.
(Onslow's) $691

HISTORICAL FACTS
Ocean Liner Posters

Whether they depict Cunard liners crossing the Atlantic or ships serving other routes there is always a strong demand for this category. Good graphics by artists such as Frank H Mason, Norman Wilkinson, Walter Thomas, Montague B Black, Odin Rosenvinge, Chas Pears, command prices starting at $500–$700 in some cases rising upwards of $1,600

John Jenkins (Onslow's)

Maurice Randall, The Blue Funnel Line, lithograph in colors, circa 1920, backed on japan, 33½ x 20in.
(Christie's) $405

Kenneth D. Shoesmith, Canadian Pacific To Canada & USA (Empress of Britain), printed by Baynard.
(Onslow's) $987

Anonymous, Allan Line to Canada, lithograph in colors, circa 1910, 40 x 25in.
(Christie's) $1,140

Norman Wilkinson (1882–1971), Cunard Line, lithograph in colors 1907, backed on linen, 29 x 36½in.
(Christie's) $1,104

Anonymous, Grace Line, lithograph in colors, circa 1925, 39 x 27in.
(Christie's) $700

Anonymous, Atlantic Transport Line, Direct to London, lithograph in colors, circa 1910, printed by The Liverpool Printing and Stationery Co., Ltd., 40 x 25in.
(Christie's) $643

Anonymous, Holland-Amerika Linie, Rotterdam–New York, lithograph in colors, circa 1912, printed by Van LL, Amsterdam, backed on linen, 30 x 41in.
(Christie's) $1,656

Albert Sebille, Cie Gle Transatlantique, Havre–New York, lithograph in colors, 1939, printed by Maquet, Paris, backed on linen, 42 x 30in.
(Christie's) $2,850

Greig, Union Castle Line Travel The Big Ship Way South and East Africa (Cape Town Castle), double royal, on linen.
(Onslow's) $559

Ralph O'Neil, Bombay Harbour, BB & CI and P&O, lithograph in colors, circa 1935, printed by The Lamson Agency Ltd., London, 40 x 50in.
(Christie's) $736

Anonymous, To USA United States Lines American Merchant Lines, printed by Dorland, double royal, on linen.
(Onslow's) $329

Jacques Rolet (1925–), Grenoble, Ville Olympique, heliogravure colors, 1968, printed by Georges Lang, Paris, backed on linen, 39 x 24in.
(Christie's) $1,288

John Sjosvard, Equestrian Games of the XVIth Olympiad 1956 Stockholm 10-17 June, double royal, dry mounted.
(Onslow's) $132

Alain Perceval, Chamrousse, photograph in colors, 1968, printed by Drager, Paris, backed on linen, 39 x 24in.
(Christie's) $736

Ismar Mujezinovic (b. 1947), two posters for the XIV Olympic Winter Games, Sarajevo, 1984, offset lithograph in colors, 1984, printed by Nisro 'Oslobodenje', Sarajevo, 27 x 19in.
(Christie's) $1,288

Herve Moran (1917–1980), Bendix, lithograph in colors, circa 1968, printed by Bedos & Cie., Paris, backed on linen, 44½ x 60½in.
(Christie's) $552

Leroy Neiman (1927–), two posters for the XIII Olympic Winter Games, Lake Placid, 1980, lithograph in colors, 1980, 39 x 20½in.
(Christie's) $1,840

Ilmari Sysimetsä (1912–1955), XVth Olympic Games, Helsinki, Finland, lithograph in colors, 1952, printed by Oy. Tilgmann AB., 39½ x 24½in.
(Christie's) $1,010

Wilhelm Jaruska (1916–), Innsbruck 1964, offset lithograph in colors, 1964, printed by Buchroithner & Co., Innsbruck, backed on linen, 37 x 24½in.
(Christie's) $589

Jean Brian, (1915–), Xth Winter Olympic Games, Grenoble, lithograph in colors, 1968, printed by Generale, Grenoble, backed on linen, 37½ x 25in.
(Christie's) $1,195

David Byrd, Moody Blues, Cold Blood, Terrace Ballroom, Salt Lake City, Utah, 1969.
(Bonhams) $352

Stanley Mouse, Timeless, serigraph.
(Bonhams) $992

Rick Griffin, 'Heart and Torch', Big Brother & The Holding Company, Santana at Fillmore West, December 1968.
(Bonhams) $304

Sätty, Fool on the Hill, 1967, Wespac San Francisco Happenings, No W7, framed and glazed, 23½ x 36in.
(Bonhams) $160

Rick Griffin, 'Flying Eyeball', Jimi Hendrix at the Fillmore & Winterland, February 1968.
(Bonhams) $1,920

Mouse, Kelley & Griffin, rare and much sought after Winterland Halloween Concert poster, 'Trip or Freak' with the Grateful Dead, Quicksilver & Big Brother.
(Bonhams) $1,312

Hapshash & The Colored Coat, The Jimi Hendrix Experience at The Fillmore Auditorium, June 1967, printed by Osiris.
(Bonhams) $768

J. Cushing, Grateful Dead and The Doors, Earl Warren Showgrounds, Santa Barbara, 1967, a Jim Salzer concert, 17 x 23in.
(Bonhams) $176

Jim Blashfield, 'The San Francisco Scene in Los Angeles', with Jefferson Airplane, Grateful Dead, Big Brother at the Hollywood Bowl, 19.9.1967.
(Bonhams) $144

R. Tuten & W. Bostedt, Fleetwood Mac, Oakland Stadium, May 1977, signed by Randy Tuten.
(Bonhams) $288

Randy Tuten, Rolling Stones, Oakland Coliseum, 9.11.1969, signed by Randy Tuten.
(Bonhams) $352

Gunther Kieser, Traffic in Concert, Frankfurt, Germany, 6.2.1971, classic poster by Gunther Kieser.
(Bonhams) $288

Gary Grimshaw, Poster for the Induction of the Yardbirds into the Rock and Roll Hall of Fame, limited edition No. 15 of 25, signed by the artist Gary Grimshaw.
(Bonhams) $928

Jim Phillips, The Doors and the Ragamuffins, August 1967, presented by the Crosstown Bus, signed by the artist Jim Phillips in silver pen.
(Bonhams) $144

Randy Tuten, 'Titanic', Creedence Clearwater Revival, Fillmore West & Winterland, May 1969, signed in silver pen by Randy Tuten.
(Bonhams) $208

Limited Edition (500) print, hand signed in black pen by James Brown for the famed 'Apollo' comeback concert in 1965.
(Bonhams) $256

The Beatles, London Palladium Royal Command Performace 1963, original 1964 printing with facsimile signatures.
(Bonhams) $176

Creedence Clearwater Revival, this is the complete poster/program for CCR's performance at the Royal Albert Hall, 14 x 23in.
(Bonhams) $277

Randy Tuten, The Doors at Cow Palace, July 1969.
(Bonhams) $448

Jimi Hendrix, original blacklight 'headshop' poster of Jimi with spiral background, circa 1969.
(Bonhams) $384

Rex Ray, Eric Clapton plays the Fillmore, November 1994.
(Bonhams) $440

Stanley Mouse, 'Edwardian Ball'. Jefferson Airplane at the Fillmore, 1967, signed with an early style Mouse signature in black pen.
(Bonhams) $352

Carson-Morris Studios, The Northern California Folk Rock Festival, May 1968 with The Doors, Animals, Big Brother, Jefferson Airplane, Country Joe, Taj Mahal and others.
(Bonhams) $416

Alton Kelley & Stanley Mouse, 'The Blue Rose', New Year's Eve, Winterland 1978, signed in gold pen by Alton Kelley.
(Bonhams) $448

Randy Tuten, Steve Miller Band, Joe Satriani, Reno, S.F. & Sacramento, December 1991, signed by Randy Tuten.
(Bonhams) $224

Randy Tuten, B.B. King, Elvin Bishop, Big Brother & The Holding Company with Nick Graventes, Selland Arena, May 1971, signed by Randy Tuten.
(Bonhams) $144

Randy Tuten, The Band, Sons of Champlin, Winterland, April 1969, signed in silver pen by Randy Tuten.
(Bonhams) $224

HISTORICAL FACTS
Travel Posters

The development of the poster in Britain was led by artists Dudley Hardy and John Hassall. Hassall designed the famous 'Skegness Is So Bracing' poster of the Jolly Fisherman in 1908. Good examples of travel posters published up to 1914 are rare and tend to be in the $800–$6,600 price range depending on the subject and artist.

Posters published by the 'Big Four' Railway companies, namely the Great Western Railway, Southern Railway, London Midland Scottish and London & North Eastern from 1923–1939 continue to grow in popularity. Subjects include resorts, golfers, architecture, abbeys, landmarks, special trains and services, industry, ports, harbors and ships, areas of outstanding natural beauty also some Continental resorts and cities. The most sought after designs are those featuring locomotives, dining cars, bathers, golf and field sports and those in the Art Deco style.

Most posters were published in two standard sizes, double royal (102 x 64cm) and quad royal (102 x 128cm). Prices very much depend on the subject, design and artist but expect to pay $800 and upwards for an attractive design and prices in the $2,400–$3,200 are not uncommon for the better designs. The dream like image of 'The Night Scotsman' by Alexander Alexeieff published by the LNER sold for $17,600.

John Jenkins (Onslow's)

New York Go By Train Pennsylvania Railroad, color photographic view of Manhattan. (Onslow's) $214

Guy Malet (1900–1973), LNER To Scotland, gouache, artist's address label on reverse, 38 x 27cm. (Onslow's) $329

D. Ogilvie, Florida Fishing Boating Swimming Attractive Residential Sites, issued by the South African Railways and Harbors and Town of Maraisburg, printed by Brown & Davis, Durban, double royal. (Onslow's) $313

Sellheim, Australia For Sun and Surf, photographic, published by Australian National Travel Association, printed by Troedel & Cooper. (Onslow's) $157

Leonard Squirrel, London Piccadilly Circus, published by British Travel & Holidays Association, double crown, on linen. (Onslow's) $240

Schabelsky, Isle of Skye, LNER, lithograph in colors, circa 1933, printed by Vincent Brooks, Day & Sons, Ltd., London, 40 x 25in. (Christie's) $643

Brenot, Montreux, published by
Klausfelder, 63 x 102cm., on linen.
(Onslow's) $314

Tom Purvis, Getting Ready For
The East Coast Travel LNER,
printed by Waterlow, quad royal, on
old linen.
(Onslow's) $1,974

D. Barclay, Knysna, printed by
Herald.
(Onslow's) $235

F. Brittain, Port Elizabeth
Humewood Golf Links, issued by
Port Elizabeth and the South
African Railways and Harbors,
printed by Herald.
(Onslow's) $612

From the studio of Alfred Lambart,
Sunbeam Motor Cycles, 61 x
81cm.
(Onslow's) $757

From the studio of Edmond
Vaughan, South For Winter
Sunshine, published by SR, Ad
1072, printed by Baynard, double
royal, on linen, 1929.
(Onslow's) $5,429

Albert Duvernay, Grau du Roi,
lithograph in colors, circa 1935,
printed by Havas, backed on linen,
39 x 25in.
(Christie's) $368

Robert Bonfils (1886–1972), Les
Alpes, lithograph in colours, 1939,
printed by Art et Tourisme, Paris,
backed on linen, 39½ x 49in.
(Christie's) $1,010

Rex John Whistler (1905–1944),
London Museum, lithograph in
colours, 1928, printed by Haycock,
Photochrom, 40 x 25in.
(Christie's) $1,656

HISTORICAL FACTS
War Posters

Before conscription was introduced in 1916 the Parliamentary Recruiting Committee issued around 200 different posters. The first of these were purely letterpress with such slogans as 'Why Aren't You In Khaki', 'Rally Round The Flag' and 'A Call To Arms'. Pictorial posters soon appeared with patriotism and fund raising appeals in mind. The National War Savings Committee produced a fair number of designs by Frank Brangwyn and Bert Thomas, famed for his 'Arf a Mo Kaiser' image. Letterpress posters start at around $30 whilst a great many pictorial examples are in the region of $60–$160. Examples of the more famous 'Daddy, what did you do in the Great War?' by Saville Lumley, E V Kealy's 'Women of Britain Say Go' and Alfred Leete's image of Lord Kitchener with his accusing finger are in the $300 to $800 price range.

The Second World War propaganda posters are popular with collectors, with an interest in military history. They cover many aspects of the war on the home front from the evacuation of children, air raid precautions, public health, salvage, fuel conservation, Dig For Victory, Civil Defence, the production of munitions, tanks, guns, ships and aircraft to those showing the allied forces in action from the Back Them Up series as well as the famous Careless Talk campaign. These generally fall into a price range of $60–$160.

John Jenkins (Onslow's)

Lucy Kemp-Welch, Forward!, single sheet on linen.
(Onslow's) $905

Anonymous, Who's Absent? Is It You, double crown, on linen; and War Loan, double crown.
(Onslow's) $90

Murray, Drink More Milk Milk Restores Energy, issued by the National Milk Publicity Council, 50 x 36cm., Dixon, Drink More Milk, two, each 50 x 36cm.
(Onslow's) $181

A U.S. WWII propaganda poster, 1944, 'Under The Shadow of Their Wings Our Land Shall Dwell Secure', 26½ x 36½in., linen backed.
(Sotheby's) $700

W.A. Fry, There's Room For You Enlist Today (railway carriage), double crown.
(Onslow's) $90

Don't Waste Bread! Defeat The U-Boat, photomontage, published by The Ministry of Food, double crown.
(Onslow's) $596

Saville Lumley, Daddy What Did You Do In The Great War?, double crown, on linen.
(Onslow's) $592

She Helps Her Boy To Victory, photomontage (artillery in action), published by The Ministry of Food, double crown.
(Onslow's) $235

W.H. Caffyn, Come Along Boys Enlist Today, double crown, 1914.
(Onslow's) $66

J.E. Sheridan, Rivets Are Bayonets Drive Them Home!, published US Shipping Board Emergency Fleet Corporation, 96 x 66cm.
(Onslow's) $39

Harrison Fisher, I Summon You To Comradeship In The Red Cross 1918, quad crown, on linen.
(Onslow's) $107

L. Zabel, Your Fatherland Is In Danger Enlist!, G Kav Rifle Division, 143 x 93cm., on linen, 1916.
(Onslow's) $300

Raleigh, Hun or Home? Buy More Liberty Bonds, published USA, double crown.
(Onslow's) $47

Baron Low, Everyone Should Do His Bit Enlist Now, double crown, 1915.
(Onslow's) $99

L.N. Britton, The Navy Is Calling Enlist Now, published US Navy Recruiting Station, 96 x 66cm.
(Onslow's) $39

Paul Ordner (1900–1969), Mont-Revard, PLM, lithograph in colors, circa 1930, printed by M. Déchaux, Paris, 39 x 24¹/₂in.
(Christie's) $920

Walter Koch, Davos, lithograph in colors, 1907, printed by Wolf, Basel, backed on linen, 35¹/₂ x 25in.
(Christie's) $2,760

Anonymous, Eisbahn, lithograph in colors, circa 1910, printed by Robert Muller, Potsdam, 28 x 18¹/₂in.
(Christie's) $736

Anonymous, Eisbahn Milchbuck, lithograph in colors, circa 1930, printed by Werkstätten Gebr.Fretz, Zürich, backed on japan, 50 x 35¹/₂in.
(Christie's) $1,563

Gaston Gorde (1908–1995), Allard de Mégève, lithograph in colors, circa 1935, printed by Editions Gaston Gorde, Paris, on linen, 39¹/₂ x 25in.
(Christie's) $1,104

Hans Thoni (1906–1980), Wengen, photomontage and lithography in colors, 1936, printed by Art Brugger, S.A., Meiringen, backed on japan, 39¹/₂ x 27in.
(Christie's) $1,379

Roger Broders, Les Sports d'Hiver au Mont-Revard, PLM, lithograph in colors, circa 1930, printed by Lucien Serre & Cie., Paris, 42¹/₂ x 31in.
(Christie's) $3,312

Mezr?, Eller's Ski-Wasser, lithograph in colors, circa 1940, printed by Kunstanstalt Caroli u. Nägele, München, backed on linen, 11¹/₂ x 9in.
(Christie's) $827

Ivo Puhonny (1876–1940), Winter Sport, Triberg, lithograph in colors, circa 1911, printed by Künstlerbund Karlsruhe, backed on japan, 35 x 23in.
(Christie's) $5,888

Roger Broders, Villard de Lans, SNCF, lithograph in colors, circa 1938, printed by l'Imp. Generale, Grenoble, 39¹/₂ x 24¹/₂in. (Christie's) $1,619

Erich Erler (1870–1946), Winter in Bayern, lithograph in colors, 1905, printed by Klein & Volbert, München, backed on linen, 28¹/₂ x 37¹/₂in. (Christie's) $4,784

Franz Lenhart, Les Sports d'Hiver en Italie, lithograph in colors, circa 1930, printed by B.V. Levi, Cortina, 39 x 24in. (Christie's) $3,128

Francisco Tamagno (1851–?), Chamonix, Mont-Blanc, PLM, lithograph in colors, circa 1900, printed by Emile Pecaud & Cie, Paris, 39 x 24in. (Christie's) $8,464

B.A. Zelenski, Womens World Ice Skating Championship, lithograph in colors, 1950, printed by Red Proletariat, backed on linen, 28¹/₂ x 39in. (Christie's) $1,011

Leo Keck, Davos Parsenn, offset lithograph in colors, circa 1940, printed by Eidenbenz-Seitz U.Co., St. Gallen, 40 x 25in. (Christie's) $1,840

Eric de Coulon, Jeunes Gens, lithograph in colors, circa 1925, printed by Money, Paris, 47 x 31¹/₂in. (Christie's) $1,747

Carl Kunst (1884–1912), Bilgeri-Ski-Ausrüstung, lithograph in colors, circa 1910, printed by Reichhold & Lang, München, 20 x 30in. (Christie's) $2,576

Anonymous, Winter Sports in Switzerland, American Express, lithograph in colors, circa 1908, backed on japan, 39¹/₂ x 25in. (Christie's) $10,120

Amish cotton piecework crib quilt, probably midwestern United States, circa 1930, the black quilted background with 'bricks' pattern marked in wool in wine, black, and moss green, 37¹/₈ x 33¹/₈in. (Skinner) $5,175

Mennonite patchwork cotton quilt, Pennsylvania, circa 1935, the overall geometric pattern worked in lemon yellow, red, navy, and olive, with orange and sky blue border, on brown calico backing, 90½ x 91⁵/₈in. (Skinner) $862

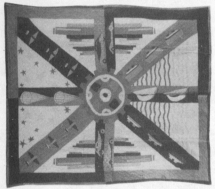

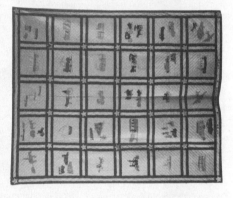

An appliqued cotton quilted coverlet, American, 20th century, worked on a white ground depicting a central wheel with spokes and radiating cars, sailboats, oceanliners, 80½ x 71½in. (Christie's) $2,530

A pieced and appliqued cotton quilted coverlet, American, dated 1939, worked in thirty squares depicting various forms of transportation, 89½ x 74in. (Christie's) $3,450

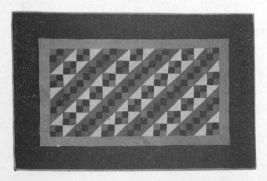

Amish cotton piecework crib quilt, midwestern United States, early 20th century, the black background with square patches worked in black, royal blue, teal, and gray with quilted violet border and surround, 53½ x 34¾in. (Skinner) $2,415

Pieced and appliqued quilt Remember the Maine, Mary Dunn Leroy, Lakewood, New York, circa 1898, the field of four American flags with appliqued letters, the outer border in concentric red and white stripes, 70 x 70in. (Skinner) $6,325

A pieced cotton coverlet, signed *Sarah E. Bosworth, Bristol, Rhode Island*, circa 1883, worked in various colored calicos and chintzes, in 144 squares each in the Kansas sunflower pattern, 88¼ x 88¼in.
(Christie's) $1,840

Hooked bed rug, probably northern New England, 19th century, loose weave butternut dyed wool ground with hooked wool floral design in green, cerise, and coral, 80 x 70in.
(Skinner) $575

A pieced and appliqued cotton quilted coverlet, Pennsylvania, third quarter 19th century, worked in red, green and yellow solids and calico cottons in the Harvest Sun pattern, 86 x 86in.   (Christie's) $1,380

A pieced and appliqued cotton crib quilt, American, circa 1845–55, worked pink, red, blue, green and mustard cottons and calicos in the Star of Bethlehem pattern, 46¼ x 47½in.   (Christie's) $2,530

A pieced and appliquéd cotton quilted coverlet, Pennsylvania, circa 1865, worked in the Star of Bethlehem pattern, 75in. x 74in.
(Christie's) $3,450

A fine pieced and appliquéd cotton quilt top, Arthur Schuman, Berne, Berks County, Pennsylvania, late 19th century, approx. 80in. x 80in.
(Sotheby's) $460

Fine crazy quilt, 19th century, in jewel-tone velvets, satins, brocades, and silks, pieces decorated with many flowers, a child blowing out cake candles, and a bird in a marsh, 60 x 70in.
(Eldred's) $715

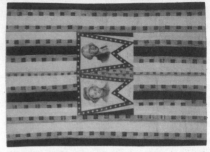

A pieced, appliquéd and printed cotton coverlet, American, circa 1876, worked in a Bars pattern and centering printed portraits of Martha and George Washington, 75¼in. x 55¼in.
(Christie's) $4,600

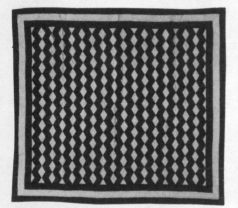

A pieced cotton calico 'Tumbling Blocks' quilt, initialed AL, American, early 20th century, composed or red, green, and yellow printed calico patches, approximately 82 x 74in. (Sotheby's) $1,035

A fine and rare Mennonite pieced cotton 'Delectable Mountain' cradle quilt, Pennsylvania, late 19th century, approx. 36in. x 35in.
(Sotheby's) $3,162

Log cabin pieced quilt, America, 1860-80, with assembly block style and multi color strips of fabric, 70½in. x 71in. (Skinner) $805

Appliqué quilt, America, 19th century, potted tulip design with border of birds amidst foliage, worked in green and red calicos on a white ground, 92½ x 94½in.
(Skinner) $978

Pieced and appliqued quilt, America, circa 1930, with repeating design of seated cats, 84½ x 63in. (Skinner) $1,265

Pieced and appliqued bow tie Amish quilt, early 20th century, with black ground and light green bow tie design, 82½ x 71½in. (Skinner) $862

An appliquéd cotton floral quilt and a stenciled cotton quilted coverlet, American, 19th century, the first composed on green, pink and red solid and calico patches on a white ground, approximately 84 x 86in. (Sotheby's) (Two) $805

A pieced and appliqued cotton quilted coverlet, American, circa 1910, worked on white ground, centering a Victorian house surrounded by abstract flowers, 86 x 78½in. (Christie's) $575

Pieced and appliqué quilt, America, 19th century, Star of Bethlehem design with various appliquéd potted flowering plants on a white ground, 85 x 88in. (Skinner) $748

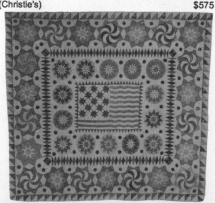

A pieced and appliquéd cotton quilted coverlet, American, circa 1865, centering an American flag enclosed by sawtooth border, 83in. x 90¼in. (Christie's) $20,700

A Sonaphone Type M6C French designer radio, circa 1952.
(Auction Team Köln) $190

A 2-valve Bausatz receiver with two reels, circa 1920.
(Auction Team Köln) $297

An SNR Excelsior 55 designer radio, 1954.
(Auction Team Köln) $474

A Blaupunkt Point Blue loudspeaker, export model, circa 1930.
(Auction Team Köln) $56

A Braun Type 100 B/54 4-valve battery portable radio, 1954.
(Auction Team Köln) $210

A Mende 98N 4-valve radio, circa 1932, case damaged.
(Auction Team Köln) $129

A Philips Autosuper Elomar RAW 4E car radio, specially for VW Beetles, 1949.
(Auction Team Köln) $541

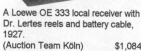

A Loewe OE 333 local receiver with Dr. Lertes reels and battery cable, 1927.
(Auction Team Köln) $1,084

A Braun BSK 239D portable radio with 5-valves and later power pack, 1938/9.
(Auction Team Köln) $257

A Telefunken 33 WL, original fascia, cover and base repainted, circa 1930
(Auction Team Köln) $224

An early English 2-valve Marconiphone V2 radio, in superb condition, 1922.
(Auction Team Köln) $1,811

A Blaupunkt radio-2 W 149, with valves, circa 1947.
(Auction Team Köln) $142

An Ozarka Senior American 5 valve battery radio, circa 1925.
(Auction Team Köln) $323

A Seibt EA381 radio with original valves, 1930.
(Auction Team Köln) $1,552

A radio Cinéphone film projector with radio and record player, circa 1950.
(Auction Team Köln) $541

A Zenith Model K 725 7-valve, 110v, bakelite radio, with built -in aerial, circa 1945.
(Auction Team Köln) $05

A Philco Transitone Model 49-602 portable battery radio, 4 valves, circa 1945.
(Auction Team Köln) $45

A Telefunken 230W 'cat's head' radio, in good original condition, circa 1933.
(Auction Team Köln) $323

A Bajazzo 51 Telefunken portable 3-band radio, battery or mains powered, circa 1951.
(Auction Team Köln) $116

A Blaupunkt B VII 3-valve battery radio with Blaupunkt reels, valves replaced, 1928/9.
(Auction Team Köln) $1,940

A Zenith Model 6 Y 001 portable radio with 6-valve battery and mains receiver, circa 1943.
(Auction Team Köln) $65

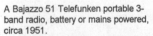

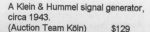

A Mende Type M 169/35 bakelite 3-valve radio with wave trap, 1935.
(Auction Team Köln) $102

National Panasonic for Matsushita Electric Industrial Co. Ltd., Japan, portable radio model 'R-725', circa 1969, plastic.
(Sotheby's) $187

A Klein & Hummel signal generator, circa 1943.
(Auction Team Köln) $129

A favourite black and white leather motorcycle jacket belonging to Jimi Hendrix, designed with three front zipper pockets.
(Christie's) $13,800

A September 1966 copy of Datebook magazine, signed by John Lennon, featuring Paul McCartney on the cover.
(Christie's) $2,070

A black satin and lycra bustier with front hook closure, ribbed back and elastic straps made for Madonna, with a letter of provenance.
(Christie's) $6,900

A circa 1970s black and white poster of Van Morrison, pictured with guitar, signed in blue ink, 34 x 22½in., framed.
(Christie's) $403

A 1964 set of four Beatles Dolls, wearing black suits with trademark bowl-style haircuts, with facsimile signatures in gold, 5in.
(Christie's) $1,150

(What's The Story) Morning Glory?, C.D., inside booklet signed in black felt tip by Liam, Noel Gallagher, Bonehead, Paul McGuigan and Alan White. (Bonhams) $512

A rare Beatles concert poster, featuring Ringo in various poses dressed in a Los Angeles Dodger baseball uniform, with an unused ticket for Press Box seating.
(Christie's) $5,520

Jimi Hendrix, a three page unpublished lyric on United Airlines notepaper, including illustrations in Jimi's hand, dated *June 5th 1969*.
(Bonhams) $24,000

Jimi Hendrix, a circa late 1960s sheet of handwritten, unreleased lyrics by the artist.
(Christie's) $4,600

A circa 1950s black and white photograph of Buddy Holly and the Crickets, mounted with square yellow paper, signed *Buddy Holly, Jerry Allison* and *Joe Mauldin.* (Christie's) $1,380

A distinctive black wool top hat worn by Guns n' Roses guitarist Slash, signed in gold marker, *Slash '94.* (Christie's) $1,380

A circa 1960s black and white photograph of the Rolling Stones, inscribed and signed by all five members of the group, 8 x 10in. (Christie's) $805

A circa early 1950s, tobacco sunburst finish, acoustic Southern Jumbo Gibson guitar, serial no. Z193328, owned and played by Hank Williams. (Christie's) $112,500

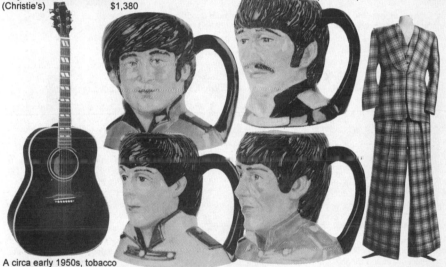

A set of four Royal Doulton Beatles character jugs showing each one dressed in Sgt. Pepper military costume. (Bonhams) $1,152

A suit worn by Elton John in the music video for 'Don't Go Breaking My Heart', his duet with singer Kiki Dee. (Christie's) $5,750

A circa 1960s letter, addressed to a fan, and signed by Paul McCartney, additionally signed on the reverse in blue ink by all four Beatles, 8 x 6in. framed. (Christie's) $1,610

A trademark work shirt worn by Bob Marley during his TUFF GOING UPRISING tour, the circa 1980 shirt is of heavy blue denim with front white metal snap closures. (Christie's) $6,900

The Beatles, the album 'Yesterday And Today', 1966, Capitol Records, stereo, T2553, with 'Butcher' cover, 12½ x 12½in. (Christie's) $1,093

Roy Orbison, signed and inscribed 8 x 10in., head and shoulders. (Vennett-Smith) $118

The Spice Girls, signed 8 x 10in., by all five, in multi-colored felt tip. (Vennett-Smith) $140

Gene Vincent, signed 8 x 10in., head and shoulders. (Vennett-Smith) $190

The Beatles, signed 8 x 10in., by John Lennon, Paul McCartney, George Harrison and Ringo Starr individually, showing them full-length all holding sunglasses. (Vennett-Smith) $2,722

A page from an autograph book circa 1963 signed in blue or black biro by *Paul McCartney, George Harrison* and *Ringo Starr*, inscribed with Lennon's secretarial signature, probably by Ringo Starr, 15½ x 9in. framed. (Christie's) $643

The Rolling Stones, scarce early signed and inscribed 8 x 10in., showing them half-length on boat on Thames, signed by Mick Jagger, Charlie Watts, Keith Richard, Bill Wyman and Brian Jones. (Vennett-Smith) $858

Freddie Mercury, signed color 8½ x 12in. heavystock magazine photograph, full-length performing at Live Aid. (Vennett-Smith) $215

Bob Dylan, signed 9 x 7½in., head and shoulders standing with snooker cue. (Vennett-Smith) $338

The Rolling Stones, signed piece, 7½ x 4½in., signed by Brian Jones, Mick Jagger, Bill Wyman, Charlie Watts, Keith Richard. (Vennett-Smith) $231

Paul McCartney, signed and inscribed 8 x 10in., half-length holding guitar.
(Vennett-Smith) $182

Personality poster of Marc Bolan, photo by Carol Sheeham, 1974.
(Bonhams) $96

Madonna, signed color 8 x 10in., overmounted, framed and glazed.
(Vennett-Smith) $165

Genesis, signed color 8 x 10in., by Phil Collins, Tony Banks and Mike Rutherford, 1993.
(Vennett-Smith) $70

Spice Girls, signed 8 x 10in., showing girls in bikinis or basque, signed by all five.
(Vennett-Smith) $190

Bruce Springsteen, signed and inscribed color 8 x 10in., three quarter length singing, 1992.
(Vennett-Smith) $100

Diana Ross, signed and inscribed color 8 x 10in., full-length in skimpy outfit, 1993.
(Vennett-Smith) $80

The Rolling Stones, signed 5¹/₂ x 4¹/₂in., by all five.
(Vennett-Smith) $660

Paul McCartney, signed and inscribed 8 x 10in., half-length seated at organ.
(Vennett-Smith) $173

The Beatles, a Parlophone Records publicity postcard, 1963, signed on the front in blue ink or biro by all four members of the group, 3¾ x 6in. (Christie's) $3,312

A two-tone blue and gray silk tailored jacket made for John Lennon for the film production of 'Help!' made by Doug Millings & Co., London. (Bonhams) $1,280

The Beatles, a rare early publicity photograph, 1962, signed on the reverse in blue biro by all four members of the group, 10 x 8in. (Christie's) $2,392

Woodstock, the original program and tickets (2) with a copy of Life Magazine covering the event, (The Good Old Days). (Bonhams) $480

John Lennon, a piece of card signed and inscribed in black biro *love John Lennon* and annotated with Lennon's caricature portraits of his and Yoko's smiling faces – 3¼ x 6⁵/₈in. (Christie's) $1,011

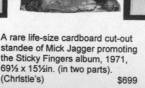

A piece of paper signed in blue biro by Jimi Hendrix, 3 x 3¾in. with a black and white photograph of subject performing at the Isle of Wight Festival, 1970, 20½ x 13in. (Christie's) $643

A rare life-size cardboard cut-out standee of Mick Jagger promoting the Sticky Fingers album, 1971, 69½ x 15½in. (in two parts). (Christie's) $699

A piece of paper signed in blue biro Buddy Holly, 1½ x 3in. in common mount with a black and white machine-print photograph, overall measurements 15 x 10¾in. framed. (Christie's) $699

An album cover 'The Rolling Stones', signed on the reverse by Brian Jones, Mick Jagger, Keith Richard, Bill Wyman.
(Bonhams) $608

Led Zeppelin, a cowhide native American Indian jacket with tassel closure and fringed front and back, decorated with multi-colored beading to neck and arms.
(Bonhams) $880

Beatles, a copy of 'Please Please Me', signed on the reverse of the album cover by all four Beatles.
(Bonhams) $3,040

John Lennon, a rare promotional display card Listen To This Dream for the single #9 Dream, 1974, from the Walls And Bridges album, signed in black felt pen John Lennon – 13¾ x 10¾in.
(Christie's) $1,840

Buddy Holly and The Crickets, a piece of paper signed in blue biro by Buddy Holly, Joe Mauldin and Jerry Allison, 4 x 3in. with a black and white photograph of the group.
(Christie's) $1,747

David Bowie, a temporary six-month driver's licence issued in Nicosia, with driver's details: David R. Jones [of] Ledra Palace and date of issue: 19th July 1971, 2¼ x 1⁵/₈in. (Christie's) $459

Ringo Starr, a two piece stage suit of mushroom worsted, 1963, the collarless, single-breasted jacket piped in black.
(Christie's) $11,040

John Lennon, LENNON, John In His Own Write, London: Jonathan Cape, 1964, first edition, 4to. front end paper signed in black ink John Lennon. (Christie's) $1,011

Queen, a sleeve for the LP 'Sheer Heart Attack', signed on the reverse by the band members. (Bonhams) $240

Gene Vincent, a short-sleeved stage shirt of chocolate brown cotton with imitation leopard skin front, given by Vincent to Johnny Carroll in 1957. (Christie's) $1,472

Led Zeppelin, 'Song Remains the Same' L.P. cover, signed by all band members. (Bonhams) $352

A pair of gold colored Ray Ban Aviator sunglasses worn by George Michael on the Faith tour, the Nelson Mandela video and the book cover 'In Praise of a Tour de Force', accompany this lot. (Bonhams) $1,600

Six original Dezo Hoffmann photographs of The Beatles, each with studio stamp on verso, mostly 8 x 10in. (Bonhams) $1,408

The Beatles, USA one-sheet for the 1964 United Artists film 'A Hard Days Night', mounted on acid-free archival tissue paper, framed and glazed, 27 x 41in. (Bonhams) $640

Bob Dylan, music sheet for 'The Times They Are A Changin' U.S.A. edition, signed on the front cover in pencil, framed and glazed, 11 x 14in. (Bonhams) $992

A large 26in. bass drum skin, painted with the black and white Queen logo, as used on the 1977 U.S. Tour and won in a Roger Taylor competition, signed *Roger Taylor X*. (Bonhams) $3,200

Sex Pistols, a copy of 'God Save the Queen' single, signed on the Queen's image by Sid Vicious, Johnny Rotten, Steve Jones and Paul Cook. (Bonhams) $512

An album The Beatles' Hottest Hits, 1965, Parlophone, 33¹/3 r.p.m., Eskimo cover, Danish, second edition. (Christie's) $827

Stevie Ray Vaughan, an 8 x 10in. black and white portrait, signed in blue metallic marker with a good full signature.
(Bonhams) $320

Crosby, Stills, Nash and Young, 'American Dreams' LP cover, signed by all four Legends.
(Bonhams) $160

Sam Cooke and others, a concert poster Supersonic Attractions presents Sam Cooke, featuring Jerry Butler, Dee Clark, The Crystals, The Drifters, Macon, Friday, May 17th, early 1960s, 35 x 22in. (Christie's) $920

Hand printed poster, black lettering on a white ground for a Beatles concert at the Azena Ballroom, Sheffield 12.2. 1963, signed and stamped by Colin Duffield who hand printed the poster.
(Bonhams) $2,720

A concert poster Supersonic Attractions Presents Jackie Wilson Mr. Excitement, also featuring Jerry Butler, Chuck Jackson, The Impressions, Auditorium, Macon, Friday, November 8th, early 1960s, 35 x 22in. (Christie's) $920

An official Queen denim jacket with the Queen logo embroidered to the back, signed on the back in black felt tip pen by all band members.
(Bonhams) $608

Oasis, LP flat, 'Definitely Maybe', signed by all five current members... Noel Gallagher, Liam (Gallagher), Paul Arthurs, Paul McGuigan, and Alan White.
(Bonhams) $640

Madonna, a half-length color publicity photograph of subject at the American Music Awards, 1985, signed and inscribed in black felt pen love Madonna, 9½ x 6½in.
(Christie's) $238

Buddy Holly and The 'Chirpin' Crickets, souvenir tour program 1958, signed on the back cover by Buddy Holly, Jo Mauldin and Jerry Allison. (Bonhams) $1,040

A Melody Maker 'Poll' questionnaire, 1969, the coupon torn from the publication and completed by John Lennon in black felt pen, 6¾in. x 10¼in. (Christie's) $4,784

A pink feather boa worn by Janis Joplin, accompanied by a photograph, 6ft. 7in. in length. (Christie's) $5,175

Fleetwood Mac, a Yamaha F-310 acoustic guitar in a natural finish, mahogany body, signed on the body *Mick Fleetwood, Stevie Nicks, John McVie, Christine McVie* and *Lindsay Buckingham*. (Christie's) $1,104

Madonna, a stage dress of aquamarine simulated silk and net embroidered with rhinestones, with shawl collar, made for Madonna for her stage performance of True Blue and Pappa Don't Preach. (Christie's) $7,360

Blondie, a pair of black stretch leather thigh-high stage boots worn by Debbie Harry. (Bonhams) $640

Jimi Hendrix and others, Ten concert and promotional posters, majority late 1960s, including a rare Marquee Club poster advertising various appearances, 30 x 20in. (Christie's) $4,416

An Aerosmith drumhead, signed in felt pen by all band members. (Bonhams) $320

John Lennon, LENNON, John A Spaniard In The Works, London, Jonathan Cape, 1965, 4to. front end paper signed and inscribed in black ink *To Victor [Spinetti] love from John*. (Christie's) $552

Madonna, a stage bra of floral cotton, the underwired cups and straps, made for Madonna's stage performance during her 1993 Girlie Show Tour.
(Christie's) $4,048

Beatles, a full set of autographs on a double album page mounted with John Lennon's cigarette butt and a lock of his hair.
(Bonhams) $1,920

A Pink Floyd 'Animals' promotional record shop display in the form of a large three dimensional pig record rack made of molded plastic, 32 x 44in. (Christie's) $736

A pair of cotton bell-bottom style pants worn by Janis Joplin, designed in a multi-color flower motif. (Christie's) $10,350

John Lennon, a rare 12-string Rickenbacker custom red GLO serial no. G.1.3950, 1967 owned and played by John Lennon.
(Bonhams) $36,800

David Bowie, an ornate multi-colored two-piece stage suit of intricately patterned worsted, the jacket signed inside on cream lining in black felt pen Bowie '91.
(Christie's) $4,784

Ringo Starr, signed postcard, head and shoulders, holding photo of himself.
(Vennett-Smith) $82

The Rolling Stones, signed color center page, 20 x 13in., by all five including Brian Jones.
(Vennett-Smith) $627

George Harrison, signed color 5 x 7in., half-length in recent years.
(Vennett-Smith) $182

An autographed photograph of Elvis as a baby, signed *'Little Baby Elvis' Priscilla & Lisa 1970*, 11 x 4in. (Bonhams) $6,636

Elvis Presley's red satin shirt, with high collar, silk pinstripe throughout. (Bonhams) $2,528

Elvis Presley's Sun record collection, 1954-55, Elvis' personal copies of his first five Sun releases in original sleeves, each signed by Elvis. (Bonhams) $23,700

A poster for 'That's the Way it is' signed by Elvis Presley, MGM 1970, the three sheet poster, 81 x 41in. (Bonhams) $711

Elvis Presley's Gretsch Chet Atkins Country Gentleman Guitar, circa 1960s, the double cut-away stained body with painted 'f-holes', together with letters of authenticity. (Bonhams) $56,880

An autographed Elvis Presley tour stop poster, 1970s, signed on a poster of Elvis on stage in the legendary 'Peacock' suit, 18 x 12in. (Bonhams) $664

An autographed poster of Elvis in concert, early 1970s, with Elvis in the 'I Got Lucky' suit on the front, (Bonhams) $822

Elvis Presley's TCB sunglasses, circa 1972, with silver-plated neo-style frames, the initials EP across the bridge in gold plate. (Bonhams) $6,320

An autographed Elvis Presley tour stop poster, 1970s, signed in black pen on a color World Championship Attendance promotional tour stop poster, 11 x 14in. (Bonhams) $980

Elvis Presley's Army uniform button, circa 1958-60, a brass button from Elvis Presley's winter army uniform, with a letter of authenticity. (Bonhams) $1,738

A figurine of Elvis Presley in concert, hand painted porcelain figure made by Royal Orleans, 9in. high. (Bonhams) $411

Elvis Presley's radio, circa 1958-60, the Phillips transistor radio used by Elvis Presley whilst stationed in the Army near Bad Nauheim. (Bonhams) $4,424

Elvis Presley's gold lamé jacket, 1950s, together with a signed photograph stating origin from Scotty Moore. (Bonhams) $8,690

Elvis' blue & white jacket from 'Speedway', 1968, the blue wool jacket with two 1½in. off-white vertical stripes on the left side panel. (Bonhams) $10,270

A poster for 'Elvis on Tour' signed by Elvis Presley, MGM 1972, the one sheet poster, 41 x 28in. (Bonhams) $948

Elvis Presley's unreleased acetate of 'Milkcow Blues Boogie, circa 1955, 12in. acetate stamped *Audiodisc 3291 Audiodisc - Made in USA.* (Bonhams) $14,220

An autographed photograph of Elvis & Priscilla Presley, 1967, signed by both on a color photograph of the honeymooning Presley couple at their Palm Springs home, 8 x 8in. (Bonhams) $2,370

An autographed photograph of Elvis Presley in concert, signed on a color shot of Elvis wearing the 'White Lionhead' suit on stage in Texas in 1971, 10 x 8in. (Bonhams) $664

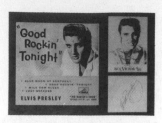

An 8 x 10in. color phototgraph of Elvis during his Vegas period signed in blue pen, *Best Wishes Elvis Presley*. mounted, framed and glazed. (Bonhams) $608

Elvis Presley's bomber jacket, the red velvet jacket with elasticated black wool trim to collar, cuffs and waistband. (Bonhams) $1,580

Elvis Presley, an early Elvis signature matted with copies of an R.C.A. promo photograph of an H.M.V. single cover, mounted, framed and glazed, 15 x 12in. (Bonhams) $608

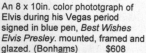

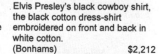

Elvis Presley, a one-piece stage suit of cream wool with high collar and flared trouser legs, the flared split cuffs trimmed with two rows of covered buttons. (Christie's) $14,720

A piece of lined paper signed and inscribed in red biro *thanks Elvis Presley*, 3 x 4in. in common mount with a single record I'm Left, You're Right, She's Gone, 1955. (Christie's) $883

Elvis Presley's black cowboy shirt, the black cotton dress-shirt embroidered on front and back in white cotton. (Bonhams) $2,212

A black and white machine-print photograph taken from a fanzine, circa 1960, signed and inscribed in blue ink *Best Wishes, Elvis Presley* – 8 x 6¼in. (Christie's) $736

A piece of lined notepaper signed and inscribed in black felt pen *Best Wishes Elvis Presley*, 2½ x 3½in., with a black and white photograph of subject in the late 1950s, 12 x 9½in. (Christie's) $515

An autographed photograph of Elvis Presley, circa 1958, signed *Best wishes Elvis Presley* on an RCA promotional photograph. (Bonhams) $948

An autographed photograph of Elvis Presley, late 1950s, signed *Best Wishes Elvis Presley* in ballpen, 8 x 10in. (Bonhams) $1,896

An RCA Victor Records Elvis' Great LP Catalog, (sic) 1964, signed on the back cover in black biro *Elvis Presley*, 7 x 3½in. (Christie's) $643

Elvis Presley, The King's autograph *Best Wishes Elvis Presley*, matted with an 8 x 8in. color photograph. (Bonhams) $240

Elvis Presley, an 8 x 10in. color photograph taken in April 1974 in Kansas City and signed in black pen *Best Wishes Elvis Presley* in Las Vegas the following December. (Bonhams) $240

A rare page of lyrics in Elvis Presley's hand for I'm Gonna Sleep with One Eye Open, circa 1959, with a black and white machine-print photograph of Elvis being interviewed by the press whilst in the U.S. Army, 9¾ x 7¼in. (Christie's) $7,360

A black and white publicity postcard circa 1959, signed and inscribed in blue biro *Thank you Elvis Presley* additionally signed on the reverse *Elvis Presley*, 6 x 4in. (Christie's) $589

An autographed Las Vegas International Menu, 1971, signed *Elvis Presley* on the souvenir menu printed with a giant close-up of Elvis in the 'Blue Tapestry' suit, 14 x 11in. (Bonhams) $948

Elvis Presley, An R.C.A. Records LP cover, 'A Legendary Performer, Vol 1', signed on the front cover in black ink, circa 1975. (Bonhams) $640

An autographed Las Vegas Hilton Menu, August 1974, signed *Elvis Presley* in black ink on the souvenir menu printed with Elvis in the 'Aloha From Hawaii' suit. (Bonhams) $664

Anatolian prayer rug, late 19th / early 20th century, empty abrashed red field, gold spandrels, 5ft. 5in. x 3ft. 8in. (Skinner) $1,150

Lotzweiler hooked rug, Germany, early 20th century, oriental design with three rectangular panels, 6ft. x 5ft. (Skinner) $1,265

Melas rug, Southwest Anatolia, last quarter 19th century, 5ft. 6in. x 3ft. 6in. (Skinner) $2,530

Serab rug, Northwest Persia, second quarter 20th century, serrated hexagonal medallion in navy and sky blue, red, rose, ivory, and blue-green on the camel field, 5ft. 6in. x 3ft. 3in. (Skinner) $633

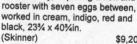

Figural hooked rug, New England, 19th century, depicting a hen and rooster with seven eggs between, worked in cream, indigo, red and black, 23¾ x 40¾in. (Skinner) $9,200

A Keiseri silk rug, the olive green lozenge-shaped painted medallion with central flowerhead surrounded by a deep red field, 89 x 53½in. (Christie's) $827

Shirvan rug, East Caucasus, last quarter 19th century, 'keyhole' medallion inset with three star-in-octagon motifs, 5ft. 8in. x 3ft. 7in. (Skinner) $2,530

Evelyn Wild, abstract rug, 1920s, wool, woven in shades of navy oyster, black, aubergine and fawn with a linear design, 53½ x 46in. (Sotheby's) $8,066

A fine Heriz rug, the navy blue field woven with a rectangular dusky pink gul, 84 x 50½in. (Christie's) $3,680

A tufted rug designed by E. McKnight Kauffer, 1930s, central design of intersecting squares and rectangles in shades of mushroom, beige and cream and mid-blue, 50 x 70½in.
(Christie's) $5,140

A silk Kashan prayer rug, the fawn field woven with a pictorial scene centered with a shepherd tending his flock, 66 x 47½in.
(Christie's) $2,024

A very fine Isfahan Serafian rug, the ivory field with a single palmette at each end issuing large scrolling serrated leaves, 5ft. x 3ft.5in.
(Christie's) $2,215

Karabagh long rug, South Caucasus, late 19th century, three large Lesghi stars in navy and sky blue, rust, light camel and blue-green on the midnight blue field, 9ft. 2in. x 4ft. 6in.
(Skinner) $1,840

An American pictorial hooked rug, late 19th century, worked in red, green, orange, blue, brown, beige and gray fabric with a steamboat in a harbour, 23¹⁄₂ x 39¹⁄₂in.
(Sotheby's) $2,300

Kuba rug, Northeast Caucasus, last quarter 19th century, Alpan design with two and a half diamond medallions each surrounded by four 'crayfish', 5ft. 6in. x 3ft. 9in.
(Skinner) $633

Floral hooked rug, America, 20th century, repeating design of flowerheads and other foliate devices, 66 x 98in.
(Skinner) $978

Tekke rug, West Turkestan, second half 19th century, three columns with six chuval guls on the rust field, 3ft. 6in. x 3ft. 4in.
(Skinner) $978

A fine Afshar rug, the shaded indigo field with rows of stylized animals, angular sprays and occasional jewelry motif, 6ft.4in. x 4ft.5in.
(Christie's) $1,201

Baluch rug, Northeast Persia, last quarter 19th century, rosette medallion surrounded by flowering shrubs, 7ft. 7in. x 5ft. 2in. (Skinner) $1,840

Geometric hooked rug, America, dated *Jan 19, 1927*, allover pattern of stars, worked in blue, red, green, yellow, gray and brown yarns, 29½ x 39¾in. (Skinner) $632

Sarouk rug, West Persia, early 20th century, floral sprays and delicate leafy vines on the midnight blue field, 4ft. 9in. x 3ft. 4in. (Skinner) $1,955

Kuba rug, Northeast Caucasus, last quarter 19th century , two columns of palmette motifs in red, gold, ivory, and camel on the sky blue field, 5ft. 10in. x 3ft. 8in. (Skinner) $633

Karachopf Kazak rug, Southwest Caucasus, second half 19th century, large octagonal medallion and four star-filled squares on the red field, 6ft. 6in. x 5ft. 9in. (Skinner) $3,565

Kuba rug, Northeast Caucasus, last quarter 19th century, three large serrated and radiating medallions and small motifs, rose, ivory double S-motif border, 6ft. x 4ft. 5in. (Skinner) $2,300

Shirvan rug, East Caucasus, last quarter 19th century, large octagonal medallion inset with diamond lattice with palmettes, 5ft. 9in. x 4ft. (Skinner) $1,725

Shirvan rug, East Caucasus, last quarter 19th century, two stepped hexagonal medallions and small motifs on the abrashed sky blue field, 3ft. 7in. x 3ft. (Skinner) $3,105

Kuba rug, Northeast Caucasus, last quarter 19th century, staggered rows of palmette motifs in red, gold, ivory and blue-green, 4ft. 10in. x 3ft. 8in. (Skinner) $1,840

Shirvan rug, East Caucasus, last quarter 19th century, 'keyhole' medallion inset with three star-in-octagon motifs, 5ft. x 3ft. 6in. (Skinner) $805

Kurd saddle cover, Northwest Persia, early 20th century, palmettes and small geometric motifs on the midnight blue field, 1ft. 9in. x 1ft. 8in. (Skinner) $230

Anatolian rug, last quarter 19th century, large concentric hooked diamond medallion on the navy blue field, 3ft. 5in.x 2ft. 8in. (Skinner) $1,610

Kazak rug, Southwest Caucasus, late 19th century, gabled rectangular medallion inset with star-filled square in royal blue, ivory, camel, and blue-green, 6ft. x 3ft. 10in. (Skinner) $690

Figural hooked rug depicting pointer, New England, dated *1901*, and titled in red, the charcoal dog with light brown ears, 30 x 35¼in. (Skinner) $4,140

Kuba rug, Northeast Caucasus, last quarter 19th century, five Lesghi stars in navy and sky blue, rust, rose, and blue-green on the black field, 5ft. 6in. x 3ft. 10in. (Skinner) $1,610

Avar rug, Northeast Caucasus, late 19th century, large red and ivory cruciform blossoming plant on the navy blue field, 4ft. 6in. by 3ft. 3in. (Skinner) $978

Tekke rug, West Turkestan, late 19th century, three columns of six midnight blue, red, and ivory chuval guls on the rust field, 4ft. x 3ft. 5in. (Skinner) $345

Fereghan rug, West Persia, early 20th century, stepped diamond medallion and matching spandrels inset with rosette lattice, 6ft. 5in. x 4ft. 8in. (Skinner) $2,645

HISTORICAL FACTS
Samplers

Samplers, from the French exemplaire, were originally a record of embroidery patterns, which could then be copied. The earliest dated one is English, made in 1586 and worked by Jane Bostock. Early examples are rare, for they were made only by the leisured upper classes. By the mid 1700s however, sampler work was spreading to all classes. By this time too, the original function of the sampler changed to become more and more an apprentice piece for young girls.

During the 18th and 19th centuries, most schools and orphanages set girls to stitch samplers as part of their general education. These could be of two types, plain sewing samplers, or embroidered examples, featuring the alphabet and numbers.

Most embroidered samplers consist of one or two simple alphabets enclosed in a narrow border, and are usually done on coarse woollen tammy, or sometimes linen. 18th and 19th century samplers often included a moralising text or some pictorial content.

One is not buying just a piece of cloth, but hours, months, sometimes even years of a person's time and devotion. By and large, the earlier the sampler, the more money it will fetch, condition, intricacy and all else being equal. The USA is a particularly rich source of samplers, and it is generally early American examples which fetch the largest sums.

Needlework sampler, 'Hannah Mosher Aged 12 Hollis 8 June 98,' dated '1798' 17 x 16³/8in. (Skinner) $1,380

An English needlework sampler, signed Margaret Littlefield, dated 1803, 16 x 11½in. (Sotheby's) $1,000

An 18th century sampler primarily in green and black worked with a verse and signed Elizabeth Mills's Work Aged 11 years, 17 x 18in. (David Lay) $311

A sampler by Rebecca Hannah Wood, 1842, with pious verse and pastoral landscape, 21 x 26in. (Christie's) $385

Needlework sampler, 'Mary L. Spearght aged 12 years', alphabets and pious verse with various foliate and geometric motifs, 17 x 16½in. (Skinner) $1,495

Needlework sampler, Wrought by Eliza Ann Hayward Aged 12 April 24th 1827, alphabets above pious verse, 17³/8 x 13³/4in. (Skinner) $2,875

Needlework sampler, *Cornelia Donaldson aged 9 years New York July 6th 1822*, 17¹/₈ x 13⁵/₈in. (Skinner) **$1,495**

Needlework sampler, 'Lydia Ritter aged 11years', probably Pennsylvania, upper panel of pious verses flanked by baskets of fruit and foliate sprays, 20¼ x 24¾in. (Skinner) **$1,265**

A sampler by Ellener Tovey, 1828, with a verse above a brick house and a lawn, 16½ x 20½in. (Christie's) **$559**

Needlework sampler, *Ruth Crandon Age 12*, upper panel of alphabets above lower panel of bands of foliate devices, 19⁵/₈in. x 13½in. (Skinner) **$1,495**

Needlework sampler, *Abigail Sawyer's Sampler Aged 11 years Phillipston June the 24, 1817. Massachusetts State*, 17¹/₈ x 17⁵/₈in. (Skinner) **$7,475**

A needlework sampler, attributed to Elizabeth Taylor, New Jersey, circa 1840, worked on a linen ground with a large yellow version of the Westtown School, 33 x 17³/₄in. (Sotheby's) **$5,462**

Needlework sampler, *Cornelia Ann Vanderveer's work July 8, 1835* alternating panels of pious verses and foliate devices. 20½in. x 17½in. (Skinner) **$920**

An English needlework sampler, signed *Mary Dunn*, dated *1797*, worked on a linen ground with a farm house, sheep and an apple tree, 14½ x 12¼in. (Sotheby's) **$1,610**

A needlework sampler, signed *Elvira Beal*, Randolph, Massachusetts, 1818-20, with alphabets above a landscape scene, 17¼ x 16¾in. (Sotheby's) **$12,650**

A George III sampler with front view of Queens Palace, trees, birds etc. by *E. Allen, Aged 11, January 23, 1818*, 22 x 17in. (Russell, Baldwin & Bright) $1,499

A needlework sampler, signed *Anne M. Dowell*, probably Delaware Valley, 19th century, worked on a green linen ground with bands of alphabets and numerals, 15¼ x 20in. (Sotheby's) $3,162

A needlework sampler, signed *Mary Beal*, probably Massachusetts, dated *1802*, worked on a linen ground with bands of alphabets, 20½ x 15in. (Sotheby's) $2,070

A needlework sampler, signed *Eliza Dutton*, Chester County, Pennsylvania, dated *1797*, the outer borders with blossoming vines issuing from vases, 16½ x 15¾in. (Sotheby's) $26,450

A fine needlework sampler, signed *Jane Hammell*, Burlington County, New Jersey, dated *1829*, worked on a linen ground with a brick house flanked by birds in trees, 17¼ x 17¾in. (Sotheby's) $40,250

A needlework sampler signed *Sally Alden*, Newton, Massachusetts, dated *June 14, 1811*, with alphabets and a pious verse above a house scene, 21¼ x 17¼in. (Sotheby's) $24,150

Needlework sampler, *Lois M. Buckminster A.*, alphabets above panel with floral spray, meandering vine and floral border, 16½ x 16½in. (Skinner) $2,070

Needlework family register, *Elizabeth H. Kay's work*, Pennsylvania, family register surrounded by foliate, bird and geometric motifs, 21⅝ x 22¾in. (Skinner) $1,955

Needlework sampler, *Mary Pollard born July 7th 1809 and wrought this June 17th 1824*, probably New Hampshire, 23⅝ x 17½in. (Skinner) $2,415

A George III child's needlework sampler, worked in colored silks with vases of flowers, Adam and Eve and the Tree of Life, 42cm.
(Bearne's) **$778**

Needlework sampler, *Mary Vallance*, probably Philadelphia, circa 1810-20, spread eagle above urns with flowering plants, 14 x 12⅝in.
(Skinner) **$1,610**

A fine sampler by Elizabeth Oxley, 1754, worked in colored silks with an angel announcing the Nativity to the shepherds, 20 x 21½in.
(Christie's) **$5,244**

An early Victorian needlework panel, by Betty Lindsey, worked with a view of Eaton Hall, enclosed by a continous band of stylized flowerheads and foliage, 23 x 24½in.
(Christie's) **$1,336**

A fine needlework sampler, signed *Rebekah Hathaway, Dighton, Massachusetts*, dated *1794*, worked on a linen ground with a brick house, 18¼ x 15¾in.
(Sotheby's) **$9,200**

Needlework sampler, *Waterford Township School Elizabeth Homer Kay's work wrought in the year 1809*, Pennsylvania, alphabets above pious verses, 17 x 16¼in.
(Skinner) **$1,725**

A needlework sampler, signed *Ann Drinkwater*, possibly New Jersey, dated *1823*, executed with a pious verse over a large pot of flowers, 21¾ x 18in.
(Sotheby's) **$5,750**

A Georgian sampler, worked with alphabet, numbers, birds and a verse entitled 'Friendship' and signed *Sarah Wheatley, May 1812*, 14½in. x 12¼in.
(Andrew Hartley) **$659**

A good William IV sampler by Merina Patten, 1835, showing in well-colored silks a Georgian house with a dog on its lawn, 16½ x 12¾in.
(David Lay) **$1,570**

Antique scrimshaw whale's tooth with polychrome decoration of Alwilda, the female pirate, 5¼in. long.
(Eldred's) $2,640

Engraved whale's tooth, mid-20th century, with decoration of a whale hunt, 6in. long.
(Eldred's) $121

Engraved whale's tooth, early 20th century, decorated with a ship on one side and horn of plenty on reverse, brass hinged lid, 5in. long.
(Eldred's) $220

Engraved whale's tooth, circa 1950, with polychrome decoration of a whale capture, inscribed *A.W. Sewell 1900*, 5in. long.
(Eldred's) $143

Engraved whale's tooth, mid-20th century, with polychrome decoration of a figurehead and bow spread, 5in. long.
(Eldred's) $99

Scrimshaw sperm whale's tooth, circa 1950, with whaleship and whale decoration, signed *Lammar*, 6in. long.
(Eldred's) $77

Antique American scrimshaw whale's tooth, with polychrome decoration of an eagle above crossed American flags above bust portrait of George Washington, 6in. long.
(Eldred's) $880

A pair of engraved scrimshaw whale's teeth, American, mid-19th century, each engraved and polychromed with a girl in fashionable dress, 5in. long.
(Sotheby's) $1,150

An engraved scrimshaw whale's tooth, American, mid-19th century, delicately engraved on either side with a fashionably dressed lady, 6in. long.
(Sotheby's) $920

Antique sperm whale's tooth, mounted as a vase, 6in. high.
(Eldred's) $303

Pair of whale's teeth 'Master of the Fleet' and 'Master's Wife', 4½in. long.
(Eldred's) $209

Antique American scrimshaw whale's tooth with polychrome decoration of George Washington, 6¼in. long.
(Eldred's) $825

A Müller No. 5 German chainstitch machine on contemporary wooden box base, circa 1930.
(Auction Team Köln) $59

An Original Bing German child's chainstitch sewing machine, on cast-iron base, with gold decoration.
(Auction Team Köln) $65

A New Home table bow shuttle sewing machine, American, circa 1900.
(Auction Team Köln) $61

A very rare Swedish swing shuttle machine by Öller, Stockholm, forerunner of L.M. Ericsson, circa 1865.
(Auction Team Köln) $1,422

A Frister & Rossmann German long shuttle standard sewing machine with painted head, circa 1900.
(Auction Team Köln) $74

An original Brunonia German swing shuttle sewing machine by Bremer and Brückmann Braunschweig with shuttle, 1895.
(Auction Team Köln) $109

A Grover & Baker type Norwegian swing-shuttle machine, with supplier's label *Johan Hammer, Trondheim*, circa 1880.
(Auction Team Köln) $142

Grover & Baker's Family Box Machine, the first portable sewing machine, with twin thread chainstitch, 1855.
(Auction Team Köln) $2,263

A Little Mother tinplate toy chainstitch sewing machine, American, circa 1935.
(Auction Team Köln) $102

A Husqvarna Model 2 standard treadle transverse shuttle machine, Swedish, circa 1874.
(Auction Team Köln) $420

A Grover & Baker American twin-thread chainstitch machine in its original wooden cabinet with cover, circa 1863.
(Auction Team Köln) $1,219

An American Florence step-stitch standard sewing machine, with elegant treadle, circa 1868.
(Auction Team Köln) $1,219

Shaker cherry case of three drawers, Mt. Lebanon, New York, 1830-40, signed *Made by Andrew Fortier Feb'ry 6th1881,* 39in. wide. (Skinner) $1,265

Shaker production cherry armless #3 web-back chair with rockers, Mount Lebanon, New York, 1880–1920, with identifying label. (Skinner) $460

Shaker cherry five drawer chest of drawers, New Lebanon, 36in. wide. (Skinner) $1,092

Shaker butternut woodbox, mid 19th century, the hinged lid with rounded edge on dovetail constructed box, 24½in. wide. (Skinner) $4,600

Shaker cherry and pine tripod stand, probably Mt. Lebanon, New York, circa 1830, the circular top with beveled edge resting on a rectangular cleat, diameter of top18in. (Skinner) $2,875

Butternut Shaker chest of drawers, Mt. Lebanon, circa 1880, the rectangular top above the case of five graduated quarter-round molded drawers, 40in. wide. (Skinner) $14,950

Shaker production maple #4 slat-back chair with rockers, Mount Lebanon, New York, 1880–1920, with dark stain, identifying Shaker label. (Skinner) $632

Shaker yellow painted pine and basswood chest of drawers, New Lebanon, New York, 1825-40, the case of four graduated molded drawers, 44in. wide. (Skinner) $5,175

Shaker one-drawer work table, 19th century, in pine with square tapered legs, ivory-inlaid escutcheon and turned wooden pull, top 21 x 17½in. (Eldred's) $1,320

Shaker painted cherry candlestand, New Lebanon, New York, 1820–40, the square top above a turned tapering classic center post and tripod base, 25¾in. high. (Skinner) $28,750

Shaker cherry and butternut sewing case, probably Enfield, Connecticut, circa 1840, on square tapering legs, 27in. wide. (Skinner) $23,000

A Shaker butternut tripod table, New Lebanon, New York, 1820–40, the circular top above a tapering columnar pedestal, 14³/₈in. diameter. (Christie's) $3,220

Shaker painted butternut and maple table with drawer, New England, circa 1820, the rectangular overhanging top with beveled edge, 19½in. wide. (Skinner) $7,475

Shaker pine chest of drawers, Harvard, Massachusetts, 1830–40, the rectangular top with rounded edge above a case of four graduated thumbmolded drawers on bracket feet, 39in. wide. (Skinner) $17,250

Shaker washed cherry workstand, Enfield, Connecticut, circa 1840, the classic one drawer stand with overhung hinged compartment, 26in. wide. (Skinner) $9,200

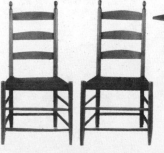

Shaker pine chest of drawers, probably New Lebanon, New York, mid 19th century, with five graduated drawers, 34in. wide. (Skinner) $690

A pair of Shaker chrome yellow stained tilter side chairs, probably Watervliet, New York, circa 1840, with three arched slats. (Skinner) $9,775

Shaker cherry drop leaf sewing case, probably Hancock, circa 1820, the overhanging rectangular top with a single drop leaf, 35½in. wide. (Skinner) $18,400

A 19th century carved shoemaker's sign decorated in black and gilt above a red sole and heel, 25in. long. (Russell Baldwin & Bright) $848

Pair of ladies snakeskin shoes with 2in. heels and pointed toes by A. G. Meek, Newport. (Christie's) $240

A lady's shoe overlaid with ivory wool embroidered in pale blue silk in chain stitch with an all over lattice, bound in pale blue silk, 1780s. (Christie's) $552

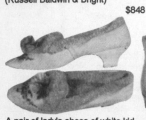

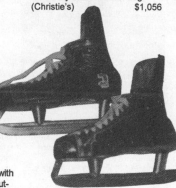

A pair of lady's shoes of white kid, lined and trimmed with self colored curly wool, with pointed toe and 1½in. Louis heel, 1880s. (Christie's) $280

A pair of transparent yellow rubberized ankle boots, stamped with Mary Quant daisy in heels, with Mary Quant carrier bag. (Christie's) $1,056

A lady's shoe of salmon pink satin, the vamp embroidered with a floral sprig in silver metal threads, 3in. heel, lined with white kid, circa 1760. (Christie's) $294

A pair of shoes of black leather with square rounded toe, the vamp cut-outs revealing crimson silk forming a stylized foliate design, probably French, circa 1860. (Christie's) $184

A pair of Red Doran's ice skates. (Du Mouchelles) $350

A pair of black velvet slippers, with square toe, no heels, the vamps embroidered in colored silks and metal threads, third quarter 19th century. (Christie's) $184

A pair of gentleman's slippers of midnight blue velvet, lined in salmon pink kid and white linen and bound in green velvet, with rounded toe and 1cm. wedge heel, probably 1860s. (Christie's) $202

A pair of black leather and scarlet canvas bondage boots, unlabeled, Boy, 1980s. (Christie's) $281

A pair of lady's boots of purple velvet with elasticated side panels, the uppers densely embroidered in gilt metal threads, rounded toe and 1¼in. Louis heel, circa 1860. (Christie's) $368

William Henry Brown (1808-1883), silhouette profile of Andrew Johnson, signed, dated and inscribed, with a silhouette profile of Mary Anne Appleton, both 1840s.
(Christie's) $2,990

Three late 18th century painted silhouette portraits, one a young boy by J. Thomason, (fl. 1786-1800) and two others of a young woman and a young man, all in gilt oval frames.
(Canterbury) $288

Auguste Day (1804-1834), silhouette profile portrait of a woman, together with a profile portrait of a woman, cut paper with ink and gouache highlights, 5¼ x 3½in. and 4 x 2¼in.
(Christie's) $1,035

Attributed to Charles Buncombe, a painted silhouette of H. Andrews, Royal Marines, half length, wearing uniform, dated 1813 on the reverse, rectangular, 10.5cm.
(Bearne's) $2,787

Mary Hana, circa 1784-1787, a pair of miniature silhouettes of the cabinet maker William Savery and his wife Mary, cut paper, 6¼ x 5¼in.
(Christie's) $8,625

American School, 19th century, Collection of eight hollow cut silhouettes, all embossed *T.P. Jones fecit*, 13½ x 9¾in.
(Skinner) $2,875

Lady Louisa Kerr, Maria, Countess of Carhampton, Helen Moseley, Thomas Bacon Esq., a group of three silhouettes, cut out on card with wash backgrounds, dated 1855, 1858 and 1855. (Bearne's) $1,760

William Miers (1793-1863), two silhouette portraits, of William Watson, shoulder length profile, and a shoulder length profile of a woman, 3¼ x 2¾ and 3¼ x 2½in.
(Canterbury) $1,216

Auguste Edouart (1789–1861), a silhouette of a gentleman, free-hand cut black paper mounted on a wash paper ground, 10½ x 7in.
(Sotheby's) $2,587

HISTORICAL FACTS
Baskets

Baskets were variously used for bread, cakes or fruit, while smaller examples were also popular for sweets and sugar.

The earliest cake baskets tended to be round, and are very rare. After 1730, however, they became very popular and it was at this time that oval forms with swing handles and pierced bodies were introduced. It is always worth while examining the piercing very carefully, as any damage is very difficult to repair.

Wirework bodies with applied foliage, wheat and flowers became fashionable about 1770, while later examples more often have engraved solid bodies, and gadrooned or reeded rims. Most cake baskets tend to have armorials on the bottom.

Early examples often lack a hallmark, but from 1760 one is more likely to find a lion passant mark, sometimes with the maker's mark as well. After the introduction of the duty mark in 1784, handles should definitely be marked. After 1800, circular gilt baskets for dessert use were reintroduced.

A silver and blue enamel cake basket, by W. H. Haseler, Birmingham, 1905, with pierced sides and border set with blue enamel flowerheads amid chased foliage, 9oz.
(Christie's)　　　　$2,105

A plated two-handled rectangular fruit basket with gadroon, scroll and acanthus leaf edging, 41cm. over handle.
(Bearne's)　　　　$194

Good quality Georgian style silver cake basket of shaped octagonal design, on a shaped rectangular base, 11 x 9in., London 1906, 24oz.
(G.A. Key)　　　　$487

A William IV silver cake basket, possibly by Jonathan Hayne, 1830, the fluted body richly chased and embossed, 11¾in. diameter, 36oz.
(Christie's)　　　　$1,747

A George III silver cake basket, Wakelin & Tayler, London, 1791, in the form of a wicker basket, with overhead ropetwist swing handle, 12in. diameter, 44oz. 10dwt.
(Christie's)　　　　$18,400

Good quality Victorian silver plated small cake basket, rectangular shaped with heavy gadrooned and shell edge, swing handle.
(G. A. Key)　　　　$119

Towle Sterling fruit basket with handle, early 20th century, pierced scroll design, on four raised feet, 10³⁄₈in. diameter, approx. 19 troy oz. (Skinner)　　　　$402

A George III silver basket, Sheffield, 1817, maker's mark *RG*, the gadrooned rim cast and chased with shells, flowers and foliate scrolls, 15¼in. long, 54oz.
(Christie's)　　　　$2,305

A George III swing-handled oval sugar basket with thread edging and bright-cut decoration, London 1795, 246gm., 8oz.
(Bearne's)　　　　$454

A William IV oblong fluted fruit basket, the reeded swing handle with acanthus leaves, foliate shell and gadrooned rim, 1837, 47ozs.
(Andrew Hartley) $1,860

A Victorian silver cake basket, maker's mark of William Comyns, 1891, the sides pierced and embossed with scrolls and lattice, 11in. wide, 18oz.
(Christie's) $911

A cake basket, of oval shape, pierced and engraved with bands of poles, bell flowers, scrolls and paterae, by William Plummer 1778, 36oz, 35cm.
(Tennants) $4,445

A George III silver cake basket, Edward Aldridge, 1766, oval and on a pierced gallery foot with gadrooned border, 14½in., 29oz.
(Christie's) $1,718

A George III silver basket, London, 1787, the sides pierced with foliage scrolls and chased with floral swags and stylized foliage, 15in. long, 23oz. (Christie's) $4,225

A George III Scottish basket with a swing handle and a boat-shaped body, by W&P Cunningham, Edinburgh, 1801, 36.5cm long, 27oz. (Christie's) $3,236

A cake basket in the mid 18th century manner, of oval form and on four scroll feet, each headed with shell-framed masks, 14¼in. long. (Christie's) $3,359

An Edward VII lobed circular cake basket with pierced sides, 25.5cm. diameter, Goldsmiths and Silversmiths Co. Ltd., London 1909, 14.7oz.
(Bearne's) $437

Victorian silver sugar basket with swing handle and supported on four scrolled feet, Sheffield 1860, by Hawksworth, Eyre and Co.
(G. A. Key) $496

Good quality Victorian silver plated pedestal fruit dish, the body pierced with foliate and floral design, circa 1870.
(G.A. Key) $118

A George III silver cake basket, William Holmes, 1787, pierced arcaded border framed by beaded borders, 14½in. wide, 33oz.
(Christie's) $2,291

Attractive Edwardian silver bon bon basket, the sides ornately pierced with scroll designs, twist swing handle, 4 x 2½in., Birmingham 1908. (G. A. Key) $176

HISTORICAL FACTS
Beakers

These stemless drinking cups are functional, simple items which were popular in various parts of Europe from the 15th to the 18th century, and they continued unchanged in shape for some 200 years from 1600. All are raised in one piece, with feet or base molding.

Nevertheless, clear national characteristics do appear in their decoration. In the 15th century Germany for instance, they were made of thick gauge metal, and usually came in pint or half-pint sizes. Early examples may have ball feet, but a molded or gadrooned foot rim was more usual. Hamburg, Breslau and Strasbourg were the major production centers.

Many fine beakers were made also in Holland, where, after the Reformation, they were used as sacramental cups, sometimes gilded, and engraved with arabesques, sacred subjects, Biblical scenes or churches. By the 17th century, they were usually engraved all over and had a molded circular foot and slightly spreading sides. 16th century Norwegian beakers, on the other hand, usually rested on feet in the form of lions or female busts.

In their typically English form, beakers tended to be simple, and uncovered, whereas the Hungarians favoured a very tall style with nationalistic decoration. In Italy, they were sometimes covered with filigree work. The earliest American examples were straight sided with flaring rim.

A pair of Scottish provincial silver-mounted horn beakers, maker's marks of James Erskine, Aberdeen, circa 1800, 6¼in. high.
(Christie's) $4,390

A late 17th century German covered beaker on three ball feet, cover with ball finial, by Johann Paul Schmidt, Leipzig, circa 1690, 15.5cm. high, 6oz.
(Phillips) $1,087

A matched set of ten early 19th century French beakers, each engraved with a Viscount's coronet and crest, two different makers, Paris circa 1800, 8.75cm high, 28oz. (Christie's) $2,115

A Danish Art Nouveau metalware beaker by A. Michelsen, Copenhagen, 1901, of tapering cylindrical shape embossed with mistletoe design, 18.5cm. high.
(Cheffins Grain & Comins)
$960

A pair of Victorian Scottish silver beakers, probably Robb & Whittet, Edinburgh, 1852, each with applied plain foot rim and applied and engraved reeded girdles, 3¼in. high.
(Christie's) $1,054

A French silver beaker circa 1890, vase shaped on domed, reeded foot, with tapering body, everted rim and presentation inscription, also a modern silver beaker by Richard Crossley, 1938, 9oz.
(Christie's) $450

An American silver and mixed metal bowl stamped *Tiffany & Co.* circa 1900, of circular form on four ball and scroll feet, 4¼in. diameter.
(Christie's) $2,155

Gebrüder Friedländer for the Bauhaus, bowl, 1915, silver-colored metal, with horizontally ribbed rim, 14¼in. diameter.
(Sotheby's) $2,812

An Edwardian silver punch bowl with shaped mask, scroll and bead decorated rim, 12¼in. wide.
(Andrew Hartley) $2,544

A Georg Jensen two-handled oval bowl with presentation inscription, 38cm. over handles, import marks for London 1931, 54.5oz.
(Bearne's) $5,022

An American silver large punch bowl with ladle, Tiffany & Co., New York, circa 1895, chrysanthemum pattern, 224oz., 20½in. diameter.
(Sotheby's) $24,150

A Japanese silver fruit bowl, late 19th century, the circular bowl of double walled construction, elaborately repoussé, 8in. 52oz.
(Christie's) $1,184

Tiffany & Co. Sterling handled fruit bowl, 1907-38, round on footed base, openwork band below reeded rim, 8⅞, approx. 16 troy oz.
(Skinner) $230

A Victorian silver monteith, maker's mark of Jas. Dixon & Sons, Sheffield, 1899, the lower body with embossed lobes and wrythen flutes, 12¼in. diameter, 68oz.
(Christie's) $2,024

An American silver two-handled punch bowl, Tiffany & Co., New York, 1912, with a matching punch ladle, 136oz., 16½in. long over handles.
(Sotheby's) $8,625

A late Victorian silver punch bowl, Mappin & Webb, Sheffield, 1895, partly fluted body with two vacant oval cartouches, 10¼in. diameter, 36oz.
(Christie's) $1,145

An Edwardian silver presentation rose bowl, maker's mark of H.A., Sheffield, 1906, on quatrefoil domed base, 10in.
(Christie's) $2,180

An early 20th century Japanese silver colored metal circular bowl, the sides decorated in high relief with iris, 26cm. diameter overall, 1693gm.
(Bearne's) $2,673

Sterling child's bowl and spoon, early 20th century, Wm. B. Kerr & Co., bowl with acid-etched design of children riding different animals from seven countries, Gorham spoon, approx. 5 troy oz.
(Skinner) $201

A Victorian silver presentation rose bowl, Job Frank Hall, 1897, the domed foot and bowl part embossed with wrythen lobes and flutes, 10in. diameter.
(Christie's) $727

An American silver two-handled large centerpiece punch bowl, Gorham Mfg. Co., Providence, RI, 1901, Martelé, .950 standard, 208oz., 20in. long over handles.
(Sotheby's) $43,125

An Edward VII 10¼in. plain circular rose bowl with applied ribband, two scroll handles on stem foot, London mark 1903, maker W. Comyns & Son, 45oz.
(Anderson & Garland) $795

An American silver sugar bowl and cover, John Burt, Boston, circa 1735, of hemispherical form with molded borders and pedestal foot, 7oz. 15dwt., 4in. diameter.
(Sotheby's) $107,000

Silver cobalt glass lined bowl, Birmingham, 1921, footed with openwork sides, swing handle, 4⅜in. diameter, approx. 6 troy oz.
(Skinner) $316

Sterling silver bowl, marked *F*, #2344, pierced cherry and foliate border, 14 troy oz., 10in. diameter, 2in. high.
(Eldred's) $248

A 10¾in. plain circular rose bowl engraved with monogram and dated 1894–1919, pierced Celtic pattern border, Dublin mark 1916, 46oz.
(Anderson & Garland) $1,727

A James I parcel-gilt wine bowl, London, 1607, marker's mark *RS*, the bowl chased with four fleur-de-lys on a broad band of punched diaper ornament, 4in. diameter, 3oz. (Christie's) $46,092

Attractive large hallmarked silver biscuit barrel of bombé sided octagonal form, 5½in. high, Sheffield 1915, 14oz. (G.A. Key) $659

A WMF cedar lined cigar box, the front and back decorated with an embossed design of a fairy kneeling among scrolling flowers, 19½cm. wide. (Dreweatt Neate) $352

An early 19th century Italian bougie or taper box, on ball and claw feet with palmette borders, kingdom of Italy marks, circa 1820 - 9.5cm. high, 7.5oz. (Christie's) $984

A small casket, designed by Alexander Fisher, circa 1900, tall 'roof' cover applied with riveted strapwork and finely chased ivy leaves, 6in. wide. (Christie's) $5,623

A late 19th century American string box of domed circular form with a pull-off, gadrooned base, decorated in low relief with trellis work, C-scrolls, shells and flowers, Gorham & Co, 1893, 9.5cm high, 4.5oz. (Christie's) $493

Attributed to Koloman Moser, for Georg Anton Scheid, Vienna, glue box and cover, circa 1901, silver colored metal, glass, black enamel, brush, 2½in. (Sotheby's) $975

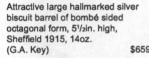

Victorian silver plated folding biscuit box of scallop shell shape, having fluted decoration and within an engraved scrolled frame, 11in. high, circa 1880. (G. A. Key) $384

Coin silver biscuit box, acorn and oak leaf finial and engraving, monogrammed *A.L.R.*, no maker's mark, 18.6 troy oz., 6½in. high. (Eldred's) $1,045

A Swiss/German guild box and cover, in the form of a seated winged ox on an oblong base, makers mark *H.H.*, 10cm long, 9oz. (Christie's) $7,578

A George II silver brandy saucepan, J. Sanders, 1736, the short V shaped spout at right angles to the later turned wood handle, 3¼in. diameter, 9oz. gross. (Christie's) $2,024

A George I silver brandy saucepan, by William Fleming, 1722, Britannia standard, of circular form with reeded borders, 6in. high. 2oz. (Christie's) $1,125

A George I silver brandy saucepan, William Fleming, 1714, plain tapering cylindrical with flared rim, 3½in. diameter, 4½oz. gross. (Christie's) $1,104

A George I brandy saucepan with a detachable, turned wooden handle and a baluster body, marks worn, 1720, 11cm. diameter, 12.5oz. gross. (Christie's) $1,265

An early 19th century brandy saucepan and cover, applied borders of anthemion and scroll motifs and chased floral sprays, probably Russian provincial or Baltic, circa 1825, 13cm diameter, 10.75oz. (Christie's) $856

Colonial silver brandy saucepan of circular baluster form with ebonized handle, detachable lid with ebonized finial, Calcutta 1848/70 by Charles, Nephew and Co. 13oz. all in. (G. A. Key) $256

Caddy Spoons

A rare George III silver caddy spoon, with shell form well, marks of Hester Bateman, London, 1783. (Eldred's) $522

Silver caddy spoon in the form of a jockey cap, Birmingham 1798, by Joseph Taylor. (G.A. Key) $266

A George III 'frying pan' caddy spoon, the circular, engine-turned bowl with central rosette, by Matthew Linwood, Birmingham, 1807. (Phillips) $400

A George III cast caddy spoon with a foliate stem and a pierced bowl decorated in relief with flowers and fruit, Edward Farrell, 1818, 2oz., 8.75cm. long. (Christie's) $640

Tiffany & Co. shell-shaped spoon, late 19th century, gold wash bowl with a floral relief pattern handle, approx. 2 troy oz. (Skinner) $373

A good George III caddy spoon with acorn bowl engraved with diaperwork, the shaped handle with central oval panel, by Elizabeth Morley, 1809. (Phillips) $480

Pair of Sheffield silver plate five-socle convertible candelabra, 19in. high.
(Eldred's) $550

A pair of silver candelabra tops on plated bases, the tops by G&S Co. Ltd, Sheffield, 1925, the bases rising from a domed foot to straight stem, 14½in. high, the tops 81oz.
(Christie's) $2,905

A pair of plated three-light candelabra, shaped square bases and detachable nozzles with scroll and foliate edging, 52.5cm. high.
(Bearne's) $680

A pair of American silver five-light candelabra, Tiffany & Co., New York, 1895, the domed bases raised on paw feet, 116oz., 17in. high.
(Sotheby's) $16,100

A pair of American silver and other metals 'Japanese style' six-light candelabra, Tiffany & Co., New York, 1879, on hexagonal bases, 137oz. 10dwt. gross, 16in. high.
(Sotheby's) $118,000

A Pair of Victorian ten-light parcel-gilt candelabra, John Samuel Hunt, London, 1846, 1848, the base with three detachable model deer, 35in. high, 1,069oz.
(Christie's) $222,945

A pair of Victorian silver-gilt seven-light candelabra, Stephen Smith, London, 1883, the fluted tapering cylindrical stems applied with acanthus foliage, 28½in. high.
404oz.(Christie's) $28,808

A pair of electroplated candelabra, by Jean Despres, each with four flat branches supporting cup-shaped candle holders, 12⅝in. high.
(Christie's) $4,686

A pair of silver six-light candelabra, by Gerald Benney, London, 1965, each with hexagonal dish with central short cylindrical stem, 19½in. high.
(Christie's) $5,623

A pair of Elkington candlesticks, the baluster form interspersed with stylized acanthus leaves and lobed middle section, Birmingham 1897, 26cm. (Bristol) $957

A pair of Edward VII Corinthian column desk top candlesticks with detachable sconces, 15cm., Birmingham 1901. (Bearne's) $502

A pair of Victorian silver candlesticks, George Fox, 1870, pierced and chased with ho-ho birds among flowering and scrolling foliage, 6½in. high, 14oz. (Christie's) $4,200

A pair of silver candlesticks, designed by Rex Silver, manufactured by Liberty & Co., Birmingham, 1906, each with slender stems applied with delicate square-section branches, 9⅞in. high. (Christie's) $37,490

A pair of George IV silver-gilt candlesticks, John and Thomas Settle, Sheffield, 1824, chased overall with scrolls, shells, flowers and foliage, 10½in. high, 27oz. (Christie's) $2,497

A pair of candlesticks, designed by Georg Jensen, circa 1918, manufactured post 1945, wrought with clusters of grapes below the pans, 5⅞in. high. (Christie's) $5,623

A pair of Sheffield plate desk-top candlesticks, the square bases, tapering paneled stems and detachable nozzles with thread edging, 15.5cm. high. (Bearne's) $340

A pair of late Victorian silver candlesticks, maker's mark of Mappin Bros., Sheffield, 1897, each of tapering square form and on a spreading foot, 6in. high. (Christie's) $933

A pair of late Victorian electro-plated candlesticks in the neo-classical style with square bases, by Messrs R & R Hodd, 30.5cm high. (Christie's) $720

Josef Hoffmann for the Wiener Werkstätte, candlestick, 1925, silver-colored metal, 8⅝in. (Sotheby's) $6,748

A pair of electro-type candlesticks, Elkington & Co., circa 1850, each on a domed circular base with three scroll feet, 12in. high. (Christie's) $458

A pair of Swedish silver candlesticks, Gustaf Möllenborg, Stockholm, 1843, each on a shaped circular base and with baluster stem and vase-shaped socket, 9in. high. (Christie's) $2,881

A pair of George III silver candlesticks, London, 1764, maker's mark *JH*, each on spreading square base and with fluted Doric column stem, 14in. high. (Christie's) $6,146

Heavy pair of early George II silver candlesticks on shaped circular bases with double knopped stems, marked for London 1734, by James Gould, 28oz. all in. (G.A. Key) $3,611

A pair of silver candlesticks, designed by The Silver Studio, maker's mark of Liberty & Co., Birmingham, 1902, stamped *CYMRIC*, 7¾in. high, 18oz. (Christie's) $11,316

A pair of Victorian silver desk candlesticks, by John Aldwinckle & Thomas Slater, 1886, of garland entwined column form on spreading square bases, 5in. high. (Christie's) $724

A pair of Louis XV silver candlesticks, Nicolas Linguet, Paris, 1740, each on a shaped octagonal spreading base, with octagonal stem and socket, 10in. high., 31oz. (Christie's) $6,338

An American silver cann, Ephraim Brasher, circa 1780, pear shaped, on molded foot with leaf capped double scroll handle, 6oz. 15dwts. 3⅞in. (Sotheby's) $3,737

A silver cann, John David, Philadelphia, circa 1770, baluster form, with scroll handle, on cast molded foot, 9oz., 4in. high. (Christie's) $9,200

An American silver cann, Daniel Henchman, Boston, circa 1760, pear shaped, with molded foot, scroll handle, 11oz. 10dwts, 4in. high. (Sotheby's) $2,587

An American silver large cann, Paul Revere Jr., Boston, circa 1780, of baluster form, leaf capped double scroll handle, 16oz. 10dwts., 6¼in. high. (Sotheby's) $31,050

Two silver canns, one by Bailey & Kitchen, Philadelphia 1833-46, the other George Walker, Philadelphia, circa 1795, 20oz., 5 and 3⅛in. high. (Christie's) $2,070

An American silver cann, Lewis Fueter, New York, circa 1770, pear shaped, plain, with a molded base, double scroll handle, 17oz. 10dwts. 4in. high. (Sotheby's) $4,025

An American silver large cann, William Holmes, Boston, circa 1760, pear shaped domed foot, leaf capped double scroll handle, 17oz. 10dwts., 6in. high. (Sotheby's) $3,450

An American silver large cann, Fletcher & Gardner, Philadelphia, circa 1815, cylindrical, decorated with reeded hoops, interlaced ribbonwork and a girdle of running leaves, 19oz. 6in. high. (Sotheby's) $4,025

An American silver cann, Jonathan Stickney Jr., Newburyport, MA, circa 1780, pear shaped, with a molded base, 14oz. 10dwts., 5¾in. high. (Sotheby's) $2,875

Fine silver sugar caster in early 18th century style of circular baluster form to a stepped circular foot, 6½in. high, London 1924, 8.5oz.
(G.A. Key) $270

Pair of Tiffany & Co. Sterling pepper casters, 1907, chrysanthemum pattern, monogram, 5⅝in. high, approx. 9 troy oz. (Skinner) $1,150

A German silver sugar caster, maker's mark probably Gottfried Bartermann, Augsburg, 1740, on stepped foot with chased fluting to body, 7oz.
(Christie's) $2,249

A decorative pair of late Victorian silver muffineers on circular domed bases, the floral and foliate chased bodies with body bands, Birmingham 1887, 4½in. high.
(G A Key) $192

A pair of Edwardian novelty sugar casters, modeled as ventilator chimneys with hooded cowls and bayonet fitting bases, Samuel Jacob, 1909, 18.5cm high, 13.5oz.
(Christie's) $1,713

Good quality pair of Georgian style silver muffineers of circular baluster form, with pierced domed lids, wrythen finials, Birmingham 1927, 4½in. high.
(G A Key) $297

A George III silver sugar caster, Hester Bateman, 1783, of baluster form, on spreading circular base with rim foot, 5¾in. high.
(Christie's) $883

A pair of early 19th century Dutch sugar casters with tapering bodies, square pedestals and pierced spool, by Francois Simons, The Hague, 1805, 26.5cm high, 34oz.
(Christie's) $4,784

A George II silver sugar caster, Samuel Wood, 1749, of baluster form, on spreading foot, with molded girdle, 7in. high, 7oz.
(Christie's) $827

Good quality mid 19th century silver plated centerpiece, the shaped square base with applied mask and shell detail, 12½in. high. (G. A. Key) $576

A WMF style white-metal two-handled fruit comport, the oval body cast with ribbon-ties and floral chains, 19¼in. wide. (Christie's) $701

An early Victorian 11½in. oval compôte, lattice-work design with applied fruiting vine ornamentation, London mark 1842, maker Chas. Reily & George Storer, 33oz. (Anderson & Garland) $1,304

An American silver épergne, Wood & Hughes, New York, circa 1870, the stem formed as a classical female head, flanked by two oval dishes, 89oz., 22in. high. (Sotheby's) $5,750

Sheffield silver plate and cut glass épergne, 19th century, open work baluster form, flower, plume and shell decoration, 16in. high. (Skinner) $2,530

An American silver figural épergne, Krider & Biddle, Philadelphia, circa 1865, modeled as a classical female figure, her head supporting a shallow frosted bowl, 183oz. 10dwts., 21½in. high. (Sotheby's) $9,775

A George IV silver centerpiece, Benjamin Smith, London, 1822, the base applied with the figure of Bacchus, with two attendant Maenads, 19¼in. high. 266oz. (Christie's) $28,808

An American silver jardinière and plateau, Gorham Mfg. Co. Providence, RI, 1905, martelé, .9584 standard, the stand domed, with a rippled edge, 256oz. gross, 23½in. long over handles. (Sotheby's) $123,500

A Victorian silver and glass centerpiece, Stephen Smith, 1867 on silver naturalistic rockwork base applied with fern sprays and lily leaves, 17in. high. (Christie's) $1,527

An American silver Art Nouveau chamber candlestick, Towle Silversmiths, Newburyport, MA, circa 1900, in the form of a daffodil, 6oz., 6¼in. long. (Sotheby's) $1,495

A Victorian silver chamber stick, R. & S. Garrard & Co., 1841, circular, with scrolled thumbpiece, gadrooned borders, 11½oz. (Christie's) $1,431

Victorian silver chamber candle lamp with shaped screen back, pierced circular base, ringlet thumbpiece, 6in. high, London 1891. (G.A. Key) $95

A George III circular chamber candlestick, with reeded borders and detachable snuffer and nozzle, engraved with crests, by Elizabeth Jones, 1798, 5½in. diameter, 10oz. (Clarke Gammon) $992

A pair of William IV silver hand candlesticks by Robinson, Edkins & Aston, Birmingham, 1835, each with circular fluted dish, vase-shaped socket, 6½in. diameter. 26oz. (Christie's) $3,092

A George II silver taperstick, by William Cafe, 1747, on shaped square base cast with shells at the angles, 5½in. high. 9oz. (Christie's) $900

A George III chamberstick, 3in. high, with gadrooned border, flying scroll handle and engraved crest, London, 1816, by Samuel Whitford II, 9oz. (Bonhams) $800

A George II silver chamberstick, the nozzle with maker's mark JC, 1754, reeded detachable nozzle and conical snuffer, 6½in. diameter, 14oz. (Christie's) $1,422

An Edwardian silver chamberstick, by Thomas Bradbury & Sons, 1904, on oblong base with plain column stem, detachable nozzle and extinguisher to oblong handle, 10.5oz. (Christie's) $655

A George III silver chocolate pot, Aldridge & Green, 1777, with reeded borders and flat domed hinged cover, 6¾in. high, 16oz.
(Christie's) $2,115

A chocolatière, the design attributed to Lucien Bonvallet, manufactured by Cardheilac, circa 1895-1900, waisted cylinder decorated with repoussé formalized leaves, 8½in. high.
(Christie's) $8,280

A George II silver chocolate pot, Jonathan French, Newcastle, 1731, hinge with detachable pin and chain, 9½in. high, 26oz. gross.
(Christie's) $8,642

Christening Mugs

A George III silver Christening mug of tapering cylindrical form, decorated with bands of reeded decoration, London 1803, 3oz. approx.
(Bonhams) $192

A George III silver Christening mug of tapering cylindrical form molded borders, London 1815, possibly by Samuel Whitford II, 4oz. approx.
(Bonhams) $400

A Victorian Christening mug, the handle modeled as a Jack Tar holding a rope, by Hayne & Cater, 1848, 6¼oz.
(Tennants) $476

A George IV silver Christening mug of tapering circular form, stylized borders, bands of relief decoration, London 1826, William Fountain, 4.5oz. approx. (Bonhams)
$400

An unusual George IV thistle-shaped christening mug on spreading leaf foot, the handle with demonic head, by Charles Fox (II), 1821, 10.2cm. high, 5.5oz. (Phillips) $608

A jeweled gold cigarette case, Fabergé, Workmaster August Hollming, St. Petersburg, 1899-1908, 4in. wide.
(Christie's) $4,600

A rectangular cigarette case, the hinged lid inset with a printed study of flowers, with chased border, Birmingham 1937.
(Dreweatt Neate) $86

A rectangular cigarette case, the lid enameled in Japanese Kakiemon style on a green ground, London 1925.
(Dreweatt Neate) $102

A jeweled gold enameled cigarette case, marked *Fabergé*, 1908–1917, decorated overall with gold engine-turned bands between narrow blue and white enamel stripes, 3¾in. long. (Christie's) $8,280

An electroplated and enamel cigarette case, circa 1900, the hinged cover with polychrome enamel panel depicting the interior of a harem, 3½ x 3¼in.
(Christie's) $858

A jeweled gold and parcel-gilt guilloché enamel cigarette case, marked *Fabergé*, 1908–1913, enameled both sides in translucent royal blue, 3½in. long.
(Christie's) $23,000

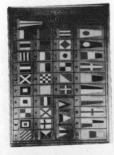

Sterling silver cigarette case, the front enameled with the international nautical code flags, hallmark for Charles Thomae & Son, Inc.
(Skinner) $460

A Continental white metal and enamel cigarette box, circa 1920, painted with a female figure in blue and white beach costume, 3½in. long. (Christie's) $843

A jeweled gold cigarette case, Fabergé, St. Petersburg, 1908–1917, the cover applied with a Russian Imperial double-headed eagle, 4in. long.
(Christie's) $7,474

A Penguin typewriter petrol lighter,
Japanese.
(Auction Team Köln) $122

A Continental table cigar lighter,
maker's mark *F.A.,* of circular
bellied form, spot hammered
decoration, 3¼in. high.
(Bonhams) $400

A gas-fuelled lighter in the form of a
camera.
(Auction Team Köln) $81

A yellow metal S.T. Dupont pocket
lighter, marked 18ct., with fine
barley finish, French, circa 1980s.
(Bonhams) $495

A Dunhill Tinder Pistol petrol lighter,
British, 1962.
(Auction Team Köln) $149

A brown Dunhill crocodile skin
covered silver plated giant table
lighter, English, circa 1931.
(Bonhams) $181

A Dunhill shagreen covered
'Unique' lighter, with silver plated
body, English, circa 1932.
(Bonhams) $281

A silver combined petrol lighter and
watch, Dunhill, No. 3679, 1927, 15-
jewel movement with three
adjustments, 54mm. high.
(Christie's) $1,840

A Victorian silver-gilt mounted wine ewer, Edward Dimes, London, 1894, the pear-shaped clear glass body on hexafoil foot, 12in. high. (Christie's)   **$4,993**

A late 19th century German silver gilt mounted clear glass claret jug, in the form of a stylized fighting cockerel, circa 1890, 34.5cm high. (Christie's)   **$2,208**

A Victorian claret jug finely engraved with fruiting vine having inscription and vacant cartouche, London 1859, maker *J.A.* (Russell, Baldwin & Bright)   **$722**

A silver claret jug, maker's marks of Garrard & Co. Ltd, 1973, with applied cast bands of fruiting vines and chased scroll decoration, 11½in. high, 28oz. (Christie's)   **$1,290**

A pair of Victorian electroplated, mounted cut-glass claret jugs, with etched decoration, engraved mounts and beaded border, 32.5cm high. (Christie's)   **$1,513**

An electroplated mounted engraved glass claret jug, the tapering cylindrical glass body decorated with foliate motifs, 28cm. high. (Bearne's)   **$243**

A Victorian cut glass claret jug of oval shape, flame finial on hinged lid, embossed in a scrolling foliate pattern, 12½in. high, London 1887. (Andrew Hartley)   **$1,472**

A silver mounted claret jug, after a design by Dr Christopher Dresser, manufactured by Hukin & Heath, circa 1881, 8½in. high. (Christie's)   **$2,674**

A Sheffield plate claret jug, vase-shaped, on square base with Greek key border, applied with male masks with drapery swags. (Christie's)   **$417**

A George III silver coaster of circular form with pierced decoration, later blue glass liner, possibly London 1775. (Bonhams) $192

A pair of Sheffield plate circular coasters with acanthus edging and on turned wood bases, 16.5cm. diameter. (Bearne's) $356

Tiffany sterling wine coaster, circa 1900, chrysanthemum pattern, everted rim, paneled sides, 16oz. 6½in. diameter. (Skinner) $4,600

Two similar George III wine coasters, London 1813 and 1814, Paul Storr, circular bellied form, ribbed shell decoration, 17cm. diameter. (Bonhams) $4,800

A set of four large silver coasters, John Winter & Co., Sheffield, 1830 and 1844, with cast vine sides and rims, 6¾in. diameter. (Christie's) $13,800

A pair of George III wine coasters, London 1810, William Abdy II, circular form, pierced decoration, bright cut borders, 11.5cm. diameter. (Bonhams) $1,280

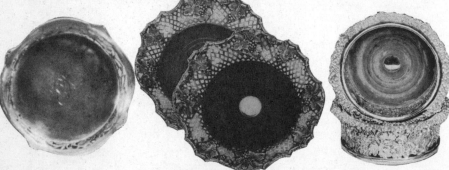

Gorham silver wine coaster, 1897, footed with openwork sides, 4¾in. diameter, approx. 4 troy oz. (Skinner) $230

A pair of Victorian coasters of openwork lattice form with vine edging, 23cm. diameter, Hy. Wilkinson & Co., Sheffield 1847, 30.2oz. (Bearne's) $2,997

A George III pair of wine coasters, Sheffield 1818, J Watson & Co., embossed with hunting dogs amidst trailing grapevine tendrils, 17.5cm. diameter. (Bonhams) $5,600

A late Victorian silver coffee pot, maker's mark of Barnard Brothers, 1896, with wicker-clad loop handle and detachable cover, 8in. high, gross 20oz. (Christie's) $342

A George II silver coffee pot, Richard Bayley, 1749, with partly fluted curved spout, domed cover with baluster finial, 9in. high, 20oz. (Christie's) $2,576

A George IV silver presentation coffee jug, Benjamin Smith 1823, the handle Victorian, the body applied with two die-stamped bands of flowerheads, 9in. high, 31oz. (Christie's) $1,747

Attractive Victorian silver coffee pot of circular baluster form, chased and embossed with foliate and floral designs, 11in. high, Sheffield 1859, 24oz. (G. A. Key) $880

Attractive Victorian silver plated coffee pot of circular baluster form, engraved with Grecian key and foliate decoration, 11½in. high, circa 1875. (G. A. Key) $144

A coffee pot, manufactured by Christofle Orfèvres, 1880, in Japanese taste with hammered ground, applied in colored metals, 7in. high. (Christie's) $5,520

A late Victorian silver coffee pot, maker's mark of H. Matthews, Birmingham, 1896, in the George I manner, 9¼in. high, gross 16oz. (Christie's) $322

An early 19th century American coffee pot of bellied oval form on a domed oval pedestal, by George W. Riggs, Baltimore, Maryland, circa 1815, 28.5cm high, 31oz. (Christie's) $1,523

A William IV Scottish coffee pot of tapering form with a tucked-in base, in the George II style, J. Mackay, Edinburgh, 1835, 28cm. high, 27.5oz. (Christie's) $2,270

A small early 19th century French coffee pot on three feet with carved supports terminating in anthemion-like motifs, Paris circa 1825, 23cm. high, 11.5oz. (Christie's) $719

A pair of silver café au lait pots, maker's mark *A.W.*, 1947, each of plain baluster form, with stepped domed cover, 8½in. high, 31oz. (Christie's) $1,527

A George II coffee pot of tapering cylindrical form with a domed cover, a knop finial and a carved faceted spout, by Edward Vincent, 1734, 21cm. high, 20.5oz. (Christie's) $3,616

An early 19th century French coffee pot with an oviform body on three paw feet, initialed, Paris circa 1825, 32.5cm. high, 20.5oz. (Christie's) $1,097

A George III silver coffee pot, maker's mark of Samuel Godbehere and Edward Wigan, 1799, vase-shaped and on oval spreading foot, with curved spout, 10½in. high. (Christie's) $1,120

Good quality Victorian silver plated coffee pot of circular baluster form, having mask to spout, on a pierced four footed base, circa 1850. (G.A. Key) $247

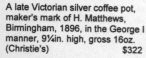

Late Victorian silver coffee biggin of tubular shape with pull lid, rope edged border, London 1897, 11oz. (G.A. Key) $297

A George V coffee pot and matching hot water jug of 18th century design with domed hinged lids, 22cm. high, maker's mark *G.B. & Co.*, Birmingham 1917. (Bearne's) $550

An American silver Moorish style demitasse pot, Tiffany & Co., New York, circa 1885, of oval pear form, 17oz., 9¼in. high. (Sotheby's) $2,070

A late 19th century German reproduction of a Turkenkopf coffee pot with a wrythen fluted baluster body, crested, 30.5cm. high, 32oz. (Christie's) $1,607

A pair of silver café au lait pots, Hamilton & Inches, Edinburgh, 1926, plain vase-shaped with canted corners and wriggle work borders, 6in. high, 26oz. (Christie's) $611

A Georgian coffee pot, the body embossed with drapes and tassels, makers Daniel Smith and Robert Sharp, London 1775, 13¼in. high. 35oz. 8dwt. (Andrew Hartley) $4,710

A George III coffee pot with leaf capped spout and double scroll wood handle, 25cm. high, Fras. Crump, London 1776, 28oz. (Bearne's) $1,101

F. Hingelberg Aarhus, coffee pot and cover and milk jug, after 1945, silver-colored metal, each piece of simple baluster form with ivory handles, 8in. (Sotheby's) $1,440

A silver coffee pot, bearing canceled marks, of pain tapering cylindrical form, on molded base, 9¼in. high. (Christie's) $1,431

HISTORICAL FACTS
Cream Jugs

The earliest milk jugs were in fact hot milk pots which harmonised with the kettles and teapots of the early 18th century. They were usually pear-shaped, sometimes octagonal in cut, with a domed lid and a short, covered spout.

The 1720s saw the introduction of a very small cold milk or cream jug, again of pear or baluster shape, on a spreading foot rim with attached beak spout. The vessel tended to become broader thereafter, on a molded foot, and the spout became an integral part of the rim, rising upwards and forwards and balanced by a scrolling handle.

Three-footed jugs appeared from the 1720s, firstly with one foot under the lip and subsequently with one under the handle. Shallow boats for cream were usually sold in pairs and could be cast in relief or sometimes shaped as nautilus shells.

The cow creamer is simply a silver cream jug in the form of a standing cow. The tail, looped over the back, serves as the handle, while the mouth is the spout. There is an oval lidded opening on the back where the milk is poured in, and this often has a fly or bee in full relief. The cow creamer was introduced from Holland around 1755 by John Schuppe, a Dutchman, and it is his name which is most often associated with the form, though later examples were also produced by other makers.

A cream jug, of good gauge, vase shaped with scroll handle, beaded border, by Robert Hennell, 1780, 5oz. 15cm. (Tennants) $953

A Dutch silver cow creamer, London import marks for 1892, in the manner of John Schuppe, the cover with fly finial, 5¹/₈in. long, 4½oz. (Christie's) $764

A Continental model of a cow creamer with horns, curled tail and applied fly motif on its back, with import marks for C. Saunders & F. Shepherd, 1906, 13cm long, 6oz. (Christie's) $947

A George III cream pail, the wirework sides decorated with applied flowering foliage and a cartouche, 1769; and a later metalware spoon, 3oz weighable silver. (Christie's) $1,370

A George III Irish silver cream jug, probably William Townsend, Dublin, 1770, on three scrolled paw supports each headed with a lion's mask, 4¾in. high, 6oz. (Christie's) $2,004

A George II baluster cream jug, with armorial and scroll chasing, scroll handle and on three C-scroll supports, London 1748 by David Hennell, 3.25oz, 10.2cm. (Bristol) $380

A Victorian silver seven-bottle cruet frame, maker's mark of Hayne & Cater, 1839, octagonal, on four pierced scrolled bracket feet, 10¾in. (Christie's) $2,846

A George III silver oil and vinegar stand, Paul Storr, 1804, the bottle mounts 1808, with gadrooned border and acanthus foliage, 11in., 38oz. (Christie's) $5,336

William IV silver cruet stand of bombé sided oval form, standing on four shell feet, five bottles, (of seven), London 1835, by Charles Fox II. (G. A. Key) $320

Large silver plated cruet stand, rectangular shaped with sloped sides and standing on four cheese feet, holding six molded glass bottles, 20th century. (G. A. Key) $120

A silver cruet set, by Omar Ramsden and Alwyn Carr, and the Guild of Handicraft Ltd., London, 1903, 1909, 1929. (Christie's) $1,030

Georgian five bottle cruet, the strapwork and gadrooned frame supported on four shell shaped feet, four similar bottles, hallmarked for London 1770. (G.A. Key) $502

A William IV square eight-division cruet stand with gadrooned border on four scroll feet, London 1833 by the Barnards, 23oz. (Dreweatt Neate) $754

An egg cruet, for six, the cups plain with scroll borders, by W. Bateman, 1836, also six spoons, of fiddle and thread pattern, 48oz. (Tennants) $1,600

George IV silver cruet stand, having wavy gadrooned edge, treen center, central carrying holder with divider for seven bottles, London 1821. (G. A. Key) $672

A massive silver prize cup and cover, by J.B. Carrington, 1899, of partly fluted vase-shape, 29½in. high, 196oz.
(Christie's) $7,636

Pair of silver egg cutter cups, American, circa 1910, hinged lid with two swing-out cutting arms, applied claw motif on handles, gold wash interior, approx. 8 troy oz.
(Skinner) $690

A George II silver gilt standing cup and cover, by William Shaw and William Priest, London 1752, 117½oz.
(George Kidner) $14,939

George III silver two handled loving cup, usual design with hollow looped handles, raised body band, 6in. high, London 1806, by Peter and William Bateman.
(G. A. Key) $215

A silver-gilt font cup, Lionel Alfred Crichton, London, 1909, circular and on trumpet-shaped foot chased with foliage and classical medallions, 6½in. high. 26oz.
(Christie's) $3,649

A 7½in. plain circular tapered loving cup with three scroll handles, on knopped fluted stem foot with circular base, modern, 20oz., 10dwt.
(Anderson & Garland) $243

George III silver loving cup of usual circular baluster form, having two reeded looped handles, 4in. high, London 1779, by John Sanders II, 5oz.
(G.A. Key) $314

A Continental silver cup, London import marks of Berthold Muller, 1902, on hexagonal lobed foot rising to short stem, 8¾in. high, 41oz.
(Christie's) $1,049

A George III two-handled cup of baluster form with an engraved body and pedestal foot by M. West, Dublin, 1769, 16cm high. 12.5oz.
(Christie's) $555

Sterling silver leaf-form dish, by Gorham, presentation inscription, 15 troy oz., 13in. long. (Eldred's) $220

A pair of Victorian silver dishes, Frank F. Fenton & Frank Fenton, Sheffield, 1873, the center of each stamped and chased with clustered fruit, 10in. (Christie's) $2,200

Victorian silver plated bacon dish, the revolving lid with half fluted decoration, having two interior trays, 12 x 8in., circa 1880. (G. A. Key) $216

A pair of American silver vegetable dishes and covers, Dominick & Haff, New York, 1886, 85oz., 11³⁄₈in. long. (Sotheby's) $4,600

A pair of George III silver strawberry dishes, Robert Garrard, London, 1815, one inset with nine Irish agricultural medals, the other with eight medals and a central plaque, 9½in. diameter, 63oz. (Christie's) $6,722

A pair of George IV silver entrée dishes and covers and Old Sheffield plate hot-water stands, John Bridge, London, 1825, the shaped circular stands on four foliage and lion's paw feet, the dishes 11in. diameter. 130oz. (Christie's) $9,603

Gustav Pedersen for Georg Jensen, coupe, manufactured 1945-51, silver-colored metal, the deep bowl with inverted rim and lightly martelé finish, 6¾in. high. (Sotheby's) $3,841

Two Victorian heart-shaped sweet dishes with pierced and embossed decoration on three ball feet, Birmingham 1887 and Chester 1897. (Dreweatt Neate) $94

A round dish, the border embossed with scrolls and bunches of hanging grapes and flowers, 10¹⁄₂in. diameter, 12oz., London 1901. (Ewbank) $400

Victorian period Sheffield plated trefoil decanter stand with gadrooned rims and standing on three cast foliate feet.
(G. A. Key) $237

Interesting Art Deco silver plated two-bottle tantalus, the two glass bottles with decorative Art Deco designs, circa 1930.
(G. A. Key) $256

Fine 19th century Sheffield plate decanter stand of trefoil form the rim repoussé with scrolls, panels of berries and foliage, 10in. wide.
(G. A. Key) $880

Dressing Cases

A Victorian coromandel dressing case with numerous silver & ivory mounted fittings finely scroll-engraved, London 1858, stamped *Mechi*. (Russell Baldwin & Bright)
      $1,952

English rosewood necéssaire, circa 1850, interior fitted with silver plate mounted glass bottles and boxes, with drawer below, 12in. wide.
(Skinner) $633

A Victorian coromandel dressing case with numerous silver mounted fittings, London, 1875.
(Russell Baldwin & Bright)
      $1,200

Ewers

A Victorian silver ewer, John Samuel Hunt, London, 1853, on circular spreading foot and short stem with knop chased to simulate coral, 17in. high. 51oz.
(Christie's) $6,146

A Victorian Scottish silver presentation ewer, McKay, Cunningham & Co., Edinburgh 1867, on spreading circular foot, with beaded borders, 11in. high. 27oz. (Christie's) $1,107

A George III silver ewer, Peter, Anne and William Bateman, London, 1802, with reeded loop handle and gadrooned borders, 12¾in. high, 35oz.
(Christie's) $5,762

Victorian asparagus tongs, London, 1861, Messrs. Eady, beaded borders with openwork scroll design, approx. 7 troy oz. (Skinner) $747

Silver grape shears, circa 1900, American, vine and grape design, approx. 4 troy oz. (Skinner) $460

Pair of silver-handled frog legs servers, American, late 19th century, reeded handles with leaf and vine decoration. (Skinner) $172

Pair of Reed and Barton large salad servers, Les Six Fleurs pattern, approximately 12 troy oz. (Skinner) $345

Koloman Moser for the Wiener Werkstätte, coffee spoon, circa 1905, silver colored metal, lapis lazuli cabochon, 3⅝in. long. (Sotheby's) $1,030

A fine Scottish silver punch ladle, maker's mark probably that of T. Finlayson, Glasgow, 1820, the circular bowl set with gilt Napoleon I coin, 17¼in. (Christie's) $4,009

An early 18th century trefid spoon with lace decorated stem and reverse of bowl, pricked with initials *R.S.* and date *1700*, maker Richard Street, Chard. (Russell, Baldwin & Bright) $820

Victorian silver fish slicer, Sheffield, 1891, Atkin Brothers, bright-cut engraved floral and scroll decoration, with carved ivory handle, 13⅞in. long. (Skinner) $345

An American silver 'Japanese style' ice cream slice, Tiffany & Co., New York, circa 1880, Lap Over Edge pattern, the handle applied with monkeys swinging and climbing, 4oz. 10dwt., 12¾in. long. (Sotheby's) $2,415

A Charles II silver trefid spoon, struck with anchor mark and skull twice, possibly Salisbury, circa 1680, the plain ovoid bowl with flat stem and trefid terminal engraved, 7½in. long. (Christie's) $843

Fine large William IV Irish silver meat skewer with coiled snake ringlet handle, well marked for Dublin 1831, possibly by P. Weekes. (G.A. Key) $349

An American silver Japanese style fish slice, Dominick & Haff, New York, circa 1880–90, chased with water plants and two bugs on spot-hammered ground, 5oz. 15dwt., 12in. long. (Sotheby's) $805

A 17th century traveling knife and fork, the ivory handles finely-carved with double figures, the elegant male and female couple on the fork each holding a scepter, probably to symbolize William and Mary. (Christie's) $3,409

An early to mid 18th century silver-mounted traveling knife and fork with tapering faceted agate handles and steel blade and prongs, in a shagreen-mounted case. (Christie's) $502

Victorian silver fish knife, Sheffield, 1880, Hy. Wilkinson & Co. engine-turned surface decoration on handle with beaded border, bright-cut engraved blade, approx. 4 troy oz. (Skinner) $143

George III silver Stilton cheese scoop with pusher, Birmingham, 1803, *JT* maker, with carved palmette-shaped ivory handle, 8½in. long. (Skinner) $373

HISTORICAL FACTS
Inkstands

Inkstands, or standishes, as they were previously known, date from the 16th century, though the earliest surviving examples are usually 17th century. The 'Treasury' type consisted of an oblong casket with two centrally hinged lids.

Throughout the 18th century a tray form predominated, in the prevailing style of the period. These could be variously fitted with inkpots, sand and/or pounceboxes, wafer boxes, sealing wax, bells and 'tapersticks'.

Glass bottles first appeared around 1765, as did pierced gallery sides. More often than not at least one of the bottles will have been replaced. How important this is to the value will depend on how well the replacement conforms with the whole.

Small, globe-shaped forms came in the last years of the 18th century, and mahogany desk models with silver tops first made their appearance around 1800. Victorian examples were often highly ornamented and included many fanciful novelty designs such as cricketers, rowing boats with the pens as oars, etc. Usage declined after 1886, with the invention of the fountain pen.

A George II inkstand on an oblong base with a reeded border and incurved corners, by Samuel Courtauld I, 1751, 26 x 16cm, 30.5oz. (Christie's) $12,883

A Victorian silver ink stand, by James Charles Edington, 1845, the well formed as an antique lamp, 9in. wide. 14oz. net. (Christie's) $1,312

A Victorian inkstand of shaped oblong form, with central taperstick flanked on either side by a cut glass bottle, W.R. Smilie, London 1854, 15oz., 11in. wide. (Andrew Hartley) $1,040

A silver-mounted tortoiseshell inkstand, by William Comyns & Sons Ltd, 1904, the base and three sides with silver harebell border, 12in. long. (Christie's) $3,654

A large matched pair of silver encased capstan inkwells of plain design, one with replacement liner, Birmingham 1911, by two makers, 6½in. diameter. (G A Key) $312

Jean Puiforcat, ink pot and cover, circa 1930, the almost cube-shaped base with canted corners in clear and frosted glass etched with geometric motifs, 4¹/₈in. (Christie's) $5,185

A George III silver mounted hardwood ship's inkstand, circa 1820, with three applied plain silver brackets to each corner, 18in. wide. (Christie's) $3,680

A George V novelty inkwell in the form of a ship's starboard light, with green glass panel, 13.5cm. high, maker's mark H.B.S., London 1926, and two pens. (Bearne's) $939

A Victorian shaped oval inkstand with chamber candlestick and silver mounted cut-glass bottles, 28cm. long, Robinson, Edkins & Aston, Birmingham 1845, 19.6oz. (Bearne's) $1,328

Victorian silver plated hotwater jug of oval baluster form, well chased and embossed with foliate and shell designs, ivory finial to lid.
(G.A. Key) $79

A Victorian parcel-gilt jug, Robert Hennell, London, 1874, in the Greek Revival style formed as an epichysis, the spool-shaped body with loop handle, 8in. high, 25oz.
(Christie's) $3,649

A George III Scottish silver mounted Chinese blue and white water jug, William Robertson, Edinburgh, circa 1795, 9½in.
(Christie's) $2,604

Designed and executed by Christian Dell at the Metallwerkstatt Bauhaus Weimar, wine jug and cover, 1922 alpaca with hammered finish, ebony, 7⁷/₈in.
(Sotheby's) $163,815

19th century Sheffield plated beer jug of slightly tapering oval form with treen handle.
(G. A. Key) $166

A George IV silver hot-water jug, Benjamin Smith, London, 1829, the melon-fluted body on spreading shaped circular rocaille foot, 10in. high, 31oz. gross.
(Christie's) $1,728

A Georgian beer jug of baluster form with leaf capped scrolled handle, William Shaw, London, 1765, 7in. high. 18oz. 9dwts.
(Andrew Hartley) $2,276

Regency silver hotwater jug of slightly compressed circular design, probably London 1816, by William Burwash, 24oz. all in.
(G.A. Key) $349

Christopher Dresser for J.W. Hukin & J.T. Heath 'crow's foot' decanter, design registered 9th October, 1878, electroplated metal, 9½in.
(Sotheby's) $6,748

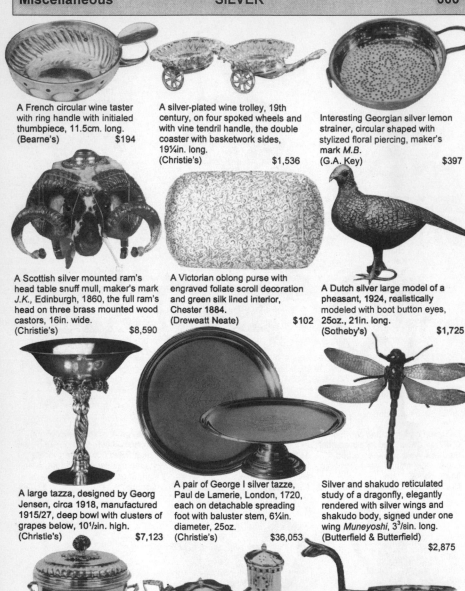

A French circular wine taster with ring handle with initialed thumbpiece, 11.5cm. long. (Bearne's) $194

A silver-plated wine trolley, 19th century, on four spoked wheels and with vine tendril handle, the double coaster with basketwork sides, 19¼in. long. (Christie's) $1,536

Interesting Georgian silver lemon strainer, circular shaped with stylized floral piercing, maker's mark *M.B.* (G.A. Key) $397

A Scottish silver mounted ram's head table snuff mull, maker's mark *J.K.,* Edinburgh, 1860, the full ram's head on three brass mounted wood castors, 16in. wide. (Christie's) $8,590

A Victorian oblong purse with engraved foliate scroll decoration and green silk lined interior, Chester 1884. (Dreweatt Neate) $102

A Dutch silver large model of a pheasant, 1924, realistically modeled with boot button eyes, 25oz., 21in. long. (Sotheby's) $1,725

A large tazza, designed by Georg Jensen, circa 1918, manufactured 1915/27, deep bowl with clusters of grapes below, 10½in. high. (Christie's) $7,123

A pair of George I silver tazze, Paul de Lamerie, London, 1720, each on detachable spreading foot with baluster stem, 6¼in. diameter, 25oz. (Christie's) $36,053

Silver and shakudo reticulated study of a dragonfly, elegantly rendered with silver wings and shakudo body, signed under one wing *Muneyoshi*, 3³/₈in. long. (Butterfield & Butterfield) $2,875

Fine Edwardian large silver biscuit barrel, the lid with pomegranate finials, 7in. high, London 1902 by the Goldsmiths and Silversmiths Co., 22oz. (G. A. Key) $608

A modern three-piece condiment set of shaped oval form with pierced and bright-cut decoration, blue glass liners and spoons, Birmingham 1976. (Bearne's) $308

Unusual hallmarked silver pouring vessel in Turkish style with animal head handle, beaded detail, Chester 1910, 7oz. (G.A. Key) $223

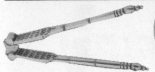

A pair of George III nut crackers, crested, John Shea, London 1807, 116gm., 3.7oz.
(Bearne's) $664

Heavy silver pap boat of usual form with lined rim and bearing a crest, London, probably 1768.
(G.A. Key) $318

Fine early 19th century child's large silver whistle/rattle/teether, (one bell missing), 6in. long, maker *J.F.*
(G.A. Key) $361

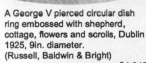

Silver evening chain purse, circa 1900, Wm. B. Kerr & Co., serpentine-form with acid-etched scroll foliate detail, 4½in. long, approx. 3 troy oz.
(Skinner) $488

A Fabergé circular cigar cutter in silver gilt and blue basse taille, enamel painted with trailing leafage frieze in white, 1.6in. diameter.
(Russell Baldwin & Bright)
                           $11,520

A George V pierced circular dish ring embossed with shepherd, cottage, flowers and scrolls, Dublin 1925, 9in. diameter.
(Russell, Baldwin & Bright)
                            $1,345

A Continental model of a standing cockerel with detachable head, realistically modeled with textured feathers and comb, by B. Muller, English import marks for 1910, 23cm high, (on wooden base).
23.5oz. (Christie's) $1,046

A Victorian plated and electro-gilt mounted brandy dispenser, late 19th century, fitted with two staved and hooped cut glass barrels with detachable mounted cork stoppers, 10½in. wide.
(Christie's) $853

A Victorian silver mounted heart-shaped mirror, the frame chased and pierced with putti and birds, 28.5cm. high, William Comyns, 1898.
(Bearne's) $810

Hallmarked silver memorial bell, well chased and embossed with religious figures and animals, 4in. high, London 1919, by C. Krall.
(G.A. Key) $412

A pair of Chilean spurs, dated *1913,* low grade silver inlay on iron.
(Bonhams) $357

Marianne Brandt for Ruppelwerk, Gotha, napkin holder, circa 1930, lime green painted sheet steel 5¼in. (Sotheby's) $1,462

A Queen Anne Scottish silver thistle shaped mug, John Luke Jnr., Glasgow, 1704, thistle shaped and on rim foot, 3³/8in. high, 4½oz. (Christie's) $3,245

An American silver cann, Richard Humphreys, Philadelphia, circa 1775, 14oz., 5¹/8in. high. (Sotheby's) $4,312

Georg Jensen mixed metal mug, impressed *Georg Jensen Design*, initials *H.K., Denmark*, 3¾in. high. (Skinner) $288

A Scottish Provincial silver mug, William Jamieson, Aberdeen, circa 1830, of plain baluster form, with everted lip and reeded scroll handle, 3½in. high, 4oz. (Christie's) $2,944

A modern silver reproduction of a late 17th century chinoiserie decorated mug, with reeded scroll handle, by Carrington & Co., 1911, 9.5cm high, 7oz. (Christie's) $518

A George III mug of tapering cylindrical form, initialed on scroll handle, 10.5cm. high, possibly Peter and Anne Bateman, London 1792, 6.6oz. (Bearne's) $292

A China trade silver mug, with pseudo hallmarks, late 19th century, chased with figures in a pavilioned landscape, 3¾in. high, 7½oz. (Christie's) $645

A George II silver mug, George Hindmarsh, 1752, of plain baluster form, on spreading circular foot, with leaf-capped scroll handle, 4½in. high, 7½oz. (Christie's) $736

A China trade silver mug, maker's mark *HC*, late nineteenth century, chased with figures in a mountainous jungle landscape, 4in., 7oz. (Christie's) $342

HISTORICAL FACTS
Mustards

Until well into the 18th century, mustard was taken dry from unpierced or 'blind' casters (on which the piercing design was nevertheless marked) and mixed on the plate.

Mustard pots appeared only after 1760. Unless they are pierced, or cut-out underneath, Georgian examples were gilded inside and liners were not required. Neo-classic vases for mustard date from the 1770s onward, and have tall reeded handles, a tall lid and a tall pedestal foot on a square base. Also in the late 18th century, legs appeared on mustard pots, and pots became solid and cylindrical, with flat lids.

Oval examples, often dipping slightly towards the center of each side, were also made at this time, before convex sides and barrel styles came in around 1800. In the 1820s forms became heavier and more elaborate.

By and large, oblong mustard pots seem less popular than other shapes.

A Victorian mustard pot with leaf capped double scroll handle and pierced stylized foliate decoration, 7cm. high, Joseph Savory & Albort Savory, London 1850.
(Bearne's) $275

A George III rectangular mustard pot with urn finial scallop shell thumb piece, London 1814, and a mustard spoon, London 1810.
(Dreweatt Neate) $320

Fine large Victorian silver mustard, octagonal shaped with foliate pierced panels, engraved domed lid, pierced thumb piece, blue glass liner, (slight chips), London 1845.
(G. A. Key) $464

Fine Victorian cast silver mustard in chinoiserie style, the sides pierced with trellis and scroll designs, 2½in. diameter, 3½in. high, London 1852.
(G. A. Key) $544

Fine large cylindrical silver drum mustard, the flat lid with shell thumb piece, scrolled handle plus blue glass liner, 2½in. high, Chester 1906.
(G. A. Key) $264

A pair of silver salts and a silver mustard pot, by Charles Robert Ashbee, London 1900, the salts each with deep hammered bowls with dot decoration around the rolled rim, each salt 1⅞in. high
(Christie's) $5,998

A George III silver gilt mustard pot with chinoiserie decoration, resting on four cast mask and paw feet, by William Fountain, 1815, 11.5cm. high. 9.5oz.
(Christie's) $1,394

George III silver mustard of slightly compressed oval design, blue glass liner and silver dredger salt spoon, the mustard marked for London 1803, maker T R, 5oz. free.
(G. A. Key) $396

Octagonal formed drum mustard with engraved design, hinged domed lid with decorative thumbpiece, hallmarked for London 1841, with a similar spoon.
(G.A. Key) $314

HISTORICAL FACTS
Nutmeg Graters

Though they were already in use in the late 17th century, most nutmeg graters found today date between the 1770s and 1830s, when hot toddy was popular. They consist of a tiny silver box large enough to contain a nutmeg and a steel grater hinged at the top for using the grater and at the bottom for removing the grated spice. They were made in many attractive shapes, such as acorns, hearts, and barrels. Also, as the outer covering of the nutmeg was sold as mace, some were shaped as ceremonial maces. The grater itself sometimes helps to date the item; this was usually of silver until 1739, with irregular holes, then of hammered sheet steel, silver framed, until the 1770s then of tinned rolled steel, and from the 1790s, of blued steel with symmetrical perforations in concentric circles in the best examples.

Peppers

HISTORICAL FACTS
Peppers

In their earliest form, pepper casters came as small, round pierced balls attached to 16th and 17th century bell salts, though they later adopted conventional caster form. In the early 18th century bun and kitchen peppers became popular. These were about 3in. high, the bun pepper of the same shape as larger casters, while the kitchen pepper, though having a similar cover, invariably has a cylindrical body and a simple loop handle. Kitchen peppers are fairly rare and now command high prices.

George III silver nutmeg grater, Birmingham, 1809, Matthew Linwood, rectangular hinged box, approx. 1 troy oz. (Skinner)   **$747**

Two silver nutmeg grinders, Birmingham, 1870s, one in the form of a strawberry, one in the form of a nutmeg seed, approx. 2 troy oz. (Skinner)   **$2,530**

A silver egg-shaped nutmeg grater, 18th century, with two engraved lines at middle, a threaded lid unscrewing to reveal a hinged and pierced iron grater, 15dwts. gross, 1½in. long. (Sotheby's)   **$1,725**

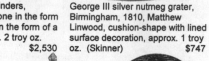

George III silver nutmeg grater, Birmingham, 1810, Matthew Linwood, cushion-shape with lined surface decoration, approx. 1 troy oz. (Skinner)   **$747**

A rare American silver matching octagonal pepper and mustard pot, John Burt, Boston, circa 1730, with projecting base band, 5oz. each, 3¾in. high. (Sotheby's)   **$31,050**

A George III Scottish silver pepper caster, Edinburgh 1814, of stylized thistle shape, on reeded spreading foot, with egg-and-dart overhang rim, 4in., 4oz. (Christie's)   **$846**

Attractive pair of late Victorian silver peppers, vase shaped with ¾ fluted decoration, standing on oval bases, 4in. high, London 1898. (G. A. Key)   **$144**

A novelty silver pepper in the form of a Toby jug, with scrolled handle, Birmingham 1911, 3in. high. (G A Key)   **$192**

American coin silver water pitcher, circa 1838–48, by Lincoln & Reed, Boston, 27 troy oz., 10½in. high. (Eldred's) $880

Sterling silver four-pint water pitcher, by Wallace, monogrammed, 20 troy oz., 9in. high. (Eldred's) $220

Sterling silver water pitcher, by Wallace, 20 troy oz., 9in. high. (Eldred's) $220

An American silver large pitcher, Tiffany & Co., New York, 1902-7, the baluster body repoussé and chased with parallel lines, foliate scrolls and clover, 55oz 10dwts., 11in. high. (Sotheby's) $3,737

An American silver water pitcher on stand, Gorham Mfg. Co., Providence RI, circa 1908, rectangular chased with masks, bands and swags of fruit, 110oz., 12¼in. (Sotheby's) $5,462

An American partly gilt and partly coppered silver 'Japanese style' water pitcher, Tiffany & Co., New York, circa 1878, 34oz. 10dwt., 8½in. high. (Sotheby's) $8,625

An American silver water pitcher, Tiffany & Co., New York, circa 1885, baluster form, embossed in Kirk style, 33oz., 12¼in. (Sotheby's) $3,450

An American silver and other metals 'Japanese style' water pitcher, Tiffany & Co., New York, 1878, of baluster form, applied with various exotic fish, 33oz., 9in. high. (Sotheby's) $28,750

An American silver Japanese style water pitcher, George W. Schlebler & Co., New York, circa 1890–1900, of baluster form, 31oz. 10dwt., 10¼in. high. (Sotheby's) $2,300

A set of twelve American silver service plates, Tiffany & Co., New York, circa 1905, the borders applied with festoons linking fluted urns, 299oz., 11in. diameter.
(Sotheby's) $20,700

A set of eleven silver plates, manufactured by Gorham & Co., circa 1900, with pierced and cast floral borders, 11in. diameter.
(Christie's) $7,360

A set of four silver octagonal dinner plates, with later chased bands of fruiting vine and foliage, 10¼in. diameter, 88oz.
(Christie's) $2,024

A William IV naturalistic dessert plate of shaped circular outline decorated in low relief, probably by William Eaton, 1831, 24cm. diameter, 10.5oz.
(Christie's) $836

A set of twelve American silver service plates, R. Wallace & Sons, Wallingford, Ct, circa 1910, the wide borders applied and chased with foliage, 266oz., 11in. diameter.
(Sotheby's) $7,475

A George IV silver dinner plate, Paul Storr, 1833, of shaped circular form, with shell and gadrooned border, 10¼in. diameter, 22oz.
(Christie's) $1,067

A set of twelve American silver dinner plates, Howard & Co., New York, 1907, with ribbon-tied reeded rims, 291oz. 10dwt., 10in. diameter.
(Sotheby's) $5,175

A set of twelve American silver small plates, Gorham Mfg. Co., Providence, RI, 1906, Martelé, .9584 standard, 93oz., 6¾in. diameter.
(Sotheby's) $7,475

A composite set of sixteen silver soup plates, nine by Heming & Co, 1913 and 1912, three by Elkington, 1896, one by Francis Higgins, 1897, 10¼in. diameter, 338 oz.
(Christie's) $4,784

A Charles II silver porringer, Edward Gladwin, London, 1682, the body flat-chased with chinoiserie birds and foliage, 4in. high, 10oz. (Christie's) $5,377

An American silver large porringer, Churchilll & Treadwell, Boston, circa 1810, with a keyhole handle, engraved script initial *S* on handle, 9oz. 10dwts, 5½in. diameter. (Sotheby's) $690

A porringer in the late 17th century manner, the lower body embossed and chased with acanthus foliage, 4¾in. high. (Christie's) $496

An American silver porringer, J. Clarke, Newport, Rhode Island, circa 1750, with double arch keyhole handle, engraved with initials, 8oz. 4¾in. diameter. (Sotheby's) $7,475

A silver porringer, maker's mark *NL* possibly West Country, the base engraved *Yeovill/Aug.st 5th 1728*, 4⅝in. high, 6½oz. (Christie's) $2,576

An American silver porringer, Daniel Russell, Newport, Rhode Island, circa 1760, with keyhole handle, engraved initials, 8oz., 5in. diameter. (Sotheby's) $2,587

Pots

An attractive Edwardian pot pourri vase and cover, Chester 1909, 184 grams total, 14.5cm. high. (Spencer's) $440

One of a pair of preserve pots and covers of tapering cylindrical form with beaded borders and applied swags and medallions, Carrington & Co., London 1912, 5½in. high, 19oz. (Christie's) $704

A pounce pot by John McKay, Edinburgh, 1798, 3oz. (Phillips) $400

Two of a set of eight George III silver salt cellars, Paul Storr, London, 1815, the bodies cast and chased with ribbon-tied floral garlands on matted ground, 4¾in. diameter, 110oz.
(Christie's) (Eight) $87,007

A set of Three Victorian novelty silver salt cellars, George William Adams, London, 1868, each formed as a coal scuttle with a foliate scroll handle and on spreading circular foot, 3¼in. long, 8oz. (Christie's) $1,824

A pair of George III oval salt cellars with pierced and engraved decoration, on four ball and claw feet, London 1785 and 1786 by Hester Bateman.
(Dreweatt Neate) $704

A pair of French parcel-gilt salt cellars, marker's mark of Charles Nicolas Odiot, Paris, circa 1850, the oblong-shaped stands chased with foliage border, 4½in. high.
(Christie's) $3,457

A set of six George II plain circular salts on hoof feet, London marks 1750, maker David Hennell, glass loose liners, 2¾in. diameter, 12oz. 10dwts. (Anderson & Garland) $858

Pair of Tiffany & Co. Sterling salts, 1907, chrysanthemum pattern, monogram, approx. 6 troy oz.
(Skinner) $862

Attractive pair of Adam styled silver salts, boat shaped and having slot pierced and garland embossed sides, Chester 1913, 3½ and 2in.
(G A Key) $160

A pair of Portuguese, cast metalware pedestal salts with round bases and bowls and slender baluster columns, by Jesus Eduardo dos Santos, Setubal, 9.75cm high x 7cm diameter.
(Christie's) $920

A pair of George II Scottish silver trencher salt cellars, John Main, Edinburgh, 1732, each of plain tapering oblong form, with chamfered corners and plain oval bowls, 3in. wide, 3.5oz. (Christie's)
$3,496

A George II silver sauceboat, Samuel Courtauld I, 1753, on three rocaille and shell feet headed with turbaned masks, 8½in. long, 16oz.
(Christie's) $2,115

A pair of oval sauceboats, with waved rims, flying scroll handles and on three hoof feet, Birmingham 1917, 10oz., 15.5cm. long.
(Bristol) $240

An early George III silver sauce boat with bowled punched rim, leaf capped flying scroll handle, London 1777, by W Grundy.
(G A Key) $304

A George III Scottish silver cream boat, James Hewitt, 1779, of squat pear shape, on molded oval foot, 7in. wide., 5oz.
(Christie's) $1,336

A matched pair of Georgian style silver sauce boats with ovolo rims, leaf capped flying scrolled handles, one Chester 1932, the other Birmingham 1933, 9oz. total.
(G A Key) $408

A George II large silver sauce boat, London, 1759, with unidentified maker's mark *RR* in script, shaped oval and on three shell and lion's mask feet, 10¾in. long. 24oz.
(Christie's) $2,784

Georg Jensen sauce boat and tray, hammered finish, openwork with berries and leaves, 8in. wide, approximately 16 troy oz.
(Skinner) $2,875

A pair of George II silver sauce boats, London, 1751, probably John Holland, helmet-shaped and on three shell and hoof feet, 7¼in. long, 20oz.
(Christie's) $3,841

Silver sauce boat in Arts and Crafts style with shaped oval base, scrolled handle, Birmingham 1934, maker JFR, 8½oz. (G. A. Key) $152

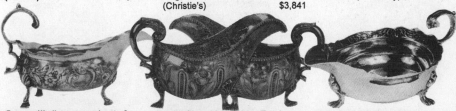

George III silver sauce boat of usual form with card cut rim, supported on three shell and hoof feet, well marked for London 1772, maker *I.K.*
(G.A. Key) $366

A pair of late 18th century Dutch sauce boats of bellied oval form with bead borders, three shell feet, probably by J.van Straatsburg, Utrecht, 1788, 20.5cm long, 21.5oz.
(Christie's) $4,416

A George II Scottish silver cream boat, James Glen, Glasgow, circa 1745, plain oval on three stylized fleur-de-lis and paw feet, 6¼in. long, 5oz.
(Christie's) $1,336

A Scottish silver mounted oak snuff box, John Lyall, Ayr, circa 1900, rectangular form, made from a piece of oak from the Old Brig of Ayr, 3½in.
(Christie's) $1,184

A 19th century Oriental rectangular snuff box with canted corners, cover chased with scrolls and leafage, possibly Malay or Dutch East Indies, 10.2cm. long, 5oz.
(Phillips) $456

A George IV 'pedlar' snuff box, of plain rounded oblong form with reeded borders, by John Linnit, 1823, 10 x 5 x 4cm.
(Phillips) $4,704

A good early Victorian snuff box, engraved all over with foliate shells, scrolls and hatching, by Charles Rawlings and William Summers, 1844, 8.5 x 6cm., 6.5oz.
(Phillips) $988

An electroplated mounted table snuff mull, late 19th century, the mount with a hinged cover, supported by a stag's head mounted hoof foot, by Walker & Hall.
(Bonhams) $563

A Swiss gold and enamel snuff-box, 19th century, maker's mark the initial *M*, oblong with rounded ends, with opaque black enamel decoration, 3¹/₈in. long.
(Christie's) $2,846

A Continental gold-mounted hardstone snuff box, 19th century, in the style of Hoffman, the cover applied with bloodstone and varicolored agate foliage, 3³/₈in. long.
(Christie's) $8,625

An early 19th century South African colonial mounted cowrie shell snuff box, engraved on the cover with a foliate wreath, by John & Thomas Townsend, of the Cape, circa 1825, 9cm. long.
(Christie's) $1,362

A George III Scottish presentation snuff box, by William & Patrick Cunningham, Edinburgh, 1814, with gold insert, of oblong form engraved with bands of floral and foliate decoration, 10oz. gross weight. (Christie's) $900

A George III Scottish silver mounted and moss agate set cowrie shell snuff mull, William Robertson, Edinburgh, circa 1795, 3¾in. wide.
(Christie's) $1,718

A Continental silver and agate snuff box, unmarked, circa 1770, cartouche-shaped with agate inlaid lid, 2oz. (Christie's) $337

A Scottish silver mounted cowrie shell snuff mull, unmarked, circa 1800, the silver mount with scalloped border, 3¼in.
(Christie's) $573

A George III tankard of plain
tapering cylindrical form, 20cm.
high, Edward Fernell, London
1783, 26.5oz.
(Bearne's) $876

A George I tankard of tapering form
with a large scroll handle, probably
by Timothy Ley, 1722, 18cm high,
12.5oz.
(Christie's) $3,128

An American silver tankard, Tiffany &
Co., New York, 1887, of large lidded
cylindrical form on four claw feet,
59oz. 2dwts., 9½in. high.
(Sotheby's) $7,000

A George III tankard of
tapering circular form with
reeded girdle and domed lid,
28.5cm. high, John Deacon,
London 1773, 23.6oz.
(Bearn's) $1,513

A William IV silver-gilt and ivory
tankard, John Bridge, London,
1831, the body with vine cartouche
enclosing a carved ivory plaque of
St. George and the Dragon, 12¼in.
high, 124oz gross.
(Christie's) $103,540

A Charles II silver-gilt small
tankard, maker's mark a key
between two pellets, London, 1669,
flat-topped hinged cover with eared
scroll thumbpiece, 4½in. high, 13oz.
(Christie's) $13,745

Late George II plain silver half pint
tankard of circular baluster form to
a circular foot, 3½in. high, London
1757, 5oz.
(G.A. Key) $259

An American silver tankard, William
Cowell, Boston, circa 1730, of
tapered cylindrical form, 22oz.
10dwt., 7½in. high.
(Sotheby's) $6,900

A Victorian silver-gilt tankard,
William Ker Reid, London, 1851,
the body applied with scrolling oak
branches and a vacant laurel
wreath cartouche, 15in. high,
124oz. (Christie's) $9,987

Louis Tardy for Tétard Frères, tea service, circa 1935, comprising: teapot, milk jug, sugar basin and cover, silver-colored metal and rosewood, teapot: 4⁷/₈in. (Sotheby's) $4,499

A George III composite three piece silver tea service, the teapot, Edinburgh, 1819, the sugar basin and cream jug, London, 1809, 36oz. (Christie's) $993

A late Victorian three-piece teaset of part fluted oblong form with gadrooned borders by Elkington & Co., Birmingham, 1899; and a similar hot water jug to match by T. Wilkinson, Birmingham, 1904, 49oz. (Christie's) $930

Victorian styled four piece silver plated coffee and tea set of slightly compressed oval design, well engraved with scrolls, leaves and cartouches. (G.A. Key) $397

Josef Hoffmann for the Wiener Werkstätte, executed by Alfred Mayer, coffee service, 1913, comprising: coffee pot, milk jug, sugar basin and cover and tray, silver colored metal, ebony, malachite cabochons coffee pot 6⁵/₈in. high. (Sotheby's) $33,741

An early four piece tea service, designed and manufactured by Georg Jensen, circa 1910/15, comprising teapot and cover, sugar basin, cream jug and oval tray, each piece wrought and chased with formalized sepals, teapot 6³/₈in. high. (Christie's) $6,186

Tiffany three-piece silver tea set, 1850-52, marked *Tiffany, Young & Ellis*, chased floral design, eagle finial, teapot, covered sugar, and creamer, monogrammed, teapot 4³/₈in. high., approx. 27 troy oz. (Skinner) $1,150

A five piece silver tea service, Finnigans Ltd, 1911, the tray 1916; the lamp Jas. Dixon & Sons, Sheffield, in the manner of Paul Storr, 251oz. (Christie's) $6,491

A George IV Scottish silver three piece tea service, J. McKay, Edinburgh, 1823, richly chased and embossed with bands of flower-heads and matted foliage, the teapot 12in. wide, 54oz.
(Christie's) $1,909

Three-piece American Empire silver tea set, marked on bottom *W. Thomson, New York, 1835*, spout in the form of an exotic bird's head, monogrammed and dated, 82.4 troy oz.
(Eldred's) $1,155

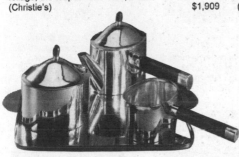

Josef Hoffmann for the Wiener Werkstätte, tea service, 1908–09, comprising: teapot, milk jug and sugar basin and cover and tray, electroplated metal, ebony, each piece monogrammed *'GF'*, teapot 5⅞in.
(Sotheby's) $10,310

A modern four-piece tea and coffee service of plain circular form with molded edging, the teapot and coffee pot with wooden handles and finials, Birmingham 1955/7, 80.262.
(Bearne's) $826

A composite silver three piece tea service, the teapot with maker's marks of Hayne & Cater, 1848, of baluster form on incurved-hexagonal foot, the body with circular panels engraved with chinoiserie scenes and presentation inscription, height of teapot 9¼in., 38oz.   (Christie's) $1,148

Durgin Sterling five-piece tea and coffee service, early 20th century, tea and coffee pots, creamer, open sugar and wastebowl, melon-shape with engraved scroll and shell decoration, with matching two-handled tray, approx. 214 troy oz.
(Skinner) $3,737

A George V four-piece tea and coffee service, of paneled oblong form with reeded edging and angular composition handles and finials on pad feet, maker's mark *S & W*, Sheffield 1934/38, 58oz.
(Bearne's) $778

Georg Jensen, a Danish silver matched five-piece tea and coffee service, of bulbous form and of hammered finish with turned wood side handles and finials, import marks for London 1923/31/38, 40.5oz.
(Bearne's) $2,673

A George III tea caddy of canted oblong form with paneled sides, by Robert Hennell, 1792, 15cm high, 12.5oz. (Christie's) $3,128

A Dutch silver tea caddy, possibly Haarlem, circa 1735, the shoulder chased with landscape vignettes framed by scrolls, 5in. (Christie's) $690

Attractive early 20th century silver tea caddy, engraved with ribbon and foliate festoons and medallions, 3½in. high, Chester 1910. (G. A. Key) $45

An American silver and other metals Japanese style tea caddy, Gorham Mfg. Co., Providence, RI, 1879, of crumpled sack form with spot-hammered surface, 9oz. gross, 4¼in. high. (Sotheby's) $3,737

A George III oval tea caddy, urn shaped finial, bright cut engraved foliate detail, London 1786, oval 14.5cm., 13oz. (Wintertons) $1,049

Woolley tea caddy, hand hammered form, impressed *Woolley, Sterling 3, The Nesmiths from the Morses, June 10, 1916*, 5in. high. (Skinner) $517

Small silver plated spirit kettle, burner and stand with engraved decoration and bearing the date of *1895*, 9in. high.
(G.A. Key) $141

A Victorian electro-plated kettle on a stand with wirework supports, the body engraved with ferns and foliage, circa 1880, 38.5cm. high.
(Christie's) $324

Silver plated spirit kettle and stand, oval shaped with half fluted decoration, gadrooned rims to kettle and stand, spirit burner, to base, 12in. high, late 19th century.
(G. A. Key) $83

A Victorian electro-plated tea kettle, stand and lamp, by J.R. Collis & Co., circa 1890, of large tapering circular form with fixed scroll handle, 16½in. high.
(Christie's) $592

Peter Behrens for AEG, Bingwerke, Nürnberg, electric kettle and cover, 1909, nickel and chromium plated metal, ebonized wood and woven cane, 8½in.
(Sotheby's) $1,593

A mid 19th century Continental kettle, on a four legged stand with burner of baluster form with lobed fluting, unmarked, probably Scandinavian, circa 1840, 46cm. high, 59oz.
(Christie's) $1,135

Coin silver hot water kettle on stand, circa 1850, with burner, by Lincoln & Foss, Boston, heavily chased, rococo style, 58 troy oz., 15in. high.
(Eldred's) $1,870

Peter Behrens for AEG, Bingwerke, Nürnberg, electric kettle and cover, 1909, brass, ebonized wood and woven cane, 9in.
(Sotheby's) $1,875

Octagonal shaped spirit kettle with ivory finial to the swing handle and hinged lid, complete with burner, hallmarked for London 1930.
(G.A. Key) $848

A Victorian teapot of plain circular form with melon finial, 17cm. high, Joseph Angell senior & Joseph Angell Junior, London 1839, 19.6oz. (Bearne's) $567

Attributed to Hans Ofner, for Argentor, Vienna, teapot, circa 1905, electroplated metal, wood, 5⅝in. (Sotheby's) $975

George II small silver teapot, Cape pattern with ebonized handle, 3½in. high, London 1756, maker *D.H.*, 9.5oz. (G.A. Key) $594

A George II Scottish silver bullet teapot, William Aytoun, Edinburgh, 1740, chased around the rim with panels of fruit, foliage and scrolls, 5½in. high. 19oz. (Christie's) $2,673

A George III Scottish silver teapot and stand, Thomas Sempill, Edinburgh, 1793, shaped oval with bright-cut engraved borders, 12in. wide overall, 23oz. total weight. (Christie's) $2,864

A George II Scottish silver bullet teapot, Coline Allan, Aberdeen, circa 1750, on stepped spreading circular foot, 6½in. high, 20oz. gross. (Christie's) $22,908

Fine Christopher Dresser teapot, Hukin & Heath, circular form with angled spout, raffia handle, 5½in. high. (Skinner) $288

A Victorian teapot of hexagonal paneled form, floral and leafage engraved, and matching jug, London 1851, maker *G.A.*, 43oz. (Russell, Baldwin & Bright) $989

Fine Victorian silver teapot of octagonal baluster form, engraved with parcels of flowers with vacant cartouches, 7in. high, Glasgow 1857, maker J M, 25 oz. (G. A. Key) $592

A George II Scottish silver bullet teapot, James Ker, Edinburgh, 1741, chased around the rim, 5in. high., 13½oz. (Christie's) $1,431

A George III oval teapot with a C-scroll handle and a swan's neck spout, Henry Nutting, 1801, 14oz. (Christie's) $1,041

Hester Bateman, oval silver teapot with bright cut decoration, scrolled treen handle and finial, angular spout, 4½in. high, London 1780. (G.A. Key) $376

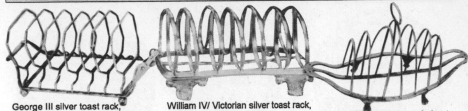

George III silver toast rack, rectangular frame with scrolled handles and having six octagonal bars, London 1806, by John Emes. (G.A. Key)   **$400**

William IV/ Victorian silver toast rack, 1837, Hy. Wilkinson & Co., scroll and shell handle and feet, 9 oz., 6½in. long. (Skinner)   **$345**

George III silver toast rack, boat shaped with seven graduated wire work bars, Birmingham 1798, 9½in. long, 7½oz. (G. A. Key)   **$303**

Fine large late Victorian silver toastrack in Gothic taste, standing on four ball feet, Sheffield 1901, 10oz. (G.A. Key)   **$240**

William IV silver toast rack, having six heart shaped divisions, Birmingham 1832, by Matthew Boulton, 13oz. (G.A. Key)   **$461**

A George III seven bar toastrack, the arched wirework divisions supported on oval base, London, 1799, possibly by John Fountain. (Bonhams)   **$400**

A Hukin & Heath plated toastrack, designed by Christopher Dresser, the arched base on four bun feet supporting six pronged divisions, 12.5cm. high. (Phillips)   **$480**

George III silver toast rack, octagonal handle and panel, engraved crest, marks of Hester Bateman, London, 1790, 7oz., 7in. high. (Eldred's)   **$1,320**

An early Victorian silver toastrack of arched form, the rectangular base on four scroll bracket feet, London 1853, George Angell, 11oz. approx. (Bonhams)   **$320**

George IV silver toast rack of seven double hooped bars to a shaped rectangular base, cast rococo style carrying handle, 6 x 4in. London 1827, 10½oz. (G. A. Key)   **$572**

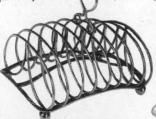

A rare Scottish Provincial silver bannock rack, Peter Lambert, Aberdeen, circa 1805, with nine double loop wire-work divisions and central ring handle, 6¾in. wide, 11oz. (Christie's)   **$3,818**

A novelty seven bar toast rack, London 1920, Holland, Aldwinckle and Slater, modeled as the letters of the name Dorothy, 4oz. approx., 11cm. long. (Bonhams)   **$320**

A Victorian salver of octafoil outline with a fern engraved center, by John Harrison & Co., Sheffield, 1873, 28cm. diameter, 20.5oz. (Christie's) $666

A George III silver two-handled small tray, maker's mark of Timothy Renou, 1796, oval, with reeded borders and handles, 20¾in. wide, 76oz. (Christie's) $9,487

Edwardian silver wine salver of shaped circular design with gadrooned and foliate edge, 8in. diameter, Sheffield 1902, 12oz. (G. A. Key) $280

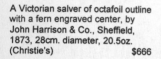

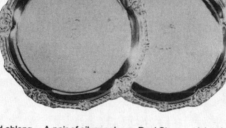

A modern tea tray of canted oblong form, with ivory handles and a reeded border, by Viners of Sheffield, 1958, 54cm long, 66.5oz. (Christie's) $2,463

A pair of silver salvers, Paul Storr, London, 1811, shaped circular and on four water-leaf and rosette feet, 9in. diameter, 35oz. (Christie's) $7,298

A late Victorian two-handled oval tray with a beaded border and handles, the center engraved with a crest, flanked by borders of Greek key and stylized drops, by W.&J.Barnard, 1879, 47cm wide, 34oz. (Christie's) $1,388

A George II Scottish silver waiter, Harry Beathune, Edinburgh, 1730, on four hoof feet, engraved with crest and motto, 6¼in. wide, 10oz. (Christie's) $1,145

A mid 19th century Austro-Hungarian two-handled tea tray of shaped oblong form with shell and scroll decorated corners, maker's mark *T & C Co, Vienna, 1857*, 69 x 43cm. (Christie's) $2,178

A George II Scottish silver teapot stand or waiter, William Aytoun, Edinburgh, 1740, shaped hexagonal on three paw feet, 6¾in. diameter, 7oz. (Christie's) $858

Attractive Art Nouveau silver dressing table tray, the centre embossed with stylized trailing flowers and foliage, 12 x 9in., Birmingham 1905, 7½oz. (G. A. Key)   **$256**

An early Victorian salver of shaped circular outline on cast scroll feet, by Messrs J.&J.Angell, 1846, 29cm diameter, 38.35oz. (Christie's)   **$1,333**

Large good quality silver plated two handled tea tray of shaped oval design, having wavy gadrooned and shell edge, 20 x 15in. by Mappin and Webb. (G. A. Key)   **$256**

A large two-handled tray of rounded oblong form with a florally chased center, Harrison Bros. & Howson, Sheffield, 1896, 77 x 46cm. 148.5oz. (Christie's)   **$3,148**

A pair of George II silver waiters, Robert Abercromby, London, 1732, shaped circular and on three hoof feet, with molded rim, 6in. diameter,13oz. (Christie's)   **$3,265**

A Victorian silver plated tea tray of waisted oblong from, the center chased with a geometric pattern, 23½in. (Andrew Hartley)   **$310**

George III silver salver, London, 1771, John Carter, gadrooned border, engraved coat of arms with heart-shaped shield and floral decoration, on four feet, 13in. diameter, approx. 32 troy oz. (Skinner)   **$2,070**

An American parcel-gilt silver and other metals Japanese-style tray, Gorham Mfg., Providence, RI, 1882, in the form of a trompe l'oeil still life, 29oz. 10dwt. gross, 11in. wide. (Sotheby's)   **$16,100**

A George II silver salver, Robert Abercromby, 1734, engraved to the center with a coat-of-arms within rococo cartouche, 12in. diameter, 32oz. (Christie's)   **$3,436**

Small silver plated soup tureen, oval shaped with half fluted decoration, the domed lid partially fluted and having looped twig handle, circa 1880. (G.A. Key) $196

Christopher Dresser for J.W. Hukin & J.T. Heath tureen, cover and ladle, design registered 28th July, 1880, electroplated metal, 8¹/₈in. high. (Sotheby's) $11,622

A George III silver soup tureen and cover, William Bruce, London, 1818, the body engraved twice with a cartouche enclosing two later crests, 16in. long, 123oz. (Christie's) $11,523

A pair of George III silver sauce tureens and covers, by Orlando Jackson, 1772, the plain body engraved with the crest of Maclean, with later ring handles, each 6in. high. 49oz. (Christie's) $4,507

A pair of French silver soup tureens, covers and stands, the tureens and covers, Jean-Charles Cahier, Paris, 1809-1819, the stands, Jean-Baptiste-Claude Odiot, Paris, 1819-1825, 16in. long, 300oz.(Christie's) $30,728

A pair of Regency silver sauce tureens and covers, Paul Storr, London, 1811, the reeded handles with lion's mask joins, 10in. long over handles, 73oz. 10dwt. (Christie's) $12,650

A Belgian silver soup tureen and cover, Mons, 1761, chased with scrolls and rocaille, 16in. long over handles, 86oz. (Christie's) $85,000

A pair of sauce tureens & stands, of ovoid shape chased with a band of lobes below a gadrooned border, with original ladles, by Thomas Heming 1769. (Tennants) $4,445

A silver soup tureen, marked *Fabergé*, Moscow, circa 1898, on four branch form feet headed by foliage, 16½in. long over handles, 147oz. (Christie's) $25,300

Georgian Sheffield plated tea urn, having stepped square base, vase shaped body, domed lid, 18in. high, late 18th century/early 19th century. (G. A. Key) $512

An early 19th century silver plated samovar, of half fluted urn shaped form, with turned foliate finial on domed lid, 18in. high. (Andrew Hartley) $800

A circular tapered half-fluted tea urn, engraved inscription, acanthus leaf border and tap with two lion mask ring handles, 21½in. high. (Anderson & Garland) $588

Regency period silver plated small tea urn on trefoil three footed base, having ivory handles to tap and sides, 13in. high, circa 1835. (G.A. Key) $157

A mid 19th century Austro-Hungarian circular tea urn on a four-legged stand with burner, Vienna, 1846, 37.5cm high, 5oz. (Christie's) $1,573

George Lecomte for G. Carre & Cie., Paris, samovar, circa 1935, comprising kettle, cover and detachable water flow regulator, with integral stand, 15½in. (Sotheby's) $2,812

George III silver tea urn, London, 1764, chased floral and scroll decoration, gadrooned rims, on four raised ball and claw feet, 19¾in. high, approx. 83 troy oz. (Skinner) $2,070

An American silver tea urn, S. Kirk & Sons, Baltimore, circa 1880-90, spherical, chased with birds and flowers, 74oz. 14in. high. (Sotheby's) $2,300

George III silver tea urn, London, 1775-76, Charles Wright (or Chas, Woodward), monogrammed center with beaded details, ivory handle, 20½in. high, approx. 78troy oz. (Skinner) $2,415

A pair of Victorian flower vases, each on spreading scroll feet, chased with foliage, 1896, in fitted case, 5in. high, 7oz. (Clarke Gammon) $576

A George II silver sugar vase, Solomon Hougham, 1795, the body engraved with bright cut stylized foliage and two vacant oval cartouches, 6¼in. wide, 6¼oz. (Christie's) $1,067

A pair of American silver vases, Gorham Mfg. Co., Providence, RI, 1900, Martelé, .950 standard, 212oz., 18¼in. high. (Sotheby's) $46,000

Fine pair of Art Nouveau silver flower vases on circular bases, the tapering cylindrical bodies joined to the bases by four stylized curved legs, 6in. high, Birmingham 1902 by Elkington and Co., 14oz. (G. A. Key) $560

An American silver and ivory vase, Gorham Mfg. Co., Providence, RI, Athenic, circa 1906, of bell shape, supported on three ivory tusks, 64oz. 10dwt. gross, 13in. high. (Sotheby's) $4,025

A pair of American silver vases, by Shreve Stanwood & Co., Boston, circa 1900, the body applied with cast and chased male & female busts, 9¾in. high. (Christie's) $2,087

A pair of modern tapering vases with round bases and shaped rims, by Walker & Hall, Sheffield, 1922, 32cm high. (Christie's) $533

A George III silver sugar vase, Burrage Davenport, 1783, vase shaped, on spreading circular foot, 5in. high, 6oz. (Christie's) $1,288

A pair of modern tapering vases with notched rims, round bases and applied vertical strapwork, by George Howson, 1909, 22cm. high, 20.5oz. (Christie's) $930

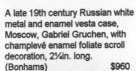

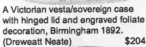

A rare California gold match safe, probably San Francisco, circa 1855, the front inlaid with gold quartz centering an enameled reserve with monogram against a leaf, 2¼in. long. (Christie's) $5,175

A late 19th century Russian white metal and enamel vesta case, Moscow, Gabriel Gruchen, with champlevé enamel foliate scroll decoration, 2¼in. long. (Bonhams) $960

A Victorian vesta/sovereign case with hinged lid and engraved foliate decoration, Birmingham 1892. (Dreweatt Neate) $204

Silver matchsafe, American, late 19th century, repoussé scrolling floral decoration with central female figure, 2½in. long, approx. 1 troy oz. (Skinner) $86

Silver matchsafe and coin purse, Birmingham, 1899, scroll foliate engraved surface decoration, compartment with two spring holders for coins, 2¼in. long, approx. 2 troy oz. (Skinner) $230

Gorham Sterling matchsafe, early 20th century, reptile skin surface design with applied United States coins, 2⅝in. long, approx. 1 troy oz. (Skinner) $201

Vinaigrettes

A George IV silver castletop vinaigrette, Birmingham 1836, Nathaniel Mills, the hinged lid with a scene of Newstead Abbey, 1½in. long. (Bonhams) $1,280

A Victorian silver novelty whistle vinaigrette, marks for 1870, S. Mordan & Co., modeled as a bugle, the other end with a whistle, 5cm. long. (Bonhams) $320

An early Victorian silver gilt castletop vinaigrette, Birmingham 1838, Nathaniel Mills, the hinged cover with a view of Windsor Castle, foliate border and sides, 1½in. long. (Bonhams) $1,120

A William IV castle-top vinaigrette, by Nathaniel Mills, Birmingham, 1837, depicting Abbotsford, of oblong form, 1½in. long. (Christie's) $937

A 19th century silver novelty vinaigrette, Birmingham, modelled as an articulated fish, 9.2 cm. long. (Bonhams) $320

A Scottish silver mounted vinaigrette, early 19th century, hinged cover applied with a foiled-back glass panel etched with a view of Edinburgh castle, 1½in. wide.   (Christie's) $1,312

A pair of American silver wine coolers, Tiffany & Co., New York, circa 1870, of vase form, 120oz. 10dwt., 9⅛in. high.
(Sotheby's) $20,700

An Old Sheffield plate gadrooned two-handled compressed vase-shaped wine cooler on a rising circular foot, 9¼in. high.
(Christie's) $760

A pair of Old Sheffield plate tapering two-handled wine coolers on rococo shell and scroll feet, un-marked circa 1810, 10in. high.
(Christie's) $1,120

Victorian period silver plated wine cooler, campana shaped with grapevine applied handles and top rim, 11in. high.
(G. A. Key) $475

A pair of Old Sheffield plated, pail shaped wine coolers with reeded hoops and lion mask, drop-ring handles, circa 1805, 20cm high.
(Christie's) $4,358

An American silver large twin handled wine cooler, Tiffany & Co., New York, circa 1865, of vase form, folding handles rising from pairs of classical female heads, 93 oz., 13in. high.
(Sotheby's) $9,200

A pair of Sheffield plated baluster wine coolers, the everted rims with a border of leaves, each with eagle head crest in a cartouche, 10in. high.
(David Lay) $1,120

Pair of Sheffield plate wine coolers, early 19th century, crested, bracket handles with foliate attachments, gadroon edge, 11in. high.
(Butterfield & Butterfield) $1,900

Early George III silver two part wine funnel with beaded edge and plain clip, London 1771. (G. A. Key) $283

A George III silver wine funnel, by Allen Dominy, 1791, of tapering circular form with reeded borders, 5½in. high. 2oz. (Christie's) $600

Early George III three part silver wine funnel with beaded edge, reeded decoration, London 1777. (G.A. Key) $761

A George III Scottish silver wine funnel, Edinburgh, circa 1800, of plain tapering form, with three applied short reeds. (Christie's) $667

A George III silver wine funnel, by Edward Capper, 1797, of tapering circular form with reeded borders, 6in. high. 2oz. (Christie's) $600

George III silver two part wine funnel of usual form with beaded edges, well marked for London 1701, maker CI I. (G.A. Key) $556

A George IV wine funnel with a squat circular bowl, crested, and a reeded border by Sebastian Crespell (II), 1825, 12.5cm high, 3oz. (Christie's) $778

A George III silver wine funnel and associated stand, the funnel by John Emes, 1801, the stand by J. MacDonald, Edinburgh, 1808, 4½in. high. (Christie's) $581

A George III silver wine funnel, Hester Bateman, 1786, the detachable strainer top with shaped clip and beaded border, 5in. (Christie's) $999

George IV silver one part wine funnel of usual form, having two body bands and reeded rim, 6in. high, London 1824, maker W B. (G. A. Key) $364

A George III silver wine funnel, possibly Thomas Watson, Newcastle, 1805, plain, with pierced detachable strainer, 5½in. high, 4oz. (Christie's) $1,049

Georgian two part silver wine funnel of plain design, the top unmarked and with beaded rim and clip, the other part bearing the London hallmark for 1784. (G. A. Key) $432

Good inside painted snuff bottle, dated *1898*, signed *Ma Xiaoxuan*, painted with fishing and pleasure boats on a river, 2½in. (Butterfield & Butterfield) $1,495

Good carved agate snuff bottle, 1800-1880, the globular body well hollowed out and carved to the front, 2⅛in. (Butterfield & Butterfield) $2,185

Good turquoise cabinet bottle, carved with a continuous mythical landscape scene showing Liu Hai and his toad, 2⅞in. (Butterfield & Butterfield) $800

Important porcelain snuff bottle in the form of a Manchu official, Guangxu mark and period, the figure captured in mid-stride, 4in. (Butterfield & Butterfield) $9,775

Very unusual archaic style russet nephrite double snuff bottle, 18th century, carved as two bottles tied up in a brocade sash, 2⅛in. (Butterfield & Butterfield) $3,162

Inside painted snuff bottle, dated *1904*, signed *Ye Zhongsan*, painted with a gathering of a young scholar and beauties in a garden, 2½in. (Butterfield & Butterfield) $800

Chinese snuff bottle, 19th century, white porcelain enameled with a cricket on both sides, Tao Kuang mark and period 1824-48. (Skinner) $575

Good rock crystal snuff bottle, 19th century, carved with sloping shoulders and a concave foot, amethyst stopper, 2½in. (Butterfield & Butterfield) $546

Fine jadeite snuff bottle, carved to the front and back with deer in a rocky pine-filled landscape, 2⅛in. (Butterfield & Butterfield) $1,265

Good polychrome painted ivory snuff bottle, late 19th century, carved and undercut with mounted warriors engaged in battle, 3¼in. (Butterfield & Butterfield) $632

Good shadow agate snuff bottle, 1800-1880, carved to the front with two roosters on a rocky outcropping, 3in. (Butterfield & Butterfield) $2,000

Good ruby glass snuff bottle, in the form of a ripe melon enclosed with flowering vines and hovering butterflies, 2in. (Butterfield & Butterfield) $920

Carved nephrite snuff bottle, 1750-1850, elegantly incised and painted with a portrait of a single blossom set off by a five-character dedication, 2¹/₈in. (Butterfield & Butterfield) $1,092

Good polychrome decorated ivory snuff bottle, late 19th century, carved and undercut with sages scroll viewing and conversing , 2⁵/₈in. (Butterfield & Butterfield) $920

Polychrome enameled molded porcelain figural snuff bottle, circa 1900, decorated in high relief with numerous children playing in a garden, 3in. (Butterfield & Butterfield) $800

Fine carved opal snuff bottle, the thin-walled spade shaped body carved to the front with a phoenix, 2½in. (Butterfield & Butterfield) $2,875

Good ruby overlaid glass snuff bottle, 1800-1880, with a leaping carp opposed by one swimming near waterplants, 2¼in. (Butterfield & Butterfield) $747

White jade snuff bottle, 1750-1825, carved to the front with a fisherman moored by a rocky promontory, 2³/₈in. (Butterfield & Butterfield) $747

A Paris mythological tapestry depicting the story of Cephalus and Procris, mid-17th century, Procris speaking with Cephalus in the left background, the two figures in the center leaning on his spear, 8ft. 5in. x 14ft. 3in. (Sotheby's) $12,650

An Aubusson gênre tapestry of boys playing, 18th century, the frolicking children playing dress-up, hide and seek and other games amidst a lightly wooded landscape, 7ft x 11ft. (Sotheby's) $13,800

An Aubusson pastoral tapestry, 19th century, depicting a lady with two young musicians seated by a tree, within trompe l'oeil framework, 5ft. 10in. x 6ft. 1in. (Sotheby's) $4,600

A tapestry of the month of September, late 17th century, probably English, two farmers emptying baskets of feed on the ground for the chickens, 10ft.5in. x 9ft. (Sotheby's) $20,700

An Aubusson historical tapestry, 17th century, a queen holding the reins of her horse and gesturing to the royal courtier to her left, 9ft. 1in. x 12ft. 4in. (Sotheby's) $25,300

A pastoral tapestry, Aubusson, late 19th century, woven with a scène galante of a shepherd boy and girl embracing, in a wooded landscape, 132 x 160cm. wide. (Sotheby's) $8,335

A Paris pre-Gobelins mythological tapestry depicting the story of Venus and Adonis, mid-17th century, Adonis in the foreground with his hunting dogs, Venus embracing him, 7ft. 8in. x 15ft. 8in.
(Sotheby's) $12,650

A Brussels tapestry depicting the 'Triumph of Bacchus and Ariadne', attributed to the workshop of Jan van der Borcht, circa 1700, the two figures sitting in a golden chariot drawn by leopards, 17ft. 8in. x 11ft. 5in.
(Sotheby's) $46,000

A Brussels mythological tapestry, late 17th century, probably depicting Diana the Huntress with hounds, a gentleman hunter with his arms thrown upwards in the center, 9ft.2in. x 7ft.10in.
(Sotheby's) $18,400

A Flemish Old Testament tapestry panel, first half of the 17th century, probably Antwerp, Saul (?) and three other gentlemen conversing, 8ft.11in. X 8ft. 3½in. (Sotheby's) $13,800

A Brussels Old Testament tapestry from the story of Hezekiah, in the manner of Bernaert van-Orley, mid-16th century, depicting King Hezekiah sanctifying the house of the Lord in Jerusalem, 10ft. 6in. x 15ft.
(Sotheby's) $31,050

A pre-Gobelins historical tapestry depicting the story of Tancred and Erminia, from the workshop of Raphael de la Planche, circa 1660, depicting the wounded Tancred being assisted by Erminia and Vafrino, 9ft. 2in. x 11ft. 8in. (Sotheby's) $23,000

Most people are now familiar with the account of how the Teddy bear got its name. This tells how, while on a hunting trip in 1902, President Theodore Roosevelt could not bring himself to shoot a bear cub which had been conveniently tethered to a post by some well-meaning aide (the President having just shot its mother). Such fore'bear'ance on the part of the noted hunter appealed to the popular press, and the incident was captured in a cartoon of the day. Seeing this, one Morris Michtom, of the Ideal Toy Corp. who had created some toy bears, asked permission to call them after Theodore, so the Teddy bear came into being.

Roosevelt obviously felt the connection did no harm to the presidential image, and when his daughter married in 1906, the wedding breakfast tables were decorated with tiny bears made by the Steiff toy company.

Margrete Steiff had been making felt animals at Geingen in Germany for some time and was joined in 1897 by her ambitious nephew Richard. They exhibited at the Leipzig Fair in 1903 and the popularity of their toys was so great that the factory simply could not keep up with demand.

Pre-1910 Steiff bears tend to be rather elongated, with pointed snouts and humps. The Steiffs had the good marketing sense to put a characteristic button in each of their product's ears, thus making them instantly recognisable.

A Steiff teddy bear with golden mohair, black shoe button eyes, swivel head, jointed shaped limbs, 12½in. tall, circa 1905.
(Christie's) $3,162

A Merrythought teddy bear, with golden mohair, pronounced clipped snout, black stitched nose, mouth and claws, 17in. tall, 1930s.
(Christie's) $280

An early German teddy bear with golden mohair, black boot button eyes, center facial seam, pronounced clipped snout, 19in. tall, circa 1910.
(Christie's) $1,210

A Steiff teddy bear with golden mohair, brown and black glass eyes, pronounced snout, hump and button in ear, 1920s, 16in. high.
(Christie's) $1,656

A French teddy bear with pale golden mohair, clear and black glass eyes painted on reverse, 29in. tall, 1930s.
(Christie's) $372

A Steiff teddy bear with golden mohair, black shoe button eyes, pronounced clipped snout, 12in. tall, circa 1905.
(Christie's) $2,418

An early German teddy bear with golden mohair, black shoe button eyes, small clipped snout, 9in. tall, circa 1910.
(Christie's) $744

A Chiltern teddy bear with golden mohair, square snout, black stitched nose, mouth and claws, 20in. tall, 1930s.
(Christie's) $595

'Isaiah' an Ideal teddy bear with golden mohair, black shoe button eyes, pronounced clipped snout, 13in. tall, circa 1910.
(Christie's) $652

A Chad Valley teddy bear with golden mohair, amber and black glass eyes, clipped snout, black stitched nose, mouth and claws, 25in. tall, 1920s.
(Christie's) $484

A brown plush covered teddy bear with large clear and black glass eyes painted on reverse, cream clipped plush pronounced cut muzzle, large cardboard lined feet and growler, 30in. tall, 1930s.
(Christie's) $1,264

A pink Chiltern musical teddy bear with deep amber and black glass eyes, pronounced clipped snout, concertina musical movement in tummy, 20in. tall, 1930s.
(Christie's) $1,024

'Billy', a Chiltern teddy bear, with golden mohair, large clear and black glass eyes, linen pads, 20in. tall, circa 1935.
(Christie's) $484

'Martin', an English teddy bear with golden mohair, white, brown and black glass 'peoples' eyes, 27in. tall, 1930s.
(Christie's) $838

A pink Dean's teddy bear with clear and black glass eyes, clipped snout and black horizontally stitched nose, 12in. high, circa 1920.
(Christie's) $1,203

A Steiff teddy bear with pale blond mohair, brown and black glass eyes, clipped plush cut muzzle, 13in. tall. (Christie's) $595

'Oliver', a Farnell teddy bear with golden mohair, swivel head, jointed shaped limbs, 12in. tall, circa 1920. (Christie's) $707

A white Steiff teddy bear with beige stitched nose, mouth and claws, pronounced snout, 24in. tall, 1930s. (Christie's) $3,348

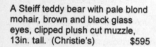

A Chiltern teddy bear with rich golden mohair, deep amber and black eyes, square snout, 19in. high, circa 1950. (Christie's) $444

A Chad Valley Magna teddy bear with golden mohair, amber and black glass eyes, swivel head, jointed shaped limbs, 21in. tall, circa 1930. (Christie's) $446

A Chiltern teddy bear with dark golden mohair, clear and black glass eyes painted on reverse, 20in. tall, 1930s. (Christie's) $521

A Steiff teddy bear with pale blond mohair, black shoe button eyes, pronounced clipped snout, 10in. tall, circa 1910. (Christie's) $930

A Farnell teddy bear with golden mohair, deep amber and black glass eyes, pronounced clipped snout, 18in. tall, 1930s. (Christie's) $893

'Fred', a Steiff teddy bear with golden mohair, black boot button eyes, black stitched nose, mouth and claws, 17in. tall, circa 1907. (Christie's) $5,952

'Bechico', a white Steiff teddy bear with brown and black glass eyes, pronounced snout, 24in. tall, circa 1929. (Christie's) $14,509

A Chad Valley teddy bear with pale blond mohair, amber and black plastic eyes, 13in. tall, 1950s. (Christie's) $280

A Farnell teddy bear with golden mohair, clear and black glass eyes painted on reverse, 17in. tall, 1920s. (Christie's) $521

A Steiff teddy bear having gold mohair plush, center seam, wide apart ears, pronounced clipped muzzle, 21in. (Phillips) $5,100

A Steiff centre seam teddy bear with golden mohair, black boot button eyes, pronounced snout, felt pads, hump and blank button in ear, 15in. tall, circa 1905. (Christie's) $5,580

A Steiff teddy bear with golden mohair, brown and black glass eyes, hump, growler and button in ear, 18in. tall, 1920s. (Christie's) $2,976

A Steiff teddy bear with golden mohair, black shoe button eyes, felt pads and button in ear, 11in. tall, circa 1910. (Christie's) $1,582

A Chiltern teddy bear with golden mohair, amber and black plastic eyes, square snout, black stitched nose, mouth and claws, 24in. tall, 1950s. (Christie's) $595

A Steiff teddy bear with golden mohair, brown and black glass eyes, cream felt pads, growler, hump, and button in ear, 17in. tall, 1920s. (Christie's) $4,694

HISTORICAL FACTS
Telephones

"Mr Watson, come here, I want you," was the first complete sentence ever spoken over a telephone in June 1875 by Alexander Graham Bell in Boston, USA.

The origins of the telephone are somewhat controversial. It is Alexander Graham Bell who is usually given the credit for its invention, though an American, one Elisha Grey, actually filed a patent on a similar device on the same day as Bell. Unfortunately, in terms of international time, he did so a few hours later, so lost his claim in an ensuing Supreme Court action.

Going back to basics, however, it was in fact neither of these gentlemen who put the first rudimentary telephone together, but Professor Philip Reis of Friedrichsdorf in Germany. For the microphone, he hollowed out the bung of a beer barrel, which he then covered with a German sausage skin to make a diaphragm. He attached to this a strip of platinum which vibrated with the diaphragm to form a make and break electrical circuit. Then he took a knitting needle, surrounded with a coil of wire which he attached to a violin to act as a sound box. This, incredibly, reproduced the sound received by the bung covered with sausage skin. The first telephone had been created!

Most early telephones found today are of the Ericsson type and originate from Scandinavia, Germany and England.

An L.M. Ericsson pointer dial desk telephone, circa 1910.
(Auction Team Köln) $840

An L.M. Ericsson desk telephone, with metal casing, 1925.
(Auction Team Köln) $116

An L.M. Ericsson skeleton telephone, with hygienic mouthpiece.
(Auction Team Köln) $1,010

A decorative Danish wall telephone with original cast-iron wall plate.
(Auction Team Köln) $373

An L.M. Ericsson, Stockholm, exchange telephone, with wooden casing, circa 1953.
(Auction Team Köln) $194

A Swedish line dial telephone, possibly by Ericsson, with two original push buttons, circa 1910.
(Auction Team Köln) $611

An L.M. Ericsson Stockholm skeleton telephone, with speaking button and horn-shaped speaker.
(Auction Team Köln) $1,293

A Danish central battery KTAS desk telephone, with coin slot, the receiver with speaking horn.
(Auction Team Köln) $203

A KTAS Model 1904 local battery desk telephone, on wooden socle, and with side handle, 1930.
(Auction Team Köln) $142

A Lolland Falsters local battery wall telephone, with wall desk, Danish,
(Auction Team Köln) $373

A local battery Allmana Telefonaktiebolaget L.M. Ericsson desk telephone, with second bell, receiver with conical grip and speaking horn.
(Auction Team Köln) $190

A Swedish Rikstelefon local battery wall telephone with receiver bracket in front of the bell, circa 1910.
(Auction Team Köln) $388

A very rare Ericsson house telephone, with receiver bracket and dial, 1900.
(Auction Team Köln) $614

A French local battery desk telephone by the Association des Ouvertes en Instruments de Précision, Paris.
(Auction Team Köln) $103

An early Hantel Präzisions telephone, with wall desk, leather covered handle, circa 1895.
(Auction Team Köln) $7,114

An RCA Victor Model 8T 243 television receiver, early postwar set by the Radio Corporation of America, 1948.
(Auction Team Köln) $122

A Wega Vision 3000L TV set, 1963.
(Auction Team Köln) $116

An HMV Model 904 combined radio and television, rare 5-tube version, 1938.
(Auction Team Köln) $2,455

A Sony Model 5-305 UW TV set, small size, for battery or mains, circa 1958.
(Auction Team Köln) $45

A very early Marconi Model 703 combined radio, record player and television, one of only eight models said to have been produced.
(Auction Team Köln) $2,328

An early English Ekco Vision portable television, for battery or mains, with 31cm. diameter round picture tubes, circa 1955.
(Auction Team Köln) $181

An Ekco Type TX 275 early British television for mains and battery, 1955.
(Auction Team Köln) $74

A Kuba Komet 1523 de Luxe combined radio and television, in working order, 1962.
(Auction Team Köln) $8,408

Sentinel 400 TV, early portable American set with small 7in. tubes, circa 1948. (Auction Team Köln) $311

A pair of terracotta blackamoor figures, standing with horizontally stretched arms to each side, 34¼in. high.
(Christie's) $1,414

A French terracotta group of a lion savaging a wild boar, by Edme Dumont, signed and dated *1768*, 14½in. high.
(Sotheby's) $28,750

A pair of terracotta urns, possibly by the Watcombe pottery, circa 1900, each with a flowers, fruit and foliage swagged urn, tied with ribbons, 30in. high.
(Christie's) $6,601

A North Italian terracotta figure of St. John, 16th century, the seated figure clad in a tunic and turned to the left, 16½in. high.
(Sotheby's) $34,500

A pair of terracotta garden urns, designed by Archibald Knox and manufactured by Liberty & Co., circa 1902, each with incised entrelac design, 14¼in. high.
(Christie's) $4,124

A terracotta head of Zeus, late 19th/20th century, probably French, 20in. high.
(Christie's) $3,018

A pair of French terracotta female allegorical figures, attributed to the workshop of Simon Louis Boizot, late 18th century, figures 30³/₈in. and 30½in. high.
(Sotheby's) $17,250

L. Hjorth: Terracotta figure of two young men fighting, bound together at the waist, stamped *L. Hjorth*.
(Ewbank) $627

A pair of French terracotta figures of Terpsichore and male figure playing a horn, the first after a model by Pierre-Francois Berruer, 18th/19th century, 14½in. high.
(Sotheby's) $5,750

An early 19th century woolwork picture of a ship, dressed overall with signal flags, 53 x 51cm., in walnut veneered frame.
(Bearne's) $1,587

Melbourne Olympic Games, 1956 silk handkerchief.
(Bill Lucas) $32

A 17th century stumpwork embroidery, 9 x 13in.
(G E Sworder) $32,800

An Italian armorial embroidery, second quarter 18th century, with metal-thread and silk on red velvet ground, depicting a central armorial shield, almost certainly that of Francesco Maria Pasini, 134 x 96in.
(Christie's) $15,180

A pair of oval embroidered pictures in colored silks with sprays of naturalistic flowers and butterflies against a tobacco colored satin ground, 1780s, 14 x 17in.
(Christie's) $1,197

An unusual horizontal needlework hanging embroidered in coloured wools and silks with a group of exotically dressed men sitting beneath ruins, possibly 18th century, Scandinavian, 74 x 90in.
(Christie's) $4,048

A woolwork picture with silk and painted details, probably depicting the flight of Mary, Queen of Scots, 27½ x 24½in., 1820s, framed.
(Christie's) $330

A pair of Beauvais tapestry cushions, the tapestry mid-18th century, woven in wools and silks, one depicting a pair of hounds in a wooded landscape, 24 x 26in. and 23 x 24in.
(Christie's) $7,921

A pair of tapestry cushions, Aubusson, early 19th century, one woven with playing children, the other with sporting dogs and a hind, 46 x 52cm. (Sotheby's) $4,048

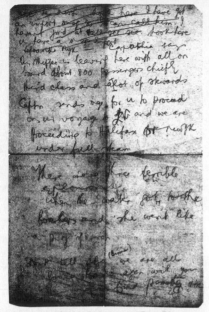

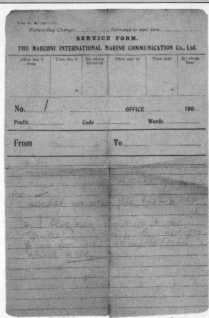

S.S. Virginian: Titanic Disaster and Post-Disaster messages, 14th April 1912, twelve messages starting (11.15pm.) *Hear MGY call CQD SOS has struck iceberg pos. 41.46N 50.14W.* The signals in pencil on Marconi headed service paper, 8½ x 5½in. (Christie's) $18,400

S.S. Carpathia Post-Disaster messages, 17th April, 1912, messages sent by survivors of the Titanic to New York, two album pages, 5½ x 8½in. each. (Christie's) $2,576

Captain Smith, a rare sepia photograph showing Smith as a member of a group of thirteen officers in White Star Line Mediterranean Day Dress, 10 x 13in. framed and glazed. (Christie's) $2,576

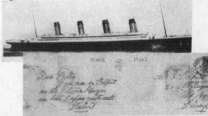

Postcard of 'The ill fated American Liner Titanic', real photographic by J. Beagles. (Onslow's) $144

White Star RMS Titanic bookpost postcard, to Mr T Perkins, 20 Montagu Road, Old Town, Liverpool 'Dear Father, I am over in Belfast on the Titanic' postmarked Belfast 9.16pm FE[B] 10 1912. (Onslow's) $1,280

Deathless Story of the Titanic (The) 2nd ed, issued by Lloyds Weekly News, 1912. (Onslow's) $96

'Among The Icebergs The Most Appalling Disaster In Maritime History', mono art, published by Valentines, with technical details of ship. (Onslow's) $272

A memorial picture of the 'Titanic' musicians, the eight musicians photographed with the title The *Heroic Musicians of The Titanic*, 15½ x 11in. (Christie's) $2,576

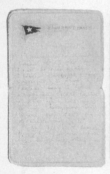

On Board RMS Titanic, an autograph signed letter on two sides on official letter card, from Eileen Gessney, postmarked Southampton 2.30pm April 10 12. (Onslow's) $3,360

White Star Line Fleet Includes 'Olympic' 45,000 Tons 'Titanic' 45,000 Tons Largest Steamers In The World, a hanging calendar on card for 1912, 30 x 50cm. (Onslow's) $3,680

The Ship That Will Never Return (The Loss of the Titanic) written by F V St Clare, sheet music No 172, published by E Marks, with port side view of the ship. (Onslow's) $112

A newspaper vendor's stand poster entitled 'The Daily Mirror Saturday April 10 1912 Hymn Played While The Titanic Sank', 76 x 51cm. (Onslow's) $752

Postcard of the White Star Royal Mail Steamer Titanic, naïve color art, published by State Series Liverpool. (Onslow's) $96

A screen printed poster for the 20th Century Fox production of Titanic starring Clifton Webb, Barbara Stanwyck and Robert Wagner, 1963, on linen, 103 x 70cm. (Onslow's) $544

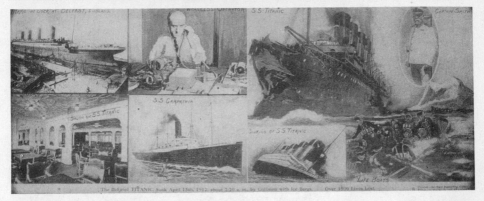

'The ill-Fated Titanic Sunk April 15th 1912 About 2.20am by Collision with Icebergs Over 1500 Lives Lost',
monochrome photographic collage of seven views. (Onslow's) $160

White Star Line 'Olympic' & 'Titanic' Largest Steamers In The World, a publicity booklet entitled Notes and
Illustrations of the First and Second Class Passenger Accomodation, 1912. (Onslow's) $8,000

White Star Line Olympic & Titanic Third Class Accomodation The Largest Steamers In The World, a publicity
booklet, 10 x 15cm. (Onslow's) $4,800

A White Star Line varnished wood stationery or publicity booklet rack, 27 x 26 x 12cm. (Onslow's) $416

Captain Edward J. Smith, Titanic, signed certificate of discharge for Seaman J.G. Raddish, from the Britannic, 5th May 1893. (Vennett-Smith) $2,013

White Star Line pack of fifty-two playing cards, lacking jokers. (Onslow's) $288

'The Last of the Titanic', three sepia photographs taken from R.M.S. Oceanic on May 13th 1912 showing the discovery and final recovery of the last of Titanic collapsible canvas lifeboats, 13½ x 21in. (Christie's) $4,600

A Titanic memorial program, dated Monday, May 20th, 1912 for a benefit concert held for the Disaster Fund with monochromes of Titanic, Captain Smith with his officers, artistes including George Formby (Snr), 10 x 7½in. (Christie's) $2,024

Titanic memorial French sheet music, Plus Près De Toi Mon Dieu (Nearer My God to Thee), published by Henry Wykes..., 7 x 10¾in. (Christie's) $1,656

On Board RMS Titanic, an unused double sheet of official writing paper with embossed company burgee. (Onslow's) $1,440

Sepia photographs depicting the recovery and embalming of 'Titanic' passengers and the loading of horse drawn hearses at a Government dockyard, 4½ x 6in. (Christie's) $2,024

The Titanic, 'How the Titanic met with disaster on her maiden voyage, The Daily Graphic 16th April 1912, front page diagram. (Christie's) $2,208

Fireman William Nutbeam (Survivor), his Continuous Certificate of Discharge No. 680419, date of last entry 8th June 1923. (Onslow's) $2,500

A circular bakelite White Star Line ashtray, Omniteware made by Fraser & Glass London N8, 15cm diameter. (Onslow's) $152

A Titanic memorial picture, Titanic photographed from a three quarter port bow position, 11½ x 16½in. (Christie's) $2,208

A paper souvenir napkin, *In Affectionate Remembrance of the 1503 Persons Who Lost Their Lives by the Foundering of the World's Largest Liner SS Titanic*, with vignette of the Ship, 37cm. square, framed. (Onslow's) $240

White Star Line TSS Titanic color art postcard, from Thomas Mudd to his mother, '*Dear Mother, Arrived at Southampton safe The Titanic is a splendid boat*'. (Onslow's) $5,760

Titanic, hardback edition of Sinking of the Titanic, ed. by Marshall Everett, 13th May 1912. (Vennett-Smith) $173

Postcard of 'SS Titanic foundered April 14th 1912 Over 1600 passengers drowned', mono art published by W & T Gaines. (Onslow's) $272

On Board RMS Titanic, an unused perforated letter card with printed company burgee. (Onslow's) $1,520

A rare Beardsley & Wolcott Mfg. Co. spring operated one-slice toaster of classic design, with wooden handles on either side.
(Auction Team Köln) $56

A ceramic Hostess Sandwich Toaster by the All Rite Co., Rushville Indiana, with original cable.
(Auction Team Köln) $38

A Degea No. 12075 swivel toaster with heating plates, German, circa 1925.
(Auction Team Köln) $102

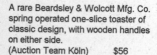

A Therma Nodel No. 3201, silvered machine with turning facility.
(Auction Team Köln) $149

A Toast-O-Lator Model J toaster, toast is inserted at the side and passes through the toaster as in a car-wash! 1940.
(Auction Team Köln) $142

A Hotpoint Model D American hotplate toaster by Edison Appliance Co.
(Auction Team Köln) $149

An early ceramic D-12 toaster with floral decoration, circa 1920.
(Auction Team Köln) $375

A Rite Electric Toaster, American, circa 1918.
(Auction Team Köln) $323

A General Electric D-12 ceramic toaster, with high wire basket, circa 1910.
(Auction Team Köln) $408

A Victorian black japanned tôle purdonium of oval form, painted in gilt and enamels with foliage, 67cm. high. (Cheffins Grain & Comins) $1,600

A tôle tray, signed *Martha Cahoon*, 20th century, painted with a sailor presenting a bouquet of flowers to a mermaid, 20in. long. (Sotheby's) $1,437

Toleware coffee pot, with floral decoration, 11in. high. (Eldred's) $495

Painted and galvanised tin birdbath, America, 19th century, the square recessed top with cove molded sides, 32½in. high. (Skinner) $2,990

A japanned-tin log bucket, 19th century, the rounded rectangular hinged lid painted with a Dutch style scene of figures skating, 19½in. high. (Christie's) $1,431

A painted tôle log bin, circa 1850, of oval form with pierced borders, swags and rosettes, on four feet, 66cm. high. (Sotheby's) $7,873

A rare wriggle-work decorated toleware coffeepot, Pennsylvania, 19th century, of ovoid diamond form with strap handle and conical lid, 13³/₄in. high. (Sotheby's) $1,495

A North European painted tôle single bedstead, 19th century, the shaped paneled head and foot decorated in imitation of mahogany and rosewood, 38in. wide. (Christie's) $1,563

A paint decorated tinware coffee pot, Pennsylvania, circa 1830, painted red with borders of yellow, green and red flowers, 10½in. high. (Sotheby's) $1,725

A sugar axe, 17in., with oak handle.
(Tool Shop Auctions)　　　$83

A 32½in. socketed axe head.
(Tool Shop Auctions)　　　$281

An early European socketed
fighting axe head.
(Tool Shop Auctions)　　　$198

A large French Coopers' doloire,
original handle, impressive smiths'
stamp.
(Tool Shop Auctions)　　　$116

A fine German side axe from The
Black Forest with ornate smiths'
stamp.
(Tool Shop Auctions)　　　$206

A beautifully balanced miniature
doloire, blade 9in. overall, marked
NAUD A COGNAC.
(Tool Shop Auctions)　　　$165

An intimidating early beheading axe
found in England although
European in style, 16 x 12in.
(Tool Shop Auctions)　　　$347

A fine Pontypool type billhook by
Harrison.
(Tool Shop Auctions)　　　$23

A superb right hand coachmakers'
side axe with forged terracing at the
top of the blade.
(Tool Shop Auctions)　　　$198

A rare Boy Scout hatchet stamped
Boy Scout Reg'd 1910.
(Tool Shop Auctions)　　　$50

A most unusual resin axe from
Bordeaux, distinctive curved blade.
(Tool Shop Auctions)　　　$132

An early French rignt hand
coachmakers' side axe.
(Tool Shop Auctions)　　　$248

A medieval socketed axe head.
(Tool Shop Auctions)　　　$330

A hand forged axe head.
(Tool Shop Auctions)　　　$347

A double edged Chairmakers' hand
adze. (Tool Shop Auctions)　　　$66

An 18th century, possibly earlier, billhook.
(Tool Shop Auctions) $50

An 18th century European side axe with various smiths' stamps.
(Tool Shop Auctions) $190

A handsome sugar axe with ebony handle.
(Tool Shop Auctions) $58

A fascinating early socketed billhook from a vineyard in Grand Champagne.
(Tool Shop Auctions) $165

An axe head with '3 pellets' smiths' stamp, possibly 16th century.
(Tool Shop Auctions) $99

A coopers' side axe by Alex Mathieson.
(Tool Shop Auctions) $53

An unusual French vine axe with massive 27in. blade.
(Tool Shop Auctions) $198

An early French right hand coachmakers' side axe, marked *J.Calle*.
(Tool Shop Auctions) $149

An elegant early European axe
(Tool Shop Auctions) $50

A fine 18th century curved froe.
(Tool Shop Auctions) $280

A 17th century lathing hammer/axe with prominent maker's mark.
(Tool Shop Auctions) $165

A rare masting axe by Mathieson.
(Tool Shop Auctions) $182

An early socketed froe.
(Tool Shop Auctions) $83

A massive elegant sugar cleaver, 18½in.
(Tool Shop Auctions) $165

A firemans' axe by Elwell.
(Tool Shop Auctions) $25

A 5-tine eel gleave, 27in. long.
(Tool Shop Auctions)　　　$231

An extremely rare Scottish
poachers' hand gaff.
(Tool Shop Auctions)　　$83

A 5-tine eel gleave by Augereau.
(Tool Shop Auctions)　　　$198

An early French 3-tine eel gleave
from the Dordogne.
(Tool Shop Auctions)　　$190

A well made 3 tine eel gleave, hand
forged with smith's mark.
(Tool Shop Auctions)　　　$182

An early 5-tine eel gleave by
Augereau from the Loire Valley.
(Tool Shop Auctions)　　　$363

A 5-tine eel gleave, 21in. long.
(Tool Shop Auctions)　　$190

A 3-tine eel gleave, 23in. long,
pitted.
(Tool Shop Auctions)　　$231

A 5-tine eel gleave, 24in. long,
smith's mark *R. Flaxman.*
(Tool Shop Auctions)　　　$446

A fine 6-tine eel gleave, 22in. long.
(Tool Shop Auctions)　　$545

A large five pronged fish spear,
16in. overall, reputedly used on
sturgeon in The Volga.
(Tool Shop Auctions)　　$66

A hand-forged Welsh four-tine eel
gleave.
(Tool Shop Auctions)　　　$83

A fine 18in. eel gleave, 5-tines,
early 19th century.
(Tool Shop Auctions)　　$165

A 19th century French 3-tine eel
gleave from the Dordogne.
(Tool Shop Auctions)　　$190

A 5-tine eel gleave, 23in. long,
smith's mark *J. Colls.*
(Tool Shop Auctions)　　　$182

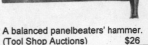

A brass veneering hammer.
(Tool Shop Auctions) $36

A rare cigar box knife and hammer by Gray of Sheffield.
(Tool Shop Auctions) $99

A balanced panelbeaters' hammer.
(Tool Shop Auctions) $26

A broom or besom makers' hammer by Dickinson & Son.
(Tool Shop Auctions) $50

A silversmiths' planishing hammer.
(Tool Shop Auctions) $50

A small all steel crate hammer by Brades.
(Tool Shop Auctions) $33

A huge claw hammer, 7in. head.
(Tool Shop Auctions) $33

A superb French 17th century hammer with chipped floral design and maker's mark.
(Tool Shop Auctions) $231

A filemakers' hammer.
(Tool Shop Auctions) $182

An unusual marking hammer with provision for replaceable stamps made by Matthews Marking Devices, Pittsburgh.
(Tool Shop Auctions) $58

18th century socketed hammer of superb style, 9in. overall, wooden handle elaborately turned in a series of flamboyant rings and circular reeds, 1769.
(Tool Shop Auctions) $4,290

A massive bookbinders' hammer by Brades.
(Tool Shop Auctions) $140

Mortice Gauges

A Stanley No. 77 rosewood mortise gauge.
(Tool Shop Auctions) $25

An ebony and brass mortise gauge by Marples. Original trade label.
(Tool Shop Auctions) $58

A fine ebony and brass oval mortise gauge.
(Tool Shop Auctions) $58

Four various dovetail gauges.
(Tool Shop Auctions) $86

A brass dovetail gauge, patent number 29191.
(Tool Shop Auctions) $107

Four craftsman made dovetail gauges.
(Tool Shop Auctions) $69

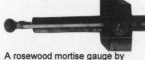
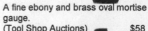

A rosewood mortise gauge by Sorby.
(Tool Shop Auctions) $66

A quality solid boxwood and brass marking gauge by Marples.
(Tool Shop Auctions) $41

A solid boxwood and brass marking gauge marked *Patent 14734*.
(Tool Shop Auctions) $66

An ebony and bone 19th century gauge, discovered in a ships carpenter's chest in Baltimore.
(Tool Shop Auctions) $305

A pretty ebony and brass mortise gauge with 8in. brass rule on the stem.
(Tool Shop Auctions) $140

A Stanley No.77 rosewood and brass mortise gauge, calibrated stock.
(Tool Shop Auctions) $50

A 22½in. dovetail steel and
rosewood Norris No.1 jointer.
(Tool Shop Auctions) $2,145

An iron sash shave by Mathieson
(Tool Shop Auctions) $50

A brass shoulder plane with golden
patinated boxwood infill and wedge.
(Tool Shop Auctions) $165

A gunmetal Scottish skew badger,
lovely overstuffed walnut infill.
(Tool Shop Auctions) $446

A small size 2³⁄8 x 7⁷⁄16in. Norris A4
with original iron.
(Tool Shop Auctions) $693

A Norris No. 2 dovetailed
smoothing plane, original iron.
(Tool Shop Auctions) $248

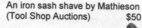

An interesting, dated side bead by
Iohn Green inscribed with the
painted inscription, *William Drydale
Pickering, 1835.*
(Tool Shop Auctions) $144

A miniature gunmetal violinmakers'
plane with round sole, attractive
front acanthus style grip with scroll
carved ivory wedge and stuffing.
1½ x ¾in.
(Tool Shop Auctions) $1,007

A 16th/17th century musical-
instrument maker's plane, 6 x
2³⁄16in., complete with toothing iron
and conceivably original wedge.
(Tool Shop Auctions) $2,021

A stem wedged beech plough by
Mathieson.
(Tool Shop Auctions) $61

A fine carved plane, this European
router in oak, 7 x 6in. is elaborately
carved into the face of a ram,
17th/18th century.
(Tool Shop Auctions) $2,393

A well made beech fillister with
brass screw arms and iron and
steel locking nuts.
(Tool Shop Auctions) $165

A lovely 22 x 3¼in. jointer in
hornbeam with apple wedge and
handle.
(Tool Shop Auctions) $66

A reverse ogee with single fillet by
Varvill & Sons, 3in.
(Tool Shop Auctions) $74

A 22½in. Norris A1 dovetailed
jointer with rosewood infill, in totally
original condition.
(Tool Shop Auctions) $3,713

A 6in. steel and brass plumb bob.
(Tool Shop Auctions) $165

A steel tipped lead onion bob, 5½in.
(Tool Shop Auctions) $66

A 5¼in. steel tipped brass plumb
bob. (Tool Shop Auctions) $99

A 19th century 36oz brass plumb
bob with steel point.
(Tool Shop Auctions) $132

An early 19th century European
brass plumb bob.
(Tool Shop Auctions) $149

A steel plumb bob with integral
pulley.
(Tool Shop Auctions) $110

A 4in. 19th century ivory plumb bob
with steel point.
(Tool Shop Auctions) $206

A Continental brass plumb bob with
spacer.
(Tool Shop Auctions) $83

A heavy 19th century steel and
brass plumb bob.
(Tool Shop Auctions) $198

A massive 11½in. brass 19th
century steel tipped plumb bob.
(Tool Shop Auctions) $545

An early iron European plumb bob.
(Tool Shop Auctions) $83

An 8in. steel plumb bob,
conceivably 18th century.
(Tool Shop Auctions) $165

An 8in. steel tipped brass plumb
bob.
(Tool Shop Auctions) $132

An extremely imposing, highly
decorative brass plumb bob.
(Tool Shop Auctions) $627

An ornate steel tipped chalice bob
with floral decoration.
(Tool Shop Auctions) $396

A C.I.J 'Les Jouets Renault' tinplate coupé, French 1930s, the two door coupé painted in French blue with yellow interior, with original key, 11¾in. (Sotheby's) $515

A tinplate lithographed machine gun position with hand lever for friction power, soldier in khaki uniform, possibly Märklin, circa 1930. (Auction Team Köln) $58

German composition rocking horse pull-toy, circa 1890, with carved wooden mouth and nose area and original mane and tail. (Eldred's) $440

Carousel horse, Charles Dare, New York Carousel Mfg. Co., last quarter 19th century, probably from a two-row portable track machine, with swirled marble eyes, 51in. long. (Skinner) $1,265

A Steiff Mickey Mouse with velvet body, green velvet shorts with pearl buttons, tail lacking, circa 1935, (Auction Team Köln) $1,492

Child's carved wooden rocking horse, 19th century, 35in. high, 44in. long. (Eldred's) $550

A Lehmann EPL 625 'Wild West', German, 1909-1945, the clockwork toy handpainted with white horse and rider with red shirt, 7¼in. (Sotheby's) $368

A Lehmann EPL 490 'Tut-Tut', German, 1903-1935, the clockwork car with bellows lithographed in cream and red, with matching driver, 6¾in. long. (Sotheby's) $920

Steiff 'Bully' on wheels with black and white mohair, swivel head, horse hair collar, original bell and swing tag, 9in. long, circa 1929. (Christie's) $558

A tinplate lithographed clockwork figure of a dwarf riding a snail, German, possibly Georg Köhler, circa 1950. (Auction Team Köln) $285

Li'l Abner and his Dogpatch Band, American tinplate clockwork toy by Unique Art, in original box, 1945. (Auction Team Köln) $408

A Wolverine 'Sunny Andy' Zilotone toy, American, circa 1931, the tinplate clockwork toy with curved gold and blue xylophone, played by a tinplate figure, 8¾in. long. (Sotheby's) $552

Victorian black lacquered papier mâché tray, mid 19th century, stamped *Jennens & Bettridge*, centered by a floral design, 31in. wide. (Skinner) $1,700

A Regency rosewood butler's tray on later mahogany stand, the oval tray with hinged sides and integral handles, 35½in. wide. (Christie's) $1,379

A parcel-gilt decorated tortoiseshell tray, probably Japanese, 19th century, 17in. diameter. (Christie's) $4,370

Victorian painted tôle tray, mid 19th century, depicting the Annunciation, with flower filled borders, 24in. long. (Skinner) $402

Continental painted tôle tray, early 19th century, depicting a capriccio amidst ruins, 30in. long. (Skinner) $1,955

An oval papier mâché tray, 19th century, center painted with an oval panel depicting children at play with various animals, 26½in. wide. (Christie's) $1,240

Painted carved wood monkey figure with tray, probably France, late 19th century, dressed in a greenish yellow smock, 65in. high. (Skinner) $10,925

A 19th century paper mâché tray by William S. Burton London, painted with a vase of flowers, flanked by birds on green lacquered ground, 32in. x 25in. (Andrew Hartley) $973

A mahogany butler's tray, 19th century, on a later stand, the tray with an undulating gallery 28½in. wide. (Christie's) $1,477

English painted tole serving tray, first half 19th century, painted with brown and green flowers on a red ground, 28½in. diameter. (Skinner) $1,955

A Victorian mahogany butler's tray on X-frame stand, the tray with hinged sides, pierced with carrying handles, 37in. wide. (Christie's) $2,030

It was as far back as 1714 that an Englishman, Henry Mill, first took out a patent for 'An Artificial Machine or Method for the Impression or Transcribing of Letters Singly or Progressively one after another, as in writing, whereby all Writing whatever may be Engrossed in Paper or Parchment so Neat and Exact as not to be distinguished form Print'. His design never went into production however, and it was not until nearly 130 years later, in 1843, the American Charles Thurber in turn patented his idea of a mechanical typewriter. From then on the concept really caught the imagination of inventors and there were numerous attempts to produce readable copy. None were successful however until, in 1867, the first practical typewriter was invented by three Americans, Sholes, Glidden and Soule. Their machine worked on a shift key mechanism, which forms the basis of more modern machines. Early typewriters demand good prices and are still to be found, mainly because of the enormous output of early manufacturers to cope with the immediate demand. In the 1870s alone, the companies of Remington, Oliver, Smith, Underwood and Yost sold over 50,000 models.

German machines by companies such as Edelmann are rarer as is the Gühl and Harbeck Kosmopolit typewriter with gilt and black finish and in a walnut case.

An American Index pointer typewriter, lacks rubber type, cylinder and type sheet, 1893.
(Auction Team Köln) $177

An Elliott Fisher overstrike typesetting machine, American 1896.
(Auction Team Köln) $813

A Typo typewriter, the French version of the decorative English type-bar machine, with round Ideal keyboard and double shift-key, 1914.
(Auction Team Köln) $746

A Typo Visible French edition of the popular British Imperial Visible Model B, French Ideal keyboard with double shift key, 1914.
(Auction Team Köln) $678

A Smith Premier No. 1., the first version of the decorative American understrike machine with full keyboard, with integral type cleaning brush, 1889.
(Auction Team Köln) $813

A cast-iron based Sun Typewriter, one of the first pointer typewriters and forerunner of the Odell, 1885.
(Auction Team Köln) $1,746

A Blickensdörfer No. 5 popular American type-wheel portable typewriter with early metal type board and original wooden case, 1893.
(Auction Team Köln) $149

A de-luxe gold version of the Royal Quiet Deluxe typewriter, designed by Henry Dreyfuss, in original case, 1948.
(Auction Team Köln) $905

The Simplex Typewriter, first edition of the American tinplate toy machine, with original box, 1892.
(Auction Team Köln) $102

A Victor Index typewriter, equipped with pointer and typebar and reverse hammer action, American, 1889.
(Auction Team Köln) $6,102

A Ludolf German tinplate toy pointer typewriter, with rotating type disk, circa 1930.
(Auction Team Köln) $213

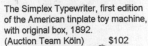

A Columbia Bar-Lock No. 10 American full-keyboard typewriter, with decorative typebasket, circa 1900.
(Auction Team Köln) $485

A Franklin No. 8 decorative American typebar machine with round Ideal keyboard and portrait of Benjamin Franklin on the carriage plate, 1898.
(Auction Team Köln) $1,762

Ajax Imperial Model B three row English type-bar machine with round Ideal keyboard and double shift keys, 1914.
(Auction Team Köln) $776

A Densmore No. 1, the first model of the classic American understrike machine, 1891.
(Auction Team Köln) $1,152

A Rofa Model IV type bar machine with 3-row Universal keyboard and vertical type-bar, 1923.
(Auction Team Köln) $646

The Emerson No. 3 American typewriter with interesting side typebar arrangement, 1907.
(Auction Team Köln) $1,592

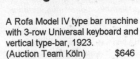

A superslim Empire Aristocrat portable typewriter, four row keyboard, with original metal cover, British, circa 1935.
(Auction Team Köln) $190

A Columbia No. 2 typewriter by Charles Spiro, New York, with large typewheel for large and small types, 1884.
(Auction Team Köln) $6,102

A Franklin No. 8 very decorative American type-bar machine, with round Ideal keyboard and portrait of Benjamin Franklin on the carriage cover, 1898.
(Auction Team Köln) $582

A rare Discret pointer typewriter with sliding bar for encoding text, with original wooden case, German, 1899.
(Auction Team Köln) $8,814

A Picht, Steglitz braille typewriter, German.
(Auction Team Köln) $72

A Merritt American pointer understrike typewriter, with fold-up carriage and original wooden case, 1889.
(Auction Team Köln) $1,338

An IBM electric typewriter, the first typebar model produced by them, circa 1935.
(Auction Team Köln) $129

A green Hammond Multiplex shuttle typewriter, with case, American.
(Auction Team Köln) $485

Frister & Rossmann Model 3 understrike typewriter, with so-called Berlin Schlafbrett, German,1900.
(Auction Team Köln) $776

A very rare Adler No. 8 double script fender machine for 180 characters, with interchangeable typebar for 90 characters, 1903.
(Auction Team Köln) $813

An Odell No. 4 decorative American pointer typewriter by Farquhar and Albrecht, Chicago, 1889.
(Auction Team Köln) $1,152

A Mignon Model 4 pointer typewriter with three additional cylinders, for fractions, script and cursive, German, 1923.
(Auction Team Köln) $226

An Imperial Model B British typebar machine with Ideal keyboard and double shift key, 1908.
(Auction Team Köln) $1,152

A Liliput typewriter, with circular non-metallic typeface beneath printed tinplate dial, 10in. wide.
(Christie's) $3,141

A Wagner Underwood No. 1 American front strike machine, produced by Franz Xavier Wagner, New York, 1896.
(Auction Team Köln) $388

A large sheet-metal rooster weathervane, American, 19th century, the silhouetted figure with comb, wattle and tail detail, 32¼in. high.
(Sotheby's) $1,725

A German iron weathervane, early 16th century, in the form of a fierce dragon's head baring its teeth, 10¾ x 15½in.
(Sotheby's) $2,587

A molded copper spread-winged eagle weathervane, possibly New York, second half 19th century, the full-bodied spread-winged eagle with articulated feathers, bill, and eyes, 29in. high.
(Christie's) $805

Sheet iron horse weather vane, New England, 19th century, the cutout figure of a horse with painted mane and muzzle, 20in. long.
(Skinner) $2,530

Doughboy molded copper weathervane, America, early 20th century, with painted flag, 36½in. high.
(Skinner) $4,600

Rare miniature rooster weather vane, J.W. Fiske, New York City, circa 1890, copper with yellow sizing, verdigris and traces of gold leaf, 12 x 10in.
(Skinner) $6,325

A molded and gilded copper rooster weathervane, American, third quarter 19th century, the swell-bodied figure with molded feather and wing detail, 22in. high.
(Sotheby's) $1,150

Rare Steeplechase horse weather vane, New England, circa 1885, maker unknown, patinated copper with verdigris surface, the fully sculpted body with applied ears and eyes, 26 x 34in.
(Skinner) $86,100

A molded copper rooster weathervane, probably Pennsylvania, 19th century, the swell-bodied ridged figure with ridged sheet copper tail, 18½in. high.
(Sotheby's) $1,035

A molded copper cow weathervane, American, third quarter 19th century, the full-bodied figure with a molded zinc head, 27in. long.
(Sotheby's) $2,185

Large cast iron horse weather vane, Rochester Iron Works, circa 1890, found in Vermont, exceptional surface of rust bleeding through paint, 26 x 34in.
(Skinner) $48,300

Molded gilt copper rooster weathervane, America, late 19th century, areas of verdigris, 28½in. long.
(Skinner) $4,600

Merino Ram, 'Ethan Allen' molded and gilded copper weathervane, attributed to J.W. Fiske & Co., New York, late 19th century.
(Skinner) $68,500

A molded copper running horse weathervane, American, third quarter 19th century, the swell-bodied figure of a stylized horse with a ridged mane, 25in. long.
(Sotheby's) $1,265

A molded copper rooster weathervane, American, third quarter 19th century, the swell-bodied figure with molded feather, wing and tail detail, 26in. high.
(Sotheby's) $1,955

Molded cow copper weathervane, America, late 19th century, fine verdigris surface, 30½in. long. (Skinner) $4,312

Small cast iron horse weather vane, Rochester Iron Works, circa 1890, vibrant patina of rust bleeding through mustard colored sizing, 18½ x 14½in. (Skinner) $31,050

A molded and gilded copper whale weathervane, American, 20th century, the molded full-bodied whale with articulated mouth, fins and tail, 19in. high. (Christie's) $2,530

A molded and gilded copper blackhawk weathervane, J.W. Fiske & Co., New York, third quarter 19th century, the swell-bodied figure with molded facial, mane and tail detail, 25in. long. (Sotheby's) $8,050

A carved and painted pine running horse weathervane, American, 19th century, the carved full-bodied yellow-painted running horse with applied white-painted eyes and yellow-painted ears, 31in. high. (Christie's) $4,600

A large molded copper and zinc hackney horse weathervane, American, third quarter 19th century, the full-bodied figure in running position, with molded tail and mane detail, 34in. long. (Sotheby's) $5,750

Glen Moray'93–Early 20th century, De Luxe Scots Whisky. Blended by MacDonald & Muir Ltd., Leith. Proprietors Glen Moray Glenlivet Distillery, etc., 70⁰ proof. (Christie's) $652

Dalmore–50 year-old, distilled 1926 and decanted at natural strength by Whyte & MacKay Distillers Ltd. (Christie's) $1,467

Glen Grant–1889, Finest Highland Malt, distilled 1889. Glen Grant Distillery Ltd., Rothes, Morayshire, green colored three piece molded glass bottle. (Christie's) $2,934

The Glenlivet–48 year-old, distilled 19th May 1883, bottled December 1931. Distilled and bottled by George & John Gordon Smith, The Glenlivet Distillery, Glenlivet, Scotland. (Christie's) $4,890

Beam's–100 Months Old, ceramic decanter formed as a Ford Corvette-1957. Bottled by James B. Beam Distilling Co., Clermont Beam, Kentucky, 80⁰. (Christie's) $277

Tomatin–10 year-old–Early 20th century. Distilled and bottled in Scotland by Tomatin Distillers Co. Ltd., Tomatin Distillery, Inverness-shire, green colored glass bottle, 70⁰ . (Christie's) $3,586

Glen Grant–32 year-old, distilled 1919. J & J Grant, Glenlivet, Strathspey. Bottled by James Catto & Co., 31-35 Virginia Street, Aberdeen. Single malt, 70⁰. (Christie's) $2,608

Springbank–50 year-old, distilled by J & A Mitchell & Co. Ltd., Springbank Distillery, Campbeltown, Argyll, pear shaped bottle, single malt. (Christie's) $3,423

Full strength Scots Liqueur–circa 1927, bottled by The Drambuie Liqueur Co. (1927) Ltd., 9 Union Street, Edinburgh, brown colored glass bottle. (Christie's) $1,223

The Very Finest Pure Malt Scotch Whisky, bottled by John Lupton & Son, Pure Produce of Scotland, brown colored glass bottle, 93° Proof. (Christie's) $522

Beam's–100 Months Old, ceramic decanter formed as a Ford V8 Fire Chief's car-1934. Bottled by James B. Beam Distilling co., Clermont Beam, Kentucky. In original carton, 80°. (Christie's) $456

Talisker Pure Malt Whisky, Talisker Distillery, Isle of Skye, green colored glass bottle, stopper cork, foil capsule. Single malt, 80° (Christie's) $1,060

Crabbie–12 year-old–Early 20th century, Special Reserve Scotch Whisky, John Crabbie & Sons Ltd., Leith Scotland, brown colored glass bottle, stopper cork, 70°. (Christie's) $652

Beam's–100 Months Old, ceramic decanter formed as a Model A Ford-1928. Bottled by James B. Beam Distilling Co., Clermont Beam, Kentucky. In original carton, 80°. (Christie's) $456

The Macallan–50 year-old, bottle number 11 of 500, distilled 1928, bottled 1983. Distilled and bottled by Macallan-Glenlivet PLC, Craigellachie. Single malt, 38.6% vol. (Christie's) $7,335

Macallan–19th century, label printed *Established 1824; Cask Sample; Speyside Malt Whisky; Macallan; Warehoused 18-4-1872; When Drawn 1-12-1899. Strength 93,6°* . (Christie's) $7,824

Beam's–100 Months Old, ceramic decanter formed as a Model A Ford Police Car- 1929. Bottled by James B. Beam, Kentucky. In original carton, 80°. (Christie's) $945

The Balvenie–50 year-old, distilled 1937, bottled 1987 by William Grant & Sons Ltd., Distillers, Dufftown, Banffshire. In wooden presentation case, single malt, 42% vol. (Christie's) $3,423

A pineapple-decorated carved pine wall plaque, American, 18th/early 19th century, of rectangular form decorated with a pineapple, 27¼in. long.
(Sotheby's) $4,025

A fruitwood lemon squeezer. (David Lay) $235

Figural carved wood pig-form footrest, America, 19th century, velvet covered body, felt ears, button eyes, 9¾in. high.
(Skinner) $1,265

A Spanish gilt and painted wood reliquary bust of a female saint, circa 1600, the veiled figure with eyes cast downwards.
(Sotheby's) $1,840

A pair of Spanish gilt and painted wood figures of male saints, 16th century, one of Saint James with the pilgrim's hat, the other with a lamb by his feet, 20¾in. high.
(Sotheby's) $17,250

A South German gilt and painted three-quarter length wood figure of the Magdalene, early 16th century, 15¼in. high.
(Sotheby's) $3,450

A carved and painted pine black bear, American, 20th century, the large stylized bear modeled seated on its haunches, 36in. long.
(Sotheby's) $2,300

A pair of Italian gilt and painted wood angels, 18th century, each winged figure with windswept hair and cloak, 19¼in. high.
(Sotheby's) $13,800

Ebonized wood figural inkwell, Continental, probably Italian, 19th century, in the form of a blackamoor head, 6¼in. high.
(Skinner) $805

A South German (probably Franconian) painted lindenwood relief of two Apostles at the Last Supper, circa 1500, 15½ x 10⅝in.
(Sotheby's) $8,625

A Regency mahogany table coaster, by James Mein of Kelso, the circular top on three brass and leather castors, 8¾in. diameter.
(Christie's) $883

A Netherlandish painted wood relief of the Deposition, 16th century, Christ lying upon the Madonna's lap, 18¾ x 21in.
(Sotheby's) $5,750

A pair of large oak reliefs of reclining figures, 18th century, probably Netherlandish, each clad in classical robes, 23 x 40in. (Sotheby's) $4,025

Red painted carved birch bowl, American, 19th century, oval form with double finger hole handles, 27in. (Skinner) $3,737

A Netherlandish oak figure of a reclining dragon, 16th century, probably from a Saint George group, 11⁵/₈ x 18¹/₈in. (Sotheby's) $7,475

A Netherlandish oak group of Saint Martin on horseback, last quarter 15th century, the figure cutting his cloak for the beggar, 33³/₄ x 26in. (Sotheby's) $25,300

A late 19th century finely carved oak goat's head, on oak shield, 22 x 22in. overall. (Anderson & Garland) $826

Carved and painted wood carousel horse, Stein and Goldstein, Brooklyn, New York, 1910–15, inner row jumper, 38in. high. (Skinner) $1,955

A carved and painted pine circus figure: The Pugilist, American, circa 1870, on a rectangular rolling stand, 64in. high overall. (Sotheby's) $4,600

A pair of Flemish walnut cherubim in baroque style, carved with curly hair, 20in. high. (Sotheby's) $3,162

A South German painted wood relief of Magdalene, early 16th century, the crowned and draped figure holding the chalice, 37³/₄in. high. (Sotheby's) $4,830

An Austrian (Salzburg school) painted wood Pieta, circa 1430, the veiled figure with her left hand at her chest, 21½in. high. (Sotheby's) $23,000

An English oak ceiling boss of a nereide, early 15th century, the mermaid holding a mirror and a comb, 11¾in. square. (Sotheby's) $4,025

Unusual wooden flagon, American, 19th century, in old green paint, four iron bands, carved handle and cover, 16in. high. (Eldred's) $1,320